WORLD WAR III
IT STARTED WITH EMP

ALBERT LYNN CLARK

The EC Publishing LLC books may be ordered
through booksellers or by contacting:

EC Publishing LLC
116 South Magnolia Ave.
Suite 3, Unit F
Ocala, FL 34471, USA
Direct Line: +1 (352) 644-6538
Fax: +1 (800) 483-1813
http://www.ecpublishingllc.com/

Ordering Information:
Quantity sales. Special discounts are available on quantity purchases by corporations, associations, and others. For
details, contact the publisher at the address above.

Printed in the United States of America

CONTENTS

DEDICATION

To those U.S. military members that died in wars and police actions because of those that said there was no need to prepare for a war between wars.

No war preparation is preparation for slavery or death. If you are a minor country you must rely on the big countries so talk peace with the best. If you are a big country you must rely on yourself and assume that you are the target for any country that proposes to be big. Are you ready?

The countries known for peace, such as Switzerland, are armed to the teeth. When nearly every home has bomb shelters, machine guns and grenades you just don't want to mess with that country. The price is too high and what do you win if you have to destroy the country to win it. Many of these armed peaceful countries have mandatory military service for every able bodied man in the country. Everyone is a trained and fully armed soldier.

In the United States many want us to give up our rifles and hand guns. Machine guns and grenades will get you arrested now.

OTHER BOOKS BY ALBERT LYNN CLARK

SCIENCE FICTION
Ancient Destiny I – SHIP
Ancient Destiny II – Escape from Earth
Ancient Destiny III – Generations
Ancient Destiny IV - Survivors

NON-FICTION
Lighting & Thunder
It is MY Lighting & Thunder
Oklahoma Blackjacker

FOREWORD

Before there was an IBM compatible personal computer, I bought my own personal computer. Nostradamus always said that someday people would figure out the sequence of his verses in his Centuries. With the aid of the computer I set out to sort these verses. I started with the known historical predictions that had come true and put the unknown into a separate stack. It did not take long for me to realize that the separate, "future", stack contained his prediction of World War Three. The adversaries, their weapons, their targets, the major battles and locations were all spelled out in detail. It was easy to put them into a logical order that showed the progress of the war from the buildup to the climax. The stilted translations of Nostradamus are not only very common, but also hard to comprehend. I also translated some verses myself and disagreed with the other translations. The outline of this book uses these verses. I added the fictional story line and characters to make it interesting to read versus very dry.

I have built this fiction novel to make the story come home to people, to show the true horror of his predictions, and to serve as a warning to our society. There are many verses from Nostradamus included as openings into chapters or sections of chapters. There are a few places where there were so many verses telling the story that I just did not bother with putting fiction with it, but let Nostradamus do the telling of the story. When you reach those sections I do not believe that you will see any gap in the action.

An earlier outline for this novel started with a minor battle with Iraq to test our response and judge our weapons. This earlier outline of this novel was used as the basis for a US Army war game that was completed in June before the Iraqi invasion of Kuwait in August of the same year. The attendees of this war game were the generals that gained their fame from the Gulf War. The tactics used during the Gulf War were straight from this war game. Since that part of my novel became history, it was deleted from this novel. The reason that I wrote this novel is because no one in authority believed that this "Gulf War" was only a test. They were so busy patting themselves on the back that they never took the rest of my prediction seriously. There is research going on to develop some of the weapons I mention herein.

Throughout history the generals and politicians believe every battle is a war to end all wars. There is always another war. Hopefully, those that read this book in its entirety will influence the Congress and friends to take my warning seriously. The more people that are prepared, the less likely this story will become true history. If the United States was actually prepared to fight any major war, this big war might get put off indefinitely. Unfortunately, we are the weakest we have been since the Civil War armies went back to their homes.

When you see a Nostradamus verse it is numbered with century and verse within that century. V95 would be century Five and verse 95. Most verse interpretations are in my own words and are not intended to be a faithful translation, but rather convey what I believe is the true meaning of that verse. While I have not intentionally twisted my interpretations, you would be better off doing your own translations directly from the original Nostradamus. I cannot recommend a "scholarly" translation, because there have been a lot of misinterpretations. Some of mine may be wrong, but the overall story of WWIII is too real and logical for many verses to be wrongly interpreted.

1 HEMP DAY

Jim Claris woke in stifling silence. The fan had stopped and the lack of noise woke him. He looked at the hotel alarm radio and couldn't see it. He assumed that a pillow or something was blocking his view. Normally, after being asleep, the city lights coming in the window would allow him to see well, but it was so black he couldn't see the window. He reached up and snapped on the bedside lamp, but it didn't work. He realized that he must be having a dream about being awake when he wasn't, but decided be needed to go the bathroom. He staggered around the bed and walls until he found the commode in the dark. When he came out, he realized that he was, in fact, awake and it was dark. He went to the window and looked out. He could see the moon was lighting the city below, but not a single electric light showed. "Ah hah, a power failure. That's why I can't see the alarm radio, the light wouldn't work and the fan was stopped." He tried to call down to the desk, but the phone was also dead. He picked up his watch from the bed table and used his lighter to see the time. It said 2 AM. He went to the hall, but it was also dark. He came back and checked the wind up alarm clock. It said, 2:20 AM. "What the hell, either it's fast or my watch is slow." He didn't know what to think, but got dressed in the blue jeans, sports shirt and soft leather jacket he normally wore when flying the airlines, put on his shoes, heavy leather belt, and pulled his pocket knife out of his briefcase and slipped it into his pocket.

Jim then felt his way down the hall to the stairs, with occasional assistance from his cigarette lighter, to the lobby. It was also dark, but there were a number of hotel employees talking, "What the hell is going on, all the hotels are dark, all the cars stopped." As they talked and looked out the front windows, an airline size plane, with no lights, like a shadow passing before your eyes, proceeded to crash into buildings near the runway and explode.

Jim rushed out toward the street, and saw the traffic stopped and deserted, the street dark except for the fires of the burning airliner, and a few people at 2:30 AM milling around. He checked his watch again and it still said exactly 2:00 AM, it had stopped. Even though he was alone he talked out loud to himself, just to hear his own voice, "Oh shit! It's happened. No, that's stupid. The power is off, the airliner crashed because of the loss of TACAN and ILS (instrument landing system), the plane didn't lose power. My watch just needs a battery Just then he saw an older car coming out of the parking garage and come toward him with lights ablaze. It was Darcy and Shelby going home from work.

The car pulled up beside him and Darcy said, "Jim, what's going on? We were just closing the bar when the lights went off. We went down to get the car and found 20 other people not being able to start their cars. This old thing started just as it usually does, a little slow, but normal. We drive up here and there are no lights on the street, there are cars stopped everywhere and that huge fire across the street."

JIM SAID, "I KNOW WHAT IT COULD BE, BUT PROBABLY ISN'T, SO I WON'T SAY. HAVE YOU TRIED YOUR CAR RADIO?"

Shelby said, "No, but ... the light came on but I can't even get any static."

Jim lied, "Looks like a city wide power failure. Could you give me a ride around to the other side of the airport where Los Angeles Air Force Station is? They may have the answer."

Shelby said, "Sure, hop in. I know where it is. It's not far. Doesn't look like we'll be watching television tonight when we get home anyway."

Jim hopped in the back seat and Shelby slowly headed for the Air Force Station. She had to weave between stalled cars and trucks and the occasional pedestrian wandering around looking at the stalled cars. Jim wanted to make plans, but none had come to mind. It was fortunate that Darcy and Shelby had been leaving the hotel just as he walked out. He didn't know anyone else. He didn't know them except for his many visits to the bar where they worked. He did know quite a bit about them from their conversations in the bar over the last two years. He had stayed at this same hotel on each and every of his many trips to Los Angeles and they had been working in the bar every night that he had been there.

Jim had nearly gone to sleep in the back seat when they arrived at one of the gates at the Air Force Station. There were portable generators running already providing security lighting of the area and a number of military moving around with guns. Jim had Shelby pull up to the gate until the two guards leveled M-16's at them and by flashlight ordered them out of the car. Jim already had his Air Force Reserve identity card out and smoothly opened the door. He continued moving forward past the car holding his

ID card like a shield as the girls just sat there frozen in their seats. One guard moved forward and looked at the ID card and immediately softened when he saw what it was and the Lieutenant Colonel ranking saying, "I'm sorry sir, but no one told me about reservists being recalled. We just went to DEFCON two and were ordered to secure this gate. Have they called out the reserves?"

Jim said, "Beats me, all the power is off and there is no radio." The guard responded, "I know. I was listening to the radio when the power died. I switched the radio to battery, but it still didn't even hiss. I then tried my brick (the hand held walkie-talkie), but it was dead too. It wouldn't even hiss with the squelch control turned off." The only thing that is working is the command post communications on emergency generator. I heard they were trying to call everyone, but the phones are dead all over town. Do you know Lieutenant Colonel Painter? He just walked in 10 minutes ago. He said, 'Shit's hit the fan now.' Are you coming in...I can't let the car in."

Jim said, "No, I have got other places to go." The guard had not looked too closely or he would have seen the "ret" after the LTCol. which meant that Jim was a retired lieutenant colonel. The guard had seen the color, red, that signified reserves. Blue/gray shows active duty and green shows regular retired. Until the reserve reaches age 60, the card is red and benefits are limited. Jim walked back to the car, and Shelby nervously did a U-turn around the guard house to leave at Jim's direction. Both girls were too scared at the guards pointing guns just minutes earlier to say anything. Both were thinking, "Who the hell is this Jim guy, and how crazy are they for trusting him to drive him here, and what the hell is going on?"

As Shelby was pulling out onto the street she had to stop to miss a speeding old farm truck that turned left in toward the gate at high speed with no lights. The truck was going too fast, hit the divider with the left front wheel, putting it in the air just as the back duals hit the outside curb. It flipped over onto its top and then rolled another complete time and came to rest pushing the chain link fence to a sixty degree angle. The guards came rushing up; Jim told Shelby, "STOP!"; Jim jumped out and yelled "GO!". Shelby drove out into the street turning right instinctively away from the crash and then stopped in half a block, uncertain as to what to do. Darcy was yelling "stop" but her mind was yelling "go".

Jim ran toward the truck yelling "Terrorists". That brought the running guards down to a crouch as they ran and their guns up to the ready. Several terrorists had been thrown free that were riding in the back of the truck. One started to raise a gun only to receive a fuselage of .223 caliber shells from the now ready guards. A third guard called from the guard shack on a portable land telephone with wires, and more security were already cautiously leaving the building inside the gate and then running toward the gate when they saw that the gate guards apparently had the upper hand. Jim scooped up a fallen automatic pistol that was laying in the street within twenty feet after jumping out of Shelby's car. The gate guards now laid out in prone firing position as Jim ran forward yelling, "Cover me!" Out of the corner of his eye he saw the other security going toward the gate had also hit the ground when the gate guards did. Jim felt exposed running, but his momentum carried him up onto the truck before he stopped his forward progress. He was on the driver's door looking downward into the sideways compartment. He could see the driver trying to turn some knob on some device with lights and shot him and one of the others in the front seat that was trying to aim a gun at Jim. In his peripheral vision, Jim saw one of the people lying on the ground bringing a gun up and shot him also. He yelled, "Freeze!!" and no one else tried moving toward a gun.

By that time the security police had moved in also and started coming around the truck to take charge of the situation. A major in uniform pointed a gun at Jim and emphatically stated, "You, drop the gun and get down slowly."

Jim did as he was told, tossing the gun to the front of the truck away from everyone then crawling off the truck toward the Major saying, "Relax, Major, I'm one of you, Lieutenant Colonel Claris."

A gate guard spoke up, "That's right, Major. I've seen his identification and he reacted when we were taking cover."

The major re-holstered his gun, and said, "Let me see your ID. Okay, so what are you doing here?"

Jim said, "I came here to see if we were at war."

The major replied, "Maybe you better come with me." Sergeant, "Bring those girls into the security building and watch them. Leave their car parked in the entrance for now and bring up some security trucks to block both the in and out side of every gate on this place. I'll be back to check." To Jim he said, "Come with me." and started walking toward the buildings. Jim obediently followed telling the girls that he would be back shortly.

When they arrived at the command post, Jim immediately recognized John Saxmore. John recognized him also and said, "Jim isn't it? What are you doing here?"

Jim said, "I still work for the Air Force. I was here working with Northrop teaching them how to use computer programs developed by our office to speed up their work on converting the B-2 technology to commercial applications. When the lights went off, I thought there might have been a HEMP event and came here to confirm it before I panicked, with good cause. I just happened to be leaving the gate after being turned away by your security guards when this truck tried charging the gate a little too fast and flipped almost right beside the car I was in. As the truck flipped, I saw people in the back of this open farm truck with guns and knew what it was. I reacted without thinking, figuring the only chance was to strike while they were recovering from the crash. I'm lucky our guys didn't shoot me, rushing in wearing civilian clothes like I did."

The phone rang, and John Saxmore was called to the telephone and stayed on the phone for several minutes repeatedly stating, "Are you sure, check it out, call in some experts" When he hung up the telephone he gave a shiver and tried to decide whether to have Jim locked up or just tell him all and let him go. John used to work for the Headquarters Air Force Material Command in Dayton, Ohio as a civilian and knew Jim had been to Los Angeles Air Force Station a number of times over a 10 year period. He hadn't been around for 5 years, but when Jim did visit back then he usually worked on their most secret stuff making a point to learn as little classified as possible while assisting their managers in managing projects. He had worked on several Star Wars or Space Defense Initiative (SDI) programs and had accompanied various generals to lecture the colonels and high ranking civilians on management techniques. He decided suspicion was stupid and returned to Jim to tell him what he knew. He wasn't going to arrest Jim at any rate; Jim may have just saved a lot of lives; and Jim was probably going to deduce much of it anyway. He motioned to Jim to follow him and went into one of the small glass offices in the command post.

As soon as the door was closed, John said, "Jim. I should not be telling you all of this, but I decided that you ought to know anyway. An Iraqi satellite with a Chinese made nuclear power plant launched by a Japanese rocket, just blew up over Northeastern California creating a major HEMP event."

Jim interjected, "I was afraid that was what had happened. Do you know how much damage there was."

John continued, "Not only that, but different satellites did the same thing over Hawaii, Alaska, Colorado, Kansas, Texas, Ohio, and Eastern New York. Others went off over Australia and Europe. Not all the satellites were from Iraq and not all were launched by the Japanese, but it was apparently a deliberate HEMP attack against the western world. Ordinary communications are out over most of the world. The phone call I just got was my first official communication outside of this command post. We were tracking the Iraqi satellite on a special, this is top secret by the way, video that gave us an image of the satellite blowing up just before the video automatically shut down to protect itself from "over exposure"."

Jim said, "What about that terrorist attack? Has a warning gone out to other bases to block their gates?"

"There are several military bases out of contact. Of those, contact had been established, but lost within 5 minutes of reporting a disturbance at their gates. Apparently, your unthinking charge saved this base. As soon as I got the official Air Force call, the security chief broke in to say the truck had what appears to be a Soviet Spetnaz backpack nuclear weapon that had a bullet in it that destroyed the timer or it would have gone off. That must have been your bullet."

JIM SAID, "YOU ARE KIDDING, AREN'T YOU?"

"We don't know what the device is for sure, but it is a backpack with very sophisticated electronics hooked to some very heavy stainless steel tanks. I got a briefing on them two years ago as part of the Soviet Détente team briefings where the Soviets were bragging about what they would have done to us if peace had not broken out. These backpack nuclear weapons have about a one kiloton explosive force. They won't blow up a city, but two million pounds of TNT would make a very big hole where an air base used to be and these things leave behind fallout also. You would not repair a runway when the whole base becomes a 200 foot deep radioactive hole in the ground. Thanks. Scared shitless, huh. Bet you won't go charging in again. You couldn't have gotten away either. Are you looking for a job here during the war."

Jim replied, "I'm glad I did stop it, but that was pure luck. I was operating on instinct. I should have been shot. The bomb should have gone off anyway. No, I'm not looking for a job. I've got a family back in Ohio and I'm going to try to get there somehow, some way."

"Well, I'll tell you what. We owe you more than just a debt of gratitude. I can't promise you any airplanes are going to be carrying any passengers that way. I can't give you a government vehicle, but I can let you take that car you came in and whatever is left of the terrorist stuff they brought in, as long as you leave us some for evidence. I wouldn't go if I were you. We don't know that this isn't the start of an all out nuclear war. On second thought, maybe you better get out of LA sooner than later."

Jim replied, "It's not my car and I think every car made after 1975 has fried electronic ignitions. It may be easier said then done to get out of here and home, but I'll get there. I have to try anyway."

John reached into his pocket, then handed Jim a set of keys and said, "What the hell. I'm probably not going to leaving this hole for months anyway. Take my MG. It doesn't have any transistors except in the radio. At least maybe you can save it by getting it out of town. You know LA is a prime target and the crazies will start looting as soon as they find out. The food supply off base will only last a day or two without transportation."

Jim said, "Hey, thanks. I really appreciate this. I'll repay you someday." With that he left the command post and went up to retrieve the girls and the MG. He took them aside and told them that he was going to take the MG, whatever guns he could carry, and take off for Ohio. The girls ask him what was going on and he gave them a brief explanation. The explanation did not make much sense to the girls, but they realized that LA would be a prime target in a nuclear war.

Darcy said, "Let me go with you. There is no future staying here and getting killed. Hollywood won't even exist anymore. We can take my Mercury. It's in good shape and can haul more than an MG."

Shelby piped in, "Me too. The three musketeers, one for all and all for one. I was getting a little tired of the rejection and obscene proposals of the movie crowd anyway. We won't all fit in an MG, and maybe this friend of yours will want it back before you can give it back."

Jim couldn't argue much with getting the girls out of here also, and he knew he could use someone else to drive. It might be much longer than the twenty five hundred to three thousand mile drive that it was in ordinary times. Darcy's old Mercury was in good shape. California people seemed to find better mechanics to work on all the old cars. He returned the MG keys. He then went through the collection of terrorist weapons from the truck crash, they were still scattered on the ground. He chose a 12 gauge riot pump gun, three Beretta fifteen shot nine millimeter automatic pistols - one for each of them, an M-16 because of its familiarity from Viet Nam times when he shot expert in the air force required training, two LAR's expendable bazooka type weapons, a half dozen grenades, a 44 Weatherby with night scope/ telescopic sight, and two Uzi's that also used the nine millimeter ammunition of the Berettas. The security police gave him boxes of extra shells for everything but the LARs then gathered up the rest of the terrorist weapons and took them into the main building.

The security guys, to show their appreciation for saving the base, also loaded him up with cases of cokes, M.R.E.s (meals ready to eat the modern equivalent of W.W.II K-rations), some clothing from the small base exchange for Jim because he had decided to forget going back to the hotel, some sunglasses, and even a couple of uniforms donated out of an airman's closet. The girls were determined to gather things from their apartment and didn't really appreciate the admiration of the enlisted security people that were assisting Jim. All of these went into the Mercury and they were off. Security vehicles wouldn't start either except for a couple of older diesel trucks that they had used to push other vehicles around the gates and fences, circling the wagon's, or so to speak.

John Saxmore came out of he building, handed an envelop to Jim, and said, "Thought this might help. Gods Speed." and started to return to the building.

"Wait, John. Here are your MG keys back. The two girls here are coming with me, so we'll take their car. I really appreciate your offering." John nodded, turned, and left.

When Jim opened the envelop he found a letter signed by the Los Angeles Air Force Base commander, a two star general, that said that Jim had his authority to carry any kind of weapon and commandeer any equipment needed for his journey to Ohio. It said he was doing a ground survey of local conditions across the country and that he was to report in to Wright-Patterson Air Force Base after his arrival in Dayton, Ohio.

Jim thought things internationally and nationally must look pretty bad for the general to give him this letter. Jim had unintentionally saved the base from a nuclear devastation. Jim didn't know what to think, but climbed into the driver's seat of Shelby's car and, with the girls, drove out to go to their apartment. The car looked loaded already, but Jim figured he could re-pack or even throw things out while the girl's packed belongings at their apartment. He had warned them to take only clothing and important person items.

It was already 5:00 AM and Jim suspected that as people woke up, there would be panic and riots followed by food riots as the city's trucked in food supply could not be trucked in. It would be a day or two before the supplies ran out. However, cash registers, bank card machines, even the banks would have an immediate problem that started when the lights went out. It would not be long before the riot prone areas would discover that there would not be any police cars or fire trucks. The question was whether these areas were so uncivilized as to immediately start looting or whether they would try to help their fellow man.

GRAND FORKS AIR FORCE BASE, NORTH DAKOTA

Colonel Henry Lakeman was sound asleep and Major Jeremy Houston was in the Visiting Officers Quarters or VOQ or "Q" for short. At 0300 hours his red telephone beside the bed rang. "Hello, Colonel Lakeman."

"Sir, Captain Lawrence, a DEFCON II Alert has just been called, you better come out. This is not a drill."

"SHIT! God!...I'll be right there, send my driver."

"Sorry Sir. Our vehicles are all dead. Every last one. Must have been sabotage and this is the big one."

Karen, Henry Lakeman's wife was awake now and tried flipping on the light. Henry could hear the clicking of the switch and could see from moonlight coming in the window. She knew better than to say anything at the moment.

"Captain, tell me that the electricity is out all over the base and downtown."

"Sir, it is out all over the base except where we had emergency generators here for the command post and out in some munitions areas. I don't know about downtown, but the telephones to town are down. I called for a full security alert from everyone on base and I sent someone through base quarters to knock on doors to tell them about the alert, but I don't know what to do about downtown."

"Take it easy son, I'll be driving down in my old Mustang. Find some people with older cars made before 1975 and send them downtown with lists of names and addresses, then transport them the same way out to the base. Call the munitions squadron and see if their old diesel dump trucks will start and use some of them for buses. Get as many airplanes manned and loaded on full alert with what we have before we send too many people downtown. Have admin. troops do the taxi work. As you contact people, ask them if they have any bicycles and bring or ride them, tell them to take their kids' bikes. Just relax and I'll be right there."

Colonel Lakeman was now out of bed and moving fast to get his uniform on. Karen asked, "Henry, is this just another alert...they never cut off the electricity before?"

"Karen...this is not just another alert. Now just stay calm and let me finish...NO! be quiet! I do not think this is the big war, but I do think that a nuclear detonation has knocked out the electricity and telephones. Yes, and don't expect them to work for days. Now just plan on keeping the kids here, your car won't work either. I'm taking the old Mustang. I'll check back with you as soon as I can. Take an inventory of all the food in the house, matches, everything that we can use without electricity and make sure it works before you include it. I've got to go. Bye, remember I love you and I don't think we're in any real danger." With that Henry went out fired off his pristine drag strip ready fully restored 1965 Shelby Mustang and with a lot of tire smoke and squealing headed for the command post. The car earned him a lot of respect from the enlisted troops and junior officers even if he didn't work on it himself and seldom drove it. It was a great ice breaker in conversations.

Jeremy was asleep in the VOQ room with his windows open when he heard a car roaring by at a very high speed and then tires squealing as it turned somewhere nearby. Jeremy opened his eyes and looked out onto the moonlit sky, expecting to hear a security police siren at chase. He heard nothing except the racing car moving further away and still squealing around corners...then silence. He was awake, so he got up, went the bathroom in the dark and then went to the open window. He saw darkness. There was not an electric light in sight. He looked back to the bedside alarm radio and saw that its dial was black in the shadow of the corner of the room. He tried the room light switch, knowing that it would not work. It didn't. He had not been a sound sleeper since his last divorce, so he got dressed and went down to the lobby. The airman on duty was checking a fuse panel with a flashlight. "No electricity? Phones work?"

The airman replied, "Morning sir, the television and lights both went out so I must have blown a circuit breaker. I assume the phones work...or have you tried already?"

"No, I haven't tried....Nope, they don't work. Is there a bus this time of night? Well, I'm going for a walk. You might as well give up and just sit here in the dark 'til the lights come on or someone comes to get you."

Jeremy stepped out into the cold North Dakota summer night air wishing he had worn a warm coat and stepped out toward the command post. He could see that even the search light that always circled above the base was out. 'That and the telephones...I'll bet that was Henry's car going to the command post to find out about the power failure. No security cops because last nights discussion came true..."SHIT and HOT DAMN. We'za goin' ta war!" With that thought Jeremy broke into a jog toward the command post. Major Jeremy Houston had known "Hank" when they were both junior captains. They had flown "buffs" or B-52 bombers together years ago. Hank had been selected for a ground job in a weapons systems program office where they were modernizing the old B-52 with new electronics. It was supposed to be for his experience, but he was never given a job where a pilot's experience had anything to do with his job. He found someone that he felt could run things for him that had more experience and gathered in some old friends and new acquaintances to help him, and then applied and was accepted to a long term graduate program. Naturally, whenever Hank needed advice in school, he had a list of friends to help him impress the teacher. When he graduated, the people he had left in his office had continued to follow his general orders of fifteen months early and had perfected things beyond Hank's dreams. While Jeremy was still flying buffs, Hank had become a wing commander. Jeremy was on Hank's base because he had volunteered to come visit with Hank by agreeing to pick up some emergency spare parts while he was here. Jeremy was in good shape and it did not take him long to get to the command post. He recognized Hank's car outside and went in the building to the door of the command post and knocked.

"Colonel Lakeman, we have an alarm at the door. There is a someone in a flight suit that claims he is Major Jeremy Houston, but we have no one on our ASCAS security roster for the base."

"Let him in. I'll vouch for him. He's an old friend here on TDY (temporary duty)."

"Well Jeremy. It's started."

"What's started?"

"An Arab satellite just went nuclear and HEMP'd our electronics. In fact make that five, just over the United States. There were three more over Europe. Almost everything is dead. We're on DEFCON II. We're recalling people by using bicycles and old cars without electronic ignitions. The news is pretty slow coming in. Telephones and electricity are out across the whole country. All radio and television stations are off the air so we can't even broadcast a recall or alert the civilian population. Most of our telephone systems are out except for those that interconnect here at the secure telephone system in the SCIF (Specially Compartmented Information Facility). I can't reach anyone that I know the number to, but Karen at my house. The on base phones are out except for the HEMP phones connected to our red switch here." Author's Note: A red switch would be a secure/scrambled military telephone system, possibly designed to protect from HEMP. A red telephone is a secure/scrambled telephone, but not necessarily red in color.

"Colonel, there is a call for you."

Henry went to the command post telephone linked directly to the airborne command post and heard a whispery wavering voice coming faintly through the UHF radio signal and scramblers, "Standby for an update. All bases being linked in broadcast mode." That meant that the airborne command post was going to broadcast a message, but that no one could answer back once they were affirmed as being on line. "Broadcast begins. The United States and Europe have been simultaneously HEMP'd by Arab satellites in low earth orbit. Most electronically or computer controlled systems have been burned out in the Free World. The Arab ambassadors and consulates to the United States are claiming that it was not their fault and that it was faulty engineering that caused the problem. Our satellites have been disabled, but recon flights over Northern Italy have confirmed Arab troop movements confronting Italian troops along the Yugoslav border. As of this time we are considering this an act of war by unknown Arab countries. Request that all strategic bomber bases launch one of each three operational aircraft in the shortest route to Bagdad. This is not, repeat NOT, the target area, only a navigation point. Airborne aircraft will be given final orders not later than 2300 ZULU, repeat ZULU. If confirmation not received by that time aircraft are to return to their original bases or the nearest base if the original base not achievable. All aircraft are to be airborne not later than 1700 ZULU. Refueling points will be confirmed prior to takeoff. Confirmation of this message is HOTEL, INDIA, TANGO, OSCAR, OSCAR, ROMEO, BRAVO, ROMEO."

That's it! How many planes have we generated so far, fifteen? Are there any problems with the others? How about air crews? Okay, we'll assume all aircraft and air crews will be available by 1700 ZULU. Twenty-eight aircraft... bring in ten air crews for briefing in the planning room, NOW! Use the land line to tell a munitions crew to break loose one of their dump trucks to haul all ten crews standing in the back...NOW! MOVE IT!"

Jeremy had never seen Hank like this and didn't know he had it in him. Hank was just a nice guy that politically moved up the ladder...maybe the real Henry had just been hiding during the nearly twenty years Jeremy had known him. Jeremy followed into the planning room unbidden and watched as Hank called in the meteorologists, flight planners, maps of the new unplanned routes, etc. Henry may not know how himself, but he sure as heck knows who does know. By the time the air crews were crowded into the room, a make shift briefing had been prepared showing the details of the general route to the Middle East, their expected fuel consumption, planned refueling points, etc. Now this, Hank was an expert at. He was a very good B-52 pilot once, and didn't forget, even though he didn't fly any more. Jeremy was not run out, but neither did he butt in or get introduced, he just sat back in the corner and watched Henry work miracles. Hank had learned to do with people what he had done as a buff pilot. He was literally flying the people and they were anxious to do his bidding. Maybe, Jeremy thought, I should take a lesson in being laid back and political. For all his bravado, Jeremy might be the best B-52 pilot, but he could only fly one plane, Hank was ready to fly all twenty-eight of his simultaneously, though vicariously. Maybe that attitude was what made Karen stay with Hank these many years while Jeremy could not keep a wife due to his job. Yes, Karen was important too. Jeremy had not said anything to Hank, but he knew for a fact that Hank had been selected as a very young brigadier general...it just had not been announced yet, and it wasn't like Hank to brag or toot his own horn. That's why Hank was selected to be the Wing Commander here...he already had general in the bag...it WAS a general billet (in other words, the wing commander was supposed to be at least a brigadier general).

The duty officer came in to interrupt the final parts of the briefing, "Colonel, sorry to interrupt, but the avionics squadron just called in to say that eleven of the twenty-eight aircraft have lost critical parts of their avionics suites. They are trying to change them out with equipment sealed in storage. Estimated time to have them back on line is 1800 hours."

For the first time Henry acknowledged Jeremy's presence with a wince and a glance. "Tell avionics to work faster, I need those aircraft at 1100 hours for a war mission, 1800 hours is several hours too late." (ZULU time is the 24 hour clock time of Greenwich, England time or 5 hours later than Central Daylight Time in North Dakota. The 1800 hours is 6 PM on a 24 hour clock.)

"We will send a minimum of seven aircraft on this mission. You will have a full load of everything. You know your refueling points. Now stay close to your aircraft, and I want engines running at 1130 hours local and lined up ready for takeoff using normal intervals...none of that MITO stuff." (MITO=Minimum Interval Take Off and can be very dangerous due to the later aircraft hitting the jet wash of the early aircraft.)"

As everyone saluted and left, Henry turned to Jeremy and said, "Don't even think about going back to your home base, you told me you don't even have a steady (girlfriend) right now. I wouldn't risk you in that aeroclub plane, and I could use an up-to-date B-52 pilot for advice, if not by filling in on one of my crews. Any heartburn?"

Jeremy said, "For a few days anyway. I kind of like knowing what's going on. Usually I'm one of the guys sitting out in some airplane being ordered around with no explanations. Can you clear me of any AWOL charges?"(Away With Out Leave which is punishable by court martial).

"Soon as I can talk with your commander. In the meantime, I'll log you in here every day. My number two was in New York City at a meeting and probably won't be returning. I need someone to fill in for me. You are now my Exec and will speak for me when I'm not here."

2 ASSESSMENT

VIII,70

An ugly, wicked and infamous villain will come to power, and tyrannize all of Mesopotamia, He will make friends by seducing them, and the land will be made horribly black.

In the air over the Middle East.

Prince Facil Saud, the Crown Prince of Saudi Arabia, was flying to Teheran, Iran for a meeting of the Moslem International League and Consortium, MILC. Saudi Arabia was not a signatory of the Consortium because Saudi Arabia had been independent for a long time and saw no reason to change. The Saud family had originally been the Saudi nomadic tribe. Today, there were around five thousand members of that tribe and they were the rulers of Saudi Arabia. Saudi Arabia was not part of the Persian Empire nor the Ottoman Empire, but had remained independent. They were getting a lot of pressure to abdicate their power to the Consortium and agree to adopt the rules, taxes, and orders of one Jabal Iscarnon, the "President of Iran". There was no way under Allah that Saudi Arabia would fall under Iranian rule. The trade was being allowed to maintain the Saudi family riches. The threat was to lose it all. Facil had friends in the United States and if Iran tried to force the issue with military, he felt that he could call on the United States just as his father had when Hussein invaded Kuwait.

Facil agreed with most of the principles: educated people, modernization, industrialization, but with ultimate subjugation to religion. The only thing he couldn't take was a religious leader in another country giving orders to the King. Facil actually ran the country now. His father was quite old and had turned over everything but the crown to his oldest son. If something were to happen to Facil, the power would transfer to one of his many uncles or cousins. They were benevolent rulers, but absolute just the same. They would, to a man, not relinquish the throne to anyone outside their family. The family had a few problems. One King had gotten a bit greedy until replaced, bloodlessly, by his brother. Another heir, like himself, had been replaced by a cousin, when the true heir was found to be mentally deficient. But never was there a question as to which tribe ruled. The country even had the name Saud in its own name. If not ruled by the Saud tribe how could it be Saudi Arabia.

His plane was beyond luxury; a Boeing 747 outfitted as a palace. It was designed for the comfort of one passenger, and included a harem, luxurious couches, a communication center operated by remote control, a hot tub, and a water bed. Prince Facil Saud was slender and just a hair under six feet. His face was hawkish unlike many other Arabs with more round faces. He was very good-natured and well versed in western ways. He could fit into western society with no problem or even an accent. However, he looked Saud with darker skin and prominent bones. He could not be mistaken for American Indian, Spanish, or Negro. He looked like an Arab.

Facil looked over the attendance list with amazement. Never had so many Muslim leaders been together at one meeting. If someone wanted to destroy Islam, it could bomb Teheran and take care of all the leaders. Some of the ones he knew personally were kings, like he would be soon, and others were dictators that might as well be called kings. The countries were, Saudi Arabia, Iran, Iraq, Jordan, Egypt, Algeria, Libya, Morocco, Sudan, Syria, Afghanistan, Chad, Pakistan, and surprisingly Turkey. Other leaders that he knew nothing about or why they were represented were from countries that had broken off from the Soviet Union. He had not wanted to go, but MILC, as it was called in the West, was getting very strong and might actually start to control the price of oil. It had been very clear that an emissary would not be allowed to attend. He was attending because it was well known that his father, the actual king, was in ill health and not running the country anyway.

Facil was still not married and needed to get married soon or lose his right to the crown. He determined to pick a bride before he returned from this trip so his father could bless his choice to satisfy the Saud family. Without a wife, one of his uncles or cousins that was married would gain the crown on his father's death. Until then he could enjoy his favorite portion of his personal harem on board the aircraft. There was Joy, from Baltimore, Suzane from Sweden, Carey from France, Kareen from his own country, and Carey from Malaysia. Each had been carefully screened and was well paid for their time. It was too bad he could not pick one from the harem to be his wife. His wife had to be of royal Muslim blood. It looked like it might be Bridget, a princess from Jordan. Once he married, he could no longer associate with his harem; it was against Saudi law. Anyone aspiring to be king had be monogamous. Before landing Facil moved into the cockpit with the pilots to do the landing himself. After the aircraft was parked, he stayed with the pilots to give them special instructions. Facil saw his own personal limo that had flown ahead being driven to the aircraft and members of his body guard get out before he gave the okay to kill the aircraft engines. He told them to not worry about refueling and post a guard to prevent tampering with the aircraft. The pilots should stay in the aircraft at all times. If Facil called on the secure radio from his car, they were to be ready to start engines for an immediate take off. He felt very uncomfortable about this meeting. He also told the pilots to have ten of his F-15 fighters stand alert in case they needed to escort his plane back to Saudi Arabia. He had told his AWACS to be aloft during the entire trip to assure that his 747 was not interfered with in the air. At the first hint of trouble, Facil would run for his bullet and land mine proof limo, call the 747 on secure unjammable radio and have them tell his F-15's to launch toward Teheran for escort home.

Facil had an uneventful ride to a veritable palace that had been built in the city. He was graciously escorted from his car inside with his body guards close at hand. They entered the grand hall and met with other leaders of the Moslem world. The snacks were first rate and served by beautiful young Arab women in revealing harem costumes. Facil noted that his country was Saudi Arabia, no other country had the term ARAB as part of its name, and yet the people were called Arabs. Moslem was a bigger term and included many African blacks as well. Many Arab families had Arab blood diluted with African black blood to the point that many Arabs looked more black than Arab. The Iranians were more of a European race and yet Moslem. The Saud family was an exception, and these girls were mostly Arabs also. There were also a number of black Muslims, not be confused with the American term, "Black Muslim". The gathering was all small talk waiting for the meeting until they were led to a sweeping staircase at the back.

At the bottom of the stairs was a vault door fully two feet thick. Other country leaders were also being escorted that way. They entered a long hall covered with marble floors and walls with many hanging oil paintings of ancient Muslim beginnings. The vault door was closed. They took turns going into an elevator. There were two elevators and one ruler and his body guards took turns until the last were safely transported. When Facil had taken his turn he discovered that it was a long downward ride that came out into an ante-chamber where they were expected to leave their body guards in a balcony of sorts that had glass windows looking down onto a very expensive conference room with a large circular table and plush chairs. There were too many armed guards for them to fight if they had to. Other rulers already had their personal body guards in the balcony, and were seated at the table. Facil quietly nodded his okay and entered the conference room ahead, while his guards moved into the balcony. The guards would have full view of anything and would be prepared to fight if they saw a signal from their masters. None of the guards had been searched and everything had been entirely cordial to this point.

After all the rulers were seated, Iranian President Jabal Iscarnon entered the room within seconds and humbly introduced himself and wished blessings on all the rulers along with apologies for the humble meeting place. Jabal explained that the table was circular to prevent any Muslim from getting the honored head of the table. All would be equal at this meeting. The table was well stocked with refreshment and all were assured their body guards were equally cared for. Facil glanced and saw that his guards were in fact snacking behind him on the other side of the glass. There were no women, as befitted a Moslem rulers' meeting.

The room slowly darkened and holographic images appeared above the hole in the middle of the circular table. It was almost impossible to tell that another ruler was only inches away, let alone see any faces. The "briefing" occupied the room. There were miraculous views of the earth taken from space and equally realistic subterranean cutaways of the earth to show the deposits of natural resources. There were LANDSAT photos of water and plant life with explanations provided by an obviously professional speaker. There were computer graphic images of stockpiles of food around the world and charts to show the future projections of all. It showed that the Moslem Combine had at least a seven year supply of canned food and fresh grain bought by its members using oil money and playing the commodities game with crop and meat prices. No pork bellies of course since they were Muslim. The briefing was very captivating and overwhelming with some humor to keep it light. Gradually the briefing turned toward the military might of the world. Facil heard some murmurs and shifting on the soft leather chairs around him, but because of the darkness could not see any faces. The briefer's tone changed to something more challenging and serious, but no one around the table said anything intelligible until the briefer pronounced, "Even as I speak, the Soviet Union's equipment is being commandeered by faithful Soviet Muslims for the Moslem cause. At the same time, Oriental troops are doing the same to support Red China who has kept the Communist faith."

It was King Ordman of Morocco that broke first, "Wait a minute here. Turn on the lights now! I demand to be heard on this."

King Hussein of Jordan also spoke out, "I also demand to be heard. Stop the briefing and turn on the lights."

Before others could speak out, the briefing abruptly stopped and the lights slowly brightened. As the lights came up, Facil looked behind him toward his guards and found nothing but a blank steel wall. He stood up and demanded, "I demand to be told what is going on at this very minute. Where are our body guards? I am leaving, NOW!"

Jabal Iscarnon was heard from one end of the room, not at the table. A room behind obviously thick bullet proof glass showed he and several of the other leaders had quietly left during the darkness of the briefing and moved to this other room. Their chairs at the table were even missing, Facil noted. He also noted that apparently their entire chair had gone down to be replaced with a trap door while the ring leaders moved to their separate room.

Jabal ordered, "Sit Back Down. I am in absolute control here. Your bodyguards are about five hundred feet above you watching what they think is the same as you were watching. They are watching a tourist film of the middle eastern countries. The conference room is actually a large elevator that descended during the briefing. You have two choices, join our cause now and follow orders. After the war you can return to your country's leadership and receive a share of the benefits of the Alliance. Your other alternative is that you lose your life now and I take over leadership of your country."

Facil realized at least some of the spot he was in, but had to ask a question, "I am not saying that I will not join whatever this Alliance is because you have not told me yet, but I have a rhetorical question to ask, 'If you kidnap me, what makes you think my father will not order our military to war with you? Or what prevents Prince Jezmine from taking over Jordan when his father is kidnapped?"

Jabal responded, "Please be seated and I will show you what has happened to put me in power. Remember while you watch this that I will usurp power from those loyal to the Alliance."

What followed was video tape of recent events in each country, that proved Jabal's point. Saudi Arabia was what Facil was most interested in. Shortly after Facil's plane took off from Saudi Arabia, the loyal palace guards were over-whelmed by other palace guards thought to be friends. Jabal's minions had been working for years for this day. The key Saudi people were convinced through bribes, brainwashed, educated, or blackmailed into cooperation to overthrow the Saud family and the military forces capable of overcoming the coup d'ta. Fighter aircraft were down for maintenance, tanks were out of gas. Each member of the Saud family, wherever they were in the world were either held prisoners in their own houses, kidnapped like Facil, and a few killed. The Saud family was at the physical mercy of Jabal. Since the Moslem countries were led by a king or dictator, the control of the leader meant control of the country. Even Egypt's President was elected essentially for life. The room was dark during the holovision broadcast with the volume too loud for the leaders to be heard. The Arab leaders conceded to watch.

At the end of the broadcast, there was a continuation of the original briefing that explained an Alliance between the Far East and the Moslem leaders to take over the world. China and Japan would rule India, Russia, and the Pacific ocean. The Muslims would rule Europe and all the southern provinces of the Soviet Union that were of Muslim origin. In addition, India would be partitioned and the Moslems given the eastern half of the country while China would have the West. The America's were to be disabled based upon a long ago plan that Japan had after World War II. The American economy was based on the transistor. The American's had invented it themselves, but it was Japan that made them so cheap that America ran on transistor technology that was highly vulnerable to HEMP or High Altitude Electro-Magnetic Pulse. When Iran had supposedly launched a series of communications satellites from Red China they had actually launched space based nuclear bombs that would detonate on command causing HEMP events throughout North America and Europe. Japan would have their revenge upon America after the Eurasian Continent was conquered. Australia and New Zealand were considered little more than Islands. The first stage was already past when the Arab countries had supposedly brought peace to Yugoslavia. In fact, Yugoslavia was over-whelmed by superior numbers of everything. The attack against Europe was to proceed from Yugoslavia into Italy. Simultaneously, China would strike at Siberia.

A series of slides were presented that showed the new balance of power after Soviet defectors took or disable Soviet equipment for the new Alliance and after the HEMP bombs were activated in space.

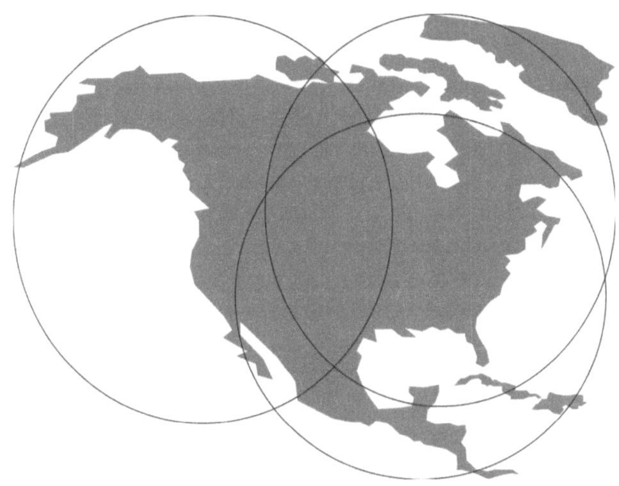

HEMP - High altitude Electro Magnetic Pulse. When a nuclear bomb explodes near the ground the effect is limited to a few miles outside the blast effects. However, at the upper part of the stratosphere it creates an unusual event where electrons in the thin air are knocked loose from the air molecules which because of the low density are going at the speed of light striking other molecules which knocks loose electrons in an ever increasing electronic storm that by the time it reaches the earth has created a major pulse of electricity. The abundance of free electrons is why they call it the Ionosphere Power lines collect these free electrons sending a major surge down the line wiping out transformers and anything else in the path. A transistor device designed for 3 volts has no chance when hit with a 100,000 volt surge. Car electronics are effected due to the miles of wire in a modern automobile. It is like getting hit by a spark from a spark plug wire. The human gets a jolt, but a transistor would be destroyed. Actually the spark plug wire would deliver far more amperage than static electricity. It is more like the shock you get from walking on carpet. A person not holding onto a length of wire is normally insulated and would only feel extra static electricity in the air, if they even felt that much. In 1969, the U.S. had nuclear tipped anti-ballistic missiles or ABMs. In testing, they discovered that the HEMP from the ABM's warhead in space might do more damage by destroying their electronics than letting a few missiles hit. Shortly thereafter, they signed the Salt One Treaty to limit ABMs because of the HEMP effect. Three ABM missiles with nuclear warheads, creating unintentional HEMP events, would wipe out all electronics in the U.S.

The Iraqi's had purchased numerous weapons from the crumbling Soviet Union. They alone had fifty nuclear attack submarines with which they hoped to find the American submarines and sink them. All of their original submarines had been equipped with the new silent anti-cavitation propeller stolen from the United States by Toshiba of Japan in the mid 1980's. These came equipped only with conventional torpedoes and anti-ship missiles. They had also managed to acquire a Soviet nuclear ballistic missile submarine complete with nuclear missiles and the permissive action link (PAL) codes to detonate them. The PAL device was invented by the Americans to make sure their own missiles could not be fired without permission and the Americans had provided the same to the Russians to prevent unauthorized use of theirs. The Iranians had also purchased one hundred diesel submarines from the Soviet Union and China. These only had conventional torpedoes and a limited number of anti-ship missiles.

The most telling slide was the one that summarized the new balance of power after defections from the Soviet military and with the mobilization of the reserves.

Equip	USA	EEC	USSR	CHINA
				ARABS
TANKS	4000	1000	2000	89000
ARMOR OTHER	6000	4000	4000	84000
INFANTRY (Thousands)	700	300	2500	350000
FIGHTER A/C State of the Art	700	500	1500	6500
- 2ND CLASS Fighter Aircraft	0	0	0	5500
BOMBER A/C	100	0	100	700
TRANSPORT Air Long Range	75	10	200	450
TRANSPORT Air Short Range	250	150	350	1297

AWACS Radar Aircraft	30	10	30	20
JSTARS Aircraft	4	0	0	0
TRANSPORT Commercial Air	100	0	120	400
OIL TANKERS	40	20	2	210
PASSENGER SHIPS	20	50	3	50
STRATEGIC MISSILES	100	0	100	230
THEATER MISSILES	100	100	400	1600

The professional briefer said, "As you can plainly see. The Soviet Union cannot defend themselves against the Chinese with a 19 times force advantage. Europe, even if they had one hundred percent of all remaining US Forces, would be behind by a 6.5 times to one advantage on our side. In reality, the US Forces will be negated and the advantage to us over Europe is actually also approximately 19 times to one. Any general knows he can win with a four to one advantage. Alexander said 4 times the enemy forces was sufficient to win a battle.

Of primary concern is that nuclear forces from the Allies will be ninety percent eliminated if they try to use them. Red China and Japan have spent years secretly launching anti-ballistics missile space based systems disguised as peaceful communications or research satellites. In the Soviet Union, many nuclear weapons lie within Moslem country borders and are hence under our control even if we cannot defeat their fail safe systems, but we can prevent their launch, Yet more were sabotaged by our Soviet Muslim and Oriental friends living within the Soviet Union. One must remember that nearly sixty percent of their military have never been European Russians. The United States being such an open country has been infiltrated for many years so that few of their bombers or missiles will ever get airborne. We have Arab and Chinese troops undercover near every major launching point for aircraft or missiles. What they miss during the launchings will be taken care of by the space based systems.

American will come to a total stand still for years after the HEMP. We also have a few other tricks up our sleeves also to keep them at home. After we conquer Europe, we may entertain taking over the Americas as well.

We have a duty to reform the West to Moslem ways. There are many Muslims already living there already that are trained and in place to do our bidding. After Europe is conquered we can teach them the ways of Mohammed and cure their corrupt societies. America is the most corrupt of all, but until we pacify Europe, we cannot consider the actual conquering of the Americas. The Americas are protected by too much ocean to be able to transport an overwhelming force that far. Once Europe is ours, we can safely invade the Americas without an enemy behind our backs. France and Great Britain have the most to pay for, since they tried to colonize us not so long ago. We fought what they call, "The Crusades". They undermined the Ottoman Empire. They broke up a great Islamic empire. We have fought among ourselves while being kept down by the Great Satan, the United States. But it was not the United States that broke us up. It was Europe and Europe we shall have. Once we have broken their will to fight, the common European will be most happy to accept Islam as their religion and Mohammed as their prophet.

We have some entirely new weapons that have been kept my secret until now. Naturally our Iraqi friends have been in charge of developing the nerve gas and the biological weapons. Much of it was stock piled prior to the battle with the Americans over Kuwait, but never used. The American news media even took pictures of the "Milk Factory" where they bred the biological weapons...who ever heard of a "Milk Factory", but it was shown around the world as anti-American propaganda by their own cable news network (CNN), by the way, a number of their overseas reporters have been on our payroll since before CNN hired them. When we sent troops into Yugoslavia to free the Bosnian people, the world heralded us as saviors, thanks to CNN. Pictures were staged of concentration camps held by all the sides and of Arabs bringing relief from war. When we were asked to intervene in the Greek civil war our Turkish friends were more than happy to oblige and that was the end of a centuries old war between Turkey and Greece. Now the tourists actually feel safe as they wander around Athens and lie on the beaches. The Turkish troops are seen as a respite from car bombings and terrorist attacks. Naturally, we were behind the terrorism, not the Greeks, but who's to know. It destroyed the already shaky Greek government. Of course, we have small contingents of Syrians, Jordanians, Egyptians and others in Turkey and ostensibly running the show, but most of the troops are Turkish, fate accompli.

Even now the stupid Italian Red Guard is playing into our hands as they follow our orders on terrorism in Italy. The tourist trade in Venice,

Florence, and other northern cities in Italy is almost at zero. Even as I speak our troops are moving to the Italian border under the guise of preventing the terrorism from spreading into Yugoslavia. Tomorrow we will be prepared to end the charade. Instead of ostensibly following the orders of the United Nations, our troops will remove their United Nations uniforms and change to our new United Moslem uniform and the Jihad will start. Then the world will take us seriously, but it will be too late.

Even the United States back in 1990 stated that Iraq alone had the fourth largest army in the world. Now add in Iran, Egypt, and the rest of the Moslem world. At the same time as we attack Europe, China will attack India and the Soviet Union simultaneously.

For many years we have educated our brightest people in the United States and Europe and they were not majoring in primary school education. They were studying engineering, mathematics, electronics and other fields to help in our war. It was hard to believe that no one ever figured out just what they were studying. They simply couldn't believe that we were any threat. We will show the world just what threat is. We should be able to conquer Europe in a few months. It will take another three years to pacify the local populations and then we will take on the Americas.

Are you worried about nuclear retaliation from the Americans? Don't be. Remember their so called "Star Wars"? I said their bombers and missiles will never get off the ground. We have purchased houses and farms near their bases within range of surface to air missiles and high powered rifles. Our people are just waiting for the signals to get ready. Not all of the people are Arabs, of course. Some are European Muslims, some are Indians from India, some are Blacks that have been converted to Moslems. They think that we will put them in charge of the United States when we're done; wrongly of course. They are still Americans. They put too much value on life. We know that the lives of commoners are too cheap to worry with. That is why there are rich and poor. The poor are camel dung to be used as we see fit. If any nuclear missiles get through, we will be safe in our underground cities that we have been building for the last twenty years. The west may have built some of our command bunkers, but did they think we could not have done that ourselves. That was just more show for them to think we were incapable. Actually, the Egyptians are quite good engineers and builders. They built the pyramids after all.

The only ones above ground will be our troops mixed in with the Westerners. Do you think the Americans will bomb Paris or Bonn or London? Of course not. All of our young men will be scattered throughout

Europe. Do you think they can bomb the world? Besides, our people will have the latest in biological, chemical, and nuclear protective gear. We have developed special bubbles for our troop encampments. There are special filters that will clean the air and fill the bubbles with clean air under positive pressure to keep things out. All of our tanks and armored vehicles will have filters installed within a few hours. All of our people were inoculated against our biological agents within the last year, even your people, Prince Facil Saud. All Muslims deserve to live. Besides in a few days you will order your people to join us in the last Holy Jihad to conquer the world. Don't speak. Remember, we have the entire Saud family under our protection. If you join us, they will be safe and you will be King. If you do not agree to join us, I'm sure we will find one of your family that will.

Prince Facil Saud would not have volunteered to join this madness, and he did believe it was true madness, but as the crown prince of Saudi Arabia, he was not too dumb to know when he was beaten. Facil replied, "You have my word, I will join you. We will conquer!"

King Hussein, not to be outdone and standing, "The prophecy has come to pass, Mohammed has returned, long live Jabal Iscarnon."

Others were standing and proclaiming their loyalty as Jabal Iscarnon raised his hands for silence. "Thank you, oh honored ones. Yes...we will conquer. Yes, we are united, but no I am not Mohammed returned, but as of today, I am leader of the Moslem faith. I speak for Mohammed. I will teach the ways of Mohammed to the world. The world will have the laws of Islam. We will have the life that Mohammed envisioned for us. No longer will we be the down trodden of the world. No longer will the West steal our resources and give us empty promises. No longer will we be encouraged to fight each other to keep us down. The Holy world started as the Arab world and will end as the Holy Arab world. The known world will be Arab property as it started. The oldest words we have started here and the words will end here. We will bring a thousand years of peace. This is not my bidding, this is the Will of Allah."

"Naturally, we, the leaders of the world will remain here, together, in brotherhood. We will use our own underground communications to order our countries and our holy troops."

Prince Facil Saud's hope of escape to Saudi Arabia was dashed. The only way that Facil, the Saud family and his beloved Arabia would come through this is with one hundred percent cooperation with this madman. Somehow, he would come through this and maybe free his country. To save his country many of his countrymen would die in a senseless and worthless war. No matter how good things looked on paper, the Europeans had more experience in war...and the Americans. They may appear soft. They may appear weak kneed, but once Americans got something in their head, they would succeed. Americans were brought up to think they could do anything any time they decided they really wanted to. These madmen did not understand how Westerners owned things and were willing to fight for what they owned. The typical Arab never owned much and therefore had little to lose. Poor people did not fight as hard when sent away from their homes at a rich rulers orders as rich people did defending their homes and way of life. Facil had spent enough time in the West to understand Western ways and Western thinking. His dream was for Saudi Arabia to become another America where his people all could be free and educated, where his people would be proud to be Arabs. Not through military might, but accomplishment and beauty. He had built up his forces to protect his country from the Iraqi's and now they and their old enemies the Iranians had his country. He would get it back someday if he could survive.

3 NUKES IN THE UNITED STATES

"Incoming message, sir..... 'Nuclear detonations, repeat, nuclear detonations have been detected in New York City, Boston, Philadelphia, Washington DC, Norfolk, Miami, Cleveland, Cincinnati, Memphis, Atlanta, Mobile, Houston, Dallas, Chicago, Denver, Salt Lake City, San Diego, and Seattle. Reports were received and confirmed that a Backpack Nuke was intercepted at Los Angeles Air Force Base, but communications were lost during the confirmation message. Recon flights show that much of Los Angeles is burning so there may have been other Nukes delivered. There were no radar intercepts of any missiles inbound before the detonations. Anyone trying to force any entry to any military facility is to be treated as highly dangerous and search for any evidence of Backpack Nuclear Weapons. If a 1 foot by 3 foot by 2 foot package is found with blinking LED lights, you must assume it is nuclear. The information on arming and disarming these Soviet devices is thought to be on CIA computers, but is not yet available. The number of casualties is unknown. Recon planes from Edward's Air Force Base have confirmed that San Diego harbor is destroyed with high radiation in the area. Los Angeles is burning over much of the city, but no bomb site or high radiation was detectable from altitude. Recon flights over New York City show that apparently what was not destroyed immediately may have been sunk into the ocean due to large quakes of 7.5 within minutes of the nuclear detonation detection. Manhattan Island can be considered gone. There were no detected detonations in the Far East, Middle East, or Europe. There were similar detonations in Moscow and several other cities. These detonations in the Russian heartland were not confirmed as we have no satellite transmissions coming in and cannot send a recon plane without provoking retaliation. Apparently the Russians are doing nothing aggressive at this point, but intelligence shows movement toward several nuclear missile launch sites."

The Colonel left the message verification to the Emergency Action or "E" "A" duty officers. "Damn, Damn, Damn, Damn, Damn, Damn, I've had Jim Claris's letter for three months now. I even remember him bouncing this idea off me back in about 1980...I didn't believe his unbelievable story... called it future history or something. Now it's too damn late. I threw his letter out two months ago. I told you all I remember. When he got into describing the battles, I quit reading...figuring he was too far out there."

Jeremy said, "My count is 29 million living in those cities give or take a couple of million. Don't know how many will glow with the fall out. How good are these detonation reports?"

"Damn good reports, Jeremy. I didn't notice a detonation report on Los Angeles, only the report of a back pack Nuke and a bunch of fires. L.A. riots revisited? No fire department, no police...the Watts neighborhood still boiling over since the early sixties. Might not have been one. I remember hearing that a backpack Nuke is only worth about five kilotons versus the twenty kiloton bombs we dropped on Japan. One fourth as big is one sixteenth the damage, but look at New York City...did they hit the World Trade Center parking garage again I wonder?

They got miscellaneous intelligence and mission message throughout the rest of the day, but none with that kind of impact. At 1645 ZULU the message came in to launch the third of the operational B-52's along with confirmation that targeting information would be sent directly to the aircraft somewhere over the ocean. The aircraft were to fly a northern route over Canada, but then stay over the Atlantic for the remainder of the flight, using Gibraltar to stay over ocean. The messages were correctly authenticated and the aircraft were launched on schedule.

As the first aircraft took off it was about one half mile off the end of the runway when it exploded in flight. The second and third aircraft were already either in the air or committed to takeoff before the fourth flight could be prevented from take off, but the second and third aircraft also exploded. Several people saw the vapor trail of ground launched anti-aircraft missiles before the B-52's exploded. At the same time rockets began impacting in the alert pad where the regular alert aircraft were and more rockets impacting in the build-up area causing secondary explosions that enveloped other aircraft, ground vehicles and people until there were only four aircraft undamaged. The base had lost twenty-four of its twenty-eight bombers and one hundred percent of its tanker aircraft. Actually only sixty percent were destroyed, the others could be repaired if they could get the electronics going again.

It took Henry four hours to get a message through to headquarters on the disaster. By that time other messages had come in confirming that all of the bomber bases were hit. Only ten bombers from the entire United States had successfully made take-offs, and of those, three aborted due to maintenance problems, one disappeared somewhere over the ocean. The remaining six bombers were recalled due to Moslem fighter cover over the Straits of Gibraltar.

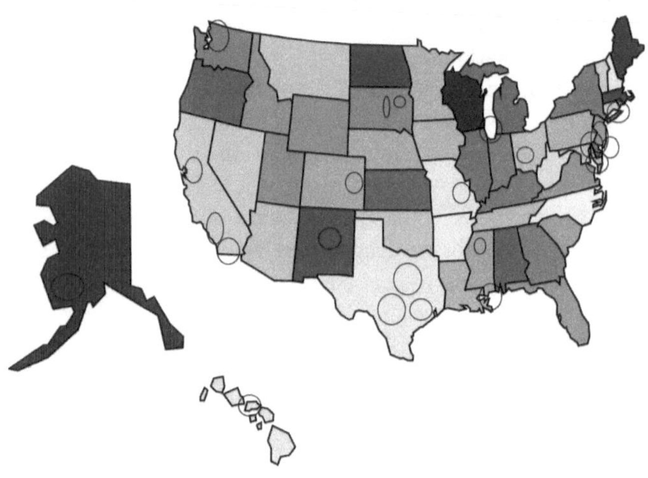

The circles represent nuclear bombs that went off in the United States. Most were backpack size nuclear weapons. These were dirty, exploding on the ground, but the damage was limited due to their size. The fallout was somewhat limited not only due to size but containment by the city itself. The missile launched bombs exploded thousands of feet above their targets creating more damage on the ground, but with very minimal fallout. The U.S. and the U.S.S.R. both have such bombs that are 99.9% fallout free.

IN THE BUNKER, TEHERAN, IRAN

Prince Facil Saud and the other rulers of the Moslem world were all housed in huge suites built underground and opening off their meeting room. Each suite included items literally taken from their home countries to make them feel at home. Prince Facil walked into his suite to find his girls from the airplane waiting for him. They were terrified from their experience while Facil was at the meeting. Most of the girls were not Muslim and Facil was a little surprised that they had brought them here.

"How did you get here?, he asked.

It took awhile before his harem accepted their relative safety with him and told him their story. The Boeing 747 was sitting on the ramp waiting for a fuel truck. The girls were watching a videotape and relaxing when they heard gunfire near the main cabin door. The pilots had rushed out of their cabin and down the stairs to main deck with guns drawn, but they were shot down by automatic weapons fire. Some Iranians in some strange uniform with an insignia that said United Moslem Forces came rushing up the stairs and the girls were told to come with them. They were herded down the stairs to a Mercedes limousine and locked in. Other Iranians were coming out of the airplane with Facil's belongings and throwing them into a truck. The limousine then pulled out and raced through the city. They were brought down in a small elevator into this place. Shortly thereafter, Facil's personal belongings were brought in and arranged. No one had mistreated them, but neither did they say what was happening. Facil recognized the fact that Jabal had killed his only military support in this country. His bodyguards that had come in with him were also probably killed. The girls were saved to make him feel comfortable and try to win him over.

Just after the girls finished their story, servants came in with a feast befitting a king. There was no wine, only fruit juices. Facil had wine in the West, but would not consider it in an Arab country, unless in trusted company. It was against Moslem beliefs to drink intoxicating beverages. It was one of the things most Arabs did not understand about the Westerners. Westerners could have wine with a meal or even stronger drinks socially and most still not be going against their religion. They could still be good people and drink. Most seldom got drunk. There were some Christians that believed against drink just like the Muslims did and were just as faithful to that belief. The Arabs did not understand because there were basically only Shiite and Sunny (pronounced suu nee) Moslems and they sometimes fought about the difference. Arabs could not understand that the Westerns were composed of Catholic and Protestant and within the Protestant there were Episcopalians, Methodists, Lutherans, Baptist (1st and Southern), Church of Christ, 1st Christian, and many many others. The Westerners had learned to live with their differences whereas the Arabs had not. He could never accept the Christian religion, but he understood them far better than most Arabs and he also believed they had their rights as Moslems had theirs. Matter of fact, how come this Iranian can be so friendly with the Chinese. At least Christians, Jews, and Moslems all started with the same Bible at one time. They had far more in common with them than any Oriental religion, especially the Japanese and Chinese. This Iranian could claim to be religious, but like so many others, he was power mad.

He understood also that many Arabs had been badly treated in the West when they went to college. Their fathers had sent them to learn the West, but they never tried. They were spoiled rich Arabs that expected to be worshipped for their wealth and could not understand how that attitude just made them outcasts in college. Facil had gotten his degree in the West and gone into United States Air Force pilot training school as a foreign student and done very badly. He was like some of the other Arabs. He made himself an outcast. He had washed back when he met Jim Claris. He realized this was the second time he had thought of Jim today. It must be because of the same high stress he had now and back then, so many years ago.

Jim had spent many hours talking with Facil around the table when the other students at their table were flying. Gradually, Facil had come to understand more about Americans and why they were the way they are. Facil had also learned English better and became more comfortable talking with other Americans. As a result he started progressing in pilot training at a rate faster than many of the Americans. He had soloed in jets at his first opportunity and even tried to drink an "after-burner", a drink made with one hundred fifty-one proof rum. The bartender sets it on fire and then you drink it. Facil had not paid good attention when the others had done it ahead of him and he tried to drink it slowly. He had a burned face and mouth and everyone had laughed at him...no with him. They explained that the secret was to throw it into your mouth dowsing the flame. Raw courage in drinking it brought less pain than his timid approach. In fact he threw another down and everyone in the club cheered, accepting his new courage.

In fact he started getting along so well that he had drifted away from Jim, becoming more one of the guys than Jim was. Jim was the thinking type. He could handle a plane as good or better than any of them, but he didn't like flying. Their mutual instructor was also the quiet thinking type and it was really a surprise when their instructor was awarded the Americans' highest honor...the Medal of Honor, for service in Viet Nam. Their instructor had never talked about it and wouldn't afterward...except to say that it wasn't his best action that he got the award for. It really made you wonder what he had done that was more courageous after reading the story in the newspaper about his medal winning actions.

Their instructor thought Jim was so good that he put him up for the final check ride in pilot training after only two hundred hours instead of the standard two hundred and thirty hours of flying. Unfortunately, the check pilot had been a bomber pilot instead of a Wild Weasel fighter pilot like Jim's instructor. Jim had scared the pants off of him. Facil had been Jim's wing man that day on the check ride. He had led the way and then Jim had to prove he could rejoin in formation after a separation. Jim had flown the craziest he had ever seen. Instead of a twenty degree cut off angle and twenty knots of extra airspeed, Jim had used ninety degrees of cutoff and one hundred or more knots of airspeed. He would have been scared if he had not known who was flying the other airplane. At the last minute Jim had cut the power and thrown the T-38 trainer into a ninety degree bank and nailed it. In other words from what appeared to be a side collision at high speed, Jim was calmly flying at about two feet of wing tip clearance. In wartime, Jim could have flown the pants off anyone. Allah, but was that beautiful. His rejoin had taken less than two minutes instead of the ten minutes normally required. It would make a difference in a war. Same thing with the trailing rejoin, Jim used about three hundred knots of overtake and rejoined in thirty seconds instead of ten minutes. Of course Jim had come in low and then climbed up with zero power and his speed brake out to keep from over shooting. The check pilot had, to use an American expression, shit a brick. When they got on the ground, the check pilot had gone into the building leaving Jim to put write up the flight log and not saying a word. When Jim came in he found that he had busted the check ride big time. That poor bomber pilot was scared shitless for the whole flight and afraid to say a word. Facil had marveled at the flying, but technically, Jim had broken all the rules. Facil just wished he would have a wing man like that if he ever went flying in a war. None of his Arab pilots were that hot. Facil always did think that Jim purposely blew it in the way he did to prove he was hot and still flunk out so he would not go to Viet Nam. Jim was the type that would not hesitate to kill to protect a friend or defend his country, but he was also the type to not want to bomb villages and possibly kill innocent people, like so many that had been killed in Viet Nam. He already knew that the United States was not out to win the war. He had frequently remarked that he wanted to bomb Haipong Harbor and Hanoi, but the American's weren't doing it. In looking back, he knew that Jim had deliberately scared that check pilot. He wouldn't have been able to scare our quiet instructor...he probably would simply have been told to save it for the war.

LOS ANGELES, CALIFORNIA

Jim turned onto the 405 freeway headed north away from this area of town. As he headed north he could see looters or at least a mob coming toward the Hawthorn shopping mall. It was after 7 AM and people would realize that there was no electricity, telephones, or policemen...at least not in their cars. Those inclined to loot were free to go about looting with relative impunity. As they drove north away from Hawthorn they saw more and more looters smashing store windows. In fact the hotels that they had been at earlier were scenes of mob violence. Jim did not slow, he sped up, especially when it looked as though some may have been pointing guns at them.

As they went past downtown it was full of people, but they couldn't tell what they were doing. By the time they got to the Olympic Avenue exit where the girls said to turn, they could see fires spreading across the valley behind them. Jim turned west toward the ocean.

It didn't take too long to realize that Olympic Avenue in Santa Monica was not a good place to exit the freeway. They immediately were swept up by a mob of people looting stores. Probably what kept them from becoming victims was the age and worn appearance of the old Mercury. They drove forward until the road was blocked by burning cars and took a side road. After a very short discussion on the increasing number of fires they had seen, the girls told Jim to just get back to the interstate if he could. There was nothing at their apartments to risk their lives for. A block off the main road there was an army/navy surplus store that was being looted. Jim gave each girl a gun and told them not to show the guns until they were really in danger and then shoot to kill. Jim jumped out and ran into the store, coming out a short time after with a small seven foot round mountain tent, and a gasoline Coleman © lantern and a couple of army blankets, some eating utensils, hunting knives, etc. Most of the looters were getting guns and ammunition, so Jim helped himself to more of the Meals Ready to Eat and emergency energy bars. He dropped them off at the car, saw the girls still had no one bothering them, so went back into the store for more supplies. Jim managed to pick up 8 boxes of 12 gauge No. two shot, 5 boxes of 5 each double ought-00 12 gauge buckshot. The 00 was like shooting 10 shots of 38 caliber ammo with one shot of a shotgun. The Number Two was like sixteen 22 caliber shots at one time. At close range, you didn't have to aim to cut someone in two. At longer range each shot was still enough to knock someone down wounded seriously. However a shotgun or pistol is worthless at anything over 75 yards unless it is at least a 357 magnum or larger. It was starting to get unruly with people fighting over shortages of guns very quickly. Jim immediately headed for the door. Just as he came outside, the guy in front of him that had been carrying four or five shotguns and rifles tripped and fell with everyone scooping up his spoils before he could recover. This started a scuffle. Jim grabbed a Winchester 1100 12 gauge automatic that slid his way and quickly moved away from the crowd. When he got to the car the girls were more than ready to leave.

As they rounded the corner to go back south to get on Interstate 10, their way was blocked by a burning building collapsing into the street. Jim quickly backed into the street, the way west was blocked with people that were getting increasingly unruly at the surplus shop. The way east was blocked by another crowd so Jim headed north away from highway 10 and toward a more residential area. It didn't take long to reach Santa Monica Boulevard, but a shopping center to the north presented more looters with an invitation to riot.

Shelby said, "turn left, we can circle toward the coast then over to Interstate 10 heading east and avoid all of these shopping centers, maybe we can even go by our apartment since we seem to be caught here anyway."

They headed west until they saw another gaggle of people blocking the main road then turned left again. Jim was not sure of the street, but Shelby picked one heading west that was residential with few stops, which Jim only slowed for, making about forty-five miles per hour most of the time.

Shelby, said, "Slow down to turn left in two blocks." Jim did as ordered as Shelby led them the back ways to their apartment. Darcy and Shelby immediately jumped out and headed toward their apartment. Jim was unwilling to leave the car, and spent some time hooking military ammo clips for the Berettas on military webbed belts. He made sure all the guns were loaded with full clips. He was just finishing his check when he heard a scream, and saw Darcy running down the stairs and Shelby fighting off a big dark skinned man that had a gun in one hand. She was not winning. Jim grabbed the Weatherby with scope out of the back seat, took aim and deliberate missed the man. The man was looking for the shot when Jim yelled, "Just let her go, NOW!". The man started to bring up the gun and pull Shelby in front of him. Jim could see more men behind them coming through an upstairs outdoor hallway also carrying something. Hesitation over, Jim shot the man in the head. Seventy five yards with that gun made a head a big target. Shelby fell away from him, quickly regained her footing and half ran half fell down the stairs. Darcy had hit the courtyard and was running toward the car by the time Shelby made it to the courtyard. Jim had moved near the open driver's door with the Weatherby propped on the roof aimed at the first man emerging from the hallway. The Weatherby spoke again, dropping another from a chest wound, and again until the girls were in the car, the men had retreated and Jim figured the gun was empty. He threw it in the back window, hit the car seat, the key, the gas pedal and an instant later the gear shift jerking the car and smoking the tires as his door closed. The other men were armed, but they were almost around the corner of the building before the first return fire hit the pavement behind them. Jim kept it on the floor until they were doing over 90 and were two blocks away, he slowed to turn left, then right, then left again, with the idea of losing any pursuit. Darcy gave him the shortest directions to get to the interstate by-passing as many commercial places as possible.

It was not until they were near the interstate that they ran into more trouble. Some people saw them coming and tried to block their way by rolling cars in front of them. By hand since they were newer. They weren't quick enough to close the gap and the cars were not heavy enough. The Mercury, (Merc) for short, caught one of them by a piece of its bumper against the big heavy bumper of the Merc and sent the Nissan flipping away to the right. The Mazda on the right scraped the side paint of the Merc and skewed sideways down the street rolling about five miles per hour from the near impact. Jim was about to relax, when he saw about twenty big motorcycles go through the same way after them. Jim hoped that they were not following the Merc. He was wrong. Jim imagined that he had just passed through an impromptu toll booth. Jim had no aspirations on outrunning the cycles, but wanted to keep a good ramming speed, if need be. He accelerated full throttle up the on ramp of Interstate I-10 Eastbound.

"Darcy..., get a shotgun out of the back seat, get at least twenty shells laying on the seat. Shelby, get in the back on my side and put a pistol beside you where you can get it if there is a problem with the shotgun. Shelby, get an M-16, yes that's one. Now reach in that backpack and get at least four clips out on the seat by your pistol. Good, now Darcy, you can't fire until they are within two car lengths, and then fire the shot gun until they drop back. Shelby, pull your head in." Jim then pointed a Beretta back at them and held the trigger down spraying shells over the top of the car backwards in their general direction. He saw one biker lose it and take out three other bikes with him. Two accelerated in their direction, and the rest caught up.

Jim yelled, "Get ready to fire. It's their lives or yours." Jim put a fresh clip off his webbed belt across his chest into the Beretta. As the bikers pulled up near them, some fired a pistol at the Merc. Darcy fired two shots from the 12 gauge and took out three bikers with three more dropping back rapidly, two more flipped their bikes over the three that fell in their path. On the driver's side Shelby opened up with the M-16 hitting nothing as the gun muzzle climbed up above them.

Jim yelled, "short bursts. Reload." Two bikes were pulling up beside them and two were right on the Merc's bumper. Jim yelled, "Hang on to something." He hit the brakes. Two bikers hit the bumper losing control of their bikes as they came over the handlebars. The three bikers beside the Merc on the left shot ahead, not expecting the braking. The tail of a fourth bike on the right was next to Jim's right fender. Jim swerved into him knocking his back wheel out from under him and then Jim had to swerve to miss the rider and the sliding Harley Davidson. Jim now was the hunter. They quickly recognized that Jim was accelerating for them with his pistol out the side window and out accelerated him, taking the next exit off of Interstate 10. The bikers decided that it might be wise to hassle someone else. That loaded Mercury turned out to be a porcupine with deadly barbs.

When they slowed down and began to look around without further pursuit, they could see that much of their area was on fire. Hollywood looked to be the center of a firestorm. Many of the older buildings had wooden structures and once fires got out of hand with no fire departments, it was a goner. There were also huge pillars of smoke to the West and South. When they approach the intersection with Interstate 405 again, they could see a huge panoramic view of Los Angeles burning. There were huge fiery tornadoes sweeping across the city. Hollywood was burning, but not like that. Darcy emphatically said we have to take the north route toward Bakersfield. We can't drive through that."

Shelby interrupted, "She's right and don't spare the horsepower, we have to get out of here now."

Jim was not familiar with that route. He had always driven into Los Angeles from San Bernadino, but they were the experts and he could see that north and west were their best bets. They had just come from the west and didn't find it too friendly, so north it was. They were heading north instead of east, but east looked very dangerous. Jim didn't tell the girls why, but he had driven the old Mercury awhile now and figured it was in really good shape mechanically and kicked up the speed to over a hundred. When the girls asked, he said he just wanted to get out of town before the riots and fires caught them and there were no cops around anyway. They accepted his answer until they realized that the smoke ahead was closing in on the Interstate, the trees and houses in the Santa Monica mountains were burning and the fires were converging on the highway.

Darcy was in wonder at what had happened in a few short hours. Why were they here in their car driving through riots and fires escaping into the country. Jim was just an honest Midwesterner that was very married and comfortable to be around. He had not propositioned either of them even though they had tried to get him to, just as a bet between themselves. He was not unattractive, but neither Darcy nor Shelby were lonely enough to want to actually take him to bed. They got a kick out of teasing him and knew he enjoyed the game too. He watched them working or wrote in his notebooks. Both knew that he thought they were a little too young, which made the game fun when he came to town. This was the fifth week out of the last two months. He gave them a safe haven and refuge from other customers that liked to pinch bottoms and make cash offers, thinking the girls were put there for that purpose, not just to serve drinks. It was sometimes demeaning work in the bar, but it paid well and Marriott customers also tipped well. LA was the only place for their dream of stardom to come to pass and the job was the means to survive without losing their self respect. Hanging around Jim between drink orders and deliveries made the other customers think they were taken for the evening and at least partially kept the wolves away. Jim was not the kind of man either she or Shelby had ever talked about dying with. Jim was physically very average. Five foot ten, one hundred ninety pounds. He was definitely not a body builder, and had a spare tire, but not pudgy and gave the impression of being very capable of holding his own and not being a pushover to anyone, although if had been an athlete it was a long time ago. He had prematurely graying hair, probably from some of the job frustrations and traveling. Now here they were about to die with this man driving their car into the middle of a forest fire.

Much to their surprise, they made it through a wall of fire that had whipped across the freeway as the firestorm met, feeling a little scorched, but with no damage done. The heat waves kept the smoke rising so Jim could see the road and no one had to inhale much. Jim took highway 14 that split out to the right with the idea of staying out of town and taking the shortest route to Interstate 40 that would lead them east across the desert.

It was 10:00 AM when they came into Palmdale. They were out of Los Angeles, and out of gasoline. The people there were out in the streets, but without any looting going on. There was a roadblock set up and some civilians with guns at it.

"WHERE ARE YOU GOING AND WHERE DID YOU COME FROM?"

Jim answered, "We're going home to Ohio and we came from Los Angeles. Is there anywhere I can get gas?"

"The civilians were not unfriendly, but protectively asked, "Who are the two girls, they are not dressed like tourists...waitresses maybe, but not tourists. Are you girls traveling with him from choice?"

"Yes."

Jim volunteered, "I have known them for some time and we all knew we would be better off away from Los Angeles right now."

"AND WHY IS THAT?"

"The city is burning from riots and no fire or police departments to stop them. Darcy is from near my home town and Shelby's home is on the way. There are no airplanes or buses, so we took Darcy's car here."

"DO YOU KNOW WHY THERE IS NO ELECTRICITY OR TELEPHONES AND WHY MOST OF OUR CARS DON'T WORK?"

Jim evasively replied, "There was a huge power surge near Los Angeles that knocked out all the power, telephones, and new cars with transistor ignitions. It will take a while to fix it, so we decided that we had better start driving. We really just need to get some gasoline and start driving. I'll pay double per gallon and siphon it out of a stalled car if you'll let me."

One of the road blockers spoke up and said, "Ah hell, Mecelroy, they can get gas out of my truck down there for all I care. You know the gas station needs electricity to pump gas. Let them go on their way, we're just wasting their time here."

The man directed Jim down an off ramp to his stalled pickup with a large farmer's type of gas barrel in the back with a pump on it. He said, "Hell, if I'd a knowed that this new truck was going do this due to some power surge I'd kept the old 72 Chevy. Here I can pump all you want since this piece of new trash ain't going nowhere soon. Reckon if you got some money I'd better sell you some of these spare gas cans." He had four gas cans rattling around in the back. Jim took them, full of gas, and paid the man double for them. He wouldn't take a good profit on the gas, but just estimated how many gallons he had pumped with the hand pump and rounded off to the nearest dime on the original purchase price. Jim offered to buy the hand pump and man originally said, "NO" until Jim offered him one hundred dollars cash. The man gave him twenty in change and said he could buy a new one for forty. "I sure do apologize for my neighbors up there on the interstate. We's not unfriendly here, just scared. This morning before the sun came up we could see the glow of the fires, and now you can see smoke. Must be one hell of a fire."

Jim offered some advice for the man's friendliness, "I can't explain and don't even know how bad things are, but I am afraid this is only the start. It may be months before things get back to normal. I think we may even have started World War III. It could be years. That truck of yours still has an old Chevy three fifty engine. Go to a parts place or junk yard, buy an old distributor and intake manifold and carburetor to get it back in business. You may never be able to drive it otherwise. Tell your neighbors, farm and emergency equipment first. Don't worry about it if it's imported, it was probably not designed for an old style ignition and carburetor. You may have to eat your own crops for some time to come."

The farmer only half way believed Jim, but thanked him for the advice and sent him back on to highway 14 with a wave to the road blockers that it was okay. Jim was glad that he had three hundred in cash from his trip and another three hundred in fifties hidden away in his billfold. He was now down to four fifty with three thousand miles ahead of him and he suspected no one was taking credit cards.

Jim had slowed down after leaving Los Angeles to save the car, tires, and gasoline. The old Mercury had decided it liked the highway that it may never have seen much of in its life and kept trying to creep up to ninety, but Jim slowed back down to sixty-five when he saw it getting up. By now he had briefed the girls on everything he thought had occurred and what was maybe still occurring. The trip to Rosamond was uneventful and Jim reflected upon his overall assessment of the world situation.

Some country or countries, probably middle eastern, and maybe with Chinese help had set off several nuclear bombs disguised as low earth orbit communications satellites over most of the free world causing a massive nearly world-wide HEMP event that knocked out every transistor device in the free world not protected from HEMP. Even most of the military equipment would be dead. Trucks, cars, television sets and camera's, radios, telephones, and electrical power relays would all be dead. A few old rotary dial telephones probably still worked if their switch boards were the old analog type, tube type or manual.

Even many of the factories that produced these items were computer controlled. Banks and other places dependent upon computers would be dead. Many factories that had HEMP protection during the cold war had allowed their protection to lapse with the advent of distributed processing and local area networks. He knew that most of the equipment in his own office would be dead. They should have had the data in protected lead lined underground vaults, but the equipment with all of its phone lines coming in would be dead anyway. A nuclear bomb going off above the earth, above the stratosphere, was the worst kind. A low earth orbit would be somewhere between 150 and 300 miles with somewhere around 200 miles being ideal. For some reason this causes something like a lightening bolt to surge through the air in all directions for hundreds of miles. This is the kind of electricity you would get from a Van de Graph generator. Lots of voltage but very little amperage. It is like the mechanic that can get shocked with 30,000 volts from a car ignition system and emit swear words, while an electrician gets killed dead by 120 volts of house wiring. It's a question of electrical path through the body and the amperage. Anyway, transistors like around 5 volts or less with very low amperage. Now throw about 50,000 or more volts everywhere not electrically shielded and you get zero electricity. Jim wondered why automobiles weren't protected for 50,000 volts figuring some mechanic or owner would accidentally short out a spark plug wire in the wrong place. Was the HEMP in excess of the 50,000 volts predicted? There was one chapter that Jim remembered very well from taking Air War College (AWC) as part of his reserve training, called the Chaos Factor ©. It mentioned some early nuclear antiballistic missile (ABM) testing in the Pacific that caused non-transistor traffic lights and burglar alarms to go off all over Hawaii, 800 miles from the test. The anti-missile's warhead was not at optimum altitude and that was before the widespread use of transistors. It was very effective in shooting down enemy ICBM's, intercontinental Ballistic Missiles, but the HEMP might do more damage than a few war heads hitting their targets. Did the Japanese sell us all this cheap transistor stuff to stop our efforts on ABM? Jim saw nothing that showed Japanese involvement in any plot.

Up ahead Jim could see a military roadblock on the highway about where Rosamond should be. He figured that it was from the military on Edwards Air Force Base and he would have nothing to fear. He had the girls put the surplus blankets over the weapons on the back seat and put his Beretta under the front edge of his seat. He pulled up to a slow stop at the guard out in front of the armored personnel carriers (APCs). The guard asked him where he was going and where was he coming from.

Jim replied, "Los Angeles and home to Ohio."

The guard asked him for some identification and when they left Los Angeles. Jim presented his reserve US Air Force Lieutenant Colonel ID card, which he already had out and replied that they had left during the morning.

The guard said, "Excuse me sir, would you wait here. I have to talk with my supervisor." The guard got on a vehicle radio that had survived the HEMP and talked briefly with someone. He then talked to the guard that walked back to Jim's window. Sir, would you mind following that APC that is pulling out. He is going to lead you onto Edward's air force base where someone wants to speak with you."

Jim complied. He would have volunteered, but this didn't look like a volunteer situation. There was no threat, just an implied order that as a good ex-military man, he followed without question. The girls were not so sure. Darcy spoke out, "Why are they taking us onto the base? Are we under arrest? Aren't they going to find the guns?"

Jim said, "Relax, I'm sure we don't have to worry. They probably will not search the car until we are ready to leave and they are probably taking us onto the base to ask about what's going on in Los Angeles."

Fortunately, Jim was correct. They were looking for some reliable source of information on Los Angeles. They had communication with the command post there, but it was buttoned up with fires raging through the base above ground. Norton Air Force Base or the Navy at Long Beach were never available by radio. The secure digital telephone links had been pretty much wiped out. It was secure, but mostly not HEMP proof. Jim told them everything that they had experienced during the past few hours; showed the commander his letter from Los Angeles authorizing the weapons in his vehicle, before they were found anyway; and asked for a place to sleep, two rooms. The commander also decided to trust Jim with the information that most of their satellites had been knocked out with HEMP, but most of their military planes were still flyable. Unfortunately, the commercial style planes such as the KC-10 tankers, the DC-10 and 747 cargo planes, and their VIP planes were knocked out due to fried electronics and most importantly their computer controlled fuel control systems were knocked out. All of their standard vehicles were non-functional, but their diesel Humvee's and APC's worked just fine. Edwards was more HEMP conscious than most of the bases due to their testing for same, and consequently still had most on base communications intact with considerable world contact. Unfortunately, all civilian telephone trunk lines were out because of the computer controlled switching and relay systems with no word on the repair time since AT&T trucks were also knocked out.

The commander had not flown any recon (reconnaissance) missions over Los Angeles due to the smoke and unknown radiation that might be there. Since it was only fires, he would fly over when the fires died to see what was left and send a relief mission to the military bases in the Los Angeles pocket as soon as a ground recon was safe. He had flown an SR-71, yes he did have a few, to the east and north. San Francisco looked as bad as Los Angeles. Sacramento and McClellan Air Force Base looked okay from the air, but there was no ground traffic to speak of and no radio communications. War had not been declared on anyone, because they didn't know who the enemy was for sure.

By UHF radio they had reports from many military bases. Since Jim was heading east, he should stay away from Saint Louis. It was nuked, but there was no missile or bomber that ever appeared on radar at Cheyenne Mountain in Colorado. He didn't know which ones may have been looted and burned or actually nuked, but fires were raging in these cities, and handed Jim a computer print out. New York City, Washington DC, Boston, Chicago, Saint Louis, San Francisco, Los Angeles, Seattle, Honolulu, San Diego, Charleston, Dallas, Houston, Mobile, Pensacola, Dayton, Cincinatti, Cleveland, Salt Lake City, Denver, Detroit. There were negative reports from military units overseas. Apparently, this attack was primarily aimed at the United States and not anywhere in Europe or Asia. However, a military Satellite had confirmed that Moscow and Saint Petersburg in Russia had nuclear explosions on the ground with massive amounts of fall out. Russia knew it was not us and has not declared war on anyone.

The general said, "I don't know the level of contact with any overseas government. We are on DEFCON TWO pending DEFCON ONE when we find the bad guys. I know of no recall for reservists, possibly due to the lack of communications like telephones, radio, and television, but you're free to go. You can have VIP quarters for tonight. If you wish to stay here, we'll find you a job. I can see your answer, good luck on your trip. I'll clear you out the gate. Just call security police before you leave."

Jim thanked him, got the girls who were nervously waiting in the outer office and took them down to the car and to the VIP quarters. The girls were surprised that these were called VIP quarters. It was a typical military ranch style four bedroom house with a carport instead of a garage. It was standard issue, bare bones living. The furniture and drapes were obviously purchased by the military...no one since 1950 would have had them. The house was probably 1960's Viet Nam war vintage. Yes, the military had more money to spend that did not go directly to the war. The kitchen and bathrooms were block asphalt based vinyl twelve inch squares and the carpet was one step ahead of indoor/outdoor carpet. It did have an excellent central air conditioner, a liqueur stocked refrigerator with a few snacks and cokes, and military clean rooms. The walls were obvious military shades of pale green, pale pink,...even the white seemed a subdued white. The bedspreads were first class comforters from the base exchange and the bedrooms had matching curtains. Not bad, but in stark contrast to the rest of the decor and the coarse starched sheets.

Jim spent the next several hours discussing what he knew, what might lay ahead on the journey, and their option to maybe stay on a nice safe air base. Jim stated that he would go on by himself whether or not they would sell him the car. They said were going east regardless. Each went to their separate bedrooms for the rest of the afternoon and night. The previous day had been long for all of them. Jim slept the sleep of the dead and the girls managed to sleep fairly well considering how displaced they felt, having gone from aspiring movie starlets in Los Angeles to fugitives on a strange military base in the middle of the desert after their night and morning long panic.

4 THE JOURNEY BEGINS

DAY 2, AUGUST 19

The next morning he emptied out the refrigerator into the car and went to the base exchange. He bought the girls some clothing using his credit card, which the military base exchange store would still take. They didn't want much, but their waitress outfits were obviously not suited to the trip since they were patterned after the classic French maid costume. Anytime they were stopped their clothing raised eyebrows and questions. The selection was not great, but as good as it ever is at a base exchange. They got shorts for the hot days, slacks for evenings and cooler days and jackets for the desert nights. Jim tried to talk them in to sturdier clothing like blue jeans, but there was too much actress/model in them to go for rough clothing. They still could not fathom the trials that may lie ahead. They would not believe Jim in that it was going to be more than two or three days driving time. Jim also picked up three sleeping bags to replace the rough army surplus blankets he had looted. He also picked up some fishing line, hooks, and lures. He bought extra jeans and shirts for himself as well as a pair of hiking boots and a pair of jogging shoes to supplement the slip-on's that he had. He picked up a half dozen six gallon gasoline cans, a case of motor oil, and other fluids for the car. A couple of books to read, hand tools including a bow saw and some extra blades for it, a self winding watch that still worked after the HEMP event, Rolaids© for his chronic acid indigestion, aspirin, antibiotic ointment, medical and duct tape, some pots and pans to cook in and eat out of, cigarettes, and other miscellaneous things. The total on his credit card came to nearly one thousand dollars, but Jim didn't expect to ever see a bill, at least not for years. Their shopping complete and their car and extra gas cans gassed up, and they were off on their journey east.

THE SOVIET UNION

Asian troops stationed in the southern Soviet Union shot their Soviet Officers and took command of their own tanks. At the same time Moslem troops in Asia shot their Soviet Officers and also took command. Then Arab and

Japanese airliners flew the Asian troops to Asia and the Moslem troops to the Middle East in a complicated exchange of tanks, artillery and other equipment.

RED CHINA, MONGOLIA

The Red Chinese army fired almost every nuclear tipped missile in their inventory. The Chinese weapons were not sophisticated and produced considerable fallout that killed thirty percent of the civilians living in Mongolia and other north Asian countries. Their long range missiles, that could have hit Moscow, simply didn't work. The ones that flew far enough simply hit the ground without coming to critical mass and not exploding nuclear. Some were shot down by Russian space defenses. None exploded with nuclear force. A typical warhead only has around one hundred and fifty pounds of convention high explosive. The biggest problem was cleaning up chunks of plutonium that were broken up by the high explosive. These can be picked up by hand if you don't breath in dust or have a cut. With a face mask and breathing apparatus and gloves, it is easy to handle like any other metal, heavy like lead. Their intermediate range missiles destroyed most of the Soviet bases in Siberia.

The Soviets responded by hurling submarine missiles at all of the major Chinese cities and major arms factories. The Soviet land based missiles had been largely sabotaged by Asian or Moslem military members who gave their lives to Allah and whoever Asians gave their lives to. The twenty largest cities became radioactive dust in the wind. The Chinese, knowing this would likely happen had evacuated their cities during the previous twenty-four hours. Even smarter, they paid attention to the weather forecast and had evacuated downwind from their cities to keep them from the inevitable fallout, even though the Soviets had perfected relatively clean nukes along with the United States.

The Chinese weapons not fired on the first day were mostly destroyed by Soviet Missiles from their submarine fleet. Their submarine fleet was compromised by the missile firings and Chinese submarines sank most of them, though too late.

The Soviet Union wasn't the only target of Chinese nuclear missiles. All the major cities and military bases in India were also hit with nukes killing upwards of two hundred and seventy-five million people. Hanoi, North Viet Nam, and Saigon, South Viet Nam were also destroyed to eliminate having to worry about the Vietnamese high command that had never gotten along with the Red Chinese. India had no retaliatory strike capability after the attack.

5 THE DESERT

Shelby, Darcy, and Jim left through the north gate to Edwards Air Force Base and headed east on state highway 58 toward Interstate 40. They were rested and eager to be going home. Los Angeles and Hollywood were quite literally in the past for Shelby and Darcy. Their dreams of stardom shattered along with the city of dreams. Their dreams now lay in getting home if possible. If you have ever driven across the American desert in eastern California and thought it was deserted, you should see it as they saw it. There were stalled cars and trucks here and there, but there had been little traffic along the road at 2:00 AM when their ignitions or fuel injections failed. All of the stalled vehicles were deserted leaving them to think someone with an older truck had picked up all the drivers from the night before and taken them somewhere.

There were no other living things along the road until they arrived in Needles, Arizona. Jim did not want to push the old Mercury hard because it was old and they had many miles to go and no idea what they might find. They kept the speed to 60. There would be no one along to help them if they broke down along the way.

As they drove into Needles, they met a roadblock manned by old timers from Lake Havasu City. As soon as the Mercury and its people were determined not to be a threat, they demanded information from Lieutenant Colonel Jim Claris about what was going on. They had no outside communications or power for over 24 hours now and were very concerned. The retired people at Lake Havasu City were actually dying from the heat without air conditioning. They had already had twenty deaths from the heat. Most of the older people were well to do and had new cars so there where almost no vehicles that were running. The road block had been set up because a motor cycle gang had terrorized some residents until people had pulled out their guns and chased them off. There were several other road blocks being manned at Yucca and Parker to keep people out that might cause a problem. They had provided working vehicles to their policeman in town to patrol and maintain order, supplemented by many retired people carrying guns on foot patrol since there were no working two way communications. Each volunteer foot patrol kept at least two others in sight to spread the word. Ten old timers had died as the result of the motor cycle gang and thirty were hospitalized with related strokes and other ailments related to the motorcycle gang. The trio were warned that the motor cycle gang had passed through Kingman at 2:00 PM that day.

Jim told them why their power and communications were off and that they were going to have to learn to do without for a long time. He spared them the information that they would not be getting groceries for the foreseeable future also and that they could not support themselves here nor be evacuated by anyone. Someone would figure that out within a few days at most. They were no one's dummies, only outside their routine experience. Their solution would probably be well planned out and better than anything Jim could suggest.

Jim drove on to Kingman, Arizona to find another roadblock, but word had already gotten through. When Jim asked how, he was told that the old timers had taken loose some power lines and created their own telegraph using automobile batteries and starter solenoids. Jim just shook his head and said, "You people are going to come through this all right; better than most will. That was very creative of someone. How far does your telegraph network go?"

A well dressed younger retired person stepped forward and provided the following verbal report to Jim. "So far everything goes through Lake Havasu City and out to the nearest town on each road, but we'll expand as necessary. We're set up with two way now. One line leading into the "City" and one line leading out so we can transmit and receive simultaneously. The "City" has two operators for each of the outlying towns. You weren't told this in Needles because we didn't know if you were really passing through on a government mission on your way home or if you were going to take all those weapons and try to raid the "City". Since you went on by and arrived here on schedule, we're to tell you so you can report back to the government. By the way, we already figured out that supply trucks are not getting through Needles or Kingman, which means that they are disabled too. General Davis, Air Force Retired, said that those vehicles needing transistors to run will be out of business for a long time. We're working on getting a supply line. We already have convinced a local rancher that we are the customer, not some far off market. In exchange, we will provide security for him and he agreed to accept our IOUs until the financial market recovers. Yes, we are planting gardens, but we'll have to see if we can grow enough. At least we won't starve with plenty of beef on the table.

Good luck on your journey. By the way, we heard there may be trouble around Flagstaff. A couple in an old pickup is sitting in the city park now that just came from Flagstaff. They said that the motorcycle gang that came through here, went right into the Flagstaff police station and took over the place and were taking over the town when this couple decided to high tail it out in their old pickup that still ran. You might want to talk with them before you head east. The park is up the road about 6 blocks on your right. It's a beat up white 1970's Ford. They were looking for information on Los Angeles where the rest of their family is."

Jim thanked the man and decided to face the delicate task of telling the couple not to go to Los Angeles for awhile at least. Jim saw the couple at a picnic table. The man was laying on one bench and the woman was reading a book on the other. Jim inquired, "Are you the couple from Flagstaff?"

"YES, WHO WANTS TO KNOW?"

Jim said, "I'm Jim Claris. I just arrived from Los Angeles and I'll trade my bad news for yours if you will tell me what's happening east of here."

The man replied, "Hi, I'm sorry I was so gruff. I'm Wilbur Steele, and we've had a very hard day so far and we're both scared and tired." Jim shook his hand as Wilbur continued, "We don't know what happened for sure, but only what we heard. We heard that this motorcycle gang just drove right into town and without stopping rode right up to the police station and the highway patrol office, walked in and took them over. They locked up all the police they could find, took all the guns, left guards at the stations and then started around town looking for off duty police. Another group had a list of registered guns in the city and started rounding them up. I was always afraid registering guns was a bad practice. They look like they are just taking over the city to stay awhile. We heard they had set up road blocks on the main roads to keep anyone from going into or leaving the city and we decided it was time to leave while we knew of some back roads they didn't know about. There was supposed to be some other people coming. We waited for them at a prearranged meeting place, but no one showed up there. We figured that the road had been closed after we went through and our friends took too long packing. We didn't take time to pack. We just grabbed and ran. I wouldn't get too close to Flagstaff. We just drove straight here before stopping anywhere. Now, it's your turn. Tell us about west of here."

"I appreciate the information. We left Los Angeles within hours of D Day...." Jim told all he knew to date.

At the end of Jim's story Wilbur was not feeling too well, "What do we do now? We can't go home and we can't go back to Flagstaff. We have nothing to trade or money that anyone wants."

Jim said, "You might try working for one of the ranchers around here, or maybe Lake Havasu City, or try getting out to the valley further north of Los Angeles where they grow all those vegetables." With that Jim turned to leave.

As Jim headed west on Interstate 40, he told the girls what he had found out and started them looking for alternate routes. Because of the Grand Canyon, there weren't any northern routes except by back tracking through Las Vegas or trying to get by on the south by taking US highway 89 south to Prescott then Arizona 69 to Interstate 79, north to Camp Verde around mile marker 285, east on some unnamed path, hopefully county road, to Arizona 89 and then north to Winslow and Interstate 40 again. There wasn't much until they got to Ash Fork and discovered that it had been burnt down. Nothing was standing except for concrete walls. They headed south on Arizona 69, glad that they had heard about Flagstaff. When they came to Drake, nothing moved except the Mercury as it passed on through to the south. The same for Paulden. Chino Valley, was a town of around three thousand people according to the road atlas, but now looked like three thousand armed men. The road was totally blocked and the street barricaded in several places. As they approached, Jim could see lookouts on every building. He said, "Relax, we're not the ones they're looking for. Apparently they've heard about Flagstaff too."

A county sheriff was in front of the first barricaded with his hand up for Jim to stop. As Jim slowly pulled up to him the sheriff walked up to the window. There were no guns trained on the Mercury, but plenty were in clear sight where they could be quickly. "Just turn off your engine and answer a few questions. Who are you? Where are you coming from? Why are you here?"

"My name is Jim Claris, this is Darcy and Shelby, we came from Los Angeles and are trying to get around Flagstaff because we heard it wasn't safe. Not knowing the roads, but only having a road atlas, we came this way to get around south and then up north to Winslow."

"Stay right here, and keep your hands on the wheel." The sheriff disappeared around the barricade and then came back shortly. Would you mind coming with me to answer some more questions?"

Jim brazenly replied, "I don't mind coming with you to answer questions, but want to keep my car where I can see it and bring the girls."

The sheriff visibly relaxed his argumentative stance. "I'm sorry, of course you can bring your car and your girls. I'm just a little tense. We'd like some news from the west and we're friends not enemies."

Jim also relaxed his on the ready posture and followed the sheriff as the barricade was pulled back to pass the Mercury. He slowly followed the sheriff to a restaurant that was apparently being used as a command post where the sheriff motioned him into a parking slot. The sheriff reached to open Jim's door and said, "Come on inside. You can see your car through the window there and it's a lot cooler than out here." As Jim and the girls went in they discovered it was air conditioned. The sheriff simply said, "emergency generator." to their questioning look.

He presented his orders made up by Los Angeles Air Force Base and he went through his now growing song and dance routine of his trip to date, remarking that, "….what used to take a few hours was now taking days of driving. He would have expected Oklahoma in two days and it had already been three and was not to Flagstaff yet."

The head of the operation here in Prescott was an Army National Guard general who had convinced the Prescott city council that severe measures were needed. If a lowly motorcycle gang can take over the larger town of Flagstaff, then Prescott had better be on guard. The general was quite aware of the seriousness of the situation and supplies. Their worst fear was that the diet of beef would not provide the vitamins needed for their health on a long term. Their medical supplies could not possibly hold out for long and any major sickness would decimate the population.

The general said, "I hate to put a damper on your happy plans, but we have sent scouts out and found that Winslow is already under the control of the motor cycle gang. However, Holbrook found out in time to arm themselves. Thank goodness that gun control has not gone too far here in Arizona. There is little military, inadequate police, and it is the towns' people that have provided the militia to keep the gang from expanding out. The gang have been joined by some dissatisfied Indians from the reservations that see this as an opportunity to gain a bargaining position to be used after the war. The tribes and most of the Indian population are not involved. In fact, they are probably just as well off as we are. They have taught their people enough of the old ways to help them survive, or at least believe that they can get by until things get back to normal. The Indians causing problems are those that were always militant. Somehow the motor cycle gangs convinced these numskulls that this is their time to make themselves and their mistaken ideas felt. We don't know if this means fifty or five thousand. We only know that at Winslow the motor cycle gang was joined by "some" Indians."

JIM QUESTIONED, "WE HAVE TO GET THROUGH. HOW WOULD YOU SUGGEST GOING?"

A civilian moved forward with a road atlas. "We don't know of course, but assuming that Holbrook is still safe, you have to get that far east before turning north. The general didn't tell you, but there is also trouble in Phoenix with the Mexican population and riots. Without an effective police and no National Guard, all they can do is control the spread of the riots. The road from Camp Verde over to 87 is okay, but at 87. cut south to 260. That will put you another twenty miles out of your way, but... turn at Payson onto 260 and I'd recommend you stay on it all the way to Show Low, then take 61 over to US 666 to Sanders. That will take you clear around any potential trouble in Holbrook. Assuming that Holbrook keeps the road closed, Gallup should be okay."

The general asked, "How are you doing for gasoline? You may not find another gas station the rest of the day, and that's not an economy car you've got there."

Jim said, "If I can get some around here, I have a manual pump I can use to fill up the car. I also have some spare gas cans. If worst comes to worst there are a lot of cars and trucks with gas that won't run that I can siphon out of."

The general said, "You can have some from that tank truck down the block. Here is a note authorizing it and someone here will wave at them when you stop there. You earned your gasoline here by giving me some news and by reminding me that unless we start draining all the gas out of all the newer vehicles it will just evaporate and gum them up. We need to collect and ration it."

Jim did as instructed and left town with twenty two in the tank and twenty four gallons in cans. They also refilled their water containers since this WAS Arizona and it might be a long time before they had another opportunity for gasoline and a safe water supply.

When Jim came to a small campground east of Camp Verde he declared that they were stopping for the night. The girls were concerned that he had not asked them. Jim replied, "I'm dead tired. I didn't want to spend the night in an armed camp expecting some kind of attack or getting trapped there either. I didn't want to stop too near the main road, just in case. I'm tired. We're on a deserted road in a national park, and this campground is off the road. It looks as safe as we're going to get."

Darcy said, "I'd like you to remember that it's my car you're driving. I might have liked to stay somewhere with running water in a motel, not out here in some tent."

Shelby chimed in, "Me too, don't cha know. But, maybe he's right. Maybe this is better. It is getting dark. This is not a good road to keep driving on in the dark. We owe him a lot so far. It may be our car, but we've used his money all the way so far. We're at least even in the life saving department. You can sleep in the car if you want, I'm sleeping with Jim in the tent. Don't look at me like that. I did say sleep. I'd feel safer with him in the tent. Might be warmer with two people too. It is getting pretty cold."

Darcy butted in, "I'm sorry. I'm tired too. Can we light a campfire and eat before we go to bed? And, Shelby, he may be the only man alive that we actually know. Maybe sleeping isn't all we ought to do."

Jim objected, "Hey I'm sorry I didn't consult. I didn't want to talk in front of them in Prescott, but I did think we needed to get while the getting was good before they changed their mind. Yes, we can have a fire here... who's to see it. I'm hungry too, but only for food. Sleeping only is just fine." Both girls turned to look at him questioningly and he tried to explain, "I think you're both beautiful. If I was a little younger and single I'd love to do it with both of you. You need someone closer to your own age. I have been a faithful husband to this point regardless of temptation. Right now I'm very tired. Sleeping together will keep as all warm."

With that they lit a fire, ate a poorly prepared outdoor meal in the cold. Talked about what they were going to do now and about what they thought was going on in the United States, the world, Los Angeles, and their respective familial homes. They then climbed into the tent.

Jim had locked the car, hung pots and pans on string to surrounding trees as an alarm, hid some of the guns and ammo in the trunk and put a lot of it in the tent...just to be sure. He doused the fire before going into the tent and waited for the steam to settle. He sat outside the tent for the girls to get out of their clothing and smoked a cigarette while watching for any signs of movement. He heard insects and an owl, but it was otherwise a typical night in the mountains in a lonely campground.

For warmth, the girls insisted that they zip two bags together and use the third over the top. By sleeping body to body it would be warmer. Jim was put in the middle since the two girls felt uncomfortable sleeping next to each other, but had both had occasion to sleep with men. When Jim got into the tent they insisted that he get down to his skivvies. They didn't want blue jeans and a sweaty shirt in the sleeping bags. Jim was uncomfortable sleeping between two beautiful, shapely, and mostly nude girls. He was not surprised that he was quite aroused by it and hoped the girls didn't notice after his monogamous speech. He stayed on his back until the girls seemed asleep. It didn't take long before they were all warm and shortly thereafter all asleep.

When Jim woke up he was only partially aware of holding a girl and being very aroused by it. He gradually realized that he was also quite aware of a shapely girl holding him also. He was a little confused and sort of froze up until he got his senses back. He had been dreaming of being at home in bed. Now he knew where he was and who he was with. He lost his arousal as he consciously did not move. He didn't want Darcy to discover his arousal while holding her and afraid to wake Shelby holding him by backing up away from Darcy. He started feeling the rocks through the bottom of the sleeping bag to the point he would have to move. In a few moments of wakefulness, his arousal was mostly over and he slowly moved Shelby's arm from around him and started her turning away as he rolled onto his back taking his arm from over Darcy. He didn't think he would get back to sleep between the girls, but he was asleep within five minutes.

GRAND FORKS AIR FORCE BASE, NORTH DAKOTA

Henry was very distraught over the loss of his command and so many of his friends flying or working around the aircraft on the ground, but was now a raging bull with no matador to gouge.

Jeremy was incredulous. He would have been one of the lead aircraft taking off from Minot Air Force Base, if he had been there instead of in the safety of the command post here.

Henry's security police had found most of the launch sites of the various weapons used against them. Almost one hundred percent had been launched from land belonging or being leased by some Muslim or Oriental. His security police had only lost four injured in exchange for killing over one hundred Arabs that had either stormed the gates or made it through some other perimeter fence. The ammunition storage dump had been breached and several facilities destroyed before the security police could react, but react they did with no one escaping. They had three live captives that could not find a way to die before being captured and man-handled into cuffs. One wounded staff sergeant had killed one Arab with his bare hands when his gun was empty and the Arab still had a loaded Uzi.

"Jeremy, I have to find this Jim Claris. He would know what to do next. He tried to tell everyone this would happen back in the mid 1980's, but everyone thought the Russians were the bad guys. Back when we were visiting the various Strategic Air Command bases, this one included, Jim pointed out to me how vulnerable they were to someone on the ground. At that time most alert pads were within plain sight of a civilian road within range of someone with a twenty-two rifle. An Arab could have parked out there on the road and taken out our entire alert force. I was only a Captain back then and couldn't do a thing about it. Eventually we plowed some dirt revetments around the pads, but we simply had no defense against any kind of weapon. Our bases were never intended for any ground defense. Our fences were only to keep out wanderers never an attacking force. Our bases should never have been so undefended. Who thought to build alert pads on civilian roads? Why didn't we have more land area around our secure areas and why wasn't the whole area protected by Army troops and outposts?"

"I'm just glad to be alive. I should have been in the first aircraft from Minot. How many enemies have we allowed to settle here. Can we trust any Arab? How many Vietnamese were Viet Cong or North Vietnamese? What about Haitians? Chinese? Japanese? Koreans? I guess we can trust the German's, Italians, Irish, and English."

"Jeremy, you think that's bad. I knew some of the ones that apparently attacked us. I thought that they were Americans first and foreigner second. I never would have believed that they were armed and just waiting for their cue."

"I think we better get all the help we can get. Apparently this Jim Claris had it figured out a long time ago, but no one listened. You say you threw out his battle plans or what ever they were? You better find him. Would he still be at Wright-Pitiful? (Nickname for Wright-Patterson Air Force Base, Ohio)."

Another message came in reporting similar problems with ICBM's. In panic the president had ordered some ICBM's re-targeted for the Middle Eastern capitols suspected to be responsible. As the missiles launched they were destroyed by Stinger type ground to air missiles or high powered rifles. Most of the perpetrators were long gone when security police reacted. In a few cases someone had gotten close enough to lob in a grenade with a grenade launcher completely destroying the missile silos along with the missiles inside. Many missile silos had been attacked the night the HEMP bombs had exploded and the missiles destroyed in the ground. Because of the delays in communicating with the submarine fleet, their missiles were never re-programmed. Over eighty percent of the submarine fleet at sea had not been in communication since the HEMP events. Apparently someone talked the president out of nuking cities at random when there was still a lot of question as to who was to blame. Good thing, since most of the missiles were targeted for Russia, and none for the Middle East. The submarines completely below the surface were impervious to the HEMP that crippled so much of the military. They could be held in reserve for more information. They were also very stealthy and could not easily be located. Of course the Arabs were way out of their league in trying to detect and sink a nuclear submarine anyway.

All military bases had the same problem in that there were very few of their commercial style vehicles running and even much of the military equipment was no longer functional. There were a number of the old munitions dump trucks and semi-truck tractors built before the electronics took over. There were a few hot rods, classic cars, and just really old cars that did not have the electronics that were immediately commandeered on the bases to provide for security forces and other critical transportation.

Teheran, Iran.

Facil did not have any of the girls that night, even though they slept with him. It had been a very very long day. Morning came all too quick.

Facil was awakened at 6 AM and served breakfast. He hardly had time to dress when they were back to get him from his luxurious quarters. He and the other leaders were led to the conference room.

Jabal Iscarnon was speaking again, "Just hours ago we crippled the United States. New York City is gone, Chicago, Seattle, Los Angeles, and others. Our HEMP attack worked perfectly. The Americans did not get any of their bombers off the ground. We destroyed over fifty percent yesterday when you were being briefed. The die is cast. Our troops have crossed into Italy. The attacks started as soon as we had you safely in our underground city. Because of our attacks, the news media and the world is still counting on some of you as allies. I would imagine the Americans don't believe how we would attack Italy with all of the equipment they left in Saudi Arabia at our soft under belly. We captured it in five hours, sorry Facil, but your ground troops ran. Apparently they didn't like the odds. With your air force crippled by simply not being fueled...it was too late to stop Hussein once his tanks started rolling. No, we didn't go through Kuwait. We all are Moslems here. There was no need. Approximately five hundred Americans died in a hopeless attempt to slow us down. The others hid. The American oil men are now our captives. Watch!"

The lights dimmed and the holovision in the middle of the conference table came on again. There were American oil executives that supervised the oil fields throughout the Middle East. They spoke of how they had been pumping the blood out of the Middle East for years and confessed how they had kept the Arabs fighting with each other and then they were executed by the hundreds. The wives and children shown being auctioned off to the highest bidder after watching their husbands executed by bleeding to death after having both hands chopped off for stealing from the Arab countries. The Arabs had used the old big guy with the huge curved sword routine.

Facil had no doubt that a video tape somewhere would leak out. The United States may have been seriously damaged, but now Allah would see the eventual end of the Arab world. Facil had no doubt that within months, the Americans would be inventing new weapons and their once mighty industry would rise from the ashes to smother whatever progress the Moslems had made. There was no way that Europe would roll over for the Arabs now that they had been attacked.

The next series of pictures were taken from space down on the United States. While Jabal ranted about the total destruction of the cities, Facil was surprised at the relatively minor damage. This was not the work of missiles that Jabal had bragged about except for Washington D.C. and New York City. Only a few blocks of downtown Chicago were destroyed, as was the case in several cities. If they were even nuked, it must have been the small Russian made backpack style nukes. New York City was gone. It must have been several missiles. How much of his nuclear strength had Jabal used?

More pictures showed massive troop movements across the Chinese borders into the Soviet Union and India. Other pictures showing Moslem tanks racing through border stations with the lead tank blowing up the guard stations before they ever got there so there wasn't anyone alive to stop them.

Jabal interrupted the show, "Gentlemen, we have already conquered Venice and are moving into the Italian peninsula. The resistance is light. We haven't found much opposition in these Europeans. Our airplanes have already attacked the American base at Vincinza. Now the ground troops are moving to take the Air Base..."

They had a lunch served by Arabian girls dressed as belly dancers. Then Jabal announced, "WE HAVE IT. I just received word that our troops have already moved into the base at Vincinza. Within hours we will be flying missions against Rome, the capitol of the wicked Christian religion."

All Facil could think of was how foolish to worry about Rome. France and Germany were the countries to worry about. He wondered if Jabal realized how big Spain was in land area. The British had not been beaten in centuries. Why wasn't Jabal bombing the French and German air bases? Range of course. He didn't have long range aircraft. His own Saudi Arabian F-15's would be hard pressed to bomb France and Germany and his weren't equipped as bombers. His were some of the few with long range conformal fuel tanks. The Russian MIG aircraft were even more short winded. They were good for defense, but not for an offense. Jabal would say that was one of the results of keeping the Arabs from being strong, and he would be right. But what country in their right mind would sell strategic weapons to any other country anyway.

Jabal then made his demand, "Now the time has come to be leaders of your countries. Each of you will be escorted to a room made up to resemble your offices. Your words and picture will be broadcast to your countrymen. You will each be given a speech to present. You will have thirty minutes to study it before the broadcast. The broadcast is a call to arms against the Western infidels. I hate to remind you, but you know the consequences if you do not sound convincing."

Facil had no choice. It was the life of his entire extended family being held hostage. Besides, some other less courageous member of the royal family would step in his place if he did not comply. It would be better for his country if he cooperated. He presumed the other rulers held hostage here would have similar thoughts and the same decision. Watch out West, here we come. Watch out Saudi Arabia, we must survive this somehow. The more I cooperate, the more I will be trusted, the better deal I can make for my country. He also presumed that even though told this would be a live broadcast, it was probably a taped and delayed broadcast to make sure there were no secret codes imbedded.

Facil gave his speech nearly verbatim with as much conviction as he could, "My countrymen. The time of greatness is upon us. The will of Allah has decreed that we no longer live in slavery to the infidels of the world. It our time in the sun. No longer will we be content to live on the handouts of the Western world. It is time to take what is rightfully ours. Our resources have been used to make them powerful. By their handouts we have also gained strength. While they have become weak, we have become strong. We have gained the military might to conquer the infidels to make them true followers of Allah. No more will the world worship false gods, but will worship Allah.

All men under the age of fifty will report to the nearest military institution to receive your training and uniforms. This is the one and only Holy Jihad. The Moslem world is united. No longer will Arabs war among themselves. No longer will we swear allegiance to a single country. We will swear our very lives to service to Allah and the United Moslem Forces that will conquer the world to make it an Islam world. No longer will we be confined to our deserts. We will now own the oases of the world. We will no longer wander the deserts, but will own the gardens. We will have great forests and grassy plains, mighty rivers and endless lakes of fresh water. It is time for Saudi Arabia and the Moslem world to unite and spread over the world. Allah and your prince are calling for your allegiance. Our children will no longer be destined to wander, but will have their home anywhere in the world.

All the leaders of the Moslem world, Saudi Arabia, first and foremost, Morocco, Egypt, Algeria, Libya, Syria, Jordan, even Iraq and Iran have made peace and joined together as Muslims to remake the world into an Islam world. The war has already started. The United States, the great Satan, has been humbled and will not interfere. Europe is bending to our will. It will take a great sacrifice on all our parts. Our men that die in battle will be at Mohammed's side with Allah. No longer will they die in infamy, but will live forever for the glory of Islam.

My Air Force Commander, General Icmon will prepare every available fighter plane for deployment to Europe. Our new air bases will be in Europe. Vincinza, the American base in Italy is being prepared for our use at this moment. The new uniforms of the United Moslem Forces Air Force will be delivered within hours, they will be worn with the pride of our faith. Saudi Arabia is but one of the many forces that will convert the world.

The military arms that were so graciously left for our use by the now defunct United States are now ours. These arms are to be moved as rapidly as possible toward the soft under belly of Europe. Huge tankers, no longer needed for shipping our wealth to the West, have been converted for transports. Our tanks will be loaded onto these great warships and moved into the Mediterranean Sea for a crushing blow to the Infidel forces in Europe.

All my commanders will report to the ranking commanders of the United Moslem Forces that will soon report for duty at all of our bases. These commanders will be reporting to our central headquarters. My commanders will follow their orders as if they came directly from me. I will be sitting on a great council of all the rulers of the Moslem world. Rather than trust to one man the orders will come from the counsel. I will be a primary member of that council and will bow only to a carefully considered decision on use of our forces.

LONG LIVE THE NEW ISLAMIC WORLD. LONG LIVE THE FORCES OF MOHAMMED, THE UNITED ARAB FORCES, LONG LIVE SAUDI ARABIA!"

It was done. The speech was finished. He hoped that he sounded convincing. He thought only through cooperation could he save his country and the royal lineage of the Saud family. If he was convincing enough for Jabal, maybe he could hold his Saudi Forces out of much of the war by having them held in reserve and save the lives of his countrymen. Already Jabal had played into his hopes by having his forces shipped by converted tanker around Africa to Europe. That would take time and keep his forces from the danger of the major battle for a little time at least. His men would stay in Saudi Arabia until his equipment was delivered to some already secured beach head. It could already have added months to their lives. If the war were to fail, it might very well be over before his forces were committed. Unfortunately, his air forces would be quickly committed. His F-15's had more range and were better fighters than most of the Arab or European forces.

Facil presumed the other leaders had performed much as he had. He wondered if he had sealed his death, or whether Jabal would allow the leaders any part in the decisions of war. He would probably be kept alive to provide more inspiration to his people if the need arose. But, would he be actually a part of the war staff?

In Saudi Arabia, Facil's commanders were incredulous. They could not believe that Facil would commit their forces in this way. They never had any aspirations of world domination. Saudi Arabia had always been neutralist. They had not been part of the Persian Empire nor the Ottoman Empire. Even in biblical times Saudi Arabia had been a country of Bedouins and the wise men of the east in the Christ story of Christendom. They had their sheiks. Mecca was not accidentally in Saudi Arabia. The most holy spot in Islam. Jerusalem was fought over between Jews and Muslims, but Mecca had always been a safe haven in Saudi Arabia. It was here because Saudi Arabia was a land of peace and safety. They thought they knew their emperor. He would not order them in this way unless for the good of his country.

The new commanders and the uniforms were obviously already in country for within two hours the new commanders and uniforms were delivered. Many soldiers and airmen walked away rather than change uniforms, but they were quickly arrested by the Saudi police and returned to duty. It was duty or death. Apparently, the religious leaders of Saudi Arabia were in consort with the religious leaders throughout the Moslem world long before their rulers were aware. It was serve for the glory of Islam or die in infamy by execution. The Saudi people were quite confused by this sudden turn of events. Many were well educated and the many of the wealthy attempted to escape to the West, but there were no non-military flights. All of the private jets and ships had been seized over night by the religious police run by the Mosques.

The Arabs already owned many airlines, especially cargo planes and these planes had already converged on the Moslem countries from around the world. All of the American and European descent pilots had been executed after landing. Some aircraft had to be forced to land once they suspected something and tried to fly away. A couple of airlines had even been shot down as examples to the others. In some cases, Arab or Oriental pilots that had been posing as baggage handlers had to fly some of the airplanes. They had plenty of airplanes to transport troops around Europe, over three thousand military cargo or civilian airliners and cargo planes compared to three hundred for the mighty American military.

When Facil got back to his suite, he went around the room searching for television cameras and microphones.

"Facil, what are you doing? What has happened?", asked Joy.

"IYihhh, he est a krazie man. He heas beeen drooged." cried Kareen.

"What are you looking for?" said Carey.

Facil ignored their entreaties and continued tearing up the room finding nothing. After thirty minutes the room look like it had been the victim of a robbery where the robbers were trying to find something or a police drug search. "I don't care, let them take their pictures and tape my voice."

"What are you talking about, Facil?" said Suzanne.

"Video and sound surveillance equipment. I couldn't find any. I'm sure this suite is bugged to get incriminating pictures to send back home and to tape my voice to be used against me. I will let them hear my secret thoughts. It might be good that they heard the word of reason. I am not yet married, and therefore cannot be breaking the law. Arab's have had harems for many years. I know how to foul them on that account. Girls! I want you to spend every waking hour decorating our suite here with a very special decoration. Kareen, write the following sentence in your most perfect Arabic: 'I am captive and they will not let me marry.' Then girls, you can all very carefully write this exact sentence on every wall and every floor such that no camera angle can fail to show the sentence. Make it big to be read from a distance and repeated many times small to be read from close up to see the entire thing. You may write it sideways, on end, backwards to show in a mirror. I do not care, but it must be everywhere. Kareen, you will inspect each girls sentence before she starts her decorating and after it is printed. Then you will inspect each wall and the floor and the sheets of the bed to make sure that it is everywhere. If the room can look nice with this decoration, more the better."

"Carey, ring for maid service. Joy, prepare my bath." Facil went to his bedroom while Joy went through the bedroom to the lavish bathroom to prepare his whirlpool bath scented with the herbs and spices that made him feel at home. Facil came into the bath wearing a silk robe which Joy slipped off him when he slipped into the tub. She wore nothing, but did not enter the bath since she had not been invited. "Will you wash my back?" While he leaned forward, she slid into the bath behind him and soaped and rinsed his back. After twenty minutes of sitting between her legs as she washed his upper body from behind, he stood and stated, "Thank you Joy, you have honored me." He climbed from the bath and she toweled him down. When he started to get aroused he stated, "That is good. You may leave me to finish. Please stand just outside the door. She did. He finished toweling himself dry and put his silk robe back on. He came into the bedroom and laid on the bed motioning her to join him. She had put on the traditional see through Harem costume from the movies and came to lie beside him. He said, "Just sit beside me, I have something to tell you. Do not be angry with me, I am also angry that I was not even consulted or I would have said do not even attempt what I am going to tell you now." Apprehensively, she sat at the head of the bed leaning against the headboard, as he told her what he had found out today about the attacks on the U.S.. When he felt her anger building, he reminded her that they were both prisoners and had to come through this together. She must trust him that he had nothing to do with this war and disapproved of the very concept of war.

He left her crying on the bed and now dressed in his familiar sheik and came into the living room. "Carey, please ring for our dinner."

6 WOLF CREEK PASS

August 21

When Jim woke again, he was still on his back with each girls one arm and one leg over him. He could feel their young soft figures against him and laid there enjoying it for awhile. After about thirty minutes, he cooled off and he became aware of a rock under the tent that was pressing on him to point of discomfort. He woke the girls, they pumped out some water from a hand pump in the campground and made hot water for instant coffee before getting on the road again.

They stopped for lunch in Payson. You would never know anything was wrong, except by noticing there were no new vehicles and the restaurant had no electricity. Without electricity, they had not heard of the problems elsewhere, but were just upset at the power company. They new car failures were a total mystery, but most people still had an older car...no rust in Arizona...so they were not without transportation. Neither Jim nor the girls volunteered any information, but ate their food in quiet and listened to the locals. Jim hated using his credit card for payment, knowing that it was no good, but figured the money the restaurant was taking might not be any better. Jim wanted to save what cash he had.

The roads had been slow going since Prescott. These were not actually mountains, but the roads still didn't go straight, and Jim wanted to take no unnecessary chances with the car or tires. They actually topped off the gas tank in St. Johns, having found Show Low and St. Johns as blissfully ignorant as Payson.

When they got to Interstate 40, it was as if there were no problems. When they got to Gallup, there was a smoke cloud still hanging over the city and numerous fires. They ran into a police road block.

The policeman explained that Albuquerque had blown up in a nuclear explosion on D-Day about five hours after the power had failed. They didn't know anything about it except that some horribly burned people showed up in the Gallup hospital telling the story. The story spread and there were some riots, but with the New Mexico people all being armed, the riots failed as soon as they could get the good people organized. Some fires just had to burn themselves out because there was no fire department since D-Day. He sent them north on US 666 and Durango, Colorado to get around the Albuquerque that was most certainly deadly.

As they passed through Gallup, there were numerous groups of armed men roaming the streets and an occasionally fire still smoldering where a lower class business used to be. The shopping mall was packed with people, mostly on foot. The bigger the city the higher the percentage of newer cars that were now useless. If you have ever been between Gallup and Durango, you know you are nowhere. It was no wonder some of the young Indian bucks were displeased. The land was too dry for anything but cactus and sagebrush. There were a few farms with some irrigation and healthy cows, but most consisted of an old beat up pickup or car next to just as old a trailer house with dirt for a lawn and broken washing machines for shrubs. The livestock consisted of chickens and dogs. This land might have been fertile at one time, but it was before the white man came to America. Now it was desert. There was no way the Indians could live here without federal assistance.

Jim commented, "The Indians should have been educating their people to get out of here to somewhere more fertile. Instead they try to teach the old ways. Those old ways don't work around this kind of land. There are no lush fields of grass and consequently very little wild game. Did you know that at one time five of the top ten ballerinas were of Indian descent? That was when the Indians were trying to be assimilated as white. Most Indians could get education and be accepted as part of the white man's community without another thought. Most part Indians can get a free college education, but don't finish high school. I had a high school football coach that was full blood Commanche. No one thought anything about it until we got a new band director that was doing a tribute to him and ran his words together to sound like "Cochese Adoah" when he meant to say Coach Esadoah. Both men were great men and a tribute to their professions. I had thought so little about the Coach's chiseled face and coloring, that I did not know he was Indian. I thought he had a good sun tan and was weathered from coaching. In talking to my Dad about the incident I also found out that the high school principle was full blooded Choctaw. The principle's wife was not seen much because she believed in wearing traditional American Indian dress and preferred to speak their own language. My Dad, that was of English descent, looked more Indian than our high school principle did. I honestly hope they will not starve without federal assistance and food being trucked in."

At Shiprock, New Mexico they had electricity from the huge coal fired generators not far to the west. The electrical grid may have broken down, but there were direct wires to Shiprock and Farmington. When they got to Farmington they got gas at a gasoline station. The station attendant complained about taking a credit card for gasoline, but since it was not on the manual look up list and he could not phone for verification, he accepted it. It had been 38 hours since they had left Edwards air force base

Jim drove on to Durango where there was no electricity. The town was peaceful and still ignorant of what had happened. They knew that Farmington had electricity and they did not. They ate dinner there at a dark tourist Mexican restaurant by candlelight. Their stoves were natural gas that would work as long as the gas did not have to be switched there through a computer controlled station. It had taken all day to get from mid Arizona to here so Jim rented a motel room with two beds, one for the girls and one for himself. They accepted his credit card rather than turn away business just because they could not verify the card. Jim tried to top off the tank, but the service stations that were still open, had no electricity to pump gasoline and Jim was too tired to try to use the hand pump he had.

Darcy crawled into bed with Jim sometime during the night, preferring a man to a girl to sleep next to.

DAY 5 - 21 AUGUST

Jim was not aware of it until the early morning hours when he woke aroused as he had the morning before. When Jim was fully awake he woke Darcy and then went over to Shelby's bed to wake her. Shelby reached up, put her arms around his neck, pulled him down to her and gave him a long passionate kiss before he could pull away. Jim passionately kissed back in automatic and lonely response without thinking and the kiss lasted until Darcy cleared her throat. Jim started pulling away and Shelby let him go with a musical, "Good Morning." followed by an affected, "Darrrliiing"

WHEN DARCY WENT INTO THE BATHROOM SHELBY SAID, "SHE'S NOT JEALOUS, IS SHE?"

You tell me." Jim was getting dressed across the room. "Would you be if you were her? I woke up with Darcy in my bed and you in the other." He had not really talked to Darcy, just gone to the bathroom, found Darcy up and dressed when he came out and had gone to wake up Shelby. He was unsure as to why Darcy had crawled into bed with him during the night or whether Shelby knew that she had. He changed the subject with, "Better get up and get ready to go, we've got a long way to go yet."

Darcy came out of the bathroom with good timing...had she been listening to see if she should stay in the bathroom and decided it was safe to come out? Shelby, abashedly, came out from the covers, a'naturale and with a wiggle, winked at Darcy, and went slowly past her into the bathroom.

Darcy laughingly said, "Teasing will get you everywhere." To Jim she said, "Shelby and I have been friends a long time, Shelby has always been more forward. She's a tease, but a good girl. I opened the bathroom door and found the two of you kissing on her bed, so I cleared my throat to see if it was clear to come out." After a pause and sitting down on the end of the bed she said, "These are very strange times. The three of us only have each other. None of us may have any family left when we return. It may still be just the three of us for a long time. At least I don't know where we would meet anyone better than you for a while...maybe never. That assumes we ever get to our respective homes of course. I know you loved your family, but at least we have sort of known each other for a long time. I think we all know each other pretty well under the circumstances. Don't you agree?"

"Yes, I agree. It is was very fortunate that we had made friends on my trips to Los Angeles and it was fortunate for all of us that I came out of the hotel just when you were there with your car. Now we are on an adventure together, but it may only last a few more days before we're all home with our families." Jim noticed that Darcy assumed that Jim knew he could find no better than Darcy and Shelby. He had not thought about it, but she might be right. He had not considered not being able to get home. He had pushed the idea of his family being gone to the back and had refused to accept the possibility whenever the idea tried to creep back in.

They stopped at a restaurant to eat. They had a sign on the door that they were sorry, but they would only accept cash. Jim needed coffee and figured that some breakfast would help on the drive. Jim was always hungry in the morning when away from home. They looked at the road atlas to study their route for the day and had light banter until they got on the road. The two girls soon were oohing and ah-ing over the scenery of the mountains that they had never seen as Jim drove past Chimney Rock toward Wolf Creek Pass.

After the last two nights sleeping with the girls and their slow progress toward home, Jim had to admit that if things dragged on much longer, his doubts about seeing his family would grow, and his willpower might fade. The girls were sexy. It had been a while since his having had sex. They were young and made him feel more sexually attractive than his wife had in years. She had an aversion to sexy clothes and didn't remember ever wearing the sexy clothes she attracted him with. The girls still wore the man attracting clothes of single gorgeous girls, aspiring actresses even. They had been on the road for four days now and would have been home by now, but were only just starting. They had crossed two states and still had five to go, with Colorado, Kansas, and Missouri being wide states that took time. Jim started really having doubts about finding his family. It would take them at least a week yet to get there unless things improved. Would his family still be alive? Were they still there? Would Jim and the girls be able to make the trip? Jim said to himself that of course his family was still okay and waiting and he would get home one way or another. At the same time he knew that he had his doubts and was getting comfortable with the two younger girls. The age difference seemed more normal after three full days of driving, eating, and sleeping together. His family was much younger even though he could have daughters near their age. He thought about past generations when the age gap would be considered normal. Girls of fifteen were married off to old geezers in their forties and fifties back then. These girls were mid twenties and in their prime..he was not that old yet.

The scenery was magnificent crossing over Wolf Creek Pass. The road was tree lined except for large boulders every so often. They saw chipmunks and squirrels and Darcy thought she saw a fawn and a doe. The trees were interrupted here and there for magnificent vistas of the mountains and the steepness of the bank on the other side of the guardrail. They were about halfway down the pass into the San Louis Valley when Jim spotted another roadblock ahead. When he approached closer he could see numerous motor cycles parked around the roadblock.   He stopped several curves above the roadblock, and said, "Shelby and Darcy get your pistols out and ready." He checked his riot shotgun and his own pistols. "Shelby, get in the back seat with an M-16 at the ready, in fully automatic."

Darcy replied, "What's the matter?"

"There is a roadblock ahead with a bunch of motorcycles. What good reason would a motorcycle gang have for setting up a roadblock on a mountain road miles from a town?"

"I see your point. Can't we just go around them?"

"I don't have a map that shows the back roads. There are only a few passes over the mountains. We can't go south through Albuquerque to get around the mountains. We could go back to Durango. Do you want to go back. I have to keep going, but I will take you back if you want."

"No. Okay. Let's hope they're friendly."

"Forget going back. Get the guns up and ready, there are some motorcycles that just pulled onto the road behind us and they're carrying guns. I don't think they're friendly."

Shelby, always the most bold, climbed over the seat and got into a comfortable position where she could bring up the M-16 if Jim told her to do so. Jim placed the riot gun and one of the Beretta automatic pistols by him on the seat with a box of 12 gauge shells, four extra clips for the his and Darcy's pistols, and an M-79 grenade launcher with three extra rounds. He also put an extra loaded Beretta under his seat.

Shelby said, "Those motorcycles behind us are keeping their distance."

Once they had made sure everything was ready, Jim continued on toward the roadblock further down the mountain. He slowed when he got on the last stretch and slowly approached the roadblock. The road block consisted of a couple of converted Harleys with Volkswagen engines. The three wheel kind where the driver sits on the engine compartment and has the big handlebars stretching back to the driver. There were around thirty Harleys parked nearby or within a hundred yards of the roadblock.

Jim stopped ten yards from the roadblock. A very large fat man with a long beard, leather vest and pants, and carrying a shotgun yelled, "Bring that thing on up here...it's tax time." Jim heard Harleys starting behind him and in the mirrors saw four to seven more Harleys coming out of the trees behind him coming toward him. He could also see that they were armed. Jim yelled at the girls, "Hang on, we're going through. Get your guns up and ready to fire."

With that Jim floored the old Mercury which responded with an authoritative screech of tires. Several of the motor cycle gang near the road block tried to get their guns aimed, but the old Mercury was already demolishing the converted Harleys used for the road block. The gang members near that point changed their minds about aiming and dove for cover from flying motor cycle parts. The motor cycles behind accelerated toward them, but half went down in a profusion of spills as motor cycle parts careened back onto the road. The Volkswagen engine and rear wheels of one bike was spinning rapidly working its way toward the tree line down the mountain knocking other Harleys into the roadway. The pursuit evaporated with pursuing bikers stopping if not adding their own bikes to the wreck. Two of the motorcycles cart wheeled onto the road after losing their front tires on the debris.

Jim said, "It's not over, they'll regroup and catch us soon." He was sliding the big Mercury from one corner to the next just barely keeping the skidding under control and throwing everyone and everything in the car from side to side. The extra ammo stayed on the seat next to Jim because Darcy was partially laying on top of it, trying to sit back up after the first corner, and still trying not to be thrown against her door on the opposite corners. Shelby had turned around in the back seat facing backward and had one leg on either side of the drive shaft tunnel and her elbows spread out behind the rear seat with her M-16 resting near the back glass. This kept her fairly stable as the car skidded one way then the other and Jim accelerated out of one turn and braked into the next, over and over. When there was still no pursuit, Jim eased off a bit giving Darcy a chance to get back into a sitting position, but still sliding on each turn. "Keep your guns ready and tell me when you see them behind us. I don't have time to watch for them and keep up our speed."

Darcy said, "I didn't know it was possible to go this fast down a mountain, let alone in this big boat."

They had gone about a mile and Jim had gotten into a routine of sliding around turns, squealing the now warmed rubber, when Shelby nervously yelled, "Here they come!"

Jim could see at least twenty bikes three turns back and gaining. "Shelby, move right up to the back of the front seat, carefully point your gun at the back glass and shoot it out when they get close. Darcy, climb back there with her. Both of you use the back of the seat for cover. Keep your heads down except for aiming. Don't shoot until I yell, 'M-16!', and then Shelby, I want you to slowly aim at the nearest biker and gently squeeze the trigger and shoot out the back glass with your eyes closed and head turned to the side and then aim and fire again just for a second and move the gun from right to left. Don't hold the trigger down. As soon as the guns starts pulling, release the trigger, aim again and fire again. Short bursts will work better. Darcy, if anyone gets within two car lengths I will yell, 'SHOTGUN!'. If I don't, Shelby, you tell her. Darcy, at that time aim carefully and shoot to kill or we're all dead. Darcy, when not using the shotgun, keep one M-16 loaded with a new clip. Shelby, when you run out of bullets just get your head down and change your M-16 for one with a new clip. Darcy, make sure that box of loaded clips is close. Remember how I showed you how to load the guns back at Edwards. Don't worry about where the empty clips go as long as they don't get in the box with the full ones. As a last resort, I will use the car as a weapon. If they get too close I'm going to hit the brakes and try to surprise them to make them come crashing into us. When I yell, 'HANG ON!', do so."

By now the bikers were only one corner behind and Jim sped up to the limits of the car and the road and still provide a semi-solid firing platform for the girls. He made it sliding around two more corners until they caught up with the careening car. As they came within 75 yards, or half the distance between mountain curves Jim yelled, "Shelby, fire a single warning shot to get rid of the rear glass and to let them know we're armed!"

Shelby did so with a couple of the bikers swerving causing a chain reaction of swerving from the others. Their advance slowed, but some were attempting to aim and fire at the weaving car ahead.

Jim yelled, "M-16...NOW." Shelby let loose too long a burst with the gun climbing right up to the window frame and hitting before she let go of the trigger. She hit nothing, but could see returning smoke from the bikers' guns behind.

Shelby yelled, "They're shooting back" and fired a more aimed shorter burst from the M-16. One biker's front spoke hit the ground throwing the bike and rider into cart wheels and taking down three other bikes before they were clear. The next two bursts did no damage because the bikers had slowed somewhat. Shelby then discovered the M-16 was empty, ducked back down and exchanged M-16's with Darcy who was sitting half in the rear floor board and half on the back seat. When Shelby raised up with the new M-16, the motor cycles were closing in again. Shelby did not take time to aim, but hosed off a series of sweeps in their general direction. This shot two bikers off their bikes and one bike exploded and crashed into other bikes. Another had an engine fire but was still pursuing them until the flames from the engine fire reached the gas tank and then really exploded throwing burning gasoline onto two other bikers who slowed to bat out the flames on their leathers. This slowed the group enough for Shelby to again exchange M-16's, but when Shelby again looked out the back she could see they were really close now. Shelby used up the clip in two poorly executed sweeps across the road. One bike about 30 yards behind the leaders went down and somersaulted off the road. Shelby ducked when she saw a motor cycle, "biker" aim a big handgun at her head from less than 10 yards. The bullet took out the front windshield of the old Mercury. Lucky Jim had on partially wrap around sun glasses that protected his eyes from flying glass that he caught up with one half second later. It also kept the wind out of his eyes. One biker apparently was not so lucky and must have taken a face full of glass because he let go of his bike to grab his face and completely missed the next corner with he and his bike arching out into empty space toward the trees and rocks below. No one saw him hit because they passed the spot too quickly.

During the same second that the windshield exploded Jim and Shelby both yelled, "SHOTGUN" and two seconds later Darcy stuck a 12 gauge Winchester automatic out the back window and started firing.

Darcy was not half bad and outright blew the four closest riders completely off their still moving bikes before using up the five shells in the magazine. She yelled, "M-16!" and then ducked back down to reload the shotgun. In the second or so that Shelby was replacing Darcy at the back window, four more cycles moved almost to the Merc's bumper and two more had pulled abreast on a short straight-away between corners.

Jim yelled, "BRAKES!" and hit the brakes hard just long enough for three of the four bikes to bend their front wheels on the back bumper and started flying forward toward the trunk. Jim swerved hard right forcing the bike on the left to fly forward in front of the car and forcing the bike to the right, that had tried to stop, off the road and down the mountain without a road. He disappeared into the treetops below when Jim floored the Merc and aimed for the bike ahead. Becoming the hound instead of the fox. The bike ahead wanted none of that and quickly accelerated away. Jim pulled the 12 gauge riot gun from the seat and roughly pointed it out the front window. He must have at least wounded the biker ahead because the bike and rider went straight up the hill through the trees at the next corner. Jim threw the gun onto the seat and skidded around a corner losing sight of the entire gang behind the bend and tree line. Jim saw that the gas gauge was on empty after the chase and shifted into neutral. Jim thought, 'Thank goodness that this is a Mercury and got a GM or this would blow the transmission.'

Darcy yelled, "Don't slow down, they'll catch us again."

Jim said, "We're out of gas." That wasn't quite true, but Jim didn't want to completely run out during another high speed chase. He had to go much slower with only brakes to steer into turns and only gravity for acceleration. They got down to about fifteen miles per hour about two miles from their last sight of the motorcycle gang when the engine coughed and died at the same time as Jim saw a gravel road exiting down to the right and back up the lower part of the hill. He braked and took it. When the engine coughed and died Jim had this terrible sinking feeling. The gauge had shown a quarter of a tank only two miles early when he shifted into neutral and was now below empty. A hole in the tank? The car rolled to a stop in front of a cabin, near, but out of sight of the road. Jim said to keep their guns at the ready while he put gas from the cans in the trunk into the gas tank.   As soon as Jim got out he looked under the car and could see no dripping gasoline at the back, but when he went around to open the trunk he saw that the back of the car had several holes in the back. The big heavy bumper had numerous dents, but nothing that penetrated. When Jim looked under the back of the car he could see where the tank had been hit by something several times, but only had one hole about nine millimeters in diameter. The other marks must have been ricochets, but one had made a hole. It appeared that the rear of the tank had been protected by the bumper, but the bottom of the tank hung below the bumper. He then opened the truck to see about the gas cans and found that only two still had gasoline... the others had holes. Jim passed out some gum to the girls and the three started chewing, "...to seal the tank..." while Jim looked at the tree line for a stick of the right size. He brought back several and the third one he tried fit in the hole by screwing it in...probably providing a good temporary fix. He broke off the end of the stick leaving an inch hanging down. Jim then used the now chewed up gum to stick around the stick and to the bottom of the tank to hopefully seal the tank.

As Jim was doing this he remembered when he was with his parents but thirty years ago. Thirty years ago his father had hit a rock and was leaking gasoline. To keep his father from going back down the mountain without camping there, Jim had unwrapped a piece of used chewing gum and stuck it over the hole in the gas tank. It worked so well that when the car was traded off three years later, it still had a piece of very hard chewing gum on the bottom of the gas tank. Jim just hoped this would work as well again.

Jim wanted the gum well chewed so he told the girls to keep chewing while he pulled out his Beretta and decided to take a look in the cabin. It would be easier to defend than the car if it came to a stationary shoot-out. When Jim tried the door, it was standing slightly ajar. When he went in he discovered a man, woman, and three kids dead. The man and kids had died quickly, the woman was naked and had been beaten to death.

"Eeeeeeeeeaaaaaahhhh!" A noisy intake of breath...sort of a reverse scream.

Jim turned to find that Darcy and Shelby had come quietly in the door immediately behind him. Darcy had a shocked look and had her hand over her mouth. Shelby had fire in her eyes, but was also frozen and staring at the sight. Jim spread his arms and grabbed the door herding the girls back out. "Please just guard with the car, and let me look."

Darcy allowed herself to be pushed back out taking small stiff steps. Shelby resisted long enough to say, "cover them, okay."

"Don't worry, just keep the guns ready, okay?"

With his assurance, Shelby grabbed Darcy's arm, and ordered, "Come on Darcy, that's only a sample of what they'll do if they catch us. Let's get our M-16's and do what Jim says, guard the car. We'll kill those sons of bitches if they come around us again. What you saw is why we must kill them. They deserve it."

Darcy looked at her like some creature from outer space, but moved to comply.

Jim went back in and found an empty gun cabinet, guns and ammo appearing to be the only things missing. He also found bullet holes in the inner walls, including around the door like the man had a gun to protect his family, but failed. The killers, probably the motor cycle gang, had simply shot in a back window and shot him in the back through a back window. Jim found a cache of commercial emergency rations in foil packs in one cupboard and another full of canned goods. He filled a laundry basket and took it to the car then went back for the rest.

When Darcy first looked at Jim carrying out food she looked at him like he had lost his mind, then decided that it was a good idea to stock up whenever and wherever they could.

Jim asked, "Well, what do you think? Shall we drive and maybe let the motorcycles find us again, or do we just walk on down the mountain and hope we can find someone friendly to help us?"

They debated on whether to take the car or just walk downhill but decided to not leave the car with all of their supplies, guns, and ammo. They pumped the remaining gasoline out of the family's Audi into their own tank and took off again. Jim decided to just coast most of the way taking it slow and easy to save the car, the gasoline, and the tires. Going slower also made less noise because the engine was nearly silent at idle and the tires didn't squeal on the turns. They saw more and more little roads going off the road that they knew probably went to many more cabins as they got closer to the tiny town of Salt Fork. If this was a vacation, Jim would have taken the girls by to see Wagon Wheel Gap and Creede, but this trip had to keep heading towards Alamosa which Jim assumed would mean a temporary haven.

The drive was uneventful until they went through Salt Fork. When they did they saw numerous motor cycles and the gang members saw them.

Jim floored the old Merc to get as much head start as possible and told the girls to remember the routines from earlier.

Jim yelled, "Darcy load in a fragmentation grenade into the M-79 grenade launcher. It's just like a monstrously big gauge single shot shotgun, and basically is. You flip a shotgun style catch and "break" the gun in the middle. The shell is put in just like in a single shot shotgun. The shell is not plastic or paper like a shotgun shell, but loads like it was. You "break" the barrel, stick in the shell, and snap the barrel back up into the armed position. If you know what you are doing, you can pull up the gun sight and actually get a range for how far you are lobbing the shell, but wait to use it until I see a good target, and then just aim it like a shotgun with no sight. In the meantime keep it on safety and have the M-16 ready. Darcy keep the shotgun ready. Shelby, keep your M-16 ready and just fire whenever you want at anyone that gets in range." They had already reloaded every clip and gun.

On the seventeen mile stretch between South Fork and Del Norte the gang held back about three quarters of a mile. Jim didn't like that and told Shelby to keep watch on them, but asked Darcy to help him watch ahead for road blocks. The cycles could easily catch Jim, but weren't trying, so Jim slowed down to around fifty to save the car. It seemed forever, but fifteen to twenty minutes later they were entering the town of Del Norte with the gang still hanging back. Jim said, "Stay low and hang on, this feels like an ambush. If there is a roadblock, I'm not stopping until we crash."

As Jim came up a rise, there it was, right in the middle of the main intersection, a road block. Jim quickly decided that he was not going to be able to break through and would only total the car and get everyone killed. He immediately locked the brakes, slid for a short distance then released the brakes and cut the wheel hard right. The car made the turn, but when it hit the gravel of the side road the back end came loose and clipped the stop sign tearing it out of the ground and causing it to go spinning to a stop in the middle of the road behind them. The tail of the Mercury sending the sign flying just like a baseball hit by a bat. Jim floored the old Merc as soon as got the sliding stopped and fishtailed to the next intersection. He slowed enough to see that the next street over was clear and then hit the brakes. He couldn't slow enough on the gravel so had to floor it in reverse to back up a bit and then hit low gear and fishtailed down the street crossing "Main???" street and continuing on for a block while doing the same thing again until he was back on highway 160 heading east. The gang had alerted the gang in the town about their coming, but without radios the gang didn't know when and apparently expected the road block right over the small hill on highway 160 to stop the people in the old Mercury. Now the motor cycles on the east side of the roadblock were in the act. It did take awhile for Jim to drive the four blocks out of the way. Jim, almost accidentally, took out four of motorcycles when he turned onto 160 by sideswiping them. The Harleys were no match for five thousand pounds of Detroit steel. He had five or six ahead of him and a like number behind. He yelled, "Get up and start shooting those bikes behind us."

Shelby immediately opened fire with her M-16 while Darcy grabbed another to hand her when the first was empty. She took them all out. Whether she damaged their bikes, one biker losing it took the others out, or whether she killed them all, didn't matter. They were laying down on the road behind instead of chasing them. The bikers ahead realized that their bikes would not stop the Mercury and Jim was firing at them with his Beretta. They were firing back, but when Jim hit one with a grazing shot, they decided he had the advantage and they were not accurate enough to shoot backwards while riding forward. They accelerated away like the Mercury had suddenly backed up. Jim surmised that the motor cycles that had followed them had not been able to get through the roadblock either and were considerably behind at this point. He kept his speed up to one hundred, but not floored. "No point in blowing the engine", Jim thought. The gang got off the highway at Torres, a few miles west of Monte Vista where Jim just kept going. He sailed through Monte Vista at a dangerous sixty miles per hour and then decided to slow down to fifty, when the town crossing was uneventful. As he approached Alamosa, he could see an impenetrable roadblock of road construction equipment manned by policemen in uniform. He and the girls visibly relax almost collapsing with relief that they had made it past the gang. Jim slowed to a crawl, then stopped as a policeman came forward. Jim kept his hands on the wheel and the girls held their hands up in view, empty of guns for once.

"We heard you were coming." At Jim's incredulous look, he continued, "There is a forest ranger that has an old tube type ham radio and a few more here in town. We discovered that they still work. We heard about one exploit with the bikers. Can you tell us where you think you're going and what you found along the road from where ever you've been.?"

"JAKE!" ... "Save the questions. We'll ask them after they're in town and then let you know their answers. The road block's not for them. Let them through!"

Jim went as directed and found himself following a Jeep into the town and downtown to city hall. He pulled into a visitor slot surprised at the number of vehicles moving around. He also had seen probably a hundred horses saddled and either ridden or hitched up to something since entering the town. He was as anxious to talk to them as they were to him.

The man that had called off the policeman that had also driven the Jeep that led them down town came walking over, "Hello, I'm Mayor John Daly, not the one from Chicago and it is pronounced and spelled "Daly" not "Daily". We're real anxious to meet outsiders. Would you come in and join us in a discussion?"

"We would be happy to, but we have all our stuff in the car and need to leave someone here to watch it."

Daly cut in, "We'll have someone watch it for you."

"I appreciate that, but, to be honest, we have some very potent firepower in the car." Jim pulled the letter out of his billfold and handed it to Mayor Daly. "I'm on a mission of sorts, and the girls were going my direction. ...not to mention that I commandeered Darcy's car from her. I have to keep the arms and food stuffs for the trip."

Daly replied after pausing to finish reading the letter, "Don't you worry about a thing. We won't let anyone close to it. Besides, you couldn't stop us from taking it anyway...if we wanted it. We'll protect it for you. Come on in and relax."

Jim acquiesced and motioned for the girls to follow him which they did after a short hesitation about leaving the safely of the car. By the time they arrived at the door, some women were there to usher the girls one way while Mayor Daly ushered him another. This concerned Jim for no reason, because they were treated very well indeed. The girls had been ushered aside to let them get cleaned up and to make sure they weren't being held hostage or abused in any way. Jim, because of male chauvinism and his letter from the general, was assumed to be the primary source of information, which in this case he actually was, but mainly because of his background versus the girls background.

Jim found out from the Mayor and several others that were in the city council chambers that they had established short wave radio contact with many in short range, but world communications were still disrupted. The HAM operators could pick up the frequencies of their around the world friends and tell that most were still trying to transmit, but could not get intelligible information more than 800 miles away and then very spotty.

The forest ranger had reported the motor cycle gang, but they had not come after him yet, and he was afraid to try to leave. He figured that if he saw them coming he would take his already packed backpack and leave the bad guys lost in the woods. He had the training and the knowledge of these mountains to survive forever, if need be, while the gang members would probably be lost as soon as they got out of hearing range of their buddies. The forest ranger did not know that from Jim's inspection of the one cabin, that the gang may have murdered everyone along the road.

The discussion went on for two hours. At the end of which, the town of Alamosa decided that their defensive perimeter needed to move out to at least cover the valley. If the good guys could control the few passes with roads, they could keep all of the bad guys out. After hearing that this was a problem all the way back to the coast, they decided that they couldn't wait for outside help. They figured that the motor cycle gang would not be so tough against the ranchers of the San Louis Valley. Tomorrow they were going to send out riders to the nearby ranches and vehicles toward Salina to get a mountain pass to mountain pass defensive line set up and to get the good guys and their weapons organized.

Mayor Daly ended the meeting by standing and asking Jim to stay over at his house for the time being. Jim replied, "We wouldn't want to do that, how about a motel?"

"You'll find the motels are full of tourists stranded here and they won't take your money either. We decided that we, the town, would put up all the good people that some way or another ended up here in Alamosa. If the time gets too extended, we may put them to work doing something to earn their keep. We decided that the US Government money is currently valueless so there is either charity which we don't have here or barter. I'm offering barter for more discussion while you're with us. I know you're capable of moving on since you got this far, so I'm not afraid of you out wearing your welcome. Besides, if you did decide to stay, I'm sure that we could find a job for you to earn your living here. My kids have moved away to the big cities and the wife and I have a big lonely house to share. How about it?"

"Since you put it that way, I'd be proud to accept your deal. I'd appreciate more discussion myself. It's been a pretty hectic week for the girls and myself. We might just stay a day or two, if that's all right?"

"Certainly. Glad to have you. The dark haired one, Doris ... no Darcy ... she looks almost like my Mindy that's living in Saint Louis now. Mindy's 24, single, and trying to establish a career before she gets married. Gladis, my wife, never considered any other career other than being my wife. She was 17 when we got married and we've never wanted to be apart yet. I'll never understand these new women."

Darcy and Shelby were already waiting in the lobby when the meeting broke up and Jim came out. They were fresh and clean looking with new clothes. One of the older women waiting with them volunteered, "We couldn't have your girls running around in dirty work clothes looking like soldiers from some trench now could we. We traded their clothing for new clothing even up. You've been told about our barter system I suppose. We even got them over to the hair dressers for a little prettying up. They picked out their own clothes. I hope you don't mind. They are young, you know."

Shelby flirtingly said, "Bet you can't resist us now, can you?" That surprised the older women that figured they were already having sex.

Darcy was not so forward, but looked like she was wanting to say the same.

Jim just stared. The girls had been wearing dirty blue jeans and flannel shirts and were smudged and messy from no mirror or shower in several days, not to mention today's excitement.

Now Shelby had her blond hair smoothly over one shoulder, with makeup highlighting her blue eyes and pale skin. Her blouse was one of those short things that looked like bandanna material tied at the waist with no buttons...and obviously no bra. Her midriff was bare down from just below her breasts to her short shorts tied up at the sides of the thighs showing skin between the ties. Her shoes had changed into lifted sandals with thin straps holding her feet on them and lacing up on the ankle. That is the only kind of shoe that Jim had thought of as sexy. God she looked good.

Darcy had been hanging back and now stepped forward breaking Jim's stare at Shelby only to be frozen now on Darcy. Darcy's dark brown hair was tied up into a loose bun which emphasized her slender neck and bare shoulders. She was wearing a Mexican style down on the shoulders natural cotton colored crop top with lace making her already look even more enticing. The crop top which didn't start without showing part of her breast ended just below leaving her midriff bare like Shelby's until they arrived at an Aztec colored mini wrap skirt leaving her legs mainly bare. She wore some sandals that were almost high heeled and had a single wide strap holding her foot in that matched the skirt. While not as brazen, it made her, if anything, maybe more sexy than Shelby.

The older woman broke the trance, "I'm sorry. I thought they were your lovers not your daughters."

"They are not my daughters and we have been together since the start and will probably be together for some time yet. No, it was just such a change from what they were wearing." That was Jim's first admission that they might become lovers.

Jim would not make the advances, but with his knowledge that finding his family might be a futile effort and these two beautiful starlets, dressed like this ... he knew his will power was absolutely out the window if they came on to him in private. In fact, Jim had to turn away to keep from being even more embarrassed as he realized he was getting aroused right in public. He thanked the woman for her care of the girls (it didn't sound as sincere as he meant it to sound, probably because of his rapid loss of will power). He started off down the steps leading the way, expected everyone to follow.

Mayor Daly caught him in two steps and leaned over to almost whisper, "Jim... do I ever envy you! If I had those two, I would never get any sleep. How did you pick them?"

Jim replied, "I didn't go into that part of my story, but it was pure chance. I'll tell you tonight after we get settled. We haven't been lovers yet, but I'm not sure whether I'm looking forward to sleep tonight or not."

Mayor Daly came back with, "Well, the whole upstairs is yours at the house. The master bed room is down stairs and the upstairs has three bedrooms and a large bath...not that you're going to be using all the bedrooms. I wouldn't if I were your age and had those two." Mayor Daly was almost laughing out loud in a man to man sort of private joke way.

It turned out the woman was Mayor Daly's wife. She was attractive and looked in good shape for her age which must have been around sixty-five putting Mayor Daly at least sixty-five also. She had white hair and a few wrinkles, but her secretly laughing eyes gave away her little impish or cupid girl nature. She had been happily married all of her life to one man so did her flirting vicariously. Jim wondered if he should tell her he was also happily married and didn't need to cave in to the situation, but now she had made that impossible. There was no use bringing out his still hiding pain that his family was either already dead, would be before he got there, or at least he might never find them if they did survive. It was only that almost sure knowledge that made the girls so attractive to him. If he was flying home tomorrow to his family without this war, he would probably have been able to ignore the girls, but not under these circumstances. Their choice of clothing could not have been worse for his virtue. He had been much safer when they were wearing the jeans and flannel shirts he had purchased at the base exchange at Edward's Air Force Base so long ago. Apparently she was overjoyed at his obvious attraction for the girls. She had probably tried so hard to marry off her own that they had rebelled into making a career before men choice.

Jim Claris was absolutely bushed. Shortly after Mayor Daly and his wife had fed them supper, Jim asked to be excused. He was extremely sleepy. The girls repeated his excuse and went up the same way. By this time they were all tired. When Jim assigned each of them separate bedrooms, no one questioned, but went on to bed.

DAY 5, 22 AUGUST

It was broad daylight when Jim woke up, got dressed and went down stairs. Mrs. Daly had pancakes ready to cook and the coffee hot. Jim ate and made small talk. When Jim asked where the Mayor was, he got the answer, "He's just out doing his mayor work."

When Jim had finished eating, she volunteered, "Actually, the Mayor is downtown organizing a small army. We're all hunters in these parts and quite a number are so called survivalists. They plan on taking your suggestion and blocking the passes into the valley to keep the bad guys out. I wouldn't want to be one of the ones hiding out in one of the valley towns."

Jim thanked her and asked that she keep the girls here while he went downtown to see if he could help. She agreed and Jim left. Jim drove downtown, since he couldn't remember how far it was. It turned out to be only six blocks. When he got there the highway was jammed with pickups and jeeps loaded with men with guns. The mayor saw him and came over.

"Hi Jim, sleep well? We're about ready to go. We're going to make sure Monte Vista and Del Norte are safe then move on up that pass to the top. If it's not clear, we'll clear it out clear on down to the bottom of the other side and set up a road block down there on the other side."

"Jim said, maybe you should just roadblock the top so you can stay in radio contact with this side of the mountain. You could have a group on the other side trapped when the snows come. Why don't you go to the next bigger town on the other side so they will keep their side of the pass clear?"

"That will work for Wolf Creek (pass), but Walsenburg has turned into an enemy camp. We'll clear the roads all the way to Durango to the West. We've already got a clear road to Salina, but we don't even know what we have over in Walsenburg. Some guys tried going over there last night and were lucky to get back over the pass. We've got about one hundred guys sitting at Fort Garland... making a fort " Mayor Daly let out a laugh, "just to make sure they don't come on over here."

"Good show. Don't mind me. You're doing fine on your own."

"Hey Jim, I'm a retired Army infantry colonel. I served two tours in Nam. Don't feel bad, this is my area of expertise. In fact we're going house to house all the way up Wolf Creek (pass) and down the other side. I suspect that gang you ran in to yesterday, will not feel so courageous when they are the ones out gunned. I'll bet they clear out before we even catch sight of them. I figure it will take about three days to search the cabins to the other side and make sure the road is open to Durango. When we get back we're going to make sure that the La Veta (pass) is closed so we don't have to worry about who is in Walsenburg and then set up a guard to make sure the road stays closed. I suggest that you stay right here for the week. I can't make you stay here, but until we've got more information, you're safe here."

"Thanks for the hospitality." The mayor was already walking off toward his mechanized civilian infantry column. Jim was going toward the house when he met the girls walking toward downtown. They thumbed a ride and they went back to Mayor Daly's house. They decided they would leave as soon as they had the old Mercury's gas tank fixed properly and some new gas cans and more gasoline. They had plenty of everything else. Mrs. Daly sent him to an old time garage down the street. It had a partially cement and partially dirt floor. It was littered with various pieces of metal from antique farm tractors and newer cars. The older whiskered man there said he would be glad to fix the car dropping his current work anytime Mrs. Daly asked. He not only fixed the gas tank, but seeing the bullet holes and hearing about how they got there, he added some extra metal to the doors and behind the rear seat, "for armor", he said. He traded their cheap gas cans for some heavy duty army surplus five gallon cans saying, "this is a gas can, that what you got is water cans. This is all we use up here. More important when you're out here on some back road in the mountains, don't cha know. Here, I'll fill yaw up with gas." He filled the tank and the gas cans.

He refused money, "You just keep that money and tell Ms Daly what I did fer y'all, okay. Her 'preciation mean more around hereins than yer dollars."

Jim thanked him as best he could and assured him he would explain all the things he had done for him. Jim returned, got the girls, thanked Mrs. Daly and asked her to thank her husband, but they didn't want to wait a week before resuming their journey. Since the road was open to Salina, they would try for Canon City and Pueblo and then on to Kansas. Jim said that he always liked to visit Colorado and would look them up in better times to come. With that they were on their way north to Salida.

The drive was uneventful. Salida had a roadblock set up at the bottom of the pass, but they were passed through without hassle. They followed the Royal Gorge Canyon down to Canyon City. The girls marveled at the beauty and could not believe that Jim had once taken a raft ride through the actual gorge. Jim could not resist and took the girls up and onto the bridge, but not in the car, on foot. Jim had driven across the bridge once and that had been enough. He had been driving a full size Chevy van with his family and some fool from the other side came on the bridge in another van. Jim had to put two wheels on the wooden two by four edge and pull his mirror to the side of his vehicle for them to pass, four inches from a thousand foot fall off the bridge. Jim swore he would never again attempt to drive over the bridge. It was enough just to walk over that chasm to the raging river below. The amusement park was still taking money and operating like nothing was wrong. Jim didn't want to take the time to take the Cog Train down to the bottom, and they were told that no raft rides had been going for days, but that the amusement park was still open to keep the tourist entertained that were stranded here. Some of the tour buses were old enough to have never had any electronics. Jim remembered the raft ride vividly. It had been his one and only and this ride was supposed to be one of the best raft rides around. The water had been quite high that day making it even better. The fear and excitement of the white water was nothing compared to the last few days since the war started.

They drove on through Canyon City and on over to Pueblo. Pueblo was at a stand still with tens of thousands of refugees from Denver that had run to the south to get away from any nuclear radiation that might be there. It took hours to get through Pueblo and on the open road again. The Colorado National Guard was in force in Pueblo checking for radio active contamination of any of the cars or occupants. Jim was passed on through since he had his letter from Los Angeles and had not come through any radiation areas. However, they were asked to stop at Pueblo Army Depot. They did and were put up in the VOQ.

DAY 6, 23 AUGUST

The next morning they were summoned to visit with the depot commander. Jim told his story one more time. This time the depot commander asked him to repeat again how he had stopped a terrorist attack at Los Angeles Air Force Base. Jim repeated that it was their bad luck to wreck their truck, he had just been at the right place at the right time to prevent the final arming of the back pack Nuke. The depot commander explained that this was the only confirmation they had of such an item being in use although it was the suspected nuclear bomb that had blown up several cities. He asked and Jim complied in writing up a detailed report on Los Angeles and what he had gone through thus far. The story was retyped into message format and transmitted to the ANMCC, the Alternate National Military Command Center. Jim was offered assistance, but took on only more gasoline and continued east.

Jim was stopped at a road block in Rocky Ford and warned that somewhere to the east was a gang of hoodlums that had come from Walsenburg, looted La Junta, the next town, set fire to much of it and headed east. La Junta was passable, but burned out. As Jim drove through La Junta, they were correct. It was burned out. There was not much standing. There were burned out vehicles here and there and some larger buildings still smoking. Jim turned back to Rocky Ford and suggested that they send someone back to Pueblo where there had been national guard troops. Jim was unsure as to what he should do, but he wanted to keep heading east. He decided to head north to U.S. Highway 96, instead of staying on U.S. Highway 50. By doing so he by-passed Las Animas and Lamar, Colorado, but when he got to Scott City, Kansas there was a semi truck overturned in the road just on the east side of town. The townspeople said it had been there for two days and they weren't concerned about it. They reported that a rain had washed out the bridge over Smoky Hill Creek the week before, so the only way out was the way they came in or south to Garden City. Jim headed south on U.S. 83.

Jim was driving fast toward the north side of Garden City and wondering about all the cars spread out across a field to the right when he drove right into a war zone. Jim saw the barricade being opened ahead of him. "Hey girls, there's the welcome wagon again, like at Alamosa."

Jim blissfully drove right on until suddenly gunfire erupted from the people on his side of the barricade, whoever they were, focused on him and the people behind the barricade started firing at the ones firing at Jim and the girls. Bullets flew everywhere taking out every last piece of glass in the Mercury and blowing both right side tires. Jim barely maintained control of the car to get through the barricade opening before he lost it completely and spun slowly into the ditch. Both girls had instinctively dived for the floor. Fortunately, the extra metal added by the shop in Alamosa,

Colorado stopped all of the lighter slugs and most of the bigger heavier shells. One thing about lightweight automatics; they don't fire heavy shells. Most people use soft lead or hollow point slugs for anti animal ammunition. If any of the larger shells had been heavy jacketed ammo, the added metal would not have stopped it. As it was there were only two or three holes and the bullets hit nothing of consequence inside the car. The girls weren't going to move off the floor boards, and Jim was laying on the seat until the shooting stopped. Jim cautiously raised his head to see he had made it through a make shift fort of cars and trucks barricading the road. Jim opened his door that was on the side away from the barricade and crawled out of the car with his pistol and a riot gun. As he moved to look under the front bumper that was still over the road, he could see several, apparently armed farmers coming his way with guns carried low for safety, not in a menacing way. Jim laid his riot gun down, hoping that it was unnecessary and waited for the farmers that quickly ran around behind his car and ducked down.

"You people okay?", they asked.

Jim nodded and said, "Yes, I think so. What's going on?"

With obvious breathlessness they replied, "Bunch of gangsters have been burning and looting towns to the west. We're stopping them right here and now. I see you have some guns, can you help us out?"

Jim thought, "Boy they just don't know what kind of firepower we got here." He said, "Yes, I think we can maybe help you out. I don't think we're going to be driving any further in this car without tires. If I help you, and we chase them off, will you help me get some tires and repairs?"

"You bet." With that, the farmers crouched ran back to the barricades.

Jim looked back in the car door and said, "Well, I'm going to take an M-79 grenade launcher and one of the LAWS (Light Anti-tank Weapons System or portable disposable bazooka) with me along with an M-16. You can grab whatever you can handle and come with me or just stay here as you choose. Jim put on an ammo strap with eight forty millimeter grenades that looked like huge shotgun shells, and the short 2 foot plastic tube that was the LAWS, and an M-16 along with another ammo shoulder strap with ten thirty round clips of ammunition and crouch ran to the barricade. When the townsmen saw him, they were more than a little surprised at his armament. He asked where they thought the most fire was coming from or where their ring leader might be. He fired one grenade which exploded harmlessly behind the strong point. This was a cluster of four by four pickup trucks with light bars and heavy bumpers parked on the other side of ditch. People were running in the open away from this strong point by the time Jim had cracked open the single shot shotgun style barrel and reloaded and fired again. The next round was short but with shrapnel shells blew up the adjacent gasoline tanks of the pickups which set off ammunition and other gas tanks. The bad guys were running in retreat toward other vehicles parked further away to the west on U.S. Highway 50. Several were making U-turns to retreat, when Jim dropped the M-79 and extended the LAWS. He had never fired one before.

"Clear a path behind me!" Jim took the time to make sure no one was from behind him as he went past the barricade out into the road and aimed and fired the small missile. It hit a pickup sideways in the road and the pickup lifted off the ground in a fiery explosion that took out the two nearest vehicles. The vehicles that had not already turned to flee were quickly emptied of people who were running west on foot. A cheer went up from the townspeople. Jim realized what had happened in the past few minutes and almost dropped the now used LAWS on the ground with his shaking. He had such an overload of adrenaline and fear now that the danger was over that he could hardly stand. He moved over to the barricade as nonchalantly as possible when your whole body is shaking like an earth quake, and sat down. He would have lit a cigarette, but was shaking too badly. Instead, to act cool and to clear the shakes that had set in, he clasp his hands behind his neck, leaned back, crossed his legs and acted like he was going to take a nap until the adrenaline had warn off. Most of the people had not moved and were watching the mad retreat of the gangsters. A few farmers were putting guns away and looking to go back to town. Some were moving into groups to talk about the action. A few started moving through the barricade toward Jim. Shelby and Darcy brushed past them and ran to Jim. They dropped to the ground on either side of him and asked if he was okay. "I'm fine", he replied.

DARCY SAID, "YOU'RE SHAKING LIKE A LEAF. ARE YOU SURE?"

Jim said, "Just give me a minute to settle down. I'm fine, just a little scared now that it's over." Jim usually was pretty cool about these things, and couldn't believe that it was a good two minutes before he quit shaking. One of farmers was saying, "I never saw anyone move so fast in my life. He came running up to the barricade carrying guns like Rambo, he asked a question of somebody and then in about three seconds fired off two shots from that big ass sawed off shotgun of his then he pulls this bazooka out of no where...nobody saw him carrying one and our battle is over. Then he goes over and takes a god damned nap like nothing happened."

He felt drained as he stood up to talk with the townspeople that had been talking to Shelby who had intercepted them before they could disturb Jim. Shelby had been very quick to recognize that Jim needed a few minutes to settle down. "Actually it seemed very slow motion. I'm not really that brave, it was just an emergency reaction."

"I can't believe you just fired off those shots and then jumped over the barricade and fired that bazooka in about three seconds." Shelby said. "Where did that rocket come from?"

"I can't believe I did that either. That was a disposable rocket launcher. It comes as a very small package just the size of the rocket and then extends out to length and the handle and sight fold down. It just seemed like the thing to do at the time."

"You must be a special forces guy, right?" one of the farmers asked.

"No, ex air force. I had never fired those things before, but I have seen a number of them."

"Well, come on in to the town. Let's get you fixed up with some tires. Those guys will not be back here again. They even left most of their vehicles behind."

"If I were you I would keep guards posted all around the town in case they try to sneak in at night."

"You're right. Anyway, let's go get you those tires and see if you broke anything." Joe, Sam, stay here and keep a watch out. If you see anything moving fire some shots. We'll relieve you by dark and post more guards."

"If I were you I'd send a couple of guys west of town to watch for them coming back to town. Tell them to stay out of sight, but keep watch on the road, and high tail it back to town if they see anything."

"Good idea. Hey, Jake, take Bill with you and go down the road to the curve west of town and keep watch there. Keep that hot rod of yours out of sight and if you see anything just make a fast run back for town. Joe, fire your gun when you see Jake coming. Jake, you and Bill stay awake now. We'll relieve you before dark."

"Girls, I'm sorry I don't know your names."

"Darcy"

"Shelby"

"Okay, Darcy and Shelby, I suggest you ride with Jim and I back into town to find some tires and someone to change them for you."

"Darcy, Shelby go on with them and get something to eat somewhere. I'm sorry, but I need to stay with the car to make sure those guns of mine stay out of the bad guys' hands and no one gets hurt by accident. I'm just not comfortable leaving them out here in the country, even with your guards. It would be a disaster if we didn't get here in time to protect these guns."

"I understand. I'll be back with a tow truck and a jack in a few minutes."

The girls went on in to the town and had a salad at a restaurant where the food was on the house. It had been days since they had a salad. The tow truck was back in twenty minutes, pulled him out of the ditch, helped Jim pull off the wheels and took them back into town. He was back in another twenty-five minutes with two new tires. "Follow me back into town and we'll get you another pair of new tires to match those. Payment for a town saved."

Jim followed him and got two more new tires. By this time what remained of the glass in the old Mercury was totally broken and shattered out. The man apologized for not having the right glass, but offered a sheet of Plexiglas off his desk. They cut it down to roughly fit the hole and then used sheet metal screws to attach it to the roof and to the metal behind the hood. It didn't wrap around or even curve like the original, but it would keep most of the wind out of your face. Jim then followed his directions and found the girls at the restaurant and had a chicken fried steak and mashed potatoes and iced tea, which he hadn't had in awhile. They thanked the people, "We surely do appreciate the free meal. I'm glad I was able to help. Have you heard anything about the road to Dodge City?"

"Sorry, you can't get there from here. After the rain last week the road is flooded. Which way are you headed?"

"We're headed for Ohio."

"Since you came south, I presume the road to the north isn't any good, we know the interstate across Kansas is blocked in several places, so the only way you can get there is to head south into Oklahoma and then head east again. Our bridge just clears the high water and the road to the south is dry for at least ten miles. Some of the farmers came that far to create our road block."

"Thanks, I guess we're headed to Oklahoma. Don't forget to post plenty of guards on all approaches to the town for several days." With that Jim and the girls took off heading south again.

"That section of Kansas and Oklahoma was very deserted and the small towns they went through didn't seem like anything unusual was happening. People were just going about their ordinary business. Some people they passed near their farm houses just waved, assuming they were neighbors or just being friendly. They stopped at a small grocery and gasoline station and picked up an Oklahoma map. Jim asked them if they got any news here. The answer was yes, John Watkins got him one of those Ham radio outfits. Everyone gathers over there every night to listen to the news. There's a war going on over in Europe and some of our cities here have been destroyed. At least it's not like the nuclear war we were afraid of with the Russians. I was told that there is no fall out danger here and most of the United States is just trying to get back to normal. Us farm communities have been asked to plant extra vegetables for the cities. There is supposed to be some radio stations working in Oklahoma City, but we can't get a thing out here since the war started. Where you'all headed?"

"We're gradually working our way to Ohio, but we've had a lot of detours and problems so far."

"Hope you're not planning to go through Oklahoma City?"

"Why's that?"

"Well according to people that's been there, the Arkansas River bridge is out so you can't get through to Arkansas on that road."

"WHAT ABOUT THE ROAD TO TULSA AND ON UP TO JOPLIN?"

"Supposed to be okay. Some people that moved up there a few years ago came back here last week. Said the road was okay, but they heard that Saint Louis was pretty bad. Shooting in the streets. Fighting over food. The bridges over the Mississippi are all gone, so I wouldn't try getting there through Saint Louis or even near it. That's why the people came back here from Joplin. They heard that people from Saint Louis were raiding every town along the interstate looking for food. National guard was setting up road blocks west of Springfield to try to stop them from coming all the way to Tulsa. Tulsa is in bad enough shape. Understand they are standing in soup lines there without much to eat. We've been sending trucks of cows there to help out, but the problem is not enough bread and vegetables. Fruit is even a big problem here, and we'll be short of vegetables before winter is over, but then we eat a lot of beef anyway. People been trying to plant potatoes in hopes they'll grow some before winter. Used to throw out the old ones that grew vines...now we plant the old ones. 'Bout out of good potatoes, so I hope they can grow some by winter. I'll get tired of steak and eggs myself. Some of the farmers been trying to figure ways to grind some wheat ourselves, but I tried some of their bread. Not too good. Anyhow, if I were you I'd stay away from the cities if I were you and anywhere near Saint Louis is mighty dangerous. Maybe you ought to head up north somewhere before you head east."

"Thanks for the information. I think maybe I'll try to go through to Fayetteville south of Tulsa and north of Fort Smith. Good luck on growing your potatoes."

Jim and the girls had picked up some eggs and beef jerky. They had a few cans of fruit and vegetables, but not enough to help anyone. They took off across Oklahoma and the open country there. Miles and miles of rolling hills, open treeless pastures. They stopped for the night in Woodward, staying at a small motel. Jim was too tired to argue when the girls asked the motel clerk for a king size bed. The clerk cocked an eye at Jim and then winked. He probably figured that was why Jim looked tired. They had a meal at Western Sizzler, but were disappointed that there was no salad bar, only steaks and drinks. Somehow they had potatoes and butter at least. After the meal they went to an outdoor play that some group in town was presenting since there was no television. Jim slept through much of it. After the play, they went back to the motel and Jim showered first while the girls went for a swim in the pool, and crawled under the covers. He never knew when the girls came in.

7 OKLAHOMA

August 24

The girls did not disturb Jim, or at least he did not remember it. He woke early, feeling rested. They took off driving early after some eggs and pancakes at a MacDonald's. The rolling prairies got more trees and less grass and then fewer trees and less grass until it was gradually turning to near desert through the Glass Mountains (large bare hills that looked like small mountains on the flat plains) until they got to Fairview and then several miles of scrub oak trees and cedars mixed with wheat fields until approaching Enid, there was nothing but wheat fields. The wheat was harvested in June and all the fields were plowed waiting for the winter wheat planting in the fall. Enid was a sun blanched town of about fifty thousand. The shopping malls were open and cars parked around. The Mac Donald's and Hardies were all open for business. They stopped for a hamburger. Jim asked the counter attendant where they got the buns.

"From the Bond Bread bakery here in town, of course."

"You mean they're open and producing bread?"

"Where are you from, man? This is wheat country. The Union Equity grain elevators are third or fourth biggest in the world. They say it is big enough to feed the United States for nearly a year. Most of it gets shipped out, but we have our own Pillsbury plant and Bond Bread bakery. This is the bread basket of the world", he said with pride.

"I used to live around here many years ago. I know where Union Equity is, now that you mention Pillsbury, I think I even remember it, but where is Bond Bread?" Jim got directions and asked, "Is the Gold Spot dairy still in operation?" He got directions for it also although Gold Spot and Bond had both sold out to bigger corporations since Jim had lived there. They ate their hamburgers and then Jim decided to make a side trip to Bond Bread.

The manager said, "Well actually we sold out to Rainbow years ago, but everyone here calls it Bond. In fact, we started running out of Rainbow plastic sacks for the hamburger buns and started using some of the crates of Bond Bread sacks we still had in the warehouse. Plastic keeps forever, if out of the sun and dry, you know."

"We just came from the panhandle, and they are completely out of bread there. They said Tulsa is out also. Can you increase production and spread your distribution?"

"We're baking all the bread we can during the forty hour week now."

"Why not go to twenty-four hours a day seven days a week while there are shortages? Who knows, maybe you can keep the business when competition starts again."

"We don't have the bread sacks to last more than six weeks even if we use up all of our old Bond Bread sacks."

"Do you have to wrap it all? There are people starving that would be glad to pay top dollar for unwrapped bread? What did you do before you had plastic sacks or wax paper sacks? I'll bet one reason its bagged is because its sliced. If you didn't slice it, it would cut out a couple of steps on your production line and the crust would help keep it fresh for awhile."

"Before my time and yours, but you have a point. But Enid doesn't have a lot of unemployed people right now. If we spread out our experienced people to supervise shifts...yes I guess we could. What about trucks? We don't have the delivery trucks we used to use to deliver to all the local towns? Rainbow had big semi-trucks that came in and picked up our bread and delivered it, but they aren't working anymore.

"I'll bet you could find someone with an old car and a covered U-Haul trailer or a old pickup with a cap who could make some extra money delivering the bread and selling it for a profit. Is the old Champlain refinery still operating?"

"Sure is, doesn't matter whether you buy Shell or Texaco gasoline, it all comes from the Champlain refinery around here...and that was before the war started. Apparently you're not from around here and are heading elsewhere. I'll pay for your idea by giving you all the bread products you can carry for free and you can sell it where ever you want if you think there's that much demand."

Bread was light weight, but with the only glass in the vehicle being some Plexiglas screwed to the sheet metal where the windshield was supposed to be, and rain on the horizon, Jim didn't take too much. He did have some large plastic garbage bags, so he filled some.

"He then stopped by the Pillsbury flour plant and gave them a similar story. They decided to send a truck out to the panhandle, another to Wichita, and another to Oklahoma City to try the market. They had a similar problem with a sack shortage. Jim suggested lining cardboard boxes with garbage sacks full of flour and selling it in bulk that way. Stores could measure it out by the pound like in the old days when they shipped flour and sold flour using wooden crates. People would bring their own containers from home.

Jim stopped by Vance Air Force Base, a pilot training base, but they were unaware of what was happening in the war and those trainees that had reported in had been told to go home for the week. It was a contractor run base, and the contractor's people decided to stay home in fear of the war getting worse. Very few of the contractors had shown up since the war had started. Without the contractor, they couldn't fly their training planes, because the contractor did all the repairs, refueling, fire fighting and most other daily operations. The military only flew the airplanes and did the weather and flight planning and training.

The girls wondered about the little town of Enid running out of wheat until Jim drove them past the Union Equity elevators and said that there probably a years supply for the United States stored there with more wheat stored on farms and small towns. It was amazing to see hundreds of Union Equity train cars lined up on the sidings. It was even more amazing to them when they saw an entire old time box car picked up and tilted back and forth like a child shaking a toy, until it was empty. Most of the cars were special cars that dumped out gates in the bottom. The girls didn't realize just how big the elevators were until they were driving east out of town and could see them for miles. The only trees were along the creeks and near buildings for miles of very flat wheat land. Since the back seat was completely loaded all three had to ride in the front seat. Darcy was sitting next to Jim which Jim was very self conscious of. It definitely didn't help that the girls were wearing their new sexy clothes they had gotten in Alamosa. There didn't seem to be any threat except for Jim glancing to his right and seeing down Darcy's top. It also didn't help a bit when she kept pulling it down further to get a little cooler. Summer in August in an almost open car in the daytime is not cool. It did not take too long before Jim was getting quite self conscious of an erection, which Darcy noticed and put her hand on his leg inching her fingers up his shorts. Jim said, "Please! It's already hard to keep driving."

Darcy coyly said, "Let's pull over and do something about it." All three of them had been too exhausted and scared to think much about sex for the past few days, but it had also been a few days in very close proximity and sharing some unforgettable, if bad, experiences.

Jim did not doubt that she meant it and the age difference was seeming more and more normal but he said, "We need to get to Tulsa before dark." and then tried to ignore her.

They took a break along the way at a gas station, and Shelby ended up sitting beside him. She went considerably further to bother him. She had this really skimpy tied together top that showed just about everything and was so thin it might as well. By this time they were all sweaty and her blouse ended up almost see through. At any rate it clung to her raised nipples. He was aroused before she put her hand on him. Jim said, "Please, this is not the time or place."

SHELBY SAID, "OKAY BUT YOU HAVE TO PUT YOUR ARM AROUND MY SHOULDERS AND PRETEND YOU LIKE ME?"

He did. Somewhere along the way, she pulled the knot loose on her top and was riding along with her top wide open and pulled back to her sides. Her breasts were large and full and whether it was the temperature or whether she was hot too, her nipples were erect. This was not helping Jim drive at all. He said, "Are you trying to drive me crazy?"

Shelby responded by saying, "It's really hot". and pulled his hand down over one breast. He let her do it and she snuggled closer.

Jim said, "I'll keep my hand where you want it if you'll move yours away before I wreck the car." She moved her hand down onto his thigh. He was still quite aroused, but that was better.

As they went further east they started running into more trees mixed with pastures, until it was mainly trees and rolling hills. They didn't stop until they reached Tulsa. When Jim pulled onto the interstate that went into Tulsa. He suggested that Shelby might like to get ready for public and put both hands back on the steering wheel. At least it broke the mood. Shortly after coming onto the interstate in Sand Springs they could see an intersection of several freeways ahead. There was a road block on the west side of the river before going into Tulsa. There were several Oklahoma highway patrolmen.

"Where are you going and why are you here?", asked the Oklahoma highway patrolmen. The police here were driving 1993 or 1994 Chevrolet Caprices.

Jim said, "We're on our way home to Ohio, but I am also performing a military mission." Jim volunteered the military mission information because he had all the firepower on board and he assumed he would have to show his letter authorizing the arms. Then to distract the patrolman, "How did you get your patrol cars running?"

"They're three fifty engines, we changed the heads and manifolds and distributor at a speed shop. They run even faster than they did before. Now, what's this about a military mission and what are you doing in this junker, and how did you get these bullet holes and dents?"

Jim said, keeping his hands in sight on the steering wheel, "It's a long story. Let me summarize. We started at Los Angeles Air Force Base and when we started, this was the best car we could get that ran. I was on TDY, er, I mean a temporary duty there from Ohio when the war started. There was nothing more I could do there so I decided I was going to get home to Ohio and my family. Darcy here actually owns the car and Shelby is her friend. They wanted to come along. The commander of Los Angeles Air Force Base provided me a letter and asked me to scout across the country to see conditions since I was determined to get home to Ohio." Jim handed him his retired United States Air Force reserve identification card and a copy of the letter. "We've been checking in at military bases along the way and passing on information to the Alternate National Military Command Center on what we found between bases. In addition to the armament, we picked up garbage sacks of fresh bread and flour in Enid, to show people here that there are some sources of food if they can get some trucks there to pick it up. We didn't bring any extra milk, but they have an operational commercial dairy too.

Thanks to the bread and flour and military identification card, the patrolman relaxed a little. "Will you please get out of the car and show us what all you have?" He was still suspicious, but had tipped his hat at the girls moving it away from his gun belt. He motioned for a couple of other officers to come over. "Excuse me, sir, but I need to confirm your story with my boss."

Jim nodded, moved to the back side window where he could reach some of the garbage bags, and waited for the other officers. Apparently he was going to be okay, because the patrolman turned his back on Jim to greet the other two officers, saluting one and repeating the story as the three stood around Jim. The patrolman nodded for Jim to show him what he had, and Jim complied by opening up one of the garbage bags wide and folding it back so it would stay open. The reaction was quite positive. The smell of fresh baked bread was overwhelming having been trapped in the bag for two hours in the afternoon sun and having been fresh right off the line before it was cool or sliced. The original patrolman said, "Man that smells good. I haven't had any bread in nearly a week and I haven't even seen bread that fresh from a bakery in my life. Jim said, "You all take a few loaves. Maybe you can help me contact someone who can distribute this and arrange for someone to pick up some over in Enid, if you want more. I also have fresh flour from there if you know of a bakery that could use it. There is a Pillsbury mill there, but they are out of sacks. In the trunk I have some of that in bulk...let me show you."

The patrolmen were completely disarmed now and were curious to see what Jim was talking about. Normally, Oklahoma patrolmen were very cautious about someone opening a car trunk and Jim had already admitted he was well armed, but they just crowded right up as Jim struggled with the bent up trunk lock. The trunk was full of bullet holes and looked like it had been in a tremendous hail storm, but the troopers had forgotten after seeing his bread. Jim got the trunk opened and opened one of the garbage sacks in one of the cardboard boxes. They peered in and the boss, Jim didn't recognize the patrolman rank ensignia, moved in and took a pinch and tasted it to make sure it was flour instead of cocaine. Suspicion was still there and the Oklahoma highway patrol was well know for finding stashes in cars passing through. "It's flour all right. Okay, close it up."

Jim did and closed the trunk...Except for the spare and their meager camping things, the boxes filled the large trunk.

The "boss" noticed the massive damage to the rear of the car, "It looks like you've been a war. Can you explain?"

Jim said, "It's been quite an adventure so far. We were jumped by two different motor cycle gangs and had a shoot out with another gang over in Garden City, Kansas. If you've got a few hours, I'd be glad to relate our adventures since leaving Los Angeles."

"I heard that Los Angeles was nuked, how did you get out? Is any of this radioactive?" The boss backed up and lowered his hand toward his gun belt, but not putting his hand on his gun.

Jim interrupted, "No Los Angeles was not nuked. You won't believe this, but I was the one that prevented the detonation of the nuke intended for Los Angeles Air Force Base. It was burned by rioters and looters. They had no fire department or police department and no water pressure. Things got out of hand and we were lucky to get out. We've avoided areas of radiation. We've been to a number of military bases since we left. We're okay."

THE BOSS ACCEPTED THAT FOR NOW AND RELAXED SOME. "DO YOU MIND IF WE SEARCH YOUR CAR?"

"I'll unload it myself if you want, but I have some touchy military hardware in there. I'd rather I handled it. In addition, I'll spill all the flour if I try to unload it here. Any chance on getting it to a bakery first?" Jim figured he might as well be up front with the information rather than to try to hide anything. If he tried to hide they would arrest them for sure and ask questions later. If he was up front, maybe they would believe he was authorized.

"What do you have?" the "boss" patrolman asked harshly.

"I was issued an M-79 single shot forty millimeter grenade launcher, a twelve shot forty millimeter semi-automatic grenade launcher with two boxes of forty millimeter high scrapnel grenades; four LAWS, disposable rocket launchers with one rocket for each, but I had to use one of them in Garden City, so there are only three left; three fully automatic M-16's with one hundred loaded thirty round clips; three twelve gauge riot guns; three Baretta nine-millimeter military fifteen shot pistols; then we have a regular twelve gauge automatic, a thirty-thirty, a Ruger three fifty seven magnum, and plenty of ammunition."

The "boss" just said, "SHIT! Are you sure you didn't steal that stuff? You're either telling the truth or you're an arms dealer."

The original patrolman held out Jim's military ID card and the letter from the general in Los Angeles, "Sir, you better look at these."

The "boss" glanced at the rank of lieutenant colonel and read the letter, and paused a moment making his decision. "Okay, I don't even want you showing all those guns. In fact, we'd better escort you through town. We've got a food riot situation brewing. You say they've got plenty of food over in Enid?"

"Yeah, but you've got to bring your own containers to carry it in and the bread won't be sliced. The bakery can put out more bread that way."

"WHY DON'T WE ESCORT YOU DOWNTOWN TO THE MAYOR'S OFFICE AND YOU CAN TELL ALL OF US WHAT YOU KNOW?"

Jim said, "Fine, lets go."

The "boss" and his sideman, led the way in his car. He had another car following Jim. Jim hoped it was for his protection versus escort to jail. The girls were asked to ride in the back of the boss's car, "for safety", and Jim was provided a patrolman to ride with him. The patrolman carried a riot gun between his legs on the trip.

They followed the interstate downtown. It was lined with occasional sandbag machine gun posts with national guardsmen manning them. The bridge had another roadblock that they were waved through because of the escort. There were guardsmen all along the bridge. The patrolman volunteered, "We found a guy planting explosives on our bridges a week before the war started. Thought it was a nut case until the war started, now we are guarding the bridges."

The downtown was sand bagged and barricaded like a fortress. They went to the federal building that was well guarded by guardsmen. The visit actually went much the same as their other visits, with Jim giving the long version of his experiences since the start of the war. Apparently, Oklahoma had not been having the power problems and there was plenty of gasoline, but they were not able to export electricity outside Oklahoma due to the power grid computers being out. Even those computers were supposed to be protected, but the HEMP overload was much greater than anticipated. The generators had popped off line as had the nuclear power plants, but they had been back on line within forty-eight hours. Some towns had been without electricity for several days because of blown transformers, but due to the high number of thunderstorms, Oklahoma Gas and Electric had worked as hard as they could after getting their vehicles fixed to run with conventional electronics and carburetors. The Tulsa National Guard unit had reported for work voluntarily assuming that they were needed, which they were. The national guard immediately dispatched trucks for Enid to pick up bread, milk, and flour. Some of their trucks were old diesel semi-trucks of Korean War vintage, but they ran fine, if you like riding in old military trucks. The local radio station announced that bread, milk, and beef deliveries would be made to the local grocery stores within the next twenty-four to forty-eight hours, and that people were to bring their own sacks and boxes to carry it home. The milk would be delivered in military water tankers. They hoped this broadcast would be picked up by enough people with old tube type radios to avert imminent riots. The guard was also making a run to Springdale, Arkansas for chicken products they assumed were there, just not being distributed. Tulsa had been out of touch with national military news.

Day 7 August 24

Grand Forks AFB, North Dakota

Colonel Henry Lakeman reorganized his base forces to provide more security for the entire base. Major Houston was staying with Henry and his wife Karen. Being the Wing Commander, Henry had the nicest and biggest house on base. He only had one child still at home. His oldest son had just graduated from the Air Force Academy and was in pilot training. Major Houston had been reassigned to Colonel Lakeman's wing since neither base had a shortage of pilots, but did have a shortage of airplanes. The military commands around Washington D.C. were pretty much wiped out. The President and most of Congress died in the nuclear flames. There had been no alert, no threat, no warning. Those that died, died in their sleep.

"Colonel Lakeman, there is another message coming in."

Colonel Lakeman read the message as it was manually decoded, "Many of our military satellites have survived and are providing pictures from around the world. Arab forces have invaded Italy. We have evacuated our aircraft from Italy to Great Britain. Italian and French forces are moving toward the Po River in northern Italy. It has been confirmed that Iranian and Iraqi satellites were actually orbital nuclear weapons designed for producing HEMP.

The destruction of New York City and Washington DC were committed by sub launched missiles from a single submarine. Four were targeted on Washington DC and five on New York City. If that is the only nuclear submarine that the Arabs have, and if it is a captured Soviet submarine, it will still have eleven missiles. Our attack submarines are attempting to find it now. The other American cities reported were not, repeat not, hit by missiles. In these other cities, there is a high level of radiation in the downtown areas indicating that a nuclear device was detonated, but only several blocks were destroyed. This may have been the result of Soviet back pack nuclear devices reported to have been developed for Soviet Spetnaz and sold to Arab nations. Due to the HEMP, evacuation has been very difficult. Fortunately, the fallout from Chicago and Cleveland was carried out over the lakes and the radiation from New York and Washington DC out into the Atlantic before it fell. Long Island showed only slightly elevated radiation levels and Delaware was mostly spared from fallout from Washington DC. The actual bomb sites are too hot for anyone to enter in all the cities."

Colonel Henry turned to Major Jeremy Houston and just said, "Just wait until the food riots."

JEREMY QUESTIONED, "WHAT ARE YOU TALKING ABOUT, FOOD RIOTS?"

Jeremy replied, "How do you think the people in any of the cities are going to get food. Do you realize that less than two percent of the population lives on farms. The farms truck their produce and beef into huge factories where the beef is fattened then trucked to slaughter houses and frozen for shipment. The vegetables and fruit are mostly trucked in to canning factories. How many trucks are still running to move this stuff around? Even the railroads use computers and radios for switching and traffic movement on the rails. Do you realize how many bridges were sabotaged. Without transport, the cities couldn't get supplied and without the food processing points working, even transportation wouldn't help. The people in the cities couldn't even get out of the cities to the farms for their food. Those that did get to the farms would not find the food they expected to. Vegetables and fruits came from basically only three states, California, Florida, and Texas. Beef came from several states, but it was on the hoof. Corn was grown in many states, but it was only ripe for cooking for a very short time. Even farmers were so specialized that they bought most of their food at the grocery store."

Colonel Lakeman said, "I guess that we had better do something right now to stock our base with groceries to maintain the military, and I'll suggest that the other bases do the same."

Jeremy enjoined, "Right on, however, I would do it carefully. You can't just go down in military trucks and start emptying stores. You better send people in civvies in private cars...and not try to buy too much at each store. Even North Dakota can have food riots. Remember, some of the farms here depend upon southern states for some of their cattle feed."

"Good point. I'll pass that on too." In fact not only did Colonel Lakeman pass that on, but he sent a recommendation to what was left of military command that getting the food flowing had to be a major priority. Military and civilian trucks need to be controlled and get busy transporting food. Canning factories and other food processors needed to be made operational, even above military defense. "If everyone starved to death, there would be nothing to defend. The United States was people, not territory." Frozen and refrigerated food were out until electricity could be transmitted around the country.

Most of the generating stations were still operational, but the electrical grid was controlled by computers that routed electricity and these computers were just so much melted plastic and wire after the one hundred twenty thousand volt surge that went throughout the power grid. The same problem occurred on the telephone grids. Every micro-wave tower and computer in the system was blown, along with most of the military communications between bases. With no television or radio, there was no way to even tell people to stay calm, that the government was working to help them soon.

If the military could get food moving quickly enough, most people had enough food to last for a couple of weeks. This meant that there could be no conventional military response from the United States against the Arabs, but with the military transports, maybe people wouldn't starve.

Jim, Darcy, and Shelby

They were put up in a downtown Tulsa hotel that night, courtesy the national guard. Whether it was the teasing of the day long drive with partially clothed girls, their attraction for him and his being flattered by their attractiveness, whether it was the fatalistic view he took of finding his family, lust or feeling young again with the girls, or what...Jim and the girls were given one room with only one king size bed, but they only needed one. The girls insisted on Jim taking his shower first, and then joining him in the shower with lots of innuendoes and brushing of bodies and the lathering up and hugging. The girls soaped Jim and he soaped them. They drove Jim absolutely wild. Then they went to bed.

8 GERMANY

Day 8

Technical Sergeant (TSgt) Walter Gaddis was officially stationed in Heidleburg, Germany, but he and his M1A1 tank were currently on station at Hahn Air Force Base in Germany to protect the gates. The war started only seven days ago and already the world was topsy turvy. The United States was out of communication with the rest of world as far as he knew. HEMP bombs had exploded over the Mediterranean and northern Norway and just east of Moscow, but many of the West European electronics had survived. Reportedly, the United States had been hit the hardest with more than enough HEMP bombs to wipe out the electronics there. There were also rumors that several American cities were destroyed by nukes, but he had no way of knowing if that was true.

The Muslims were incessantly bombing Rome and had moved to the Po River where French and remaining Italian troops were building up for a major battle. There seemed to be little doubt that the Muslims were coming that way into Europe. He was only a TSgt, but he had a Master's degree in Political Science that had been paid for by the United States Army. It had taken a lot of night classes, but he had done it. He only had six months left before retirement at thirty-eight, with his degree, to go get a job, and the war had to start. He had joined the Army right out of high school. There had been no word, but he suspected that he would not be getting out of the Army for a long time now.

He was stationed here because there had been hundreds of bombings throughout Europe, many of which aimed at American bases. There had been car bombs driven through the gates at several bases that made it to somewhere important before blowing up, driver and all. His job was to sit inside the gate with the engine running. He would move his tank out of the way after the outer guards had waved them through and then move the tank back into position blocking the gate at other times. Pretty dumb duty. There were no tanks to fight. A nice steel beam on a pivot would be more logical. But they didn't have time to get one in place, so here he was. He was using a tank as a gate, burning fuel; for what?

Actually, it was not bad duty. He had enjoyed visiting on the Mosel River. Hahn was right above Zell, the home of Black Cat Mosel wine. By going down river he could visit the quaint brick brack town of Bernkastle and upriver was Cochem with its fine restored castle on a pointed hill overlooking the town. Cochem was one of the towns that had survived the bombing of World War II and was pretty much original. Even the bridge was before the war. The wine from there was much better than Zell or Bernkastle wine, but you didn't find it in the United States. There was a small town just up river from Cochem that had the very best wine, but it was hard to get even if you were German. Further down river toward Koblenz was a marvelous achievement of modern engineering where the autobahn crossed over the Mosel Valley on a bridge sitting on impossibly tall tapered rectangular concrete pillars. If you drove up out of the valley from Cochem you would get to Buchel German Air Base and then on to the autobahn between Trier and Koblenz. At this halfway point you could go past the edge of Ulmen and to the famous Nuburgring racetrack. They weren't having any races because of the war staring, but they did allow people to go driving on the track. Walter wished that he had a sports car of some type.

Koblenz, for him was known as the place where the beautiful and awesome 'Rhine in Flames' was celebrated several times a year. You could take off from Koblenz on a river boat that would go upstream toward Weisbaden and then turn around and come back as the sun set. The villages along the way would be lit by burning red flares to simulate the burning of the castles by the French last century. At some of the castles overlooking the Rhine river you would see these flares lit sequentially from the village up a narrow walkway to the castle and then the castle walls would be lit by flames. At Koblenz was a phenomenal display of fireworks to simulate a tremendous battle. Rockets are fired by barges on the river and fire is returned by the castles overlooking Koblenz. Marvelous.

The people in this area were friendly. If you went further north you would get to Bitburg Air Force Base which was a bigger American Air Base than Hahn. Bitburg even had their own high school. American high school kids here at Hahn were bussed to Weisbaden where they spent Monday through Friday at a boarding school.

France and Italy had asked for German assistance fighting the Moslem forces, but Germany had sent no help. They believed that the Moslem forces might have done okay against the Yugoslavs, but were not capable of fighting European forces. Germany had rules against sending German forces outside of Germany since World War II. Besides, Germany had dismantled most of their forces since the Soviet Union had crumbled from within. France had the largest standing force in Europe.

Germany was well protected. The Muslims had to come through France or up through much of the old Soviet Union. There were two ways to attack Europe. Though the north and Germany or through the south and the Po River valley, north or south of the ALPS. Anyone trying to come through Switzerland would pay dearly. Switzerland had always been an armed camp. All males served in the military. Active duty for a year and then reserve forces until age 55 with one or two weeks of training each year. Rather than gun control as starting in the United States, these reserve military kept their machine guns and grenade launchers in their houses along with the appropriate ammunition. All the corporate or bank officers were reserve officers of their military. The mountains were full of command bunkers and buried miniature air bases. They had no air bases. Their airplanes were buried in the sides of mountains and used the straight-a-ways of their autobahns through the mountains for runways.

Sweden and Switzerland were considered neutralist because they didn't take sides. Most Americans assumed they were pacifist countries. Actually they were armed camps. Population for population, the United States would have to have five times the military they had during World War II and this was peace time in Switzerland.

Actually he lied, he knew the brass were in touch with military brass in the United States, but there were no news broadcasts on radio or television. The brass were specifically blacking out information and keeping something quiet. It was not helping morale, imagining what might have happened, but he couldn't imagine what was so bad. The Arab's didn't have much of a nuclear force, they might have made a few bombs, but nothing serious, and no delivery vehicles. They didn't have long range missiles or bombers capable of hitting the United States, so what could it be that they were keeping secret? What had really happened.

German television was showing nightly news of the battle in Italy. It wasn't much of a battle. The Arabs were bombing Rome, gradually reducing it to rubble. Any vehicle trying to get out of town was strafed and bombed. The train tracks were all destroyed. The Italian air force was no match for the Arab air force or whatever they called it. Why the Arabs were so intent on destroying all of Rome and all of its people could only be traced back to very old history which he studied in college. The Romans had conquered the great empires of the Arab world from biblical times, including Egypt. The Arab countries had never recovered. Then centuries later when the Arabs were again in charge, the Crusades had begun, led by the Catholic church, which was the only Christian church at that time. The British Empire had been the final downfall of the Arabs, but they couldn't just attach Great Britain without taking Europe first. Italy was easy for them to hit in comparison and could lead to taking Europe on their way to Great Britain.

Back in the seventies when the German economy was so strong, they needed more workers and had imported literally millions of Arabs. Most were only on short term work visas, but tens of thousands stayed after the reunification of East and West Germany. Then the East Germans provided the cheap labor. Now it didn't matter East or West Germany, it was finally just Germany again. Every German got paid the same for the same work. The Arabs that stayed were relegated to garbage workers, house keepers, servants, waiters in restaurants and a few small shop keepers. Thousands more had gone underground and were now resurfacing to cause mayhem. There had been hundreds of bombings in the last week. Whenever they went sight-seeing he wished he had his tank. Several castles had been seriously damaged killing numerous tourists. All of the American tourists could not just return to the United States and had migrated away from the war to points north, like Germany. Every hotel, campground and guest house was full of tourists stranded in Europe. Roads and bridges had been destroyed throughout Germany by Arab terrorists. Air bases had been of particular interest. Probably to keep the planes away from Italy. That was why he was at Hahn American Air Force Base in Germany.

Buchel German Luftwaffe air base just across the valley had been hit by a car bomb attempting to run the gate. The Germans were smart. They had substantial gates compared to American bases and their entrance road took a ninety degree turn just inside the gate with an earth berm built up to keep a car from driving up to it's alert pad. That was what? Three days ago. The car was going fast, but hit the gate and exploded. The gate was bent and scorched, but still serviceable. Two German gate guards had died.

The day before yesterday, a car had blown up on Bitburg American Air Force Base right by the base exchange killing over one hundred Americans. It was apparently one of their German workers that was probably of Arab descent.

Hahn Air Base was vulnerable to that kind of attack. It was someone who just drove onto the base as a foreign national employee of the base and was waived right in. Now the American military was searching the back grounds of all foreign national employees for Arab relationships. In the meantime, every foreign national car was carefully searched for explosives complete with explosive sniffing dogs. Their cars were pulled off to the side outside the main gate where he was, but inside the outer temporary gates.

He had ten minutes until quitting time, assuming his relief came on time. He watched another batch of cars being let through the gates. One of the dogs in the main gate area started barking at the cars going by and jerked away from his lounging handler. An officer's Porsche had to slam on his brakes to avoid the dog. The dog then jumped up on the driver's side door as the officer instinctively leaned away from the window. The dog's handler came running out. TSgt Gaddis could only make out a few words above the combined engine noise of his tank idling and the cars going past. The dog handler was asking the officer to get out of his car saying something about never seeing the dog act that way unless there were explosives. He didn't hear it all, but he did hear that the officer was a munitions officer on the base and his ID card checked out. The gate guards called someone and the officer was allowed to continue.

Finally TSgt Gaddis' relief showed up fifteen minutes late, and TSgt Gaddis headed for the non-commissioned officer's (NCO) club. As he drove, he saw what looked like the old Peugeot that had been just ahead of the Porsche at the gate turning at the street where he would be turning for the club. It had been an NCO sticker on the car, so he was probably going to the club first. He wondered where the car had been since TSgt Gaddis had gotten this close to him. It must have been wandering around somewhere. He was driving into the parking lot at the club when most of the club exploded in a ball of fire. He slammed on his brakes and just sat their watching bits and pieces float in slow motion to the ground, some pieces hitting his car fifty yards away.

He was still sitting there when he heard sirens of security police and the fire department. He pulled his car out of the way of the parking lot entrance and took off running toward the fire. As he got closer he discovered charred pieces of people and decided that he would go back to his car where he got sick in the grass next to his car. The fire department trucks came racing in driving over pieces of the club and body parts and started hosing down the club. Security quickly set up a perimeter around the club. Now some of the firefighters had discovered the body parts and were retching in the grass too. In a few minutes the fire was nearly out, but he could see what was left of a full size car sitting inside the perimeter of the club building.

A SECURITY OFFICER DROVE UP AND ASKED HIM, "SERGEANT, DID YOU SEE WHAT HAPPENED?"

TSgt Gaddis saluted and salute was returned, "No sir, I just drove into the parking lot entrance when the club exploded." He paused a minute looking at the car body where the club ought to be, "But I think I know what happened. If you check, I'll bet you find that hulk is an older Peugeot. White. I saw it come on the base a few minutes ago. Then, I saw it again, turning down the street toward the club ahead of me. I got here and boom. If my relief had not been late I would have been in there." That was a shocking revelation that took his speech away.

The security officer was saying, "Would you repeat that? Are you sure that car just came onto the base? What were you doing at the gate? Did you just come onto the base too? Sergeant, are you listening?"

TSgt Gaddis had backed up and was almost sitting on the hood of his car, his face had gone white, but now the words of the officer were sinking in and his color started returning along with his senses, "I'm sorry sir. I got a bit dizzy for a minute there. I am a tank commander. I just got off gate duty and was heading for the club for supper and a few drinks."

"Do you know what happened to cause this? How could he just drive through the gate with a carload of explosives?

"SIR! I do know what happened! An explosives sniffing dog caught wind of a scent. He was in the gate shack and pulled away from his handler. The dog was apparently alerted by the Puegeot, ran outside and, since the Puegeot was already gone cornered the wrong car. The car with the explosives was ahead of the car he stopped and just kept going. I'm sure the car had an NCO sticker on it. It was a white Peugeot. Now that I think about it, the driver was dark complexioned. I thought maybe he was Mexican, but he might have been Arab. To top it off, when I saw the same car ahead of me, I wondered where it had been that I caught up with it fifteen minutes later. I'll bet he was not familiar with the base and was looking for something and either found the NCO club on purpose or decided to hit it rather than get caught just driving around."

"Well you might as well go to your quarters. You will be restricted to quarters when not on duty until we have investigated thoroughly. I just got word that we are calling a curfew for the base. All recreation services are closing until further notice. Personnel will be restricted to the base. When you go back on duty, you can plan on stopping and searching every car going on or off this base from this time on. It's good to know that the explosive sniffer dog caught the scent from a passing car. The dog should not have been in the building. From now on we will be stopping each car and give the dogs their chance to identify which car has explosives."

Jim. Darcy, and Shelby

The three had slept together in the king size bed and spent for some time without sleeping until all three were fully awake. Finally Jim had regained enough energy to wiggle his arms, one pinned under each girl, and said, "Time to rise, we need to make some more miles today."

When they got down to the car, they found the mechanical tower clock on a nearby meeting hall said 11:00. Jim asked one of the guardsmen if that time was correct, and he answered that it was as far as he knew. They had spent a lot of time and were getting a late start. Jim did not know if they were actually going anywhere on this trip, but was determined to eventually get to Dayton, Ohio, to see if his family had survived. At the rate he was going, and with reports of no bridges, it might just take another month to get home. He hoped his wife would never know about the girls, and if she found out, he hoped she would understand, but he felt like a widower that had just rediscovered other women. He only wanted his wife, but if she were dead...she wouldn't want him to be alone. The girls had revived his old youthful sex drive. Jim and the girls were escorted to the edge of town the next morning with their things intact and full gas cans again. The police did not want anyone to get their hands on the arms in his car.

The drive to Springdale, Arkansas on U.S. Highway 412 was uneventful except for passing several Army trucks going empty, and other trucks returning, not empty. He could tell, because they only had canvas tops on the trucks. The ones returning had Tyson ©chicken boxes. When they arrived in Springdale, they found the town jammed with over one hundred thousand people that had moved into town to get away from the crazies that had come from Saint Louis. They were told that Fayetteville was even more crowded. There was plenty of gasoline coming from the refineries in Oklahoma and the gasoline stations were open and taking credit cards. There was no bread or milk, but plenty of eggs and chicken on sale. They followed an Army truck going to a chicken factory (?) until they got on through the traffic in Springdale.

They decided against going down to Interstate 40 at Fort Smith, Arkansas, because U.S. Highway 71 was reportedly blocked by a massive landslide set off by explosives. Apparently their little Arab friends living in the United States were also sabotaging highways. They decided not to go north because there were supposedly people from Saint Louis as far south as Branson, Missouri and had ransacked the town and were trying to head south. Apparently they were trying to get around the Oklahoma national guard that had set up roadblocks just west of Springfield, Missouri. That left Jim, Darcy, and Shelby heading east on U.S. 412 for Harrison, Arkansas uncomfortably close to where the looters from Saint Louis had gravitated. Once they got through Springdale, Arkansas, it was already turning dark and the road was totally deserted. When they got to Huntsville, Arkansas, there was a sign along the main highway that said, "No Vacancy". That meant forget going into town. There was a sign pointing north away from Huntsville that said, "Withrow Springs State Park". Jim went there and found a deserted campground. They camped.

"Should we have stayed back in Oklahoma?" Darcy asked.

Jim answered, "I think maybe you girls should have, but I am still trying to get through to Ohio. I have to. Do you want me to drive you back? I'll bet you could catch a ride with one of the Army trucks just a few miles back down the road. This is still your car, if you want to keep it and I will find another way to get there."

Shelby said, "I didn't leave anything in Oklahoma. Whither you go, I go."

Darcy said, "Me too, I was just asking. Jim, if you're going to keep trying for Ohio, so am I. It's still my car...or what's left of it."

Jim said, "Are you absolutely sure? It doesn't sound too pleasant ahead. We're getting closer to Saint Louis and that seems rather inhospitable. It's the first really large city we have approached, unless you count Denver. We could wish we were back fighting motorcycle gangs in Colorado. They may have been mean and well armed, but there weren't that many of them."

Darcy said, "I don't care. I'd rather not have to fight, but if we die together, we die together fighting."

Jim said, "I don't know if I like the sound of that. I hope you're not doing this just to be with me. I'm still too old for you, despite what happened last night, and I am still married as long as I don't know that my family is gone." He refused to use the word dead, because he was a naturally married man that loved his wife and family...even though he now expected them to be dead. He expected never to see them again. If Saint Louis had a mob this far away ransacking the countryside, imagine what it would be like just outside Dayton, Ohio, with Columbus and Cincinnati, Ohio being so close. People in that area must really be starving to death and killing each other for food, and not necessarily just the poor people.

Darcy replied, "No, not just to be with you...although that is one factor. If I can't stay with you, then I want to go home. I should have gone home after the first year in L.A. when I couldn't find an acting job. California was a crazy place to try to live before the war. Arizona is nowhere unless you're a land owner. Colorado was down right dangerous. Kansas was no where. Oklahoma, was too rural. I'm really not a farm girl or cow town girl. Arkansas??? I'd just as soon go back to Colorado. At least it was a pretty place to die. I'm heading for home in Ohio."

"Shelby, I'd like to hear your reasons for going on to Ohio and whatever dangers we may face. Don't forget it sounds more dangerous ahead than what we have seen so far."

"Well, Jim and Darcy. Los Angeles is gone, my life was in Los Angeles. I haven't seen anything to stop for. Remember, I'm from Saint Louis. I don't figure I can go home either. With Hollywood gone, I would try Broadway, but I we've heard that Broadway is a radioactive hole in the ground. There hasn't been anything of interest to me except for the adventure. I've always dreamed about adventures, and this is great. I feel like an explorer ... maybe like a pioneer moving west during the Indian wars except we're heading east and the Indians don't just have bows and arrows. I'd pay for this adventure, if I had the money. This is the most exciting thing in my life. I'm loving every minute of this. If this were one hundred years ago, I would have gone west on a wagon train. If I die on this trip, well, at least I will have had a more amazing adventure than I thought was possible in today's world

There were adventurous women back then and very few today. How many chances does a girl get to go on a dangerous adventure? By the way, you probably think I've been loose. Actually, I've only had sex with one other man before in my life. I was in love once back in college, or thought I was. He dumped me for a rich girl with a BMW and I went to Los Angeles to become a rich girl.

I just like the feeling of turning men on. It put excitement in my life. I'm a born flirt. I like to give them the come on and then dump them like I was dumped. I like that power over men. Since I was dumped, it gives me a good feeling to be wanted even if only physically. I would never have done it with any of them unless they wanted me for more than my looks and they were willing to commit. Yes, I've been hungry for a man I wanted to actually do it with, I have been turned on for most of my life. Many men have turned me on, but any man that tries to pick me up in a bar or any movie producer that thinks he can get something are not the men I'm looking for. Jim, if I had met you in college, I would have had you for myself. I respect your desire to find your wife despite the odds. That's a major factor that made me decide I would have you physically. You were always different from many of the men when I talked with you in the bar. I could tell you were attracted, but that I couldn't have had you then if I wanted. You were just looking for conversation and company."

Darcy started to interrupt Shelby, but Shelby held up her hand and continued, "Don't interrupt, I'm on a roll here. Even Darcy probably thought I had more men. I've deliberately given that impression to people, because it turns men on to think they are with a loose woman. It also is more of a put down to them when I say no. I have used them to take me nice places like concerts and Vegas, but then I would refuse to go all the way. I really haven't met anyone since college that I cared enough for. No Jim, I don't think I'm in love with you, but your attempts to be loyal to your wife when the odds are so slim of finding her, turns me on. I'm jealous of her in a way; that she could find someone as loyal as you when I've found no one that might even be like that. I will be happy for you if you find her, but I would also like to be with you if you don't. I might even learn to love you, and I would be as loyal as you have tried to be to a wife you may never see again. I think maybe I do love you. I do. But if you do find your wife, I'll just go looking for someone like you. I won't be heart broken; I'll be happy for you and maybe just a little disappointed that I couldn't keep you for myself."

"Wait...you asked, and now I'm going to spill it all. Darcy, I don't mind sharing Jim with you. In fact, if it were for a life time I still wouldn't mind. You were my best friend even before this adventure. Maybe this is how the Mormons used to do it; share their men and have another woman to share the duties of housework, farm work, crafts and childbearing with. They needed the men in pioneer times for their strength, but there were more women than men. There are still more women. If you only count the good men, it makes sense that they are shared. Especially in a war, the men die more than women do because they go off to war. Which means to regain our population, we need more than one woman per man. At one per man it takes nine months for each child to be born, if a woman could get pregnant immediately. With two women per man, only four and half months. Don't worry, Darcy and I got a years supply of birth control pills from Mrs. Daly back in Alamosa. I'm not about to get pregnant without a husband to take care of me.

Anyway, I haven't had much actual sex in my life. My adventure in Los Angeles was a failure and Los Angeles and Hollywood is gone now. I plan on having as much sex as Jim can provide me and as much adventure as I can while I'm still alive. If my life is short, I have to live fast for awhile. We don't even know how much of the United States is left. We don't know how long we've got to live. We have to live as much as possible while we can. Don't worry, if I see somewhere that looks like I might be able to live, I'll say 'good-bye'. Otherwise, I'm not stopping until I get to Ohio. If I had to go alone, I would still try. Well I guess that's it." Shelby looked at them, and added, "I'm sorry, Jim, I shouldn't have said you'll never find your family alive. You still have to try."

Jim said, "Yes, Dayton, Ohio was one of the places that was nuked, and my house was near the air base. Don't feel bad, I've not had much hope for awhile, but I do have to still try. My wife is very stubborn and tough. She knew that I thought this was coming and I did make some small preparations such as laying in two or three guns and some ammunition. She never knew that both of our houses were on the hills around Dayton instead of the valley with the idea that a blast would be deflected by the hills."

"While we're talkative," said Darcy, "I've got a few confessions myself. Before this all happened and every time I met Jim, I wished that Jim was single, younger, and lived in Los Angeles. Don't mean to admit you are too old for me. Women have always liked mature men. Young women marrying much older men is just not in fashion right now. In fact, it has only been in this century that women married men their own age unless it was an arranged marriage. I knew I didn't have a chance with you until this happened."

"Darcy." Jim said disapprovingly.

"Let me talk. Shelby had her turn, now it is my turn to bare it all. I'm not sure what love is, I agree with Shelby, let's have sex while we can. I always figured Shelby did do it more than I did, even though I didn't know for sure, I just assumed those trips to Vegas and other places included sex. I just haven't even found that many I wanted to be with for even a play or trip to Vegas, let alone going to Hawaii with a man like you did Shelby. I have to feel comfortable with someone before I will even date them. I had sex with a boy in high school, because everyone said it was so good and natural. I felt dirty and it was not even fun. I got involved with a hunk in Hollywood that I thought was going somewhere and felt the same as I did about things, but he made it and dumped me. As soon as he got a role in a movie, I was forgotten. We lived together for about two months not long after I got there. We vowed to help each other. Ha. He got one minor part and our apartment was not good enough. I wasn't good enough either. As soon as he felt he was in, he started running with starlets that had minor parts in movies. The last time I saw him was last year and he was strung out on drugs and already a has been. I wouldn't have stuck it out except for Shelby. Yes, I can share Jim too. I agree, if the United States survives this we need to double up with the men. With all the homosexuals and crumbs around...

Then there is another factor I have wondered about. The white European people of this country have been giving up the country for some time. Birth control is a conspiracy against the Europeans. Women's lib has been a plot against the rich Americans of European descent. The non-white races of the United States have six and eight kids on welfare while European women have been having near zero. The average for white Americans has been one point two per couple. We need two per couple to not have a decline in whites. If the non-whites are having six and eight, we need six and eight just to maintain our plurality. Then you count the fact that the United States has been letting in more non-white immigrants than whites, and democracy is doomed. It is the whites that have made this country. It is the whites that have been paying for the welfare that has allowed the non-whites to reproduce at prodigious rates. That's not completely true, I was concerned when they let all of the Vietnamese in, but many of them have turned out to be workers also. They may appreciate this country more than most of the whites these days. Some of the Cubans have even made it and are hard working...but then they are of European descent also. I don't mean to sound so prejudiced. There are a lot of blacks that have been major contributors, but it is the lazy, uneducated of any race that I am prejudiced against. I don't know if I'm more disgusted

Jim cut in, "If you met the blacks that are in the military, you might think differently toward them. If we had mandatory military service, maybe we could get all of them out of the Ghettos. I agree with being prejudiced about the lazy people on welfare, milking the system. What we need to do as a nation is to eliminate the welfare that takes away their spirit. Would you work if you could get more money for not working than by working? There are people that need more assistance, but we need to be far more selective in who gets welfare. Unemployment payments are fine, but if it is because of alcohol or drugs, we need to get them help, not pay for their addiction. When immigrants come in we should provide them some help in getting work, but not cash."

Darcy came took her speech back over, "A country cannot survive that has a declining number of people paying the way of a growing welfare crowd. I was afraid the United States was going to be lost in my lifetime, without this war. Now? I simply don't know. The abortion rates are absurd. Who gets the abortions, the poor people? NO! I had hoped to get famous to get power to bring this message to the American people."

"Should women get paid the same for the same job? Of course. Should they be restricted from doing things? YES. Should divorce be so common? NO. One reason that marriages haven't lasted is that women put careers and things ahead of their children. Our morals have been pretty bad. Pioneer women stayed by their men as the men also stayed by their women. Pioneer women had lots of children to help with the farms. The men needed the children to help with the farm. There were a man's job and a woman's job. Men didn't want to do women's work and vice versa. The men took pride in supporting their family. The wives took pride in their husband, even if he didn't keep up with the Jones. During World War II many women took what would have been men's jobs. Then women wanted to continue working when the men came home. And then families started getting two wage earners and pretty soon it was keeping up with the Jones and that required both to work. Then women wanted equal pay, and then they wanted men's jobs. Then women wanted to boss men who had always been the boss. Now the women's libbers want to take away the man's job and men lose their manhood. To prove their manhood they take other girls on the side. And women wonder why it's hard to find a good man. Tell me Jim, have you ever felt put upon because of women's lib? Have you ever had a woman promoted when you deserved it? No, don't answer."

"Anyway, I was ready to move back to Ohio and find some man to start having kids with. I was never going to be famous and powerful, but at least I could start living my beliefs. Now I don't know whether it will ever be possible. What do I have to lose? Jim is the kind of man I hoped to find, but married, maybe. He is my only ticket home at the moment if it doesn't work out with him. Yes, I am sexually turned on and, yes, I do love Jim, but if it doesn't work out. Well, I am on my home. Safety, where? We could think some city was safe and then it gets nuked. I don't know any farmers, and I'm not quite ready to live on a farm anyway, yet. I've got nothing to lose and everything to gain by going. If we don't make it we tried."

They were all silent then until Jim broke the silence, "Well, I guess it's time for me to come clean too. Yes, I love my wife. I am afraid that she won't have made it, but our house was out of town and might have survived. I'm hoping that the survivors in Dayton are not reacting like they did in Saint Louis.

My wife doesn't care much about sex and has this thing about not being sexy or wearing sexy clothes. She made sex seem unpleasant. To the point that I wasn't really enjoying it so much and I was feeling old. I probably can't provide as much as you want. I am getting older. In fact, there were times when I thought I was horny only to have my wife say something that turned me off and then when she said, 'okay', I wasn't up to it. I don't meant it to sound so bad. I love her because she is a good person who always tries to help others and makes me feel good about myself. She is old fashioned and not a women's libber, and happy with what I can provide. I love her, and I would never have cheated except, I am afraid she's gone."

"But to still be honest, both of you have always been a turn on for me. I enjoyed talking to you because you were friendly faces when I traveled to L.A., and I could imagine being young enough for you to actually like me. It was flattering to have you around. You are both gorgeous girls. I mean, I have seen very few girls ever to compare with your looks. There's Shelby with her surreal figure and Darcy that has the classic shape sought for by women around the world. And to top that, neither are you are dumb like some good looking girls. When someone meets Darcy they are dumb-struck by her beauty and Shelby, well, you just almost expect something to ruin the magnificence, like a little squeaky voice. Any man would like to be around the two of you."

Even under the circumstances, I would have felt like a dirty old man making any advances toward you, but when you were insistent under the circumstances, my weak resistance quickly broke. If I can't find my family, I would be crazy not to want to spend my life with either or both of you if that were possible. I don't expect to be able to hang on to you and I'm afraid of you getting hurt on my probably insane attempt to get home."

We may have to "hole up" somewhere. If there is no way across the Mississippi, we may have to wait for a bridge to get built. I know approximately where they used to have some ferry boats across. I'm hoping once we get there, there will be a way across. We don't have much money and I don't know how long we can use my credit cards. I have a total of three checks that I probably can't use. I would presume that I am getting a paycheck from the government somewhere, but I don't know where or how.

It was direct electronic deposit into the bank in Dayton and we know that there is no longer any electronic deposit or a bank in Dayton. The money must be going somewhere or at least sometime I may be able to get it. Not that it does me any good."

"I agree with Darcy on her thoughts on birth control. If times were normal, we, even the men, want to keep up with the Jones. You are right, it takes your family being proud of youOne reason so many women work is that college is so expensive. It would be impossible to send eight kids to college, unless you were wealthy."

"Well, I don't want to lead you somewhere where you get hurt. I have to admit, L.A. wasn't the place to be, and maybe not Alamosa, or Pueblo, but a lot of Oklahoma seemed pretty well off. Now we're heading into what may be the most dangerous yet. Let's assume we do make it, but I don't find my family alive. The two of you will meet someone more your age. I can't imagine it ever being legal to have two wives and it's frowned upon to have multiple kids with two women, and how would we buy the clothes to make them look good in school and then go on to college?"

"There is no way that you girls will not find someone younger that can make you happier than I can. If I can't find my family, I still don't expect to keep either of you. I was at my peak in my mid-twenties, not now. If I was twenty-five again, I could use two girls, if the two of you could remain friends and share me. Now at forty, I can't imagine being able to keep it up. At fifty, no way. At sixty, you girls will be in your late thirties and still want to have sex. And then I will be seventy, if alive, and you will be in your forties. Then you will wish you had ended up with a twenty-five year old instead of me. Well, there you have it. Well, we've eaten, the tent is set up, we have no television or radio. Do you think we can sleep?"

"Sure we can," Shelby winked. "Let's head for the tent."

Jim laughed, it felt good to laugh. He checked that their pots and pans alarms were set between trees around the campsite. He locked the spare armament in the trunk of the car. He checked the riot guns and Berettas for ammo. This was the pits. Two beautiful girls on a camping trip and all these guns and still not feel safe. They shouldn't need a gun. He was afraid of getting in the tent with the girls and being ambushed. It was one thing in the safety of the hotel in Tulsa, but they were the only ones here and mobs not far away that had already moved this far from Saint Louis. The only real alternative was to stay in Los Angeles, and that would not have been a good option. They would most likely be dead now. So maybe continuing was the best for all of them.

They all awoke with the banging of pots and pans in the trees near their tent. He yanked his hands loose from under the girls and he quickly whispered, "keep the lights off."

He felt for and grabbed a riot gun and handed a gun to each girl whispering, "Quiet, I'll investigate. Don't cock the guns until you know you have to. He grabbed also a Baretta and, as quickly as he could, silently unzipped the tent enough to peek out. He saw nothing of danger other than bright moon light that would highlight his every movement and wished he had put the tent in the shadows. He unzipped the tent enough to crawl out naked in the night. He made sure he knew exactly where the Baretta was by his feet and wished he had told the girls to lay flat. The tent was no protection at all. He put one hand on the trigger and the other on the pump action and slowly raised his head above the tent. When he could see. He saw nothing. He did not move, but tried to look into the shadows under the trees. He slowly turned around and saw nothing. He then bent back down and told the girls he saw nothing and to lay flat so they wouldn't get hit if someone started shooting. He said, "Hand me a flashlight."

He moved off into the shadows and leaned with his bare back end against a tree straining to see anything moving. He waited and then moved to where he thought the pans had fallen. He stopped between the trees where the pans were lying on the ground. He waited looking into the dark again. He still saw nothing moving. He finally turned on the flashlight, holding it away from his body, ready to dodge away from the light if someone fired at the light. Nothing. He then shined the light away from the tent toward the darkness of the trees and saw nothing. He then used the flashlight to find the pans and as he brought the light to the ground he could see where a deer had walked up and then apparently madly dashed back the way it had come. A deer had broken the string holding the pans. There was no one. He called out, "It's okay, only a deer."

The girls came out into the moon light, also stark naked and very shapely. Moon goddesses. They timidly came toward Jim's flashlight in fear. He didn't want him to realize their nakedness or see his so he kept the light on the ground. When they arrived they put their arms around him, one girl on each side and said, "Where is the deer?"

Jim bent down and showed them the deer tracks and gave them an explanation for what he said must have happened. They continued to hang on him as he tied the broken string to reset their alarm system. As Jim turned back toward the tent, Shelby reached down and grabbed his maleness. Jim said, "I don't think that we should all do it together again. It was wild, but a little dangerous. Good thing it was only a deer. We really should post a guard."

Shelby said, "I'll take the first shift, you take over here."

Darcy didn't understand at first until Shelby looked down with emphasis, and Darcy took over. Jim said, "Really girls."

SHELBY SAID, "WE DON'T WANT YOU TO CATCH COLD, NOW DO WE?"

Shelby went into the tent and dressed, "Okay people, I'm dressed. Get with it."

In a few hours, Shelby came in, woke Darcy, and Shelby laid down clothed and went to sleep without waking Jim. Darcy let them both sleep until after daylight. She then woke them both and lit their propane camp stove to heat some water from the campground hand pump for coffee. Fortunately, none of them were breakfast eaters. They were on the road by 9 AM.

DAY 9, August 26
Jim, Darcy, and Shelby

The trip was uneventful until they got to the intersection with U.S. 65 near Harrison, Arkansas. The road was thick with old cars and motorcycles moving south toward Harrison. Jim said, "Don't tell anyone, but I think we just drove into the exodus from Saint Louis. Maybe they aren't as bad as we heard they were."

The majority of the people were minorities, but with a fair number of whites. No one had paid them any attention, probably because the old Mercury was even more beat up than most of their cars were. Their cars were almost as packed as theirs. However, rather than personal items their Mercury was loaded with guns that they could easily get killed for. Jim said, "We're stuck following the crowd, I only hope we can continue right on through this group or find an intersection with a major road where we can get away before we're found out. I wonder how many have radiation poisoning from the Nuke that went off in Saint Louis."

"Jim, " Shelby said, "find somewhere to pull off. I'm scared. Darcy and I need to change into something less attractive, and quick."

"You're right." Jim hadn't looked at it from their perspective. Jim had only been worried about them coming after him for the guns. They might attack the girls because they were beautiful girls. Both girls were trying to shrink down into their seats out of sight. Jim heard shots ahead off to the right. He just kept the pace of the crowd. When they came to a house near the road, it was being ransacked. What appeared to be happening was that the husband and another local had been shot and his wife and maybe a daughter were being raped right there in the front yard of the house. No paid any attention.

"Jim, do something."

"Like what, tip everyone off that we're not one of them. We're too outnumbered with no where to run." The girls saw the implications of discovery and looked toward Jim silently, but with horror at what was happening so close. Both girls tried to hide under the dashboard near the floor. They were spotted anyway.

"Hey, you in the Mercury, STOP!."

Darcy yelled at Jim, "GO GO"

Jim floored it pulling out from behind the car ahead. It tried to run him off, but it was a newer smaller car and suffered a missing fender without much apparent damage to the old Mercury. Jim turned on his lights and laid on the horn. Several cars behind pulled out behind them while cars ahead just moved out of the way. Apparently, every so many cars was a gun car. A car several hundred yards ahead pulled out at a ninety degree angle to the traffic creating a road block. Jim yelled, "Get out your guns and this time use one of the grenades in the M-79 grenade launcher to take out the nearest car that is chasing us. Shelby and Darcy crawled into the back seat and took up the positions they had used in Colorado. This time though, Shelby picked up the M-79 grenade launcher and cautiously loaded a round. Jim said, "Hang on tight!" Both girls dropped down to the floor. Jim slowed to fifty and put two wheels in the ditch to try to get around the road blocking car. He couldn't make it, but when he clipped the blocking car it sailed up in the air and crashed into the cars down road as Jim pulled back onto the road flooring the old Mercury again. The right front fender was pulled loose in front and was bent backwards slightly past ninety degrees. It was hitting everything sticking out on cars in the right lane.

The pursuit was coming on again. Jim yelled, "Get ready with that grenade launcher Shelby, here they come again. Darcy get another grenade ready to reload if she misses." Shelby aimed too high the first time. It probably would have hit the lead car the first time except they were all moving at nearly one hundred miles per hour. The grenade hit about the tenth car. It leapt into the air in flames and pieces, but the nine cars ahead of it kept on coming. They were faster than the old Mercury and handled better on the corners. Jim also had the problem of passing cars that were maintaining their positions in the right lane until he flew past, but after he went by they were pulling over intentionally to give the pursuers more road to corner on.

Jim said, "Wait for a clear section of road and aim just below the bumper of the lead car." Shelby did and the lead car exploded and flew backwards taking out all of the pursuit."

Jim slowed and got back into line, again trying to hide. But he saw more cars pulling out of line behind him with guns pointing out the windows. "No good, we've got to keep running." As he pulled back out he accidentally hit the car ahead with the remains of the right front fender taking off the fender but sending the car that was hit on the rear bumper sliding sideways behind him, where it was hit by two of the pursuers again blocking the road. One car pulled right into the rear door of the Mercury as Jim flew past; another pursuer. It destroyed the front of the car that hit him, but also knocked Jim into the ditch at over seventy. As Jim swerved back onto the road he smashed into two cars in the right lane then slid back into the ditch ripping loose the left rear bumper and part of the rear fender. Jim regained control and kept right on going. No one else tried to run them off the road.

When they came into Harrison, the traffic was stopped, blocking both lanes of traffic all trying to go the same direction. Jim turned on a dirt street to the left and then back to the right again to try to get through town. As he came to a main street they could see a roadblock to the right on the main highway, but Jim flew past on the side street. He kept on going for a few blocks until he came to a school. He swerved to take the right hand turn on the side road and came back onto the main highway just in time to sideswipe a pickup that was racing to cut them off. The pickup went crashing into a store front through the glass. The car behind the pickup crashed into the right rear bumper giving a whole new angle to the rear of the old Mercury, but smashing the radiator on the car that hit them. Gunfire erupted knocking numerous holes in the Plexiglas that had replaced the windshield.

When Jim came to where U.S. 412 turned to the left away from U.S. 65 he turned left. He was hoping that the people behind were moving toward Little Rock instead of back toward Saint Louis and the river.

Jim kept on driving fast until they came to Mountain Home, Arkansas. There were more road blocks in the town, but they seemed to be manned by towns people instead of bad guys, so Jim slowed and stopped. He got out of the now crumpled Mercury with his hands up and said, "Thank God, some friendly people. We ran into a mob at Harrison. Almost got us. Can we rest here for awhile." Jim was a Mason and he had seen a Masonic compass and triangle entering the town. He gave the Grand Hailing Sign for help in hopes that they would recognize and acknowledge it.

ONE OF THE ARMED FARMERS SPOKE UP, "DID YOU RUN INTO A MOB AT HARRISON?"

Jim replied, "Yes, I think they were refugees from Saint Louis. I think they were headed to Little Rock."

"Is that how you got your car all torn up?"

"Yeah, they tried to hijack us."

"Come in peace brother. Are you a mason?"

"Jim answered a couple more questions with strange stilted answers, and was truly welcomed into the town."

The girls did not know any of what was going on, but Jim was shaking hands with everyone like they were old friends. The girls discovered that neither rear door was working and climbed out the rear side windows. They held their questions. Darcy surveyed what was left of her car. The right fender was missing. The right side of the front bumper was pushed back about ten degrees. The right doors were about four inches less thick than they were because the metal was mashed and torn. The right rear bumper was bent forward about twenty degrees along with the fender being mashed in. The left side was not bent but torn loose from its mounting where the welds had failed and what was left of the fender bounced freely about two inches below normal. There were more holes in the trunk than metal. The right rear fender was ripped and torn. Both left doors were better than the right hand ones, but didn't look much better. The left front fender looked good in comparison, but had its dents too. The left front corner was okay.

Jim called out, "Darcy...Shelby...come on over and meet the people." By now there were a number of wives showing up. They were invited to several houses for lunch and Jim didn't want to offend anyone.

It was settled, by one man speaking up, "Gentlemen, as Worshipful Master, I have the solution. Everyone will have one hour to whip up some quick lunch and meet at the Hall for pot luck and information. Jim, will you do us the honor of joining us and telling all of us of your adventures?"

Jim couldn't refuse. Several men were posted down the road to warn of anyone approaching, just in case the mob turned back north and east. The roadblock of farm machinery was moved just outside the city limits on the east side of town and another set up on the west side. Jim and the girls had a choice of many fine dishes and were asked to take the leftovers. They did take some. There was no shortage of anything that they could see. Jim told the story of their adventure, leaving out the racy personal lives they had the last couple of nights. The girls were seriously asked to stay in their town where it was safe, but they refused.

When they got back to their car, they discovered that the rear bumper had been re-welded, still crooked, but attached. The front bumper had been replaced by a heavy duty off road pickup bumper with deer guard. The right front fender had been replaced with the wrong fender, but it would work to keep water and rocks from flying up on the windshield. The left rear fender was somewhat straighter having been welded back on. Under the circumstances it was a very pleasant surprise. Darcy and Shelby just walked around the car looking. One of the men opened the right front door to let them in, "Sorry, we couldn't get the back doors to work."

DARCY ASKED JIM, "WHAT IS THAT EMBLEM THEY PUT ON THE FRONT AND BACK OF MY CAR?"

Jim said, "That's a Masonic emblem. I'll explain later." Jim turned to the townspeople and thanked them profusely, but he had explained in the Hall where they were going and why and they understood why they were going to put as many miles as possible behind them. After they got back on the road, the girls asked why the town had done what they did.

"They were anxious to get some outside news. They haven't had any news at all since the war started. They have had no telephones or electricity and no one coming through town except the people that live around here. They have already taken in a lot of strangers from surrounding towns."

"Yes, but they went so far out of their way for us, fixing the car and all. And what was that strange conversation you had when we first came to the roadblock?"

Jim explained, "I saw a Masonic sign on their city limits sign and figured that in a small town like this probably everyone was a mason. I let them know I was also a mason. Why do you think the mayor was so friendly in Alamosa? Same thing there. And at the bakery in Enid, and to the Oklahoma Highway patrolman that had first greeted them at Tulsa. The patrol chief was not paying attention or he didn't believe me at first. Mason's are the world's largest fraternity, but they are not like a college fraternity."

"But I heard that Masons are bad. In fact I heard one preacher on television claiming that they were devil worshippers." Darcy said.

"Hardly." Jim interrupted, "Masons are similar to the Lions Club except that Masons cannot have a meeting without a Bible being opened in the middle of the meeting room. Many of their teachings are related to the Bible. The "G" in the Masonic Triangle stands for God and Geometry.

You know of another religious fraternity? The Knights of Columbus is a Catholic fraternity open to only Catholics. The Masons are open to all religions, including Catholics."

"Then why are some churches preaching against the Masons." Darcy asked.

Jim said, "There is a long history. Back during the crusades some organizations, that are part of the Mason's, escorted pilgrims through the Moslem lands for a price. At the end of the crusades, the York Rite Masons had more money than the Catholic Church or the King of France. The York Rite also had a better army than France did at that time. The Catholic Church and the King were both afraid of them. The Church came out verbally against them saying that they were pagans because people were starting to think more of them than they did the Church. The King sent his armies while some were inspired against them by the Church. The leader of the York Rite, Jacques DeMolay, disbanded his army rather than have to fight his own king. It was against the rules of masonry to interfere with government or church. His army disappeared along with all the riches supposedly with the York Rite. Jacques DeMolay was tortured to death in public without giving up any information that would lead to other York Rite members. That's why the young men's Masonic organization is called DeMolays."

Darcy interrupted, "DeMolays? I know them. They are made up of the better nicer kids in my home town. They're Masons?"

"Not full fledged Masons. DeMolay is to teach patriotism and reverence to God to young men too young to be Masons. Anyway, no one has ever found the treasures. Some say that the York Rite gave it to the poor as fast as it was gained. Others say it was smuggled out of France and helped finance the British Empire that was so powerful for so long. No one knows."

SHELBY INTERRUPTED THIS TIME, "WHAT HAS THE BRITISH EMPIRE GOT TO DO WITH MASONS?"

"That's another story, but it was Masons that brought about the Magna Carte to establish the rights of the English. From that time on, all the crown princes of England have had to be Masons to be the crown prince."

"But what about the churches here. I remember when the Southern Baptist church publicly called for a vote outlawing the Masons."

"The vote failed. The leader of the Southern Baptist church had petitioned for membership once but was never made a mason for some reason. If someone is not accepted for any reason, the reason is buried to protect the person that failed. Anyway, he claimed that people were attending Masons instead of a recognized church and he wanted some of the money that is donated to the Masons. Did you know that the Masons give more to charity than any organized religion? You've heard of Shrine hospitals."

"OF COURSE, WHO HASN'T? ARE THEY MASONS?"

"Did you know that all Shriners must have been made Masons first and then the Scottish Rite or York Rite before they can become Shriners?"

"No, I didn't."

"Did you know that Shrine hospitals for crippled and burned children have never billed anyone. People are told how much they should donate based on their income, but the donation is voluntary."

"I've always heard of the hospitals, but I figured they were only for Masons...I know some people that were not Masons that sent their kids, but he joined the Masons after that. I figured he had to." Shelby said.

Darcy said, "I know that's not so. One of my cousins was horribly burned and was sent to a Shrine burn center. They weren't Masons. A friend of mine that I went to school with told about how the doctors told her parents that she would never walk, until she went to a Shrine hospital."

"Being a Mason has nothing to do with taking your kids there. It only takes a doctor that recommends it because the kid cannot be helped by ordinary hospitals." Jim said.

"I didn't know that. I have always heard how successful they were. I didn't know they only took the bad cases." Darcy was carrying on the conversation with Jim. Shelby was just listening.

"Anyway, Masons is not a religion, but a religious organization. Another reason that many Christian churches don't like Masons is because all Masons must recognize God, but do not have to be Christians. They can be Jewish or Moslem, as long as they recognize one supreme being, God. In fact the Scottish Rite implies that Christ was a mason. At least he spent a long time with a Masonic organization. How do you think Paul, the Disciple was able to travel over the Roman Empire spreading the word without getting arrested every place he went? He stayed with Masons and they helped him get to the next city and so on. Don't be confused though, the Mason's is not a secret organization. They advertise on city limits signs in small towns, their meeting halls are well marked. Masons frequently wear jewelry that can be recognized. It is an organization with secrets versus a secret organization. The secrets are secret signs and terminology that will identify one mason to another throughout the world. Any mason asking for help from another is supposed to be provided help. Usually any obvious help is given without having to ask. That's what happened in those towns I mentioned. Ever heard the term, "a penny for your thoughts." Some lodges have a copper penny unique to their lodge. If you are in real need you can go to them and trade your penny for anything you desperately need."

"I've heard that there is a secret power structure that destroys our ideas of democracy."

"Contrary to that, let me give you a Masonic American history lesson. Remember the Boston Tea Party? Well the Masonic lodge in Boston has minutes of every meeting they ever held in Boston since long before the revolutionary war ... except for one night, the night of the Tea Party."

"NOoooo."

"Not only that, but the people who signed the role call for the meeting would be a who's who of the American revolution. In fact many were the same ones that signed the declaration of independence. The United States is the first country in modern times established on the fundamentals of masonry. The guy back in Mountain View that said he was the Worshipful Master? Well he was the elected president of the Masons of that town. Just like we elect a U.S. President. Members vote on rules, like our congress. Masons predates the United States. You've studied how the King of England gave up his power to the British Parliament an the Prime Minister. Did you know that since then, the kings of England had to achieve a certain level in the Masonic lodge before they can be crowned king? Did you know that the Constitution was written by a Mason and most of the signatories were Masons? Did you know that George Washington was a Mason, in fact the Worshipful Master of his lodge? Did you know that Franklin Delanor Roosevelt was a mason? Why did Gerald Ford become President when Nixon and his vice president had both resigned? Was it because Ford was a Mason? He was you know. Why did Lafayette bring his fortune and French troops to help our revolution? He was a Mason. The Germans troops that came here to help fight in our revolution? Masons. Did you know many of the ring leaders of the French revolution were Mason's that had served in the United States during our revolution? Alexander Hamilton, Paul Revere, you name them. Mostly Masons. This is a country founded by Masons with Masonic ideals. But, once founded, the Masons try to stay out of intervening except as necessary. Alexander Haig? Mason. Get the picture?"

"Yes, but why don't we hear more about these good things?"

"Masons have this thing. You've heard about people wanting to rewrite the Constitution? Most democratic countries pattern their constitution after ours. Well it's because it was written by Masons. There are only about six million Masons in the United States out of our two hundred and fifty million. Most are just common people, too generous to be rich. They can only be powerful by working behind the scenes to further what we Masons consider to be good for the future of our country. I try to be a good person first, then I try to be a good family man, then I try to be a good American, and then comes being a good Mason."

"What about being racist, although I am?" Darcy said.

"There have been Black Masons since before the revolutionary war. One of the principles that are repeated as part of the ritual of all meetings is that everyone meets together on one level symbolizing that all men are equal under God's law. It was intended that Jews, Gentiles, Moslems, Kings and commoners were all equal under God's law. Some time, right after the civil war, Black separatists asked for permission to form Masonic lodges for Black people. They were turned down by the American lodge at that time because of our determination that all men are equal, but they were granted their own separate Grand Lodge by the Grand Lodge of England. The lodges originally formed as Black lodges are not just for Blacks. Since they have their own Black lodges, the other Masons simply don't get Blacks wanting to join. We have American Indians, and Spanish in our lodge, but no Blacks, at least not that I know of. There has been talk about combining the lodges so all American Masons will be equal, but that would amount to closing down the Black lodges because the Blacks would be assimilated into the more common lodges. Well you've had the lecture, you can join. No, women can't be members. But if you are the wife, mother, daughter, sister...can't think of the other one, but one of five relations of a Mason you can join the Eastern Stars that is a woman's Masonic organization. There are also corresponding organizations to the Shrine and others. Job's Daughters is an organization for young daughters of a Mason and DeMolay for young boys. Rainbow Girls is for any girl recommended by an Eastern Star or Mason. That's it."

"Well, I never knew that about the Mason's. Is that the only reason those people have been helping us?" Shelby asked.

"No. It's just that I identified myself as a Mason, but Mason's are good people that help many others including non-Masons. They would help anyone in need. The fact that I identified myself as a mason meant that they could trust me and I was not a looter spying on them. In Oklahoma, for instance, every child in the state is tested for hearing and eyesight at least twice during their twelve years of public school and hundreds of pairs of eye glasses are provided for those unable to afford them. The cost of the eyeglasses is paid by the local lodges and a local ophthalmologist donates his time and sells the glasses to the lodge at his cost. We did receive extra special help though because I was a mason."

By this time they were all the way to the intersection of U.S. 412 where U.S. 62 continued to Jonesboro. They came upon another road block, but this time they were on the back side of it. The men on guard turned around to look at them as they drove up, but did not look threatening. One sauntered over and said, "If I were you, I wouldn't come this way. They's havin' a race riot that started over in Blytheville then spread to Jonesboro. They's been shooting up Jonesboro all day. We's making sure they don't come thisa way. Where yah goin'?"

Jim said, "We're heading home to Ohio, do you know the best road?

"Ain't heerd no rawdio, but I know'd the bridge over'n at Memphis ain't no more, I seen that there ain't no bridge at Caruthersville and I heerd that there ain't no Saint Louis no more. I heerd that they're a tryin' to get some ferry boats going again up north of Cape Girardeau. If'n I were you'all I'd head up thata way. If'n I were you I wouldn't go through Paragould. That riotin' bunch of idiates mightin' gone up there by now. Ida head up this here state road to Missouri."

"Is there anywhere around here that we could spend the night? It's getting dark and I don't know these roads. Besides we've had a big day."

"Nah, there ain't no place to stay, but ifn you wanna, you can just stop along here 'bout anywhere. Nobody'd care as long as you got that Masonic emblem on yur car."

Jim thanked him and took his advice. It was a narrow road that went through several small towns. There were no motels and the streets were patrolled by men carrying guns. It was long past dark when they got to Poplar Bluff and the motels were full with people sleeping in cars on side streets. The gasoline stations for miles had said "Closed Out of Gas". They found a roadside park on the edge of Dudley, Missouri and pulled in for the night. It was just big enough to get behind some trees out of sight of the road. They had eaten some peanut butter sandwiches along the way by light of the dome light as Jim drove. Jim was unwilling to stay in a tent so close to the road with rioters so close and the girls were unwilling to stay in a tent without Jim so they decided to take turns staying awake with everyone sleeping in the car. The watch person sat at the wheel and the other two stretched out as well as possible on the seats, with the one sleeping in the seat using the watch person's lap. Everyone was too tired to consider any sex.

Day 9

Grand Forks Air Force Base, North Dakota

Henry was sent a message from a Lieutenant General (Lt. Gen.) Gates that thanked him for his suggestion and asked if he had more. Shortly thereafter, Henry's and every other military post and base was ordered to report on all food processing facilities within their area and to send people there to find how they had fared and what the military could do to help, from getting parts from point "A" to point "B" or just in transporting their food. The military had decided to void all contracts that required one company to ship food across country if there was a closer supplier. The brains of the military planning were tasked with the job of shortening as many civilian supply lines as possible. When the local food producers were working and distributing, the next priority was helping the farmers, the ultimate producers.

Henry and Jeremy discussed a response and more suggestions they could make. Henry said, "I wish Jim Claris was available. He thought all this out long ago, and even told me once what we should do to prevent each of these major problems. It's too late to prevent it, but he did have ideas for how to react assuming that we didn't prepare in advance. It was too many years ago and I didn't take it seriously enough."

Jeremy Houston responded, "Why don't you make that a suggestion to headquarters? To find Jim Claris and get him into the central planning?"

"Okay, but we still need to make suggestions. We don't know where to find him or if he's still alive. We didn't lose as many people as I was afraid we did, and he may still be working for the government. I will suggest that and tell them why."

"That's why I kept you around, Jeremy. Ideas? How about telling everyone to loan out their emergency generators to grocery stores, gas stations, and Ham operators for the good of their communities. It's more important to keep big food coolers operating than someone's individual refrigerator. Thank goodness this didn't happen in the winter when electricity would have been needed for heat."

"See, Hank? You've got good ideas too. Here's one. Let's get our spare military generators out there in towns to help out too. And, let's try to get some radio stations working on AM and FM for those people whose radios may have survived somehow. If protected by the trunk of a car or in a fishing tackle box. In fact, my brother has some old tube type radios that he might be trying out if he can find some electricity. Here's another, I can't believe we didn't get this idea first. Let's get electricity out to the water pumping stations so fires can be fought, people can have running water and sanitation, and some trucks to the fire department for them to carry hose. The police need transport too. Maybe we can commandeer some old cars at the junk yards and get them operating. We may not need police for crowd control here in North Dakota, but can you imagine the people that survived the Chicago Nuke? I would presume the National Guard has been called in already. Actually, you may have to drive out and get them for them to go on duty. That will take some active military help."

"That's enough ideas for now, lets get this on paper spelled out well enough to explain our ideas in full. We'll already saturate the system. Unless we come up with something more important than these ideas, we won't submit them until these have had some action. Let's try to prioritize these and recommend a sequence of action."

They spent the next two hours getting the words down and reading it to each other to make sure it was right. Colonel Lakeman didn't get to be a Brigadier General selectee for his ideas. It was his ability to get others' ideas on paper.

Many brilliant government workers were never recognized for their brilliance and their ideas not accepted because they never took the time to explain their ideas for other higher ranking, but not necessarily smarter government employees. Promotions were sometimes based partially on golf games or parties organized, not on government work ability or productivity. Many were promoted because they were promoted by other Catholics or graduates of the same school, or members of the same college fraternity, or because the government needed to fill quotas of some race or sex. In fact, during the sixties and seventies the government stressed the promotion of minority races, during the late eighties and early nineties they stressed the promotion of women in disproportionate numbers. During the drastic military cut-backs of the mid nineties the government wanted to get rid of the older government employees and started reducing retirement benefits while offering incentives to retire without losing benefits. The result was that the military civil servants that retired were the experienced male military veterans. What remained were females and minorities that had an anti-military attitude and little concern for what was good for the country...only what was good for their own careers. Even many generals were promoted, not for their intelligence or experience, but their ideological beliefs. Any officer that argued for continued military strength was shoved aside into a back room job until they retired. If they spoke out publicly, they were told to immediately retire. Colonel Lakeman was being promoted because he was quiet about his beliefs for military strength, his golf game, his wife's ability to entertain, and his ability to get other people to produce ideas and get them on paper. He was also a graduate of the Air Force Academy

9 MISSISSIPPI

August 27

At the first daylight, Jim started the car and started driving. At Sikeston, they came upon a military road block. They checked Jim's ID card, then let him pass. When he got to the interstate they met another road block, where they checked his ID again. They explained that the military was blocking all access to the south due to the rioting in Blytheville and Jonesboro. The military did not have the strength to stop it or the food to pacify them.   Jim told them how they had come, and was informed that they would send some military to reinforce the civilian road block on the this side of Jonesboro. He was also told that he would run into road blocks at Perryville, Missouri to keep the Saint Louis people north. They were trying to repair the Interstate 57 bridge, but the estimated completion was not until October. There were no bridges between and none expected to be open for months.

He had heard that they were trying to get some car ferries across, but was told that right now the river was up near flood stage due to heavy rains all across the Mid-West from Wisconsin down to northern Missouri and all the way over to Ohio that had flooded the Ohio rivers and forced a big flood of the Mississippi below the Ohio river. The Mississippi above this point was near flood stage. Actually it could have flooded north of Perryville, and they would not know it, because of the lack of communications. Their commander was in Cape Girardeau, lieutenant Colonel Smieth. (Pronounced with a long i)

He got on Interstate 55 and headed north towards Saint Louis. After about five miles he had to stop and shift gasoline from the spare cans to the gas tank. They were on their last tank of gasoline until they could find more.

Cape Girardeau was crawling with people. He eventually found the Armies field command headquarters and got in to see the commander.

"Hello, Colonel Smieth."

"Lieutenant Colonel, now why am I supposed to see you?"

Jim handed him his ID card and said, "I'm Lieutenant Colonel Jim Claris, recalled to active duty, but unable to get a new ID card, sorry. I'm on a mission explained in this letter." Jim handed him the letter from Los Angeles Air Force Base.

"I thought L.A. was destroyed by a bomb?"

"No, I disarmed a back pack nuke on the air base. As far as I know they are still okay at the base, but the city was burning from riots and uncontrolled wild fires when we left."

"How did you leave and how did you get here and why are you here?"

"Believe it or not we drove all the way across the country in a POV (military term for a privately owned vehicle). We got to this point looking for a way across the Mississippi. We had intelligence indicating the bridges were gone, but were hoping to find a ferry boat in operation or maybe a military pontoon bridge."

"Okay, say I believe you. The estimated date of October to get a bridge open is a joke with this flooding. And, because of the flooding there aren't any ferry boats or pontoon bridges and won't be until the levies dry out a little. There is a serious food problem. You wouldn't believe how much is imported into towns that is not produced anywhere in a hundred miles. Of course we have excess of some things, this is a farming area you know. There's few vegetables, but lots of beef, pork and chicken. There's fruit, but no citrus fruit. So what do you want from me?"

"Well, you gave me a status report. Were you ordered to this position?"

"What the hell do you think? We have no radio. We can't just drive up to Saint Louis, we might keep them out of here, but I don't have the forces to go there. I don't even have the forces to go down to Blytheville and quell the riots. My only orders were to go here from Fort Leonard Wood to protect the eastern approaches to the bridge on Interstate 57 that they are going to try to fix when the flood recedes. There is supposedly more military on the other side of the bridge doing the same thing. This is the closest major town that could put us up while the bridge is being built. I was told to just sit here until relieved. The men are upset because they left their families there and can't go back to check on them. The damn idiots from Saint Louis are reportedly south and east of there and we don't even know if our families are alive. I might not even have the forces to get that far if we tried, but I got some guys about to go AWOL (away without leave). What can you tell me about Fort Leonard Wood?"

"Nothing I'm afraid. I do know that the Oklahoma national guard has troops west of Springfield to keep them from getting past there and the

Arkansas national guard has troops in Springdale, Arkansas to keep them from coming south. I also know we had a serious run in with them in our car coming here as they were coming down from Branson, Missouri."

"How many people have you told this to?"

"No one in Missouri, except for you."

"Keep it that way." Lieutenant Colonel Smieth looked very forlorn. Apparently his family was back in Fort Leonard Wood too. But he had his orders and the intelligence to know there was nothing he could do with his forces if Fort Leonard Wood had been overrun. "So, what are you going to do now?"

"Well, I guess we're stuck here for awhile. Is there anywhere we could stay for awhile? Do you have any way of getting me some back pay?"

"Yes. No. And no. Yes, you are stuck. No, every room in town is full including the gymnasiums and churches and private homes. There is a tent city south of town at the airport. That's where most of my troops are staying too. We're working ten hours a day seven days a week. Keeps them out of trouble. If there is any booze in town, it must be in private homes. We must have half the white and quite a few black people from Blytheville and Jonesboro, Arkansas, and a lot of people from the south side of Saint Louis that got here before we set up the road blocks. Hell, when the mobs hit our road blocks we must have killed a thousand before they withdrew. Fired off half our small arms ammo and a third of our tank ammo. We've only got four tanks. Fuel's short. Every town around here is just as full of people. I'm surprised my men let you through. The whole area is out of gasoline except for what I commandeered for my own vehicles. There's not supposed to be anyone driving anywhere without permission in my jurisdiction. This area can't be supplied across the Mississippi or from the north, south, or west. It's going to get mighty cold here before that bridge gets finished or we get some other supply lines open. You may have heard that the central natural gas pipeline from Louisiana to Northeast United States has been cut off. Apparently, their computer controlled switching station was HEMP'd or sabotaged along with their spare computer. Would you believe that a lot of their equipment isn't even manufactured in the United States. How could the government have allowed that? Without natural gas for the entire winter millions of people in the Northeast will freeze to death."

"Colonel, you said airport. Are there any airplanes there that could fly us over the Mississippi?"

"Sorry, but most of the people flew their own planes out of here before we got here. There are a couple of small old planes there, but we don't know of anyone that can fly, or if the planes even fly. You're in the air force, do you fly?"

"I don't have a license, but I could probably fly them, if I could get one started. I know I could if the planes have a flight operations manual in them that would tell me such things as take-off speed, stall speed and how to start it.."

"Here, let me write you a letter so the airport guards will let you past and give it a try. Isn't this a crap not even having a typewriter. You'd think this was the revolutionary war, having to write orders in handwriting. Even the old typewriters had transistors in them for memory correction and such. Now they don't even work."

Jim went back to his car and headed back south toward the airport. "Remember, I don't know if the airplanes are flyable. Besides, you might not want to fly with me. I can probably take off okay, but I'm not much of a navigator and I don't know whether I can land the plane. I'm serious, I always had a hard time with my landings and that was after hours of help in a new airplane I had not flown before. I did flunk pilot training. I might fly all the way to Ohio, just to crash and die. The airplanes may not have the range to fly that far."

Shelby said, "Where you go I go, remember."

"Okay."

When Jim got there, he found a Piper Cub, a tail dragger. He had flown in one once, but had never taken off or landed any tail dragger. The other airplane was nice to see, a Cessna 172 or something like one. At least it looked like what Jim thought was a 172. It was four passenger with a wing on top of the fuselage. He checked the oil. It looked okay. He got in and found a mechanics manual that told about starting the engine. He tried. Nothing at all happened. Dead Battery. He hooked the car battery up with jumper cables and let it charge for awhile. The engine turned over, but still nothing. Jim hated to waste his gasoline, but this was such a good opportunity so he let the battery continue charging with the car running while he checked the starting procedures. Magnetos...both in the green. Carb heat on...check. Full choke...check. Throttle....... The engine turned over, but nothing happened. The battery was near dead again. While he let it charge he checked out the Piper Cub. It looked pretty good for a Cub, but it was only a two place plane with one behind the other seating and practically no instruments. "This one won't work, because it can only carry two people and no luggage. It probably doesn't have much range."

By now it was near dark. The hangars were packed with people sleeping blanket to blanket. There was an empty area of the airport with a porta potty sitting on the grass. They set up camp there. They talked about what Jim might do to get the plane running. He had checked and it was full of gasoline. "It could be a bad engine although not taken apart, it could be the carburetor, or the ignition. No, magnetos should not have been affected by the HEMP, so it's probably not the ignition."

Eventually they went on to bed. All were too thoughtful about their plight to be interested in sex. With all of the people around, they also felt funny about going naked. They all kept on their full underwear. Actually, Jim felt more safe than any other times in the tent. He was concerned with the problems of getting over the Mississippi. He had no desire to spend the fall here waiting for a bridge to get built or the levees to dry out. He was in love with both girls, but not true love like for his wife. He felt good with them. He wanted to protect them. They had become very close like men to in combat, except this was women and a man relying on each other and intimate moments taken from the heat of battle. His love with his wife had been built over many years, he had to find out if she was still there for him. The girls were going for him like a patient goes for a psychiatrist. He was wrong to let them. He took advantage of them and the position they were all in. Or had they taken advantage of him? They wouldn't have given him the time of day in normal times if he had come on to them.

He had to correct that situation and somehow do the things he knew was right. Saving them and keeping them with him to this point had worked out for their best. His trying to get home was the best thing. Getting them home was good too. But somehow he had to back off from them. True, they were both well over twenty-one, but he was old enough to be their father. They should have someone their age.

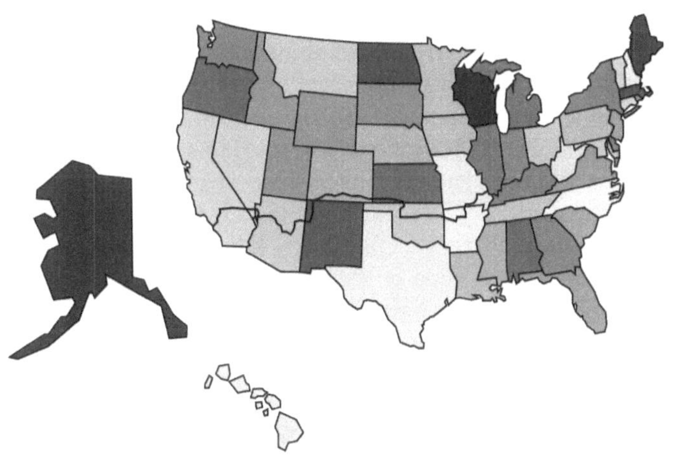

The line represents the path that Jim, Darcy, and Shelby took across the country until being stopped by the Mississippi river.

GRAND FORKS AIR FORCE BASE, NORTH DAKOTA

At twelve noon there were explosions on the flight line and in the munitions storage areas. These were followed by calls for Broken Arrows. A Broken Arrow is a destroyed nuclear weapon. Henry immediately asked, "What's happened?"

"All of the cruise missile just exploded. We have Broken Arrows all over the base. Half of the B-52's that we had left are burning."

"Cordon off the entire side of the base with the alert pad and the storage area. I'm on my way."

There were only four B-52's left now and two of those had been cannibalized for parts before this had happened. His base was basically defunct. He had the base and the area around it searched, but could find no explanation for the occurrence. What was really strange was that those missiles in storage had exploded.

The hardy farmers and store owners in North Dakota never panicked. They were used to stocking extra amounts of food in case of blizzards in the winter and because their larger towns were associated with major strategic bases, they were used to cooperating with the military.

There was a vegetable cannery outside of town. When the Colonel and Major visited the cannery to see if they could help, they discovered that it was almost totally automated and consequently dysfunctional. They had used four VAX computers to operate the assembly lines, wash and de-hull the vegetables, but three were protected by steel walls and UPS systems (un-interruptable power supply-UPS). They were in sealed steel wall rooms because of the military's preoccupation with HEMP protection. The local sales rep that sold them had been indoctrinated by the military. In fact, he had been retired military. The fourth was installed later in an unprotected area and the static charge of HEMP that killed it did not come down the power line. That portion of the canning process could be operated manually with people doing the work of the machines. Of course there was no power and it would take several days to convert that one portion of the line to human workers.

The locals had never been big on small foreign or even new American cars and many drove older American made vehicles that never had electronic devices. Many that did have newer American cars and pickups had chosen the ones with standard V-8 engines that had already been converted with older point type distributors and intake manifolds and carburetors instead of electronic ignition and fuel injection. In fact there were more pickups and jeeps than passenger cars. Because snow was a way of life in the winter, they didn't bother with salt. It wouldn't melt the ice with their temperatures anyway. Snow would blow or stack, you didn't want to melt the snow to get ice. Another benefit of no salt was that their cars didn't rust.

The Colonel didn't want to stay gone long, because their portable radios had gone the way of most transistors. Upon his return to the base, the Colonel received the news that he was to turn the base over to his second in command and report to the Alternate National Military Command Post (ANMCC). The National Military Command Post no longer existed since it had been in the Pentagon that had been a primary target. The ANMCC was like Cheyenne Mountain or NORAD or whatever you wanted to call it. It was a metal city mounted on shock absorbers inside a granite mountain protected by giant blast doors. It was far enough away to not get hit by any stray missiles aimed at Washington DC and yet close enough that people could be evacuated to there by helicopter, if there had been warning. There had been no warning so the ANMCC was far from being fully staffed. Lt. Gen. Gates was apparently the ranking officer in the United States, or at least he was in charge of the ANMCC and wanted Colonel Lakeman there also. An F-15 would land soon to take him to a civilian airport near the ANMCC where a Humvee would be waiting for him. General Gates must really be in a hurry to get him there. He told Jeremy to stand by and he would call him to the ANMCC as soon as he could. He wanted him there for advice. There was not time to contact the ANMCC before the scheduled time for the F-15. Now there was a plane. Designed in the late fifties, tested in the sixties, it had been the reason the United States and Israel had enjoyed total air superiority since the early seventies. Being an ex-bomber pilot, he had not had much chance to fly in a hot fighter. He went home, packed a bag, asked Major Jeremy Houston to stay at the house and take care of his wife and left. The F-15 was already waiting for him.

It took two hours to get back on the ground and an hour and a half to get to the ANMCC. Due to tight security it took an hour to get into the ANMCC through the blast door and down the tunnel and finally into General Gates office.

General Gates greeted him and then informed Brigadier General Henry Lakeman, that he was second in command of the ANMCC. Muslim assassins had executed a number of Naval admirals in Norfolk, Virginia and San Diego, California that were not killed in nuclear attacks. The same had happened at the Air Combat Command, also in Norfolk. Scott Air Force Base, Illinois had also been hit as had a large number of major United States Air Force Bases worldwide. United States Air Forces in Europe (USAFE) headquarters building had been blown up by a bomb during duty hours. Air Force Materiel Command (AFMC) had been destroyed by a back pack nuclear device. Hanscom Air Force Base, Massachusetts had been hit by a number of apparently pre-planted conventional explosives in various buildings wiping out the generals there and the Lawrence Livermore Laboratories. Pacific Air Command Air Force at Hickam (PACAF), Pacific Army Command (PACOM) overlooking Honolulu, several other places around the Island of Oahu, FORSCOM at Atlanta, Georgia. All contact with United States European Command (USECOM), Panama, South Korea, and SHAPE headquarters and all other Pacific and European bases had been lost. There were several Navy admirals at sea with the aircraft carrier flotillas, but contact was sporadic and unreliable. It appeared that Lieutenant General Gates might be the ranking officer in the United States military ... at least among the bases in contact with each other in the continental United States (CONUS is the military term). From satellite photographs, it appeared that most United States forces should have survived OCONUS (outside the CONUS), but without communications, ANMCC had no command over them. It was assumed that the undersea telephone lines had somehow been cut.

There were several submarines that had not checked in and no contact could be made with them. Extreme long wave through the earth radio was extremely slow, but should have gotten through to them to surface and report in, but it was assumed that somehow we must have lost some submarines.

DAY 11, August 28
Jim, Darcy, and Shelby

Jim woke at first light and quietly got dressed. The girls had slept all night for a change, but had stayed up so late talking that they slept through his getting dressed. He left a note on the car to explain he was walking over to the airplanes to check them out some more.

"Okay, little Cub, let's see what you've got." It did not have a fuel gauge. He climbed up and used a stick to measure gasoline level and found it full. "That's a good sign." He checked the oil and found it new. "That's a better sign." He turned the prop through a couple of revolutions by hand because he had seen others do it when they flew Cubs. "One, two, ah three for good measure." He crawled into the cockpit and tried the controls. Everything worked and felt tight like a new airplane. Not that Jim was much of a pilot. He pulled out the choke and pumped the throttle knob a couple of times, "Well, here goes nothing. The original Cub did not have an electric starter, but this one did. He pushed the starter button and the engine turned over for a couple of seconds and then fired up with a roar. He pulled back the throttle and pushed in the choke slightly. It hummed. Maybe he could fly one girl over then come back and get the other girl and then trade the appropriated airplane for a vehicle, or buy one or steal one. Maybe he could get the Cessna running to where they could fly nearly all the way if they flew light and carried their gas cans. While he thought he checked the meager instruments. The oil pressure was good, the temperature started to rise toward normal, he pulled out the throttle some more and the engine settled down to an impressively smooth idle. He shut the engine down by pulling the throttle all the way out to a slow idle and pulled the choke all the way out to flood the engine. The engine died as expected. He had one plane at least.

Lieutenant Colonel Smieth drove over in his Humvee. "Colonel Claris, I see you got one of them running. Good, I have a mission for you. I want you to fly over Fort Leonard Wood, and see if it's been overrun. If it has, then report directly to me and no one else. If it is intact, then fly back here and tell everyone you can. It might prevent some mass desertions. Is there anything you need?"

Jim was taken aback. He had only planned on getting away, but he wouldn't have known about the planes without Colonel Smieth's help. Last night he had decided he would try doing 'the right thing' again. He said, "Colonel, I'm not sure of the range of this airplane and I have never flown a tail dragger, but I understand your position, and I will give it a try. What I want in exchange is for my two women to be given a secure place to wait for me and if I don't get back safely, I want your personal assurance that you will continue to provide them a safe place to live with a roof over their heads and security and food, and if you can, a way to their homes in Ohio."

"Woah, I didn't realize I was asking so much. Is it that dangerous?"

"With my flying experience it is, but I'll have a go at it if you will give me your promise as an officer to take care of them."

"Fair enough. How long did you say its been since you flew?"

"How about eighteen years, and I washed out of Air Force pilot training. I've never flown a tail dragger and it's a lot different than one with regular tricycle gear like that other one that would scare me anyway."

"Couldn't you get the other one to start. Maybe I can get a couple of my mechanics over here and take a look at it. Okay? If we can get it going maybe you won't have so much to fear."

"Sounds good, Colonel."

"Call me Sam. I think you've just given me a little more respect for the Air Force. I always figured you guys were a little chicken, but I wouldn't fly in that thing with your experience. I cannot order you to fly. Will you?"

"Call me Jim, and I wouldn't fly it except that I need a way across the river anyway and this will give me a chance to try flying it without having one of the girls with me if I crash it."

Jim could see the girls walking over. Apparently the airplane engine had awakened them. The colonel had driven over to a truck, and shortly the truck started toward him. The truck arrived before the girls did, so he was talking with them when the girls arrived on foot. "Yes, this uses a magneto instead of a conventional or electronic ignition. It is a combination generator and distributor. You use the battery to run them up to speed and then flip on the ignition that provide spark to the plugs somehow. I'm not much of an aircraft mechanic. The engine is similar to a flat Volkswagen engine, but puts out somewhere over one hundred horsepower. It's made by Continental here in the United States, but it is air cooled like a VW. It's made only for use in small airplanes. Think you can do anything?"

"Hey man, if it is internal combustion, I can fix it. I'll get it running if I have to take it apart and put it back together again." Softly the corporal asked, "Are those your daughters ... or girlfriends?"

Jim replied, "Girlfriends. We've been together since the war started."

"Sorry man. Didn't mean nothin' by it."

"Forgiven, just see if you can get this thing running."

Jim turned and walked over to the girls, "They're going to try to get the Cessna running."

Shelby and Darcy both threw their arms around him and Darcy said, "That's why I love you, Jim, you always find a way."

"Girls, I want you to listen now. I'm going to be leaving you for a few hours about 10 AM. Lieutenant Colonel Smieth is the commander of the Army around here and he has promised to take care of you while I go on a little errand for him."

The girls looked thunderstruck. Shelby said, "What are you going to do?"

Jim explained his arrangement with Colonel Smieth and his short mission down playing the danger with his flying. The girls pleaded, "Please, Jim you can't go. It's not that important to get across the Mississippi, we need you with us. We should have a say in this too. You are our protector, you took us on and now you can't leave us in this nowhere place that could be overrun at any time. What would we do? What will we do?

"Hey! Settle down. I'm going on a test flight for a few hours of flying and then I'll be back. Maybe we can get out of this place as early as tomorrow instead of months from now. Besides, Colonel Smieth will take care of you until I return for however long it takes me to get back. I will get back to you here before crossing the Mississippi. Now relax, here comes the colonel."

After introductions, Colonel Smieth was beaming, "Darcy, Shelby, I have found you an actual apartment. One of my guys was from around here and he his parents have an empty apartment above their garage on a farm just on the south side of town, over looking the river, but high enough to be safe from any flooding. Jim will be back by nightfall and you can get cleaned up and have a clean bed instead of a tent to sleep in tonight. And, I'll bet my men over there will have that plane humming to take you over the river tomorrow after that good night's sleep. Jim, I'm loaning you a Humvee. If one of the girls will follow me in the car, you can ride back here with me. When you get back to the airport, I'll loan you a Humvee to drive until you leave."

They followed him to the farm. It was everything they could wish for. It did have a view of the river and the all brick garage not only had a nice big furnished apartment, but space to park the car in the garage.

09:30 DAY 11, 28 AUGUST

Jim left the girls and rode back with the colonel to the airport. "Jim, I was wrong to ask you to take this mission. If my guys get that Cessna fixed, you should just fly on home and forget the mission. The troops will make it with the ammunition we still have. I was being selfish and wanting to find out about my own families safety. I'm not going AWOL, and my men won't either. They are good troops. It's just that it is frustrating being so close and yet so far. By the way, to make matters worse, I sent a patrol out and they ran into a mob about ten miles west of here."

"No, I'm going. Your men need to know that their families are okay if they are okay. From what I have seen, you will need a lot more ammunition. Matter of fact, I may find a place to land over there and let your commander know of your position here. Why don't you write me up a report? If the fort is okay, and I don't find a place to land, maybe I could drop it in some kind of metal canister that they would know was a message."

"If you're sure. Well, okay, and I appreciate it. It will mean a lot to all of us here. We desperately need resupply of fuel for our vehicles and ammunition if we are going to have to hold off looters for months. The girls will be safe, because any mob would have to go through here to get to the farm. In fact, the town could be overrun and the mob never find that farm. Why are you taking all that armament with you?"

"I've been living with these so long, I wouldn't be comfortable without some guns. I'd rather be over prepared. I don't expect to have any problems except with my landings." Jim laughed, "but just in case I have to walk back." and he patted his armament which consisted of his Beretta, his Ruger 357 magnum, a riot gun and a bag of ammunition.

The colonel wrote up a message, long hand. Jim added one of his own that he let the colonel read and then he put both in a courier bag and handed it to Jim. Jim's part of the message told of the troops lined up in Springfield, Missouri and Springdale, Arkansas and suggested that if he could not contact some headquarters, it was time for the military to move out on their own to bring some law and order. He couldn't sit by and watch rioters destroy an entire state and move off into other states. He had control of the ground troops right in the middle of everything and had a responsibility to act correctly, even without orders. Lieutenant Colonel Smieth could not talk that way to his boss, but Lieutenant Colonel Claris, U.S. Air Force, on a special mission, he could. The fact that it was included in the same bag, gave it more credence.

The corporal had not made any progress on the Cessna, but had managed to take out a lot of parts. "Sorry, sir, this may take awhile. This ignition system is something else. Another thing, this engine has not been started in a long time. I'm going to have to take it apart some. There is something wrong inside. The valves don't move when the engine turns over so the timing gears or chain or whatever this thing has is broken. We found another old engine in that hanger over there. Between the two, we'll have it running in a couple of days.

Jim decided that they not only needed to get the message to Fort Leonard Wood, which he figured was sitting back waiting for orders, but the small one hundred man force here in Cape Girardeau, needed some aerial reconnaissance to see just how hemmed in they were. Jim realized just how important getting the bridge fixed must be to the welfare of the country. If this force was overrun and the engineers on this side of the river killed it might be even more months to get the bridge reopened. Saint Louis and Memphis were both radioactive, which made the opening of bridges there remote.

Jim added another note to the pouch that suggested trying to get a message through to some headquarters to start shipping in food, ammunition and troops to Cape Girardeau to make sure the force survived.

Jim fired up the Piper Cub the same as he had earlier that morning. He had already pulled the chocks and released the ground straps that held the airplane on the ground in case of wind. He let it run for a few minutes to get up his nerve until the engine temperature quit climbing just below the middle of the gauge and figuring it was okay, he started taxiing for the runway. He found he had a hard time seeing out over the engine and ended up opening the side window and clipping it onto the wing. He started taxiing toward the runway again looking out the side around the engine. He found he was not good at taxiing without nose wheel steering. The rudder didn't do anything unless he had enough power to force wind past it and with that much power he over controlled.

Lieutenant Colonel Smieth could not look. Jim was not kidding when he said he was not a qualified pilot, especially not in a tail dragger. Jim sat on the end of the runway for awhile. The taxiing experience had not been good, but he decided to go for broke. If successful, he would be off the ground and flying. He knew the plane would fly like most airplanes once off the ground, but if he didn't get it off the ground he would probably die right then and there. Right now, he was wondering why he was attempting this, but "What the Hell!" Jim pushed the throttle slowly in to the fire wall. The cub started taxiing faster and faster. As it gained speed the plane was easier to control. Jim held the wheel back to keep the tail on the ground, but it wasn't seeming to fly so he decided to let the plane do more of the work and released back pressure. The tail rose and he was now accelerating down the runway gaining speed. Jim pulled back slightly on the wheel. He felt like the little plane was going to dig its prop into the runway and it would be all over. Finally Jim decided that the Cub would not go much faster on the ground and added a little more back pressure to the wheel and the little Piper Cub was flying. Jim was now talking out loud, "Thank you God, one more time. There is no way I'm going to be able to land this thing, I might as well go for broke. I'll fly the mission and drop the message to Cape Girardeau in his ammo bag without landing. When I get back I will try my first landing in a tail dragger. At least that way they would get the news that I am flying to deliver ... just in case my landing is slightly worse than my take-off."

Jim did not have a flight map, but he had a Missouri road map to navigate by. He would have to try to follow roads and use towns for identification ... and hope he was over the right towns. He rocked his wings to the ground people that were probably amazed he got off the ground and that he was okay. He did not over fly them, because that would waste fuel and he had no idea of fuel usage. He pulled back the power to the upper edge of the green area of the tachometer and found the plane showing a relatively steady eighty miles per hour. He pushed in more throttle and got to ninety-five, but backed it back down to eighty figuring that it was a good airspeed for fuel economy and not hurting the engine. He climbed as fast as he could, but the airspeed dropped to sixty. This was definitely not a jet interceptor. By five miles out he was about a thousand feet off the ground. The T-38 trainer he had flown in pilot training would be at 30,000 feet and broken the sound barrier by now. He wish he knew the barometric pressure, because he just realized it made a big difference to the altimeter. He did remember that when in doubt 29.92 was a good average setting that all high altitude jets used when under radar traffic control.

He flew over the interstate north until he could identify state highway 72 and turned northeast. Since he didn't know the winds, he would just have to follow highway all the way there. There were many people on U.S. 67 heading south. He figured they were from Saint Louis, and hoped they would not turn east, but keep heading south. He continued until he flew over what he hoped was Irontown and then north to state 32. He had figured it was around one hundred forty miles to the army camp. He wondered if a Cub would fly three hundred miles without refueling. The little plane flew nicely, but was very slow. He wondered how much head wind he had. If the upper winds got to eighty, he would actually fly backwards.

As he flew over the countryside he saw numerous burned out towns and farms. He, luckily, did not see any looters, because he was flying low. What he did see as he swooped down over a burned town and a couple of farms were what appeared to be numerous burned corpses of people in the rubble. The Piper Cub seemed to fly just fine at fifty as he flew over only a few feet off the ground. The power lines were down due to the fire so he didn't have to worry about hitting one.

He found Fort Leonard Wood and identified the Army post. He flew low over the Fort until he saw what he though must the headquarters building. He couldn't know for sure, but there was a flag pole and a nice wide street that looked like it out to be. He had plenty of attention. It had probably been awhile since seeing any airplanes. He suddenly realized that it was probably a forbidden air space, but it was too late to worry about it now. He was afraid to try a landing there at the fort, so he added yet another message to the pouch explaining that the troops in Cape Girardeau were completely surrounded and possibly in trouble. He opened the left window and slowed to fifty five miles per hour. He was flying very low, just high enough to make sure he didn't hit any buildings and threw out the message bag trying to hit the street in front of what he hoped was headquarters. His aim was off and it hit and dented a staff car in front of the building and bounced off onto the sidewalk and then tumbled through the grass to hit the building. Everyone on the ground threw themselves to the ground thinking they were being bombed.

He figured they would call the bomb squad before they found out what it was. He would be halfway back by the time they read it.

His guessed his fuel was down to less than half a tank, but he hoped that he had been fighting a predominantly western head wind and would have a tailwind on the way back to help the fuel situation. He also hoped the second half of the gas gauge lasted as long as the first half of the gauge. "Oh SHIT! A storm's coming."

He could see a line of heavy clouds coming from the southwest with a wall of heavy rain and lightning. It had come from the southwest while he was looking for the right place to drop his message. He didn't know if he could stay ahead of it. For a while he thought he was pulling away, but as the storm grew he was making less and less ground speed. The storm was drawing in air near ground level and sucking it into the storm. The storm was moving east northeast and the wind near the ground was moving in the opposite direction. He decided to try to fly above the ground wind so he climbed for altitude. It helped, but it was also harder to gauge his ground speed. He could see dirt being blown to the west and the storm getting nearer. Eventually, he decided he had better get back down to the ground and try to find a place to land the airplane and ride out the storm on the ground. He knew he was past Taum Sauk Mountain which at only seventeen hundred and seventy-two feet was the highest point in Missouri. His guessed his fuel was also down to less than one quarter of a tank and he didn't know without a fuel gauge or any idea how much the airplane held. He had lost sight of the road he was following and the storm was right upon him now. He went ahead and pushed the throttle in and started a sinking dive toward the ground and trying to find somewhere to land. He saw a meadow near a stream and decided to give it a try.

He dragged in the landing using lots of power and powered the little plane in to the ground, literally flying it at sixty miles per hour down until the wheels were hitting the grass and then cut the power and started pulling back. He climbed, not good. Rather than stall and pancake back in, he put the power back in, flew around the meadow. The rain was starting to hit the plane now. He came in a little slower with still lots of power and this time came in nose high and tail low. At forty-five and the tires hitting grass again, he pulled off the power. The little plane sank quickly through the grass and hit slightly tail first, then the front wheels banged down. Jim kept pulling the wheel back to keep the nose up even though the plane had no flying speed at all. He had a fear of a plane with no nose gear pitching forward onto the prop, but the plane landed and came to a stop.

When he discovered he was safe on the ground, stopped with the engine ticking over at idle, he looked around and saw a small shanty and barn not far away. He was afraid the little Cub would get flipped by the coming storm so he taxied crookedly up toward the barn hoping to find some way to tie the plane down. He had to taxi at full power to get up the gentle slope to the buildings. He pulled right into the yard between the shanty and barn and then cut the engine and ran into the barn. Sure enough he found plenty of rope and things he could use for stakes. He went back out and using a the back of a large wood splitting ax he had found, he pounded his stakes into the ground and tied the airplane down. He used some old boards he found in the barn to put on the ailerons and then wrapped rope around the board and aileron to keep it from flapping in the wind. If the control surfaces are not tied down properly they may flap in the wind to the point that they break the hinges or bend or possibly tear completely off. By putting a board on top and underneath and tying them together, the surface is fixed like it would be when you are holding the controls. Sort of like putting on a splint. He attempted the same thing with the rudder and elevator on the tail. He then decided to head to the house for shelter for himself. It was a full fledged rain now and getting worse. He was wearing his Ruger 357 and his Beretta, and got his riot gun and ammo sack out of the airplane then closed it up as good as he could remembering to close the little cool air vent that blew in air to the pilot.

He went to the house and found the door locked. It had curtains on the window. He knocked for a while, but the storm wind had come up now and was blowing rain onto the porch. He hit the door with his shoulder and the door frame gave way admitting him to the little house. He was surprised when the little house looked lived in with furniture in place and pictures on the walls. He propped a chair against the door to keep it shut with its now broken door frame. He went into the kitchen and found the cabinets stocked with food. It was getting cold and he was drenched, so he went to the fireplace in the living room that had been in use for years. It had wood stacked near it and old newspapers. He opened the fireplace damper then put paper under the old cast iron grate and stacked smaller pieces of wood above that on the grate and then used his BIC lighter to light the paper. It caught quickly and the dry wood looked like it was going to burn. At that point he sat down in a chair in front of the fire and reflected on how lucky he had been to get the plane on the ground in one piece and even find some shelter.

DAY -11, 28 AUGUST

It was eight hours later that the following transmission was received. "Any United States forces, this information must reach the Alternate National Military Command Center (ANMCC) please relay any means possible. This is the TRIDENT submarine Spokane, we were attacked by ten repeat ten submarines simultaneously. SONAR indicated eight diesels and two nuclear submarines. We did not hear them until they opened torpedo tubes. Twenty-two torpedoes were fired at us with no warning. Five hit our decoys, three hit their own submarines, we evaded eight, we intercepted three with our own torpedoes, three hit our submarine. We lost them by blowing all ballast at flank speed while firing all torpedoes. We surfaced, but are rapidly sinking and abandoning s......" Transmission was lost at that point.

Lt. Gen. Gates asked, "Colonel Lakeman, what assumptions can we make from that transmission?"

Colonel Lakeman did not like to commit himself without conferring with the experts he usually had around him but replied, "Sir, I am without a staff to properly evaluate the message, and I am not an expert on Navy matters, but I would say the message is genuine coming in the radio that it did and relayed to us here. I would also say that I did not know the Arabs had more than a half dozen submarines. Either our estimate of their capabilities are grossly underestimated, or the Arabs have someone else in this war helping them. I would also say that the Spokane is probably not the only American submarine that was attacked."

"Not bad, considering you did not have the current intelligence reports. There have been reports of upwards of ten thousand Arabs in Red China attending submarine schools and seen around submarine training bases there. CIA provided a list of ten thousand names so we must presume that there were more that the CIA did not get names for. The Red Chinese have almost exclusively diesel submarines, but if we assume you train one hundred men to operate one submarine than ten thousand men equates to one hundred submarines. Diesel submarines are not as fast as nuclear submarines especially when operating on battery while submerged, but their electric motors are actually quieter than nuclear submarines running steam turbines. The Chinese have come a long way in making them even quieter than the old diesel submarines. Remember the nuclear submarine propeller design stolen by the Japanese company Toshiba in the eighties? Well Red China was the recipient of that propeller. They have dramatically advanced the state of the art in conventional powered submarines. The old World War II diesel submarines that we think of are a long way from the Red Chinese diesel submarines of today. They can stay submerged for as long as six months by using fuel cells to generate electricity for heat, light, and ventilation. They use electrolysis of sea water to generate hydrogen for the fuel cells and oxygen for their people. Their newer batteries allow them to move fast under battery power for up to two weeks without surfacing. If they keep their speed to a crawl and stay with the currents instead of fighting them, some of them have been detected moving nearly four thousand miles without surfacing. We managed to track one that far due to exceptionally good weather and Chinese submarine took no evasive maneuvers. It was like they were showing us what they could do. Their diesel submarines are much simpler than the nuclear submarines, their diesel fuel weight approximately balances the weight of the nuclear containment vessel. Their main draw back is that their top speed submerged has not been clocked above twenty-five knots. One of our submarines could easily outrun one if they knew they were being tracked."

"Sir, excuse me." said Henry, "why don't we send a message to all of our submarines that are in open water to accelerate to top speed for a few hours to lose whatever may be hunting them down and then change to a random course for awhile, just in case their planned course has been compromised."

"Good, Henry. That's what I brought you here for, ideas and quick thinking. Our submarines may have been found because their routes were pre-planned and compromised. At top speed, a diesel on battery may be quiet, but a lot slower than a Nuke sub. If they even try to keep up, they will have to surface and go to full diesel. Our subs get away anyway, and find out if they were being hunted at the same time."

"Captain, prepare a message giving the order to all submarines to accelerate to flank speed for two hours in any one direction and during that two hours plot a new course to keep them away from their original course, but still meeting the mission parameters. Tell them to report tomorrow on whether they discovered intruders following them."

The Navy Captain prepared the orders and after General Gate's okay, transmitted it to the submarines using the slow long wave, but reliable radio.

10 LOOTER WARS

DAY 12
August 29

Henry had discovered that there had been no communications with nearly forty percent of all CONUS Navy and Air Force bases or Army posts since the HEMP attack. Communications with the Navy fleets were difficult. Finally, the ANMCC received an updated intelligence briefing on what was happening in Europe. Without the CIA headquarters in now smoldering Washington DC, it was difficult to assemble the satellite photographs and figure them out. The information was several days old. There were no real time television transmissions, but some of the satellites took photographs and then ejected film rolls on a schedule that were fired out of orbit and captured by special C-130 aircraft. These film rolls then had to be developed and analyzed. Unfortunately many of the people and places that used to do this work were no longer available. These were the updates over the next few days:

"The United Arab Forces are composed of troops from most of the Moslem countries. There are currently ten thousand first line tanks and thirty thousand other armored vehicles in the northeast quadrant of Italy.

With a population of nearly three billion, it is easy to field a four hundred million man army. The Soviet Union had not been so military since World War II. Even Stalin did not spend as much money on their military as the Red Chinese. The Japanese provided the engineering and western technology, not to mention manufacturing capability to include Japanese made U.S. F-16 fighters and Japan's own design main battle tanks. The Chinese manufactured lots of out-moded fighter planes, bombers and tanks of their own. Which will win a dogfight? One F-16 or MIG 29 or twenty old MIG 15's? Add in sophisticated air to air missiles and the Red Chinese aircraft in large numbers were very potent and over-whelmed the remains of the Soviet Air Force in the region. Add in the hijacked Soviet equipment now in Chinese hands, along with a four hundred million man army, and the Soviet forces were on the run. The Red Chinese army had moved three hundred miles into the Soviet Union.

At the same time Red China had moved into South East Asia (SEA) where they met serious opposition from the North Vietnam and Thailand. Thailand fell quickly with the King fleeing the country to Mexico. North Vietnam did not seem to care that Hanoi was dust. They were fighting to the bitter end.

The most ambitious, it appeared was attacking India and moving mass numbers of people and equipment through the Himalayan Mountains. Bangladesh fell immediately as it was agreed that Pakistan would take northern India and allow Red China to have the remainder. Arrangements had already been made to move the Muslims living in Bangladesh to Northern India as soon as possible to make all Pakistan and new China lands contiguous to prevent any future arguments between Pakistan and China like the ongoing wars between Pakistan and India. India had been close to civil war between Hindu's, Moslems, and other religions for several years, and was expected to be an easy conquest regardless of their population.

The submarines that we contacted checked in except for five (5). We received confirmation of long wave radio contact from only twenty-two (22) of our submarines. Thirty of those reported that they were being shadowed by unknown submarines. Of those six (6) of the thirty (30) were fired upon with torpedoes but escaped undamaged. We must assume that the five (5) that did not report in were sunk when attempting to get away from their shadows. All subs are now under standing orders to accelerate for two hours per day if there is no known surface or air forces that might detect the acceleration. The purpose, of course, is to get away from any enemy submarines that may have found them.

Cape Girardeau

Darcy said, "I don't like Jim flying off and leaving us."

Shelby responded, "Hey, he'll be all right. He knows what he is doing. I wish I had know him before he met his wife. If any one is going to survive this whole thing, it will be Jim. He may not be a body builder, but he has smarts that make up for any lack of strength, but he's no physical weakling either. Look at it this way, we get a nice apartment to get cleaned up. Jim will be back in time for dinner. We can have some fun tonight in our own place for a night with plenty of privacy and yet safety. This is better than a hotel you know. The Army will have the other airplane running tomorrow, and Jim says we can fly it most of the way home. In fact if we get rid of everything but gasoline cans, Jim thinks we can make it all the way home. Jim will find that his family is gone. In fact, he will be able to fly over and see that there is nothing left. They probably wouldn't let us in on the ground due to radiation, but Jim would insist on seeing for himself. This way he will see. Then, we can get on with the rest of our lives."

"Sounds good when you say it. You're probably right. Jim is a survivor. I'll take the shower first. Why don't you go down and get some more things out of the car? Then I'll fix some lunch while you shower."

"You got it, Darcy."

Darcy took her shower and cooked a hot lunch while Shelby took her turn in the shower. They went out the back after lunch and lay in the late August sun watching the Mississippi flow past far below their vantage point on the hill. The garage blocked the view from the farm house so no one could see them. The sun felt good and they were soon sun bathing in the nude. It was around 4 P.M. when they were awakened by a rumbling noise.

Shelby responded first, "Darcy, I hear something."

"Yeah, it woke me up. Sounded like thunder, but there isn't a cloud in the sky, which reminds me. I think that I have cooked all four sides and better get out of the sun. I don't usually sunburn, but it has been almost two weeks since I last had time to just lay in the sun."

"Me too. Will you fasten my bra for me?" Shelby said after pulling on her panties and positioning her bra.

"When did you start wearing a bra? This is the first time since this started that you've had one on, although with this little thing, why bother?"

"It was more like a swimsuit. You had that bare shouldered thing to sun in. My tie front shirt covered my shoulders, and I wanted to be more like sun bathing in a swimsuit. I wasn't planning on going nude like we both did. We could have been caught, you know."

"Yeah, that soldier whose parents own this place might have come out here with some of his horny buddies knowing we were alone with no man around. I wonder if Jim knew that the farm was deserted with the parents having gone to Memphis when the war started."

"Let's go on inside now at least, that wind is really picking up now." The girls picked up the blankets they had spread on the grass and headed around the corner of the garage apartment.

"Shelby, look at that storm coming. I hope Jim's made it back."

"Sure he has. He's just briefing Colonel Smieth on what he found. He was flying a plane, now walking. Jim told me that little plane would do nearly one hundred miles an hour. I haven't seen a storm yet that moved one hundred miles an hour. A tornado may have three hundred mile per hour winds, but only moves about thirty. It was less than three hundred miles round trip. That's three hours. Let's add an hour for messing around. If he left within an hour of his planned time of ten, he would have gotten back at two. It's four thirty by that watch the sergeant gave me."

"What sergeant?"

"That guy that is working on the other airplane. I mentioned not knowing the time of day since the war started and he slipped off this government watch and gave it to me saying he could get another easy. He said it was manufactured by the military to be cheap, but survivable in a nuclear war. You have to wind it up every day." Shelby showed Darcy the phosphorescent dial, black watch with its camouflage cloth strap. She had it in her bag because she said when she tightened the band to the last notch it still slid off over her small hands.

"You're right, they would have told us if he had not gotten back on time. He's probably spreading the news to everyone. He thought that Fort Leonard Wood had probably just let the rioters pass through destroying the town because they didn't want to interfere with civilians without orders. He expected to bring back good news. Let's see what we have in the car that we can bring upstairs and cook a big meal for when Jim gets here. If we get busy now, we should have something scrumptious by six thirty and you know Jim will be here by then. You know what they say, 'the quickest way to a man's heart' and all that."

"Sounds like fun. We've never been able to cook him a real meal before and we have the time and a kitchen range that actually works. Do you think we ought to see if we can get into the main house for some spices?"

"No, I don't think we should. We're guests here. Let's not be less civilized than we have been since this started. This is someone's home and for all we know they will be coming home soon. At least their son may come out here to check on things, and the house was locked when we got here."

"You're right. It was just an idea. We have some provisions, but no one thought about spices. Maybe we can make our own. I saw some wild parsley growing back there."

"If you're going to pick flowers, you better hurry. That storms rolling in fast."

Shelby did feel a little silly and giddy as she danced barefoot through the grass looking for parsley. She saw another weed that she recognized as wild sage, and picked some, but she was wearing only bikini pants and a very skimpy cloth bra. If Jim saw her now he would get a good laugh. She felt more naked than she did when they made love. She got back in just after some large cold rain drops started pelting down on her. She got wet from only about twenty or thirty of the large drops. They were very cold.

They cooked up a large dinner and even had some wine cooling outside in the rain that was the coldest thing around. It got very dark and stormy very quickly, but they lit some candles and had the light of the propane kitchen range to cook by. They had a marvelous time cooking and were looking forward to Jim's surprise when he got back home.

"Shelby, it's completely dark outside. Would you check that watch of yours and see what time it is?"

"It's seven. Time flies when you're having fun, huh. I haven't had that much fun cooking in a long time. I think I could learn to be a domesticated wife. I think I enjoyed it more because I was cooking for Jim and had you there to share the fun with."

"Where is Jim? He should have been here by six."

"Relax Darcy, he may be on his way now and late due to the rain. We should've gotten dressed up in something nice before he got here anyway and here we are running around in short shorts and skimpy tops. I don't have a sexy low cut cocktail dress except for our bar girl dresses, but at least they are French maid kind of sexy, and a little more sophisticated."

Time passed as they dressed up, brushed their hair, and continued waiting. Shelby got one of the wine bottles and poured each of them a drink. "Might was well have some while we wait."

"I'm worried, Shelby. Check your watch again."

"It's eight thirty. Maybe he was forced to eat in town with the Colonel, or maybe he just can't find the little dirt road we're on in the rain. Relax, Darcy, he got back here two or three hours before the storm got here."

"I hope so. It's not like he can call on the telephone to say he's late, but now I understand how a wife can get very frustrated when the man doesn't call home to say he's going to be late. We spent two hours cooking for someone that doesn't even show up. It's already ruined. We might as well re-heat some and eat some of it ourselves. If he's not here yet, he missed it. I'm going to be really pissed off at him if he ate in town just leaving us out here in the country, not knowing. I don't understand why some wives would get a divorce over it, but I can see how they can fret and worry and take it out on their spouses when they do get home, ruining a marriage. I'll never do that at least, but it is worth the fretting and worrying part."

"What time is it now Shelby?" They had finished eating and finished the bottle of wine in silence. They had even lit some new candles since the others had burned away to stubs.

"Darcy, it's eleven. I don't think Jim's coming home tonight. Maybe they made him stay in town with this storm and all."

DAY 12, AUGUST 29

Jim woke at first daylight. It was still raining heavy, but there was no thunder that he could hear at the moment. He knew he was going nowhere in this rain, but he was curious about what happened to his plane. He couldn't go back to sleep, or so he thought,

It rained for two weeks all day and all night. It was sometimes too heavy to see the barn let alone the meadow. Some of the tall grass was covered with water, it was starting to look like a pond. The house and barn were well up the side of the valley and the water didn't seem to be rising for the last three days even though the rain never let up. Every time the rain seemed to let up, Jim would start seeing lightning or hearing thunder and the rain would drum down again. The milk cow had come to the barn to get out of the rain even.

CAPE GIRARDEAU

The girls drank the other bottle of wine and both slept the sleep of the drunk. They were out of it. A clap of thunder the next morning woke them both. Darcy was holding a hand over her eyes, "Shelby, what time is it now?"

"Ten in the morning. I feel like something the cat drug in."

"I'm getting up. Maybe Jim came in and found us passed out and slept on the sofa, that would be like him."

"I'm getting up too. Just give me a minute to find the floor. I keep telling myself I will not get drunk on wine. I still feel drunk." Shelby leaned on the bedroom door frame while Darcy searched the small apartment and looked out the front window. She then went downstairs to the garage. Shelby could see the rain still driving at the front window and the rolling of the thunder. It was quite a storm.

"No one has been in the garage. Only our foot prints on the dirt floor around our car. Anyone coming in that road would have left some ruts. Something has happened to Jim. He didn't come back. He went on without us. God, why did we let him go?"

"Relax Darcy, it may have rained in town before it rained here and the road out here to the farm just got too muddy. He'll be out when the rain stops."

"Shelby, the colonel was going to loan him a Humvee. It can drive almost anywhere. If the farmers that lived here could get up and down that road, a Humvee would have. We're alone in this God forsaken place. Jim is either dead or left us."

"Listen Darcy, I was left by a fiancee. I was really in love with him, but I had bad vibes. That's why I was pushing to get married...before he left me. I may not have known Jim for a long time. He would not voluntarily leave us here. I feel as if some extra sensory perception would tell me if something bad had happened. I feel as if he is alive, but maybe he is in trouble. Maybe he screwed up his landing in that little airplane that had no nose wheel, as if he was afraid he would, but he said he thought it landed at about forty-five miles an hour. Maybe he's in town with a broken leg or something and trying to get the colonel to have someone drive him out here. Even if Jim has no true love for us, he is too good a man to just leave us here. I agree with you, something has happened to him or he'd be here by now."

"Let's drive into town and find him."

"It's too muddy and our car has no windows except for some Plexiglas over the hole where the windshield out to be and it's full of bullet holes. Let's at least wait until it quits raining. I'm having some coffee. Join me?"

"Darcy, it's noon, it's not going to quit raining, let's give it a try. I saw a roll of clear plastic sheeting down in the garage. We can use some of Jim's duct tape and seal up the car some. At least the car is dry so the tape should stick. But Jim didn't just leave us here."

They taped up plastic over the windows, pulled out of the garage and turned around on the grass, but had not made it past the main house before the car was hopelessly mired in the mud. Shelby was putting rocks and boards under the wheels and then pushing while Darcy drove and then they changed places. They could make it about one car length only to get re-stuck. They were covered with mud from head to foot when they heard the roar of an engine coming toward them down the long muddy driveway from the main road. They were both wearing jeans and jackets that were more brown from mud than any other identifiable color. Even their faces, hands and hair were streaming down muddy water. Darcy said, "Cut the engine, I hear something."

"I do too. I told you Jim would make it back!" Shelby said excitedly.

"Oh God, make it true." Darcy said, as she clasped her muddy hands together waiting for the vehicle to appear through the driving rain.

It was only Lieutenant Colonel Smieth driving his Humvee by himself. He handed Shelby a long heavy nylon strap with a big metal hook and said, "Hook this on your car and I'll pull you back to the garage."

"Where's Jim?"

"Shelby? Right? I'll tell you what I know when we get your car back to the garage."

"Darcy, you drive the car, I'll watch the strap to make sure it holds without tearing the bumper off the car. He said he'd tell us after we got the car back in the garage. At least he knows something. Maybe Jim had to land at Fort Leonard Wood and couldn't take off again until after the storm. At least there is some news, so he must have gotten that far.

When they got the car pulled backwards about fifty feet it's tires started hitting gravel near the garage and no longer needed the tow. Shelby unhooked the tow strap and Darcy drove the car into the garage. The door was more than wide enough to get two vehicles through and inside you could park four plus other equipment. Colonel Smieth drove the Humvee in beside their car. They were conscious of the mud streaming off both of them. It would take awhile just to clean out the inside of the car.

Both girls where shivering from the cold wet rain and mud and looked truly miserable as they waited for Colonel Smieth to tell them something. He only said, "Why don't you get cleaned up and get something dry on. I'll wait in the living room. I have to tell you the long story and refuse to just tell you something you can jump to the wrong conclusions on. I'll only say that Jim got to the fort. Do you have any coffee?"

Darcy was truly embarrassed about here bedraggled filthy appearance and was shivering uncontrollably. Between that and just being nervous she made a beeline for the inside stairs and the bathroom. Shelby walked up with the colonel. "So Jim's all right?"

"I'm not saying any more until both of you are dried off and you are both sitting down so I can tell you the whole story. Now go on." Shelby moved on up the stairs ahead of him and to the bathroom. She found she really needed to go the bathroom and pulled off all her clothes and went to the bathroom while Darcy was showering.

"Hurry up Darcy. I'm freezing out here."

"Jim's all right, right?"

"The colonel didn't exactly say that, but said we had to be dried off and ready to listen to a long story. Maybe Jim did have to land there and can't get back. Maybe his landing there was worse than his takeoff and he damaged the airplane or is hurt. We won't know until we're both ready to sit down with him, so hurry."

"Okay, I'm coming out now." Shelby slid past her not touching her wet cold muddy body against Darcy's steaming warm clean one. It had been awhile since the last hot shower. Neither girl had any more jeans to wear and didn't feel their cocktail waitress's dresses were befitting so they were back to their shorts and sexy tops, which they felt were less of a come on than the dresses. They both realized that they had been dressing for Jim and needed some more modest clothes, especially now that it looked like Jim might be delayed for ... two or three days??? They rejoined Lieutenant Colonel Smieth who was sitting at the kitchen table with a cup of coffee. They noted he had made a pot on the kitchen range.

"Get a cup of coffee girls, and then sit down and I'll tell you everything I know." The girls were scared and still anxious to find out something so they did his bidding and sat down around the table with their coffee in hand. It did help with their shivering. The shower had helped, and the coffee hit the spot. "Okay, Jim did make it as far as Fort Leonard Wood. While on the way there he spotted mobs from Saint Louis directly to the west of us here. He bombed the headquarters at Fort Leonard Wood with his message pouch and it took them three hours to figure out that it was not a bomb and to get the messages to the commander. The commander immediately dispatched four more tanks, six armored personnel carriers and two hundred more troops to hold this position, protect the approaches to the interstate bridge over the Mississippi, and maybe be able to use some forces to bring order to Blytheville and Jonesboro. At any rate, we should be safe here now. The reinforcements arrived this morning about two hours ago. They found either burned out towns and farms or deserted towns and farms. They saw no signs of live looters, although they did see their handiwork. I tried to come by last night, but couldn't find the road in the dark and the soldier that owns this place was out on duty at one of the more distant road blocks, so I decided to try again this morning and then the reinforcements arrived and this is the earliest I could get here. I'm sorry I didn't get here earlier, but I'm glad to be able to tell you that Jim got that far at least. I will keep my promise to keep you safe here, and you can keep this place for as long as you need to or I will try to find you a place in town if you want me to. I promised Jim that I would provide for your care and protection if he didn't"

Darcy almost screamed her interruption, "Are you saying Jim is not coming back? What happened? Is he dead? He did this for you, you know? What's going to happen to us without him? Why didn't he put us ahead of your insane mission?"

"Settle down, ah, Darcy. We don't know that he is not coming back. We don't know that he isn't okay and wasn't just forced down due to the weather."

Shelby interrupted this time, though not as hysterical, "It wasn't weather, he said the plane would do one hundred miles an hour and he would have outrun the storm."

"Whoa! The Piper Cub will only do about ninety-five to start with and cannot cruise at much more than eighty-five for any distance. Based on the time it took him to get to Fort Leonard Wood, he was only averaging about seventy. We're talking the difference between air speed and ground speed."

"So." Darcy and Shelby said together accusingly.

"So. The speed his airplane was going through the air might have been eighty-five, but because of head winds of fifteen miles an hour he was only going seventy miles over the ground for every eight-five mile through the air. Do you remember the east wind that came up before the storm last night?"

"Yes, but it was maybe only forty miles an hour. That means he should have been going forty-five ground speed at normal cruise speed instead of the eighty-five, right."

"Very good, Darcy. But there is one more factor. The buildings, trees and hills slows down the wind on the ground. About a hundred feet up, that forty mile per hour wind could easily have been one hundred miles an hour or more. That would mean that if he got caught in winds ahead of the storm he could actually have been flying backwards unless he found a place to land. If he hadn't found a place to land, that storm would have demolished that little plane if he didn't fly it into a hill before the storm tore up the plane." He saw their terrified looks. "I'm sure he headed back and saw the storm on his way here and found a place to land. The weather has stayed too bad for him to take off again, but I'm sure he is all right. The storm was not visible at Fort Leonard Wood until two hours after he had flown over and left the message. The commander there figured that Jim had not made it back ahead of the storm so he told my reinforcements to look for a little airplane on their way here, but of course could find no one in the storm.

He could have set that little airplane down almost anywhere. A short stretch of straight road, a field, almost anywhere. He'll fly in when the rain stops, unless he finds another way in. Regardless, I gave him my promise to take care of you and I will. In fact, I figure he made it over half way back before he would have had to land. Of course, I can't say for sure, because I don't know what the winds were except on the ground. I'll bet he's here within four hours of daylight with no rain. In the meantime you are my personal guests. If there is anything you need, just let me know.

"I won't take that bet, because I want it to be true more than you do. We were just commenting on the fact that we could use some more moderate clothing, if you know where we could find some really cheap. We have no money, but if we get home and can find you, our families will be glad to send the money with interest."

"Well, I hope Jim doesn't get mad at me, but I'll ask one of my WACs, ah, female Army soldiers, to see if they know of anywhere in town that has any. I'll bet there is a seamstress or a ladies store somewhere in town. When I find out where, I'll send out an escort for you. I think this is the safest place for you right now."

"Thank you Colonel."

"Call me Gary. Colonel is for the military."

"Thank you, Gary. I'm sorry for what I said about Jim doing it just for you. He likes to help. He is obsessed with doing what he considers the right thing. We've all risked our lives a few times on the trip. It's just that this time we're not with him and don't know what's happened.

After Gary Smieth left, Darcy and Shelby were very lonely out in their garage apartment on the farm southeast of Cape Girardeau, but it was peaceful and scenic. During the two weeks of rain, Colonel Smieth made it out three times to bring food. During the second week a WAC came to pick them up to take them to town for some shopping. The girls heard it coming and opened the garage door so the colonel could get in out of the rain. At the same time Shelby had picked up the M-79 grenade launcher and Darcy had picked up an M-16, just in case in wasn't who they thought it was. The couldn't even see the vehicle due to the heavy rain until it was within the farm yard. They could tell it was only one driver and the Humvee had the silver leaf of a lieutenant colonel on the bumper. They were surprised when a woman in uniform got out.

Army Captain Jane Gray had been driving Lieutenant Colonel Smieth's Hummer. The girls laid down their guns and came down into the garage to meet her.

"Hello. You must be Darcy and Shelby? I'm Captain Jane Gray. Just call me Jane."

"No, I'm Shelby and she's Darcy." Shelby replied. "I presume that you have found somewhere for us to get some more modest clothing?"

"As a matter of fact, that is not a problem. There is a shopping mall on the edge of town that's loaded. The population of Cape Girardeau may have multiplied since the start of the war, but so far, no one is ready to go shopping at the mall spending money when they don't know if money will be good next week or if good whether they will get much more for a long time. For most people, buying new clothing and other mall type things, is just not a high priority. I've come to take you shopping. Colonel Smieth will be supplying the credit so let's go shop 'til you drop."

"That's great. Let's go." Darcy said. They all got in the Hummer and went to the shopping mall. They made small talk with Jane and told their story of how they came to be here and the fact that Jim had flown for reinforcements.

When they arrived, Darcy and Shelby were surprised that they had first run of the mall before it opened. There were some Army guards posted at the doors to the mall to discourage looting. They could not have slowed a mob, but their presence kept the honest people honest.

"Look at this, Darcy." Shelby said as she modeled a slinky glove leather outfit. It fit like it was her own skin. It consisted of long leather pants down to the ankle and a long sleeve, big collared crop top leaving about two inches of midriff showing.

"That looks hot, but maybe a little expensive. How about some blue jeans." Darcy replied.

"You've got to be kidding. This may be my last chance to buy real clothing. I'm going to wear them while I've got the figure. I'm serious, do you think Jim will like?"

"If he doesn't, he's crazy. I think I'll go for something more practical. Winter is coming you know. We may not have heat. If we are driving that old Mercury of mine, it has no windows to keep out the cold."

"Fine. See if I care. I'll just snuggle up to Jim in the middle of the front seat and you can keep my other side warm. Okay. How about this fur coat?"

"That, I know is too expensive."

"Relax. It's rabbit fur, not mink or ermine."

"Hey, Shelby, what do you think of this?" It was Darcy's turn to model in front of a mirror. She had found some tapered blue jeans, a long sleeve low cut blouse, an fleece lined matching blue jeans jacket, and some denim colored high heeled fleece lined boots with a rim of fleece showing at the top. There could be a lot of debate on whether Darcy's outfit was sexier than Shelby's.

Jane, their escort, said, "Either one of you would make anything look sexy. I couldn't pick between the outfits and can understand why this Jim of yours likes you both. I want to meet him when he returns."

"THANK YOU, JANE. DO YOU REALLY THINK THIS DENIM LOOKS AS SEXY AS SHELBY'S LEATHERS?"

"Yes. Maybe more so. The leathers might have the edge on pure sex, but they look like a come on. If I were a man, I would think yours are more sexy because it doesn't look like you are trying to look sexy, but your clothes make your figure just as revealing."

Shelby came over wearing a black felt Mexican style cowboy hat with tasseled balls hanging down. He tan skin and blue eyes denied her a Mexican heritage, but she could pass for a few of the nobles of Spain. "What do you think with this hat."

"Perfect. It provides direction for your outfit. Without the hat you looked, pardon me for saying it, but you looked like a lady of the evening that you see on Hollywood street corners. The hat changes it to the Spanish nobility that still quietly owns a lot of California. I like it."

"I do too, but I would suggest that with winter coming on you might want something warmer than that jeans jacket." Jane volunteered.

"The jacket will be quiet warm when buttoned up. Apparently you've never owned real fleece lined clothing. The manmade stuff just doesn't compare. After all the rain we had, I do think we could both use some full length water proof over coats though. They would also stop the wind. Shelby, that leather you are wearing is not fleece lined. It's nothing more than a second skin." Darcy said.

Shelby replied, "You're right about the second skin. It's incredibly thin and smooth inside and out. You're forgetting the rabbit fur coat. I do need some boots though. These spike heels with spaghetti straps will never work in any snow. Where did you find those you are wearing?"

After selecting their clothing, they went to the Sears © store to look for some things Jim might think they needed. The store was out of camping equipment, and anything to cut wood with, but they did have a small one hand baby sledge hammer that looked cute that would help drive the tent stakes in the ground. They also picked up some tools. They were still shopping when the mall officially opened. Jane had wandered away to bring the Humvee around to the Sears door.

Darcy and Shelby both looked up to find that they were surrounded by some large burley country boys leering at them. Darcy froze, Shelby spoke out, "What do you think you are staring at. Move-it."

"I'll move it honey." One of them said as he moved forward and put his hands on Shelby. Shelby tried to slap him, but he was too quick and strong. He just grabbed her hands and forcing them behind her back he picked her up and started carrying her toward the storeroom door nearby. "Oh, this is going to be fun. I like them spirited."

Darcy ran at his back wielding the baby sledge hammer to hit him in the head. Two of the other large men grabbed her pulling her jeans jacket back and down on her lower shoulders toward her waist where she could not effectively move her arms.

"Johnny is just havin' a little fun with your friend there. How about you and me joining them in the back room?"

Darcy let out a blood curdling scream that brought some nearby soldiers, store clerks, Jane, and an older copy of the burly men that were manhandling the girls.

One of the soldiers that had been a door guard yelled, "Freeze! Let go of those girls NOW!" and pointed his M-16 at them aiming down the barrel.

The older copy of the burly men came up behind the soldier aiming the gun and with one hand pushed him aside as he came forward. The soldier went flying to the side losing his M-16 and taking down a merchandise table as he went. Jane had pulled out her military issue sidearms and was running in their direction thinking, "The soldier must have not chambered a round or had his M-16 on safety, thank God, or the wrong people might have died." With that she chambered a round and checked that the safety on her sidearm was off as she quietly but rapidly moved closer.

The older burly man grabbed the shoulder of one of the ones surrounding the girls and threw him to the ground while the others scattered. Johnny, carrying Shelby and the other man carrying Darcy dropped the girls and turned to face the man in fear. "John, Jess, just what the hell do you young boys think you're doin' I want you down on your knees NOW! Now apologize to these young women and tell them you was just foolin' them. NOW!"

Both "two boys" dropped to their knees and sincerely apologized to Darcy and Shelby like their life depended on their sounding sincere, which it might have. The older man said, "Boys. Get out to the truck, NOW! I bring you'all into town one god damn time and see what happens. I swear to God that when we get home I'm going to finally follow your mother's advice and tear up everyone of those girlie magazines that you read. You boys are plumb uncivilized." His seven "boys", if you call a 20 year or more old 300 pound 6 foot male a "boy", high tailed it toward the door. The soldier had retrieved his gun and just got out of the way of the boys as they headed for the door. Jane was stopped, watching in amazement as this powerful mountain man reigned in his high spirited youngin's and now turned almost gracefully to the two girls and sincerely apologized for the actions of his son as his failing as a father, "They're not bad boys. We've just lived out in the country too long. They dropped out of school after the 6th grade cause they don't need book learnin' or maybe they would be a little more civilized. We just heard about them city folk from Saint Louis coming down here with guns and hurting people and stealing their women. We came into town for safety with our neighbors. I reckon the boys forgot which side they was on. I sincerely apologize and I promise those boys will never do nothin' like that to no woman again."

Darcy, as usual in these circumstances, was silent, but Shelby told the mountain man, "No harm done since you chased them off. If I were you, I would tame them down some though. If you had kept them in school, maybe they would have learned more than just book learning. Maybe they would have learned how to be human."

"I'm sorry, Miss. You may be right. It's a little late to send them back to school now though. You better believe they will be learning real fast how to get along with others." With that the mountain man turned and headed toward the door.

Jane came over to the girls still holding her pistol in the proper two handed grip, but with the barrel absentmindedly pointed at the floor as the three girls now and everyone else in the store watched the huge back of the mountain man retreat out the Sears door of the mall and on toward a fifty year old farm truck.

After the spell broke, all three girls were ready to head for home and away from the mall. What was this world coming to. These barely human, uncivilized, huge, strong mountain men were moving into the city to live with other city folks in fear of another group of city folks.

DAY 15
The Bunker in Iran

Facil and the other leaders were briefed on what was happening with the same sophisticated hologram briefings with speeches by Jabal. They lived in luxury, they ate like the kings they were, but most had no real say so in the events going on in the world. Facil supposed he as well as the others were being kept alive as some form of inspiration to his loyal followers, and there were many.

They had many times as many troops as the Europeans. Whereas the Europeans, and especially the Americans had become soft, the Muslims were work toughened and whereas the Christian religions taught peace, the Muslims had their Jihad to spur them on. Whereas many Muslims in peace time had only a glimmer of hope of getting to heaven, sacrificing your life in war time was a guarantee of heaven. Whereas a man deformed in any way could never get to heaven, wounds in battle were holy. In peace time a man missing a hand would be assumed to be a thief and despicable. In the Jihad, the man was a saint. Whereas some Christians found it difficult to kill, even in war, a Muslim could have no greater glory.

In today's briefing, King Hussein of Jordan spoke up and said, "Jabal, how can you prosecute this war with Israel in our midst?"

"I wondered when you would ask. It seems that their water supply was tainted, or was it the wind. As soon as we knew everyone was on the way here, we released a biological toxin in a variety of mediums. Those that drank their water died within twenty-four hours. Those that breathed the air died quicker. Since most were air breathers, Ha, I made a joke, were too sick within an hour to present any resistance. There may have been some in underground shelters with their own air and water, but we have already seized their military equipment for our Jihad. Wasn't it nice of the American's to stock pile so much military equipment for us?"

Facil's face would have turned white except that his skin was naturally swarthy. Yes, the Saud family spoke of anti-Semitism, but that was only rhetoric, actually Facil had made some close Jewish friends in pilot training. While he had become part of the American class and was accepted by them, and he honestly liked the swaggering brash pilot trainees, he discovered that he and the Jew in his class were actually much closer in background. They had much more in common. Both were darker skinned, knew some of the same places, had close religious beliefs. Why couldn't the Arab and the Jew get along?

If this latest announcement was true, that meant that every Jew in Israel was killed by a manmade sickness without regard to man, woman, or child. What glory was there in killing children? To meet an enemy in the air was so much cleaner. Man and machine versus man and machine. No civilians were put in any great danger and the two men were fighting. A good fight could even win honor for the vanquished. It was not unheard of for the loser to be allowed to fly home in a crippled airplane. It was uncouth to shoot a pilot in his parachute. The chivalry of the air war prohibited such acts.

Ground war was different. There was still tank to tank and man to man, but frequently it was reduced to artillery duels that killed man and machine unseeing. It also resulted in killing innocent civilians that were near the battle, but the civilians would have had to know it was coming in time that they could have moved away when the battle reached their front steps.

Strategic bombing was another story. In World War II most bombing was aimed at factories and railroads and bridges until Hitler decided to bomb London daily. That actually hurt his chances of winning the war because in bombing London and trying to kill civilians, he was allowing factories, airfields, railroads, etc. to not be destroyed. Fire bombs and nuclear bombs were different. They were used to force fear into your opponent. The threat of mass destruction was far less human than most war activities.

Again, even though the United States was the only one to use a nuke before this war, everyone had them because Hitler pushed so hard to get his first. This fear drove the Americans to hinder his progress through strategic bombing while rushing their own nuclear bomb development. The Russians used the German scientists after the war to get their own. Now many countries had learned to build them.

Hitler also developed nerve gas to kill the enemy. Mustard gas went back to World War I and was used to kill soldiers, not civilians. Gas warfare was outlawed because it sometimes killed as many of your own as theirs. Now an off shoot of gas, was to produce a biological agent that could be dispersed as gas, but which your troops would have immunity to. What scared Facil was the idea of spreading a deadly disease that had been mutated to make it quickly spreadable and more fatal than the original. Ideally the disease would be made to self mutate to a harmless bacteria within hours or days, but what if it went the other way and started multiplying and mutating into something that your own people were not inoculated against.

That night Facil went back to his suite and his girls with a heavy heart.

"Facil, what's happened now?" asked Carey.

"I will tell you. Today I learned that Jabal has done what Hitler tried to do and what Egypt tried to do many times in history. He has annihilated Israel to the last child. He used biological disease to quickly kill every Israeli. The Jews of the world would be declaring vengeance upon all of the Arab leaders when the news got out to the world as it must already be doing. You cannot go in and annihilate an entire country, an entire people and not have the wrath of Allah upon you. Mohammed was a man of peace and our savior. The Jews turned away their savior and now Jabal has turned away from ours. I dare Jabal or anyone to repeat my words to the Moslem Empire. I will cooperate to save my family and my country. I will direct troops to win battles with the west, because I must, but I cannot condone cowardly acts of genocide against mankind."

His Harem bombarded him with questions. Most of his girls did not understand what he meant when he talked of biological disease. "How can man control a disease? How can Jabal, or any man, be responsible for the will of Allah? Is this not Allah's way of finally punishing the Jews?" asked Kareen.

Facil tried to explain how man could do this. Joy was familiar with the terminology, but surprised that Facil seemed to think it had been so successful. From what she had learned, things like this did not really work that well.

Suzane said, "Biological agents are against the Geneva Convention, how can they be used?"

Facil replied, "Only the naive. Treaties are fine to have between two countries to establish the terms of peace between two countries that want peace, but when someone is out to conquer the world, the only rules are the winning of the war. The winner will establish any future rules to protect himself. When the United States won the last world war they established rules for everyone to follow if there were to be another war. Korea didn't use chemical and biological weapons because they didn't have any. At the same time they did not follow the Geneva Convention in many other matters. North Viet Nam broke every rule in the book that they had the capability to break. In the so called Gulf War when Iraq took over Kuwait, Iraq used some chemical and biological weapons, but got by with it. Everyone knows they were used during the Iraq Iran war that went on for ten years. Where was the world community to arrest the user?"

11 GROUND WAR

THE BUNKER

The Italian Air Force or what remains of it has given up defending Italy and has retreated into France to support the French defense of the greater European continent. The Italian commander of the Italian Air Force has vowed to retake Italy and punish the Moslem forces.

"As you can see gentlemen, Italy has fallen to us in only four weeks. Rome is on its knees. Our tanks even now are moving to take over when our Air Force has done all the damage it can. The only thing holding back our tanks is the driving time from here to there. We want to build up our tank force to commit at least fifty percent of our tanks to the battle before we move into the heart of Italy and into Europe. We have had only one setback, 'The Pope has escaped to the coast and left Italy.' Vatican city is in ruins along with the artifacts of old Rome when they ruled the Arab world. They will never again rise from the ashes. The Coliseum is rubble, the Pantheon is a hole in the ground. Haydrian's villa outside Rome can no longer be called ruins, it is unidentifiable. I spared Venice only because, as Arabs from our dry deserts we might find amusement in that city in the water, or our home away from home after the war." Now please sit back and watch our overall assessment of the world.

"The United States. That country is in total disarray. The forty million beggars on their welfare roles were joined by another thirty million down trodden people to create a new class referred to by other Americans simply as the looters. Our Chinese friends were more than happy to supply millions of their old outmoded automatic assault rifles and pistols to them. They are now in the midst of a civil war with seventy million looters against one hundred and sixty million weak kneed civilians. Gun control, hah. We financed millions of dollars of gun control legislation. It took millions of guns out of the hands of law abiding civilians. It made millions of them think that they could control guns. It made millions not even want a gun in their house. They are now faced with millions of well armed countrymen that are to reverse the classes there. The rich will be hunted down and the so called looters will be in charge of the country. Then we will have nothing to fear since unemployed uneducated people cannot hope to run a country. There have already been reports of cannibalism in wide spread parts of the United States. Their military of only one and a half million is helpless in the face of seventy million armed looters. Even if order is achieved there, it will devastate their country. Before they could possibly become strong again, we will have taken Europe and will hold most of South and Central America. We will be able to build up our forces there and simply move across their southern border to conquer the remaining Christian outpost. Then Islam will be worldwide.

France. Their forces are hopelessly outnumbered. They do not even know that they do not have a chance. There has been no resistance to our forces what-so-ever except suicide attacks by some Italian forces. The French have bottled up their main forces along the Po river in northern Italy and do not even know they are in a trap that we are going to close on them.

In a desperate attempt to win a hopeless battle, they have massed most of the ships of the Italian and French navies and are now sailing around the boot of Italy in a vain attempt to cut our supply lines by landing forces near Venice and then blocking the land between there and the Alps mountains. Tomorrow the world will see. The American Mediterranean fleet has withdrawn near Barcelona to be held in reserve. As inventors of the first successful air to ship missiles, the French think they can defend their fleet while they land their forces.

Africa. The African forces are allying themselves with us. They do not contribute much equipment, and most do not understand Islam, but we can use their forces to clear minefields if we herd them ahead of us when we do move into Europe.

Spain. The forces of Egypt, Libya, Algeria, Morocco and others have been moved up to cross into Spain as soon as we have dealt with the French and Italian navies.

Germany. The long time historical enemy of France has not lifted a finger to help anyone. They are hoping that the French forces will win, but be reduced to the point Germany can just demand their surrender without a fight. We have moved our forces into Czechoslovakia and rolled over any token resistance they may have put up. We are not foolish enough to attack Germany through the Soviet Union, but the threat should keep both Russian and German forces frozen there.

Soviet Union. Starvation, their military is in shambles after the Muslims and Asians took their equipment. What force they do have was on the European front and is attempting to cross over to the war front with China, who has already taken much of Siberia and the oil fields there.

China is reporting pacification of South East Asia has been completed. Vietnam, Burma, Laos, Thailand, Malaysia, and Indonesia surrendered almost without a shot. There are large battles with India, but India cannot stand long without support from Europe, the United States, or the Soviet Union, and none of those have support to give. Pakistan has almost succeeded in retaking their originally land in India and have been joined by the Muslims throughout India in over throwing the Hindu's. India will be divided up between Pakistan and China.

III,12

Due to the confusion on the Ebro and Tagus river in Spain, the Po River in Italy, the Rhone river in France, and near Lake Geneva and Arezzo Italy. Two leaders and the cities of the River Garonne will be captured, killed, and drowned.

VI,54

At the second hour after daybreak, the Arab forces of Tunisia and Algeria along with the guerrillas in northern Morocco will capture the king of Morocco.

WEEK 4

Communications in Europe are much better than here. Most of their telephone lines are working as well as many of their radios. Some television stations are carrying live pictures of the air action over Rome throughout Europe. We have received some video tape flown here by F-15 courtesy our American Air Base in Spain. A copy of this video tape will be delivered to the ANMCC ASAP (as soon as possible). There is a news blackout on the French and Italian buildup on the Po River, but plenty of live broadcasts from Rome. Apparently CNN is broadcasting out of Venice, but without satellite relay, there has been little on television. The video tape is of little intelligence value other than it shows large numbers of fighter bomber aircraft dropping bombs, the Pantheon and Roman Coliseum being destroyed, and bombs exploding inside the walls of Vatican City. The aircraft represent mainly Arab countries, and are of French, American, German, and Russian manufacture.

V,47

The great Arab will march on, but the Turks will undermine him and the Greek navy will move against him.

II,52

The Greek and Turkish Navy will meet on the seas and war will erupt between them.

III,89

The Greek navy will suffer losses and will receive help from the United States, after the Arabs announce their intentions, but not enough.

IX,91

Greece will be hit with disease from an artificial dust. A leader named Anthony will refuse to help Greece.

V,91

Greece will be invaded from Albania.

IX,60

Yugoslavia will be threatened by Albania and a conquered Greece led by an Arab with a black hat, but the attack will be delayed because of an allied attack launched into the Mediterranean from Portugal.

VI,68

When rebel soldiers fight furiously with steel weapons against their chief, the Albanian enemy will also be working to conquer Rome by bribing officials.

VIII,11

Refugees will swamp Vicenza. Venice will die in the war. The Duke of Valence (Prince of Monaco) will be defeated near the Lunigiana valley.

DAY 30, SEPTEMBER 16

Technical Sergeant (TSgt) Walter Gaddis had heard the news broadcast out of Venice by CNN. It was really a mess. The four main parts of Yugoslavia: Serbia, Croatia, Macedonia, and Bosnia had fought throughout history except when Tito had brought them together to fight a guerrilla war against the Germans first and then against the Russians. They had been a communist country, but fiercely independent of the Soviet Union. They had a very strong military.

Then Tito had died. When the 1984 Winter Olympics were held in Yugoslavia, the ethnic groups had cooperated and put on a good show showing their different cultures as the world wondered about the peace between these divergent groups, especially those that knew the history of Yugoslavia. With the breakup of Russia and Soviet Block countries declaring their independence from Russia, Bosnia tried to declare their independence from Yugoslavia as did Croatia. With Serbia being the ruling class, they decided not to let Yugoslavia break up and demanded that Bosnia and Croatia come back. Shortly thereafter Bosnia and Croatia started throwing out the Serbs and taking their property. Guns started firing. Croatia and Bosnia started mobilizing military forces against each other and Serbia. Then all sides started committing atrocities on each other with every group blaming the other groups for having concentration camps and mass murders. They were probably all correct. Anyway, the Allies took the side of the Moslem Bosnia against the Christian Serbs, but weren't willing to commit military forces. Eventually, the Arabs volunteered to loan troops and equipment to the United Nations peace keeping forces in Bosnia. Before long the civil wars spread to the Kurds in Turkey and the Turks in Greece. Albania got involved somehow. A real mess. Walter wasn't sure whether to call the Arabs good or bad, but it appeared they were taking on the strong man role held by the United States since World War II. Right now it appeared the Arabs had gone too far in attacking Greece.

Venice, Italy was swamped with refugees from Yugoslavia that came by land and Greeks that had come by sea. Most of the military cargo aircraft from the United States Air Force had been very busy ferrying food to the hundreds of thousands, if not millions, of refugees in the camps.

Technical Sergeant Walter Gaddis had learned more about what was happening in the United States and the news was not good. He heard that nuclear bombs going off in space over the U.S. had destroyed all the transistor devices and there were no communications and very little transportation. There were people rioting and killing for food from their neighbors. He was worried about his parents in Biloxi, Mississippi, but had no way to get word to them. All telephones and telegraph in the U.S. was out and the military in Europe had suspended mail service to the U.S. because apparently the postman was no longer making his rounds. Dark, nor rain, nor snow couldn't stop the mail, but their vehicles and automated mail sorters weren't working. Apparently, the U.S. was not a very safe place. There were estimates that more people had died from Americans shooting Americans than died from the nuclear bombs that went off on the ground, which was more Americans than had ever died in a war before. He was glad he was in the relative safety here in Europe. The war hadn't actually gotten to his location.

Security at Hahn was at the peak. Reports were coming out of the Arabs destroying Rome, Italy and moving toward Germany through Hungary and Czechoslovakia and then toward the Austrian border. TSgt Walter Gaddis's unit had been moved to the German border near Berne,

Switzerland to prevent an invasion of Arab forces currently moving into Switzerland. TSgt Gaddis was still guarding the gate at Hahn with his M1A1 tank. He was now working twelve hours on and twelve hours off, seven days per week. He was due for a three day pass next weekend for the first time in nearly a month. It had been three weeks since his last day off.

Traffic had been snarled at the gate entrances as workers living off base had to have their cars inspected before coming onto the base. There were complaints about the average waiting time during rush hours that was over one hour. He saw a Mercedes coming down the highway fast, but he turned in at the gate and was coming fast. The new heavy metal pipe gate would stop him, but TSgt Gaddis saw another car turn off and follow the first. He ordered his continuously idling tank to move fast to block the gate. The treads ground, temporarily losing some traction due to the huge torque suddenly applied, but the tank leaped forward blocking the gate. It was a good thing too because the first car exploded destroying the pipe gate. The second car exploded impacting the front of the tank. The tank driver was temporarily blinded and ground up and over the debris almost to the main road before disengaging the clutch and stopping the tank until he regained his vision and hearing.

TSgt Gaddis had quickly dropped down into the turret pulling the hatch down as he dropped. The explosion had deafened him then the vacuum after the over pressure of the blast yanked the hatch from his hand since he had not had time to dog it down. His ears were ringing very loudly as he cautiously raised up to peer out of the hatch. He ducked just in time to keep from being set afire as a nearby car gasoline tank exploded. He reached out and pulled the hatch down and dogged it down now. He also turned on the full chemical and biological filtering system to protect them from fumes of automobiles burning. He was surveying the damage by using the periscope when he became aware of someone down in the tank tugging on his pant leg.

He looked down and said, "What is it? Speak up, Bill, I can't hear a word you're saying."

He could see Bill's mouth moving and then some other crew members mouths. Then he became aware of being able to "hear" his tank commanders chair squeaking which he had never heard before. He could hear the bearings in the periscope. He could even hear the bearings in the engine turning. He could not hear voices. He was deaf. He started talking for the crew's benefit not knowing how he sounded to them, "Relax, we are all right. It would appear that I have temporarily lost my hearing. What just happened is that I saw cars trying to run the gate from the outside and ordered the tank to block their entry. The first car blew up the pipe gate and the second one blew up on impact with the tank. We're a little scorched, but his explosives didn't scratch the tank. The explosion destroyed the gate shack and every car that was sitting in line to get in the gate. There is a lot of fire and some secondary explosions as gasoline tanks explode in the fire. The tank is sitting out almost to the main road. Bill, since my hearing is not so good, will you radio back to security to tell them what happened and that we need relief immediately? I can not hear you, make a head movement, 'yes', if you will radio. Thanks. I will keep watch through the periscope if there are any additional problems coming. Bill, can you understand me and am I speaking too loud?" Bill said something back, then realized I couldn't hear and simply made an exaggerated 'yes' with his head.

Bill, came back and tugged his pant leg again and handed him a note. It said, "The radio seems to be working. I could not contact anyone. I put out the secondary antenna and still could not contact anyone. I then changed frequencies to the Buchel German Luftwaffe Air Base and they said there had been a rocket attack here on Hahn Air Force Base and they had not been able to contact anyone either, until we called."

"Bill, call them back. Ask them if they can see how much damage was done to the base, then write me another note."

TSgt Gaddis swiveled around the periscope and could not see any fires or damage of any kind behind him on the base or anywhere except right here at this gate. The bearing in the periscope were very loud, but the scope appeared to still move as easily as always. When Bill handed him another note he asked, "Can you hear the bearings in this scope when I swivel it?"

Bill shook his head, 'no'. The note said, "What the security police saw from Buchel were rockets fired from outside of Hahn that blew up above the base with puffs of what appeared to be smoke. No, they could not see any damage or fires on Hahn."

"Oh Shit."

Bill tugged on his pants asking something.

"Bill, I still can't hear, but I am thinking that the base has been gassed with something. Because of the fires around us, I sealed the tank and turned on our CBN (Chemical, Biological, Nuclear) filters to protect us from gasoline fumes. I may have saved our lives. What say we stay buttoned up in here and take a tour of the base?"

Bill said something to the other crew members and then gave a visible 'yes' motion.

"Okay driver, take us where ever you want to go. You use your port, keep the vent closed; I'll use the periscope. Bill, I'll give a running commentary on what I see. Grab my foot if you can't understand or if you see any indication of a problem with the filters. They protected us this far, but if they start stopping up or you get any signal of anything coming through we've got to make a run for it immediately."

The tank took off making a round of the air base. TSgt Gaddis was worried that they would find people dead everywhere but a few live ones that would want them to open the tank. He had no idea what had happened and therefore no idea as to whether he could open the tank yet. Was it chemical or biological? Was it persistent or had it already dispersed or evaporated or changed to something harmless?

He called out his commentary. "We are heading in on the main road. We are now going down the main road. There are vehicles that have run into trees and buildings. There are vehicles out on the lawns. The drivers and passengers are slumped over and presumed dead. Some managed to get doors open and are lying half in and half out, dead. There are pedestrians lying about near sidewalks. We are at the Commissary. There are twenty or thirty people outside that just collapsed where they were. Same at the base exchange. We are turning onto the flight line now. Just go through the gate."

The driver drove through the chain link security gate onto the flight line. If TSgt Gaddis could hear it scrape on the tank with his strange hearing, then there was probably no detection of crashing through the gate for those that could not see. He noticed the gunner looking through his infrared gun sight. There were some aircraft just landing on the runway. He turned up his magnification and could see controllers in the tower slumped over their equipment. The aircraft were taxiing in his direction now. He pointed the turret at them and moved in left and right. He hoped they would recognize that he was trying to warn them away.

They kept on coming. "Gunner, fire warning shots near the aircraft. Do not damage them, but try to warn them away. Good shot. The aircraft have all stopped where they were. Fire again. Good. Driver accelerate directly at them. Good, the aircraft are turning around and going back to the runway to get away from us. Gunner fire again. Good, I think they have gotten the message and are taking off again. They are. I can see into this hangar and can see bodies. There are some more bodies at base OPs. Driver take us toward the command post. It may have been sealed with some people still alive." As they approached the command post, some officers came out and tried to wave them down. "Driver, go up to them and stop."

Bill hit his shin and made a motion as if speaking into a microphone. "Good idea, Bill, but you take my position and do the talking. Remember, I can't hear you."

Bill took the tank commander's seat in the turret and looked through the periscope while talking on the microphone. The tank had a public address system and microphones outside that would allow two way communication. He was glad that Bill thought about it. He had probably forgotten because he couldn't hear whether it was even working or not if he had tried.

Bill wrote him a note which said, "Gas, they think it has dispersed now. Shall I open the tank?"

"Everyone, you can hear and see better than I can at the moment. Raise your right hand if you think we should open the tank?" Everyone raised their hand, and then he did too. "Okay Bill, open her up." They lived. The airplanes that they had scared away, were called by the command post and they returned to land once again.

MISSOURI

Jim woke in the morning to find that the rain had finally stopped and it was sunny. He had been about to go crazy in the cabin alone in the rain. He had been eating fresh chicken eggs that he gathered from the hen house and had fresh milk from the cow daily, but the diet was getting a little old. No time to worry about the cholesterol he had been eating. The plane looked sodden, but undamaged. Sam had cleaned the weeds and grass out of the axles and struts and guy wires and could find nothing wrong, except his makeshift runway was under several feet of water. As he was looking at the pond he saw a couple of horses in the pasture that he had not seen during the rains. Jim thought, "It might be days before the natural pond drained so I can take off in the airplane. Even then, the grass might be too tall for the little airplane to power through with enough speed to fly. I have been here for two weeks. I need to get back to Cape Girardeau and the girls. If those horses are not too wild, maybe I can find a bridle or some rope for a halter or something so I can ride back to Cape Girardeau rather then sit here in the country. It looks like this place was lived in before the war, maybe there is some tack in the barn."

Jim found a saddle in the barn and managed to catch a horse in the pasture. It took five days of riding to get back to Cape Girardeau. He passed by several burned out towns and farms. At the third town, he realized that of all the horrible, sickening burned corpses he had seen, none were young women. He said to the heavens, "Most of the bodies have been men. Some were young kids, girl or boy, I couldn't tell, but kids. I've seen some overweight female bodies, but I have not seen any obviously female corpses of the more slender variety. To me that means that the looters are going through the farms and towns collecting the young able women and destroying the evidence when they leave."

On the third day of riding he had gotten more used to riding and was beyond the pain of the first two days. When he came over a hill he stopped and turned the horse back over the hill. He found a place to tie the bridle so he could leave the horse and laid down at the top of the hill with his head just over the rise where he could see, but doubted that anyone on the road below could see.

What he saw was that he had come across a small army of looters that seemed to be heading for Cape Girardeau. He spent the day under some trees when not watching from the hilltop and used the night to sneak across the road on his horse. After he got across the road that the looters were using, he found a garage to hide he and the horse in until morning. He could get lost all too easily trying to ride any distance at night. "If I go stumbling about at night, I might ride right into a looter camp before I know it, or the horse may step in something and get hurt. That's all I would need.

CAPE GIRARDEAU

After the rains stopped and a week had gone by with no Jim, the girls were giving up seeing him again. Darcy asked Gary to find them a place in town if that were possible. Gary had to admit that with good weather somebody would question putting guards out along the road and him going down this road to, where? He found an old apartment above an old drugstore. The Drugstore had gone through numerous modernization, but the old apartment had been unused for fifty years. At one time the owners lived there, but after World War II bought a house in the suburbs. With the housing shortage they were willing to rent it out if they could find people they could trust not to rob the place, and provide a little additional security. They had come to the Lieutenant Colonel to see if he had any recommendations right after Darcy had asked about an apartment in town.

Darcy and Shelby moved the next day. They completely unloaded the old Mercury for the first time since the start of the war.

"Thank you, Gary, for your fast reaction. With Jim gone, I just couldn't stand being out there in the country alone."

"I'm not so sure, but if Darcy wants to I follow. Without Jim around, and after the incident in the mall I'm afraid of everything. On the other hand, maybe living in town will make me more comfortable being around people."

"I'm glad I found this place for you. It will be a lot easier to watch out for you and you can be the burglar alarm, not that anyone will be breaking in with a military patrol on the main streets. You'll be a lot safer here."

The girls settled down to wait their fate. Would they go on when the bridge was finished? By themselves, not likely, at least not until things, society, were rebuilt a lot. It was a scary prospect.

12 THE EUROPEAN FLEET

DAY 35

WEEK 6, DAY 35, SEPTEMBER 21
The Catholic Pope has fled Rome and gone to England for safety. Thousands of refugees are packing the roads from Rome to Naples, Pisa, and other coastal cities.

Facil had almost forgotten about sex. He told his harem everything he knew and at first they blamed him for the war and what was happening. But he also expressed his feelings about what was happening. He was now on the war staff as it were. He had input into the battle plans, but still had to be careful about what he said. Gradually his harem began to understand the position he was in and Facil, never a big man, was wasting away. His harem, that had signed on for very good pay had resigned themselves to the fact that he was every bit of the captive that they were. He had always been kind and treated them as intelligent, something many girls in their line of work would never see.

Joy, for example had hired on for one year at one hundred thousand dollars and had agreed to extend for another year. She had figured in another few months she would have one quarter of a million dollars, tax free with which she could go back to the United States, get an advanced degree or two and maybe marry some college professor who would never find out about her previous job for Facil. She liked Facil, she was not promiscuous and would marry Facil if he asked and been his queen and remained true to him. She could never be a Muslim just as he was not a good Muslim. She could follow the public rules as well as he could. She could accept that adultery would mean her death, once married, he would be obligated to never stray and she would accept the same.

Joy had been hardest on him, because she was the most educated of his Harem. She initially blamed him for the plight of the United States. She blamed him for annihilation of the Jews and placed him in the same category as Hitler. She stayed completely away from him and would not answer his bidding in any way for weeks. As she watched him, she realized that Facil could have had her killed for her actions as part of his harem. She finally realized that Facil really had no choice in this war. He had no power other than that he was alive and inside the enemy camp. She was also there and she saw nothing she could do to harm the enemy. Facil was in not much better shape. Finally she went to him when he came back to the suite.

"Facil, may I speak freely."

"Yes, please do, Joy, my dear. I only want you to understand that I am powerless to do any good in the world at the present time except to try to stay alive and wait for some chance."

"I do understand. Girls, gather around, I think you should be with me on this. You know my lack of action with Facil the past six weeks. Kareen, you, being Arab yourself, were the only one to even speak to Facil. We were wrong. I truly believe that Facil has been truthful with us. I think he had decided on the only right course. We are all prisoners. If Facil did not cooperate he would have been killed immediately. By staying alive, maybe some time he can save just one life, or maybe millions. Maybe he will be the one to negotiate a peace when the Arabs lose this insane war. Maybe he can only stop the slaughter of one tiny village. If he were dead, his country might die with him, or he might be replaced by someone far worse. I have known Facil for nearly two years now and have never found him to be anything other than a kind person with unlimited money to buy anything. That has been his only fault, but the reason I came to him. There are powerful people who buy and sell sex slaves, but Facil hired all of us and pays us well. We have a contract with a definite expiration. The only stipulation is that we cannot talk of what we did during this time and the knowledge that our very existence here will be denounced if we were try to go to the news media, but we are being paid well.

Now you see Facil suffering more than we are suffering. We may not have any blame, but we must support Facil and try to relieve his burden, by making him as happy as we can. He is not one of them or I would have been executed long before now. How about it girls? Let's make him as happy as we can while we're all stuck here together. Hate is getting us no where."

Joy's speech lifted the dark cloud over all their heads. They had long since decorated the suite with his disclaimers. They had made some into designs with the writing going in all directions to form pentagons and stars, and Aztec designs. There was no way to zoom a camera in or out without getting the disclaimer in the picture.

That was the first genuinely fun dinner they had since their arrival. Afterward, they drew straws to see who would accompany Facil to bed for the night.

II,26
Paris will celebrate their top general but he will soon lose on the field of battle and retreat to a defensive position along the Po river after the Ticino river is flooded first with water with and then blood, fire and bodies in the second battle.

II,33
The Arabs will go upstream to where the Adige River, joins the Po River and by crossing the two rivers before they combine their strength will cross and will wreck the French. The enemy near the Genoa will march against France.

VI,48
Florence and Sienna will be turned to desert by the enemy.

VIII,7
News will come from Milan that man made disease will be found in the Seine.

I,37
Shortly before the setting of the sun, the battle-cry will be sounded and a great people will be left in doubt. Destroyed the marine port will be silent and graves will be uprooted.

VIII,17
Those who thought themselves secure will be suddenly destroyed. through three powers at war the world is in trouble. The enemy will seize the marine city and inhabitants will suffer from famine, fire flooding, disease and every evil will be multiplied.

II,59
A French fleet will be supported by an impressive land force. Also from beneath the sea Neptune and his sea forces will come. Province (southeast France) will be reddened to be occupied by a great host. destruction of Narbonne because of flying projectile weapons.

II,78
The forces of great Neptune will come from beneath the sea. When North African and French blood are mixed in battle. The isles (Corsica and Sardinia) will bleed, not reached in time. This setback will hurt him because of a secret not well kept.

V,23

Two powers contented because of conquest will be united together, and together will be joined in Mars (symbol of war), but then the great leaders of Africa will shake in terror, when the union will be broken by the opposing fleet.

September 23

There still had been no direct battles near the Po River. The French and Italian forces on the West side were digging in for a solid line of defense. The combined French and Italian fleet was sailing northward along the east coast of Italy. The Italian ground forces from southern Italy had moved northward on land and were approaching the northeast quadrant. They had been ordered to hold until the amphibious forces had landed near Venice and to remain hidden until ordered to counter-attack.

Colonel Henry spent most of his time monitoring the progress of reestablishing law and order around the major cities in the United States and getting the supply lines of food moving into the cities. Communications had improved to the point that there was a Ham radio news network operating around the country. The AM/FM radio broadcasts reached a few, but a very small percentage. Telephone service had been re-established within most cities, though not between cities. Electric power was coming back on line across most of the country.

A very serious problem had surfaced that was not immediately reported as military action. Every river bridge on the Mississippi river had been destroyed. Not just damaged, but destroyed. This cut off all road and rail traffic between east and west United States. A pontoon bridge had been established north of Saint Louis, but the roads to and from the bridge were not adequate for semi-truck traffic.

There had been several flights of truck parts from South America to the United States to get trucks with electronic parts going again. Luckily many of the diesels were still pre- electronic fuel injection. Fully sixty percent of the semi-trucks of the United States were reportedly operational and in use. One hundred percent of the rail traffic had been restored except for missing bridges here and there that had been sabotaged. The Mississippi was the major obstacle. Everything had to be routed north through Brainerd, Minnesota creating a terrible traffic jam on the two lane roads into and out of that little town. The government was working on getting several new bridges in on better roads to the south, but bridges would take months to build. There was also an effort to buildup side roads to points where military pontoon bridges could be accessible from highways so commercial trucks could cross them. The Mississippi was not the only problem river without bridges, but it ran from north to south and was a large river. The downtown Saint Louis, Missouri area near where all the roads come together for what used to be bridges was too radioactively hot to use anyway. Those bridges, and downtown Saint Louis would never exist again, but the Interstate 270 bridges north of Saint Louis were being feverishly worked on. Estimated completion was late November.

Suddenly there was a squawking noise that filled the command post. An automated voice announced, "Nuclear Detonation Report! Nuclear Detonation Report." A light lit an area on the world map on the wall that showed the Adriatic Sea south of Venice.

Colonel Henry blanched and quivered. General Gates said harshly, "Colonel Lakeman. Your assessment?" It was not a question it was an order.

Henry recognized the General's voice and slowly relaxed. He looked at the General, but no words would come immediately. "Well...What is it?" General Gates asked.

Henry managed to say through suddenly welling tears, "Sir, I know what it is. A sub launched nuclear missile has just destroyed the combined French and Italian Navies with few men getting ashore."

"Do you know something I don't? I have not seen any assessment as to what the detonation report was. How do you know what it was?" questioned General Gates almost accusingly.

"Sir. It's a long story. Remember me saying that you needed to find a Jim Claris? Well, he told me this would happen now, but he told me years ago, trying to warn someone."

General Gates angrily cut him off, "What kind of garbage are you feeding me? You knew this and did nothing to stop it? How did you know this was going to happen?"

"Sir, I heard this years ago, and had forgotten that I had heard it until it happened. Would you believe someone that told you in 1980 that this was going to happen now? I passed it off as science fiction. I didn't believe it and forgot most of what I was told about some future war. That is why we need to find Jim Claris. He knows this stuff. I don't know how, but he told about this happening over fifteen years ago. He claims to have gotten this information from reading Nostradamus, but so far he had been one hundred percent accurate."

"Sorry Colonel. But the loss of life that must have occurred. Who is this Jim Claris and where do I find him? I heard from him about a month ago after years of not even thinking about him. Out of the blue, he writes me this letter warning me that the war is imminent. He was living in Fairborn, Ohio and working as a civil servant at Wright-Patterson Air Force Base. He was a reserve mobilization augmentee. I think he was a lieutenant colonel when he left the reserves."

"Good, if he survived the Nuke at Wright-Patterson we can recall him to active duty and bring him here. We have no contact with Wright-Patterson, but the bomb there was a small one. But, isn't Fairborn the town right outside the gate? It may be gone too."

"Sir, Jim built a house out in the country on a hill without direct sight of the valley. He may have survived. There used to be a guard base over in Springfield, Ohio, can't we contact them and send someone over there?"

"Fine, we'll do it. How did you say he knew this?"

"He claims that he interpreted Nostradamus and found a detailed road map of World War III. He said the Arabs would do what they are doing right now. He warned about them taking Yugoslavia. I couldn't imagine us letting them conquer Yugoslavia and Greece without a war, but when they did it as a United Nations peace keeping force, I didn't realize that the force was primarily an Arab force. It wasn't until I got Jim's letter last month that I started questioning things. I really don't remember too much of it, but after things happen I remember that he had told me they would. In fact the night before the HEMP attack, I was talking about Jim with another friend of mine I would like to get here, a Major Jeremy Houston, that is at Minot. He and I prepared the suggestions together that laid out the recovery plans so far."

"Fine, we'll send a plane for him. Anyone else you think we ought to have?"

Colonel Henry thought for a moment and replied, "If this is the main command post of the military, and if our communications from here are as good as we will get, I think we need to bring in the top key men from the Army and Navy and start figuring out what we do now?"

"Done." said General Gates.

Fortunately Jim Claris's house and family were in place and safe, but unfortunately, Jim Claris had been on a government TDY to Los Angeles when the HEMP hit. Then there was a report that Los Angeles had been destroyed. There had been several reports to the Alternate National Military Command Center over the past two months from Jim, but nothing for a long time now. The crew sent to get him brought back his wife and family to the ANMCC.

II,32

The allies will build up near Ravenna, Italy, but are hit with biological weapons while the Arabs take Yugoslavia.

II,84

Northern Italian communists will receive Yugoslavian advisors. Rome asks for US help. A civil war breaks out between the Red Communists supported by Arabs in Northern Italy and Rome.

IV,98

The Arabs will send reinforcements come from Albania and will carry all the way to Rome

I,9

From the Orient (what Nostradamus called the Middle East) will come the raids into Venice and Italy supported by a Libyan (Arab) fleet. Malta will be afraid of the raid and most of the Mediterranean islands will be evacuated.

III,38

French and the forces from some other nation march around the mountains (along the coast toward Italy) to die and be captured near harvest (autumn) and contrary month (January) by the Muslim leaders.

III,43

People of the Tarn, Lot and Garonne (French rivers) beware of passing the Apennine mountains. Your graves will be near Rome and Ancona (eastern coast of Italy). The enemy with the straggly black beard will erect a trophy of his victory.

II,72

The French army will be flanked in Italy with the enemy attacking from all directions. The Italian army will retreat destroying the French army's attacks near the Ticino and Rubicon rivers.

III,23

The French fleet will come to Italy and will sail out of southern France and follow down the western coast of Italy, but will get trapped among the islands of the Adriatic off the coast of Yugoslavia when the Arabian fleet cuts off the supply routes to the fleet.

VIII,6

French fleet, do not approach Corsica or Sardinia, you will be sorry. Everyone of you will die without help from land. You will either swim in your own blood or be captured, but you won't believe me.

I,29

A creature that is both terrestrial and aquatic will land upon the beach. It will be terribly frightening but pleasing to the eye of a military man as it quickly reaches the Italian defenses.

IV,90

The French and Italian navies will not be able to unite and Milan and Pavia (northern Italy) will be afraid of being overrun cut off from resupply from the navies who are themselves in trouble.

V,63

An unsuccessful compromise will bring honor to some, undue complaints for others. Ships will be engaged in Latin seas to suffer cold, hunger and great waves. far from the Tiber (Rome) the land will be stained with blood, and diverse diseases will inflict everyone.

II,5

When iron and a letter are enclosed in a fish, one will leave to make war. His fleet will be well propelled by sea, appearing near Latin land (Italy)

III,21

Where the Conca River flows into the Adriatic Sea a submarine will appear.

II,43

While the Italian and French navies are attempting to engage the Arabian fleet a Ballistic Missile will cause the earth to quake struck from the sky. Where the Po and Tiber rivers flow into the Gulf of Venice and Rome an amphibious creature will land on the shore.

II,86

The fleet will be destroyed in the Adriatic after the earth and sea is thrown into the air, leaving the Arabian fleet controlling the Mediterranean. This will allow the Arabs to build up their sea forces in the Red Sea to protect the southern approaches to the Mediterranean.

Facil woke in the morning feeling the best he had felt since his captivity began. He no longer felt the guilt of the previous six weeks. His harem, led by Joy from the United States had absolved him of the sins of this war. Now that they recognized that he had no choice he could also quit wondering if maybe there had been some way he could have gotten out of his involvement to date. He was also bolstered by a new inner strength, that he would not succumb to the dark power of Jabal. He would keep his quiet, for months if need be to be able to have the smallest power for good when there was an opportunity that might not get him killed. The longer he appeared to be a co-conspirator, the longer he could live for having the power to just say,

'NO', to further blood shed. Yes, he had become Americanized. Yes, he was like the Israeli, but maybe he was more western than all but a few Arabs.

His new resolve was apparent to the other Arab leaders that knew him. His very appearance was more Sultan-like than captive. He had that inner power that only a few leaders possess. He verbally supported Jabal, but it was now a concession versus fear. He was giving a little in exchange for a lot. Even Jabal recognized this, but Facil was too powerful among all the leaders to do anything about without having to fight all of them. Facil had provided a lot of funding to many of them through the years. He could threaten as a group. He might even get by with assassinating two or three to control their countries, but he could not assassinate all of them without the Muslim alliance destroying itself from within. With Facil giving lip service to the cause, he could not hurt Facil without having a minor revolt on his hands. Even some of the Arab leaders like Colonel Hadifan of Libya might mistrust him, if he raised any hand against another leader that was at least verbally in support of the cause.

He had hoped to use the harem as blackmail, but Facil had out thought him on that one, unless he could get Facil and his harem to some other location not yet decorated in the disclaimer. He knew from voice recordings that Facil was not a supporter of the cause, but as long as he played along he had to remain safe. Playing a secret recording to anyone would have gotten Jabal nowhere. He couldn't use the private tapes on the media without showing the true thoughts of Facil.

"Gentlemen, I have a holovision broadcast I would like to bring you live right now from the Adriatic sea. Please give it your undivided attention as it is extremely important to our Holy Jihad."

The lights went down and the air over the center of the conference table crackled then a picture came into view. "One of our satellites is passing from north to south over the Adriatic Sea. The first point of attention is the Adriatic Sea about one hundred kilometers south of Venice. You can see over one hundred ships. This is the combined French and Italian navies that I mentioned were coming to cut off our supply lines from Yugoslavia to northern Italy."

Facil saw a very sizable force. He could tell that the French and Italians had confiscated a number of civilian container ships for this armada. This sizable force, if landed, could indeed cut off the vital ammunition and fuel supplies for the Muslim forces already in Italy. The end of the war may be coming much sooner than depicted, except that Jabal seemed to have no fear of this sizable force. He knew he must have something up his sleeve.

Now watch as we zoom in on the mouth of the river. As we zoom in you can almost see a nuclear submarine launching a missile. Now we quickly shift back to the armada and watch the fun."

The streak of flame from the falling war head came down from the sky toward the middle of the fleet. Then it hit the ocean. A millisecond later that seemed like several seconds, and another sun seemed to blossom from below the water. The camera instantly closed its iris to lessen the light and filters went into place. The ball of flame rose partially from the ocean and everything nearby vaporized. A mighty cloud spread out over the ocean obstructing the view, then it was seen that ships had capsized with some hulls even burning in the light of this new sun. Ships that escaped the cloud did not immediately capsize, but first their superstructures caught fire, blazing like magnesium. Then the rolling cloud caught them sending them over past horizontal.

The fleet had been nuked. Facil found it hard to believe that he was watching the almost instantaneous, but seemingly slow motion death of an Armada. Was this what it was like when Aristotle had defeated a fleet sailing toward Greece by having the citizens hold mirror polished metal shields like lenses to reflect and focus the sun on the wooden ships of the time? This was not mirrors, this was a nuke. Just like the focused light of the Greek mirrors caused the sails and wooden ships to catch fire and burn, the light from the nuclear sun caused the aluminum decks and superstructures to instantly flame setting off secondary explosions even before the sound and water waves hit. The sound wave traveled the next fastest and ships within five miles were capsized if they had not already exploded, then the tidal wave of a submerged nuclear bomb hit them. Facil could imagine everything at sea being destroyed until even the coastal cities were inundated by water from this man made tidal wave.

The picture shifted back to the submarine and Colonel Hadifan of Libya could be seen looking up at the invisible satellite and waving, knowing where the satellite would be. How many men had just died in that armada, one hundred thousand? More? The Europeans would go down to defeat now. Facil would never support the wholesale carnage that was going on, but his decision to go along for now had been the correct one. The Muslim forces might just win the war and dominate the world. At the same time he wondered how long it would be before the Chinese decided they didn't need Arabs any longer.

IX,94

Weak navies will be united, but secretly, the enemies will penetrate the strong defenses. When the weak navies will be attacked, Bratislava (Austria, Czechoslovakia and Hungary) will tremble. Lubeck and Meissen (East Germany) will ally with the Arabs.

WEEK 6 DAY 39, September 25

The Italian Army has suffered major defeat. The United Muslim Forces have a major new weapon enabling a very small Muslim force with to destroy over two hundred tanks and five thousand men. Defeat of this Italian force has left the door open for Muslim forces to take Rome un-contested.

Jabal came on the speaker, "Now for the demonstration of the ultimate in landing craft. One unique invention of our own. The Italian Army in the south was moving north along the east coast to catch our forces between the French and Italian fleets and cross with the French forces across the Po river as we were moving west along coast. With mountains to the north they expected to spring their trap. The fleet was destroyed yesterday and today as the Italian army was still moving along the coast to reinforce the south side of the Po River.

What Facil saw was a huge submarine type of vehicle, or landing craft. It crawled up onto the beach. It was huge. It had multiple cannons on turrets like a tank, but it made a tank look like a toy. The Italian tanks fired on it with gouges into the armor, but no actual penetration. The multiple turrets on the submarine lander fired and twenty Italian tanks exploded. The tanks fired putting one turret out of action, but another 19 tanks exploded. Italian helicopters tried to attack, but were quickly shot down by a combination of gatling guns and missiles. The firepower of this behemoth was astounding. Then another picture appeared of French landing craft that escaped the nuke in the Adriatic and yet another behemoth submarine lander or submersible tank, or whatever it was, landed behind them annihilating the French landing within thirty minutes.

Jabal explained. We were building tankers before. We built a submarine nearly tanker size. By blowing ballast we can come into very shallow water where monster tank treads take hold on the beach and pull the craft up on land. It cannot climb hills or mountains, but it works quite effectively on a beach or over any relatively flat land. The tank treads are the same as used on the largest cranes in the world. The treads, big as they are, are internal to the shell making them impervious to most damage. As you can see it has armor plate far thicker than a tank and since Iraq and Iran had plenty of disabled tanks we simply mounted multiple turrets. Air is blown through the turrets and cannons to clear them of water. All turrets are automatic loading. Everything is automated and actually has a quite small crew. It is protected by a fleet of diesel submarines. So far it is only capable of going ten knots in water and five miles per hour on land, but we will improve if need be.

This is the first time forces will be truly amphibious. The vaunted United States Marines must come in ships which off load landing craft that crawl only a few feet up the beach with no offensive capability and then their marines go running out into machine gun and artillery fire, if their landing craft even made it to the beach. After taking the beach then they land tanks. These tanker size submarines will come in below water rather than be subject to air, missile, and artillery attack until the tracks land on sand, the power to the screws or propellers is then shifted through a gearbox to the caterpillar treads so the ship can climb up onto the land. It's extremely heavy armor and its firepower allow it to destroy any coastal defenses until the more mobile normal tanks and infantry can disembark. It is capable of carrying one hundred tanks and three thousand troops. If carrying only troops that number may be increased to ten thousand. That is why we started building our own tankers and then closed off the ship building docks to prevent spying. It has its own air system far better than a tank could have so it is impervious to chemical and biological warfare.

Obviously, this is the first time we have used them and caused total panic on the Allied troops already there. There is nothing to stop it on near level ground except for nuclear weapons. The number of these vessels is currently being kept from you until we are ready to release it. More are currently being built and new weapons are being developed for its defensive and offensive capability.

Can you imagine one hundred of these moving from the beaches in the United States. On some of their flat ground there in Florida or Texas the tanks would only run behind the inexorable power of these land ships to mop up small pockets. Five hundred U.S. M1A1 Abrams main battle tanks would be no match for our amphibious creature. The middle of the United States is key to conquering them. If we could land these on the beaches of Texas they could roll all the way to Canada between mountain ranges destroying everything in their path. Because they are submarines they can go around the world undetected. But wait. That may be for the future. We conquer Europe first. We will not have the numbers to take on the United States yet.

Facil took the story of these huge sea monsters crawling on land back his harem. He had never confided in harem girls before, but he did like them educated. He did want more than prostitutes. He wanted truly beautiful girls that understood the contract they were signing with him so he would not be accused of taking advantage of some poor uneducated girls. He had nothing but contempt for any Arab who would buy from the white slave trade. He knew there were hundreds of girls and too many young boys who disappeared into the white slave market each year. He had publicly vowed to execute any from Saudi Arabia connected with white or any slavery. We have the money to buy what we want without lowering ourselves to buying and selling without all parties consent.

"I saw the most monstrous killing machine ever devised at work today. When you see an oil tanker, you only see that part above the water. You must know that there is far more under the water. You think an American aircraft carrier with three thousand crewmen and one hundred planes is big. You should see an oil tanker size ship that can beach itself and then climb on the land as some giant sea creature with stingers to destroy life on land. It is actually an oil tanker size submarine that has tank treads to crawl on the land and has many tank turrets firing cannon shells at the enemy. The last resistance in Italy failed today against only two of these. The only remaining obstacle is the Po river and the French forces trying to defend the Po have been flanked by the one that landed south of the mouth of the river. Girls, the United Moslems are conquering Europe. I cannot stop it any more than the Italian tanks could stop the behemoths that climbed out onto their beaches.

I'm sorry to say this, but I want to make you feel as comfortable as possible. Words fail me. I want you to know that I will provide a comfortable home for you even after I marry, if something happens that you have no home to go to. If you need protection, I will provide all the protection that I am able to give for as long as is necessary. Will you forgive me for what my people are doing?"

Joy spoke up first, "Facil, you are a good man and I appreciate your offer and will be most happy to take you up on it for as long as necessary, but The United States is not defeated yet. I do not believe it is to be defeated this time either. I respect you, but I think your Arab friends are overly confident and that you are not getting the whole story. Are you sure that you are not watching some Hollywood production?"

"No, Joy, it is not a Hollywood production. People are really dying by the thousands if not millions. I agree that I don't think my Arab friends realize the size of the hornets nest they stirred when they attacked the United States. Many of them think it is no bigger than England and smaller than Germany. They do not realize that western Europe will fit in the eastern half of the United States. Jabal talks as if Europe is the danger and the United States is of no consequence once Europe has been taken."

Carey said, "What of France? The Muslims haven't touched France yet have they?"

"No Carey, but it will be soon."

Suzane said, "I do not know about whether the United States is that strong, but won't your forces recognize our neutrality?"

"No. They recognize only their own law and treaties are for the weak. It would be better for your people if they were fighters."

"But they are. Don't you know that in my country, as in Switzerland, military service is mandatory of all able bodied men? These two countries have more military per capita than any countries in the world and more military equipment. Every airplane has its own separate runway and bomb proof mountain to hide in. Every person is armed. Every family has survival gear and shelters to go to. Taking France would be far easier than taking on Sweden, or didn't you know."

Facil respected the girls, but Suzane was getting a little high and mighty all of a sudden. He initially felt the hot Arabic blood rush to his forehead in anger, then his calmer Saud blood of the diplomat took over. "Suzane, please don't talk that way to me. I am not the one commanding anything here. I have simply promised to protect you. Who will protect me? Are you?"

Suzane saw the hot rush of anger and then the calm words and felt guilty for speaking to him as she had, "I'm sorry I blurted out like that, Facil. I really appreciate you and I know that right now today, my life is literally in your hands and I can do nothing to thank you. You have just proven that you are the more civilized of the two of us. I promise that if I am ever in a position to protect you, I will. In the meantime, please accept my apology and my gratitude for your protection now. The only payment I can give will be a special night when you deign to chose me."

Again, thought Facil with pride, the power of diplomacy wins the prize, the family blood runs strong in me, stronger than the Arab blood. Maybe it is because my family blood is purer Arab. I must find a wife whose family blood is worthy for my successors. These European and American women have good blood too, but they are not Arabic. I am proud to be an Arab despite the loonies in power at the moment. Providing I use my blood wisely, my family will outlast these loonies in charge. Kareen is Arabic, but not of Saudi Arabia and not of the noble bloodline I will need to keep the future generations strong. Joy, the American is so typically invincible American. You can defeat me, but America will win. The Swede, so incredulous that their treaty means so little and so arrogant... not confident like Joy, but arrogant that her country is right in its armed neutrality and yet dependent upon a king just like his country which he has let down. Kareen was brought up subservient as a good Arab woman, but has learned from the others. Carey is so French, pretty, shy, snobbish versus arrogant or confident. Kareen, beaten back as a country and as a woman, committed to making a man happy, but without the fire to make him truly pleased, devoid of passion. Yes, I can gauge the world with my little harem. Oriental, Arab, south and northern European, and that newer experimental breed, the American, so far the most successful of all having some inner power not present elsewhere. The unbeatable confidence of a country that feels it will succeed, that knows no defeat. Even in defeat, it can find a victory in the long run. Dangerous to cross. I'm afraid my Arab brothers will find that out and I fear for Islam.

After dinner, Suzane said, "Facil, come here, you're mine. I'm going to make it up to you." She did. Facil kind of liked European and American women. Kareen and Sara were both too anxious to please him, and it didn't have the honest passion of the Europeans. But, as the crown prince, he had to chose an Arab wife. When this war was over, if he still had a country, he would choose an Arab wife and give his harem a bonus they would not believe. They were fast becoming his only close friends and he rewarded friendship. He wondered if there was any way he could keep Joy as an American advisor after this was over.

Jabal thought he would have western Europe to include France, Spain, Germany, Denmark, Belgium, Poland, Austria, Czechoslovakia, Rumania by winter and northern Europe and Russia by the end of the first year of war. The next year he planned to take the Americas. China would have all of Asia and Siberia and India all the way to the country of Russia which was his.

That night Facil's sleep was disturbed by nightmares of sea monsters rising from the sea breathing fire and having a knight in silver armor wearing an American shield swinging a sword and beheading the dragon. When he woke in a sweat, Suzane was shaking him. He shared his dream with her and then went to Joy and told her of his dream. They commiserated with him until he was ready to go back to bed.

This time he spent the rest of the night dreaming that his kingdom was gone, but Joy was arguing with an American general to spare his life and return him to power.

IV,48
The fertile and spacious plain of Ausonia (south central Italy) will see many flying creatures. The sun will be clouded by their numbers. They will destroy everything and great disease will originate with them.

WEEK 6 DAY 40, September 26
When Suzane woke him, it was late. He went to the conference room barely making it in time to take his seat.

"Facil," greeted Jabal, "that harem getting too much for you?" That brought a round of laughter from around the table. Facil turned a slightly darker color than his normal deep tanned color.

He replied, "Jabal, when this war is over, let's keep the European women."

Jabal said, "We all know that you are sowing your oats now, but you will take an Arab bride as law demands and remain true to her."

Facil had gained his composure and replied, "Praise be to Allah, I could not take nights like last night as an old man."

That made the room laugh with him.

The holovision briefing today was the Muslim air force bombing Rome like a horde of locusts and Muslim tanks destroying every town and village as they moved toward Rome. Facil was revolted. They could expect no mercy when the Allies regained the upper hand. Were they trying to annihilate the Italian people? No one had ever succeeded in annihilating a people. What Jabal was doing was preparing every enemy to fight to the death. There was much more to be gained by defeating the armies and the governments and then try to make friends with the people. That's what Rome did. Conquered armies and pacified the people. In many cases the conquered were allowed to seemingly govern themselves to keep the people happy with Roman rule. The Siamese at one time ruled China, then escaped to Thailand. The Japanese didn't try to kill the Chinese or the Koreans. Common people are content to be common people as long as they can retain some semblance of normalcy.

Even if Facil were in favor of the war, he would point out the error in this, "Jabal! Point of order. I am in this for better or worse, I would rather it be for the better."

"Facil, you have the floor. I will listen to your advice then make the decision. Speak."

"Jabal, we may not have the ammunition to kill all the people in the world. We must save a few for slaves if nothing else." That got a round of laughter from the leaders around the table and credence to the rest of Facil's point of view. "No, what I am really worried about is putting the spirit of fight in the commoner. If the commoner can still farm his farm or work in his factory and go to his home, many do not care who controls the country, but if you try to kill everyone, the word will spread that everyone must fight for their lives. Italy and France combined would be hard pressed to field three million military, but if the entire population is fighting for its life you suddenly have an enemy of seventy million. Europe contains three hundred million people that know how to shoot a gun. I recommend that you roll through the towns and villages that do not try to prevent you. Leave them alone."

"I don't want to leave a guerrilla war behind our lines."

"Jabal, you are our illustrious leader, but I have studied the history of war. No army has ever succeeded in annihilating a single people, but many have conquered countries. After the war you have farmers to do our farming and factory workers to provide us with goods. Please, do not cause us to fight an unlimited number of fighters. In a town of ten thousand there may be two hundred that hide out and fight our supply lines. That is better than fighting the whole ten thousand. If you continue killing Italians, soon there will be fifty million French on the front line fighting for their existence instead of two hundred thousand along the Po river."

"Point taken." Jabal was smart enough to see that most leaders agreed with Facil, and maybe Facil was right. "Facil, you may be right. If we move through fast instead of trying to totally eliminate resistance, we can get our army to Rome faster."

Facil interjected, "Why don't you move on the French forces and move into Europe instead of going for Rome? You will be leaving the French forces behind your lines of supply. If you don't move west to meet them they could move east to cut the supply lines."

"Facil, the whole point is to punish those who throughout history have kept us down. It started with the Roman Empire then the Catholic Church. This is a Holy Jihad, not just a play for power. I am not worried about the paltry French forces.

When Facil got back to his suite he told the girls what he had done.

Sara asked, "Why would you take the risk? If you get into trouble, we are history."

Suzane said, "I'm very pleased, Facil. You saved possibly millions of lives, but why did Jabal go along with it?"

"It made sense. If you go along methodically killing everyone, the common person runs from you. Then you either have that many guerrilla fighters behind you or they join up with the opposing military force and fight you. Either way trying to kill everyone just multiplies the number of people you are fighting."

"I guess you realize that you helped Jabal win the war." said Joy.

"Yes, but I did save lives as Suzane said, and maybe reduce the retribution to be levied against my people when we lose this war. I didn't do it to help Jabal win. He could have killed millions of civilians and won the war or only fought the armies and win the war quicker. Letting them live makes sense regardless, it saves innocent lives, it saves the lives of Arab troops by reducing the enemy by millions of untrained but still dangerous guerrilla fighters, it would provide a work force after the war for whoever the winner is. The dumb thing was starting this unwinnable war." He did not tell them the last part about the warning about the French forces. They might really take that wrong.

13 THE DEPTHS OF ANARCHY

DAY 44
September 30

He overslept in the morning and got his still tired horse from the garage and started riding again until he got to a military roadblock at the tiny town of Gordonville which was only three miles from Cape Girardeau. They had no radios and didn't believe his story of an attack or that they should let him use a vehicle. They wanted to detain him until shift change.

"Listen carefully, as Lieutenant Colonel Claris, I order you to let me take a Humvee in to see Lieutenant Colonel Gary Smieth. This is extremely serious and delaying me could mean the defeat of your Army unit and even your own deaths. I flew that Piper Cub all the way to Fort Leonard Wood to try to get reinforcements and that was a month ago when no one seemed to be interested in attacking here."

"Hey Sarge. I thought he looked familiar, he was that guy that flew that little airplane out of here a month ago, and we did get double the force we had here. I remember seeing him and Colonel Smieth riding around together and someone pointing that he was going to try to fly out for help."

"You sure of that Corporal, that was over a month ago." Turning to Jim he asked, "If that was you where's your airplane and where have you been for the past month?"

"I had to land the airplane because I was running out of gas and because of the storms coming in. I've spent this long trying to get back here."

"I know some guys that have been pulling guard duty around those girls you brought with you. Everyone thinks you're dead 'cept them. Turned down every Tom and Dick in town. Colonel said he promised to protect them and he was goin' to. If you're him you should know their names."

"Darcy and Shelby. Darcy is the dark haired one and Shelby's the blond."

"Maybe you are him. Okay Corporal, you say you know him, you drive him. Don't give him his cannon back until Colonel Smieth says it's okay.

Private Jones, you ride in the back to guard him so he won't try'. We'll keep your horse here."

It took about twenty minutes to find Lieutenant Colonel Gary Smieth. When he saw Jim he exclaimed, "Well, I'll be damned, you got back. Did you fly in?"

"No I had to make a forced landing on a meadow for lack of fuel and the storm that I couldn't outrun. The rains started right after I landed, and the meadow turned into a lake. I rode in on a horse until I ran into one of your roadblocks, but I came straight here to give you a warning. Yesterday, I saw thousands of people that appeared to be moving toward here along state highway 34 from both the north and the south. I cut across on a county road until I got here.

Gary volunteered, "We got reports that the Saint Louis bunch in this area of the state had linked up with the looters from Blytheville and all of Osceola county in Arkansas. Somehow, every last one of them have gotten their hands on Chinese automatic rifles and lots of ammunition. We're talking about five thousand blacks from Arkansas, ten thousand blacks from Saint Louis, ten thousand Mexican Americans, six thousand apparently white Americans, and all of them with guns. That's thirty-one thousand potential enemy just in this area of Missouri that could be moving on my reinforced rifle company.

Thank God you got the message through to Fort Leonard Wood. The commander sent four M1A1 tanks, ten armored personnel carriers and two hundred total people with plenty of ammunition "so he wouldn't get any more complaints from me." You might be interested to know that he decided that he would move without orders to link up with the Oklahoma and Arkansas national guard units and reopen the Interstate from Tulsa at least to the edge of Saint Louis. My orders are to hold this town, period. If he gets fired, I'm going down with him, he says."

"Glad to help, can I get a ride to see Darcy and Shelby?"

"They're not there. I moved them into town for their safety once it appeared you were not going to get back.

"I'll have someone take you over, but first I need to deploy my forces. What about toward Blytheville? Is there another group there or are they shifting to have a mass attack from the north only? I need some aerial reconnaissance. I wish I just had some old balloons. I'll have to send out some patrols and try to find out where they are."

"The ones I saw were northwest of here, not straight north. There is no way I could see the south and north from a horse. Did your mechanics get the Cessna running?"

"No! I won't ask you to go flying again. Yes, he did get the plane running, but we don't know if it's flyable, since you are our only pilot. The mechanic says the engine is running great but he wouldn't even try to taxi it. He completely rebuilt the engine and has been running it up several times a day. We found the airfield had a whole underground tank of Avgas, it's a five hundred gallon tank and we think it's half full, so there is plenty of gasoline for it. Most of our military vehicles prefer diesel. That 130 octane would burn up our engines."

"Can I take the plane?"

"Only to get those two girls out of here. They think you're dead and they're pretty upset. In addition, Shelby had a run in with a hillbilly. No, she's fine, she was with an escort nearby and they intervened quickly, but it scared her. That's why they're in town now. I found a place for them, but just wait over there, Jane will take you over."

"Major Holly, Captain Gray, come in here, we have some serious planning."

Jim had already made up his mind what he had to do. He wanted to see the girls, but he didn't want to see them and immediately leave on another dangerous flight. It would be better for them if they didn't see him at all. He went back out to the corporal and Humvee that had just driven him into town and seen the warm welcome of his commander. "Corporal, start it up we have a mission. Take me to the airport ASAP (as soon as possible), I have another mission to fly for the Army. Hey, and thanks for believing in me."

"Yes sir. You get in there and I'll take you anywhere you want to go."

He drove them to the airport and helped Jim get the things he wanted for the mission. Five, five gallon glass jugs which Jim filled with AVGAS and a half dozen thermite grenades, a new riot gun and ammunition, an M-16 with a half dozen thirty round banana clips, and a new Barreta with ten clips of military ammo. Jim talked with the mechanic and checked over the plane.

Jim started the plane and checked all the control surfaces after a thorough walk around. He got in and the engine fired immediately. He taxied out with no problem and just took off from the empty parking ramp. He flew to the south toward Blytheville first and discovered not only was there no attack coming from that direction, but the entire town and the old strategic air command base was underwater from a break in the levee.

In fact it looked like the whole land was under water all the way to West Memphis. He didn't fly far enough to see that far, but there was water for as far as he could see. The Cessna was making an airspeed of one hundred thirty-five miles per hour, so the Mechanic must have done a very good job. He knew he shouldn't be keeping a rebuilt engine near the redline, but he wanted the speed. Besides, he figured that the RPM was so much lower than a typical automobile engine that it would do no harm. He circled around toward Jonesboro still seeing nothing but water.

He flew north along state highway 91 and then turned east at Marble Hill and followed state highway 34 until at Jackson, he discovered some smoking Humvees and hundreds of vehicles either on Interstate 55 heading south or lining up to head south. There were vehicles all over town. They probably couldn't hear him because he could hear their vehicles over the plane engine himself, but they saw him and started shooting. He could see the puffs of smoke on the ground. He swung away to get out of range and followed along the interstate until he could see the front of the pack. They were lining up eight abreast heading south on both sides of the Interstate. They were still close to the intersection of U.S. 61.

Jim made sure his glass jugs of AVGAS were close at hand. Put the thermite grenades on the dash where he could reach them. Then he put one five gallon glass jug between his legs and lined up going south on the interstate, flying at maybe three hundred feet.

No one saw or heard him coming until he was almost over them, and then they did not have time to get their guns and aim before he was past them. He slowed to eighty and started dropping jugs on the intersection of U.S. 61 and the Interstate 55. He had the airplane trimmed for almost hands off flying. He would pull a pin on a thermite grenade making sure he had a good hold on the handle and then drop a one gallon jug and the thermite grenade at the same time. They would fall at close to same rate. The grenade would start burning before it hit the ground with it's hot white phosphorus fire that would melt thin armor plate and when the gasoline jug shattered it would ignite from the white phosphorus and the fire would be spread further. He saved two for the front of the line where they were stopped lining up vehicles. He threw in full power and climbed to get away from any small arms fire and flew over the town of Cape Girardeau just above the buildings and then flew back north. He pulled the pin on one thermite grenade holding the handle tight and flying with one hand with full power still in. It took about five minutes to get back to the intersection.

As he circled in a one eighty he could see gas tanks exploding everywhere and people on the run. He could also see small fireworks that were probably small arms ammunition exploding in the fires. No one was paying him any attention as they were running away from the roads and the vehicles. With all the cars parked so closely getting ready for their mass attack, they were perfect for a modified napalm attack. The heat flying over the intersection pitched the little Cessna 172 up so badly he almost stalled even at full throttle as the plane pitched straight up for awhile. Jim rolled to an eighty degree bank to get the nose down.

He rolled wings level and climbed for more altitude and then looked the situation over. While the plane was running, the attack broken up, for awhile at least, and plenty of fuel, Jim headed up north toward Perrysville where the Army had a roadblock set up. He saw four tanks and three armored personnel carriers and maybe seventy five people. He continued north for ten minutes or about twenty miles then made a big circle back without seeing anything of interest. He flew back and landed on the interstate and then taxied up to the roadblock. He was very pleased with his smooth as glass landing after all the years since he had flown any kind of airplane. It was a breeze compared to his one hairy landing in the Piper Cub a month ago which had been his first landing in any airplane in many years.

As hoped, they recognized the airplane and since Jim was flying it they recognized him too. They might not, riding a horse, but flying the plane they did. He told them to move their forces back down the interstate toward Cape Girardeau and to be prepared for anything. He told them what he had done and why. They could see a black column of smoke from over twenty miles away.

As soon as he was assured they were going to follow his direction, he flew back over his inferno and then low over the town and on out to the air strip south of town. The colonel already had a reception committee waiting for him. He landed and taxied up to them. As he stopped and killed the engine he saw Darcy and Shelby running to him. It was a warmer day today and they were wearing the same short shorts and skimpy tops he was familiar with. He got out and ran toward them also.

They would have knocked him down except for hitting him from two different angles. They smothered him with kisses and tears of joy. He was very relieved to see them also and it took him awhile to remember and acknowledge the military greeting. While he had flow up around Perrysville, the colonel had already seen the devastation he wrought on the looters. The attack seemed to be over before it started and the colonel wanted him taken to headquarters immediately to report on what he had seen. He had to pry the girls loose as he got into the Humvee to take him to the headquarters.

"Jim, you flew anyway. I admire your courage after losing the first airplane. What in heck happened out there?"

"Well I went straight to the airport convincing the corporal that I was following orders and he complied. I filled up five one gallon glass jugs of gasoline and the corporal got me five thermite grenades. I first flew down to Blytheville and found everything under water from a levee break from somewhere toward Memphis all the way west of Blytheville. I then skirted Cape Girardeau looking for more looters until I found where they were massing for the attack and dropped my homemade napalm. I dropped them in pairs on the columns of looters that were lining up for an attack, one glass jar and one thermite grenade at a time. After buzzing the town to make sure people noticed I flew back over and saw groups of cars and trucks burning and ammunition cooking off. As one car would explode it set fire to the next. I'll bet there were five hundred vehicles burning out there. I then flew on north of Perryville to make sure there were no masses around your roadblock up there and told the force there to move south to mop up the looters. They could see the smoke all the way up there. I then flew back over again and landed. Here I am. Did I do good?

"Hell, you did more than I might have been able to do with my tanks and stuff. My troops from Perryville and here are out rounding up looters now. The ones that didn't get caught in your little holocaust high tailed it back to Marble Hills. We haven't tried to attack it yet, because we're swamped with prisoners. Those looters close to the fire are throwing down their guns, if they haven't lost them and surrendering. I think you convinced them that the Army is in charge and they have to pay attention to authority. There hasn't been a shot fired since my guys got there. At last count we were up to over ten thousand prisoners walking toward town. Say, could you land your airplane somewhere on the highway instead of at the airfield, that would make a good prison with its high fences and hangers for shelters? I'm really hard pressed to figure out how to guard that many people and still maintain any roadblocks."

"Sure I could, but the AVGAS in on the airfield."

"No sweat. I'm sure I've got at least one empty tank truck that can haul away the AVGAS. I'll have my mechanic round up any parts that might fit your airplane too."

"Say, Gary, while I'm moving the airplane over to the Interstate for parking, why don't I recon Marble Hills and see what's going on there. I could use someone with a good camera to take some pictures that we can blow up."

"We haven't had time to count the number killed or captured, but we figure there are several thousand that were in town that retreated to Marble Hills. I'm also concerned that they'll scatter out again. I sure would love to capture them, but don't know how to do it and guard all those prisoners we already have plus maintain local security, plus maintain roadblocks. Sure I'd love to know what's going on over there. I'll send Jane with you. She's a WAC and our company photographer. She brought a portable dark room and can do blowups for photo intelligence."

"Jane, get your best camera and some film and go with Lieutenant Colonel Claris in the airplane to take aerial photo recon pictures."

"Yes, Sir. Give me five minutes." Jane drove him back to the airfield where he checked over the airplane carefully, checked the oil again. The mechanic had refueled the plane. Darcy and Shelby were still there when Jim got back to the airfield. They had been told he would be back soon, but it had been over two hours. It was already 2 PM and they didn't want him taking off again and were not particularly interested in hearing how safe it was. They berated him for being gone a month the last time he took a short flight then coming back and not even saying hello before taking off again. They had hardly seen each other and here he was going off again. Jim promised he would be back before dark and that he was not going so far that he couldn't walk home if he had to. He reminded them that he had gone twice and did make it back unhurt both times. He waved good-bye as he taxied out, and then rocked his wings at them after he was in the air.

"You know, both Darcy and Shelby are really in love with you. I don't mean puppy love, it is not just the war, although that might have started it, I mean deep long lasting love. It nearly broke their hearts thinking you weren't coming back."

"They may think they are in love, but I'm nearly twice their age."

"So, a lot of women throughout history have married older men."

"Maybe so, but that was then and this is now."

"Do you realize how many young men will die in this country before this is over. Do you realize how many men have died in this country already. If young women don't marry older men, they may have to be spinsters or wait for the little boys to grow up and marry younger. So is there any sense worrying about them getting what they want? Don't you care for them?"

"Yes, of course I do. I just feel the age difference will lead them to find younger men and tell me good-bye. And, I still don't know about my wife in Dayton, Ohio, and the young men haven't gone off to war yet. Besides, I may not be what you call a young man, but I may be going off to war also. If I'm too old to fight, I'm too old for the girls."

"Good. Yes you do know about your wife. You know the young men Darcy and Shelby's age are prime cannon fodder and you're a more senior officer even if you did go to war. No you're not too old for the girl's. How's that for catching every single one of your arguments?"

"Not bad, but try to see my point. They're young and I probably can't keep up with them in bed for long. When I'm ready to sit in a rocker they will be ready to go traveling. I'll die of old age while they're still young."

"Okay, so they'll be later middle aged widows. What's new about that? At least they won't have been spinsters."

"They're both beautiful girls. If I was their age and this was earlier this summer, I wouldn't even get the time of day from them. I'm not rich or famous, or handsome and I don't have that athletic build."

"I don't think either care about rich or famous. You don't understand women. They can be attracted to a handsome man and at the same time be turned off by him. When I see an athletic build these days I think the guy is probably working out to show his muscles to some other guy. Muscled guys date slender guys. Slender probably means AIDS. Do you realize how many big muscle men love themselves first, another guy second and really don't care for girls? We girls know that too. When we see athletic we think, "too bad they're probably gay". I'll bet you can still get it on pretty good." The airplane's front seats were designed for two slender people in comfort or if one were bigger a cozy friendly shoulder to shoulder fit, even though Jane was a girls and Jim not all that big. Two big guys would be cramped. A one hundred ninety pound man and a one hundred twenty pound woman were cozy.

"There is Marble Hill ahead, I'm going to come across fairly low so have that camera ready."

She was all business. She grabbed her camera from the back seat, opened the window as she had been shown and started clicking off pictures as Jim circled the town in a narrowing spiral. At first, all he could see was that the town was jammed with vehicles with more being parked on all roads leading to town. As they circled closer, he could make out a town park that was crowded with people. As he got closer, he could see that the town park appeared to be full of people trapped in the park by others around the park. Some were running from others.

"Jim, you better get out of here, I see gun fire aimed at us." Jim quit the circling and dived for speed toward the outskirts of town. The plane was apparently okay so far. He made a low circle out of sight of the town due to rolling hills and trees then passed right over the town and the town square at tree top level at full speed, which isn't really that fast. He could see that the people in the park appeared to be naked women running from a few men inside the park. He could see some down and apparently hitting and fighting men on top of them and that the perimeter of the park was lined with men. He could also see gunfire up close and personal and heard a few thumps as slugs hit the airplane. He kept on going making a beeline for the airfield. The engine seemed to be fine, but he could see fuel leaking out of the wing tanks on both wings.

"I told you to get away. I told you. I told you. Are we going to catch fire?"

"Not if we're not already on fire, the engine is in front and the gas is blowing behind us. The holes are far enough out that I don't even think its hitting the tail section, not that would hurt."

"You mean we're going to crash anyway."

"No. We're not going to crash. We have two choices. Set down on the road somewhere and try to find something to plug the holes or just try to fly back to the airfield leaking all the way. We're not that far and we have a full tank of fuel. We'll be back home in fifteen minutes minus a little fuel. I wouldn't smoke around the airplane if I were you."

Jane immediately calmed down and said, "I feel a little dizzy." She laid her head on his shoulder and put her right hand in his lap.

From looking at Jane getting out of the plane with her camera, you would think that it was just a routine aerial photo session. Jim waved everyone back from the airplane because of fuel running out of the tanks. He must have lost ten gallons on what should have been a one gallon return flight.

"I need something to plug some holes in the wings, they're leaking fuel badly."

The mechanic yelled back, "I got just the thing." and ran for his truck coming back with an epoxy gas tank sealer kit. It had a special tape to put over the holes for instant leak proof repair and designed to stick even stronger where metal was covered with gasoline. "The gasoline softened the adhesive to its maximum stickiness." the mechanic said as he taped up the holes. He then mixed the epoxy sticks and spread the mixture over the tape to where the tape was completely under the epoxy. "Developed for battlefield repairs, just what the doctor ordered."

"What did you do? Anything else hurt?" The mechanic was now going over every inch of his adopted airplane to survey for more damage. He could see Jane and Jim were walking, so he was only concerned about possible airplane wounds.

"Where are Darcy and Shelby?"

"Colonel made them go back to their apartment when those prisoners started coming. Says after you refuel, you should fly on closer to town and he'll send out some ground transportation."

Jane grabbed Jim's arm with both arms holding his arm between her breasts, and said, "Why don't we fly south for awhile and land, and then go back to town?"

The mechanic wasn't supposed to hear or notice but said, "Sergeant, you're to take that Humvee over there and get right back to the office and develop that film immediately while I check over this plane and refuel it."

"Bye bye now. I'll get you later." Jane softly teased and French kissed his ear in parting. She then ran to the Humvee with her "feminine swaying hips run".

Jim watched her run and then drive off and then turned to the mechanic. "Well, is she okay?"

"She's dynamite. Oh, you mean the airplane. Yeah, she'll be all right too. That fuel tank repair sets up in ten minutes. You could fly it now as soon as we refuel. By tomorrow it will be the strongest part of the plane. However, it will cut your speed. I tried to be smooth, but you've got some new added bumps now. The fuselage has some holes too, but I can't find any damage inside. You've got twenty holes in the elevators back there, but if she flew okay, I guess it still works okay. I can't see any major structural damage to any spars or control wires. Your tires aren't flat. Nothing hit anywhere near my engine up there. Let's refuel it and get you going before it gets dark."

When Jim landed on the last straight section of interstate highway before the town, he was immediately met by a Humvee to take him to headquarters where he was met by Lieutenant Colonel Smieth. "Jim, Jane says you got her some great pictures and it looks like all the looters are holed up in Marble Hills. She said they have a number of female hostages too. We're going to try to organize a quick strike tomorrow but to plan it out we need some good photo interpretation. I explained to Darcy and

Shelby that you were okay, but I had to have your services for one more day before I turned you loose. Jane's not used to taking aerial pictures and says she needs your help to explain angles and altitudes so she can make a large photo map of the town that we can use tonight to plan our quick strike tomorrow. If you get any sleep, I'll also need you to make one more over flight just to verify that things haven't changed and to keep us out of an ambush. I sent some dinner to the dark room already, just go down that hall to the stairs and then when you get to the basement go straight ahead to the door facing you at the end of the basement hallway. I need that map up here as soon as you can get it.

He paused before knocking on the door, unsure as to what to say. The building had an Army trailer portable generator providing electricity for lighting. The last couple of hall lights had been removed to put one in semi-darkness before arriving at the darkroom. He knocked.

"Don't open the door, I have film out. Who's there?"

"Jim."

"Hang on a minute, Jim, I'm getting it ready for you. Three minutes and then we can have hours of fun."

When the door opened Jane was in a white lab coat spotted by her developing chemicals, her hair was mussed from working. "Welcome to my den of iniquity. We have work to do. Just sit yourself at that big table over there and I'll start giving you pictures to arrange as if you were looking from the west."

Jim did as he was bid and soon had an aerial map of the town of Marble Hill and the approaches. Some pictures were overlapped and there were a few holes between pictures, but it was surprising good detail. It wasn't close enough to count people, but you could count cars. She had apparently blown up distant pictures more than closer pictures to put them all on a similar scale. "How many pictures did you take anyway?"

"Three hundred and fifty-seven."

"That's going to take hours?"

"First of all we have to tape this together as best as we can, take some pictures of it for posterity, and then take it up to the planning room, which is the old city council room. Here, you work on that side and I'll work on this side." The entire picture was five feet by four feet when finished, but didn't show much detail, only general layout of the town and you could count the number of cars.

She took some pictures of the completed collage and then ordered, "Take this on upstairs to the colonel and then get back down here, but knock before entering again."

As the pictures he was watching started becoming clear, he could see that they were pictures of the park he had flown over. The park had been full of women that the looters must have captured along the way and now were bidding on or something. They were making a spectacle of them by corralling them like cattle in the city park. "These look like they are getting sharp, Jane."

"Let me see." She put one arm around his waist, but otherwise just looked at the pictures and said, "very good, pick some up like I'm doing and place them in this next set of trays. These trays cause a chemical reaction on the paper that brings out the picture and these next trays stop the reaction to "wash off" the previous chemical."

They finished the pictures and found some girls that were barely into their teens. They saw one young girl being raped by a large man with others looking on and apparently cheering. The oldest woman in the park was probably not much over forty, meaning that they just killed the older ones with Jim's knowledge of the burned out towns he had gone through. How many men had died protecting their women, and how many women have died was the unspoken question. The more pictures they developed the more their hate grew. He considered himself civilized and had never forced himself on a woman and would become a celibate rather than do so.

By the time they finished they both just wanted to take guns and kill as many of these monsters as possible. It wasn't a racial thing, there were a significant number that appeared to be white Americans. These must have been the unemployed and criminals that had filled so much of Saint Louis and some small towns around. They were the animals being kept at bay by the trappings and handouts of civilization. Once the telephone and radio calls for help were silenced and even the police cars could not respond, the animal was let loose to plunder the countryside. Because of anti-gun sentiment and gun laws in many towns, these animals were the only ones with guns.

Jim recognized another hate, that he could never touch, and that was for the countries that apparently had been smuggling in guns to the poor. Why is it that it is illegal to have a gun in Washington D.C., but a child in grade school can get his hands on an Uzi in minutes? Fully automatic guns were illegal to sell in the United States except to registered collectors, the police and military, but every child in a city gang had automatic assault guns, and Jim was talking Uzi's, Automags, AK-47's, and others, not some hunting rifle that could only fire on semi-automatic. What's even more crazy, is that kids that cannot legally buy a gun anywhere can buy an outlawed gun cheaper than an honest citizen can buy a legitimate gun. Maybe if it had not been for gun laws, the average citizen could have banded together and protected themselves. AUTHORS NOTE: 2 million fully automatic Red Chinese assault rifles were actually smuggled in by the Red Chinese secret police between 1989 and 1991. Who got them? Was that all?

There were a few states, like Oklahoma, that had not been overrun. That was probably due to lack of gun laws. The average person had at least one gun in the house there. Oklahoma had never changed the law that said you could carry guns anywhere as long as they were not concealed. Oklahoma in the late 1980's had passed a law that said a home owner could even shoot someone outside his house if in self defense, and some had done so and won in court. Oklahoma, being such a poor state, with a poor pay scale, and a low average education, probably had more than their fair percentage of ex convicts or would be convicts. Look at every crime statistic. High number of women in prison, gangs roaming the streets of the cities, high teenage pregnancy, but when the police could not respond after the start of the war, the people had been together, armed to protect their own property. That state was the nearest to being normal that he had seen thus far.

Arizona might have been okay, except for the gangs coming from California. California had gun laws and Arizona very few, but he had seen even an old folks' community taking up arms to protect themselves. Jim could hardly imagine some eastern cities where people were not allowed to legally have guns, but the gangs and crooks had fully automatic, illegal to sell anywhere, assault weapons running out of their ears. Dayton, however, might be typical of some eastern cities. Dayton had a gun law, but comprised only two hundred thousand compared to a million in its suburbs, and the suburbs had no gun laws. Many people were hunters or at least hunter sympathizers and many had guns for protection only. They were, in fact, similar to a lot of Oklahoma people. In Ohio there were more rich people and fewer really poor people, but the poor ones were even poorer than the high number of poor in Oklahoma. Maybe he would eventually get home and find out for himself.

"Jim, the pictures are dry, let's get them upstairs and spread some hate. I printed enough copies that some can be circulated around."

"I'm going to recommend that a town meeting be held and the pictures be shown to local men who may very well form their own posse to help the military get rid of this scum."

"Good idea. The colonel wouldn't listen to me, but he will listen to you. Jim, if you take the airplane up again, I want to go along." She coquettishly smiled and said, "and I promise to keep my clothes on and my hands off." I deserve to do some damage to them too. Most women will never see those pictures, some women would hide in fear, but I'm in the Army, fully trained to fight, and stuck with mainly an office job. If they want more pictures or if you're going to bomb them, I'm your man...er .. woman."

"I don't have any say so in that. We'll see."

They took the pictures upstairs and stood back to let the pictures speak. They were passed around the planning staff in silence. Occasionally one man would look up at them in question. You could see a grim determination building as one by one they all saw all the pictures.

"Colonel Smieth. You've said you were short on troops. You've also told me how most of the people here were gun toting law abiding citizens. You want some reinforcements? Call a town meeting at dawn and show the pictures around. I'll bet by noon, that you have a good sized volunteer force that can hold any flanks or weak points or guard your bridge, or even be the other half of a pincers movement if that's what you need. In the meantime, I'll be flying over making sure their positions are the same, making sure no one gets into an ambush or bombing if necessary. I do suggest that you get me some long delay or contact armed satchel charges or whatever I can drop from altitude without blowing myself up. I'll do mainly recon, but I'd like the option of being able to break a choke point or an ambush."

"Done. Jane get some more film in your camera. I want you to go along on the recon flights, these pictures are worth their weight in gold."

14 RULE BY THE PEOPLE

DAY 46
October 2

There were many extra people in town that came there early, or to escape the looters, before the Army arrived to set up roadblocks. Most had some form of guns and ammo that they had brought with them. The town meeting was called at 0900 after spending from 0700 to 0830 spreading the word about the meeting. Photographs were posted up and down main street for everyone to see. Only men had been asked to come specifically recommending that the ladies stay home, but Missouri ladies are not stay at home types. The crowd had an angry buzz before Lieutenant Colonel Smieth got up on the Marquee of the old theater and asked for silence through an old fashioned megaphone borrowed from the high school. Everyone stopped the angry talking in expectation except for one outspoken man, "Who put those obscene pictures up here on main street?"

"I want everyone to be quiet while I explain. You know we were nearly attacked less than twenty-four hours ago by the looters that had a vastly superior force."

"SO, ARE YOU TRYING TO SAY THEY DID IT?"

"Please let me finish my short speech and then we will open it up for questions and I will point at you for the first question and then repeat it for everyone. People in the back can pass notes to the front. Please let me speak before anyone starts any questions. I think I will answer everyone.

This superior force was severely damaged by one Jim Claris flying over in a small private airplane and dropping gasoline on the leading cars that caused the cars to explode catching the car next to it explode and so on until the rest of the looters fled and gave up on the attack. We have not cleared the road to the west of the interstate because the burned cars have made a good roadblock to prevent another attempt to attack us.

Yesterday afternoon, Jim Claris flew over the town of Marble Hills. The town park there on the highway is full of captured woman prisoners between the ages of eleven and forty that are being raped and killed by the looters gone absolutely crazy. The pictures were taken by a photographer riding in his airplane and developed last night.

HEY! Please hold it down, I want everyone to hear and the people in back can't here if the people in front won't be absolutely quiet.

The Army people here number only three hundred and there are possibly as many as thirty thousand of them, but with our tanks and other armor everyone down to the last man or woman has volunteered to try to free those captive civilian women and get rid of as many looters as possible doing so."

"YEAH. HEAR HEAR!"

Gary waved his arms for silence and when the cheers died down some, he yelled, "QUIET! PLEASE! I will continue when it's silent then you will know whether to cheer or not.

With the forces I have, I will have to make a quick concentrated run at the park with my tanks going top speed followed by the armored personnel carriers and infantry to protect the tanks and to collect the captive women and try to protect them while we fight our way out. This would take everything we have leaving nothing to protect this town or the bridge they are working on across the Mississippi. We cannot do this without your help to man the barricades on the highways and to guard the engineers working on the bridges. Since you don't have any armor, we ask that we have at least ten of you for each one of us that was pulling guard duty. We normally had one hundred people on guard duty so I need one thousand civilians with whatever guns and ammunition you possess. We still are not able to go in there and try to kill or capture all the looters, we don't have the forces. We also need some people to guard the side roads as we go by to make sure we are not cut off from behind. There are sixteen possible side roads and I need four hundred armed civilians that are willing to die if necessary to keep us from being attacked from behind by looters coming down these side roads. To keep the looters from simply heading west out of Marble Hills with the women, we must go around on those same side roads and set up a road block outside town to the south, west. The Army will block the road to the north as some of the people I have at the Perryville road block are going to attack from the north as a diversion at the same time as my main force hits from the east."

Before everyone steps forward to volunteer, the Army people are considering this a near suicide mission that is worth it, but they joined up to protect our country and women like these captives. The ones that volunteer must also be willing to die if need be to protect whatever they are assigned to protect. Some of the more timid that are not willing to die for strangers, but would die to protect the town will be kept for town defense duty. Others will be assigned to the other missions I listed. I will repeat them.

1. Town defense duty.
2. Protect the engineers at the bridge. The bridge must be fixed before this country can get back to normal.
3. Block the side roads with their lives to protect our backs as the Army passes a side road.
4. The most dangerous, work around on those side roads to block escape routes to the south and west of Marble Hills. It may not be possible to get west of Lutesville unless someone knows a hidden road around it.

We cannot do any of this without two thousand of the twenty thousand able bodied men in town. If we fail we may get all the women killed as well as most of the Army here leaving you to your own defenses. We must be assured that the bridge will be protected as it is more important than anything in the state or all the lives in the state. The bridge is critical for the United States. If successful, I may get court marshaled for leaving my duty to protect the bridge. At worst we get wiped out and they overrun the town and the bridge. You have one hour to decide. Those of you willing to die for your country go five blocks west to one of the trucks there with your guns and ammunition.

Now, I'm open for questions and I promised you would be first." He pointed at the man that had made him stop twice.

"To repeat his question so everyone can hear it, he asked when we are going to go. We will decide at precisely 1100 hours or 11 AM depending on how many volunteers we have. We will leave as soon afterward as we can get people at least moving to their positions. Jim Claris will over fly the town for more photos every few hours. We may decide to go at night just before dawn, if not this afternoon. When we go it will have to be quickly. Next question?"

"Will you be providing any weapons?"

"Only at our fixed locations were we have some fifty caliber machine guns. We also have extra grenades. However, we will insist that veterans with experience man these machine guns and have the grenades. We don't want any one hurt by accident."

"If there are as many as thirty thousand of them and twenty thousand of us, can't we defend ourselves behind barricades?"

"They have automatic weapons while you have shotguns and rifles."

"Couldn't a long time hunter with a rifle take out several before they got close enough with an automatic?"

"Yes, as long as you can see them in daylight before they get too close, a hunter with a scope on a 30-30 could take out twenty or thirty before they got close. Another thing to remember is that they are basically city people that have somehow been supplied guns by an outside source. Every gun we found has been Red Chinese. There are probably no more than five hundred that are experienced with guns."

"What do we need you for?" followed by a loud coarse of laughing from the crowd in general. "Just about everyone here is an experienced hunter and most of us have two or three guns and several boxes of ammo."

"You need us to break a concentration and because you should not have to fight."

"Damn it soldier. A good sixty percent of us are veterans and we know how to handle guns. We can pick them off. It's about time we started acting like men. I think I'm speaking for the men of this town and the surrounding towns. It's time we banded together instead of hiding. We'll protect our own town from now on, and yeah, we'll protect the bridge, and yeah, we're coming with you. AM I RIGHT?."

"RIGHT!" the crowd shouted.

The military didn't bother to sign up volunteers, they were coming out of the woodwork. The whole town turned out. There were five thousand that took the first shift around the town, a thousand that went to the bridge so they could have five hundred on alternating shifts without coming back to town. They had fifteen thousand volunteers that wanted to come with them if they didn't take women. Another five thousand women had their own guns, and it was decided that they would join the five thousand men guarding the city, twenty-five hundred people per shift. The really scary part was that there were another ten thousand armed men and women that were considered too important, too old, too frail, or too pregnant to pull shift duty. In defending their own homes, they should be able to hold off a force of one hundred thousand if given some professional leadership.

Lieutenant Colonel Smieth would have to stay in town and trust his officers to carry out the raid, not out of any cowardice, but to provide that leadership to the town just in case their raid failed. The people were determined that once the women were protected they wanted to either kill or capture the remainder of the looters.

DAY 45, OCTOBER 1 - GERMANY

TSgt Gaddis's tank had received orders to wait for a tank transport to take them to Berne Switzerland. The German army had been invited in to help defend Switzerland. He had gone to the U.S. Army hospital in Landstule, Germany to have his hearing checked. There was definitely no shortage of vehicles. They didn't arrive for two days after he lost his hearing, and it had already returned enough to be able to hear voices and he had lost his ability to hear gears and bearings. He presumed that the hearing loss was temporary.

At Landstule he was told that he had a fifty percent loss of hearing in both ears, but he was likely to regain eighty percent within a few weeks. Music would never sound the same.

A security team had taken over the base and the aircraft removed to another operational airbase. Their mission was just to protect the base and its assets until a new wing could be brought in from the U.S. They had no need for his tank.

They met their tank transport outside the gate and were trucked to just south of Berne, Switzerland, where they rejoined their tank company that was already there. The Arabs had been tearing up Italy, but had made no moves toward the rest of Europe. The days were pretty boring. Fuel was strictly rationed and therefore they did not even train except for dry firing their tanks on battery power only and going over and over their manuals and tactics. Every day was classroom. Every night was freedom to roam around the town. Typical G.I. bars showed up overnight with dancing and strip tease girls and ladies of the night.

Missouri

During the speech Jim had found Darcy and Shelby's apartment, which was sparsely furnished, but which they had painted before Jim came back. They drank coffee and listened to the speech through the open window. The girls beamed with pride when Jim's name was first mentioned, but got nervous when it was announced that Jim would be flying over the looters again.

Shelby said, "Do you have to? I saw those patches on the wings and the airplane had a lot of bullet holes in it. You were lucky that you didn't get killed. Okay, but you don't have to fly low this time do you?"

Darcy said, "I understand why you're doing it, but remember Shelby and I. What would happen to us? Gary has been taking care of us and Jane has been a regular visitor with us, but he will not be around forever. He may be reassigned at any time. If the town can take care of itself, he will be leaving, and then what happens to us? The owners of this building said we are welcome to stay here as long as we need to for no cost. Gary bought us some clothing, but what do we do next year stuck here if something were to happen to you?"

"Nothings going to happen to me, hopefully. I have to, just like the men of this area are now banding together for their own defense. I can't be less. I shouldn't need to get so low this time. Jane is going to use telephoto lenses for pictures. We also need to protect the airplane so we can keep flying over the area almost continuously during the entire operation."

"That's good. I do understand," Shelby unconvincingly stated. "Speaking of Jane, has she been a bad girl?"

"There's the high sign from the colonel. Time for me to go. I promise that I will make every effort to get this behind and then start working on getting us on our way again."

Darcy said, "You had better." and gave him a long passionate kiss.

Shelby took her turn, grabbing his buttocks with one hand and his neck with the other, pulling him down to whisper. "Remember, next time I see you, I want you to be the aggressor with me. But first get back safe."

Jim went to the plane, it had been refueled by the tank truck where they had pumped it out at the airfield. There were miscellaneous munitions and more glass jars collected near the interstate runway. Jane was there with a camera and a very large telephoto lens. Jane said, "Don't forget that our orders are to stay out of their range and just take pictures for recon."

"Right on. Let's get this thing going." Shortly they were off the ground and heading toward Marble Hills to see if the looters were staying put from yesterday evening. Jane immediately went through her routine and this time stripped to her bikini underwear immediately and then tugged off his shirt which he reluctantly cooperated with rather than get it torn off. She then took off her bra and said, "I'm ready for work now. That was lovely last night. I had no idea it could be like that. I am really looking forward to doing it with you again. Did you talk with Darcy and Shelby?"

"Yes, but I didn't have long."

Jane said, "If I had the opportunity, I would take you to bed myself. Maybe in wartime the women just get more horny because they feel the need to reproduce the human race. How do you like these?" When Jim looked her way, she had opened her blouse and was bra-less with a very nice set.

"Perfecto, but I think you better get your camera ready.

She became all business, as he circled the town shooting many many pictures. He couldn't see anything moving at first except occasional people. He could still tell there were a lot of people around and in the park, but he couldn't tell from this range. "Do you need to get in closer?"

"No this is fine. Once I develop these we will be able to see faces. I have enough, unless you see something."

"No, it looks like everyone is still there and sleeping late." He flew back over the dangerous intersections to make sure there were no ambushes waiting for the Army. She turned toward him again, put a hand in his lap and asked, "Any chance that we could do it when we get back?" But with his being distracted by trying to spot things on the ground, she wasn't able to get him to respond even..

She dressed buttoned her blouse as they came in to land. They took the pictures to be developed and spent the next three hours developing film and delivering it. The pictures showed women and girls being brought into the park from where ever they had been during the night. Some were being carried apparently unconscious. Jim and Jane felt their blood run hot, full of vengeance. They really were treating them like some kind of animal to be used.

The Army was on its way and would be there in less than an hour when they took off for the second time. This time Jim had some satchel charges with two minute fuses that were rugged enough to be dropped from an airplane. He had his regular M-16, riot gun and Barreta. She had a heavier machine gun that he was not familiar with. She even kept her clothes on.

They flew the route the tanks were taking and this time could see over a hundred old trucks and pickups going away from Cape Girardeau and moving down roads to go around Marble Hill to prevent a rear attack and possibly a pinchers action to actually conquer the looters. They had found some old tube type radios with a ten mile range from hilltop to hilltop to communicate between the Army and the civilians. All the civilians had been instructed to wear white cloths on each arm to make sure they could be identified. When they flew over the town, there still wasn't much movement.

The park looked fuller with even less movement in the town than the other times they had flown over. Jim said, "I want to fly low just one time to see if the women are by themselves in the park and not being guarded with guns where they can be gunned down."

"I agree. My job is to just look, right."

"Affirmative. I will build up speed and then come in very low to get less exposure to ground fire." He did. She did most of the looking.

"The women are mainly in the center of the park. Some seem to be tending to others that are laying down. None of them have any clothing. I hope we kill every one of those looters."

"I just hope we can get the majority of the women out safely without losing our troops and equipment. Then maybe we can worry about getting some of them."

Their job was to stay back and watch from above for concentrations of looters that could stop the rescue or that might otherwise do serious damage to either the Army group or the townspeople that had joined the fight. This flight allowed no time for any hanky panky in the air. They could see the people from town going through a field on the other side of Lutesville to prevent a breakout to the west and a roadblock formed to the south by parking heavy farm machinery on the road with townspeople surrounding the roadblock.

They could see the tanks leading the way followed by armored personnel carriers. Behind them were townspeople in their pickups, cars and farm trucks breaking off in large groups at each intersection. The could see some of the looters had heard the tanks getting close to town on the east and were running that way with guns and starting up larger trucks and heading that way when the group from the Perrysville roadblock started shelling the north side of town and moving into town at high speed. They only had two tanks and two armored personnel carriers, but they were firing tank shells and machine guns down the street into the town. The looters that had been looking east turned to go north thinking that their ears had deceived them. Obviously, the ones responding were supposed to be providing security. Two minutes later the tanks to the east sped up to around fifty miles an hour. Some looter managed to get a pickup started and pulled in front of the tank, bad mistake. The tank literally knocked it out of the way sending it flying into the air and the tank did not slow because Jim could see the spacing between tanks didn't change. Four blocks ahead of the tank they managed to pull five or six cars into the street. The drivers got out and ran. The lead tank smashed the first car and jumped two more still without slowing. The tanks behind finished the job of smashing the cars flat. It looked like only the engine block if anything was more than a foot thick after the eighty ton tanks went over them. The armored personnel carriers had no problem getting over the remains of the cars.

Jim flew closer to the get a good view of the park and could see the women huddling in the center of the park and the looters nearest main street running for their cars.

"To the right! To the right!" Jane yelled, "They're going to shoot the women." They had the windows open on both sides of the plane. Jane stuck her machine gun out the window pointing down. "Get me closer!"

Jim dived right down to within ten feet of the trees and below some of the larger buildings with the water tower looming above them. Jane opened up on fully automatic. Jim didn't know the rate of fire of the machine gun, and it didn't seem to have much kick, but he could see men and guns flying everywhere with car and truck windshields exploding and tires blowing up with the vehicles tilting. They totally lost interest in shooting the women and went running away from the park or firing at the airplane. Jane moved her aim of fire at the far side of the park until she almost shot off the wing spar on that side of the plane, but then they were past.

"Jim, I shot the wing support. Are we going to crash?"

"Depends on how much you shot it. I'll try not to pull many Gees for the rest of the flight. How bad does it look?"

"There are about ten dime size holes in it."

"Are they in one place or spaced out?"

"No two are within six inches if that makes a difference."

"Should be okay, but watch where you're shooting."

Jim had climbed to get back up. He felt several impacts on the back of the plane as they climbed out away from the park, but everything seemed to be working okay. They could see the tanks were nearing the park now with their turrets swinging around shooting anything moving outside the park. The armored personnel carriers were moving into the center of the park now. Jim was flying in a large left hand circle so he could see what was happening and gradually climbing to get more out of range and see more. Jane was straining to see out the right side of the plane.

"There are a large number of vehicles going towards the west side of town. Can we slow them down with a satchel charge?"

"Not yet, I want to make sure the Army gets back out of town with the women. They have the armored personnel carriers (APCs) open and some Army guys are herding the women into them."

"The tanks from Perryville have backed back out of town and are firing into the edge of town blowing up cars trying to come their direction. I can see one tank stopped just inside of town. I couldn't tell, but it looked like it lost a tread."

Jim looked that way when it came into his view as he circled and could see fire on the top and one side of the tank. Then the ammunition inside started blowing up.

Jim tried to turn away from the blast, but it caught a lot of the plane flipping it completely over. The plane was ceasing to fly and losing all airspeed. As it gained speed and starting spinning, Jim forced the nose down into more of a dive. Jane was screaming, but Jim had to gain airspeed to get it to fly. Finally the ailerons started biting and he was able to put wings level though upside down. As it gained flying speed, he rolled it over and pulled out of the dive swooping low over the town.

Jane continued screaming until he started climbing back up obviously under control again. "What happened? Why did you do that? I wet my pants."

"Sorry about that. The tank that was stopped exploded and the shock wave caught the airplane and flipped us over killing our airspeed. I had to dive to get it to flying speed. I guess you didn't do too much damage to the wing or it would have fallen off by now."

"I'm sorry. I lost my cool. I'm okay now, let's get back and see what's going on."

The little plane didn't climb very fast, and Jim wanted altitude because he still wasn't sure there wasn't more serious damage he hadn't felt yet. He had gone several miles from town after the almost crash. When he got back into town he could see that the Armored personnel carriers were loaded. As he passed through the middle of town he could see that when the tank blew up it had destroyed the buildings surrounding it spreading fire in the buildings around them.

As he looked ahead to the east, he could see that the looters had set up a good roadblock by towing out some semi-truck trailers and other vehicles. They were trying to bottle up the tanks. "Satchel charges, NOW!"

Jane responded immediately arming the charges and dropping two at the same time right on target, Jim turned the plane and returned as quickly as possible and Jane dropped two more wiping out most of the roadblock when Jim started feeling many hits on the airplane and the airplane started flying slightly sideways or as a pilot would say "crabbing". (To keep an airplane flying straight east when there is a strong north wind the airplane must be "crabbed" to where the nose is actually pointing east north east. If an airplane must be crabbed to fly in the desired direction when there is no strong crossing wind, that means something is catching wind and disturbing the aerodynamics of the wind flowing around the airplane. On a glider, just opening an air vent can cause the airplane to seriously crab. The pilot does this like he would in a car, turning into the skid.)

"See if you can see something wrong with the wing or tail on your side, we took some hits."

"The front wing is fine, just a minute, let me look at another angle. JIM!, the metal on the right side of that thing that sticks up is ripped badly, I can see the bracing inside. Can we still fly?"

"Hopefully although a little sideways or crabbed." Jim sang a couple of bars, 'Crabs walk sideways but lobsters walk straight.' Anyway, we're crabbing."

"It's not funny. I've never flown in a plane that had something wrong with it."

"So. Neither have I, and I'm the pilot."

"Thanks for telling me. I think we'd better keep our altitude."

After the satchel charges went off, much of the roadblock was cleared, but the tanks seeing the airplane drop their charges, decided that was a signal that they needed to blow up something too so the lead tank fired his cannon over and over into the debris on either side of the street. "Jim, I see some people rolling barrels toward the main street. from the right."

"Gasoline? Get your machine gun and see if you can't discourage them." Jim brought the airplane down low once more and Jane fired into the barrels which erupted into a fiery inferno.

"Yep, gasoline all right. They must have been trying to roll that out in front of the tanks and then set it afire to stop the tanks. Ooooohhhh!"

"Are you okay?"

"Yes, but it scared me. We have some new ventilation in the door."

Jim could see several tears where bullets must have come from almost directly below and dealt a glancing blow to the lightweight aluminum of the door.

"Jim, I hate to say this, but the tire on this side is gone too. It's in shreds. I don't mean flat, I mean shredded. There isn't much left on the wheel. What does that mean?"

"Well I guess that means I get to land on one wheel?"

"Jim, you're not being funny. Can we land?"

"You have a better idea? Would you rather jump out now?"

"JIM! What now?"

"Well I suggest that we try to stay out of the battle below as much as possible. Thank God that we are sitting on and wearing flak vests, and that we laid more of them on the floor. I can land on one wheel, but I don't know what will happen when I drop the other wheel on the pavement as we lose speed. I suggest that we keep flying around and get rid of more gasoline in the airplane before I try to land."

"I hadn't thought about that. You better keep flying."

"It looks like the Army is getting out of town okay now, let's see how the civilians are doing on the west side of town since we're going that way." There was a solid line of vehicles going west from the center of Marble Hills all the way to Lutesville where their way west was blocked by a good sized bull dozer that did not allow room for cars to get by without going in the ditches. On the south of Lutesville, about a mile south, the road was full of farm machinery and there was one heck of a fire fight going on between towns people from behind rocks and farm equipment and looters in the ditches along the road.

"Do you agree that the places for the remaining satchel charges are on the town side of that roadblock to the west in the town and the other would be right here in the middle of all those looter cars near the roadblock?"

"Yes, but that would mean flying low again, wouldn't it."

"I don't see any high altitude bomb sights on this baby or any aerodynamic bombs for that matter. Do you?"

"Jim, I mean will this airplane continue flying if we get any more damage, or will we die?"

"All I know is that the looters are giving those townspeople a hard fight and will kill a lot of them. There is only two of us. The airplane giving one last bomb run right now is more valuable than we are, but we may not survive the landing with that blown tire anyway. I figured we might as well get rid of the last two charges before we try landing."

"I'd rather not, but where you go, I go, since I can't get out and walk. No, I see your point. If there is a good chance we might die on landing, we ought to do more damage before we land."

Jim flew low, taking more hits on the plane. There were now trickles of fuel coming from numerous holes in the wing tanks. There were numerous holes in the cockpit. The airplane now wanted to tilt to one side in addition to crabbing. The satchel charges were superb. The cars on the road both south of town and on the west side of town exploded causing a chain reaction of cars catching fire and blowing up due to their close proximity. This was better than during their attempted attack on Cape Girardeau.

These cars were jammed in so tight that the chain reaction spread up the road from south to north for the entire mile until it intersected with the already past chain reaction headed east through town toward Marble Hills.

Along the road south of town, flaming gasoline from the exploding fuel tanks not only set the blacktop on fire with horrid rancid black smoke, but poured into ditches, burning the looters that had taken up positions there. The blacktop was burning brightly along with car and truck tires long after the gasoline tanks exploded. The town of Lutesville was going up like a tinder box as whole blocks seemed to erupt in flames. No one would sleep there tonight. The chain reaction of fiery explosions stopped on the east edge of Lutesville when some pickups managed to get through the ditches into the fields and leave a gap the flames couldn't pass. By now, Jim's fuel was going down quickly due to bullet holes in the internal wing tanks, again.

"I hope we've done enough, now its time to head home before we run out of gas."

"Is there anyway we could do it one more time just in case we don't make it?"

"Do what? Oh, that. Sorry Jane. The airplane is not exactly flying nicely. Just tighten your seat belt and when I yell NOW, bend over and wrap your arms around your legs to keep your body from flopping around and hitting the sides of the plane."

Jim came in as slow as possible. His flaps were not working so he had to come in with no flaps, which meant faster, but he dragged the plane in on power at the verge of a stall, flying catty angled, to keep one wing and tire low while still staying lined up on the interstate highway they were using as a landing strip. The one wheel touched down, and Jim tried to hold off the right tire, but with the damage to the vertical stabilizer and rudder he just couldn't do it long. When the one wheel hit Jim threw everything to the left, but the right wheel drug them to the right until it looked like they were going to hit a vehicle parked on the shoulder. Jim suddenly hit the brakes, which only worked on the wheel with rubber and turned the wheel all the way to the left and the Cessna 175 ground looped like a race car spinning out at a racetrack. As soon as the skid started, Jim locked the brakes. The other two tires blew also, but the airplane came to a stop toward the middle of the interstate, missing the vehicle on the shoulder.

Jim and Jane sat in their seats not moving, just looking straight ahead at the charcoal colored dust settling around the plane. Finally the smell of burnt rubber got them moving. The dust was settling and the vision was clearing now where you could see the crazy skid marks of the plane drifting right and then suddenly veering left in a mixed up pattern of a tricycle leaving rubber while spinning. They were reaching for the doors before anyone on the edge of road started moving toward them. Jim and Jane were standing on opposite sides of the plane surveying the damage and the skid marks as the Army mechanic came up in his Humvee. "Sir. You killed it. You killed the airplane. Just look at it. Half of the tail is missing. You must have five hundred holes in it this time. What happened to this strut. Sergeant, did you do this?"

Jane sheepishly admitted that she had done it firing at looters and it had taken her a moment to realize she was shooting the airplane. Jim said, "Can you fix her?"

"No. How can anyone expect anyone else to fix this. You destroyed it." Calmer now, he said, "Well. Unless you bent the landing gear. She'll never fly straight again. She'll never be trust worthy again. Even some of the elevator spars are ruined and I can't replace them. What do I use to replace aluminum skin on it. I don't know. I can try."

"You'll figure something out. Just make sure its not too heavy. If necessary leave the holes in the fuselage to keep weight down, or maybe just put some duct tape over them. I'll check back with you later."

Jim and Jane went straight to headquarters to find out what was going on. Jane went straight to her room to change into a fresh uniform. Jim went straight into the operations and planning room. Gary looked up when Jim entered. The guards had not bothered to check his identification by this point.

"Jim, you made it back okay! Great, you saved the entire operation and with fires on three sides of them they are surrendering in droves. Some of the women that are able to talk said the looters looked like they were going to execute the entire lot of them when this airplane came swooping down and started killing them by the dozen. Then I got another report from the lead tank that you blew up a major roadblock that might have trapped the tanks in town and then blew up the gasoline barrels they were going to spring the trap with. Then a third report that you set half of Lutesville on fire dropping bombs on the looters vehicles that were parked too close together. It looks like we control this part of Missouri again. It will take us a couple of days just to get everyone into the old airport, but with the help of the civilians here, we should have no problems. It looks like the Army's primary job can be down scaled to just guarding the prisoners and the bridge. The civilians can take care of the town and the countryside from now on. Where's Jane?"

"Glad I could be of assistance. Ah, Jane is changing uniforms. I don't think you will be able to get her in an airplane anytime again soon."

"OH, WHY'S THAT?"

"Well, you weren't there to see what we were doing first hand. Probably no one on the ground knows what happened to us. First the tank blew up when we were too close and the airplane just quit flying when the shock wave hit us. That's when Jane wet her pants."

"She what?"

"She wet her pants. She thought we were crashing."

"But you weren't?"

"Well, I thought we were too, for awhile. I wasn't sure whether I could get it to fly again, but I was too busy trying to recover the airplane to worry about the consequences. Anyway, we were totally out of control for a while with the airplane totally stalled and flipped upside down. Then I got enough airspeed to at least get it pointed nose down to gain speed and eventually pulled it out of the dive close to the ground. Let's see, Jane shot up the right wing support shooting at looters that really did look like they were going to execute the women. Then the tank blew up, then we blew up the roadblock the looters were trying to form to trap the tanks in the town and got the tail of the plane about shot off, then Jane shot some more that were rolling barrels of gasoline toward the main street presumably to burn tanks or APCs. That's when one tire was shot off the airplane with some more bullet holes in the cockpit. Then we dropped some satchel charges on a looter roadblock south of Lutesville and dropped some more at the western side of town, where we got holes shot in the internal wing tanks such that we had to head straight to our landing point before we ran out of fuel. Then we came back to a rather hairy landing where I had to ground loop the airplane to keep from totally crashing the plane since we were missing a tire. When we stopped, we had no tires left. The airplane is pretty much of a mess."

Gary chuckled, "Jane wet her pants. I can understand why, but Jane tries to be so cold and aloof. That must have really chagrined her to wet her pants. I'm not going to let her live that one down." Gary was in very good spirits. He had taken a risk with his entire career and his military force and had won handily. Then he got solemn, "The operation was a huge success, but I lost twenty men of my own today and thirty civilians on our side were killed and another two hundred injured in some way. None of mine were only wounded. The tank that blew up had a crew of four inside it. Some looter managed to get a large angle iron in the tracks and broke a track stopping the diversionary force. Twelve of the military that were supposed to be inside the APC's gave up their space to the captured women and were riding outside when picked off by small arms fire. You didn't see it apparently, but the last APC to come into town got hit with burning gasoline and cooked all four troops inside it. The fire had burned out before we made our rapid exit. Naturally the looters that have surrendered so far have claimed they had nothing to do with kidnapping and raping and torturing women. Most claim they didn't even know there were any captured women. Most of the civilians killed or injured were at the south roadblock before you dropped your satchel charge on them. The civilians are reporting that they have counted two thousand burned looters along that road and in Lutesville.

Anyway, we stopped the tanks outside of Marble Hills to use to keep looters from following by using cannon at long range to discourage following right away and the APC's came on into town. The refugees in the high school were cleared out and we took the women there. Some of them are in pretty bad shape physically, some are nearly crazy and won't let anyone come around them, some just sit there like they don't know where they are and can't speak, and some are mad as hell and want us to execute all the looters. Other women are just confused, probably not crazy or clinically depressed, or physically hurt, or even mad, just don't know what they will do now. Some of the town's women have been bringing spare clothing to the school to provide to the women, but are afraid to go in. Some of the women, now that they are in a building don't want any men to come near them. They went in the personnel carriers to keep from being shot knowing the APCs were safer than in the open. Once the APC's were opened and the women got in the building they aren't letting anyone else near. My soldiers want to help. I have male medics, no female nurses, that could help the physical problems, but some of the women are holding the doors and attacking any man that comes close. I haven't been able to get any of my females in there yet.

Would you take Jane, Darcy, and Shelby over there and see if you can get in for an objective opinion to report back to me? I know they need help, but I'm just out of control of the situation. As far as the civilians, Cape Girardeau has a minimum of medical doctors and no psychologist types at all. They are at a loss too. They are standing by to help, but totally unsuccessful. The women at the school haven't even allowed any of the clothing in. There were five hundred sixty-three women that we rescued. We've also come across some more among the looters that claim they were kidnapped and forced to go along too, but since we can't tell, we have segregated them at the airport by assigning all of them to one hangar. That's another three hundred twenty women, but they will have to wait. They are at least clothed and none are serious physically. We have reports about several other towns that were being used by the looters to hold women in reserve. We're going to start visiting surrounding towns looking for them now that we have broken the main gang of looters. That could be hundreds more women who were kidnapped after their husbands or fathers were killed. Over at the school, some of the women could be dying because they are refusing help. I'll have you all driven over there in a large van that will also have some medics standing by with medical supplies. Okay?"

Jane walked in just then looking a little sheepish. I guess Jim told you what we were doing today?

"Yes, Jane, every bit of it, but now I have another mission for you if Jim agrees to it."

Jim said, "Of course I'll try." at the same time as Jane said, "You're not getting me back in that airplane."

Gary laughed at Jane, "No this is ground work only. Take along a camera for inside work with lots of film, but don't shoot any pictures that you don't have permission to shoot. Jim will explain."

"You're presupposing that Darcy, Shelby, and Jane will come along to help and that we'll be successful."

"You have to be successful, Jim. The alternative is that none of them are going to get any better and many may die."

"Oh, you must be talking about the women. Of course I want to help. What kind of pictures do you want, Colonel?"

"Documentation of their condition, how they were kept, how they were not clothed, their wounds, their psychology too, if you can. You're not taking pictures for Playmate, more a civilian court of law and history books. I can see Jim has caught on. He'll explain more while you're picking up Jim's women and getting there."

Jim walked over to Darcy and Shelby's apartment above the pharmacy and told them the results of the battle that they were elated at. He then told them what they were being asked to do. Although it was only sixty-five degrees outside, they decided to wear their short shorts and skimpy tops to look semi-nude rather than go there fully dressed with all of the naked women. As they were coming out, they met Anne with her camera equipment. They were all transported to the school. Darcy and Shelby went up first and gathered up some of the bags of clothing that had been donated by the women of the area.

"Go away, you're not welcome here."

Shelby answered, "We're not staying, we are just here to bring in some blankets. It's supposed to get cold tonight and some of you may get cold."

"Go away. You are not getting in here."

Darcy and Shelby set down their stacks of blankets near the door and walked back to the truck. The door opened so those inside could see the blankets, but they were not coming out naked to get them. Darcy, Shelby, and Jim carried bags of clothing donated by the town's women up to the door and knocked again.

The door opened and arms stuck out to get the bags that Darcy and Shelby were holding. Darcy and Shelby went back to the stack and picked up two boxes of clothes next. The door opened and the arms came out again, but this time Darcy spoke up, "This isn't going to work ladies. There are men out here, you have no clothes and these are boxes. It just won't do to have you open the door wide enough for us to hand you the boxes and then just stand there in your all in all with boobies to the world to carry these boxes while the men watch."

"WHAT DO YOU EXPECT THEN?"

"Just leave something in the door to keep it open so I can get a foot in the door and then back up away from the door so we can bring the next load in."

"AND WHAT'S GOING TO KEEP THE MEN OUT?"

"The door. I'm sorry to be so flippant, but there is only one man with us and he is ours. We can open the door and close it behind us. You can watch through windows to make sure there are no other men. Okay?"

Silence, but then the door opened and something was put in the door, wedging it open about four inches. Darcy pulled the door open with her toe until she could catch it with an elbow and open it enough for Darcy and Shelby to come in. "We're in. Does someone want to remove the broom?"

Shelby put down her box and pulled out a long country style dress and holding it up to herself said, "First I shall model the early American style for that modest woman from the country."

Apparently this was the first thing these women had found humorous in some time and they broke down laughing and crying. "That one looks good for me, do you have any underwear there."

Darcy dug into the sack she had first brought to the door and pulled out a nylon full panty and a French bikini style, "We have modest and ....."

"Ladies," said Shelby, "I have one favor to ask of you. The Army would like to bring in one more woman to document what happened to you to help keep the Army commander from being fired for rescuing you."

"What? That's absurd."

"No. He had orders to guard some bridge construction south of here and risked his career and his entire force and possibly the rebuilding of the United States to pull his forces away from that critical bridge to rescue you. He used every last one of his forces and organized the town to help you. Surely, you can let in one woman."

"Okay, but she comes by herself."

"Okay, I'll get her from that van out there while we bring in more clothing. Could we get some help from the man that was flying that airplane that saved your lives. He can carry a lot more than we can and he will only come as far as this first room here."

"NO! NO MEN!"

"Was he the one flying that plane? Listen ladies, if any man is allowed it ought to be him. He risked his life for us flying that plane and saved every woman's life here. I'm surprised he is still alive after all the bullets sent his way."

Darcy paled, "What? Bullets? He was low enough to get fired at?"

"Yes, he was very very low. I can see he means something to both of you."

Shelby improvised, "Yes, he has saved our lives many times and gotten us here through many gangs of looters since leaving Los Angeles months ago."

"He brought you all the way from L.A.? Did you fly?"

"No we came by car...or what's left of it. He found the airplane here and was going to use it to fly the three of us across the river over a month ago, but he won't quit helping the people here. There were two airplanes but he lost one over a month ago trying to help out and it took him a month to get back here riding a horse. That was another mercy mission. The day he rode back into town, he didn't even tell us he had returned and he was out in that other airplane and saved the town from an attack by that same bunch of looters. He found you when he was flying over to see if another attack was being planned and then helped organize your rescue, but he told us he would stay high away from more gunfire."

"Ladies," said their apparent ringleader, "If we are to ever say anything to any man alive again, I want to thank him personally. Are we agreed?"

Both Jane and Jim came in helping to carry the next load of clothes.

The looters had kidnapped all of them. Those that were lucky and quickly surrendered were taken by men and traveled with the men that had taken them. They had been raped and beaten, but not like the others. They had also been properly fed and clothed because they had done much of the cooking for the men. There were quite a few that had come from Saint Louis. As the looters got away from the city they came to expect that there would never be any law and order to come after them so they allowed the women to live to be used. From the number of towns they had seen when you added up all that all the interviewees had seen probably ten thousand men had been murdered trying to protect their loved ones. All young children under ten had been murdered and all the men except for a few that managed to sneak into the mob. A man would hide out and then join in some attack as if they had always been part of the looters. They never noticed the additions, but some of the women knew what had happened because some of the men had known the men that joined later on. Only the best looking women were kidnapped. Those that did not meet standards were just shot. Some had quit living like the twenty catatonics there in the school. There were apparently thousands of women from Saint Louis and some surrounding towns being held somewhere in reserve. Apparently, some of the leaders of the looters had some grand plan for the women. They had all been treated like cattle.

There had been many acts of heroism where men had died protecting women from the looters. There was the high school cheer leader that had a high school boy considered to be a fairy that had used his saxophone to club three looters unconscious before he had been shot trying to protect her. He had yelled while fighting that she had never noticed him, but he would die rather than let anyone hurt her. She knew who he was, but never knew his name or the fact that he had cared for her.

Most of the women had husbands that died protecting them. Most of the girls had fathers that died protecting them. Actually only their leaders were against men. Most of the women were just afraid of strange men that might be as bad as the looters.

Jim and Jane both assured all the women that their names and pictures would be protected to keep their trauma a secret after the war. Jane said that she and only she had custody of the pictures. When showing pictures on main street before the rescue raid, the faces had been intentionally blurred except of one child that had been alone and looking straight up. Jane had personally collected every last picture during the speech and during the volunteering to make sure no man took one home for his private pin-up collection. Each picture had also been serial numbered and a warning to return it placed on the back, but the warning was unnecessary since no one took one.

Most of the women wanted to just stay in the school. They knew no one here. They had no money. They had only clothes given to them by the women of the town, many had no underwear to their names even. They didn't want men in the school, except for Jim, the doctors, and the medics. They wanted anonymity from everyone. This went on for about a week with Jim and the girls living in the school only leaving to get things or to make a report to the colonel. Jane was spending more time away now as she developed and cataloged her pictures.

15 HOME

DAY 60
October 16

"Well Gary, it's been fun, but your bridge is still two months off. Everything is under control. The Cessna is flyable again, and we're ready to be on our way at long last."

"The mechanic thinks it will fly, but he wouldn't buy it himself if he were a pilot. You could just stay here until after the war. We've won our looter war, at least in this small area. The townspeople will treat you like royalty. There are ten thousand extra women that all owe you their lives."

"As I said, weeks ago, I'm not hopeful, especially after all this time, but I did love my wife and I have to know."

Darcy and Shelby were already at the airport. They had not seen the airplane after its last flight two weeks ago. Now they understood why it couldn't have been flown. It seemed to have more patched holes than original metal. The mechanic had said that he had removed forty-two slugs from under the flak jackets that Jim had taken along to protect from ground fire. Altogether there had been over three hundred bullet holes in the plane. He had to modify some metal to make new spares for the vertical stabilizer and had used some aluminum roofing material that had to be hammered to the right shape to cover the vertical stabilizer and one side of the elevator. He had found a full new large roll of stainless steel tape at a parts store that had been donated to fixing the airplane that had saved the town. He explained that it was thinly rolled steel with an adhesive backing on it. You strip off the wax paper and stick it on the aluminum. The fuselage had very little aluminum showing since much of the tape overlapped.

As Jim left the building, a cheer went up. The sarcastic thought crossed his mind, "They must really be glad to see me go." He knew the cheering was in his honor. There were several thousand people along the streets. He recognized some of the more courageous women that had left the school to join the extended community that Cape Girardeau had become after his ordeal in the dark room. It wasn't even a blip on the scale of what they had undergone, but it brought home what can happen when people are not working for the good of everyone else. Another thing that had made things easier was a barge of canned goods that had floated down the Mississippi and beached itself on a bend of the river. Enough food to last a couple of months if you didn't count what was already in town.

The Mississippi was close to being back below flood stage, the bridge had not washed out and repairs were underway, just two months behind schedule due to shortages of material. There was still no way to get the old Mercury across the river, the airplane was the only thing that could cross. When the river got down to normal they were working on having some ferry boats ready, but they weren't ready and the river wasn't down.

There was someone's classic convertible for him to ride in and Jane took his picture sitting on the back trunk lid with flowers around him. He felt very foolish with people cheering him for what he didn't think he had a choice about doing. Courage? Hero? Civilized was more the word, what any civilized person would do if they could.

Jim arrived at the interstate they were using. The mechanic had the airplane fueled along with four five gallon gas cans of extra gasoline. They had to travel light due to the size of the airplane. They each had their Barreta, M-16's, extra clips, Jim's riot gun, and one M-79 grenade launcher and a dozen grenades. Jim had his one pair of well-worn blue jeans, a flannel shirt and the leather coat that he had started with no extra clothes. The girls had left behind their shorts. Shelby was wearing her leather slacks and bolero leather jacket with her skimpy tied together top from Alamosa. Darcy was wearing tight blue jeans, her ski jacket, and because Shelby had kept her skimpy top she had hers on too. They hoped they would not need camping gear, but Jim had three space blankets. They each had a backpack with food. Shelby and Jim had most of the heavy ammo in theirs and Darcy had some small camping pans and a metal disk and cup for each of them.

Jane was there too and after hugging Darcy and Shelby, came and nearly attacked Jim with a French kiss to the mouth while holding his head and then slipping another hand into his jeans. Jane had been sharing him for the past two weeks. "Jim, I am going to miss you. I love you, but not like Darcy and Shelby do. You take care of them. When this is over maybe I'll find you again, or someone like you. Darcy, Shelby, you give him some for me too." With that a tear started to come and she turned and ran back toward the well wishers that had come out to see them off.

The engine sounded good, but the aerodynamics were not very smooth with all of the repairs. Jim had to use a lot of interstate to get off the ground and then climbed slowly until he had altitude to get over the hills and trees then they crossed the river. He was hoping to make it six hundred miles with one landing to refuel and then maybe trade whatever was left of the plane for a vehicle or find some more gasoline for it. Jim now had five hundred dollars in paper money that was scraped together by donations from the troops whose lives he had saved. Gary offered him two thousand dollars from the paymaster funds, but Jim turned it down. Gary had come out okay so far bending the rules, but no point in pushing it.

They were flying low over the countryside. Jim was keeping the RPM's down to around two thousand instead of the full twenty-four hundred revolutions per minute to conserve fuel. He used the magnetic compass to head east northeast to eventually intersect with Interstate 70 and follow it into Dayton. By the time they intersected with the interstate they were two thirds of the way to Terre Haute, Indiana on the Illinois border. They were also down on fuel. There were cars and trucks spread out on the interstate, hundreds in all directions. Many of them were burnt. As they flew low there were bodies next to many of the cars or what was left of them. When Jim found a flat section free of power lines and vehicles he landed and refueled. He took off again flying low over the interstate wondering about all of the dead people by their vehicles. When he flew over Terre Haute everything seemed to be normal. There were cars on the street and people walking around. Jim flew lower toward the airport to land and see about some additional high test gasoline commonly referred to as AVGAS.

"Jim, there are no women down there." Darcy said.

"She's right, Jim. I had been thinking the same thing, there are no women."

"You sure?"

"Yes."

"Maybe I shouldn't land?"

"You got it, let' get out of here." Darcy said.

Jim climbed out. Now that they could see behind them, they could see a collection of vehicles following. Whereas seventy was a slow approach speed to an airport. Seventy for fifty vehicles on city streets was a break-neck speed. Jim put in the power and climbed. Darcy was in the front by Jim, "They're shooting at us now. I see them pointing guns and puffs of smoke."

Jim turned sharply and put some buildings between them and headed east out of town. He went across town at an angle because they were trying to follow down side streets and that didn't give them time to aim as he disappeared around buildings. He headed out along the interstate at a top speed of one hundred and twenty miles per hour. Within a half hour he saw in the mirror vehicles gaining on them. He turned to the south flying away from the interstate at a forty-five degree angle. Darcy started to ask, but as he turned Shelby spoke up, "How can they catch us in an airplane?"

Because a lot of cars and trucks can go just as fast. The advantage of an airplane is a much higher speed limit and the fact that an airplane can go in a straight line when the road doesn't. This interstate is straight. After an hour of flying he angled back to where he could see the interstate again. They gradually got closer and closer, but could see no pursuit. Jim said, "I'm going to have to land soon. We're running out of gas."

"What are we going to do? This is nowhere. Don't you have to have special aviation gasoline?"

"I'm trying to find...ah there we go, a Porsche."

"Will it run? It's so new."

"No, but I bet it has high test gasoline in it." Jim landed and then taxied back to the Porsche and siphoned gasoline into the gas cans that he then poured into the airplane. "Well, here's hoping."

Without pursuit and a nearly full tank Darcy started talking. "I'll bet that Terre Haute was full of looters from Chicago or Indianapolis. That's why there were bodies everywhere."

Shelby asked, "What about the Porsche driver?"

"Didn't see one. He probably just left his car and walked somewhere or caught a ride in an older car."

"Thank God." Darcy said.

"I hate to say anything, but east of the Mississippi has a lot more cities than the west. If all of the cities went crazy due to lack of food in the cities, this may not be a good place to be."

"I hate to say anything rude myself, but our gasoline is getting low again and we will have to get more gas before Indianapolis because we have to go way around the city."

"Why?"

"Because they got one of the small nukes and we don't know where there may be radiation. We don't have that much gas."

As they were traveling east they came to a military vehicle column headed west. Jim let down and landed headed west in the east bound lane beside the column also going west but in the west bound lane. He was hoping that since he was on the other side of the meridian, he would not be considered a threat. He taxied along faster than the column until he caught up with a vehicle he though may be a command vehicle and stopped. They all got out of the airplane and waved both arms at the Army. A major got out and said, "What do you want? You are holding up a whole column here."

"I'm Lieutenant Colonel Jim Claris, United States Air Force Reserve Retired, recalled to active duty. I have information you need before going further. I'll come over." He said softly to the girls, "Better stay here for now."

Jim went through the meridian and came up to the major and showed him his identification card and a now tattered copy of his letter from Los Angeles Air Force Base. "Major, I just flew here today from Cape Girardeau, Missouri where they are trying to get a bridge open across the Mississippi. and found that there are dead people all along the interstate getting into Terre Haute and Terre Haute has apparently been taken over completely by looters. I was going to land to gas up the plane since everything looked normal until the girls over there realized they had seen no women on the ground in Terre Haute and then that we were being followed by about fifty vehicles with guns. They shot at us and followed us out of town on the interstate. That little airplane wasn't fast enough so I went away from the interstate until we lost them. There could have been thousands of them. At Cape Girardeau the Army there was attacked by about thirty thousand looters from northern Arkansas and Saint Louis. We won."

"That's where we are headed. The number is estimated at one hundred thousand and we are looking for them. When the riots started in Indianapolis we declared martial law, but an estimated twenty thousand took off to the east. We couldn't pursue until we had Indianapolis under control. They met up with an estimated eighty thousand from Chicago. The Illinois national guard is moving south. We have air support available if need be, except we don't have much helicopter support. The Cobras and Black Hawks lost all their electronics and are worthless. We expect to confront them, have a fly over by A-10s and then a massive surrender. They don't want to surrender and we will lob in a few shells and have a firepower demonstration by some A-10's. That ought to make them surrender."

"You're probably right. Make sure you have plenty of hardware and plenty of ammunition, that's a pretty good force you're facing. In Missouri they were killing everyone except desirable women and then keeping them like cattle." Jim told him the story of why they were beaten and how.

"Your little airplane won't be any help to us when we have real airplanes. You'd better get on your way. Where did you say you were going?"

"I didn't, but I am on my way to Dayton, Ohio.

"I didn't know there was any Air Force there after the nuke?"

"My family was there."

"I'm sorry. Stop at the airport on this side of town, tell them I told you to refuel there. Don't stop flying until you get well past Columbus. The east side of Indianapolis is radioactive and about forty miles south of the nuke, and with Dayton, Columbus, and Cincinnati so close there was no way they could get enough food in there. We have had reports of cannibalism. Then with the other big cities of Cleveland, Toledo, Detroit...Well Ohio is not the place to be. Wright-Patterson Air Force Base is a smoking hole and the fallout went straight south creating a path of radiation poisoning all the way south of town. We had good surveillance. Some military people managed to get out of there before the food riots started. I'd recommend that you just fly south to Kentucky or go back the way you came. Pennsylvania is safe. The military has a big force to keep the rioters from leaving the state to the east and the Ohio river, with no bridges has made an ideal roadblock to the south. I am really sorry, but there is no use looking for your family there."

"Thanks for the advice, but I have to go. My orders are to report what I've seen across the United States. Do you have any communication with any national command headquarters?"

"Yes. The Alternate National Military Command Center is in charge."

"Who do I talk with in Indianapolis? This is my first contact with any military that had a link to national headquarters."

"Talk to Colonel William Alexander. We have a telephone established at the airport on the west side of town. By using land lines we have started establishing pretty good communications, at least for the military. You can call for military transport. I have to get going. We have a battle to go to."

DAY 61, OCTOBER 17

Jim flew the little airplane on to the airport outside of Indianapolis he had been told was held by the military and came in for a landing. It took some talking but he got a ride to the other side of town to see the Colonel with the telephone.

Jim and the girls finally got in to see the Colonel. Jim got through on the telephone, but was told they didn't need any more reports because they were establishing so many communications with their military units now. "If you can wait around there for a few weeks we can catch up your pay. In the meantime I'll clear it to get you some quarters. We have instructions to try to round up as many government workers as possible to get the country back on its feet."

"If its all the same, I have to get on to Dayton to find out what happened to my family."

"There's no point in going there. Wright-Patterson Air Force Base is gone. I can get you partial pay quicker. If you insist on going east, check in with another military unit in a few weeks. Maybe we'll have a job for you then."

"Thanks, Sergeant. I'll check in when I can."

Jim thanked the Colonel for the use of his only phone to a headquarters and excused himself.

Jim went back to Shelby and Darcy. "Looks like we're free. They don't want any more reports. I'm supposed to check in when I can to see if they have a job for me."

"So. We go on?"

"Guess so. Let's see if we can get someone to take us back to the plane."

When they got back to the plane, Jim got some AVGAS from the military there. They took off heading east again. It was only one hundred miles to Dayton. He flew over at five thousand feet to stay out of small arms range and to stay away from any radiation nearer the ground. There were large areas of town burned. Darcy said she could see large groups of men carrying guns through her binoculars. He flew over the city to the east side and then came down to a lower altitude. As he flew over the ridge where his house had been, he could see that all the houses had been burnt.

DARCY ASKED, "JIM? ONE OF THOSE IS YOURS ISN'T IT?"

"Yes. See that one with the pool near the end of the cul d'sac? That was it. I want to land and see if someone knows what happened to my family, but it doesn't look good. We might as well go look for your homes. Can you give me directions?

"Well Columbus is sixty miles east, but it is on this side of the city and north of the interstate highway." Darcy replied.

"We'll be there in about twenty-five minutes."

Jim didn't say anything, but it was not looking good. Darcy could see it too. Every farm had been burned along the way. There were carcasses of cows and pigs that had been butchered where they were caught.

"A little further north, Jim."

"There it is and look the farm looks okay. Go lower and see if you can find a place to land."

The farm really did look like it had survived. Jim pulled the power back and flew low over the farm. There was a paved road only a half mile past the farm house, so he flew around the farm, lined up and landed the plane on the paved road. They got out and Darcy was running ahead of Shelby and Jim who had stayed to get their guns and things, just in case.

Darcy wasn't looking back, but what Shelby and Jim were looking at were guns. Shotguns, hunting guns, and pistols. They were surrounded. Apparently, the Corn field had been full of people. There was no use fighting so they just held their hands up and started backing away from the airplane toward the farm.

"What are you people doing here?" A spokesman from the crowd asked.

"We were attempting to bring Darcy home." said Jim.

"Is that Darcy running toward the house?"

"Yes." Jim took the opportunity to look around toward Darcy and saw her stopped in a semicircle of armed people.

"What's her last name?"

"Williams. She said this was her parents farm."

"The names right. Lay your guns down real slow. We'll put them in the airplane for you. You can have them back if that is Darcy, and we'll apologize for our poor welcome. We're all local people here and we've had a lot of problems with looters. You came in from the west so you should have seen the farms. We just kept retreating until we took our stand near here. This farm just happens to be our headquarters. If that is Darcy, we have some bad news. Her parents were killed before we could get here."

By the time they had gotten to the house, Darcy had gotten the news and was being comforted by some of the neighbors that knew her. The people were now very friendly to Shelby and Jim as well. One of the men Jim's age took Jim aside and asked, "What are you doing with Darcy? You're too old for her."

Jim gave him a sketchy story of their escapes and close calls coming across the country.

The man seemed semi-satisfied with his answer but added, "I can understand your attraction for younger women. I also know that Darcy was never interested in any of the local boys, but you do realize you're too old for her don't you?"

"Yes. I was also concerned that her feelings were due to the circumstance, like a psychiatrist and patient. We were in a war and fighting for our lives. Actually I had casually known both girls at their jobs in Los Angeles before the war. Since the war started, we've been running. The girls got the better of my judgment after so many weeks together."

"Well. We're going to insist she stay here for awhile among friends."

"Could you keep Shelby here also, I'm going back to try to find out what happened to my family at Dayton."

"Certainly, and you're welcome back here too."

Darcy did not want him to go and Shelby did not want him to go without her. Jim had to promise that he would come back regardless of what he found, "Darcy needs her closest friend right now It's best that I go on this trip alone. It was fortunate that I found a safe place for you and Darcy." He took off and flew back to Dayton.

He came straight in and landed the Cessna on the road near what had been his house. He already had his guns at the ready when he landed. The area was not wooded and on the top of a ridge over looking the Dayton suburb of Fairborn. He kept an eye on the nearby woods and slowly walked toward his house, or what was left of it. The whole neighborhood was pretty well destroyed. There was no evidence of what happened to his family. The remains of his cars were still in the remains of the garage. He wandered over to a couple of the other houses.

"Jim? Is that you?"

"Eva?" Eva was the attractive wife of the real estate developer that had developed the housing area.

"Yes. I know you're looking for your family, but I don't know where they went. One day they were there defending your house, and the next day they were gone. They were not home when the big mob from Dayton arrived."

"What are you doing here in the middle of this disaster? Where's Buddy?"

Eva clouded up and started crying, "They're all dead. Your wife helped fight them off, but she was gone when the rest arrived. We were overwhelmed. Buddy had been killed the day before so I was at your house when the mob arrived. I haven't been able to leave if I knew where to go."

"Where did my family go?"

"I don't know. They were here the day before Buddy was killed. When Buddy was killed I ran to your house, because I knew you had guns there and a wife willing to fight. They were not there, but your guns and ammunition were out in plain site. The only thing I recognized was missing were some of your pictures. Therefore, they escaped somehow."

"Thank you, Eva. Surely there is somewhere you want to go. You can't stay here. How did you survive?"

"I know I can't stay here. My parents are dead. I have a sister in Florida, but no way to get there. I might as well go where you are going, if you'll take me with you. I survived by hiding in your shelter under your house as it burned. The mob from Dayton left sometime during the fire. I had to stay there until after the metal door cooled and found no one alive."

"Of course you can go. You can't take much with you though."

"This is all I have." She shrugged her shoulders to show that what she was wearing was it. Jim looked for the first time. She was covered with soot from the burned out houses. She was wearing dirty and torn blue jeans and a torn, long sleeved blouse. She was just as attractive as before.

They got in the plane and took off. "Right now we are going to a farm just on this side of Columbus and north of the Interstate."

"Why?"

During the short flight, Jim explained Darcy and Shelby to Eva with a short version of their trip from Los Angeles. When he finished they were coming in for a landing on the road near the farm. They were met by Shelby's brother, Joshua and some of the farmers. Jim introduced Eva and as they walked to the farmhouse Jim told about his visit to his home and finding Eva there.

DAY 62, OCTOBER 18

They stayed there for a couple of days. Joshua was saying, "One thing that had caused the destruction of the cities was the gun laws. People could not defend their homes. Many of the people from the northwest side of town joined us in stopping the mobs coming from the poor areas of Columbus and Dayton. We don't know if the mob is gone for good or where they went. We have a difficult time patrolling our boundaries which cover most of this county. Jim, I'm not sure how to say this. It seems to be the consensus that Darcy is in love with you and you didn't take advantage of the girls. If anything, it was the other way. What are your true feelings?"

"It's difficult at best. I know I am too old for them. I have a wife and family that I love. I have fallen in love with both Darcy and Shelby. I've tried to tell them that they should be looking for younger men when this is over. I thought my family was gone, but I was driven to find out for sure. What I found out in Dayton is that they disappeared before the mobs destroyed my house. They took only pictures and not the guns so they apparently escaped somehow on short notice. I have no idea where to look for them, but there is now every chance that they are still alive somewhere. Eva, the woman from Dayton has family in Florida. My wife had family that may have been in Florida also. It's possible that her brother in law, a pilot may have somehow flown in here and whisked them off. So, for want of direction, I'm heading for Florida, Fort Myers Beach in particular."

"ARE YOU GOING TO TAKE DARCY WITH YOU?

"I would rather leave Darcy here among friends, but the decision is hers. Shelby can decide for herself, but Darcy is her only tie to this place. Her family died in Saint Louis."

"Jim. You may and may not find your family. You probably won't. They were probably kidnapped by someone. What I'm trying to say is that the people here have taken a vote and decided that Darcy and Shelby are better off with you at the present time. We are within range of Columbus, Dayton, Toledo, Detroit, and conceivably Cleveland. There is no guarantee for Darcy's safety either here or with you, but she chooses to go with you. We will give you a choice of whatever we have. What we have most of here is food. We have some summer sausage that needs no refrigeration as long as it is sealed."

"Sound great. The summer sausage that is. I don't suppose you have some Grey Poupon Mustard."

"As a matter of fact, we don't, but we have an unlimited supply of French's standard mustard. We found a whole truck load of French's products. I might suggest that you also take some barbecue sauce."

"Thank you, we will. However, we can't take much. How about two bottles of each and twenty pounds of your summer sausage."

"Is that all?"

"The plane can't carry much and we are up the maximum of passengers already. We don't have much weight left to carry."

They managed to gas up the plane and they were off for Florida. They flew past Columbus not wanting to get too close. The southern side of the city was ashes. They flew near enough to see Ohio University at Athens that looked serene and peaceful and undamaged. Jim wondered about that and supposed the students had held off the mobs from Columbus. Jim would love to know what happened.

They continued on down toward Kentucky. They were approaching the Ohio River when Eva asked, "Jim, can you fly low over this town down here, I know some people that used to live there. I think they have an airfield nearby too."

"Fine." Jim buzzed lower over the town and gunfire erupted from below. Jim climbed for altitude but the engine sputtered. He almost stalled the plane. It shuddered and the stall warning pealed its sound, but he got the nose down. He glided down.

"There's the river. I'm going to try to glide across. I think I have enough altitude to make it."

Eva said, "I'm sorry. It's all my fault. Are we going to die?"

"Not if I can find a place to land before the plane decides it's going to come down on its own." Jim cut the now smoking engine. It was silent except for the rushing of the wind. They were coming down, but they had no problem crossing the river. The problem was finding a clearing . This part of Kentucky was on the edge of the Smoky mountains and forested. Jim didn't have much choice now, they were coming down. There was a clearing ahead, but not big enough to make a safe landing. He told the girls to bend over using a backpack for a pillow and grab their knees. He came in over the trees and decided to go for broke. He figured it was better to fall thirty feet down then hit the other side of the clearing at eighty miles an hour. He brought in at tree top level just above stall speed and then pulled back hard just before they cleared the trees. The airspeed dropped to sixty and then stalled and dropped to about thirty as they hit the ground. The nose had not had time to fall from the stall so they hit tail first, bounced onto the wheels and bounced hard then tried to roll onto its nose, but didn't.

Jim had hit his head on the wheel and was only semi-conscious. No one moved for several minutes. Jim must have been out for a few minutes because Eva that had been sitting beside him was holding his head and Darcy was holding his shoulders. He didn't remember having been knocked out. The trees were in a line at the nose of the plane. Jim looked from side to side. The clearing hadn't big as big as he thought. He said, "Everyone out and get everything out. This plane is going nowhere again."

"How did you land the plane here?" asked Shelby in wonder.

Jim looked around the small clearing and the airplane and replied, "Beats me. How about a controlled crash? Is everyone all right?"

"Except for you we're all okay. Does that hurt much?"

"Ow! Only when you touch it. Let's get what we can in our packs and start walking. Keep your bags light. Let's try to keep it to food, guns and ammunition."

"Good thing the farmers fitted me with new clothing back there. Thanks to Darcy."

It was very slow going. They were in the mountains of northeast Kentucky. The forest has unforgiving underbrush and they were carrying heavy packs. They had no tent or sleeping bags, but they did have a lot of weight. Added to that and it was getting cold. They stopped frequently during the day and early in the evenings to light a fire while there was light to find a place and wood. They were making only maybe fifteen miles a day at best with some days probably not covering more than five air miles. They by-passed towns since they were on foot and could not possibly get away from any bad guys. They did approach a few farm houses out in the open very cautiously. They were welcomed and had good food to eat. Apparently, Kentucky had not had the looting since they did not have big cities that ran out of food. The variety of food was limited, but they did have enough food for their small population in Kentucky. Consequently, at least northern Kentucky was civilized as was West Virginia.

III,64
When an Arab from Persia occupies Olchades (southeast Spain), a fleet will be formed to fight the Arab fleet. The (Arab) chief will pause the attack after sacking Crete and rest in the Ionian port (Syracuse, Sicily).
IV,98
The Albanians will come to Rome, but the multitude hide because of locusts (aircraft) in the sky. Italy will be hit with germ warfare and destroyed crops.
IV,56
Neither the germ warfare nor weapons will destroy Rome completely until the death from the sky comes to the top of the hills. Then a Church leader will realize that is the end.
II,81
Through fire from the sky the city will be almost totally burned while at the same time there will be great flooding. Sardinia will be ravaged by the Arabian fleet and the Church will have to evacuate.
VIII,99
By the power of the three "temporals" the Pope will have to leave the Vatican to try to re-establish the Church elsewhere.
II,93
Rome will counterattack the Libyans, just before a great flood. The Chief of State will be captured and the Vatican burned.
X,65
Rome will be destroyed when the blood and substance of the people is destroyed. A leader will give the harshest commands to leave his mark and Rome will be utterly destroyed.
II,41

The great star will burn for seven days and the clouds will cause two suns to appear. A dog will howl all night when the grand Pontiff will change countries.

V,88

A marine creature from foreign seas will land on the beach and hold Savona (north west Italy) to make Turin its prisoner.

V,62

Blood will be spilled on the rocks near Orgon (southeast France). The great evil will be recognized when Rome falls and the seas taken.

VII,6

Naples, Palermo, and all of Sicily will be made uninhabitable by the Arabs. Corsica, Salerno, and Sardinia will be cut off from supplies and disease will be everywhere.

WEEK 10, DAY 63, OCTOBER 19

There was not enough of Rome left to quarter troops. The Vatican, Walls and the Roman artifacts including the aqueducts were no more. No more would a tourist be able to throw three coins into the fountain, because the fountain was a crater. Much of the city had collapsed down into the catacombs built to carry sewage by the original Romans.

Muslim troops moved up the coast to the Po River. The French had months to dig in there and had fortified the south bank of the river as an impenetrable defensive position to keep the Muslims out of the rest of Europe. The surviving Italian troops were there with the French. The remains of the Italian air force were flying side by side with the French to provide an air cap over the allied forces on the Po.

There were American troops fighting with the Spanish against the invasion from Africa to defend the Iberian peninsula. The Germans had not gotten involved because they were afraid of an attack through Austria and had never fought along the French side of anything. The U.S. Mediterranean fleet had been withdrawn into the Atlantic to provide air support for the Spanish and American troops fighting in Spain without being in as much danger from land based Muslim aircraft and to prevent being trapped inside the Straits of Gibraltar, both sides of which were now under Muslim control. There were regular submarine patrols in the straits to keep out allied naval forces.

Without the French, Italian, or American fleets, the Mediterranean had become a staging point and almost a private lake for Muslim forces. The battle at the Po River was underway. The air battles raged over head with neither side able to commit much toward close air support of ground troops. The Arabs were firing tank shells across at dug in artillery positions and French and Italian tanks were being used as reserves to bolster any potential weak points in the defensive lines.

Facil had gotten into a routine now. He still didn't support the war, but Jabal had begun to trust his comments. Facil did not lie. He was always weak toward saving lives, but his comments frequently won when he stated his reasons. Jabal had wasted too much time on the total destruction of Rome, and allowed the French too much time to prepare. Facil ate his meals and visited with his harem girls. After two months, the various country leaders were being allowed to congregate and Facil's suite had become a favorite place to discuss the politics of war and the possible aftermaths. The girls enjoyed being hosts since their bodies were off limits to the other rulers. They enjoyed the appreciative stares and teasing the visitors. Jabal's kitchens supplied the catering and janitor service so the work was limited to the serving duties.

Facil had decided that Jabal had plenty to hang him on, but was so confident of his jail that the rulers speaking sedition and power control were beneath his concern. He had no doubt that every conversation was recorded in both video and voice. His people would love Facil for his private conversations while under the eyes of his captors. This would probably be true of the other leaders as well, so Jabal couldn't use them for blackmail or for proving complicity in the war crimes that would be sure to follow. Jabal had no doubt had every word analyzed for value. Their conversations could only be used against them if the Muslim forces did conquer their half of the world and were not then conquered by the Asians.

DAY 66, KENTUCKY

On their third day a farmer gave them a ride into town where they caught a bus into Lexington and from there to Knoxville, Tennessee. They even accepted Jim's credit card. Luckily, the bus terminals did not have the metal detectors like the airports of old. They had to sell their rifles and regular shotguns for almost nothing to a pawn shop. They kept their shorter riot guns, the M-79 grenade launcher, pistols, and ammunition. When they got to Knoxville, Jim found a military unit. They read his letter and agreed to assist. Better yet, they resupplied his money with another pay advance until the pay could get straightened out. They were advised to stay there rather than continue south.

"We've come all the way through Kentucky and Tennessee with no trouble, why can't we continue? There wasn't any bomb damage in the South."

"Alabama and Georgia have several large cities and over a million people on welfare. Most of their cities are burning and there are looters everywhere. We have the Ohio River protecting Kentucky on the north, the Mississippi on the west and mountains on the east and south. We have a good portion of our combined national guards along the southern Tennessee border. If you have to go south I would avoid the cities and towns whenever possible."

"What about Florida?"

"We don't know anything about it. There were refugees fleeing the mobs from Georgia, Alabama, and Mississippi that told us about what was happening before we closed our borders. Would you like to talk with some of the people we are processing through the border here?"

"Yes, I would. As I told you part of my mission is to report on conditions back to the Alternate National Military Command Post that is charge of the military. In fact, if you have a phone line to there, I would like to use it."

"We have a line here in Knoxville, but you'll have to come back here to use it after you visit the refugees."

"Well, is there any military transportation we could take to Chattanooga?"

"There are occasional battles with looters just south of Chattanooga. It's not safe. That's also where we process a lot of refugees."

"I've got to go that way anyway to get to my destination in Florida."

"Well, I've got a mail run you can go on if you don't mind riding in the back of canvas truck. I'll also need to give you a letter of passage in case you cross into Georgia and want to come back this way."

Jim, Shelby, Darcy, and Eva had a bouncy cold ride south to Chattanooga from Knoxville. When they got there they found a huge tent city of refugees north of the town with military guards around the fences. Jim was assigned a tent outside the fence. He left the girls there to rest up and get warm by the small coal heater in the tent while he went to interview refugees.

"I lived in a suburb north of Atlanta. After the electricity went off it was only hours before we could see fires in downtown Atlanta. We didn't know what was going on, but one of my neighbors had an old car that would start. We took it toward town to see what was burning. We almost got caught in the riots and looting. As we were heading back home, I knew I had to get my family out of town and stopped by an old car lot and bought an old used car that would start. All of us did except for the neighbor with the old car. We packed what we could and headed out of town just as the rioters were approaching our suburb. We drained the gasoline out of our new cars and drove north. We stopped at a barbecue grill at Roswell, north of the beltway and were just finishing eating when we saw riots starting there too. We got back in our cars and kept going until we got here."

"Same type of thing here, but we, my wife and children and I, came from Birmingham, that's Birmingham, Alabama. I kept stopping in motels along the way, but then we heard that those crazy welfare people were converging on us from both Huntsville and Birmingham. We spent three weeks in motels and ended up here before we were stopped by the military. These tents are not like home, but it's safe and we have food. We've been told that they're not quite sure what to do. Every motel in the state is full and many people have taken in boarders. I guess it's not their fault. Refugees like us have been coming from both the east and south."

"You think you had it bad? I came all the way from Montgomery, by way of Mobile. At least we tried to go to Mobile. We were lucky to escape with our lives. I used to travel all over Alabama as a salesman so I knew all the back roads and had a lot of old clients that helped us along the way. I spent three weeks running as fast as I could go. The looters seemed to be sticking to the main highways and cities so far. Of course you gotta remember that small town people are pretty well armed and not used to having police protect them. They also stick together."

"Do you think it would be possible to get through to Florida, if someone stuck to the back roads?

"It might be possible, but I wouldn't try it. Problem is that people don't know how to work. There are generations that have been on welfare. They sit around watching television in their subsidized or completely public housing, go pick up their welfare and disability checks then go to the grocery store and buy their food with food stamps and spend their welfare money on booze and drugs. All of a sudden the grocery store is out of food, they can't get their welfare checks, and the drugs run out with no more being smuggled in. Then they go crazy for lack of drugs, and storm the hospitals and drug stores looking for more. When they can't find them anymore they burn their own houses and the businesses downtown and then head for the suburbs."

"Nah, in Atlanta, they started looting and burning as soon as they found out the cops couldn't respond. They headed straight for the suburbs, just burning as they went."

Jim left them arguing and went to talk to the commander of the camp. "How many refugees do you have?"

"Twenty thousand so far. They are still coming, but it has slowed down considerably."

"What about the military in Alabama and Georgia?"

"What about them? There weren't that many active military there. We're in contact with the Navy in Mobile and the Air War University at Maxwell Air Force Base in Alabama, they are secure, but have no orders. The looters are turning away from them as soon as they find the military presence. Then of course, there have been no problems from around Pensacola to past Eglin Air Force Base."

"Why hasn't the military moved in to keep the peace?"

"There have been no orders."

"Are you telling me that not one single commander has had the guts to do something without orders? Why are you doing what you are doing?"

"The governor ordered it. We sent runners to call up the guard and the reserves in the state and it spread word of mouth. At any rate, not even Memphis suffered much damage from looters. We were there within hours with the military and things never really got out of hand."

"That's the way it should have been in every city. What's going on in most of the country is absurd." Jim went on and told about his trip across the country so far.

DAY 70

The commander helped them get a good vehicle from one of the refugees and helped him get it fixed up and armored somewhat. They replaced the glass with Plexiglas that would not shatter if shot. Added boiler plate around the engine compartment and gas tank. They added a boiler plate bumper and a layer behind the back seat with more welded to the doors. All this required heavier springs which they didn't have, but they did find some air bags to put in the coil springs. The car was a full size Chevrolet with a four hundred cubic inch engine in good condition. It even had good tires.

They did not go straight through Chattanooga, but went east to U.S. Highway 19 out of Murphy, North Carolina, because it was relatively safe in Tennessee and it was known to be bad just south of the mountains near Chattanooga. It was a scenic drive through sparsely populated mountains and forest. They took the Y in Georgia and turned on U.S. Highway 129. They cautiously approached and then sped across Interstate 365 watching their rear to make sure they weren't seen. So far so good. They also made it across Interstate Highway 85. The turned right onto State Highway 11 at Jefferson. There was no one at all in the town, but there were burned out cars in the road and all the windows were smashed out. They were trying to get to Warner Robins, Georgia where the Air Force Base with the same name was. When they went through Winder, the town had been burnt to the ground. There were bodies lying around being picked at by wild dogs and birds with the horrible stench of burned flesh. Eva came apart and cried. Darcy and Shelby had become more hardened and although upset it put them on their vigilance with their guns in hand. Jim drove as quietly as he could through the town and when the road opened up he quickly sped out of town. He stopped about five miles out of town to console Eva. She clutched him tightly and cried and blubbered onto his shirt as he put his arms around her. She was unable to talk intelligibly.

"Darcy, Shelby, be ready for anything. Eva, just lie down on the seat. I don't want to sit here on an open road." With that he pushed Eva away and drove on down the road. When he felt they were close to Monroe he stopped again. "We are very close to Atlanta and this town is large enough to have a bypass around on the north. We don't know if it will be like the last town, whether they defended themselves, or whether it is controlled by the looters. Do you think we ought to just go into the town, or try to bypass it? Remember that if we take one of these little side roads we could end up trapped on a dead end road, or wander too close to Atlanta."

Shelby spoke first, "Take a side road, but go left around the other side of the town away from Atlanta. That way if we take a wrong turn we don't find ourselves in Atlanta by accident."

"There was a road back about one hundred yards. Let's go."

"I'm okay now Jim. Darcy, will you show me how to load this shotgun?

"I think you might be better off with this Glock automatic pistol. Here, see you push this button and then grab the clip here and pull it out. Here is a bag of loaded clips. You grab one, slide it in, and give the butt a little hit to make sure the clip is locked in. This button is the safety. Pull the top of the gun back like this. That loads a clip into the chamber and cocks the hammer. As soon as you push the safety, it will fire. Now you try it."

"Very good. Have you shot a gun before."

"Yes, but someone else loaded it for me. Thanks. I'll do my part now. I'm sorry about that last town. Everything just kept rushing in on me. My husband and parents were killed. My neighbors were killed, but those people were being eaten and the smell."

"That was worse than anything we have seen so far ourselves."

Jim drove easily to keep the tires from squealing and drawing attention. They saw a lot of destruction, but made it all the way to Macon, where they ran into the military in force. Macon was untouched. There was a roadblock near the edge of town. Jim stopped short, got out with no guns and walked toward the military uniforms with his hands in sight, with the girls following him in like style. He asked for the person in charge, gave his name and made it obvious he was someone that they should not question. They were not going to let him past, but they called for their Non Commissioned Officer In Charge, NCOIC. He came forward and Jim identified himself as Lieutenant Colonel Jim Claris, who had a letter for the commander that explained his mission.

"Sorry Sir, but your transport does not exactly look normal and you parked it well back from the roadblock. Do you mind if I take a look?"

"Yes, I do. You will find it is full of guns, ammunition, and grenades. We started in Los Angeles when the war started. I'd like to tell you the whole story, but I need to talk to at least an O-6. We've driven all the way from Chattanooga since early this morning and seen some very unpleasant sights. Will you please just either escort us there, you can ride with us if you want, or call him out here?"

"Let me call back to headquarters." He did and came back shortly. "I'll ride with you, but we have an Armored Personnel Carrier, APC, coming to escort you." They waited for the APC and then the Master Sergeant got in the front seat beside Jim with the girls in back. Jim was escorted into the Colonel's office with the girls held in a break room in the building. Jim presented his letter. The Colonel called the ANMCC who verified Jim's identification. The Colonel visibly relaxed.

"Well. It seems as we are supposed to give you VIP quarters and that someone there wants to contact you about something. We're also supposed to catch up your pay in the amount of ten thousand dollars. I guess I can let the guards go. I'll write a note of identification. Do you know how to get to Warner Robins Air Force Base?"

"I have been there a number of times although the last time was fifteen years ago. In fact we used to drive down from Atlanta rather than take the puddle jumper."

"You'll find the way perfectly safe, so please keep your hardware out of sight. I'd love to hear your story if you're going to be here for awhile." Jim went down to the base, got paid, and was put up in the VOQ. The manager apologized for not having better quarters, but they were given two rooms with a living room. Darcy spent the night with Jim while Eva used the other bedroom while Shelby slept on the sofa. When Jim woke up, Shelby was there. "My turn. It's been several days you know. Darcy and I agreed to share as long as you're around."

DAY 71

At breakfast in the officer's club the girls were stared at surreptitiously by all the officers passing through and eating there. Eva said, "I think we had better get moving again or they may hold us here for some reason. It has been easy so far and we're over half way to Fort Meyers already. Does everyone agree?"

"Yes, I'm ready. Let's eat a big breakfast, then go by the commissary to see what we can get and be on our way. I can't take you into the commissary so I'll drop you by the VOQ to pack and I'll see if I can get some groceries." They all agreed and by 10:30 AM they were on their way south again. They went by the roadblock of the Warner Robins defense area on highway 129 heading for Florida.

They ran into trouble at Hawkensville where roads came in from seven different directions. One minute they were feeling comfortable after their visit at Warner Robins and the next they were driving through crowds of looters. No one was paying them much attention in their old car, but they were petrified. Eva didn't know what to do, but Darcy handed her the bag of clips and the Glock automatic. They handed Jim one of the riot guns and another automatic. They had the grenade launcher loaded and handy and riot guns and automatic pistols loaded. They kept them all down as out of sight as possible. They were in traffic which gradually got heavier. They were nearing the center of the town and all of them were praying they could get through town without getting stopped. When they got to what must have been the conjunction of all the highways at the town square, some large thuggy white guys came up to the car and yelled, "Hey, this guy got three girls in here. Don't you know you aren't allowed to take your own girls? Hey! Are you listening to me? Hey Joe, this guy got girls in his car. Aren't all the girls supposed to be locked up over at the school?"

Jim remembered that time over in Missouri where they had all the women corralled in the city park, naked. This must be another place like that. Were all the looters totally uncivilized? He knew he had to get out of there and get out now. There was a pickup ahead of him. If it wasn't for he boilerplate and heavy bumper the back end of a pickup would cave in the front of the car, but he floored the old Chevy and turned the wheel slightly, He shoved the backend of the pickup up and over out of the way into parked cars along the side of the street. He then hit the back end of a smaller car and did the same to it. He shoved another ahead of him into the intersection. He saw the road to the left was mostly clear, turned, and floored it.

There was a lot of yelling behind them. Darcy yelled over the roar of the engine, "Here they come, get ready!"

Shelby unhooked the fold down rear Plexiglas window and got the grenade launcher ready. Jim yelled back, "Don't use the grenades unless you have to, we only have twenty. We left the others behind."

The old Chevy was pretty fast, but with its extra weight it would only do about one hundred and five. Some of the cars were gaining rapidly. They were approaching a narrow bridge, and Jim yelled. Shelby try to hit one just before it gets to the bridge. Darcy, you get the other Grenade launcher and you try to if Shelby misses."

Both girls were pretty good at it by now and Shelby hit the lead car just in time for it to explode and flip to a sliding stop against a guard rail. The next car hit it and crashed into the other guard rail. The car behind them tried to stop and crashed into the backs of the other two creating a perfect road block. One of the cars burst into flames sealing their getaway. Jim kept the car going and had Eva get out a road map to figure out what road they were on. "I think we're heading southeast."

"We're either on 129 or State 46. We're on 129 if the next town is Abbeville."

"It is. We're on the right road. It's only five miles ahead. Wait, I see a roadblock ahead."

"Can we break through it?" yelled Darcy.

"We might ..." Jim hit the brakes, stopping for the roadblock. "I think they're friendlies." Jim stopped the car, got out and held his hands partially in the air as he walked toward a brace of shotgun barrels. "I'm an Air Force officer and I have three young women with me. I'm just trying to get to Fort Meyers where my wife was during the war. Will you let us through?"

"If what you're saying is so. Tell the women to get out of the car slowly."

"Eva, Girls, they're friendlies. Get out of the car and hold your hands up so they can see them." The girls complied.

One of the men said, "Come on Jake. He don't look bad. He's not a looter. Show us some identification."

Jim took out his military identification car and held it out to the man. "See, Jake? I told you he was okay."

Jake said, "Oh all right. Go back and bring you car on through. Where you comin' from?"

"We just came through Hawkinsville that was completely full of looters that you're worried about. They chased us for awhile, but we lost them."

They passed on through the town and several more along their way that seemed almost normal. At Thomasville, Georgia they were stopped at a roadblock just to tell them to stay away from Jacksonville and stick to the coast road, U.S. 19 and 98 until they got past Ocala. Jacksonville had been hit by heavy rioting. Miami was in flames with a near war going on as the military was attempting to retake the town from the rioters who were well armed. They drove on to Tampa and on to Fort Meyers getting gasoline at a military post along the way.

DAY 73

When they got to Fort Meyers Beach Jim found the street going to his sister-in-laws house. There was no one there. Jim went to the neighbor next door. When he explained who he was and why he was there, the woman recognized him from the one time they had visited Florida and from pictures.

"I have a spare key. I'll bet you'd like in. I'm sure Shirley wouldn't mind in the best of times. OH! You have company? What was it? Oh yeh, which one is Shirley's sister?"

"Uh, none of them?"

"Well...I guess these are strange times. Did you lose your family?"

"Sort of. I can't find them. I have been traveling from Los Angeles since the war started. I finally got to Dayton, and they were gone. I mean they were gone before the mobs got to our house. Eva was the only one in the neighborhood still alive, but she says that my family had disappeared the night before the mobs killed everyone. Her car was in the garage and all of my guns were in the house when they disappeared, but the family pictures were missing. Shelby, the blond, and Darcy, the brunette, escaped from Los Angeles with me the day the war started. After discovering she wasn't in Dayton, I decided to try here in Florida. Now I am at a total loss."

"Well, might as well make yourself at home." They did. They all went down to the beach and bought swimsuits. Shelby got one of those tee string suits that had nothing in back but a string top and bottom. There wasn't much in front either bottom or top. It was a light tan. When Jim first saw it he thought she was naked. She bought another slightly more modest to keep from getting arrested if in a public place. Darcy picked out a similar suit but in bright yellow. Eva was ten years older and more modest. Hers almost covered her breasts and did cover her buttocks. It had a fringe from the string and the bottom. It still was quite small, but legal.

Eva said, "I couldn't go quite as far as Shelby and Darcy, but how do I look?"

Jim replied, "Very good. I mean very good."

"I still haven't thanked you properly for getting me out of Dayton. I would have died there you know."

"Relax, Eva. I just got there at the right time." Darcy and Shelby came out of the dressing room wearing silk short shorts with their bikini tops.

"Jim, can we get these?"

"Sure."

"We're going to walk back along the beach. This is the first time we've felt safe in months. Okay?"

"Certainly." Eva and Jim drove back to the house while the girls walked back.

"How long do you think it will take them to get back?"

"An hour and half to two hours. Why?" When they got back to the house, she showed him why. Jim didn't have a chance. He had always been physically attracted to her since meeting her for the first time. They were asleep when Shelby and Darcy returned. When they woke, Shelby and Darcy had left a note in the kitchen. It said, "We came and went. Meet us down on the beach at the end of the street when you're ready. Welcome to the Claris Club, Eva."

Eva was quite embarrassed. "I guess they came back early. Shall we go join them at the beach and grab some rays? My suntan has faded badly since last summer. Jim, I wasn't just thanking you for rescuing me. It's been awhile for me too. Let's go." They all went to the beach. It was idyllic to be lying in the sun, soaking up rays, and not having to carry their guns and food.

This went on until March. Jim made occasional trips to MacDill Air Force Base south of Tampa for money from the military and food from the military commissary not available in the local stores. The Air Force did a good job of transporting condiments by air to their various Air Force Base commissaries. The local stores had plenty of food since Florida was a net exporter of beef, vegetables, and fruit, but spices and things not grown in Florida were in short supply. MacDill had no communications with the Alternate National Military Command Post as it was all burnt out during the initial HEMP attack. They carried mail on their flights, but had no live communications with the ANMCC, until December. Therefore, the ANMCC never knew that Jim Claris was near MacDill Air Force Base. Most of the other bases around the country had been notified by voice to be on the lookout for Jim to bring him to the ANMCC. As a result, Jim did not know his family was safe there.

WEEK 20

Red China had no problem moving through Siberia except for weather and poor roads, except that North Korea had decided they didn't like the Red Chinese controlling all of their back door and had attacked the Red Chinese. They were supposed to have attacked and taken South Korea without American help, but instead turned on their Red Chinese brothers. Their Russian made MIG-29's, possibly with Russian pilots, were superior to the Japanese made and flown F-16's or the Red Chinese MIGs and were they were shooting down twenty Red Chinese aircraft for every MIG-29. That could not go on forever, because North Korea was limited on aircraft versus an almost unlimited supply of Red Chinese MIGs. When the Red Chinese tried to invade North Korea, they discovered that the North Koreans had laid nuclear land mines. People could cross, but a tank not on an approved road would be heavy enough to set one off, destroying everything within one mile of the land mine and poisoning the land with radioactivity. The Red Chinese had tried to march their men through radioactive bursts from the North Koreans, but within a week their attack on North Korea ground to a halt due to radiation sickness among their troops who were dying by the tens of thousands. Red China's nuclear stockpile had been pretty much wiped out by the Soviet counter attacks, so nuking North Korea was not an option.

At the same time the poisoning of the land on the North Korean border served to seal in the North Koreans so after three months Red China decided to just let them live on the other side of the poison line and move their troops and aircraft out of range of North Korean aircraft.

Japan had built an impressive ship building business before the war and had produced more convertible tankers than the Arabs had. These were made available to Red Chinese troops who spent two weeks taking all of the Philippine Islands that had conveniently kicked out the American forces in the late 1980's. They were defenseless. Of course some escaped into the jungle to continue a jungle warfare as in World War II. The difference here was that there was no strong United States to smuggle in arms and ammunition.

ii,100

Within the British Isles there will be a horrible uproar. Only the faction demanding war will be allowed to be heard. They will come as plunderers and so taken insult, that others will want to join in the great league of the conquered.

Those Brits calling for intervention get carried away in their anti-Arab demonstrations and start breaking Arab windows and otherwise destroying their property. As a result, more Brits join with the Arabs in calling the Arab "Peace Keeping Force" the good guys in revolution to the lawlessness of the anti-Arab goods.

v,93

By means of those of the moon (symbol for Arabs), when Mercury will be dominating the sky, the island of Scotland will have a knowledgeable leader, one who will put the British into confusion.

It did not help the British when the leading Scot also supported the Arab "Peace Keeping Force." He said they needed the Arabs to fight the trouble makers in south eastern Europe because of the danger from the Chinese invading much of Asia. Britain was not strong enough and whatever force they had need to be more concerned about British holdings in Asia. Whether he was in the pay of the Arabs, or misguided, or what, but he led a rebel faction that was every bit as radical as the Northern Irish. Whereas the British could blockade Belfast, there was no way they could do much about all of Scotland and the rebels appeared to live here and there throughout Scotland and England, although all the members of the rebel group were Scottish.

ix,48

The great city of the maritime ocean, London, will be surrounded by a flood of shallow water and covered with ice. In December and in the spring it will suffer from hurricane winds.

The Brits had mobilized their forces to assist at the Po River, but a massive storm had hit. Ice in the Thames River had caused massive flooding along the river. Hurricanes normally spawn straight south of Britain off the African coast and travel west as tropical depressions gaining strength at the Americas. This one came straight north in the winter instead of traveling west hitting Great Britain with one hundred and fifty mile an hour winds causing massive damage and ice thick enough to cave in many buildings not made for heavy ice loads. Digging out from the ice and drying out from the flooding and repairing the damage took priority over a foreign war that was not threatening direct British interests. All British and American flights originating out of Great Britain were grounded for most of the winter and spring. These aircraft not being available for the Battle of Italy was a major set back.

16 PITY LUCERNE

The deadlock on the Po River had still not been broken. Jabal had not used nuclear HEMP due to potential damage to his own equipment. He could not use chemicals or biological poisons because of the proximity of their forces and the prevailing winds that blew from the west and European side of the Po to the east and Muslim side. Despite his huge air force, the French and Italian Air Forces augmented by British and American Air Forces controlled their side of the Po River even though he controlled his side.

Jabal announced, "Gentlemen, I have decided that tomorrow we will commit every fighter plane we have to destroying the allied air forces in order to gain control of the battlefield. Does anyone see a problem with this?"

Facil, as the former commander of the Saudi Air Force, was the expert who had not been asked to this point, "Jabal, it would be very beneficial to have total air superiority over the Po River Battlefield, but let me remind you that whereas we have no production facilities for airplanes on Muslim lands, the French, British, and Americans can produce more and more airplanes to replace their attrition's and spare parts. I for one believe that we have been right up to this point to mainly provide protection for our own forces to prevent air strikes through maximum use of all airplanes as interceptors. Losing air superiority over our own troop areas would be a disaster. Remember the bombing of Iraq, not so long ago."

"Yes, but Facil, let me remind you that the United States will be incapacitated by civil wars until we will come as a peace force. Let me also remind you, that every Muslim troop has at least one air to air missile of the latest fire and forget technology (The famous Stinger missile was fired out of a tube and the user had to keep the crosshairs on the airplane the whole time the missile was in flight. The new missile was aimed fired and then the user could hide.) Before when you asked me to spare Italian lives to speed up our progress you were correct and it was unfortunate I did not ask you sooner. This time, you are asking us to slow our progress. Winter is upon us now. The time table has slipped. It is time my troops got away from the cold of northern Italy to the more moderate coast land of the Riviera of France."

The rest of the day was a discussion as to how to use their air power. Facil did manage to keep the Saudi F-15's held in reserve for use in France after the breakout of Muslim forces.

MONTH 5, DECEMBER 25

Jabal had picked Christmas day for perverse reasons and hoping to find the Christians napping, but their allied air force made a good accounting of itself. The pictures of the day on holovision were of incessant dogfights between fighter planes with considerable live gun camera pictures. It was hard to assess what was happening or who was winning. It was especially difficult since the airplanes were largely of the same manufacture. Both sides flew F-15's and F-16's and F-18's of the United States and French Mirages of different models, and British Tornado's. The Tornado did not make a good dog fighter compared to the U.S. and French made airplanes. Only the Russian MIGs were distinguishable, but even then, to an untrained eye, the Russian copies of American airplanes made them hard to identify. Facil had no problems, being a fighter pilot himself, but he could imagine the problems his colleagues were having.

VIII,21

Three ships will enter the port of Agde (southern France). They will be carrying an infection, a disease. They will bypass a bridge and carry off millions, but to break the bridge, they will be resisted by a third of a million.

I,11

Logical, physical and emotional action, work in Naples, Leon (Spain) and Sicily but will be effected by fiery weapons and flooding at the time when Rome falls because of weak thinking.

X,60

I weep for Nice, Monaco, Pisa, Genoa, Savona, Siena, Modena, and Malta. The new year's gift will be blood, metal, and fire as the earth shudders and floods because of unwillingness.

III,10

Monaco will be under siege with the Arabian fleet coming in close to pound them 7 times until Monaco surrenders. The great leader will be led away in a large metal vehicle.

II,4

From Monaco to Sicily, the west coast of Italy will be pillaged by the Arabs.

VII,37

Ten assassins will be sent to murder the captain of the ship but he will be warned by another captain. The fleets will engage, but the leader fight each other and many ships will be sunk near Antibes. The Arabs will capture Frejus.

X,23

Land and sea forces will devastate Frejus, Antibes, and towns around Nice with locusts (airplanes) coming from land and sea and break the laws of war.

VII,19

The defenses of Nice will not be engaged in battle, but destroyed by a some new frightful weapon of shining metal that is new to Europeans.

III,90

A great leader, known as the Satyr and the Tiger of Hyrcania, North Iran, will be presented with a gift from those of the great Ocean. A chief of a fleet will set out from the Persian Gulf. He will be the one who will invade the port of Marseilles

IV,94

Two prominent brothers will come out of Spain, the eldest will be defeated in sight of the Pyrenees mountains. The sea the River Rhone, Lake Geneva, and Germany will be reddened with blood. Narbonne and Beziers will be contaminated from Agde

III,75

Pau(France), Verona and Vicenza (Italy), Sargossa (Spain), will be soaked in blood by those from distant lands. A very great disease will come in giant shells. Relief through death will be near and remedies far off.

II,96

A strong glowing flame will be seen in the sky at night from both ends of the River Rhone (Marseilles and Lyons). There will be famine, steel weapons, and relief will come too late. The Persians will invade Macedonia (northern Greece).

V,46

Two enemies will be defeated after great punishment from the Chinese scepter. A fleet from Africa will appear before the Pannonians (Balkan nations of Romania, Bulgaria and southwestern USSR) and by land and sea horrible deeds will take place. A great Asian leader will come by land and sea with a great army. In blue and gray uniforms they will pursue those of the cross to death.

MONTH 6, JANUARY 7

The dogfights were becoming obviously less vicious with fewer and fewer airplanes on both sides. The allied losses were put at ten thousand which Facil knew were probably less than one thousand, while the Muslim loses were put at one hundred, but were probably closer to fifteen hundred. There was no way of knowing for sure, but Muslim pilots had come out very poorly compared to American pilots in the Gulf War or during the Israeli wars. Thank goodness for the capture of the Israel air forces.

The reports from Spain were discouraging to say the least. Most of the northern Africa Muslim air force had been committed there against a very small number of American airplanes based in Spain and Great Britain. Again, the reports were distorted, but President Mosmorin of Egypt was groaning about having lost two hundred F-16's, two hundred F-4's, and one hundred MIG 21's and 23's in the last two weeks. The official holovision reports told of only one hundred losses compared to two thousand American losses. Facil knew that the United States did not even possess two thousand fighter planes in the world, at least not flying with the American Air Force. Most good airplanes were of U.S. manufacture, but the American Air Force only had a small number of the ones manufactured. He was more afraid that the losses had been reversed from the reported numbers. The Arab forces had landed six thousand tanks in Spain along with two million troops, but had been unable to take Spain after all these months. The Muslim's controlled the coast line on the Mediterranean side, but had been unable to progress into the mountainous regions.

The build up along the Po River now added to eight million Muslim troops and twenty thousand tanks, but these forces had been unable to get across the Po River to fight face to face with the allies. In the meantime, these tanks and men required an extensive supply line from the Middle East to Italy. Their converted oil tanks were no longer bringing more equipment or troops but were heavily committed to keeping supplies moving.

MONTH 7, FEBRUARY 10

TSgt Gaddis's unit went on full alert. The Arabs had just crossed into Switzerland. The Swiss air force shot down one hundred and fifty Arab aircraft before pulling back due to the high number of their own losses. The combined German, Swiss, and American army units spread out to defend Berne. There were rumors about advancing south into the heart of Switzerland. French units moved into Switzerland along the Rhone valley to Lucerne to join the French there. The Swiss also concentrated much of their army there also.

Now you have to picture a country where every man is drafted into the military and every family keeps military guns, ammunition, and grenades in their homes. Where every new home and office building has a nuclear bomb proof shelter. Where every man stays in the active reserve until age fifty-five. That is Switzerland. A very well armed country with an unfriendly terrain.

Telephone communications had been re-established and there were radio broadcasts across the country. The looters had been pretty well rounded up and food was plentiful again. There were even limited television stations in operation. Televisions were pretty much public devices for multiple families. There was no television production except in Mexico that was available for American consumption. Most families had at least a portable radio with earphones. People were not taking long trips so the tourist industry had not started. Banks were operating with manual accounting procedures using computers only for backup.

The civilian crisis was over. The military industry was just coming up again. Between the cut backs in defense and all the closures and de-militarizing of the defense industry, there wasn't much. Add to that the fifty percent of the industries that were destroyed by the relatively few nukes that destroyed cities and there was a severe shortage of defense industry. General Gates would wait no longer. He ordered a re-deployment of the meager U.S. forces in Germany to come to the aid of the French. He ordered a re-deployment of some forces to Berne, Switzerland, to prevent an Arab attack into Germany from Lucerne, Switzerland.

VI,98

Volcae and Toulouse are invaded by disease producing weapons when Rome is being plundered.

VIII,51

The Arab Turk says a prayer after conquering Cordova (south Spain) but while at sea will be captured by the British from Gibraltar.

V,55

One powerful in the ways of Mohammed will be born in Yemen. He will trouble Spain by conquering southern Spain and he will be the one who lead the Arab ships against the Italian navy.

III,20

By the Guadalquivir River he will beat back the Spanish deep into Iberia.

VIII,94

Near a lake a leader will be killed and after resisting for seven months they will be beaten for hesitating to fight without their leader.

VI,88

The Spanish realm will be desolated. The Spanish will retreat and use the River Elbe in northern Spain for defense with the Pyrenees mountains at their backs to hide in and fortify.

I,20

Tours, Orleans, Blois, Anger, Reims and Nates (east central and north central France) will be harassed by encampments of foreigners.

iii,58

Near the Rhine river from the Austrian mountains, will come a great leader, but he will arrive too late. He will plan a defense line through center Europe to Southwest Russia. His destruction will be so complete, that they will be unable to find him.

ix,90

A captain of Grand Germany will secretly aid the enemy. he will give away the Balkan defenses and his treason will cause a great flow of blood.

MONTH 7, FEBRUARY 15

"General Gates, there has been a new development reported by the French. The Arabs have started using germ warfare. We are now operating in a complete Chemical, Biological, and Nuclear or CBN environment. Apparently this germ was really a microscopic bacteria too small to be stopped by the CBN filters on our M1A2 tanks."

"How can that be?"

"Sir. May I speak?" Jim asked.

With a disgusted look General Gates replied, "You might as well. I haven't been able to keep you quiet yet."

"Sir. We have a new filter in testing now that exceeds the requirement for this new bacteria, but we need your authorization to go into production."

"Who ordered the new filter?"

"I did, sir." Jim said.

"God Damn it. Oh hell, you did good. Go ahead and start producing and ship as soon as you can. We'll have to try to withhold our forces until they get the new filters."

Jabal was speaking, "The amphibious lander could not go to Rome due to the rough terrain from the coast in Italy, but our tanks are pulverizing what the airplanes left. We have destroyed police and army forces, but we have skipped the towns and villages that did not try to fight back. Facil, you were correct, the French are attempting to cut our supply lines, but we have hundreds of airliners from the world's airlines that we own that are being used for cargo, not to mention the hundreds of cargo planes that we jointly own.

In the meantime our forces are moving northward through Switzerland to move into the heart of France, Paris. The Swiss Air Force is not what you would expect from a neutralist country, nor their armor. They are putting up a good fight. The French forces are pulling back away from our supply lines to reinforce the passages to France from Switzerland. Italy is ours, Facil. I told you not to worry about the French forces. They managed to kill five thousand of our troops before they realized we were flanking them through Switzerland. Tomorrow our forces will move into Lucerne, Switzerland and within days will enter France near Geneva. We already have significant forces in the Rhone valley near the inland sea of Switzerland.

Our tanks near Rome are moving up the west coast of Italy to surround the French forces that attempted to cut our supply lines. We control the north side of the Po and area moving through the Rhone valley toward France. We are nearing the Austrian border on the southeast. The German forces along with the few American forces in Germany is moving toward Austria and Switzerland in a vain attempt to slow us down. Now we are moving to cut off the French with them trapped on the south side of the Po. We control over half of Spain. The paltry Spanish forces cannot fight a fixed battle with us. The American Air Force is holding its own for now with help from their Mediterranean fleet, but they will run out of ammunition soon with the United States embroiled in a civil war. Once we capture the French forces on the Po we will be unopposed moving into France.."

"Jabal, may I speak," said King Hussein of Jordan.

"Of course, the King of Jordan, does not have to ask to speak."

"Jabal, you know that I have always supported our causes. I stood against the Israelis with the Palestine Liberation Organization. I think maybe we are going to far, spreading our forces too thin. How can we move through mountains in Czechoslovakia and Austria and at the same time move our forces through mountains in Switzerland, and still defeat the French forces at the Po?"

"Because we have them out numbered by that much. We can prosecute all of these fronts and we still have plenty of reserves, as well as a few surprises."

Facil went back to his suite with mixed feelings. He did not want to be involved in a war. He was against killing and war. But, he was beginning to think they might win this war. To save his country and his royal position in that country he was going to have to sell himself to the Muslim leadership. Rather than sit here feeling like a hostage, he was going to have to take a more proactive part to retain his country. He would have to become a valued part of the leadership. He was no fool on prosecuting a war, he had been to all the right American schools and was a student of history. Since Mecca, the most holy place of the Muslim world, the capitol of Islam was located in his own Saudi Arabia, he should be able to become a powerful member of the ruling class of this new Muslim world. At the same time that he was providing leadership to the military process, he might bring some reason to the process and save millions upon millions of civilian lives.

Mohammed was a peaceful man. He would want Facil to save lives if he could. Facil was having a new experience in his life, like a born again Christian from the United States. He was getting religion. He was going above the compliance of a Saudi Arabian king who had to follow the rules of Islam, he was becoming converted to the true beliefs as he saw them. He had studied all the writings of Mohammed but they were just now sinking in. He could not stop the war, but he could bring order to it and save millions of lives. There was a problem however. He had a harem of mainly non Arabic girls. It was time that he married, in spite of the war. He would meet no girls here, but he was living in sin. He was not turning against his girls, he loved them all.

"Facil, you are so deep in thought. What has happened now?" Kareen interrupted his thoughts.

"We are winning the war. I must prepare to accept my new position in a new world order."

"Facil, are you becoming brainwashed? What are they doing to you in these so called meetings?" said Joy.

"I am not becoming brainwashed, Joy. We sit and watch our forces destroy whatever they want to. We are winning in Italy, Spain, Czechoslovakia, and Switzerland. There is no one to stop the Arab forces. I have to accept the destiny and worry about the destiny of my Saudi Arabia. I will have to join as an active part of the leadership or lose my country."

"Bull Shit!" said Joy.

Facil's Arabic blood suddenly took over, "STOP! I will have none of this. I am a king. I am the king of Saudi Arabia, one of the richest and largest countries in the world. I have a duty to my country and a duty to my religion. I have been a playboy too long. I should have already married and secured my son's future. I do not even have a son, nor do I have a wife. I will have no more to do with you. Leave me!"

"Facil, I thought you loved us." said Suzane. Kareen was crying, Sara had fear all over her face, Carey looked mad, Joy looked full of her American conviction and pride and defiance.

Facil blood cooled as his Saud royal blood overcame the Arab Bedouin inherited blood. "I'm sorry. I didn't mean to speak that way. I do love you, even you Joy, maybe you most, but I can see the writing on the wall. The Muslim forces are almost unopposed. They are winning. If I don't hurry up and become a part of it, they may get rid of me. If that were to happen, I would not want to be one of you, and my country will be taken over by religious zealots with crazy ideas. I have come to really believe in the laws and teachings of Mohammed. He would not have approved of the wholesale killing. By joining them, I assure my future, the future of my country as a calmer more reasonable country, I assure your lives, and, I may be able to save millions of innocent European lives."

"Do you really think that you will not be beaten?" said Joy defiantly.

"Please, Joy, let me speak. I will try to keep my temper because you are an American and I understand Americans."

"Do you really." Joy said it not as a question but as a cynical statement.

"Please, Joy. One more time, let me speak. Yes, I do understand Americans and I do not expect to ever conquer America. Americans would never submit to foreign rule and have not since your revolutionary war. You have become too soft and have reduced your military in a false security that the world would understand that America simply fears no one. But, the Arab leaders do not understand the inner confidence and strength of America. There is no way that the Arabs can cross the ocean and conquer America. Even if we managed to invade your country, we would have to fight every last man, woman, and child. Those that are pacifists now, that espouse an abhorrence to violence would suddenly become very violent. Revenge upon us would be the word of the day and you Americans would probably find a way to win."

"Thank you." said Joy.

Facil continued, "But Joy, their are few American forces in Europe and the Europeans have never understood the inner freedom of Americans.

Most of them will simply try to hide from the war. When Rome conquered so much of the world, the commoners acquiesced. When the Huns attacked Rome, the commoners submitted to foreign rule. When the Catholic church took power over kings, the people joined. When Napoleon moved through Germany, the great German people entertained the French when their Army was defeated. During two world wars, the French people surrendered when their Army was defeated. Now the British, maybe that is where the Americans got their attitude. But again, too many have lost that attitude that it takes to rule a world. At one time Great Britain extended from America to China, and they gave it up, bit by bit. Behind the scenes the rich of England own far more than the Japanese ever dreamed of having, our Arab ownership was nothing. But again, it is the old royal families that still control the vast holdings, not the people."

Joy, you are an American. Look at you. You are a meek little girl who has rented her life to me. A weak American."

Joy interrupted, "I'll show you weak you little twerp."

Facil's Arab blood showed in his eyes and Joy sat back down. "No Joy, you are acting the part. I am illustrating my point...or is it you that is illustrating the point. I am trying to say that you show your good American blood. Here you are, a total captive, in an Arab stronghold that a king cannot get out of. Your life is forfeit if I were to blink an eye. I, as a king of a wealthy country may not be able to defend you, and yet you are defiant. I was trying to say, when you got huffy, that you are weaker than many Americans. You are a woman. You are a woman that rented yourself to me rather than work at a normal career to get ahead in a society that allows you to get ahead. Most American women would have rebuked the offer I gave you, rather than make easy dollars. Yet here you are defying me and the position you are in as a result of your weakness. My point was that even a weak American, such as yourself, in a position of total slavery with no hope of escape, cannot be conquered. Surely, if my Arab brothers were to know you they too would know that America is not the country to consider messing with.

Maybe centuries from now, the American pioneer blood will have cooled, but it still runs hot. I let my Bedouin blood show a few minutes ago, before my calmer royal blood brought the diplomatic reason back.

Who are Americans? They are the rebels and adventurers of the world. They are criminals who rebelled against taxes and rules in England that were offered a suicidal chance at some freedom, by coming to America. They are religious rebels who wanted to break away from the large religions.

They are adventurers that would sell themselves into a temporary slavery to come to an unknown country where they might be able to become their own people. They are rich people, bored with the civilized European lives and the greedy that saw the opportunity to get in on the ground floor of an expanding economy of a new world. They are fortune hunters after gold or land. They are the people that came to a new world and with a very small number fought millions of American Indians that knew the land and had a majority. In our older societies, we have learned that you need a four to one advantage to win a battle. All the way back to earliest American times you Americans attacked Indians that grossly out numbered you relying on the technology of guns versus arrows and working together you won.

The American Indian should have learned your ways and then pushed you back into the ocean. They had two hundred years, no three centuries from 1492 to 1800 to learn about guns and gunpowder. They had the land and the majority of the resources under their control from 1492 to 1800. They could have learned to make their own gunpowder and steel to make guns,, but were too busy fighting among themselves. Just as Europeans have been kept weak for centuries of fighting each other.

The Europeans should have realized that they were the world minority in numbers, but with their technology that somehow came about, they had the power. The British might have, but messed up their monopoly on America, just as the Spanish had earlier. The Spanish tried to take the gold from America and killed Indians that welcomed them to try to find more gold. The Indians thought they were Gods and if the Spanish had been smart they would have ruled all the Americas.

The British had North America, India, China, and could have had unbreakable world power, except that they were selfish toward other Europeans. Napoleon was fighting Europeans from greed and unreasonable hatred and nationalism. Then England tried to draw cash from America to fight Napoleon instead of enlisting their aid. France and Germany provided forces to fight against the English or the English might have put down the revolution.

America almost blew it during your civil war, Americans against Americans with no one an innocent civilian. The revolutionary war where most were united, the war of 1812 where most were united. Even the civil war brought the futility of fighting each other, but taught everyone that war was everyone's war. Then the real Indian wars and the Spanish American war. In World War I and World War II, Americans banded together as a terrible force. You had little to fear, and yet you volunteered to work in aircraft factories and fight in foreign places.

Your only defeat was in Viet Nam where Americans knew they were in no danger from abroad, and yet got involved in a war. You expected the North Vietnamese to surrender the minute Americans showed they would get involved, but in that war, Vietnamese were willing to kill each other and Americans. Most Americans wanted to go in and kick butt, which you could have very easily, but America was in no danger and didn't push your own government to win over the poor little backwards people. You were too afraid of killing civilians. You had forgotten the lessons of a real war, because it was not you against them, it was simply a question of destroying them or pulling out.

In this war Americans will not be able to simply pull out and will know that they are fighting for their lives. Our attacks on the continental United States will have raised the ire of America. Americans will eventually unite and become a fearsome force. America did not expect attack on their own continent and yet in the World Wars became the most powerful force in he world, twice. This time we have shown them that America is in danger.

Our only hope for survival from American retribution is to take all of Europe before the United States can gear up again. There is no danger of us getting it done in time to conquer your country. Even if we did, Joy, you show what it would be like to try. Women in America would pick up guns beside the men. The children are brought up in war games. America is not a country to mess with.

"Then why are you going along with the other Arabs?"

"Because, Joy, all of you. I have talked about Europeans fighting among themselves. Even now, they are not fighting as a cohesive group. The Germans worry about Germany. They didn't immediately send troops or aircraft to help. Where are the British in Italy. The French are only helping Italy to keep us from France. Europeans were content to let us take Yugoslavia and Greece without a shot.

Switzerland and, sorry Suzane, Sweden profess to be neutral. In World War II, Switzerland was far from neutral. They banked the conquered riches of the world. They manufactured the German's dreaded 88mm cannons for their artillery and Panzer tanks. They build armored personnel carriers for Hitler. When the war was being lost, thousands of German rich moved to Switzerland and thousands more put the treasures of Europe in Swiss banks. Did you know that at the end of World War II, The United States embargoed Switzerland for six months until the American people, thinking the war was completely won insisted on bringing home the troops. The American blockade meant that no food or oil or anything went into or out of Switzerland. The American government wanted the Swiss to give back all the gold and art that the German's had captured and stored there. The Swiss could have cared less about the moral of the situation. They burned much of the forest area of Switzerland in the form of firewood to not freeze in the winter and were down to eating the dairy cows and goats that was to provide their milk. Another few months and the entire country might have either starved or given up their riches. As a result, now Switzerland is the banking capitol of the world and their riches have purchased businesses and land around the world. The financing of all this was the treasure of Europe, but the Swiss didn't care.

Sorry again Suzane, but Sweden did this too, but the King kept a lot of the valuables for his own."

"That's not true." said Suzane, "How would you know anyway?"

"I told you that I was a student of history. This is part of the history. The Arab countries are far from being without fault. At one time the Arab empire covered all of North Africa and most of Spain, not to mention Greece, Yugoslavia...why do you think Bosnia was a predominantly Muslim country on the far side of Yugoslavia from other Moslem countries. The Soviet Union's south half was part of the Arab empire. There are many Muslim mosques in Spain.

Then we got complacent. We started bickering among ourselves, just like the Europeans. We allowed the Europeans take Spain back. We allowed the Czars of Russia to take our northern countries. We didn't stick together. Our biggest failing was that we did not progress in our military science. With our power, we should have had cannons and guns before the Europeans. The Chinese already had gunpowder and our influence extended all across India to China. Why didn't we have cannons to conquer the rest of the world? Why did we fold from within? Why did Rome fall? Look at us. It has been centuries since we worked together instead of fighting each other. Why did the meek Lebanese people allow the civil war to go for years when all they wanted was peace?

The United States is classic. At the end of World War II, a few nuclear bombs would have brought world domination. Whereas Hitler spent months shelling Leningrad, the United States could have reduced Moscow to dust in seconds with no fear of retribution. The world could have been united under one government policed by Europeans and Americans. No,

France wanted independence from everyone. The United States wanted to just go home from a foreign war to their loved ones in America.

The cold war came to an end because the United States scared the pants off of the Russian government. They showed how their cruise missile could be programmed to hit anywhere with absolute pin point accuracy. Their stealth technology totally baffled the Russian made defenses in Iraq. Their Star Wars or Space Defense Initiative (SDI) technology was not put in place, but it was demonstrated to be well on the way to making nuclear missiles and bombers obsolete. It was easy to see how the United States were on the verge of controlling the ultimate high ground, space. If the United States could fly a cruise missile two thousand miles and hit a tank, how much harder to hit a tank from a satellite that was only two hundred miles away. But then the United States quit working. They put aside their military technology.

At the same time, we have been independently building up using our oil money to defend against each other. The west wanted to sell to get their oil money back and keep their military establishment going. Since the United States quit buying new stuff, it was expedient to sell it to the Arabs who were willing to buy anything. The west fomented wars between us to keep us down from uniting and to sell more arms. They didn't force us, we were anxious to fight each other. Saudi Arabia was a big buyer. We bought our own and financed equipment for other countries. We did not want war and couldn't be enticed. Saudi Arabia was working for a united Arabia, but not to fight war. We wanted to earn our place with factories and modernization. The Shah of Iran wanted that too, look where it got him.

We couldn't unite for peace, but we are now united for war. Europe is not united. Joy, right now the reports are that the United States is in a civil war, poor against rich. Red China provided millions of guns to America's black market in guns which resulted from gun control laws. The law abiding sold their guns out of guilt and the law breakers and fringes of your society were buying more and more on the black market. We Arabs, not my Saudi Arabians, but the Libyans and others, were secretly in the midst of America to cause confusion and fight against America. In America, many of us were treated worse than you treated your blacks and Chinese. We stock piled the Chinese guns for the day the war started and then passed them out for free to the looters that inevitably went to work in your corrupt society.

Jabal doesn't expect the United States to survive. He thinks we will be able to come in and take over and welcomed for the peace we bring, as in Yugoslavia. I don't believe that's true, Joy. I think he has awakened a hornets' nest."

"I will never break my word. I will take care of you to my dying day, but I will be sleeping alone until I find my wife and queen, who you know must be from Saudi Arabian royal blood. Good night."

V,85

Through the Swiss and neighboring lands there will be war above the clouds. The fighters will come from the sea escorting bombers and Geneva will make mistakes.

IX,44

Leave Geneva, everyone of you. Saturn will take your gold in exchange for iron. Zopyra (deceiver of Babylon) will exterminate all who oppose him. Before he comes there will signs in the sky.

II,83

When traffic on the Lyons is blocked and its trade in ruins and prey to soldiers, the Arabs will come from the mountains in a drizzle.

VI,81

One will hear and see the tears for the Arabs will have inhuman hearts who have attacked the Mediterranean islands and Genoa and now Lake Geneva. Switzerland will be in famine with no one to help.

VIII,62

When the holy temple is plundered (when Rome falls) they who hold the greatest power on the Rhone (in France) will profane sacred things. From them will come a deadly disease and a leader will not be condemned for retreating.

v,73

The church of god will be persecuted and the holy temple will be plundered. A child will turn against its provider, the Poles will be Arab allies.

MONTH 7, FEBRUARY 16

"Now that's scary." Said TSgt Gaddis. "Did you say that the Camel Jockeys used germ warfare to kill the defenders in Lucerne?"

"Yes." said his major. "I want all of you to remember to button up your tanks and get on filters at the first sign of attack or before initiating an attack yourselves. Sergeant, tell them your experience."

"We were fending off two vehicles making a run at the gate at Hahn Air Force Base in Germany, The first one exploded, wiping out the gate, and the second one exploded against us. I had pulled the hatch down, but had not secured it. I was holding it by hand. The explosion sucked open the hatch and deafened me. I managed to close the hatch and then I turned on the filters because there were automobiles exploding around us. When we got every thing under control and started looking around we discovered everyone on base was dead except for us and the officers in the command post. We found out later that it was nerve gas. Major, will those filters stop germs?"

"We think it will. We have tested it in the laboratory, but we don't know what the Arabs may be using. There may be some bacteria that are too fine to be stopped by the filter. I've been told we are testing a filter add on that will periodically spray the filter with an antiseptic to kill any germs that get on the filter, but can't get it out of testing since we don't know the long term effects of the antiseptic that you tank drivers will be breathing for long periods."

"YOU'RE SAYING THEY DON'T CARE ABOUT SHORT TERM DEATH IN A WAR IF THERE MIGHT BE SOME LONG TERM EFFECT?"

"That's about it." said the Major with a crooked smile cracking his face.

"I suggest that we get all of our tank drivers to sign a petition to get that thing over here now. We can agree not to sue the government about long term effects. I'd rather have something that will work now and keep me alive short term before I worry about long term effects. It won't do any good to protect me from something that might hurt my quality of live at seventy if I'm dead at thirty."

"You write it, I'll sign it." was the chorus from the assembled tankers.

The major said, "Okay. I'll get the JAG (military lawyers) to draft us up something if you guys want me to then you can sign or not sign as you see fit. Sound okay?"

MONTH 7, FEBRUARY 20

Today's holovision briefing was terrible. The Moslem forces had met a mass of forces in Lucerne Switzerland from the combined countries of Switzerland and France and were completely stymied. The German forces had moved through Austria and were at the Czechoslovakia border to defend Austria from the Arabs. The United States Air Force and the German Air Force had complete air superiority and were destroying Muslim forces in wholesale amounts. The Muslim forces had gotten too far to be in range of their own relatively short range aircraft sold to the Arab countries and the Arabs had no air to air refueling capability. Just as Facil was being to speak up, the Muslim forces opened up with man packed ground to air missiles and fighter bomber aircraft began falling out of the sky everywhere until the air attack was called off.

"Facil, is that better. We were pulling them in to destroy them. We have taken American stinger missiles and improved the guidance system to be a fire and forget missile. The man aims it until he gets a tone, squeezes the trigger and one second later it's on its way and cannot be deterred."

The Holovision screen changed to a view of Lucerne, Switzerland. The Arab tanks and infantry in the Rhone valley were pinned down under heavy fire from in and around the city. There were tanks in the back of the column burning and more in the front. Now it looked like the Arab forces were trapped. They fired back but their shells burst in the air over the city doing no apparent damage. The guns from town destroyed more Arab tanks. Again the view switched to show the Arab shells bursting over the town. Then it became apparent that the cannon fire from town was rapidly diminishing. Then it ceased and the Arabs started clearing away their ruined tanks to move on into the town.

After the lunch of dates and other Arabic foods served by beautiful Arab girls, the scene returned to Lucerne where the holovision showed the three dimensional bodies of tens of thousands of bodies of people that had died a horrible suffocating death.

Jabal explained, "I told you we had a few more things. This came out of the Iraq Milk Factory." He had a good laugh. Facil noticed that not all of the leaders thought it so nice. "Any time that we are faced with a concentration of troops, we can just wipe them out. Our men are immune from the disease. No European or animal will ever live in that city again."

Facil remembered Lucerne well and had many a meal there in the past along with many on the boats on the lake. It was one of the most beautiful spots in the world. If Jabal was telling the truth the city had been poisoned forever. He thought that most biological weapons were created to decay in a short period of time.

"Jabal, you said never. Don't these biological weapons have a decay life where it is safe for animals to return?"

"Facil, I am displeased with you. Why should that be of concern to us? Do you still ride camels in the desert? As long as you have the proper inoculation you can pass through with, pardon the pun, immunity." Jabal had just destroyed a very beautiful place and didn't care, which disturbed Facil, but he was already on Jabal's bad list. Facil was determined to find some way to get back in his good graces. He still had not slept with his harem. They ate together in silence now. He would keep his promise to try to keep them safe.

MONTH 7, FEBRUARY 20

"Here is your petition to get those germ killers added to the tank filters." said the Major. "You can sign or not sign. I'll pick it up tonight at 6 PM, that's 1800 hours for you military war mongers. I found the office to send the petition. I'll get it in tomorrow's mail."

Every tanker to the last man lined up and signed the petition. No one had to pressure anyone. TSgt Gaddis did not doubt that sometime after the war there would be people whose life was saved by the device that would probably sue the government for long term effects of the device that might and might not cause any effects.

Mail service had resumed to the U.S. now and there were a few people that had gotten through to relatives on HAM radio, but he had not heard anything from his home yet. He had written several letters, but had no response. He didn't know if they were alive, or had just moved as a result of the war. According to the military newspaper, many people had moved. Anyone living in a city that had been nuked had moved to get away from the radiation. Many people had simply moved away because their homes had been destroyed by looters. There had apparently been a mass exodus of people from both coasts moving to the center of the country where few people would ever consider becoming looters. Oklahoma had come through in great shape. There were some incidents, but apparently they had quickly adjusted and never really lost anything. The population had doubled and housing was a severe problem with over two million people living in tents, but there was plenty of food and apparently work.

Oklahoma was typical of several states in that area of the country. During the Arab oil embargo of 1973, the U.S. had only imported twenty-three percent of its oil. When this war started, over seventy-five percent was imported. A lot of it came from Venezuela, Canada, and Mexico, but with the war and submarines sinking ships it became critical for the U.S. to produce their own oil. The oil fields of Oklahoma and Texas were booming trying to make up for years of neglect. If TSgt Gaddis could, he would invest everything he had in the Anadarko Oil Region of Oklahoma. They had said for fifteen years that the one area had more oil than the Middle East, but never got the support for oil prices to make it worth while exploiting. Now there were over one million people just in Oklahoma working in the oil fields. Then when you add in the people building houses for these people, and the grocers, and the telephone men getting the system back up. It was no wonder the population in that area of the country had doubled. In addition, there were few cities with a nuclear radiation problem.

Very few factories had been damaged in the war and all were back in production now. There were few cars being produced, so transportation was a problem. Many factories were only producing war materials. There were reports that soon there would be one hundred M4 tanks a week coming off the assembly lines. These were supposed to be generations ahead of the old M1A1 tanks that he commanded. They had better armor, more speed, better guns, you name it. They were supposed to be the tankers' cats meow. He would believe it when he saw it. That production number alone would mean thirty-six thousand tanks per year. There were only about ten thousand M1A1's in the entire world under the control of the U.S. army. At that rate, the United States would have more tanks than the Arabs in less than two years if the Arabs didn't lose any. Of course the tanks were there and the war was here. He'd just like to see those germ killers added to the old tank's filter.

The Arabs were firmly entrenched in southern Switzerland now and TSgt Gaddis had little doubt that he would soon be in the shooting war. Because of the M1A1 tanks speed, his unit was one of several American units being held in reserve in case the Arabs made a break through somewhere. Winter was definitely a dumb time for a tank assault on Switzerland. He had this mental image of tanks driving under or plowing through the snow and falling off the mountain roads since they couldn't see where they were going. How was the infantry keeping up? Riding on sleds pulled by tanks somewhere under the snow?

MONTH 7, FEBRUARY 22

The major came into the briefing room. "The French have launched their own CBN (Chemical, Biological, (or) Nuclear) attack on Lucerne and chased out the Arabs. The Arabs weren't totally destroyed like the Swiss and French were before though. They did take major losses. We are expecting orders at any time."

17 THE U.S. FLEET

Month 8

By this time Jim had just about given up finding his family again and had settled in with his three women. MacDill kept paying all military and civil servants in their area, including those that had technically lost their jobs while on vacation when their bases were destroyed. There were only seventy-six in Florida. There were another two thousand that were eventually transported by air back to their homes and their duty stations.

Florida had been pretty well pacified. The ones guilty of looting were moved to the Miami area that had become somewhat of a large concentration camp. There were few ways to get across to the west coast of Florida and these were easily blocked. The military simply set up a defensive line north of Miami to keep them there. Food was brought in by the military, but there were too many looters imprisoned there to try them in court and the U.S. government had not made any decisions as to what to do with them. By this time it was assumed that anyone that shouldn't be imprisoned there was either dead or had escaped before the area was cordoned off. Homestead Air Force Base had become nothing more than a feeding area. It was fortified to keep it safe and food was flown in for distribution. There was discussion around MacDill of opening up civilian airports in Miami for food supplies. The looters would probably eventually be incarcerated more formally somewhere, but for now Miami worked just fine. In fact, looters from Georgia and the Carolinas were now being shipped in there. The temperature was such that heat was not required. Summer might not be comfortable without air conditioning, but the people could survive the heat. The water system had been restarted using emergency generators for the water pumps and sewage system. With water and food, the looters could survive. There were constant gang style wars between the various factions. There was a lot of discussion about letting the looters being located there with their guns to defend themselves from other ethnic groups that had guns. Others argued that they were getting their just deserts. They had killed innumerable unarmed or poorly armed civilians to loot their valuables and their women. At any rate, the military had not sent them in armed, but if they stayed near their entry point, the nearness of the military provided security and easier access to food. The military did not allow any actual gang wars within a mile of Homestead or any of the entry points. Any sustained gunfire brought in tanks and armored personnel carriers to restore the peace. In fact, there had been some times when an air strike was used to bring the peace. The sound of a jet plane generally stopped any war starting.

There were a number of cities that had become concentration camps for looters. There was not enough military to maintain peace within these areas. Los Angeles was one of these areas. The Los Angeles airport had become a military airport to fly in food. The hotels had become barracks for military to keep the peace within a few blocks of the airport. Again, the temperature had made Los Angeles a good area.

Most of the women had been allowed to leave because there was no such thing as law and order except as provided in different ethnic areas defending themselves against other ethnics. Most of the women were left wherever the looters had been captured, but that left tens of thousands of unattached women just in Florida. Nationally there were millions. It was a major struggle, but like the Mormons back in their early days, the men were being asked to take several wives based on their ability to provide for them. Like in World War II, women were doing work that was normally men's work, but like the Mormons there were incentives for these new extended families to have multiple children to repopulate the United States. Once a woman became clearly pregnant she was expected to refrain from sex, leaving the man more time with his other women to get them pregnant also. Like his wife, Eva could not have children either. Darcy and Shelby were both pregnant for lack of birth control.

Their house, Jim's sister in law's house actually, was only about three blocks from the beach and on a canal that eventually opened to the Gulf of Mexico. Shirley had left a boat in the boathouse that had an old points type distributor and carburetor making it perfectly serviceable. Jim preferred to take the boat much of the time to get out because walking to the main drag along the coast meant getting accosted by all the single women.

Jim had become used to constant sex with three women and now that it was only one, he missed it somewhat, but was afraid of AIDS. His three women had all been AIDS free and had the same concern. They had learned to share a single man even before the official push toward polygamy. Reports said that AIDS was running at forty percent of the population.

Among women under forty, the percentage was nearly fifty percent. Among the women that had been forced to be with the looters the percentage was nearly eighty percent. One hundred percent of the looters were assumed to have AIDS now. The percentage of non-looter men with AIDS was now up to sixty-five percent also, corresponding to the percentage of women under forty. That meant that in addition to the people killed in the war, in addition to the millions killed by looters, forty to fifty percent of the population was going to die of AIDS within the next ten years.

AIDS had been spread by the looters. All it took was for a few to share the same woman to spread it among the entire group of looters and their women. In addition, with the excess in women, many men took more than one partner, even if just on a one hour fling. Without knowing which ones had AIDS, it was spread through the non-looter population, though not as badly.

There was fear that even if the spread of AIDS could be stopped, the U.S. population could dip below forty million people before it could start growing again. As a result the men being drafted into the military were largely AIDS carriers, in an attempt to keep more healthy men in the U.S. to father children. There had been discussion to develop huge sperm banks to keep healthy women pregnant and producing children without men, but there was a revulsion by most people and a fear by men of a new set of Amazon women that lived without men like the rumors that had pervaded history for years. Jim's three girls had already warned Jim that he should stay away from any sperm banks that had started.

There was, of course, a danger that AIDS would not stop spreading and the human race might disappear.

There were reports in the newspaper that the Arabs and Chinese had a rapidly spreading AIDS problem as the result of the marauding. The captured women had been passed around among the men, spreading AIDS to many of their millions of military. Unlike the looters in the U.S., the invading armies had discovered the rapidly spreading AIDS and were making it a capital offense to take the women for themselves. Women were becoming an official spoil of war. The captured women under forty, of child bearing age, were tested for AIDS and tattooed on ear lobe if they had it. If they didn't, they were shipped back to the Arab countries and held in camps for breeding purposes. What this amounted to was stocking the harems of the wealthy powerful Arabs. The official rule was that the older women were to be bred first and then the younger ones. At menopause, the women were then to be given to the troops. Reportedly, they were actually housed in brothels for the profit of their Arab masters.

On the other front, there were not many women being captured by the Chinese and China could not see ever having a shortage of people. All they had to do was reduce the restrictions to having children. Three or four hundred million fewer Chinese was seen as a benefit. Chinese women, free of AIDS, were moved to the fronts and women were killed rather than captured in Southeast Asia and Russia. The Chinese did not take captives. They had already eradicated forty percent of the population in Southeast Asia and forty percent in India. The Vietnamese and Thais were proving difficult as they were fighting for their lives in difficult terrain. The Russians were difficult, because even with the mass defections to the Chinese and Arabs, the Russians are good and well equipped fighters, especially in defending their home country. Add that to the Siberian winters, and the Chinese were moving slowly.

During the next week there were a number of newspaper articles requesting that one hundred percent AIDS testing be administered in the U.S. and those with it to be branded with a tattoo. Annual or even semi-annual testing would reduce the spread of AIDS. Over the next month there were more articles calling for the mandatory AIDS testing which came to pass midway through April. Hospitals had a new AIDS testing that could be done with certainty in minutes. There could still be a latent AIDS, but those with any significant amount of the virus could be detected quickly. The hospitals in Florida had touched peroxide on the heads of people with AIDS and within days more and more people on the streets with AIDS had a light blond patch on their heads. Some people combated this by cutting their hair short enough to cut off the bleached hair. Others became blondes. Many just took mates with AIDS to keep it from spreading and they went around arm in arm with their own bleached spots that they renewed regularly to show their pride in living with it and letting people know that they were not going to spread it to the non-infected. There were more newspaper articles calling on all AIDS infected people to advertise their status out of patriotism.

With the AIDS infected people branding themselves with blond patches, many even took to tattooing an "AIDS" on their ear lobes. That made it handy for the ones with like tattoos to know that their partner would have no compunction against the possibility of AIDS and free sex was becoming the reality talked about in the early seventies, at least among the AIDS community.

One drawback was that the people with and without AIDS started segregating themselves. Their were restaurants for AIDS, housing areas for people with AIDS. People were selling their houses in some areas because of the number of AIDS tattoos around them. Their houses were bought by people with AIDS. Some people wondered about a coming civil war. Others said that was unlikely because the people with AIDS would die before it came to that. Another problem was beginning to surface with employers losing fifty percent of their workers to AIDS. Consequently, many were only hiring non-AIDS people. This led to long hair for both sexes getting popular. The people with AIDS were wearing it long to hide their tattoos. A sex partner would find it quickly, but an employer would not. Many without AIDS were wearing their hair long in sympathy. Jim had never worn his long at any point in his life.

MONTH 8, MARCH 18

The Muslim forces in the Rhone valley had been held up with mine fields, high altitude air attacks, and destroyed bridges and roads. The tanks could go only as fast as their fuel and ammunition could be carried on trucks. A large bomb in the pass from Italy to the Rhone valley had blocked the road for the supply trucks and the tanks had not gone far from Lucerne. As soon as they would almost get the pass open, another high flying airplane would drop more bombs destroying roads in the pass and bridges. As they were watching the party making in Lucerne by the Arabs, they began bleeding from the eyes and ears and screaming in pain.

King Hussein of Jordan stood and asked, "What is happening? Why are we seeing this?" The holovision died. Jabal was hurrying from the room through a security door. Minutes later, the council room was cleared and the rulers escorted to their suites.

Joy greeted him at the door, "It's only 1 PM what are you doing here? What is it? I know something has happened. Please Facil, we know nothing about this strange new world if you won't tell us."

He hadn't been talking with them much. He didn't know what to talk about now. "I'm sorry. I can understand, but I don't know what happened today. It appears to have been a set back. Maybe I'll find out tomorrow."

MONTH 8, MARCH 20

The major was giving another briefing, "The Arabs left behind some kind of biological trap with some form of very potent germ that kills every animal. Even the inland sea and the Rhone river are poisoned with it. The

Arabs are pulling back out of Switzerland. Apparently they have given up. We have new orders, "We are to load up on transports and will be transported back across the German border for another mission."

VI,79

Those of the Loire, Garonne, Saone, Seine, Tarn and Gironde will set up camp in the mountains near Ticino. When the attack comes the Po River valley will rise and flood.

I,90

Bordeaux, Poitiers (western France) will hear the warnings as the enemy fleet gets as far as Langon (on the River Garonne). They will use the North wind against the French, and a hideous monster will appear near Orgon (south-east France).

IX,31

The earth will tremble at Mortara (north-west Italy), Tin St George (Southern England was once known as Tin Island) will be half submerged when the temple (Westminster was built on the site of a "Temple of the Sun" destroyed in 154 AD) will rip open with cracks during Easter

III,70

Britain will be flooded with water when southern Italy is at war.

II,94

When the French prepares for battle in the Po valley, Britain will be in terror from the flooding and a quarter of a million will not escape it.

Great Britain was preparing to send troops to Italy to assist the beleaguered French and Italian troops at the Po River when a massive earthquake struck in both Northern Italy and in the south part of England. The British had not entered the war earlier because of the presumption that France and Italy could handle the Arabs. Now the earthquake had destroyed the fortifications built up by the French along the Po and the Arabs had succeeded in establishing a bridgehead on the west bank. It was too late to send British troops to that point in the battle.

In addition, the troops were needed to help the British population that was suffering a disaster of their own. London had received major earthquake damage including a total blockage of the Thames River running right through London. This, added to the torrential rains that had hit Great Britain over the winter and there was major flooding. Between the earthquake and the floods, over one quarter million Brits had died. The British military were engaged in massive rescue efforts of their own people unrelated to the war.

Again, the British aircraft and the American F-111 bombers, tankers and the American AWACS radar planes were all grounded. During the winter with the ice storms and hurricane winds, the aircraft were grounded. Now the runways were cracked and destroyed. The damage would have been less from deliberate runway bombing. There were ridges twenty feet tall sticking up. Many aircraft had been damaged on the parking ramps from the tarmac shifting and hangars falling. Even reinforced hangars designed to withstand a near miss by a nuclear bomb were torn asunder in the earthquakes.

MONTH 8 MARCH 21

They had been left alone for two days. Now another briefing, without the holovision. Jabal was briefing them without pictures. Gentlemen, we are having some problems and I would like your advice. Our troops at Lucerne were killed by some form of biological poison not of our making. Our tanks were sealed better than theirs were and seventy percent of our forces survived, but they were chased by French tanks apparently also sealed against our original biologics. We have come to a total standstill in Czechoslovakia at the Austrian border. The French pulled out from the Po River, but are now dug into the mountains along the northwest side of Italy and Monaco.

"Jabal, our troops are at risk in the Rhone valley. They can be easily trapped there and worn down. I am more widely traveled than many of you. I think that the Coasta Del Sol of northeastern Spain would be a good place to bring in our beach landers and move up into the soft underbelly of France. One problem with that is that we would have to get our troops through another narrow area between impassable hills and the coast. The best place is probably Bordeaux. The beaches are flat and the land is flat for many miles. There the landers could move across France much as you say they could across Texas and the middle flatlands of the United States. Our troops now are in mountains which is not where tanks can be of the best benefit.

Of course if we could land troops in Marseilles we would be in the flat lands of France very quickly. The port there is easily defended and would be an ideal spot to keep our troops re-supplied in France. You should only leave enough troops in Italy to defend what we have and use our transports to carry them to Marseilles, if we could capture it first."

"Thank you Facil, that has been the best advice you have given us. Now you are sounding like an Arab Prince. We will study your proposals to see if they have merit. If we decide to go with one of your proposals we will bring you in on the detailed planning. Gentlemen, that is what we need from all of you. Show your leadership."

"Jabal! He is no Moslem leader. He sleeps with an international harem. How can he be showing leadership for the Arab world when he has this kind of harem? Facil, aren't Arab girls good enough for you?"

"I no longer sleep with my harem. I am a devotee' of Mohammed. I have had a new beginning with Islam, but as a Moslem, I cannot break my word and I have promised to protect my harem from harm until they can be returned to their original homes."

"I am sure Jabal can find another place for them. Let's see you get rid of them."

"I have a contract that includes my personal protection. I will not become a liar and a cheat. I will provide them personal protection unless I can return them to safety."

Jabal entered in, "And what do you deem safety, Facil. We are conquering the world today. Would you suggest Marseilles? Or Paris?"

"I agree that we are conquering the world. I will discuss this with them tonight. Jabal, you know my loyalty to Saudi Arabia. I would die before abdicating my throne. Will you let me select a place anywhere in the world and then let me take them there? You may send an escort to make sure I return. I must keep them under my personal protection until they are returned to a place of their choice."

"Gentlemen? What do you say?" This caused a babble of unintelligible sound from around the table with some for it and some against it. "Okay, Facil, make your choice. I will fly them to the place of your choosing and then you will return immediately."

Facil was escorted back to his suite to study a hideaway for the girls where they might be safe. He would return for the good of his family and his country, but he needed to get the girls out of here for their safety before someone decided to kill them here. He had no more use for a harem.

"Girls, I have a world map here. Gather around the table, we are going to find you a safe haven outside of this prison."

Joy spoke out, "You've planned an escape!"

"No. I will return, but I have promised you your safety and Jabal is allowing you to go."

Suzane spoke next, "You don't really believe Jabal, do you? He will just take us out and have us killed, or worse."

"I will escort you there, personally."

Carey spoke up, "You will stay with us then. We will get word to the French government and they will destroy this place."

"No. I will be coming back. This place is impregnable except maybe on the ground and cannot be attacked unless Teheran falls into allied hands at the end of the war. It is totally bomb proof and well stocked for the war with its own underground water supply. This is a complete underground city. No, it will do you no good. Jabal has no fear in releasing all of us. If I run, my family and country is forfeit."

Joy said, "Then obviously, the United States is the place to go."

"No. Remember, according to our reports they are in a state of total chaos if not outright civil war."

"Then make it Malaysia."

"I wouldn't even want to take you there with the Red Chinese invading."

"I suppose France is out?" Everyone gave Carey a look that said, NO.

"South Africa?" said Joy.

"Possibly. The Moslem forces are not moving on them. They have aims on Europe. The Chinese are after Asia including Siberia and India. They have a modern country with wealth. They import a lot, and can't get imports now, but I would presume that it might be safe for awhile."

Suzane said, "I think Sweden is the best place. The war is taking place in southern Europe and Asia. The United States may be in a civil war and there may be no safe places. South Africa is surrounded by black countries wanting to wipe them off the continent. A few arms delivered by your Arab friends and they would be more than happy to inundate them."

Sara said, "Bermuda is an island and away from any war."

Joy said, "Or Jamaica?"

Sara said, "Australia?"

"Okay, let's list them out and then make a list of pros and cons." said Joy.

"Australia is on the list of countries that Red China wants." said Facil, "and remember they have nuclear weapons to take what they want."

"Bermuda lives mainly on import and export. With who?" said Suzane.

"The same for Jamaica." said Joy.

"Or any island, even Hawaii or Tahiti." said Suzane.

"How about Canada?" said Joy.

"Canada might be a good choice." said Facil.

"Hey, don't forget Sweden." said Suzane.

"Sweden would be okay for awhile at least, but I'm afraid we could not fly an airplane there with the war going on in Europe. We could try." said

Facil. "I suggest that you girls discuss it and make a decision. All of you have to go the same place. I want your decision in the morning. Wake me at 6 A.M. and I will approve if I see no reason not to.

MONTH 8, MARCH 28

Rio in Brazil was the choice. Facil informed Jabal and Jabal arranged for an airplane and a guard to make sure Facil returned. They would fly to Morocco and from there to Brazil. It was a long flight, but they were all glad to be out of captivity. They landed in Egypt and saw the Pyramids, then miles and miles of more desert until they landed in Morocco. Then miles and miles of ocean. Finally after many hours they sighted land and flew in around the famous mountain view of Rio. The girls were let off the airplane and Facil and his escort went to a bank where Facil withdrew money and gave each girl a half million dollars in local currency and each a handful of jewels worth at least that much more.

Joy exclaimed, "Facil, I think this is more than our bargain called for."

"Joy, girls, when we made our bargain, it was with the presumption that I would return you to your countries of origin the same as you left. My Arab brothers changed the bargain, so I owe you more, and I hope that you will have a good life. Remember, I have never seen any of you before and regardless of how this war comes out, I will not acknowledge knowing you."

Joy said, "Thank you, Facil. I knew you were a good person. I will be going back to the United States you know."

"Please, not yet. Stay here awhile and help get everyone settled. Make sure you know what you are going back to before you go. I love you all, but this is good-bye. You know I will do my best to reduce the killing and yet everything I have to in order to preserve my kingdom."

The plane they were flying was a large private jet with a complete bedroom. Facil had slept coming over and was now sleeping on the return. This time he was not blind folded going to and into the shelter. It started under the sports arena about a mile from the old American embassy that was seized by Komini's people. It went down fifty feet then moved sideways like a subway car then down maybe thirty floors or maybe 300 feet, then sideways another fifty feet. Each change of direction brought the opening and closing of huge blast doors.

"Welcome back Facil, I didn't know whether you would be coming back."

"The only time it crossed my mind was when your so called guards let me go into a bank to withdraw money for the girls to live on."

"They did?"

"Yes, and the girls came with me."

"And you still came back?"

"Yes. I am an Arab. Saudi Arabia is my country. I was not kidding when I said, that I am ready to act like a king. I am ready to marry to start having sons to inherit my place when I am gone. My place is here. You have committed my country to the war and now I must see it through to assure the survival of my country. But now I wish to go to my suite and clean up and get some fresh food."

"Of course, Facil. You now have free rein of the place. You may go where you wish and when you please. But since you are now single, your time would be appreciated in our real planning. I have studied your recommendations and decided that you were right. Mountain passes are no place for our tanks. Anyway, go rest up. Tomorrow's briefing will show our progress.

The holovision showed a chemical attack on Lucerne, Switzerland by the Arab forces which caused an immediate pull out by the allied forces followed by an advance of Moslem tanks, followed by a biological attack by the French forces. The Moslems retreated, leaving behind biological booby traps.

Jabal explained, "We decided that we could not advance through the Rhone valley and Lucerne, so we left behind a potent new biological weapon that even we do not have a cure for or an inoculation against. No one will ever return to Lucerne and live. Even the lake and river is poisoned. We are pulling our forces out of the Rhone valley with over seventy percent losses. It is a big defeat."

Several leaders spoke out, but finally they deferred to one leader to let him speak a consensus of the group. "Jabal, you have gone too far. We want no more poisoning of rivers. We have always been thirsty for water in our desert and here you have poisoned an entire river. What might be the impacts down stream? Water is more precious than oil. We want no more poisoning of the waters of the world."

Jabal was silent during a round of angry applause from around the table. Finally he raised his hands for silence, "You are right gentlemen, I will not poison the water again. It would do no good to inherit a lifeless river or a lifeless world. I am sorry."

Facil spoke out now, "Jabal, gentlemen. We have enough forces to conquer the world without resorting to mass destruction. I suggest that we disperse our forces to discourage the allies use of biologicals and that we refrain from using them ourselves or there will not be a world to conquer. We can do it with our conventional forces. Everyone loses when mass destruction is used."

"Facil is right. From now on we will grind it out. If our attacks are repulsed in one area we will attack in another. I spoke with Facil upon his return and will value his advice on how we can do this. You heard his ideas last week, now we will make the detailed plans."

TSgt Gaddis's tank unit had just unloaded in Germany and they were settling into their more permanent quarters when a hasty recall was made for all members of his unit to report to the post theater. He and his crew immediately hoofed it (walked) over there and took a seat. The major waited until all were seated.

"I have a videotape for you to watch that was taken from a mountain in Switzerland looking down on Lucerne. It is pretty hazy due to the distance, but it has been computer enhanced and edited to give you a picture of what's going on. By the way, this is a new technology that has been provided to us that will continue to be provided in the future. Every major battle will have one of these taken, enhanced, and edited to put each battle in perspective. There are orders that all military members that might be in a similar battle will be show these tapes on a regular basis from this point on. We'll discuss the tape when it's over. Enjoy."

The tape started as a very distant hazy view of some small city near a lake in the mountains. It zoomed in until you could plainly see the buildings in a gray fog of telephoto zooming in. Then the picture cleared and continued zooming in until you could see tanks in the town firing at something in the distance. The quality was good enough to see the French and Swiss markings on the tank. You could not make out faces of tank commanders watching the impacts of their shells The angle changed to where you could see where the shells were hitting and then zoomed in over a distance of several miles to where you could see the targets were Arab tanks.

The picture angle changed again and zoomed out to where you could plainly see roughly half of Lucerne, Switzerland. It looked almost like an actual photograph on a sunny day except that the yellow sun light could not be seen. The day was overcast. Then you could see puffs of smoke above that section of the city. The picture suddenly showed the same French and Swiss tanks that were firing at the Arabs before. The tank commanders that had their heads sticking out suddenly looked very stiff, then slumped down into their now silent tanks. Some tanks continued firing. Then the tanks started turning around to retreat through the town. Many of them crashed into buildings and sat there motionless. Others crashed through a wall of a building and kept on going. One tank was singled out and followed as it crashed through several walls and then came to a stop at an extreme climbing angle with its treads slipping, unable to get traction. A percentage of the tanks made successful turn arounds and could be seen rapidly driving through the streets of the town. The narrator was saying, "This is an example of a chemical attack. Those exposed died instantly. We believe it was a form of nerve gas. You can see that some tanks were buttoned up, but their crews just died slower. You can also see that some tanks successfully retreated. The difference was when their filters were last serviced. It is essential that every tank filter in a combat zone be changed every ninety days. All of the tanks that had filters over one hundred and eighty days old were lost. There were some with less time on their filters, but this has been traced to poor rubber seals on hatches and viewports. These should be inspected every ninety days and replaced if they do not look as new. Before going into battle every hatch seal and periscope should be greased with number six silicone grease. If the grease is not wet to the touch, it should be re-greased. The combination of these two items should be one hundred percent effective."

The video showed these maintenance actions in detail then switched back to Lucerne again. It showed Arab tanks moving into the town again. As soon as all of the tanks became bunched together on the entry into the town, more puffs of smoke appeared. This time it was the Arab tanks that died. The narrator commented. "This was a French biological attack. The disease used should have been stopped by any decent filter, but obviously infiltrated the Arab tanks. Due to a slight breeze that came up, the majority of the Arab tanks were not infected and managed to retreat back towards Italy. In fact the Arab tanks never stopped until on the Italian side of the ALPS. from this we anticipate that the Arab tanks have not had filter changes during the life of their tanks, or at least since the war started. Unfortunately, Lucerne is too deadly for us to inspect their tanks, but we suspect some crews may have removed their filters entirely. It is common for them to buy the best and then not maintain it. When they get plugged with dust, some crews remove the filter rather than replace it.

The French and Swiss troops came back into the town wearing biological equipment to try to rescue some of the Swiss citizens known to have been trapped in bomb shelters since the initial Arab attack. The shelters worked, but many Swiss starved. When some of the shelters were opened by rescuers, the occupants died within minutes. After more study it was discovered that timed devises had been planted that opened canisters of some very toxic biological mess that kills everything. Even the large lake or as some call it, the inland sea, at Lucerne was poisoned with this germ agent before the Arabs left. It has apparently killed every fish in the lake and is currently killing fish downstream in the Rhone river. Switzerland is safe and Lucerne is a dead city for the foreseeable future.

vii,10

A foul smell will come out of Lausanne in western Switzerland. none will know which side will have launched it. They will cause the armies from afar to withdraw. Fire will be seen in the sky, the foreign people will be defeated. He launched it.

MONTH 10, MAY 15

Jabal announced, "We have withdrawn fifty percent of our forces from Italy and have transferred them to ports and ships for an end around attack. We will leap frog the French forces. Facil wanted our landers on the east coast of France, but we could not get past the American carrier forces in the Atlantic so we are going with our alternative."

MONTH 10 AND MONTH 11

Red China had moved down to take Indonesia, Borneo, and getting ready to invade Australia. TSgt Gaddis and his tanker company watched the latest video tape taken by Australians that had been provided the proper new video equipment and then hidden out on the various islands as they had during World War II. The tape showed that the Red Chinese simply overwhelmed all opposition with numbers. The screen went blank except for a waving Australian flag and the Australian narrator continued, "We see here that the Red Chinese are conquering in our part of the world like the Arabs are in Europe. We have reports that the Red Chinese have taken about thirty percent of Siberia, or the eastern part. There have been nuclear battles between Red China and the Soviet Union and between Red China and North Korea. Some of our northern observation posts were abandoned because of high background radioactivity as the result of fallout. The background count at the equator in our half of the world is registering four times the normal background radiation. It is not unsafe yet, but shows an alarming trend if nuclear attacks were to continue."

I,73

Because of France's negligence they will be attacked in five different areas. Tunis and Algeria will join the Arab alliance. Leon, Seville, and Barcelona will fall because there will be no Allied fleet to help.

X,88

A horse's hoof heard at the second watch, the enemy will force an entry by sea, devastating all. He will enter the port at Marseilles.

VII,40

Within the containers with smooth surfaces 21 will be closed up outside the port. At the second watch, they will be killed in their performance, They will secure an opening and then be felled by enemies.

I,72

There will be a complete change of people in Marseilles, the others will flee as far as Lyons. Marbonne, Toulouse (southwestern France) will be threatened by the enemy at Bordeaux. They will kill and capture a million men.

VIII,6

A bright fire will be apparent in Lyons France. Malta will be taken by this shining weapon then extinguished. Deceit was used in Sardinia. The Swiss will exile themselves to London which the French will see as treason.

v,35

The English fleet will land on the bay of Biscay, Bordeaux, with its rocky coastline in drizzly weather and establish a beach-head. The Arab leader will declare war on Great Britain.

MONTH 11, JUNE 4

General Gates issued the order, "Gentlemen, the Arabs have made an end around run on the French by landing in and taking Marseilles. They are now trying to cut off the retreat of the French military from the Riviera. We are going to pull most of our tanks out of Germany and England and land them in southeast France to retake Marseilles to cut off their supplies and prevent them from landing more troops and tanks. I am ordering all available landing craft to take on tanks in Bremerhaven and Liverpool and move to Bordeaux. This operation is Top Secret, especially the location of the landing. I do not want that information to leave this room until our ships are assembled for the landing. I want every anti-sub airplane in the air to protect the landing ships. I want every submarine under our command in the English Channel to protect our forces. We will have to suspend our escort of ships across the Atlantic in the meantime. We will resume it after our forces are safely landed. Now I want everyone to get busy planning the details and writing the orders."

Hank did not interrupt General Gates, but tried to catch him before he left the room. Brigadier General Henry Lakeman was glad that Jim Claris hadn't been found yet. He would have lit into the general and probably gotten fired over it.. You told me this would happen. I disagree with the General. It's a suicide attack. Maybe you can't stop it all the time. At any rate, you're not going to stop General Gates and he outranks me by two starts so I can't stop him either.

When Hank got the general alone he said, "It would be better if we stood back and took out their tanks at long range and then retreated as soon as they turn toward our tanks and make sure that we have a good line of retreat and full tanks of fuel. We simply can't afford to lose any tanks."

The general ended the conversation with, "Colonel, there you go quoting that Jim Claris again. You and I both know he doesn't exist, so let me lead. Now go and get people moving."

MONTH 11, JUNE 10

Henry Lakeman had given up finding Jim and wondering just how long he could keep Jim's family on base when he got an idea. If Jim were still alive, he may still be getting his pay somewhere. An inquiry into the pay center that had finally gotten back into computerized operations found that he was being paid out of MacDill Air Force Base in Tampa. A satellite call there confirmed it. He asked that they send a vehicle for him and bring him to the telephone.

"Jim Claris? The Jim Claris from Wright-Patterson AFB? Do I have some news for you. I am here at the ANMCC and I have your family here. You tried to warn me about the coming war and I put you off. I have been looking for you since I got here. We need you here to fight a war. How quick can you be ready to travel?"

Jim was flabbergasted to hear that his family was still alive. His mind was going through all the ramifications of his wife finding out about his sexual activities of the past months. He would soon be the father of children from two different women that he had been living with and was also living and sleeping with what used to be a neighbor's wife. What would she think? "Hank, would you keep my existence a secret until I call you back? I am living with three girls and Carolyn would never understand. Two are pregnant. What would she say?"

"I think we had the news here. I'm not sure how to ask this. Do you know if you have AIDS?"

"No I don't. I have been with two of the girls since the day the war started and neither was promiscuous before the war. The other was a neighbor's wife that had been hiding out alone in the ruins of our old neighborhood for months before I found her. They have been, would you say monogamous? At any rate I have been their only man."

"That's a relief. I propose I tell your wife. I'm sure she will understand, given the situation. My wife and yours have become good friends. I got her out of Dayton by helicopter not too long after the war started. There are more women than men even here. She will understand, believe me. I'll bet in a few more months you wouldn't have a choice in the matter. I'll give you a couple of days, but if you don't call, I'll send the troops for you anyway. I am kidding, but I do need you here. If you want to hide there, I'll let you, but consider that you're being called back to your job to earn the salary you've been earning. Also consider that I don't know how much longer I will be able to keep your wife here when you're not. I'm surprised that I have been able to this long. I'll be talking with you. You and I both know your decision. You would come even without your family. You would also come because you owe me for your family safety."

When Jim was delivered back to the house, all three girls were waiting to find out what had happened. Jim waited until they were all comfortable and after a few moments of silence, he started, "We're moving to Pennsylvania." After ignoring the questions and complaints he went on, "I am being called to work at the ANMCC. You know what it is. You also have heard me tell you that is where the military commands all its forces. It is also, because of the war, the main seat of government. Well, it is time for me to start earning the money they have already paid me and the money I will make in the future. It has been nice here in this peaceful surrounding after what we have all been through, but it will be nice there too, if a little colder. When the war is over, we can come back here on vacations. No Pennsylvania is not where I would choose to live if given the choice. There is one other thing...my wife and kids are there."

That news hit like a lead brick on a picture window except there was silence. There was a stricken look. Eva broke the silence with, "That's great, Jim. Now we know where they disappeared to. Can we stay here in the house?"

"I thought maybe you might like to come with me."

"What about Carolyn? I can't see her agreeing to all of us living in her house."

Darcy broke in, "I'll come with you. How would we survive here without you? Even if we had the money, we might be forced to find some other man to have children with. I'd rather get AIDS so I wouldn't have to."

Jim jumped in now, "That's not logical, Darcy. You are going to have a child to worry about soon. Abortion is not only illegal for those without AIDS, but there aren't many doctors would do it anyway because everyone knows how important it is to have children. You'll have to come with me so I can support you and maybe be a legal husband, depending on the law. Hank, the guy that rescued my wife and wants me there, thinks that she will understand. I can't pretend that I don't love my wife the most, but I do love you three too. We've been through too much together for too long for me to just forget you and leave you here for whatever happens to you. You have to come with me."

"That's a relief." said Shelby. "Eva, you have to come with us too. Since you can't have children, you wouldn't last long here by yourself. Besides, you were already friends with Carolyn and you being there would make it easier for all of us."

"Maybe make it worse too you know. Because I knew her from before the war she might feel even more like it was infidelity."

"We'll just have to take that chance, Eva. It's all settled. Pack your bags. We'll be leaving in a day or two."

MONTH 11, JUNE 14

The defensive line was holding and the Moslem attacks had been reduced to artillery barrages back and forth in the lightly populated rocky coast of northwestern Italy. The forward headquarters were in Monaco with the main lines forty miles further east into Italy. There were no buildings standing for thirty miles on either side of the line. It appeared the war was stalemated in Italy.

The battle of Switzerland was at another type of stalemate. The French still had a significant force in Geneva, Switzerland along with remnants of the Swiss forces. The city was devoid of civilians except for thousands of doctors and nurses treating the one hundred thousand soldiers that had been sickened, but not killed by the biological and chemical warfare in the Rhone valley around Lucerne. All water was trucked in since the Rhone river was poisoned. Fortunately, Europeans were never big on drinking water or bathing or more would have died before the word was spread to stay away from the river. The hundreds of thousands of dead fish were a testimony to the poison of the river.

The front in Czechoslovakia had gradually moved halfway through Austria along the Danube river. The American Air Force had maintained air superiority over the area despite hundreds of Moslem air craft flying out of old Russian air bases. The Moslem forces there had also expanded to the east moving over the south half of Poland in an attempt to force the allies in Germany to move forces from Austria.

In Spain, most of the lowlands were controlled by the Arabs, but the Spanish forces were holding the mountains. The American Air Force had moved to Germany, but the U.S. Navy Mediterranean fleet in the Atlantic provided the air support necessary to hold off the Arabs. In the meantime, the Arab Air Force had to fly from Morocco and without refueling had no fuel for dog fighting. However, the U.S. Navy had ceased to bomb the Arab army leading the Arabs to believe that they were out of bombs and must be running low on air to air missiles and ammunition for their gatling guns.

It was two o'clock in the morning on a warm moonless night. The port at Marseilles was very quiet. With the demise of the French navy and with the total control of the Mediterranean being in the hands of the Arabs, there was no shipping. The port city was a lively place with French troops rotating from the defensive line near Monaco to party here. There was a midnight curfew so it was very quiet in the harbor. The harbor had submarine gates closed to keep submarines out since the Arabs were known to have a substantial fleet of submarines.

The Arab submarines controlled the Mediterranean and were roaming in the Atlantic ocean to keep ships from leaving the United States or Great Britain. They completely controlled the North Sea and the inland waterways all the way to Leningrad, or St Petersburg, or whatever you wished to call it. They had also been trying to get at the U.S. Navy aircraft carriers, but had not had any success. They had lost twenty-two submarines in sinking three destroyers, two supply freighters, and one AEGIS cruiser. On the American coast, they had sunk fifty ships with the loss of only two submarines. Eight U.S. nuclear missile submarines had been hunted and sunk by the quieter and cheaper diesel submarines, eighteen of their own submarines had not been heard from for a month and were presumed lost. With forty-two of their submarines gone the Arabs decided to let the fleet go until they could get an airport within range so they could launch one of their hundreds of anti-ship missiles.

The guards around the port of Marseilles were dutifully walking their posts all around the port. The radar at the entrance was searching for anything moving on the water as anything had to be assumed to be Arabic. There were regular patrols of AWACS airplanes flying over the Mediterranean keeping track of all surface ships and aircraft flights. There was nothing unusual.

"Hey what's that sound?" The submarine nets were ripped from their moorings and a huge dark shape began surfacing as it came into the port. A patrol boat tried to intercept it, but was crushed by the huge shape.

The guards turned on all the flood lights around the port. Something huge, like an American aircraft carrier, was rising up out of the water. Suddenly it started spitting fire from all sides quickly killing the guards and the lights. The dark shape came to the nearest large dock and began disgorging main battle tanks and infantry. Then another dark shape and another.

The town was awake and sirens were going off everywhere, but no one knew where the threat was. Men raced to their vehicles and tanks to repel, what? Then there was the unmistakable sound of hundreds of tanks rolling through the streets from the port.

When the Arabic tanks started meeting resistance they opened fire, but they were not destroying the town, only snuffing out resistance as it was met. The allies lost fifty tanks and two hundred personnel carriers and over five thousand troops before they retreated from the town letting the Arabs have it, figuring that they could get it back after getting reinforcements. But as seen by the AWACS aircraft, the seemingly random passing of oil tankers and other ships all altered their courses toward Marseilles. By eight o'clock there were a hundred ships either there or converging on the port. The tanks were unloaded first and by that time there were over a thousand tanks guarding the approaches to the town. Civilians were given the opportunity to evacuate or, if they refused, they were gunned down.

MONTH 11, JUNE 17

The videotape at today's briefing showed a brief exchange of artillery between the French and Italian armies just east of Nice, France. The narrator said, "This sequence shows that the Arab invasion of Europe almost stalemated with the French holding a line along the Riviera and with the Arab attack into Switzerland stopped, the Arab invasion appears to be stopped. The Rhone river valley of Switzerland has been declared a dead zone. No one is allowed to enter due to biological poisoning. If one did enter, he would be dead within four hours. With proper equipment it is possible to traverse the area, but several additional booby trap biological mines have been set off making matters worse. All Swiss civilians that took shelter in bomb shelters in the valley are now presumed dead of the germs or starvation. The Rhone river water all the way to the sea is considered to be poison, but it has not spread to the land around it. It is not recommended for bathing even after boiling and treatment as long as the lake at Lucerne remains poisoned.

The view changed to a beautiful picture of the Danube river flowing past a convent perched on a high hill over the valley. It looked very peaceful and quiet until Arab tanks roared around a corner of the road along the north bank of the river. Then American A-10 aircraft came swooping down firing their 30mm (millimeter) gatling guns destroying the tank column. Then infantry took up positions along the ruined tank column and fired shoulder fired missiles at the A-10's who dodged down behind the hills and fired flares to escape the missiles. The videotape continued showing the first of what would be lengthy efforts to clear the wrecked and burning Arabs tanks from the road.

The videotape then blinked and started in the middle of an active shooting war. There were explosions and smoke everywhere. The video zoomed in on a dark harbor somewhere, lit only by cannons firing and flares the sky. There were huge dark shapes like oil tankers spitting fire from multiple points around its bow and, as the tape zoomed in more, disgorging tanks and troops onto the docks. The tanks were coming out firing and the troops running for cover in the town. The narrator said, "This is our first look at a new weapon the Arabs and Japanese have produced. We think it is Japanese technology, but both the Arabs and Japanese are producing these. It is an oil tanker type of ship, but rounded on top and made water tight and stronger to act as a submarine. It came into the port of Marseilles, France two nights ago ripping right through the submarine nets and quickly taking the port area. Within twenty hours the Arabs had the entire town under their control. It was not spotted on radar because it was underwater. Its sheer size and weight allowed it to rip right through the anti-submarine nets. As soon as they took the port other tanker size ships carrying more tanks and men started converging on the port and unloading. The Arabs have out-flanked the French military who are now caught along the rugged French Riviera caught between their forces in Italy and Marseilles. We have found our tanks are no match for these submersible landing craft. Their armor is too thick and they have too much firepower."

The tape ended and the major spoke, "Gentlemen. We have orders to get back on our transports again and report to the port at Bremerhaven, Germany in two days. No one is allowed to leave the post. There will be no telephone calls or mail on or off the base starting one hour ago until sometime after we have gotten to what ever our destination is."

MONTH 11, JUNE 23

TSgt Gaddis's tank company was loaded onto LST's (standard marine landing craft) along with several other tank companies on other ships a good number of infantry and munitions and other supplies for every thing and every one.

Once they were loaded and out of the port, all ships received a mission briefing that included detailed maps, terrain maps, intelligence photos, and all the information for an invasion of France. They were to be taken by ship around to the southwestern coast of France. The U.S. Naval Mediterranean fleet with it's augmented three air groups were to provide air cover to keep all aircraft out of the area. The French and British air forces were to also be involved in providing total air cover to the operation. No one even wanted a civilian aircraft to over fly the operation until the tanks and infantry were on the ground in France.

The situation had turned critical with the Arab beachhead at Marseilles, France. The French forces that had been holding the Po river valley and the French border were suddenly outflanked and cut off from major north south roads into the heart of France. At the same time these vital roads converged on Marseilles, that was controlled by the Arabs. The French along the French Riviera were sandwiched between mountains to the north, Arabs in the Po valley to the east and Arabs behind them at the west end of the Riviera. The French forces would have to fight their way through Arabs into the heart of France while being pursued from behind by more Arabs. The French had committed too much of their force to the Riviera and could not defend their heartland, unless given some time to fight out of the trap.

The American forces were to land at Bordeaux, France. With surprise and stealth, they should be able to unload at the docks instead of a beach landing and a drive through bogs and wetlands along the coast of southwest France. By driving straight east they could cut off any Arab northern advance. By staying just east of the main route to Paris, the Arabs would have to come to them. To ignore the American force and drive north would be an invitation to having their supply lines cut. By pulling Arab forces west they pulled forces away from the battle to the east with the French. The intent was to get the French forces out of the trap.

The U.S. Navy admirals were saying that this would result in a pinchers movement with the Americans on one side and the French on the other that would destroy the Arab invasion at Marseilles. They said that without naval transport the Arabs could not build up their beachhead sufficiently to fight on two fronts. The U.S. Army generals were mixed on the subject, but the command for this invasion had no illusions. The converted oil tankers gave the Arabs as much or more transport capability than what was owned by the U.S. Navy. This would be a close fight.

18 AUSTRALIA'S DEFENSE

MONTH 12
July 1

The French forces in Italy were already moving toward France abandoning their defensive positions along the Po. The Arabic forces there quickly took the Po valley behind them completing their conquest of Italy.

The French spread their forces between Nice and Toulon with much of their Air Force retreating further north into France to better attack the Arab forces when they tried to break out of Marseilles and to get out of range of the Arab aircraft in Italy. Unfortunately, this also left their armor and infantry without air cover. The Muslim Air Force immediately took advantage of this by bombing the allied forces incessantly day and night like hornets attacking an intruder. Nice and Toulon were being bombed like Rome was bombed.

Facil broke into the holovision broadcast, standing, and calling for the lights. "Cut the broadcast! Turn on the lights. I must have the floor, NOW!"

Jabal was taken aback by Facil's sudden demand to be heard, but did as ordered, "You heard him, cut the broadcast and turn on the lights. Facil, you have the floor. Give us your wisdom." The holovision died immediately and the lights came up to full brightness.

"Jabal, Gentlemen, we are doing it again."

"Doing what Facil?"

"We have misdirected our forces."

"How? We have secured a good port in southern France with an Autoroute to Paris and the rest of the heartland of France. We have broken out of the Po valley and are moving along the coast. We have pulled out of Switzerland except for defensive forces. Aren't we performing to your satisfaction yet." said Jabal sarcastically.

"Yes and Yes, but why are we bombing cities and civilians again when the French forces are primarily lined up along the roads in between?"

"Facil, Facil, what's the point in sending in an airplane against a tank when we can destroy another famous French city?"

"Because Jabal, the whole point of this is supposed to be to conquer Europe, not destroy it. Why kill women and children when their Army is roaming free to destroy our forces and prevent us from moving?"

"We are moving, we have broken free of the Po valley."

"Like Hell you have. The French forces have only retreated to France and are creating another block to our forces from moving in. You have to re-direct our air forces onto the enemy. Why destroy cities that our people could move to? Why are we taking Europe? To destroy it or to rule it? If we are going to rule it, then we need to move people there permanently. If we are the rulers then we will need servants. Remember, you can't kill all the people, only the armies."

"I capitulate. You are correct again. We will redirect our forces to killing tanks and soldiers. It will take until tomorrow to re-plan our missions. Facil, will you help?"

"Yes, I will plan your air sorties. I am a trained Air Force commander. I now have a chance to apply my training to making our Air Force efficient. I hope there are enough air munitions to do the job."

"May we continue the holovision broadcast, while you are in the air room doing your planning?"

"Yes, but please inform them that I am in charge of the air forces now."

"Yes, Yes, of course. Gentlemen, men of the royal guard, Facil is the new general of our Air Force. He has total authority over our air forces as long as he will support our ground forces."

"Thank you, Jabal." Facil left for the air planning room to start what would be an all night job of planning tomorrow's air sorties.

C25-Pacific

I,55

In the place at Antipodes to the Middle East (South Pacific), there will be a great outpouring of blood. Evil forces will come by land and sea, by air in the and they will cause confusion, famine, disease among nations.

IX,97

The forces fighting at sea will be divided among three nations. the second of these will run out of supplies. Surrounded by the third and trying to reach the Ian fields (America). But the first will find an opening in the encirclement and together they will win a victory.

VII,59

Twice raised up, twice lowered, the Orient will enfeeble the west. Its adversary after several battles, they will be defeated at sea and ultimately fail.

The Red Chinese had an invasion force of one hundred converted oil tankers, each one transporting fifty thousand equipped troops. An invasion force of five million equipped troops plus three of the submarine monsters used by the Arabs and five hundred tanks should be more than enough to destroy Australia. This giant Armada was now shown live as it approached one hundred miles from the Australian continent. It would be only hours before the invasion.

Missiles started firing from the fifty fire support ships and from the decks of the oil tankers. This was then joined by anti-aircraft fire with smoke rolling off the decks as the rapid fire guns fired their long range shells. Within seconds there were puffs of smoke on the horizon with something either firing at them or getting hit. Then the holovision zoomed to show A-6 Intruder aircraft launching anti-ship missiles. The announcer described them as Australian Air Force aircraft. There seemed to be over a hundred aircraft and at least twenty percent were destroyed outright.

Facil thought, "For the love of Allah, they have launched their attack on Australia with no air cover whatsoever. The Australian Air Force will destroy the entire fleet. If he saw right, that only twenty of one hundred missile carrying A-6's were hit, then that meant eighty missiles heading for the Chinese one hundred and fifty ship armada. Then the scene shifted to behind the armada and more French Virage aircraft were releasing missiles.

Then bombs started landing around the Armada. Tankers are really not all that strong. They have a strong keel, but mainly they rely on the oil inside the hull providing an opposite pressure to the water outside. The decks really have very little strength. Sure enough four tankers were hit from above with large bombs that apparently blew large holes all the way through the ship and out the bottom. The entry hole was relatively small, but one ship immediately mushed into the water and started sinking. A delayed fuse that had not gone off until the bomb was near the bottom of the ship as it crashed through to the keel. The bomb had then gone off near the keel and had apparently broken the ship to where there must have been an immediate flood of water to slow the ship. Another ship had a large explosion that ripped out a huge section of deck where there had been only a small entry hole. Two more were hit, but were continuing on with smoke coming from below decks.

Then a support ship was struck by a missile, probably an American made Harpoon. It leaped clear of the water and a large section of deck exploded upward with the entire superstructure above the main deck catching fire from the heat of the explosion. Then a tanker was shown where the missile literally ripped right through the hull ten feet above water line and exited the other side of the ship twenty feet above the water exploding upon exit and opening a gapping hole in the deck and upper hull. Another tanker was struck and started sliding sideways as water rushed through a large hole in the hull that admitted huge amounts of water.

The anti-missile fire from all the ships was cascading everywhere. The entire fleet was smoking either from their own gun fire or missiles striking or bombs dropping. The view switched to a satellite view that showed high altitude Australian aircraft releasing bombs. They were the mid-range bombers like the Canberra that Australia preferred. The view from below showed geysers of water and deck explosions from the bombing while the missiles were still coming in. The picture showed two destroyers that accidentally crossed fire shooting at incoming missiles killing everyone on deck until the firing ceased with both ships listing in the water only to be struck by the incoming missiles which quickly sent them to the bottom.

The attack stopped. All the missiles had either been shot down or hit their targets and all the bombs that had been dropped had either exploded harmlessly in the water or done tremendous ship damage. Remember that American General Billy Mitchell or Doolittle or someone that had shown after World War I that even battleships could be sunk by and airplane. Munitions are more potent now.

Just when Facil was imagining how the American fleet had felt at his paltry little missile attack the guns on the ships started again. Apparently, the surviving Australian aircraft had refueled, rearmed, and were attacking again.

The scene changed to the coastline near the beaches at Sydney, Australia. The scene was inside the control cabin of one of the monstrous submarine landers. The lander was going very slow, but had a view of the ocean nearby through a view port. The lander was moving through open water in its submarine mode. There were other large shapes moving. Finally one could be seen as a conventional diesel submarine, of which China had two hundred or more.

A camera zoomed in from a satellite to the surface of the ocean showing the scene to be about fifty miles off the coast. There were twenty destroyers dropping depth charges. There were twenty airplanes and thirty helicopters carrying anti-submarine torpedoes and another five helicopters flying low and trailing something in the water that Facil assumed would be sonar buoys looking for submarines. Obviously the Australians knew they were under a submarine attack and had probably had some warning about the Monster submarine landers from the European theater. Torpedoes could also be seen racing toward the destroyers from several directions.

The announcer said, "Obviously, we are not getting full surprise, but I think you can see that we are over-whelming their defenses. There are fifty conventional submarines involved in this attack. There are an estimated two hundred and fifty torpedoes in the water going after the twenty Australian anti-submarine ships. They will not survive. Watch."

The ships did not survive. They were each hit by multiple torpedoes. There were two ship collisions only to have both hit by four or more torpedoes as they stopped in the water. Obviously many of the torpedoes were either duds or couldn't find a target as there were not two hundred and fifty explosions, maybe only one hundred, but that meant each submarine was hit by an average of five torpedoes each.

There were numerous underwater explosions from the air dropped torpedoes, but then many of the submarines surfaced to fire anti-aircraft missiles and guns at the helicopters and airplanes attacking them. So much for sonar. You don't need it when you can see the submarines. Men ran out onto the decks of the submarines and fired shoulder fired missiles to supplement the submarine anti-aircraft fire. The helicopters that didn't run had no chance. At least ten aircraft were shot down before the others ran out of range.

Now the distance to the beach was down to only five miles when anti-ship missiles came flying in, but the submarines had all submerged again and taken evasive maneuvers. Finally, five, repeat five landers pulled up onto the beach. They were met by tanks, but the tanks could not breach the landers thick hull and the landers put out intense fire that eventually sent the Australia army tanks running. As soon as that happened the tankers opened up and disgorged their men and tanks on the land beyond the beaches.

The satellite cameras zoomed out and zoomed in to show Melbourne with another five landers. Then zoomed out and back in to the west coast of Australia with five more landers. The Australians had fifteen landers ashore and a thousand tanks and seventy thousand troops safely landed.

Then came high altitude bombers that destroyed all five landers near Melbourne, two near Sydney and three on the west coast, but the tanks and soldiers were running free.

Then the hologram went dark and the lights came on.

"Facil, will you explain what happened to the Chinese invasion of Australia?" Jabal was asking.

Facil was disoriented and surprised by the question and then realized what Jabal was wanting. "They did not have air superiority for their invasion. In modern times, every beach landing has been made with air superiority. Submarines may hide under the ocean, remember that ninety percent of the world is under water. Ships may do well against ships, but when ships meet aircraft, the aircraft can be nearly immune to the ships while the ships are at the mercy of the aircraft. The Chinese tried going too far from home and tried to make an invasion without controlling the air. The Australian Navy is not very large or well equipped, the Australian Army is very small though well equipped. Against the landers the Australian Army simply didn't have the firepower. But the Australian Air Force is one of the better air forces in the world. While not large in comparison to a super power, and while not having much offensive capability, they are very well equipped. They have taken many American and British aircraft and improved upon them or had them custom made. They even make a few of their own. They fly more training hours per pilot than any Air Force including what the United States used to. They're good. Without any Air Force to contend with, they have destroyed the Chinese attack. The Chinese were too far for their land based fighter planes to provide any support. They would have been well advised to have just ignored the Australians until they had built air bases within range of Australia. They could have built bases in Borneo to attack northern Australia and then after taking some of northern Australia, they could have launched aircraft from northern Australia to cover southern Australia. I believe we just saw five million Chinese go to their deaths."

Jabal said, "That's why Facil has become an important part of our leadership. We have made the same mistakes ourselves. First we control the air, but air cannot conquer a country, only destroy it. Then we can use our army to conquer the country. Facil, will you stay and meet with me after today's briefing?"

"Of course, Jabal."

The holovision continued showing how the Chinese fleet was nearly destroyed before getting back under Chinese air cover. The last Australian airplanes to attack were the F-111's and Canberra's that had a longer range than other aircraft and could bomb from high altitude. Australia had air to air refueling, but did not want to risk their tankers. All Australian flights were directed and monitored by Australian AWACS aircraft of American manufacture.

The submarine landers were destroyed by air power where tanks could not have done it. Two thousand pound conventional bombs dropped from high altitude did not always penetrate even the lighter upper armor, but eventually found their way to the interior. All was not lost however. They had landed a significant tank force that moved into the Australian cities to escape the airplanes that did not want to bomb their own cities to get the tanks. This effectively disrupted business causing evacuation of both Melbourne and Sydney. The Chinese infantry and tanks fought roving battles in the suburbs against Australian military elements and random attacks from special forces explosives that didn't let the Chinese rest even when in the heart of the city. The question remaining was resupply of the Chinese forces.

At the end of the day, Jabal and Facil had a very open and frank discussion of the Chinese successes and failures. It was rather obvious that controlling the air was essential. Jabal confided, "The Red Chinese had lost eighty of their total of one hundred converted tankers and all fifteen submarine landers. They had lost five million troops in that air sea battle alone along with four thousand main battle tanks and ten thousand lighter armored vehicles.

In the Siberian campaign, it had been going well, but the Chinese had lost forty million troops to radiation poisoning and the Siberian weather. The Russians had destroyed half of the Chinese Air Force before withdrawing to defend the heartland of Russia. Siberia had turned into hordes of Chinese foot soldiers being attacked by roving bands of Russian tanks. While no one now had air superiority, the Red Chinese aircraft were doing very poorly at finding the Russian tanks before they roared in killing and running away.

In India, there was no real defense, but road conditions were terrible. Many of the Chinese soldiers were not ready for the hot weather encountered in India and the summer had not actually arrived yet. The Chinese tanks and armored vehicles had no air conditioning and tank crews were dying in their vehicles from the heat. The Chinese foot soldiers were not doing much better and were hard to control. They were chasing Indian women and trying to drag the women with them as their military columns tried to move through jungles without roads. Much of the country was mountainous and the local people were destroying bridges as the Chinese approached them. In many cases, these bridges were built over large chasms over which it would take months to build a new bridge. Most of their military had come to a stop there due to weather and impassable terrain.

North Viet Nam was fighting as they had fought the Americans, but now with South Vietnamese added. Where no one was fighting for their homes against the Americans now they were fighting for their homes. The Chinese were being handicapped by having to move their supplies through mountain passes to their troops in Viet Nam. Food was a major problem. How do you supply twenty million troops through mountain passes that are being bombed regularly. The Chinese Air Force quickly won the air war, but the remaining Vietnamese aircraft were flying one way suicide missions just to block a mountain pass for a few hours. In the meantime, the Vietnamese people had plenty to eat as they retreated southward a few miles per day, but the Chinese ate every grain of rice left in the fields and still needed tons more brought from a depleting Chinese stock. Because of the food problem, the Chinese troops were some times attacking without ammunition just to try to get food from their enemy. Ammunition was a problem, because an army dying of starvation doesn't need ammunition, so food has the priority, but one hundred percent of the Chinese transport can't even provide the food let alone the ammunition. China now has millions of troops carrying sacks of rice over the mountains without guns. The idea is that they will deliver food and pick up the guns of the Chinese that have died from starvation or are too weak to carry a gun.

The Chinese lost twenty million trying to invade North Korea before they gave up. At least they feel that Korea has been sealed off for several years due to radiation. There is a strip on the continent fifty miles wide that is too radioactive for anything to live for the next twenty years. It separates the continent from North Korea, so no attack is expected there. Everyone thought that their only ambition was to take South Korea.

The Red Chinese were so strong and so close they came west instead of going south. Now they are too weak to take on South Korea. The danger is that the allies might have a foothold on the Asian continent through Korea, if they could figure out how to get through the radiation zone.

Probably the biggest problem facing the Chinese is Siberia. The Russians have built underground cities and stock piles that allow their tanks to roam around doing hit and run attacks on Chinese infantry and then disappearing again. Of the four hundred million Chinese military, there are twenty million soldiers and two hundred million coolies carrying food through Siberia. No one may ever know their losses in Siberia.

I have some very good news for you, Facil."

"Oh, and what is that?" asked Facil.

"The Red Chinese are shipping two million bombs to us through the Indian Ocean around the tip of India right now. In addition they have promised to ship ten million artillery rounds to us. It appears they have the manufacturing capability that we do not have even after the Soviet nuclear attacks."

"That's great. When it gets here we will need another month to get it to our fighting Air Force units. How long until it arrives and where will it arrive?" asked Facil.

"The bombs should be delivered directly to our ports in the Mediterranean by the middle of September. They are coming through the Suez canal after crossing the Indian Ocean."

"That is a long way to come and there are a lot of submarines in the world besides ours."

"DO YOU THINK THERE ARE ANY IN THE INDIAN OCEAN OR THE RED SEA OR THE MEDITERRANEAN BESIDES OURS?"

"I wouldn't know for sure, but I suspect that there are allied or Soviet submarines around somewhere between here and there. I would not be surprised to find there are still some lurking in the Mediterranean. We must make sure this shipment stays very secret until it has been unloaded, just in case."

"It is already on our formal scheduling board."

"Then I wouldn't count on it ever arriving. We should remove it immediately and ask for another shipment immediately. Keep the second shipment completely secret. Maybe we could report the first shipment lost in a storm."

"Well, if you really think so. I will order it done."

MONTH 12, JULY 2

Technical Sergeant Walter Gaddis's unit was part of the twenty thousand infantry and three hundred tanks that the U.S. Navy landed at Burgundy and they were now moving to cut off the Arab advances out of Marseilles. Other than getting sea sick in the North Sea, the mission went without a hitch. Everything had been routinely off loaded in the port without the Arabs knowing that it had been done. Between the French Air Force, the U.S. Navy aircraft, and the U.S. Air Force from England, and the British Air Force, the Arabs did not fly a plane west of Marseilles.

The troops received an update on World War III while waiting for their equipment to be downloaded from the ships in the port.

The Red Chinese had an invasion force of one hundred converted oil tankers, each one transporting fifty thousand equipped troops. An invasion force of five million equipped troops plus three of the submarine monsters used by the Arabs and five hundred tanks should be more than enough to destroy Australia.

EUROPE

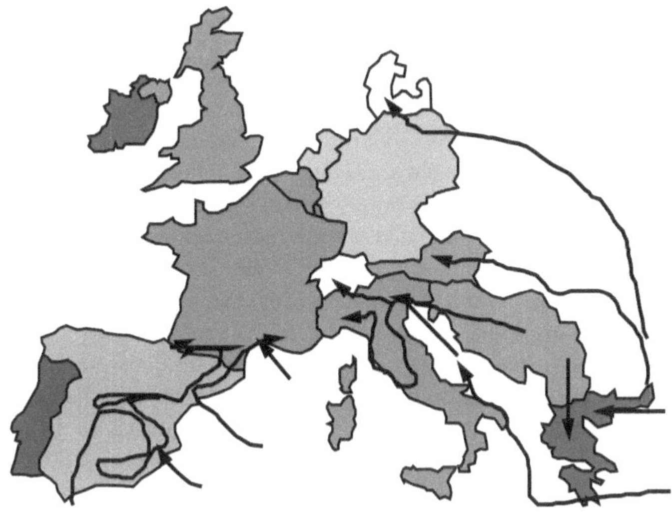

Lines represent Arab activities up to the point that the American tank force was landed in southern France.

MONTH 12, JULY 4

The infantry did not have to contend with attacking anything since the people of France were more than happy to see them. Their only job was to protect the tanks from other infantry. The tanks job was to harass the Arabs as much as possible. The American tank crews were far better trained than the Arab counterparts and the generally was also much better. During their first engagement with Arab forces they destroyed over three hundred tanks with only three American tanks put out of action. Their crews were unhurt. As soon as the Arabs mounted a counter attack, the American tanks retreated until the Arabs stopped pursuing. This resulted in the Arab forces getting spread further and further west in southwest France and drawing forces away from the French forces trapped on the Riviera.

It came just in time because the Arab Air Force had switched tactics from bombing French Riviera cities to bombing the French military between the cities. The further the Arab forces were lured from the Riviera the less air support they had.

TSgt Gaddis had to write a report on one battle, "My tank was in the second row of tanks. We had infantry positioned within four hundred yards of the Arab tank column, but off to the side of the small valley that we were in. The Arabs never knew we were there until we came over a rise firing as we came. The laser ranging gun sight worked perfectly and we were hitting Arab tanks from six thousand yards out. The additional long range firing training worked. My tank hit three Arab tanks before they could react. One at six thousand yards, one at five thousand yards, and one at four thousand yards. At that point the Arabs tanks whirled in mass to give chase. There was an estimated seven hundred tanks in that one mass. They held their fire, apparently wanting to get closer. We stopped as a group and I hit another tank from that position, although three other tanks were apparently aiming at the same tank. It was a British made Chieftain tank and simply exploded from the four nearly simultaneous hits. We then reversed engines and fired while running away. My tank had at least a part of destroying three more tanks. By now we were back to the small hill top we had come over and the Arab column had come two thousand meters in our direction, still not having fired a shot. That was when our infantry opened up with TOW wire guided missiles. Can you imagine four hundred guided missiles in the air simultaneously? Tanks were exploding everywhere. We stopped on the hill. Our range to their lead tanks was only four thousand meters, but we could not find an operational tank to shoot at. The Arab tanks spread out behind the leaders went into an all out free for all retreat with tanks bumping into tanks at fifty miles an hour. I would love to read the report on tankers being killed by jostling other friendly tanks. We gave chase, because we knew what would come next. Thousands of Arabs infantry were swarming onto the battlefield. Our infantry high tailed it in their humvees. The Humvee may not have a very high top end or good acceleration, but can you imagine the sight of two thousand French and British and Russian made vehicles trying to keep up with humvees off the road. They were tipping over and slushing to stop in mud churned up by the tanks and crashing into each other while the humvees just motored away. Then to cover our infantry retreat, we opened up on the light vehicles and infantry of the Arab forces. We were careful to stay at least two thousand meters away in case they also had TOW missile. We had two M1A1's damaged by TOW missiles fired at extreme range, before we got the order to retreat again. The crews from the M1A1s jumped onto other tanks and we were off again. The Arabs were content to let us go with no pursuit this time. We lost six humvees to enemy fire and twenty troops plus the two tanks, but we must have destroyed a hundred of their tanks and two hundred other vehicles and maybe a thousand of their troops. I'd say that was a good exchange. We then pulled back to get resupplied with fuel and ammunition for another day tomorrow.

MONTH 12, JULY 4

The hologram for today was the current status of the war in Europe. The American tank force that had been performing so well with air support from the American carrier group now retreated into northern Spain to hide in the mountains with Spanish and other American forces in Spain. The Coasta Del Sol from Gibraltar to France belonged to the Arabs. The Arabs had taken over the remains of Torrehon Air Force Base and in theory ruled Madrid. At night the Spanish ruled the streets hiding in narrow alleys and using Molotov cocktails and rocket launchers against Arab tanks and infantry. The Arabs were faced with either killing everyone or congregating at night behind an armed ring of sentries.

The war in eastern Europe that had met little opposition was now developing headaches of its own. The old Soviet block countries had rolled over and surrendered to the superior Arab forces, but now there were millions of people that needed food. The Arabs had come to realize that two billion rounds of small arms ammunition is nothing in a war of this scale. They were averaging three thousand rounds of ammunition for every enemy known killed. In some places they had tried to round up local civilians and then shoot them down with machine gun fire, but now the civilians in that area not only ran from any Arab, but would come back at night and sabotage or blow up equipment slitting throats, stealing guns and ammunition.

Facil interjected in today's briefing, "I have said from day one that you simply cannot kill everyone. You don't even want to. Many people don't care who is in control as long as they can continue their little way of life. Continue farming the farm, milking the cows, working in a textile plant, or whatever. What good would it do to conquer the world if there were no one left but Arabs to do all the menial work?"

Jabal shot back, "Look what good it does us to leave people alive, they are killing, destroying, and stealing. We should have just killed everyone if we had the ammunition."

"Jabal, that is the point. If the Arab army just came rolling through town waving instead of shooting the civilians would wave back in friendship. When we had passed up a city or town with minimal military, that town would have become part of the support of our troops. Look in France. We have developed a reputation of killing so everyone simply ran from us.

The French weren't starving when there army was here. We simply do not have the farmers producing the food behind our lines to provide food for our army. The Arab countries have never produced even what we need on an annual basis. Much of our food has had to be imported for many years. We built up some stock piles, but how long will these stock piles last when we no long produce any food anywhere. One advantage of conquering Italy should be that we inherit their food production. How much are they producing now? How much are the French in the south producing? Who stayed behind? Young men who want vengeance and trained saboteurs from the French military, assisted by British commandos.

The eastern Europeans have never produced enough to support themselves, which was one reason the Soviet Union let them go. Keep in mind that the Germans left most of the civilians alone when they passed through and when the Russians pushed out the Germans they left them alone also. For many years the Soviet Union tried to support those countries as part of the Soviet block, but it got so expensive they decided to let them go. Of course there was the other factor. At one time the Soviet Union was interested in conquering all of Europe and needed to keep their troops on the allied line for a quick attack. Gradually, they lost their will for conquest, but kept troops there to keep the allies from attacking them by threatening an invasion of allied countries. Eventually, it became purely a defensive posture. As long as those countries could be made friends of both sides the Soviets did not have to worry about them attacking Russia and the eastern block countries still served as an ideal buffer for defense. The allies could not attack Russia without attacking Poland or Czechoslovakia or some other semi-neutral country. By cutting them free, the Soviets made friends, reduced the support for those countries, but kept them as a buffer. Now we have many of those same countries."

"You're partially correct, Facil. What if we start moving our common people to those countries? They will consider it a very rich move. They will control many acres of well watered rich land. They can help control the civilian population by giving them jobs in the fields."

"You are still taking away the possessions of the local people. Some will be pacified, but others will want their homes and land back and may fight to do so."

"Anything we can do to reduce the opposition will be a help. If the working class are our working class, we can print more money and make it look like we are paying better than their previous masters and make them loyal to us. Will that work?"

"It might, Jabal. The more you kill, the more lifetime enemies you are producing. The more you befriend, the easier it will be to keep the land. I have said that from day one. Defeat their armies. Don't even try to destroy their countries. If you defeat their armies you may be able to rule the countries. If you try to destroy their countries and kill civilians, we run out of ammunition while creating more enemies."

MONTH 12, JULY 8

The United States had landed twenty thousand infantry and three hundred tanks at Burgundy and were moving to cut off the Arab advances out of Marseilles. The Muslim Air Force had destroyed seventy five percent of the armor holding off the Muslim forces along the French Riviera. The Arab forces had by-passed Monaco that had been evacuated by the French. Most of the civilians had also fled before the Arab forces arrived. Many Arab commanders moved into Monaco and Monaco was turned into a rest area for Muslim troops.

MONTH 12, JULY 10

Telephone communications had been re-established and there were radio broadcasts across the country. The looters had been pretty well rounded up and food was plentiful again. There were even limited television stations in operation. Televisions were pretty much public devises for multiple families. There was no television production except in Mexico that was available for American consumption. Most families had at least a portable radio with earphones. People were not taking long trips so the tourist industry had not started. Banks were operating with manual accounting procedures using computers only for backup.

The civilian crisis was over. The military industry was just coming up again. Between the cut backs in defense and all the closures and de-militarizing of the defense industry, there wasn't much. Add to that the fifty percent of the industries that were destroyed by the relatively few nukes that destroyed cities and there was a severe shortage of defense industry. General Gates would wait no longer. He ordered a re-deployment of the meager U.S. forces in Germany to come to the aid of the French. He ordered a re-deployment of some forces to Bern, Switzerland to prevent an Arab attack into Germany from Lucerne, Switzerland.

vi,44

At night a rainbow will appear at Nantes in northeast France. By knowledge of the sea they will stir up rain. in the Gulf to Uraba (Venezuela), a great fleet be sunk with swiftness, when Saxony (the old East Germany) united with foreign powers.

MONTH 12, JULY 15

The Moslem advance was turned into a defensive battle with the small American force destroying ten Arab tanks for every American tank stopped with the Arabs having lost over three thousand tanks in only a week of fighting.

Facil was behind the main podium now. "Jabal, gentlemen. We have lost this war without drastic measures. I have ordered fifty of my Saudi Arabian Air Force F-15's with conformal extended range fuel tanks to go after the American Mediterranean fleet with Exocet missiles. I fear it will be a one way suicide mission as they may run out of fuel and fall in the ocean without finding the fleet. With luck, they may find the fleet and be shot down by superior U.S. Navy pilots flying inferior F-14 fighters."

Jabal interrupted, "I thought they were out of range of our airplanes."

"They are, but I have modified some C-130 cargo planes with bladder tanks for an attempted aerial refueling."

This caused a clamor from the crowd. Facil waited it out showing that he was not going to be ruffled or answer until the babble died. He then pointed at one who was also a pilot and calmly stated, "You may ask the first question."

"I thought bladder tanks were aircraft cargo pallet mounted emergency fuel tanks to be unloaded on the ground, and do you mean that you have never tried doing this when there is such an important mission?"

"You are correct on both counts. However, in inventorying the munitions left by the Americans in Saudi Arabia after the gulf war, we found some drogue refueler lines for refueling American helicopters from C-130 bladder tanks and some pumps for same. We have removed some refueling nozzles from some American helicopters and mounted them on our F-15's. We have test flown these, but my pilots have never done mid-air refueling. We have not tested this because there was no time and I would just as soon lose an F-15 due to refueling on a mission as on a test flight. If it doesn't work we fly until the fuel runs out. My men are ready to die for Allah if that be the case. There is an additional problem lest you consider this routine. That is that we are using almost one hundred percent of our conformal long range fuel tanks for the F-15's. There will be no more long range missions of more than a single formation."

"Why are you doing this then?" Jabal asked.

"Because that American unit and the Americans in Spain may turn the tide of this war unless we can take care of the Mediterranean fleet that is resupplying them and providing air cover. I consider this an all or nothing opportunity. If we can sink the fleet, we have a chance of winning the war. If not, then we may lose the war. If we lose the war, I could lose my throne. Therefore, I am going for broke. This may be the single most important mission of the war."

Jabal said, "You are sounding defeatist. We will mop up Europe before the snows come."

Facil brazenly said, "No, you won't. We have spent over a year taking Italy and some leftovers of the Soviet Union. We have wounded, but not taken Spain or France. Germany is gradually retreating, but we have not breached their border defenses. The rest of Europe is unscathed as yet. It may take two to three more years."

"So what if it does?" said Jabal.

"We do not have the munitions for the Air Force to continue mass bombings. We have used up the American stock pile in Saudi Arabia. We have used up the Israeli stock pile. Egypt and most of Northern Africa have shipped everything to their front lines and are already running out of some weapons. Iran, Iraq, and Syria used everything against Rome. We are currently trying to modify Soviet air munitions for use on European aircraft.

"We have an additional problem in that fully fifty percent of our aircraft are grounded for maintenance problems and parts shortages. Parts from these grounded air craft are all that is keeping the air forces flying. All of our Cargo and Commercial aircraft are approaching time for major depot overhaul, but the only depot we have is for C-130 aircraft in

Egypt and in Israel, or should I say Palestine now. With the current rate of bombing wholesale ground targets we will be without close air support for our ground forces within three months."

Jabal forcefully said, "Facil, your mission to sink the U.S. Navy is approved, but your briefing is over. If what you say is true, everyone knows that you have not been the Air Force commander long enough to have caused shortages, but you must show me in private why you say we have a problem before we change our strategy. I am hoping for your sake that you are telling the truth, and if you are I will take revenge on my previous commander for not warning us of the problems."

"Jabal, it is not entirely their fault. They were not trained to plan and organize an air war. In addition, they were following your orders to bomb cities without question. True, I was trying to save lives originally, but now I know that it was a mistake because we simply did not have the air munitions for concentrated bombing. We have no air munitions production facilities to produce our own or the skills to do so, because the munitions were so easy to buy. All of us," indicating the entire room with a sweep of his hands, "are guilty of buying showy air craft and tanks, but inadequate spare parts and munitions. I would lay a bet that your ground forces have the same problems that have not been reported to you just as the air problems were not being reported."

"Facil, that is enough. The briefing is terminated for the day. Facil you have three hours to convince me you are correct. Report back to this room in one hour to prove your point."

"Jabal, I have all the data right here." raising a stack of papers and loose leaf books, along with a remote control for briefing charts.

"You heard me. Clear the room. Facil, go back to your air room. Do not talk to anyone outside your Air Force, and report back here in one hour."

Jabal was quite forceful with these statements and everyone did as ordered. The conference room cleared in minutes and Facil returned to his air planning room to wait the hour and review his briefing materials.

"Jabal, here are the numbers, we have only ten thousand iron bombs, that's convention bombs, of all types from five hundred to two thousand pounds. We have only three thousand air to air missiles, and no guided bombs left. We have plenty of cannon shells for close in fighting. We have all four hundred anti-ship missiles that we started with. We only have enough for anti-armor. We started this war with over one hundred thousand bombs."

"How can we have used so many? Are you sure you're right?"

"Yes, I am right. I had them counted twice. If this war is not over soon, you will lose your offensive capability for the Air Force."

"How did the allies drop so many bombs during World War II?"

"They were manufacturing bombs faster than they used them. They had so many left over that they were still using them during the Korean war and the first few years of the Viet Nam war. What they used during the Gulf war were leftovers from the Viet Nam war."

"What does it take to manufacture bombs?"

"I couldn't answer that except it takes steel processing equipment to make the cases and fins, sophisticated explosives manufacture, and electronics for the fuses."

"How long would it take us to get into manufacturing like that?"

"I'm not an engineer and I wouldn't know, but I would suspect a year, if we had the basic steel manufacturing. I'm not an engineer nor an expert in development of munitions. You need to ask someone else."

"What about artillery ammunition? Is it just as difficult?"

"Are we low on that too?"

"Just answer the question."

"No. An artillery shell doesn't need the aerodynamics. It is basically a big rifle shell with an exploding bullet."

"Maybe we can do that. No we are not low. We started with a total of twenty million artillery shells and have used ten million rounds. That can't be right can it?"

"Think about it. We started with fifty thousand tanks total. If each fired only one hundred shells, that is five million. How many shells do you think each tank fired, two hundred? How many artillery pieces do we have, twenty thousand? Two hundred shells each times twenty thousand. That is another four million rounds. That is only nine million and I think the rounds fired is probably very low. Even though we have probably lost five thousand tanks, I would be surprised it we still have ten million rounds. I'll bet you aren't being told how bad it really is."

"Will you oversee the manufacturing?"

"No. I can't. I know nothing of manufacturing."

"I will have our best western educated engineers working on it. I need someone to tell me the truth."

"I must control our Air Force, but I will look over the plans and stop in at the plants from time to time to see how it's going on. I will have to have total freedom to move around."

"Okay, you have your wish. I will give you that freedom, now that I know I can trust you."

MONTH 12, JULY 30

The attack of the American tanks landed in southern France had been going very well. The Arabs were confused and losing tanks by the dozen. The three hundred American tanks were down to two hundred and fifty, but the Arabs had lost five hundred tanks. The American infantry had lost only two hundred men to date. A-10's from Germany had also joined in the fun accounting for many of the Arab tanks. The official estimate was that the Arabs had lost fifty thousand people just to the Americans in this three week period of hit and run attacks. It was certainly nice to have air superiority. American forces had maintained the record of losing no ground troop to enemy air since World War II, unless you count the two killed by a burning pilotless MIG 15 during the Korean War.

MONTH 12, JULY 30

The refueling from the C-130 aircraft to the F-15's worked and it was nine hours after take-off that the American fleet was found on AWACS radar which vectored the aircraft in toward the fleet. Eight F-14's met the flight first. Six of the thirty F-15's were downed by long range Phoenix missiles from the F-14s. Only four more were shot down before the F-15's shot all of the F-14's down. Fifty miles from the fleet, they were intercepted by U.S. Navy F-18's that shot down three more before the remaining seventeen released their missiles and six more were shot down before the F-15's regained altitude and speed. All twelve F18's were shot down, which didn't matter because all three carriers were damaged to the point nothing could take off or land. One of the carriers ended with a fire getting to the munitions storage areas which scuttled the ship. Of the seventeen missiles, seven were shot down before reaching their targets. Five destroyers and two AEGIS cruisers were sunk by putting themselves between the missiles and the carriers. All seven sank gracefully allowing most of their crews to be evacuated. One of the carriers was scuttled by the crew prior to being abandoned. The other carrier limped home to the United States. During its return it came upon two wolf packs of Arab submarines sinking ten submarines at the cost of only three escorting destroyers.

Facil was overjoyed. Exclaimed to the conference table, "Success! We have done it. We have destroyed the U.S. Navy Mediterranean fleet that was in the Atlantic supporting both the Spanish and the American force that was holding up our advance in France. Four of the F-15's were unable to refuel and crashed in the ocean when their fuel ran out. Of the thirty Saudi Arabian F-15's sent on this mission, only seven returned, but an exchange of twenty-three fighters for twenty U.S. Navy fighters, possibly all three aircraft carriers, and seven support ships was definitely a good exchange. In addition, most of the American fleet aircraft would be lost."

"Good Job."

"Three cheers for the skill and leadership of Facil and his Air Force."

Facil was holding up his hands for quiet. When it got quiet, Facil announced, "We were very fortunate. Allah helped us. It was very good luck and the fact that Naval surface forces are obsolete with Air Force airplanes properly equipped. Thanks for the Americans that sold us their old AWACS airplanes that found the fleet. Thanks for the French that sold us their Exocet II anti-ship missiles. Most of all thanks to the U.S. Navy having to stay close to shore near the land forces landed at Burgundy to provide air support. One more thanks. Thanks to the U.S. Army that left us those

C-130 refueling lines and the helicopters that were refuelable. Thanks to our western educated engineers who converted them to work on F-15's."

Jabal shoved Facil gently aside, "I agree with you gentlemen. Every particle of this great victory was Facil. He is the one with the idea. He is the one that planned it out and directed the engineering and commanded it."

That brought about a standing ovation from the assembled Arab leaders. It lasted for several minutes before Jabal silenced it. "Now gentlemen, let's watch the holovision broadcast to see what is happening in the world."

The holovision started in the Far East. This was the first real news they had of the eastern front and the Chinese. The voice said, "This is a holovision summary provided by the Red Chinese government that covers from Day one to the present."

MONTH 12, JULY 30

The attack had been going very well. The Arabs were confused and losing tanks by the dozen. The three hundred American tanks were down to two hundred and fifty, but the Arabs had lost five hundred tanks. The American infantry had lost only two hundred men to date. A-10's from Germany had also joined in the fun accounting for many of the Arab tanks. The official estimate was that the Arabs had lost fifty thousand people just to the Americans in this three week period of hit and run attacks. It was certainly nice to have air superiority. American forces had maintained the record of losing no ground troop to enemy air since World War II, unless you count the two killed by a burning pilotless MIG 15 during the Korean War.

The line represents the total trip of Jim, Darcy, and Shelby across the U.S.

The helicopter arrived early. The pilot allowed Jim to take Eva, Darcy and Shelby along because he had no orders except to take a Jim Claris and his belongings to Tyndall Air Force Base, Florida, as quickly as possible.

When they arrived at the base, they were whisked on board a VIP jet. As with many Air Force planes, it was older and did not have the sophisticated electronic controls, but did have HEMP protection on much of its equipment. Again, they had no orders except to take Jim Claris to a remote civilian airport in southeastern Pennsylvania. The pilot explained, "I'm sorry Mr. Claris. I only have orders to fly you to a civilian airport. Now please, get on board. My orders say it is urgent. We are at war you know."

"Okay then. Let's go. Colonel, where you go, we go."

They were off. It was a long flight. The pilots didn't have any knowledge about why they were going or where the final destination would be. The only thing Jim could think of was the Alternate National Military Command Post or ANMCC that was in a mountain somewhere around that general area of the country. Jim had never been there before, but he had been hearing about it for nearly thirty years. With Washington DC destroyed, the ANMCC would be the main command post of the U.S. military. Why he would be so urgently required there, he didn't know.

They flew above the clouds and could not see much. They skirted Washington D.C. and New York City, but close enough that they could see the city was largely gone. There were fires burning everywhere including what looked like small towns. Jim asked the single flight attendant who replied, "I don't know where you have been sir. I though everyone knew about the food riots and the looters. The poor people that survived in the cities looted everything they could in the cities and then moved into the country side in search of food and loot. Imagine, millions of looters in every major city moving out into the country. It's as closest we've come to a war inside the United States as anything since the civil war. There have been tens of thousands already killed by other Americans. It's a lot worse on the other side of the Mississippi River."

Eventually they arrived at the airport in Pennsylvania where they were met by another helicopter that flew them into the mountains. They landed at night. As they were getting off the airplane, Jim saw a woman and two children waiting in the terminal. Was it? Yes, it was his wife and children. He told Eva, Darcy, and Shelby who thankfully held back and let him run ahead. He never expected to see his family again. He hated not having been faithful, but thought they were dead ...even if he lived, now, here they were. He didn't know exactly what he was going to tell her. She would believe that they were together by pure chance, but would she believe that nothing had happened. She figured she would believe in him. He would never have cheated on her if he had not believed his family was gone...even under the circumstances.

Would Eva, Darcy and Shelby keep quiet?

The biggest question was whether he could stay quiet about it. He was much like his wife, too honest for his own good. He should keep it secret, but he had never kept anything from his wife before.

He was allowed to spend the evening with his wife and children, but he had to report to work at 7 AM or 0700 in the morning. "Carolyn, Nataly, Billy! I never expected to see you again. How did you get here?"

"Jim. You are alive. I didn't expect to ever see you again either. Where have you been?

"It's a long story. I've been all across the United States. It took me months to make it to Dayton, but you were gone when I got there. The remains of the cars were there so I didn't know whether you had just been kidnapped or whether some had rescued you. I then went to Florida and you sister's summer home. That's where I was when they found me and flew me here."

"Don't you mean flew us here?"

"What do you mean, us?"

"I saw those girls get the same airplane."

"So."

"One of them was Eva."

"Oh. ... I can explain."

"I only have one question."

"What's that?"

"Do you love me?"

"You know I do. I spent months trying to get to you. I had given you up for dead. Eva was the only one still alive in our old neighborhood in Fairborn. She hid out in the fraidy hole under our house. That's where I found her. I couldn't leave her there."

"What about the other two?"

"They rescued me initially and then we drove their car out of Los Angeles all the way to the Mississippi River before we had to leave it."

"Relax Jim. Things have changed. I have spent over a year without you, wishing you would come back, and knowing things would be different. Men are expected to take multiple wives now. I have prepared myself for that day, if I ever saw you again." They continued on and Carolyn made it plain that she expected the girls to move in with them. She really wasn't as upset as she was glad to see Jim. There was a lot of question about how much longer she would have been able to stay there without Jim. It was only because of Hank that she was allowed to stay, but that time had been running out as the base got more and more crowded. There was no way for her to earn money, and without the military help, they would have starved.

Jim told her of his adventures which further helped Carolyn understand his relationship with the girls. She had them to thank for his being there as well. She already knew Eva and thought she would probably like Darcy and Shelby too, although they were a lot younger, and from what she had seen a lot more attractive too.

Morning came quickly. There was a knock at the door and a Brigadier General was standing there. "Jim? Remember me?"

"Hank Lakeman? What's happening and why are we here?"

"Later. If you're ready to go, then let's go. I'll explain later."

On the way to the mountain command post, Henry filled in Jim on what was happening and why he had been brought here.

"Did you bring my family here?"

"Yes."

"I thank you very much, but I am surprised."

"I knew how family oriented you were and since I plan on you being here for the remainder of the war, I figured it was only right."

"Well. I really appreciate it. I really do.

The first thing we need to do is to get our communications up. Get as many radio stations operating as possible. Forget television because almost all televisions were destroyed. Once you have nationwide radio coverage you can worry about television. All of the radios on the shelves of stores and warehouses should be okay because most are wrapped in plastic and inside Styrofoam that should have protected them. Batteries will be the biggest problem. Most people probably wore out their batteries on dead radios. Battery manufacture and distribution is very important. People need to have communication with the outside. The ones doing or considering doing bad might change their mind if they realize that they will have to pay soon.

The good guys need to know there is hope and to fight back against either the bad guys or just to keep from starving. You might consider air dropping at least one radio and some batteries for it everywhere there is a group of people across the country. I would destroy the cassette playing part to make sure the batteries aren't wasted on playing tapes. Make sure there is a radio station in range before you waste any radios.

The old analog telephone switching systems should be unhurt. The new digital switches probably weren't HEMP protected, but the spare parts were probably stored in EMP bags to prevent damage in shipping and handling so they should be okay. Glass fiber (or fiber optics) is susceptible to HEMP because unless its protected it turns dark and doesn't pass light waves any more. All of the millions of miles of fiber have to be replaced by either protected fiber or copper to get the telephones and cable television operating again. Fiber looked cheaper because a small piece could carry so many separate transmissions through coding and decoding with very little power going into the light waves, but now it is costly in the long run because it is destroyed."

"Slow down Jim, where are we going to get all that copper on short notice?"

"You said that millions of people were killed, right? Strip it out of their homes and apartments for now. In particular the homes that are destroyed anyway. Now, take control of the junk yards and parts houses so you can get automobiles and especially trucks back on the road with the old points type distributors and carburetors. Any Ford 302 or GM 305 or 350 was originally made for them anyway. We've got to get the transportation system moving food and other goods before everyone starves.

The farms have to be protected so they can farm and raise cattle for the people again. If there are that many dead, there should be more than enough food if we can get it distributed properly. If you have to, use military pontoon bridges to get the rivers bridged for trucking. Get the canning factories going as a top priority.

Naturally, the power companies have got to start distributing electricity. The HEMP shouldn't have hurt the generating capacity any, only the distribution of power.

You have to get the looters under control, even if you have to send in tanks or fighter bombers. A few bombs could definitely turn back a bunch of rabble, not to mention the morale value. It would show that the government is still operating. In fact it might be a good idea to just take some pictures of them for future reference when order is restored."

"What about the military situation in Europe? Don't you think we need to mobilize our forces to get over there as soon as possible?"

"Not really. We need to get the United States back on its feet as quickly as possible. Since you said that our missiles didn't get far and our bombers were shot down on takeoff, I assume that nuclear weapons are out."

"You've got that right. It's worse now. The Arabs have anti-missile satellites overhead right now. If we launch a missile it gets destroyed during the boost phase causing the remains of the five to ten warheads to get scattered around the country side. We have cleared out the areas off the end of our runways to make sure that no one can shoot them down by either arresting the Arabs and Chinese or moving them away. The only ones allowed to stay we did background checks on to make sure they were on our side. However, we don't have many planes left and Saudi Arabia has nearly complete air superiority. Our bombers wouldn't stand a chance."

"What about our cruise missiles, especially the ACM?"

"How did you know about the stealth cruise missile?"

"Jane's All the World's Airplanes?"

"Right."

"What about our hypersonic spy planes? If they can fly over at Mach Eight, couldn't they also deliver a nuke?"

"The Chinese, Japanese, Arab Star Wars system was deployed in secret and can shoot down most any missile or high flying aircraft. Our cruise missiles were all sabotaged during manufacture. All of the defense contractors had so many foreign born scientists, even many in the military. They planted miniature radio transmitters in the electronics so that when they received the right frequency other electronics in the fuel controls exploded the fuel pump that was made with explosives inside. Every building and airplane with a cruise missile went up in smoke along with the fuel. We don't have any cruise missiles."

"Oh. Well my point is that we are too outnumbered and the United States has been grievously damaged. We have to save what's left of our own country and get organized before we can do anything. Do you realize how out numbered we are?"

"We have the technology."

"Had, you mean. The Arabs have the very best fighter planes and tanks in the world including a lot of ours. The have stocked up missiles and parts for years. They had twice what we did before we cut back our military. Now they have four or five times as much."

"What about the Kuwaiti thing a few years ago? They folded quick."

"Very carefully listen and let me describe what really happened. The Iraqi's, by themselves had the fourth largest military in the world. They took Kuwait in hours and then stopped. Wait. Let me finish. Why would they just sit there and wait for us to build up for six months? Saudi Arabia only had twenty-six thousand troops against four or five hundred thousand Iraqis. Why would they wait for us to get ready? Was it a test? Did they expect us to park all that equipment in Saudi Arabia so they could come take it when they wanted? I think they wanted to see our capabilities. They found out about our cruise missiles, the F-117 Stealth Fighter, AWACS, JSTARS, our B-52's. They discovered our B1B's were ineffectual. They found out how vulnerable their command posts were. They found out about our jamming equipment. And then they managed to save most of their equipment. How many first line tanks did they lose? When they parked their airplanes in towns, did we destroy them? How many Arabs graduated from our universities? Do we still call them too dumb to do anything? What have they been doing with all of those engineering and physics degrees? We've got to get enough strength to do some good and not just throw it away."

"That's why I brought you here, but there is a three star General Gates that is in command of all U.S. Forces. He has it in mind that we need to get our troops and tanks involved. I went along, because it seemed like the right thing to do."

"Okay. I understand. We need to talk him into some special tactics. He can't just charge in and attack them. We have to have hit and run attacks and the ultimate in technology on our side. We don't have the technological edge everyone imagines. Therefore, we can only go for tactics."

"You can argue, but I would go slow. General Gates is convinced that the Army runs the Army. He is sending more fighter planes to England to support American troops even as we speak.

As a result of the nuclear bombs and riots the population of the United States had decreased dramatically. Because so many men died protecting women in the riots whereas the women were saved for the survivors. Then there were the pitched battles between looters and the military, again killing mostly men. There were tens of thousands of looter men killed and hundreds of military. Then even more thousands of looters were herded into huge concentration camps until they could be processed and tried. Because most of the east coast cities were destroyed either by nukes or by looters, burning their own cities for greed, and because of the severe shortage of food on the east coast due to the total lack of imports and the shortage of farms in the northeast meant that all of the military moved onto the bases instead of living in private housing.

As a result, there was no where for Eva Shelby and Darcy to stay. Jim's wife insisted on them staying in one of their bedrooms. Jim didn't know how she felt, if she resented them being there, but she seemed to just accept the girls as part of the war and the inevitable future.

19 DEFEAT

MONTH 13
August 1

TSgt Gaddis's tank was one of one hundred approaching an Arab tank column. As they came over the rise in their standard attack mode, they were surprised to see the Arab tanks already heading in their direction at less than three thousand meters. He yelled into his microphone, "Reverse engines, something's gone wrong. Get us the hell out of here."

Five meters in front of them, where they would have been an artillery shell exploded. Another hit the gimbals on the 105 cannon on the front. The gunner yelled, "Sergeant Gaddis, my gun won't aim and something's knocked out my laser aiming system."

There were sounds of explosions all around them now, with metal pinging off the armor on all sides, until they got out of sight over the rise. None of them knew which explosion had actually hit them. TSgt Gaddis had a rather narrow view from his periscope, but still managed to see many of his tanker friends go up in smoke as their tanks were repeatedly hit. He discovered the turret was also out of action and that his periscope was jammed. "Driver, turn this thing around and head at top speed for the rest area."

He hated not to be able to see what was happening, but his tank was out of the battle. The engine and tracks were only good for running away now, so that's what they were doing. When he got back to their refueling and armament point he found that it was afire with many secondary explosions. He had the driver go around them heading back for Bordeaux for lack of a better destination. Even though they had not been in the tank battle but for a few seconds the fuel was near empty from the high speed driving. He commanded a slow down and saw a HMMWV coming toward his tank. The passenger was his major and he was waving them down. He ordered a stop and opened the hatch. The jeep type vehicle stopped beside them with the major jumping out before it was quite stopped.

Both the major and TSgt Gaddis simultaneously asked each other, "What the hell happened?"

The major said, "We had an air attack. We thought it was our guys buzzing us again. It was Arab F-18's that dropped bombs and strafed the place for fifteen minutes. Now, what happened to you, and why are you running from the battle."

"What battle, they were waiting for us. They knew we were there. We came over the rise as planned, and they were less than three thousand meters away coming at full speed."

"Why didn't our infantry warn you and how did you get away?"

"Beats the hell out of me, unless they were dead. There were several hundred tanks running full speed at us. When I saw them, I had my driver get us the hell out of there. A shell landed where we would have been if we hadn't stopped and our turret got... Jesus Christ, look at that ..." He had just seen his mangled tank. The shell had completely twisted the gun and had almost gone through the armor. The shell had hit right at the base of the gun, missing the reactive armor. If the gun had not have caught a lot of the blast, the shell would have exploded their tank from within."

"I saw your tank, now go on."

"Shells were landing all around us with metal pinging off the hull of the tank. The gunner discovered he had lost control of the gun and lost his laser sight. I discovered the turret was frozen and even my periscope was stuck. I ordered a turn around and fast run back here. I didn't know how much damage we had and thought it could be fixed or that we could pick up a new tank. How'd did the battle go?"

"Hell if I know. I lost contact immediately. What you told me is all I know. All of our fuel and shells are gone along with most of our food supplies and trucks. This is only one of three HMMWV's that didn't get blown up. Have you ever seen what an F-18 cannon can do to light armor?"

"No, and I don't think I want to be on the receiving end to find out."

"I've been in contact with headquarters in Bordeaux, they have ordered us to get back there in two hours or they are leaving without us. Apparently, something's happened that the Arabs have beaten us again."

"How can that be? We were kicking some ass, and now retreating?"

"We've apparently lost our air cover. How else would Arab F-18's be able to find us and strafe the supply dump?"

"Makes sense. We don't have the fuel to make it back to Bordeaux. Can we get some gas?"

"No, what we have in the tank is it. The HMMWV can make it, but forget your tank. It's a waste anyway."

"But sir, I've been with this tank for five years now. We know its every peculiarity, strengths and weaknesses. It's never let us down."

"You going to push it back and then fix it yourself?"

"I see your point. Do you have room for us? I'm sorry, you'll be on foot. This is the only HMMWV that isn't loaded down with wounded, and it will be. Don't look so down, I'll be on foot with you."

They heard the familiar rumbling of more tanks approaching from the battle. They could tell they were M1A1s. TSgt Gaddis pulled out his binoculars. "Get out of here now, sir. Those aren't our M1's. Those are Arabs."

TSgt Gaddis dropped back down closing the hatch, "Driver, the Arabs are here, turn thirty degrees right and floor it."

Shells started landing around them. They drove into a town with shells destroying buildings around them. "Sergeant Gaddis, the engine just missed, we're out of gas."

"Turn into that house, driver." The driver knew he was serious so he drove into the house through the concrete block wall. He kept going until TSgt Gaddis yelled, "Stop. Everyone out. Head left up this alley and don't stop until I tell you to. If anyone shoots at you, take cover. If I'm hit, it's every man for himself."

They all gathered their meager small arms and took off running. TSgt Gaddis threw a grenade into the open tank hatch and followed them as the grenade went off in the tank setting off the other explosives there. The pursuing tanks could not see them and TSgt Gaddis had seen no infantry, so they had a decent chance of making at least a temporary escape. When the Arabs found the tank, they lost interest in pursuing further and TSgt Walter Gaddis, Bill Makleroy, Joe Danza, and Brad Dorset were free to run and hide. They were afraid to leave the small town because they would be too easy to see. The town was deserted but for them. They found an attic full of boxes and hid behind the boxes to wait for nightfall.

Bill said, "Walter, what now?"

TSgt Gaddis said, "We wait for night and then we head out for Bordeaux. I don't know what else to do. Anyone else have an idea?" No one did. "Well, this town we are in is Lacepella. We are almost straight north of Toulouse and straight east of Bordeaux. I think that we should head as straight west of here as we can staying out of towns. As soon as we are sure we are safe, we find some wheels to take us the rest of the way."

Brad said, "Sarge, we can't walk half way across a country."

TSgt Gaddis said, "From now on call me Walter. We need to get rid of these uniforms and find some civilian clothes. Joe, dig through these boxes and try to find us some clothes to wear. Brad, we are only as far as from Little Rock to Fort Smith, Arkansas. Free Europe would get lost in the west half of the United States. Hey, Joe, better find us some civilian shoes too. I wear a size eleven."

"Sorry, but these shoes are metric. You'll have to try them on."

"Okay, every man for himself. Let's get some new duds."

The Arabs didn't even bother with the town. They had seen it had been evacuated and they were not interested in finding the tankers once the tank was destroyed. When night came, the four tankers stole out of the town in their borrowed clothes.

MONTH 13, AUGUST 1

Major General Henry Lakeman was now in charge of the Alternate Military Command Post (ANMCC). He was speaking to the hushed audience. "Gentlemen, Ladies, our forces in southern France have been destroyed. The Arabs used their reconnaissance forces to lay in wait for our attacks on their columns. They were ready and waiting for us. We are still trying to get reports. We have lost contact with all headquarters in southern France. Without air superiority the Arabs started to make their air superiority work for them. Our Stinger IV missiles kept them from making close air bombing. They never had the high altitude bombing and with our mobility their aircraft were not an offensive factor against our tanks, but they knew exactly where we were at all times. It was only a matter of time before they just got ready and waited for us. The only transmissions have been from one unit making a run for the mountains in northern Spain. They said they were warned by transmissions from other units that were ambushed as they were attempting their own ambush. It may be some time before we can mount any form of offense. We don't have much left and what we do have will be protecting a limited number of air bases essential for air cargo. What I want are ideas about how to multiply our forces."

MONTH 13, AUGUST 3

Walter Gaddis's clothes were too small. He wore the pants low, tied together with rope so he wouldn't have to button the top button and so they would look longer. He ended up wearing his boots. He had found some brown paint and painted them to hide the fact that they were black military combat boots. He brought the can of paint to touch them up if it peeled. He also wore a light winter jacket with no shirt. The jacket was large enough to hide the lowliness of the belt line. He couldn't find a shirt he could button. He only did the bottom part of the zipper to keep it closed. His chest was exposed. He wore a bandanna around his neck to look more French.

Joe Danza's pants, being the same size as Walter's, were too big. He used some of the rope to make suspenders. He wore a loose knit shirt to hide his waist band. The driver had been selected small to give him more room in the driver's seat of the tank.

Bill Makleroy had it best. The clothes fit him perfectly. He had a suntan from living in Arizona before the war that gave him a darker skin tone he still hadn't lost. It helped him look like a weathered French farmer. Even the shoes fit. The drawback was the clothes were winter clothes and it was August. He solved that by wearing his dirty white tee shirt and carrying the other coat tied around his waist.

Brad Dorset might have looked more the part of the French farmer in that the clothes were loose, but fit him such that he might very well have been a farmer wearing loose clothing intentionally for comfort. He had been in Germany for most of two years and had lost his suntan. He also did not look French.

Actually many southern French had Italian, Spanish, or even Arabic blood and were darker skinned than the northern French that had German or English blood. Is there such a thing as true French. Walter said it was an attitude, not a blood line.

They made it to Gourdon before noon, but found the north bound road full. They hid in brush near the Dordogne river. Bill said, "Why aren't the vehicles moving? The road looks like a big parking lot."

Joe volunteered the answer, "The bridge is out. I talked with some guys on the ship that had the mission of wiring all the major bridges with explosives. If we were beaten their job was to make sure there was nothing left of the bridges going north."

Bill said, why can't they simply string a pontoon bridge like we do?"

Walter said, "They don't have as many rivers in the Middle East. Besides there is a lot more status to owning a tank versus a pontoon bridge section."

"Yeah, I guess you're right. How are we going to get across the road?" said Bill.

"I'm afraid we're going to have to come up with a new plan."

"Oh?"

"I don't think we're going to be able to head anyway but north, unless we really want to get caught. Once we get on the north side of the river, maybe we can find some transportation to Bordeaux.

Joe said, "I heard what they do with allied prisoners... Let's just say they don't have a problem with too many."

Brad said, "We don't know that. All we know is that there have been no prisoner exchanges and we simply don't know where they keep their prisoners."

"Regardless, we need to head north. If this river has them stopped, let's cross it at night and get north as fast as we can."

Joe asked, "And just how are we going to cross? It may not be the Amazon, or the Mississippi, but it's a good two hundred yards across and the water is moving pretty good."

"We'll build a raft and swim it across. Besides, I don't think it's over one hundred yards."

Brad said, "We build a raft and we'll just drift right down to where the Arabs are."

"You're right, let's get over into the tree line and work our way further east."

Joe said, "What do you propose we use for a raft?"

"Okay, so maybe it's a couple of big tree limbs tied together with some of this rope we've got."

"Let's get going. It gets dark around 8 PM and it's already 1 PM."

They walked east for three hours going back nearly the way they had come. At 4 PM they figured they had come far enough and were afraid they would be seen if they went much further. They found some limbs that they could move and tie together. They put their things on the raft and swam in their underwear across the river. They were not seen, but had gotten away.

MONTH 13, AUGUST 3

They walked for about an hour when they saw a village. Walter had brought his binoculars. "It looks like the people are still in their village. Anyone speak French?" No one did. "Oh well, maybe someone speaks English."

People stopped what they were doing when they saw them. One called out to them, "Hey Amerikan, Parle vu Francis'?"

Walter was taken aback that they had been called Americans but replied, "No, Parle vu Englesh?"

He got an unintelligible answer. They ended up at the town square surrounded by French. They were hemming in the Americans who had pulled out their guns with everyone knowing that they wouldn't fire them at French. A very pretty young woman wearing a short skirt and halter top stepped through the crowd. "What are you doing here?"

"You speak English. Good. We are trying to get away from the Arabs."

"Where are they?"

"They were being held up trying to cross the river without a bridge."

"Where are you going? Did you desert?"

"We are heading toward Bordeaux to rejoin our division. No we didn't desert. Our tank was destroyed. We jumped out and hid. Now we're trying to get back in the war. Can you help us get some transportation to Bordeaux?"

"Sorry. The American's pulled out of Bordeaux. The American aircraft carriers were attacked and sunk. Those Americans that could not get to Bordeaux were supposed to join the resistance in Spain. That's were most of the American troops went. You must have been in that last attack where the Arabs were ready for you. If you want to fight the Arabs, I'm afraid you will have to join me in the French Resistance. My grandfather was in the Resistance during World War II. I have joined it now. We got the news that there were no survivors of that last attack. It was an ambush. You always attacked in mass. They had already sunk the American aircraft carriers. The French and British air forces were pulled back away from the Arabs to defend Paris and London. They watched you coming from the air and then timed there attack to surprise you. So what do you want to do?"

"What do you mean?"

"Do you want to join the Resistance or just run?"

"How about we fight with you until we can get back to our American forces?"

"Okay, but the nearest American forces are in Germany now. Most have moved all the way into Austria. We have radio contact. If you wish, I will report to them that you are with us now?"

"Yes, do that. At least our families will know we're alive and the military won't call us dead or deserters."

"Where did you get those clothes? They look ridicules. This is summer, not winter."

"We found them in the attic of the house we hid in to get away from the Arabs. They were the best we could do. At least we got out of our uniforms."

"Well, come with me. Let's see if we can do a little better."

"I'm sorry, I didn't get your name. I'm Technical Sergeant Walter Gaddis."

"My name is Bridget. Yes, I was named after Bridget Bardot who was a big star when I was born. Don't they call you Walt for short."

"They would, but the government makes you sign your full name. I've been going by Walter for years now. You seem to know a lot about American's and speak English with almost no accent.

"Okay. Walter. My grandparents went to the United States after World War Two. My parents were born here, but raised as Americans. I studied French after learning it from my grand parents. I was just here on vacation when the war started and just sort of got trapped here. I was accepted when the war started because of who my grand parents were. I had already been trying to retrace his footsteps during the Resistance of World War II and met many people who either knew him or knew of him. When the war started, I was taken in. So far we have not been able to do much to help France or hurt the Arabs. Can't we destroy the Arab's bridge as soon as they get it built?"

"It wouldn't be easy. The land around the bridge is pretty flat without much place to hide and the Arabs have too much fire power to confront them."

"The Resistance of World War Two faced insurmountable odds to sneak in and hurt the Germans when they weren't looking. They had to steal their explosives from the Germans to use against them. We have our own explosives this time, provided by the government. Now come on and let's get you some clothes.

MONTH 13, AUGUST 4

General Gates issued the order, "Gentlemen, the Arabs have made an end around run on the French by landing in and taking Marseilles. They are now trying to cut off the retreat of the French military from the Riviera. We are going to pull most of our tanks out of Germany and England and land them in southeast France to retake Marseilles to cut off their supplies and prevent them from landing more troops and tanks. I am ordering all available landing craft to take on tanks in Bremerhaven and Liverpool and move to Bordeaux. This operation is Top Secret, especially the location of the landing. I do not want that information to leave this room until our ships are assembled for the landing. I want every anti-sub airplane in the air to protect the landing ships. I want every submarine under our command in the English Channel to protect our forces. We will have to suspend our escort of ships across the Atlantic in the meantime. We will resume it after our forces are safely landed. Now I want everyone to get busy planning the details and writing the orders."

Jim did not interrupt General Gates, but tried to catch him before he left the room. Brigadier General Henry Lakeman grabbed Jim's arm and said, "Hold up Jim. I already told him your opinion and was over-ruled. Save your silver bullets. Didn't you tell me this would happen. Maybe you can't stop it all the time. At any rate, you're not going to stop General Gates and he outranks me by two starts so I can't stop him either. You've known me for many years and you know I don't go out of my way for promotion. I would do something if I could."

"But Hank, thousands of men will get killed and we can't afford to just throw away tanks either. We're outnumbered a hundred to one on tanks. All we could hope to do is some hit and run attacks to slow them down."

"Okay Jim, let's try to change the tactics to hit and run then instead of one big losing tank battle."

"It would be better if we stood back and took out their tanks at long range and then retreated as soon as they turn toward our tanks and make sure that we have a good line of retreat and full tanks of fuel. We simply can't afford to lose any tanks."

As a result of the nuclear bombs and riots the population of the United States had decreased dramatically. Because so many men died protecting women in the riots whereas the women were saved for the survivors. Then there were the pitched battles between looters and the military, again killing mostly men. There were tens of thousands of looter men killed and hundreds of military. Then even more thousands of looters were herded into huge concentration camps until they could be processed and tried. Because most of the east coast cities were destroyed either by nukes or by looters, burning their own cities for greed, and because of the severe shortage of food on the east coast due to the total lack of imports and the shortage of farms in the northeast meant that all of the military moved onto the bases instead of living in private housing.

As a result, there was no where for Eva, Shelby and Darcy to stay. Jim's wife insisted on them staying in one of their bedrooms. Jim didn't know how she felt, if she resented them being there, but she seemed to just accept the girls as part of the war and the inevitable future.

MONTH 13, AUGUST 8

The Arab's pontoon bridge had finally arrived and was being set up in the river. The boats making up the bridge were maneuvering into position.

Walter was watching through binoculars. Bridge's group had buried explosives in the river banks on both sides of the river. The last boats had been linked up after three hours of maneuvering. The tanks started rolling across. Just before the first one got to this side of the river, both banks blew up along with the first and last pontoon boats. The remaining boats started drifting down stream and breaking apart as the tanks weight shifted on the waves and the tanks started capsizing the boats. It might be weeks before they could replace the pontoon bridge.

"That was great." Walter said.

"Not only that, but the same thing happened many places in France today. They can see another tank. They can detect airplanes trying to attack their bridges, but we sneak in where they aren't looking. They'll be a long time trying to go north of the river."

"I wouldn't count on that. I'll bet that next time they check the banks out better before they set up their bridge. I'll bet they bring out some infra red detectors too."

"Who cares what they bring up? What are infra red detectors any way?"

"They allow people to see at night. They will be able to see you sneaking up at night, just like it was daylight."

"How does it work?"

"It detects heat. People show up quite well, especially in the cool of the evening."

III,93

At Avignon in the southern France, the chief of all the Arab prince will stop before proceeding to the remains of Paris. Troyes in northeast France will be occupied by the angry North African, and the remaining people in Lyons will be under an army of occupation.

C18-allied offensive

II,61

Bravo, those of the Thames, the British, occupying Gironde and La Rochelle on the southwest coast of France. oh French blood! war will come to Toulon. on Garonne river the city will be the assaulted with flame-throwers and small arms killing many Arab and Chinese defenders at the breakthrough.

V,34

During the flooding of London, much of the British navy and the government moved to safety in Canada. because of the war in Europe, they will raise enough money to buy "hidden fire in containers", (tactical nuclear weapons).

II,1

Toward Aquitaine will come those of the British Isles making an important invasion on their own. Rain and frost will make it difficult for the Arabs and Chinese to move armor. They will use the port of Genoa as an important base.

III,85

It is rapidly recaptured by a young Arab leader during an Arab counter attack along the Robine and Aude rivers. The Arab counter attackers will die in the attack along with their leaders.

IX,64

The occupants of Macedonia, the Arabs, will attack across the Pyrenees from Spain. Narbonne will not offer any resistance (due to the size of the British commando force.) Secret plans of the Arabs will be carried out on land and sea leaving the free French with little land to live on.

IV,70

Quite close to the Pyrenees mountains, one will command against a great army against the forces of the eagle, USA, that have sent a few forces to help the British invasion. The forces of both sides are nearly exterminated and the American leader is chased into Pau, southern France.

MONTH 13, AUGUST 25

Major General Henry Lakeman was now in charge of the Alternate Military Command Center (ANMCC). He was speaking to the hushed audience. "Gentlemen, Ladies, our forces in southern France have been destroyed. The Arabs used their reconnaissance forces to lay in wait for our attacks on their columns. They were ready and waiting for us. We are still trying to get reports. We have lost contact with all headquarters in southern France. Without air superiority the Arabs started to make their air superiority work for them. Our Stinger IV missiles kept them from making close air bombing. They never had the high altitude bombing and with our mobility their aircraft were not an offensive factor against our tanks, but they knew exactly where we were at all times. It was only a matter of time before they just got ready and waited for us. The only transmissions have been from one unit making a run for the mountains in northern Spain. They said they were warned by transmissions from other units that were ambushed as they were attempting their own ambush. It may be some time before we can mount any form of offense. We don't have much left and what we do have will be protecting a limited number of air bases essential for air cargo. What I want are ideas about how to multiply our forces."

IX,93

Before the Arab-Chinese alliance are in position to strike with a leader named Hercules, the allies will use airborne troops and equipment to set up a defensive line near Bourgeois, France.

X,7

A great battle will be planned against Nancy in northeast France and the Easterner will boast, "I will conquer everyone". The British will be in trouble raising popular support for an expensive war to help France.

VI,80

From northwest Africa (the Fez) the invaders will penetrate further into the center of Europe whose cities will be burning and inhabitants killed. The Philip will not be able to hold two positions at Metz for long.

II,63

The French have failed to defend Ausonia in southern Italy and at the Po valley in northern Italy, and now the Arab-Chinese alliance is at the Seine near Paris. Many will die at the weakest point in the defensive line around Paris.

V,30

All around the city soldiers will be positioned to attack Paris when the Romans are coming out of their shelters and the Vatican being pillaged.

IV,52

Men and Women will both be in the defense line with the Arab leader demanding surrender. Wind will carry riot gas against the defenders who will have to fall back.

III,50

Paris will not submit to the severe surrender terms, but the French President leaves as soon as the attack starts.

III,7

The battle starts with tremendous air battles and air attacks on the artillery batteries. The enemy forces will approach the defense line.

VI,34

The French chief will worry about the device of flying fire and within the city there is panic and disorder.

IX,86

Seven crafty men appearing as Martyrs will offer surrender terms to turn over Paris when the supply lines are cut and the city surrounded, but will refuse to let the main enemy army enter Paris.

IX,96

Paris will still not surrender, but during the negotiations with the seven Martyrs, the enemy has penetrated the weakest points of the city.

III,6

A shell will land in the Notre Dame and the citizen defenders will be injured. Even the weakest are armed to defend Paris along with navy seamen that escaped the fleet.

III,13

Lightning will come through the Arch of Triumph so hot it melts gold and silver. The leader will be killed and a mini submarine fleet will enter Paris in the Seine. River in Paris when the important leader is calling for help.

IX,82

The city was besieged for a long time with many defenders killed in hand to hand combat, but the civilians were not harmed.

VII,18

Paris will feign a surrender, but a week later they will launch a counter attack, which will fail. The Arabs will execute the seven Martyrs with the guillotine and the lady who negotiated the peace held prisoner.

V,33

The leaders of the city will want fight to recover their liberty, but the men were cut up during the disastrous counter attack. And at Nantes, another battle is going on (preventing reinforcement).

I,92

The Arab-Chinese army pulled back without much entry into Paris. They pillaged the surrounding areas and captured many civilians.

X,68

The Arabs were apparently bloodied in the French attack for peace was proclaimed in Paris. But, because the city refused the peace term offered, it will be invaded with one third of million dead or captured.

I,41

The city will be attacked at night with few escaping. The enemy brought reinforcements from the sea during the apparent peace. There will be so few survivors that a women will faint to see her son alive, but poison and secret codes and radios will be hidden from the invaders

VI,96

The great city is abandoned by the soldiers. never has such a great battle been fought so near to it. The calamity will draw closer as the Chinese reinforcements arrive from the sea and after the French counterattack that killed many Arabs, the army knows nothing will be spared.

III,84

Paris is thoroughly desolated and all inhabitants either fled or were killed. all the buildings and especially the churches were violated.

MONTH 14, SEPTEMBER 20

Walter and Bridget had grown very close in the past few weeks. They were not lovers because their concerns were made up entirely of ploys to stop the Arabs. So far they had stopped the Arabs coldly at the river. Much the same had happened all across France. The French military had retreated to the area around and in Paris, but had set up a roving artillery unit that regularly shelled the Arabs across the river on a daily basis. After each barrage of thirty minutes they spent two hours moving away from return fire. Then another thirty minutes of artillery shelling on Arab positions. Bill and Brad had crossed back to the south side of the river and were spotting for the French artillery. They knew it was dangerous, but both were qualified and had insisted.

The Resistance had destroyed two bridges here. The Arabs had become more cautious on their second bridge and had only sent over one tank at a time. After six tanks had crossed singly along with four hundred troops, the Resistance had blown the bridge, but without sinking all the bridge sections. It had only taken a week for the Arab's to replace the boats at each end. The tanks and troops that crossed set up a perimeter near the bridge head to prevent any further sabotage.

The Resistance had destroyed all but two of the tanks with anti-tank missiles, but the infantry still guarded the bridge head. The other end of the bridge head was solid people. The Resistance tried to float some explosive down the river, but it didn't work. Now the Arab tanks were moving north again. The Resistance moved ahead of them blowing up roads and bridges as they went to make it difficult for the Arabs to come quickly. Their trucks got stuck in the mud trying to drive along the sides of the road. The Arab troops were constantly covered with mud and sleeping in the wet.

The Arabs had acquired plenty of infrared optics. In World War II the Resistance was able to sneak in under the noses of the Germans to destroy what they could, but with infra red optics, the Resistance had a very difficult time sneaking at night. The Arabs could see them better than in the day time. Hiding behind a bush was no good when body heat lit a person up on the infra reds.

Whole villages were wired with booby traps and Arab troops were afraid to try to sleep in the villages. If the door didn't blow up when opened, there might be a land mine under the carpet. If you did go to sleep, a timed explosive in the mattress might blow up. The Arabs in turn blew up all the villages as they passed through. The displaced French many had times had no where to go so they joined an ever growing Resistance that far out numbered the pre-war French military. Every Frenchman had an automatic assault rifle with all the ammunition that could be carried, except those that carried the anti aircraft and anti tank missiles that prevented any further low altitude bombing by either side in the battle.

MONTH 14, SEPTEMBER 22

The Arabs were advancing on Paris again. The French had totally destroyed every aircraft runway in southern France and ripped up the highways including the Auto-routes as they retreated toward Northern France. Consequently, the Arab army had to either rebuild all the roads and bridges or walk and drive through fields and ford rivers. The roads were worse to travel on than the fields because the broken slabs of concrete and blacktop worked almost as effectively as tank traps and walking had to be redefined as climbing. The fields were muddy this time of year which made for vehicles being stuck and people being wet and miserable. Every time they came to a stream they either had to wade or drive through it, or put up a temporary military bridge. It appeared that the French used some of the Durandal explosive approximately every three hundred yards to make sure that no one used the roads again.

The civilians had been evacuated from every village along with every useful item and morsel of food. They did not destroy any buildings so the Arabs had plenty of dry places to spend their evenings, but minimal food. The Arab military had a problem developing just like the Chinese. How do you keep the troops fed? If you have forty million troops in the field and each one needs two gallons of water for drinking, cooking, or bathing each day, that is eighty million gallons of safe water not polluted by chemical, biological, or nuclear radiation. If each one needs one pound of food, that is forty million pounds of food each day that had to be transported from storage in Arab countries to Europe by sea and then overland to the troops. Tanks and armored personnel vehicles (APVs) and even jeeps may be able to drive through the fields, but supply trucks need roads.

Once the American tank force had retreated, supplying the troops became the top priority. Dry clothing was essential. Arab troops from desert countries did not do well wet and cold in the mud of France. Military opposition had ceased, but now the elements were taking a toll. Winter was not even there yet and already the weather had become a major factor.

V,43

A great ruin and destruction is not far when it will be in province (south France), Naples, Sicily and to the Holy See. then it will come to Germany, against Rhine river at Cologne by forces coming from the Mainz.

X,62

From Sorbin (East Germany) a force will assail Czechoslovakia and Hungary. the Arab chief will attack from Albania.

X,31

He will march into Germany and Austria. The Arabs will find openings the defenses. At the same time destruction will come to Carmania (southern Iran) defenders buried in the earth.

III,53

Once a leader will win the prize of Nuremberg, Augsburg, and Nasle (Switzerland). Through Cologne, the chiefs of Frankfort taken. they will march through Flanders (Netherlands, Belgium) into France.

V,94

After marching into Grand Germany they will march against Brabant (Netherlands), Flanders (Belgium) and Boulogne (north France). and, after bluffing east, the eastern duke will attack Vienna and Cologne.

The United States forces had been pretty much wiped out in Europe. Not that there was that much there. Since the Early-1980's, the United States had been pulling troops and equipment out of Europe. During the Gulf war with Iraq, most of the equipment in Europe had been sitting in Saudi Arabia and was now in the hands of the Arabs. Other than the Air Force, the only benefit gained by having the small U.S. forces in Europe had been the temporary delaying actions in southern France and in Austria. Those forces had been pretty much destroyed.

The Arab forces had taken all of Austria, what we used to call Eastern Europe except for Poland that had been siding with the Arabs anyway. The Rhine river had held up the Arabs for awhile, but eventually they crossed and moved on to take much of Belgium, the Netherlands, and the remaining part of France. Because of their preoccupation with Paris that was determined to hold to the last French man or woman, there were areas of northern France and Belgium untouched.

IX,92

An army commander will want to march into the New City (New York), but he will be captured without reaching the city. he will not be able to get help from his countrymen. He will act and speak falsely.

IX,61

The attack will be made on the sea coast at the New City, relatives brought forward. They will be confined with no compensation.

The United States had not been expecting an attack when several huge Arab submarine landing craft landed on the gentle shores of Long Island and moved on the remains of the city. The Arabs captured all of the people they could round up and put them in concentration camps. Those that escaped were typical Americans, well armed. That led to guerrilla attacks on the Arabs which hindered their progress. He had wanted to march unobstructed into the remains of New York City and instead, he was having a difficult time taking Brooklyn and Queens to the north. He had eight hundred tanks and thousands of soldiers. He was determined not to let these Americans hold out like the French in Paris. He had moved forward to lead his troops, but the guerrillas captured the Arab commander of the invasion which dramatically slowed their approach.

IX,100

Naval battle, when night is ending, fire from ships will cause ruin in the west (America). Against them will come ships camouflaged in a new way. The vanquished enemy angered, victory in a drizzle.

Jim convinced the ANMCC commander to commit every stealth aircraft and ship in the American military to the battle. The Arab firepower was simply too great for their meager conventional forces, but Jim reasoned that at night they couldn't see them and by being stealth they would not appear on radar either.

The Arab landing ships were coming in with reinforcements when they were attacked from both the air and sea by aircraft and ships that did not appear on their radars. It was still dark and they couldn't see anything until they were hit with missiles or high caliber gunfire. The sky would briefly light up with the flare of a missile, but when they shot at the origination point there was nothing. Night was the perfect time for stealth attacks. Both the surface ships and the aircraft were painted black with shapes to spoil the radars being aimed at them. When the Arabs fired their radar guided missiles they went into seek mode and found other Arab ships to hit.

This attack failed completely. Eventually, they got enough American military into the New York City area to clean up the remains of the Arab military. Actually, they surrendered pretty easily when their supporting fleet was sunk.

VII,74

A military commander will invade deep into the new world and some people will welcome him, but when they realize his treachery they will cancel their welcoming activities.

X,69

A newly elected statesman will be placed in high position. Against South Aquilon (South America) will come a great military force. The statesman will be led by his sister, a leader of great crowds, but fleeing he will be murdered in the forests of Brazil.

Intelligence reports from South America showed that the Arabs indeed had established beach heads in several places. The Arabs moved into southern Brazil unopposed, even welcomed by many of the people. Since the HEMP attack there had been no western news to tell them of the European war. They didn't realize that they were being invaded. The South American news media were everywhere. South America had not warranted a nuke. Since they were not being shot at, the Arabs simply started unloading their troops and tanks peacefully.

A Brazilian welcoming delegation led by Senator Elconzo met with the Arab commander. In near perfect English Senator Elconzo said, "Sir, I see you are the commander here."

"Yes. I am. And you are?"

"Senator Elconzo. I am the leader of the welcoming committee. Do you have news from Europe?"

"No."

"Aren't you here as some form of relief party from Europe?"

"No."

"Well, Sir, just why are you here with all of this military equipment?"

"To acquire new property of course."

"What do you mean by that? You're not planning to take territory by force are you?"

"Not as long as you keep cooperating."

"Sir. We will not cooperate as you say. You will find our military is quite proficient and you are a long way from home."

"Abdul."

"Yes Sir."

"Take this infidel and lock him up."

"Yes Sir."

"You can't do this. I am a Senator of the Brazilian Congress and maybe the next President."

"You won't have any more Presidents."

The unloading continued. The only thing slowing them down were the throngs of Brazilian well wishers. The Arab commander rightly assumed that as long as the Brazilians weren't shooting they might as well keep it peaceful. Not that the pitiful South American forces could hinder them, but the longer they could put off the military confrontation, the more equipment they could get on the ground and the better positions they could get. The beaches were wide open here which made it a good landing place, but there was no cover from air forces. They could shoot down their planes easily enough, but the Arabs had no air craft carriers. It was the Armies job to take air fields where their aircraft could fly to from Africa. It should only take a few months to take South America and then they could simply move up through Mexico to take the United States itself.

There had been talk of pacifying the people, but it was decided that they would only pacify the women. The men and children, they would kill. But right now the idea was to just continue unloading. He shouldn't have told the delegation their true intent, but it had been a show of power. He had no fear of them, but they should fear him. He hadn't had them killed because gunfire might alert the new media sooner than necessary.

"Where is the delegation?" shouted some woman. "Where are they?"

"We are taking care of them." shouted the Arab.

"Where are they?"

"They have been arrested."

"Why? What did they do?"

"They threatened to call in military forces."

He didn't anticipate the reaction of the Brazilians. Instead of a welcoming committee they turned into an angry mob. It turned out that apparently the Senator's sister was really the popular one. The mob was intermingled with the troops who were not prepared to be in the very middle of a riot. Many of them were overcome quickly and their guns taken from them. The mob surged forward into the ship until they actually succeeded in rescuing the delegation and then withdrew. By then the Arab forces had recovered and started a wholesale slaughter on live Brazilian television. The Senator and his sister managed to make it to his limousine and escaped down the highway.

They left behind a wholesale slaughter. Every last Brazilian was killed, even the young women. The cameras kept rolling even after the cameramen died. The Arab general used the opportunity to put on his own broadcast where he warned the people of Brazil and South America not to oppose his superior forces.

He had been right and had conquered most of the cities of South America, destroying most of the military forces. True to his promise he had killed most of the men, children and women over forty, keeping the young women for the Sheiks back home. He had them rounded up and kept them in concentration camps until South America was completely theirs. Then the Arab leaders would move in, rebuild the cities and have ready made harems. All this land with all this water. They would all be rich.

IX,99

Aquilon (northern nations) will use the wind to end encirclement. beyond their defense lines they will launch forms of dust. Rain will also spread it, which once used against them. This will be a desperate effort against their frontiers.

HANK SAID, "WELL, JIM. WHAT DO WE DO ABOUT SOUTH AMERICA?"

Jim replied, "Obviously, we can't send any help to Europe when our own back door is open. We don't have the forces to beat them head on. There is only one choice, we will have to use one of their own weapons on them, biologicals."

"Jim. You can't be serious. We signed the Geneva convention."

"As long as you think that way we won't have a chance. We are talking about ten thousand tanks and a million troops in South America moving our direction killing everything in sight. We have biologicals that will kill quickly and then disperse quickly. We have to use weapons of mass destruction to beat that force and quickly. The Arabs have done for us what we couldn't do, separated the civilians from themselves. Most of the civilians that haven't been killed are hiding in the jungles. The Arabs are a little afraid of the jungles. Their tanks can't move. Their Air Force is ineffective in finding people in the jungle, and their troops can be picked off too easily. Therefore they have moved most of their troops into highly fortified cities making them easy targets for biologicals."

"Jim. Since they have been using biologicals, surely they know how to protect themselves."

"Yeh. From their own. They are sitting there fat dumb and happy and not expecting anything like that from the South Americans."

"Wait a minute, Jim. There is one more problem."

"Oh?"

"What about the estimated ten million young women in concentration camps there?"

"I reviewed the locations of the camps from satellite photos and our hyper sonic spy planes. They are keeping them away from the cities to keep them away from their own troops to prevent the spread of AIDS as happened in Europe. These guys are planning to stay here. For the camps nearer the cities I thought maybe we could halo jump some Air Force Pararescue guys in there with the antibodies against it. If we do it at night and jump right in the middle of the camps, the Arabs won't even know they are there until the shots are administered."

"HOW DO WE INOCULATE TEN MILLION PEOPLE THAT QUICKLY?"

"We can't, but there are only a few thousand near the cities and the toxin that I want to use will dissipate too quickly to reach the other camps. That won't kill all of the Arabs of course. They have ninety thousand or so protecting the accesses to the cities and guarding the concentration camps. I thought we could use our stealth aircraft to spread the toxin without them even detecting us."

"You're right that we have to do something. I think you are right. Let's go for it."

The mission was pretty much of a success. All but a half million Arabs were killed by the toxin. The Halo jumps by the Pararescue worked great although they had to be supplemented by Navy SEALS to carry more of the antibody. The Pararescue administer it. They feel out of the heavens into heaven. Can you imagine a hundred young very very healthy men jumping into a camp of ten thousand of the younger better looking women. There were only eight camps within range of the toxins being sprayed on the cities. Three days later the Stealth fighters flew in with the toxins. The one bad spot was that over seventy percent of the Stealth fighters were shot down because the Arabs homed in on the spray itself to shoot down the fighters that had to fly low to get the toxins on the ground. Overall, the mission was a success. The South American forces spent the next three months hunting down the remaining Arab forces and freeing their women. The American military that had dropped into the camps were glad to be rescued themselves.

20 COMMANDO TEAM

MONTH 18

It was a war of retreat. The French had lost a half million of their trained troops already while the Resistance did not have the heavy equipment to hold or push back the Arabs. This was far different from World War II in that there could be no surrender. The Arabs killed everyone caught behind their lines except for young women, girls, and young boys that were given to the troops for sex. There was no collaborating with the Arabs. The vineyards and farms produced wine and food for the Germans, but the Arabs killed everyone.

The Resistance in several areas tried to make a stand with help from French and British artillery and armor, but each stand was only temporary and resulted in huge loss of life by the Resistance. Walter retreated with the French. They had not heard from Bill or Brad since the Arabs crossed the river. Walter could only hope they were safe. Bridget, Joe, and Walter were the only ones left in their original Resistance group.

They were sleeping in a small village ten miles from the Arabs. They were getting up in the morning to wire the village. They had their first snow two weeks ago. It was early for the flat lands of France to have snow. Walter could not imagine having to sleep in tents without heat as the Arabs were doing. Bridget and he had grown closer, but the war kept them from becoming lovers. They were always on the move and always sleeping in a group with other people in the room. Many of the French couples made love during the nights together in a group when they thought others were asleep, but Bridget was American and more reserved about sex. Bridget had taken to sleeping beside him since it got really cold, but they were both fully clothed. Walter had messed his jeans several times during the night in his sleep as Bridget had snuggled against him. She regularly pulled his hand over her and put it under her blouse for him to hold her. She knew what she was doing to him, and seemed to enjoy it. They might as well be married except for the war and not consummating. They had never kissed, with

Bridget resisting his attempts with, "There's a war on. You know it can't be. We're not in love. We wouldn't know if it was real or the war."

Walter was not getting much sleep. He liked where Bridget put his hand each night, but he had just had another wet dream. He thought he heard something outside and was now fully awake and listening closely. Then he thought he heard some other language. It wasn't English or French, but he had never heard Arabic languages. Did they all speak one language? He pulled his hand from Bridge's blouse. She tried to pull it back, but he grabbed her hand and pulled her over with a, "Shhhhh. I hear something strange."

Bridget was awake now. She reached for her gun as Walter reached for his. Where were their village guards? There were guards posted out on the roads and on the streets to prevent surprises. Bridget and Walter rolled out of their blankets and started waking the others. When the doors burst open, there were twenty guns ready. The Arabs were shot immediately, but a grenade spun lazily on the floor.

In slow motion Walter grabbed Bridget and picked her off the floor and with a twisting motion jumped with her behind a large sofa. Walter saw Joe lunging for the grenade, grabbing it and was in the motion of throwing it back out the door. Walter's view was blocked by the sofa just as the grenade went off blowing blood and plaster to all corners of the room. Walter's ears were ringing as he laid on top of Bridget as chunks of this and that fell around them.

Before things had stopped falling in the room, there were people bursting in though the doorway. Neither Walter nor Bridget moved. It sounded like the people left the room. They could hear voices that must have been just outside the now destroyed door for the next ten minutes that seemed like hours talking in what must have been Arabic and then the voices moved down the street. Walter was still lying on Bridget and had become aroused even with the Arabic voices just outside the doorway.

Bridget whispered, "They've left you can get off me now."

"Not until they get out of hearing. I have something laying on my back that might fall and tip them off to come back here."

Bridget reached her arms around and to feel over his back in a hugging motion. It felt like a sexual caress until she came to what was lying on his upper back and right shoulder. "I'm sorry. You're right, there is a board laying on your shoulders. It has something on it at the other end that almost tipped when I tried to pick it up."

"There is also something heavier laying on my back end."

"Oh. You mean you are not just trying to grind your pelvis into mine?" She was getting into the spirit now. She knew nothing could happen without making a noise that could be heard. She had also recognized from Walter's response that he liked having her arms around him. She moved them deliberately down and felt over his backside. "There's what feels like a four by four timber laying there. Does it hurt?"

"No, but it's a little heavy."

"Let me massage it for you." She put her hands on his buttocks and grabbed a handful of each playfully. He kissed her and she kissed back fervently until he broke it off.

"Now I will have to say this is the not the time or the place. We have to try to get out of here. I'm afraid that with winter, the Arabs may be planning to move in here. I don't hear anyone, can you see if you can get that board off my shoulders quietly?"

She almost did. Plaster or something fell to the floor. They both stayed very still. Walter kissed her again and she kissed back as fervently as before. Walter was afraid to move and make any noise, as was she. Walter wondered if she was being this way because of the very close brush with death. When no one responded to the noise, Walter pushed himself up push up style. "See if you can wiggle out from under me quietly."

After she was free they both discovered that her blouse was practically ripped off her by Walter's rough handling getting the two of them behind the sofa before the grenade went off. She tied the remainder together in front and then she picked up the four by four wall beam so he could pull out from under it and they were both free. They didn't even whisper now, but went about picking up ammunition and arms to prepare to fight if necessary. Walter went to the doorway and carefully peered out and up and down the street, then whispered, "Let's try to get to those trees west of town and hide. If you hear or see anything or if I make a motion, move into a doorway or alley out of sight. Let's go now while their infra red sensors can't help like they would at night."

Bridget simply nodded. They spent nearly an hour getting four blocks to the edge of town. Walter motioned her down in the ditch as he got down on his stomach and started wriggling down the ditch toward the tree line. It took thirty minutes to get to the trees. When they got there Walter continued crawling another ten yards further into the underbrush and then stood and turned to help Bridget up. "Hold me, I'm freezing to death."

Walter didn't doubt it, and was very sorry that he hadn't thought of it sooner. He had been so scared of the Arabs he hadn't given her time or told her to find something warmer and apparently, she had not thought of it either. He was wearing both a long sleeve shirt and a light jacket. "I'm sorry I didn't realize." While he talked he quickly removed his jacket and put it around her and then he opened his shirt and held her nearly frozen breasts against his relatively warm chest. He held her for a while that way and then said softly, "Let's get further into the trees."

They walked sideways further in until they were a mile or more from the village. It was getting dark now and Walter was very cold except where his skin contacted hers. "We were pretty stupid not to bring some blankets or something. What I wouldn't do for a space blanket. We can't build a fire, but lets try to find some sheltered area and make us a warmer spot by piling up some branches and pine needles."

She had buttoned up the jacket he had given her and he had buttoned up the flannel shirt including the collar. They each had sub machine guns and over one hundred rounds of ammunition apiece in their small back packs and three grenades apiece. Their pine bough shelter was just big enough for both of them to climb in. They had found a thick bush that had not lost all of its leaves before the snow and had a semi dry place without snow under it. They had then piled up some loose branches and pine boughs that Walter had cut with his pocket knife and then both had piled snow on that. Their hands had gotten so cold that they had to frequently stop for several minutes and put their hands in their pockets to warm them. It was dark when they quit. Maybe their little shelter would hold in some of their own heat.

Walter didn't have much heat. The flannel shirt was some protection, but his skin was bloodless and icy to the touch. Bridget was still not looking for sex, but insisted that she lay on top of him and opened up her jacket that he had given her and then his shirt and guided his arms around her waist. "God, that's cold. We have to get you warmed up."

Walter didn't realize how cold he truly was. Even though he was bare chest to bare chest with his arms around a beautiful girl that he found himself very attracted to and she was lying on top of him trying to cover his legs with hers, he didn't get aroused, only colder. He must have near frost bite on his hands and arms and his body must have been near a hypothermia shutdown. He went to sleep in about ten minutes with the feeling of her warmth going into his own body as he could feel her growing warmer also.

When he woke, he could see some daylight starting to creep into small holes in their make do shelter. He was warm and aroused. He could feel her bare breasts on his own. Her head laid on his shoulder with her warm breath on the side of his neck. He didn't want to move, but discovered after an indeterminable time that probably was only a half hour, that there were numerous hard spots under his hips and shoulders that had become unbearable. They had both been asleep like that for perhaps eleven hours without waking. He began rubbing her back under the jacket to awaken her. She purred and then said, "Was it as good for you as it was for me?"

"Yes, but there are rocks and things under my back that are about to poke through."

He rolled her over discovering that their little shelter wasn't quite large enough for them to lay side by side. It sure felt good to get his back off the hard things on the ground. He kissed her and she kissed back as fervently as yesterday in the ruined house. Her hands moved on his back and then started stopping at all the dents from the sticks and rocks on the ground. She pushed him back. "My turn. This still isn't the time or the place, but we will. I promise you."

He was no longer as warm. Her body had warmed his whole body and his back had warmed the spot on the ground. It was still pretty dark in their shelter, but he could see that her bare breasts and stomach were covered with slimy mud that she had gotten crawling through the ditch from yesterday and had stayed moist with moisture from their bodies during the night.

She said, "Besides, you need a bath."

He looked at his chest that was covered with the same mud and replied, "Where do you think I got so dirty?"

She looked at her breasts and then pulled the coat together. "Oh."

They had eaten nothing since noon yesterday and now it must have been mid morning the next day. They had no rations so they needed to get moving and find something to eat. They had used a lot of mainly nervous energy since their last meal and both were near having the shakes. He said, "We have to get walking. We don't know how far we'll have to go to find a friendly to give us some food and we don't know how slow or fast we can go without being found by the Arabs. I hate to leave our warm little love nest, but we can't stay here without food."

"Here, Walter. Let me stuff some leaves and pine needles into our clothes for insulation." He found it a mixture of pleasure to feel her hands moving around on his upper body and itchy unpleasantness of the stuffing she was using. Pretty soon they looked like some clowns with stuffed shirts. It probably would keep them warmer, if a whole lot dirtier and itchier.

"It was around 4 P.M. when they came to an out of the way farm cottage. They took their time sneaking up to its outbuildings and then hid. After seeing no movement around them, they crawled to the house itself. After looking in several windows, Bridget tried the door and found it unlocked and empty. They found some canned goods in the kitchen and a small gas range. There was no electricity and they were afraid to light a fire in a fireplace because of the smell and smoke that could bring Arabs down on them. Bridget made them a meal of heated canned goods while Walter brought some blankets and a mattress into the now gas stove warmed kitchen. The rest of the house was somewhere below freezing. After they ate, Bridget warmed water on the stove so they could both take baths. The water came from a hand pump by the kitchen sink. Walter was hoping and Bridget did not disappoint him when she asked him to join her for a bath. She moved away when Walter tried to undress her, "Undress yourself and turn your back until I say ready."

Walter undressed with his back to her and stood there until she said, "Ready." She was already in the old style hawk legged porcelain tub. Walter was self conscious being naked in front of her and his arousal was already there.

She giggled, "Come on in. The waters fine. I can see your are ready for your bath."

That wasn't the only thing he was ready for. They scrubbed each other's front and back leaving the water nearly brown. He wanted to do it right there in the tub, but she didn't cooperate although she seemed to enjoy his attempts. He would not force himself on her if she didn't want to. She told him to settle down and put his back at the sloped end and then she laid back against him putting his arms around her with his hands on her breasts. "Now isn't that all warm and better?" She asked.

He said, "Yes, this is very comfortable." When he really felt like he would explode. He forced himself to relax and enjoy embracing her. When he woke up he had she was moving to get out and break the embrace.

She said, "The waters getting cold. Time to wake up and get out." She wrapped one of the old towels around her top and tied it in a half knot.

This was the first time he had seen her without clothes in their time together. It was the first good look he had of her. Her breasts were nearly perfect. Maybe a thirty-four C-cup. Her shoulders and upper body would appear very delicate and small except her waist that had to be only nineteen or twenty inches. Her buttocks were rounded behind in a very sexy way and her hips were relatively narrow. Her legs, which he had never seen before were quite muscular. Not too large, not skinny at all, but sinewy like a runner or body builder. Now that he noticed her legs he noticed her buttocks were also well muscled, as was her flat stomach and abdomen. She was a vision of a perfectly physically fit young woman without looking muscled and manly like a body builder. "You have a fantastic body. Were you a dancer or weight lifter?"

She looked at him with a shy crooked and still coy smile and said, "No, aerobics instructor in my spare time. It shows?"

"God does it show. I've never seen such a perfect body."

"THANK YOU, I GUESS. ARE YOU SURE THAT YOU'RE NOT JUST TRYING TO TAKE ADVANTAGE OF ME OR THE SITUATION?"

"No. I mean it. I have never seen such a lovely body."

"And just how many bodies have you been with?"

Walter blushed and said, "No. I didn't mean that... I mean not very many. I mean every guy has a mental picture of how a woman should look. You're my definition of perfect."

"What about my personality? Doesn't count much, huh? Put a sack over my head? Isn't that what you mean?

"No. I mean, yes. I mean I was attracted to you from the start because of your pretty face. I thought we were getting close psychologically before I saw your body. Now I really want close."

"Well come here then and let me see your body without the mud camouflage."

"It's not much, but it's all I've got." Walter was just short of six feet. Not tall, but not short. He used to feel his feet were too big. He was not flabby, but neither was he muscled. He was far from a ninety pound weakling weighing one hundred and seventy pounds, but he was a long way from belonging on muscle beach. He was not a weight lifter or runner. Next to her perfect body he was self conscious of his own rather undefined body. He was not in bad shape in that he liked walking a lot and could do any two peoples' physical work, but he did nothing to make his body look good.

She inspected him as he came to her. He had nothing to hide behind except his hands. She said, "We can't do anything with your hands there. Now turn around, raise your hands and let me dry your back. She was five six, only five inches shorter and probably weighed no more than one hundred ten pounds of delicious girl. She dried his back and sides and then his legs and said, "Turn around now."

He did. He was aroused again. She only had the one towel and was using the ends of it to dry him. As she got to his shoulders, her front was bare and he couldn't resist any longer. He pulled her towel free of her body and embraced and kissed her, leaning her body to the floor while her hands were clasped behind his neck. It was mutual and both released the wartime and sexual tension of the past weeks. He was on top of her and she rose to meet him until they were consummated and satisfied. He lay on top of her until she rolled over onto him and lifted her face to inspect his face for a while. Then she just laid on him as on the previous night with his arms around her tiny waist.

It did not take too long until he started to get aroused again. She attacked the side of his neck and his ears with her teeth and tongue. He was helpless to resist and became very aroused. They did it again with her on top this time. She slid off and snuggled beside him curled under his arm with her front to his side. "Your body isn't so bad either."

They both dozed off until she stirred. "It's cold in here. Let's get to the kitchen." They picked up their dirty clothes and the towel and stole to the warm of the mattress and gas stove of the kitchen. They slept the rest of the night. The next day they both dressed in their under shorts while Bridget washed their clothes. Then she washed their undies, by hand, while they wore their clothes without underwear. There were no clothes to be found in the house. Apparently the farmer and family had fled with their belongings. That left Bridget without a blouse and/or Walter without a jacket. Bridget took down some curtains and used them for stuffing Walter's shirt to keep him warmer. Neither had room in their jeans for insulation. Bridget used a torn section of the towel they had found to make a halter top to wear under Walter's jacket. Walter found a tarp in the barn that they decided to take a section of to use as a tent. They emptied the farm of all food and took along a kettle to heat it in.

MONTH 18, JANUARY

They had been walking in a northerly direction all day after leaving the farm house. They hoped to somehow walk through the front line into French territory. They ran out of woods and decided to spend the night in the woods out of sight rather than attempt crossing the open land ahead at night where infra red spotting scopes could easily see them. Walter explained that both sides had them and made night more hazardous than day for someone without a night scope. They weren't sure which side of the line they were on and either side might shoot if they saw someone crossing an open area at night.

They had sex for their third night together as lovers versus friends. They each had the other and no one else. They were both Americans. Both were willing to fight for their lives and for good causes. There was a chemical attraction between them from the very start.

Bridget didn't know if she would ever be able to return to her family in America. She had not been looking for a man, but her family thought it was time. She was college educated herself, but didn't feel that her husband necessarily had to be. She had gone to France to do her master's thesis that was the only thing separating her from a master's degree in French. After her graduation, she was expecting to go to work and find a man to have children and live with in the United States, not France. She was not interested in French men except as a subject to write about. Was Walter the right man?

Walter had been separated from his unit for months and his tank crew were all dead or at least lost from him. He didn't have any other close friends outside his unit and his unit had been destroyed in southern France. He had no family to go back to in the United States, but had been looking forward to going home to maybe find a wife to settle down with. He had been going to night school for several years and had completed over one hundred hours of college credit. Unfortunately, he would be lucky to be called a junior in most colleges because too many hours were not for any particular degree. He had entered the service at seventeen with his dying dad's permission. His mother had died when he was in grade school. His father had approved of the military because he didn't have a big life insurance policy and he knew the military would take care of his son. He died while Walter was in basic training.

Bridget and Walter might not have gotten so serious in normal times, but it was the right time for each of them to meet the other. Walter was thirty-two and Bridget was only twenty-four. Walter could retire in six years though he would still have to work to make a living. Bridge's family was not rich, but she had never had to work. Walter was working full time during high school and then joined the military. Bridget was close to her family. Walter had no family to be close to. Bridget was educated. Walter was working on it but was a long way away from her education level.

War. Americans being thrown together in a dangerous environment. Relying on each other. Walter had saved her life by throwing her with him behind the sofa in the grenade attack. Bridget saving his life when he was freezing. But then she would have died without his coat that was why he had come so close to hypothermia. They owed each other their lives and they were now totally alone behind enemy lines. It was natural to become lovers.

MONTH 18, JANUARY 14

Bridget and Walter took off walking north again staying away from hill tops or crawling slowly over hill tops on their bellies to not be silhouetted against the sky. They came to a village that was surrounded by at least five hundred tents and they could count one hundred tanks, but without binoculars they didn't know who was who. It was late afternoon, so they looked for a place out of sight to camp. They set up their makeshift tent. They used short sticks for poles and broke down someone's grape vines to hide their tent in the grape yard. The grapes were long gone. They were camped before dark. They ate their body temperature food from their cans and made love for lack of any other entertainment. They had nearly twelve hours of darkness and only needed maybe six for sleep.

MONTH 18, JANUARY 15

They spent the better part of the day trying to get close enough to the village to find out if they were friend or foe without being seen themselves. It was afternoon by the time they found that the village was full of Arabs. It also appeared that the Arabs had stopped their advance again. Were they waiting for warmer weather. The tents looked to have floors as if they weren't planning on moving them for some time. The tanks were deserted. There were plenty of guards out, but the guards changed every two hours.

It was night when Bridget and Walter got back to their tent. Their cans were frozen now and had to be heated with body heat. It had been a very tiring and discouraging day. Their canned goods were almost gone and they were still behind enemy lines. They stayed up and talked in the dark. The sky was clouded and it was total blackness.

"Walter. What do we do now? We're almost out of food. We're not sure where we are. We probably can't make it to another village and the Arabs have that one tight."

"Maybe not so tight. You know we cannot surrender to them. I would be killed outright but you would not be, even if you wanted to be killed. We are going to have to sneak in there and at least get food."

"In broad daylight. There is no where to hide approaching that village."

"No, we'll have to try it at night. Hopefully they won't be expecting us and won't be wearing their night goggles because they are uncomfortable.

It would be better if only one of us went, because one can sneak better than two and it should be me."

"And just why is that? Don't give me any of that macho stuff, or I want to protect you, or it's my job to provide for you."

"Do you have any training on slitting throats at night? How about breaking a man's neck silently? I thought not." He didn't have any training in that either, but he couldn't use the arguments she had already shot down in advance.

She believed that he had the training and was content to let him go in alone. "I'm coming in close to town though so I can help if you get in trouble. I'd rather die quickly fighting than get captured out in the tent waiting for you to get back.

He could tell she was going to come in close regardless of what he said, so he cooperated. "It might be good. If we could steal an off road vehicle maybe we could make a run for it. I'll try to find a place where you can hide and watch me. If I fire a gun straight up in the air three times, get ready to go. If I take off running out of town, sneak back to the tent and wait for me. Okay?"

They spent from before daylight to the first signs of daylight getting to within sight of the town. As the sun started to rise, they moved in closer hoping that the guards would be looking for the sun while most were asleep. Like most ancient villages it was built by a stream to carry away sewage downstream while providing cleaner water upstream. They followed it to stay out of sight and found some bushes near the edge of town right close to the tents where Bridget could hide.

Just as the sun peeked over the distant horizon, Walter moved quickly along the last part of the stream. He found a guard watching the sunrise and came up behind him. He grabbed him and slit his throat. It worked like in the movies. He drug the body into the stream bed and used his hands to bury it in the snow. He kept the unique Arab helmet, gun, and coat to look more like an Arab and to get an extra coat rather than his flannel shirt stuffed with curtains.

Walter walked over to the other guard across the road. He kept his face turned away as he walked past the other guard. The other guard said something unintelligible in Arabic and Walter backed up toward him. He was counting on coming out of the sun at the other guard. The other guard never saw it coming but was hit in the face with the rifle butt, hard enough to knock him cold. Walter dragged him off the road into the ditch, slit his throat and buried him in the snow. He then took a walk near the side of the village nearest Bridget and found a truck full of U.S. C-Rations. He then looked in some more trucks and found one full of plastique explosives. There were also backpacks in the truck. He filled a backpack with plastique and then grabbed another backpack and took it to the truck with C-Rations. He was filling it when three guards came up behind him. He heard their order to turn around or what are you doing or something in Arabic. As he was trying to think how to get out of this, he knew he would be shot as soon as they saw his face.

The unmistakable sound of an M-16 on fully automatic rang out from close range and the Arabs jerked and fell jerking from more hits with 5.56 millimeter ammunition. Walter grabbed his bag of C-Rations and his bag of plastique and jumped from the truck in a run to the truck loaded with plastique. He threw in a grenade and ran back toward Bridget that was covering him with her M-16.

Walter spotted a motorcycle and fired it up just as the grenade went off along with several thousand pounds of plastique exploded and then raced toward Bridget. Luckily, the motorcycle was parked around the corner of a building that took the brunt of the explosion. The building collapsed toward the explosion as the shock wave was too much for even the four hundred years old stone. Arabs were stirring in their tents and coming from houses in the village as Bridget was getting on the motorcycle. They had considerable speed by the time the assault rifles behind them started firing. They made it over the hill without getting hit.

They were still behind enemy lines, but they had food and wheels. Walter circled around the town trying to stay far enough that they would not hear the motorcycle. He could not make much speed going off road through the snow. Luckily the snow was not too deep. He slipped and slid over the gentle hills. He came to a small creek and tried to drive through. He killed the engine and they left the motorcycle lying on its side in the creek mostly under water.

MONTH 18, JANUARY 16

They walked the rest of the afternoon and into the night. They wanted to get as much distance as possible between them and the Arabs. "Hold it a minute. That sound is a helicopter. It's getting louder."

They could not see it, but as they were looking in the direction of the sound they saw and heard a heavy machine gun firing from the helicopter to the ground. "They must have spotted a deer or dog on infrared and shot it hoping it was us. Quick, lie down in the snow. I said NOW."

BRIDGET OBEYED HIM BUT ASKED, "WHY?"

"I'm going to cover you with the tarp and then shovel snow on you to try to hide your body heat. Then I'm going to run as far as I can and try to find a place where I can bury myself with snow. You must stay completely still until the helicopter is gone, and still wait awhile and I'll come back for you." He completed the job and took off running. He found a small drift and dived into it. He pulled his feet in, making sure they were under the snow. He then hollowed out an area around his head to breathe and a hole to get air.

Bridget had air under the tarp. The helicopter stayed in hearing range for about two hours. Several times she heard the heavy machine gun fire at something. The first time she almost took off running in its direction thinking they had found Walter, but she lay back down realizing it was hopeless and it might have been another deer they were shooting at. She wasn't sure if she loved Walter, but he was the only American she had gotten to know in over a year now. She trusted him. She depended on him. She tried to be a brave Resistance fighter like her grand father, but she was terrified most of the time. She didn't really know much about all this. The Resistance was not a professional trained group and she was the least prepared of the lot.

She had learned to shoot a gun as a girl, but she had never thought she would ever have to shoot anyone until yesterday. When she had seen the Arabs coming up behind the truck Walter had been in she had run up behind them and shot them down from behind. They didn't have a chance. She had been so terrified that she had fired short bursts until the clip went empty. She had the strength of adrenaline and enough experience to keep the M-16 generally on the target. Then it was running. Was she totally alone now behind Arab lines. Would they find her and shoot her or much worse?

As long as the helicopter was within hearing she had to stay put. What if it left, she got up and then it came back. Well, she knew what to do now at least. Did she love Walter? Could anyone know love in this circumstance? What if she got pregnant? She had long since run out of birth control pills. Walter was her only lover in two years. Had she just given in to him out of fear?

Walter was nine years her senior. Her parents were five years, no nearly six years, apart in age. Was he too old? He was strong and virile now. Would he be able to keep up with her in years to come? Would she have paid him any attention if it had been peace time back in the United States? He was a very nice man. He was strong and intelligent, if under educated. No, she probably would have considered him inferior due to the difference in their educations. She now knew him as intelligent, but too poor to go to college. That's why he joined the military, to pay for his education. He had spent eight years getting two years worth of college by going to night classes and correspondence courses when he couldn't attend night classes. There had been many times that he enrolled only to be sent where he could not attend. He might be smarter than she was and she now knew that if he had the money he would have gone to college instead of the military.

She decided that she would never have paid him any attention if not for the circumstances, but now that she knew him, he was a good catch. Maybe it was foolish. The war had caused it. Her loneliness as the only American in French world threatened by Arabs had led her to be attracted to him initially. All the reasons were wrong, but she had gotten to know him. Yes, she did love him. She would have to be careful not to get pregnant, like the Catholics. This was the wrong time and place. If they got out of this and he was willing, she would be his bride. Her parents that would have objected last year would just be happy to see her again, if they were still alive. They would love him to for getting her through this ordeal.

The ground was very cold under the snow. She must have gone to sleep for suddenly she woke with terror as someone was pulling the tarp off. "Walter! Thank God. I must have gone to sleep. You're all right."

"Yes, but we need to find as a more protected place where we can get warm and stay hidden."

"I know those hills over there. The Resistance had some caves there where they hid people from the Germans. I saw some of the caves last year when I was doing my research."

"Great. Let's get there before daylight and before we're found." It was starting to get light by the time they got to the hills. They were very rocky, with many cracks and crevices. They stopped looking for a cave and ate some cold rations from one of the kits. They heated it with body heat only and ate tepid spaghetti and meat sauce, a cookie, some crackers and cheese. Walter looked at the instant coffee with longing, but all they had for water was snow melted in their mouths. Not great.

Shortly before noon, Bridget was apologizing for not being able to recognize any land marks to find a cave, when she slipped on some loose rock and slid down a slope. "Walter! I found a cave down here. I'm going to look in to see if it's big enough for us to get in."

Walter, afraid for Bridget climbing into some small hole and getting trapped, scrabbled down the slope. He didn't see the cave, but he didn't see Bridget either. There were sparse bushes growing here and there and he started looking behind them when Bridge's voice came from behind.

"Over here Walter. I found a great one. This is man made."

He saw her peeking from behind a bush and went over there. The entrance was so small he had to get down on all fours to get in. In fact he had to take off his pack and drag it after him. When he had gone a few feet he discovered he was entering a large room supported by ancient wooden beams and a wooden floor. The room had a fireplace and a stack of wood next to it. The room came complete with a table and chairs and a rough wooden bed with the remains of an ancient cotton filled mattress.

"What is this place?"

"This was one of many that the French Resistance of World War II had."

"How come this place doesn't fill up with water with the holes in the ceiling?"

"I guess you are talking about the good condition of the wood floors. The light slits are actually channels to carry off water. There is a slight draft in here, which is coming down the natural cave from somewhere under ground and causes a positive air pressure that forces air out of the holes and keeps this place dryer. In case you haven't noticed, it's almost warm in here. Apparently there is some volcanic activity that keeps air flowing into this chamber and out the holes. Apparently the natural part of the cave is a volcanic vent that magma maybe flowed through when the volcanoes were active here. Shall we light a fire and get warm?"

"No. If the Arabs see smoke, they will come find us."

"I suspect that the German's would have too. I'll bet the builders found a way to vent the fireplace where smoke doesn't show on the outside. Shall we try it?"

"Well, okay, but I'm going to go up on top and look for smoke. We have to get some snow melted for water so we can put out the fire in case there is smoke."

"Water is no problem. Look here is an old hand pump. I'll bed it still works." She pumped an old bucket full of water and placed it by the fireplace. "I'll give you ten minutes to get out on top before I light the fire."

He waited for thirty minutes trying to look everywhere for smoke, but didn't find any smoke. He crawled back and forth on the top of the cliff, but didn't see any smoke. He finally went back down to see if she had started the fire. When he crawled back into the cave he found a very smoky fire.

Bridget had poured oil on the wood to light the fire and black smoke was pouring off. "Quick. Put the fire out."

She worriedly replied, "Did you see smoke?"

"No, but the fire is putting out black smoke, not just a wood stove."

More relaxed she said, "You should have seen it before I added the wood. It was really pouring out smoke then."

"You mean it was putting out more smoke before?"

"Yes. Now will you relax?"

"That was pretty nervy of you to burn oil."

"Not really. Wood would steam when I put it out. Versus the oil would go out immediately."

"Maybe so, but it was risky."

"Let's break out some rations and see if we can't have a hot meal for a change."

"Good idea. I'll heat some water in the bucket so we can sterilize these dishes and pans a little. I hate to think what's on them after fifty years, or however long they've been here since the last people used them."

"I'm not sure whether I want a hot meal or get out of these stinky clothes first. After we eat we can wash the clothes. Let's see what kind of condition these sheets are in." They ripped when Bridget tried to pick up a corner. Laughing she said, "I guess that answers that. I wonder about the bed. Well, the mattress is as rotten as the sheets were. Suggestions."

"SURE. WHY NOT JUST GO BACK TO THE VILLAGE AND GET SOME?"

"Right. I'll pass. I certainly was hoping for a bed to sleep on. It looks like the floor or nothing. I'm still going to get out of these smelly clothes." She took off Walter's jacket she was still wearing and her jeans. Since her shirt had been ripped to shreds she was down to her panties after removing her jeans. "Merry Christmas."

Walter was staring dumb founded. "You're right. Maybe this is going to be a Merry Christmas. It is getting warm, very warm." It wasn't really, but Walter quickly shed his clothes and they made a bed of their clothing and made love. As they laid side by side afterwards, Walter said, "Water's hot."

"WANT TO WATCH WHILE I DO THE DISHES?"

"Silly question." It was quite enjoyable watching an attractive athletic, shapely young woman of twenty-four do the dishes in a pan of hot water naked while he watched. She was not large busted, but she had enough to sway as she worked. He watched her buttocks' muscles and thigh muscles work while she washed. He got aroused again watching her. As soon as she had washed up some dishes and put in some plastic pouches of C-Rations he said, "Come here a minute."

She did. She came over on all fours and kissed him upside down leaning over his head. She then moved down to his tits and he put his arms around he back and grabbed a mouthful of tit himself and sucked. She leaned down into him. In a few minutes she made love to him and then lay on top of him a few more minutes while they caught their breath. They ate at the table and had their warmed C-Rations that were quite good or they were hungry. "Isn't this cute? Sitting here naked eating our meal in an underground room like two kids playing some kind of adult house game."

They rested and made love and rested and made love for most of two full days. They both professed to having never had any sex like it before. Neither could believe it could be so good. The morning of the third day, they were ready to come up for air.

As they got dressed in their clean clothes and came outside to the now brown winter day, Walter said, "We ought to find some way to hurt the Arabs until we get out of this."

"Why don't we find us a nice ammo or fuel dump and blow it up? We have plenty of plastique."

"We have no blasting caps."

"Oh."

"I suggest that we take only some guns and reconnoiter the neighborhood and see what's here. At least with the snow gone they can't follow our tracks."

"I'm with you. You say walk, I walk. I suggest that we continue north. I would not want to walk back into that village again. Maybe we can find some friendlies."

They walked north. They crawled across hill tops to not be silhouetted against the sky. They were going through a band of trees when they heard voices nearby. Walter pulled her down in some underbrush as whoever it was came toward them. Bridget whispered, "French. They're speaking French."

"Shhh. Arabs might speak French too. Let's wait and see."

They were European. They were not in uniform, but they were definitely not civilians. "Commandos."

BRIDGET CALLED OUT TO THEM IN FRENCH. THEY ANSWERED IN FRENCH. "WHAT WAS THAT?"

"They said, 'stay where we are, they will come to us.'" It was very quiet. Suddenly from a circle all around them they heard the simultaneous cocking of guns and saw the commandos had them completely surrounded.

They said something in French and Bridget answered them back. The only word he caught was, 'Resistance' "What are they saying?"

"They wanted to know what we were doing here. I answered them that we were in the resistance and trying to get to French lines." The commander of the group gave orders in French and the guns around them were lowered and safed.

"Excuse the reception. I'm Captain Rourke, French Commando's at your service and I speak excellent English. I spent three years with your Delta force in cross training. Can you tell us where we might find some Arabs?"

MONTH 18, JANUARY 27

"Well, three days ago, we ran across a village full of Arabs. We stole rations and plastique explosives, but then the Arabs almost shot Walter and we had to run without any blasting caps for the plastique."

"Can you find it again?"

"Why?"

"Because we are commandos my dear. What is your name?

"Bridget. I would be most happy to lead you to the village. Ready Walter?"

"That's what the Resistance is for isn't it?"

They walked back to their cave. It was crowded this time with twenty commandos plus the two Americans. Captain Rourke was uncomfortable with burning a fireplace, but relented. The commandos shared some of their food with Walter and Bridget. The French rations were not as good as the American variety, but provided a new experience. There was even wine in a small plastic carafe.

The next day they led the commandos within sight of the village. After a couple of hours of reconnaissance, the French Captain was satisfied. The next night, the commandos used the Arab plastique against the Arabs and their own shape charges on the tanks.

Walter explained to Bridget, "Shape charges are explosive made in a particular shape that direct the explosion in one direction. By placing it on a tank hull in one of the thinner places the explosion is directed in a find point to the hull and blasts through exploding any explosives inside the tank. A similar explosive like plastique would explode in all directions with only a very small part of the explosion hitting the tank."

Bridget had asked how the commandos were going to just walk in when the Arabs had infrared optics to see them. Captain Rourke explained that they had new uniforms made with Mylar plastic that reflected their body heat back inside their uniforms. That was why they stayed warm in the winter with apparently very light weight uniforms. The biggest advantage was that by reflecting their own heat back, very little heat escaped to be seen on infrared optics. It turned them into stealth commandos that could walk through infrared sensors almost invisibly. It put the modern night time commandos back to the same advantage as in World War II.

The commando raid was wildly successful in that they destroyed thirty tanks and fifty truck loads of supplies. Bridget said, "Why doesn't the government provide those Mylar suits to the Resistance. That would have saved many lives and allowed us to keep the Arabs back further."

"They are new and just provided by Great Britain. In fact with the help of the winter and these new suits we expect to stop the Arabs for the winter."

MONTH 22, APRIL 10

It appeared that the Arabs were very frustrated by the commandos. They had helicopters flying every night searching with infrared to find them, and had widened their defensive perimeters to where the Arabs had over a thousand troops just standing guard at night. Each guard was within sight of another guard. They had stopped the normal commando attacks, but the commandos had added mortars to their inventory. They were out of range of the infantry guards and the helicopters could not be everywhere. As soon as the helicopters moved away from an area a group of six commandos would start firing with three mortars into the village. When the helicopters or tanks started to get close, the commandos ran to another area and hid out while another mortar attack started from the other direction. With their camouflage infrared invisible suits they could lie on the ground right under a helicopter using either spotlights or infrared and not be seen as long as they didn't move and as long as the helicopters didn't fly really low.

Then as the helicopters found and killed one group of commandos the commandos started positioning another group to protect the mortar team. This protecting team was equipped with personnel fired ground to air missiles to shoot down the helicopters. The Arabs had not moved much all winter because the Arabs were not really equipped for winter. Even though the French winters were mild this one was colder and wetter than normal. Without roads to travel on, because of being systematically destroyed by retreating French troops, and the fields a quagmire of mud, the war came to a stalemate.

March had dried out the land enough that the Arabs were able to start moving supplies to their front line and start moving their front line north again. The commando troop had grown to forty and the cave was packed with people even though some were always outside. They were now a good fifty miles behind enemy lines and supplies were air dropped at night to a different location each time. They had also been joined by over one hundred Resistance fighters. Their clothing and tents were all made out of infrared invisible Mylar. The suits were becoming quite hot to work in with the coming of spring. Many of their large group were living in tents around the area. The cave was only the headquarters.

Walter and Bridget were out walking away from the cave to get some privacy when they heard and saw a large explosion from the direction of their cave.

"What was that?" Bridget said.

"I don't know, but I hope it wasn't our cave. Let me get on the radio and contact them. This is Walter calling Rourke. Rourke, if you hear me come in. I'm worried, Bridget. I'm not getting anything even with the silent code. If anyone can hear this signal please answer."

"Walter, there is a solid line of Arab troops five deep and as wide as we can see. They are coming over the cliffs. They blew up the cave. If you can hear this and are north, you better keep on moving."

Their secure short range walkie talkies had a five mile range over hills and twenty miles line of sight. It could not be intercepted except by an equal radio. Everyone that had one knew the button that would turn it into a grenade to make sure no one could steal one.

Bridget and Walter were on their own again and running from the Arabs behind enemy lines. They were wearing their Mylar suits because it was cool and the Mylar was light. They were wearing side arms, but nothing else and no rations. At least they knew where the front line was, fifty miles north or eighty kilometers. Back before the war in a good car on the now destroyed Autoroute that would only be thirty minutes of driving or less. Now it was days or weeks away if even achievable.

When they heard helicopters they looked for natural cover and then pulled the hood over their heads and laid still until the helicopters passed over. They caught several views of the lines of Arabs moving from the south toward them. They were not moving fast, but between hiding from helicopters and crawling over rises to hide their silhouettes, they were hard pressed to stay ahead of the lines.

Night came and they were still running. Both were bathed in sweat under their Mylar suits, but they had to keep them on to hide from the helicopters. Now that it was cooling off at night they would be found quickly without their suits. They could plainly see the lines of Arab troops, because they were using high powered flashlights. They wanted to move obliquely to the Arabs to try to get out from in front of the Arabs but were having a very hard time just staying in front of them. They could see now why the Arabs were making such distances on foot. The lines were being replaced by personnel carriers delivering fresh troops constantly moving. The headlights were readily visible. Apparently the Arabs were intent on clearing the areas behind them to stop the commando attacks.

They were both suffering from dehydration due to the Mylar suits and when they came to the stream they drank deeply hoping the water wasn't too polluted or even deliberately poisoned, but they had to get water to replace what they had swatted away. At 10 PM, the Arabs started shooting flares in front of their lines. When they were too close, Bridget and Walter had to lie down which had mixed blessings. They were able to catch their breath, but the Arab lines got closer. One time they didn't get down in time and some helicopters spotted them. Fortunately they were not too far from some trees and managed to get out of sight, still running. Their muscles were failing quickly now. Even with months of being on foot, there is a limit to what the human body can do. They had been walking, jogging or running for thirty miles now. They had sprained ankles and twisted knees from tripping over logs and fences and rocks in the darkness and still the Arab troops came toward them moving north. They could not move further and made a blind of fallen limbs and sticks to hide in the woods. They had no doubt that the Arabs would tear into it when they got there and shoot them both, but they simply had to stop. Where a marathon is usually held on streets, they had run further stumbling through creeks and over rocks and fences, sometimes crawling over hills. They laid together in their sweaty slippery on the inside Mylar suits and held each other to wait for inevitable.

"Walter. I want you to shoot me before letting me be captured. Okay?"

"Don't talk like that. We have a chance."

"I'm serious. I don't know if I could do it myself. I might miss and not die. Will you do it for me?"

"Yes, but don't talk like that any more. Okay."

"Okay. Walter, would you have married me after the war?"

"If you would have married me, I would. Any man would be attracted to you like a magnet. I have fallen very deeply in love with you. You are more than I ever expected to meet, let alone have a chance of being with. I would have contentedly spent my life with you."

"IS THAT A PROPOSAL?"

"Yes. If we get out of this and can find a church I will marry you at the first opportunity, war or no war."

"I love you too. I decided that night last winter when you hid me under the blanket with snow on top to hide. I had two hours to just think. I decided I did not want to be without you, if you wanted me. I didn't tell you, but before we die I want you to know that you're a father."

"WHAT?"

"I figure that I'm two months pregnant. At least I haven't had a period in that long."

"WHY DIDN'T YOU TELL ME? HOW COULD WE HAVE LET THAT HAPPEN IN THIS CIRCUMSTANCE?"

"Well. I didn't have any contraceptives. Accidents happen. We've been living together for since mid December. We made it through January and part of February, but that night in February when we spent the night in the Mylar tent. Maybe if I had been raised Catholic I could have counted better. I was afraid it might have been the wrong time, but we had so little time alone since the commandos moved in with us. Aren't you happy?"

"Of course. But this is bad timing. Well, maybe not. If we die here it won't matter. If we can get out of this mess to a safer place where you can have the child it will be a very joyous happening. I do love you."

It was past 1 AM when the inexorably approaching Arab line stopped and made camp only a hundred yards from their blind. Some Arabs even took part of their shelter for firewood without finding them. They had two hours rest and now were somewhat recovered. They forced their complaining muscles to move out. Now they moved in close to a ninety degree angle and got around the line of Arab troops. They even found a remote farm house with a wine cellar. They found that it had four levels to the cellar under the house. They decided they were not going to move until they had regained some strength. They found some wheels of cheese in the second basement and a stock of bees wax candles. They moved down to the third basement and built a hiding place with empty wine kegs and racks. It didn't look like much, but they had wine to drink and cheese to eat. It was silent for hours. They heard several large explosions and felt the ground shake and plaster falling from the ceiling.

They stayed put for another eight hours afraid of a house search since the Arabs had apparently been shelling close to their house. Finally they took some candles and tore down some of their hideaway to get out and went up the stairs. What they found was rubble and a blocked staircase. The first basement had some fallen beams and smashed wine kegs. The first basement had a mostly collapsed ceiling. It took two days of working, eating and sleeping to see daylight. It took another day to get out of the house. The house was totally destroyed. The shells must have been the Arab method of making sure there was no resistance. The artillery battery had not considered multiple wine cellars. It was daylight. Bridget didn't have a watch and the battery had died in Walter's watch so they could only estimate the time. It was afternoon from the position of the sun. They could see a major Arab encampment only a couple of miles away down the hill. Was it time for a repeat of their December raid to find food?

It was. Walter had the suit for his advantage plus the Arabs had thought they had cleared all the resistance. They were down to minimal guards like the village Walter had first raided. They only had side arms and knifes this time. No extra ammunition or automatic rifles. They used the same tactic as before except this time while Bridget watched his back he spent hours crawling into the town and carefully looking for stores. He found more rations and some grenades. This time he didn't bother with explosives as he was planning to get the two of them north as quickly as possible to some relative safety. He wanted rifles, but he didn't want to disturb the guards. Bridget was pregnant.

He stole back to Bridget and they went back down into their basement. There they ate some of their stolen rations.

"Walter, how are we going to get out of here? We can't possibly get past the Arab camp without getting caught. If we wait for them to move on we will just have that much farther to go to get to our lines."

"I don't know. We have food for a couple of weeks, but you're right. The longer we wait, the less unlikely we will get to safety. I haven't seen the Arabs have a single set back so far. The keep moving forward. We have slowed them down, but there have been no set backs. I suggest that tomorrow night we move out at dark and see how far we can get. Do you agree?"

"Absolutely."

The next night they took off walking. They circled wide of the encampment and headed north once more. They walked or jogged most of the night. Again, their Mylar clothing caused them to sweat profusely, but this time they had wine bottles with them. Not that wine is very good for replacing water. Because of the alcohol it made their mouths dry, but they at least had liquid to cycle through them. Despite the alcohol they swatted most of it off and didn't have to relieve themselves often. They were nearing exhaustion when someone yelled something in French. Walter assumed it was "HALT WHO GOES THERE?"

They froze and held up their hands. They had made it to someone friendly. They didn't know who, but if they spoke French, they must have been friendlies. They were. They had made it to the French. After telling their story of the past months they were given a ride into Paris.

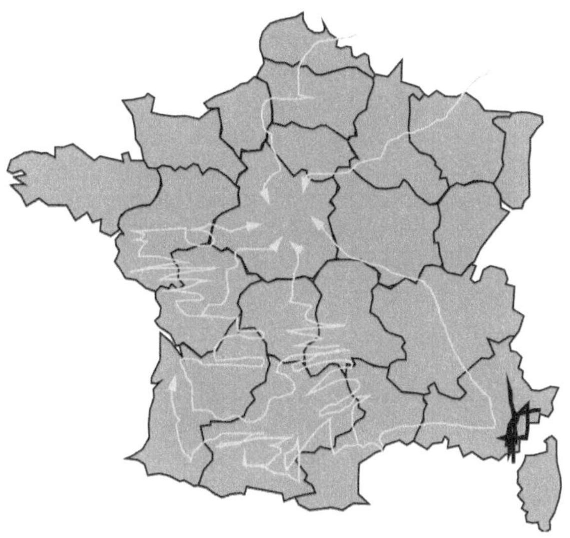

The difficult path the Arab advance made through France due to the destroyed roads, the commandos, and the tank battles with the American tanks before they were defeated. Most forces ended at the siege of Paris.

21 PARIS

MONTH 23
May 1

Walter and Bridget made it to Paris. Because of all the check points and other stops for the French military truck, they took several days to get there, but here they were. They rode in during the mid-morning. The city was surrounded by a two mile deep tent city. The streets were packed with three times the normal population of the city. Most of the villagers and farmers from the south half of France had moved to Paris.

The truck took them to the American embassy. They were stopped by marines until Walter dug out his wallet with his military identification card. There was a long wait and then a senior master sergeant came out and talked with Walter. He asked a series of questions about his unit and where he had been for the past months. It was wartime and some Persians in particular could pass for European and due to years of living in the west could speak very good English.

After several minutes of questioning, the senior master sergeant took their guns and their backpacks and escorted them into the building. A marine Captain asked, "And just who do you have there sergeant?"

"A technical sergeant Walter Gaddis and his French girlfriend Bridget. He's okay. He seems to know all about his unit. They were part of the group that tried to counter attack the Arabs to keep them in Marseilles."

"I thought most of them escaped to Spain."

Technical Sergeant Gaddis spoke up, "My unit was the one ambushed when the carriers were sunk. I didn't know which way to run. I think I am the last one of my unit."

"Hang on Sarge. If my sergeant says you're okay, you're okay. I have a list of Americans known to have been trapped behind enemy lines. Ah, here it is. Oh here you are all right. The only tank to escape like you said. Spent a long time keeping the Arabs from crossing a river. Then the French commandos picked you up and you worked with them for quite a period of time. Then we lost contact with the commando unit, and here you are. And, ah, Bridget. What did you say your last name is?"

"Bonalade."

"Just a minute. Yes here you are. We have a request from the United States to be on the look out for you. Your parents said you have been missing for over a year. Don't worry. We told them you were with the Resistance last fall. No. You can't call them. We lost all of the satellites and most of the hard lines, the under ocean telephone lines. All communications to the United States are controlled by the government due to extreme shortages. However, we do have several HAM radio operators in Paris that may be able to get through to your parents. They were last known to be in Providence, Rhode Island. Tell the HAM operator who you want to talk to and where. Here is a list of them in Paris and their addresses. Do you have any place to stay?"

"No."

"Yes we do. I found some of my parents cousins here in Paris. I stayed with them for three months while I did research here in Paris. Now if we could get some money to replace these Mylar suits."

"I can help there. Sergeant Gaddis, you are still counted as on active duty since we at least thought you were alive and fighting with the Resistance. You have several months of back pay coming. I'll give them a call. Go to room 252 on the second floor. They'll pay in Francs. With the economy the way it is with half the country under Arab control, you are quite rich. I don't know what you will find to buy though. Most of the economy has switched to strictly military production. Food is short too. Check in here once every two weeks to pick up your pay and to see if we have orders for you."

Walter collected his money and they took off for her second cousin's house. One thing they discovered very quickly was that there were no taxis due to the extreme shortage of fuel. They had to take the underground Metro. With three times its normal population and the almost total lack of automobiles, the Metro was a mad house. The average waiting time was over two hours and then it was standing room only. Typically you had to wait for three trains before you can get on one. The normally rude French had mellowed out and were as courteous as they could be under the circumstances. Walter was uncomfortable carrying over fourteen thousand dollars in Francs which at an exchange rate of eight to one was one hundred and twelve thousand Francs in a country that had imposed total price control at the pre-war prices to prevent run away inflation. With most of the countries military and police in one place, a black market was not allowed to get started. The French people facing death at the hands of the Arabs if the military lost were eager to follow directions on the elimination of crime.

The French that didn't get along well together in peace were brothers in war time. The main problem was shortages. They arrived at her relative's house and they were welcomed in. Every room had someone sleeping in it. They explained that everyone in Paris had taken in numerous boarders due to the tremendous housing shortage, but they could share the master bedroom with them.

"We're getting married as soon as we can make the arrangements." Walter said.

They were well educated and like most Europeans in the cities, spoke good English. They were over joyed. They were made to sleep in blankets on the floor on opposite sides of the master bedroom that night. The next morning they were separated. The husband took Walter out to make arrangements and find clothes to purchase. The wife did the same with Bridget.

They were married by the end of the week.

MONTH 26, August 11

The Arabs had finally made it through the French defenses and were now in sight of Paris. The French military had lost seventy percent of their original military but had five million new recruits. Their training was inadequate and they had little experience, but they fought valiantly because their lives did depend on their stopping the Arabs.

New from Germany indicted that the Arabs had also conquered Austria and the Balkans and were into both Russia proper and as far as Munich into Germany. The Arabs did not attack right away but took the time to surround Paris. The Arabs sent emissaries to ask for the surrender of Paris. The answer was no. Fully half the French population was now inside the city. The tent city around the town was now vacant.

MONTH 27, SEPTEMBER 7

The Arabs attacked with infantry and tanks. Bridget was now six months pregnant and not going anywhere. Her relatives had made her and Walter an apartment in their basement. Walter had taken guns that he had acquired on the streets and had gone to fight for the city. He was gone for four days and Bridget feared the worst.

Walter burst in, "We beat them. The Arabs tried a mass attack on the south side of the city and the west simultaneously, but they were beaten back."

"HOW?"

"The Arabs sent tens of thousands of infantry followed by tanks toward the city. There were thousands of French that withstood their fire and killed thousands of Arabs to where Arabs were walking and driving over a sea of dead Arabs. Once the first group of tanks got into the city, the French blew up whole rows of buildings trapping them inside the city where they destroyed them. The rows of collapsed buildings created a wall of rubble where Paris is now a walled city. The burned out Arab tanks make an excellent roadblock against other tanks."

"They'll try it again or they will bomb Paris to rubble."

"That's something I don't understand either. They have effectively destroyed the French and German air forces, but they are not bombing the cities. No one knows why not."

MONTH 27, SEPTEMBER 14

Exactly a week later the Arabs started shelling the outer ring of the city. The French Army effectively had ten million armed men to defend the city. They were dug in trenches around the city, stationed in buildings facing outward and on top of buildings. There were blocks upon blocks of evacuated buildings with many of the defenders permanently living in the outer blocks of the city to defend it. The French had months to lay in provisions so even though fresh food was hard to buy, there was plenty of sustenance foods such as flour for bread, rice, canned meats, etc.

The Arabs had a habit of not bypassing cities but conquering each one as they went. A stand in Paris might waste the Arabs fighting forces. It was evident that the Arabs did not have the airplane bombs and artillery shells to systematically destroy a city as they had done in Rome. It was known that the Arabs did not have much production capacity for anything on their own. The stockpiles from before the war had been wasted and now much of their ammunition was being shipped from Red China through the Suez Canal to Arab forces in Europe. This left a lot of ocean for allied forces to sink their ships before they made it to Europe. Whereas the German U-boats had to hunt for their quarry, modern submarines were assisted by radar and radar planes that pinpointed surface ships along their entire route. With anti-ship missiles, any surface ship was exposed to long range weapons.

A very serious problem was that the Arabs controlled the air. The small European air forces were pretty much out of action now with only a few hidden airplanes to be put in at a crisis. The surrounding of Paris was not a big enough crisis. A break through into Paris might warrant the risk of the remaining air forces.

Great Britain was saving its own air force for defense of the Island as in World War II. The Arabs had not yet attacked the Island country except for terrorist attacks. The German Air Force was mostly destroyed. The Spanish Air Force was non-existent. The French Air Force was worse off than the German Air Force. Switzerland and Sweden were providing limited air support from their hidden air bases in the mountains. Switzerland had lost a lot of their forces during the battles there. Because of that they didn't have much left for the allied support, but because of the poisoning of so much of Switzerland, what they had was provided with vengeance in mind. Switzerland probably still had the best stores of munitions in Europe. They had not really used much before the germ warfare had occurred. The germ warfare or biological warfare killed a lot of their population, but did little against their stores. In fact, Switzerland had been a major source of packaged foods now stocked in Paris for the stand to the death.

MONTH 27, SEPTEMBER 18

"Look to the north. I see movement." shouted Technical Sergeant Walter Gaddis. Fifty binoculars swiveled north. There were thousands of Arab infantry marching south toward Paris. Artillery and tanks from Paris fired shrapnel into their lines killing thousands but they kept coming. Artillery and tank fire ranged down on the Paris artillery, but two thirds of the remaining military of France was scattered around Paris. The Paris artillery rotated firing to prevent accurate spotting by the Arab return fire. As the infantry came under small arms fire, Arab tanks raced ahead firing into the outer ring of buildings to suppress the fire. There must have been over one thousand tanks committed to this one massive charge. The tanks kept moving to reduce hits from the French artillery. At least some of the Arab tanks still had operational American made laser gun sites that could point their 105 howitzers while moving at fifty miles per hour. The defenders had to retreat from the outer row of buildings, but the fire from the French trenches was still cutting down many of the ever advancing military. When the distance was cut to a hundred yards between the attackers and the defenders, the trenches fell silent. The Arabs now advanced at a run and dived into the trenches looking for French survivors.

It was then that the trenches started smelling like natural gas. The Arabs had not decided what it was when the flash fire as an explosion traveled for a mile in both directions down the trench. The gas in the bottom of the trench for a two mile stretch had detonated in less than three seconds killing anyone near a trench.

The estimated Arab casualties thus far in this attack were estimated at twenty thousand soldiers and fifty tanks. Then the soldiers hit the city and went house to house for six blocks routing out defenders and killing them before the tanks started entering the city. After two hundred tanks had entered the city, the outer block of buildings exploded, and the roads and streets cratered making a tank trap that would take a week to clear without any opposition. The troops and tanks within the city were then attacked with Arab military men trying to climb back over the rubble that was once the outskirts of Paris. The Arab forces still outside the trap roved around looking for an entry, but their infantry trying to cross the mountain of rubble was exposed to hidden gunfire from the buildings further into the city. The tanks simply could not cross the mountain of rubble. They retreated, and the Parisians had won again.

V,81

The royal bird (the eagle, the United States) will be over the city of the sun (Rome). It will appear as an omen that seven months later the oriental defense fall amid lightning and noise. For seven days the enemy will directly attack its gates.

In a show of force the United States flew a very long range symbolic mission against the Moslems near Rome. The big B-2 Stealth bomber now being manufactured in numbers had evaded the Arab radar planes, and flown all the way from the United States to carry on a conventional bomb raid on the Arabs. The intent was no so much to do damage as it was to show capability, and to give heart to the Italian guerrillas still fighting from the hills and mountains of Italy. The Arabs fought well when they had the overwhelming number of armor, but their infantry was not really that brave. The Arab armor could not traverse the rough terrain over much of Europe. It was hoped that this raid would show that the United States was once again going to liberate Europe, and that the few remaining people should not give up hope.

X,86

Like a winged griffin will come the commander of the exiled European forces. Accompanying him will be the commanders of Aquilon (US &

USSR). They will lead a army of red and white and they will go against the commander of Babylon (Arabs).

For the first time in history all of the forces remaining in Europe, Russia, and the United States are not just allies, but cooperating as if they were all from the same country, with one hundred percent cooperation. Even in World War II they were called allies, but Russia in particular took help from the United States, but fought their own war with no actual cooperation or joint efforts. It was to the Allied advantage to help Russia fight the Germans in World War II, because it took German forces away from France to fight the Russians. The Russians not only used that help to regain their own territory, but in the process conquered Eastern Europe for their own purposes. This time, the powers of the European races were totally united against the Arabs and Chinese. This was the war for the dominant race. The Arabs and Chinese had made it clear they were out for the extinction of the European race. The Allies were fighting not for racism or even religion, but for their very survival.

II,22

The incredible army of Europe will return from overseas and mass itself near the submerged island (England). The fleet will defeat a weak army and at Rome a leader will speak.

Many of the Europeans that came to the United States and Canada to get away from the war were now fighting mad and had joined their absentee military overseas. The fleets of Great Britain, France, Italy, Norway, Sweden, all of Europe had evacuated to the new world to get away from the Arab air superiority over most of Europe, but had now come back from the United States and Canada carrying newly trained troops and equipment converging near the coasts of England.

VII,80

The western powers will liberate the British Isles. The recognized leader will return to power. The discontented and sad rebel Scot, will attempt rebellion more, in a warm season.

Due to the riots, terrorism from the Arabs living in Great Britain, and the Scottish rebels, terrible weather, earthquakes, and long range bombing of England, the royal family had gone to Canada. With the allied forces the royal family returned to England. The Scottish leader decided it would be best to stop their assaults on the British government. The United States involvement along with Russian ships in the same naval armada brought a new spirit to Great Britain. The return of the Royal family brought throngs of patriots to the forefront. The average people of Great Britain were now cooperating with Scotland Yard to hunt down and capture the Scottish rebels that had caused so much confusion.

III,78

The chief of Scotland, with six prisoners from Germany, will be taken captive by Oriental seamen. They will pass Spain, through Gibraltar, to be presented to fearful new leader in Iran.

There were plenty of witnesses that saw him and six German statesmen in Britain taken aboard a Red Chinese ship. The British Navy had gotten rid of their last aircraft carriers and had no aircraft or ships that could find the Chinese ship that they had assumed had escaped into the Atlantic. It was the British living in Gibraltar that saw the Chinese ship as it sailed into the Mediterranean. The British long range aircraft and their ships were all searching the Atlantic and were not in a position to track the ship once found. The final destination was unknown. At least the Scottish rebel leader was out of their hair.

II,68

The efforts of the Aquilon (US & USSR) forces will be great. They will gain an entrance on the ocean coast. The British will be restored to their island. Those occupying London will tremble being discovered by ships.

Through terrorism combined with the hurricanes and earthquakes the Scottish rebels and young hooligans ruled the streets of London when the Royal family returned, but with tens of thousands of Americans, Canadians, Russians, French, and others Allies showing up those that had ruled the streets yesterday were now hiding while the average citizen that had been hiding in fear were identifying the bad guys for arrest and imprisonment until after the war. There was no time for trials now, only arrests.

VI,7

The enemy in Norway, in the Balkans and the British Isles will be hit by the united brothers (US & USSR). A Roman chief of French blood and his forces will receive a setback in the woods.

IX,29

A leader who never retreated before anyone, will want to abandon a place he had just occupied. fire from the ship igniting swamps, combustibles at Charlieu Clais. Saint Quentin and Clais recaptured.

The major Allied landing of this new combined force was at Clais. This time however, there were no enemy guarding the beaches. The Arabs were concentrating their forces on Paris and were so sure of themselves that they posted no major troops along the shores. The landing went without a hitch. To be perfectly honest the Germans knew the force preparing for them. There had been landings in Africa, Sicily and Italy already during World War II. There had been continuous bombing for years from England into Germany. This time there was no similar warning.

MONTH 33, MARCH 1

The Arabs had wintered surrounding Paris trying to starve them out. Because of all the dust raised by global warfare, the winter was very wet and cold again. The entire earth had a cloud of dust encircling it that reduced the sunlight over land enough to cause abnormal cooling. The dust had been raised by the bombing during the war in both Europe and in the Far East. Because of the cold air in the northern hemisphere there was an imbalance of temperature between the south and north areas of the earth. This caused the south half to be extra humid as cool winds raced southward over the oceans evaporating water. Currents normally level out around the equator, but the moisture spilled northward. The Arabs tanks and troops that tried to attack Paris bogged down in the mud of the now plantless moon like landscape around Paris. The tanks and troops that attacked Paris in the fall destroyed all vegetation for miles. When the rains came there was a fifteen mile wide mud pit around the city. Tank treads either spun helplessly or dug in burying the tank requiring that it be towed out. Troops slipped and slid or sank to their boot tops in the mud. It didn't take long and the Arabs decided to wait for spring and hope to starve out the city.

Paris was starving. Their huge stocks of rations were almost gone. So many people hungry for meat had knowingly or unknowingly eaten every dog, cat, and horse in the city. Unfounded rumors were that any meat offered now, might have come from the hospital. The diet was pretty much restricted to moldy rice and old bread.

"BRIDGET, IS JACK OLD ENOUGH TO TRAVEL YET?"

"He is six weeks old, and healthy, thanks to the money and foresight you had to lay in months of supplies, and could if this were normal times, but how can we travel anywhere with the city surrounded?"

"If we don't get out of this city soon, it will either be overrun by the Arabs or we may all die of sickness. Due to the water shortages and the failure of the sewage systems a sickness is starting to fall over the whole city. It may get to us at any time. I think we should try to sneak our way out of this, like we did last spring."

"WHERE WOULD WE GO IF WE COULD SNEAK OUT?"

"I was thinking maybe north toward the Netherlands and then maybe find a way over to Great Britain."

"HOW ARE WE GOING TO SNEAK OUT WITH A CRYING BABY?"

"I found a two place ultra light at Orly field and have arranged to take it out of here."

"I didn't know you could fly."

"I flew some ultra lights back when I was single and fancy free."

"What makes you think we won't get shot down immediately?"

"It is made out of wood and cloth and can't be seen on radar. If we fly out at night to where we can't be seen, but early enough for ground noises to cover our small engine, I think it can be done."

"HOW FAR CAN WE GET IN AN ULTRA LIGHT?"

"Only fifty to seventy-five miles, but that might be far enough to get north of the Arabs since they seem to have wintered here."

"I'll think about it."

"You don't have long to think. The attacks could start again anytime. The ground is drying out and grass has started growing again over the mud fields. Besides, I may not be the only one with an eye on that ultra light."

Bridget talked with her relatives for hours about their scheme. They were all in favor of it. The thirty million Frenchmen in Paris had pretty much resigned themselves to a fight to the death. They were starving. If the Arabs didn't attack soon, the French just might try to take the battle to them and die in battle versus starvation and sickness. "Bridget, because of your pregnancy and the supplies that Walter provided to this house before the real shortages started, you just don't know what it is like outside of this house. We have many friends that have lost thirty percent of their body weight over the past two months alone. The only reason we didn't share Walter's stores with them was because of your pregnancy and the need for you to provide your own milk for your baby after it was born.

Her cousin's husband chimed in, "Thank goodness for Walter's foresight, but even his stock is running low now. The more well to do like ourselves that lived in Paris are still healthy, but thousands of the immigrants from the villages are starting to die of malnutrition and unsanitary conditions. You couldn't have known it, but this neighborhood walled itself off from the rest of the city two months ago because of Typhoid and Cholera in the city proper. A major attack by the Arabs might be fought off one more time, but eventually the French will do what Walter said and attack them just to be able to die a quick suicide death without having to call it suicide. There is talk of a million martyrs making permanent history by charging into the cannons and dying at the hands of the Arabs. If that were to happen, there would be no saving Paris. By now we had hoped that the Arabs would waste their munitions and energies to just go home or that some other country could come to our aid, but neither has happened. Go with Walter and save your baby while you can. Don't worry about us. If something happens to us, it would also have happened to you. Keep the family going by getting out of here and having many more babies."

Bridget and Walter made final plans. The ultra light could not carry much so they kept their load to six meals of C-Rations apiece and one eighteen shot automatic pistol and one extra clip apiece. Grenades were left behind due to their weight and metal content that might be spotted on radar. They opened the C-Rations and disposed of all metal. That night they went to the airport and Walter took the little ultra light aloft alone to make sure it would fly and that he could fly it. When it was not shot down, Bridget felt safer. It was a small side by side seating with no cargo space. It had a cabin that should have had zippered doors, but they were missing. They had blue jeans and jackets to keep semi-warm and blankets for the baby. They would have liked to have the Mylar uniforms, but they would reflect radar in the air so they left them out. Hopefully the minimal metal of their guns and the small aircraft engine would not be seen on radar.

Just after they took off an Arab artillery barrage began. So much for anyone hearing or seeing the small ultra light airplane. The sound was deafening, and every shell carried more metal than their airplane. They could not get much altitude with the small engine and could plainly see the Arab tanks and infantry mustering for an attack. The noise coming up at them made talking impossible, so Bridget hung onto her baby, and Walter hung on to the controls, as they blindly flew in the general direction of north. The bright artillery flashes would blind people on the ground enough so they would not see them flying over. Walter could only use the flashes and his inborn feel of where he was to judge where and how he was flying since he was night blinded also.

They flew past the Arab lines by maybe ten miles before the gas gauge showed empty and Walter flew low to find a field. Their night vision was partially restored now, but the sky behind them was lit by artillery and flares to the point that the moving shadows on the upcoming ground were hard to tell from solid objects. Regardless, Walter made a pretty good landing and came in almost stalled at a very low speed so when the wheels hit and dug in. They were not injured as the ultra light flipped onto its back.

"BRIDGET, ARE YOU OKAY? HAVE YOU GOT JACK (THE BABY)?"

"Yes to both, except that I'm hanging upside down by the seat belt. Here, take Jack and lay him down on the ground and then see if you can get my belt loose without me landing on my head."

"Thanks Walter. Looks like we made it. We had better start walking. This crashed airplane will get the wrong attention when it gets light. How did you get out of your seat belt without help?"

"When we started to flip, I ducked. When the airplane quit moving I discovered my head was already touching the top of the plane so I did a head stand while I flipped loose the buckle."

"ARE YOU OKAY? DID YOU HIT YOUR HEAD HARD?"

"I don't recall hitting my head. It was just touching the top of the airplane where the roof collapsed. I don't think I even have a bruise. I ripped my jacket on something though and got my arm wet with some fluid from the engine. Probably oil."

"Let's stop and let me see with a flashlight."

"No. We're too close to the Arabs. I'm fine. Just keep walking away from the artillery until it starts getting light."

They took turns carrying Jack. It was fortunate that Bridget was in such good shape before the baby. Although no one would let her out of the house until now, she had been working out in her room only a few days after Jack was born. Jack was easy. It was her grandfather's name although he spelled it 'Jacques'. They were in France, Jack was born in France. It so happened that Walter had a great uncle that was a 'jack' also.

They walked all night stopping one time to rest, drink, and nurse Jack. In the morning they were another fifteen miles from the known position of the Arabs and decided to take shelter in a road culvert out of the weather. It was dry and stopped the wind although not tall enough to stand in.

MONTH 33, MARCH 4

Walter and Bridget were free. They had not walked far when they came to a small town. The sign said Boutoncourt. Neither of them were knowledgeable of where it was except they knew they were north of Paris. Walter approached the town alone to make sure it was safe. There didn't seem to be anyone home. He knocked on a door of a darkened house and got no response. Bridget followed him into the town carrying Jack. She called out for anyone to answer, and got no answer. Apparently the town had been evacuated. Jack felt the uneasiness and like any six week old baby cried. He was crying as they walked down the street in the early morning.

Then they heard a noise behind them as a shutter banged open and then a woman's voice calling out to them.

They were welcomed by the townspeople, once a mother gave in to the babies cry. The attack on Paris was still going on with terrible losses for the Arabs which was good news to Frenchmen everywhere. They were fed a good meal by the French. The French explained that they were near the north shore of France.

"DO YOU MEAN THE ARABS HAVE NOT COME THIS FAR NORTH?"

"Not yet. We are ready to run with the first signs that the Arabs are coming this way. If you keep heading north the British are still operating the ferry to England."

"I wouldn't stay here if I were you. The Arabs could come at any moment."

Bridget spoke up, "I thank you for taking us in, but I have to ask. What are you doing to the Arabs to help your brothers in Paris?"

"What can we do?"

"Do you have any living members of the World War II Resistance?"

"Yes. Well, he can tell you. Do you have any of the Mylar suits the French commandos were passing out?"

"Walter, they wore them all winter for their warmth, but now it is too hot. The purpose was to be invisible to the Arabs infrared. You could sneak in and destroy fuel and ammunition dumps. If you can destroy enough un-armored trucks the tanks will run out of fuel and ammunition. We are Americans and have fought our way from southern France. Walter fought the Arabs in Paris, and you are French, you should be fighting the Arabs, instead of sitting here waiting for them to come and get you, which they will."

The lecture did nothing except make the French unhappy with them. They headed north, and after two more days of walking, found the ferry to take them to England.

They found the English coast an armed camp with artillery and tanks built up to where it would be extremely difficult for any country to invade them. Walter discovered that his French francs were nearly worthless at the English exchange rate. They took a bus to London. Along the way Walter kept seeing more and more American equipment to the American embassy where he was given got some more pay in English pounds sterling. They helped him arrange for a small efficiency apartment. They discovered that England was short of everything except people that had left the continent to get away from the war. They decided instead to stay in a small village away from London, where it was cheaper.

MONTH 36, JUNE 15

Lieutenant General Lakeman was speaking, "Supplies had been shipped for months into England and Northern Europe from the United States, but now we are ready to mount a counter attack. I know we had hoped to have more equipment in Europe before the invasion, but we have a chance at saving what's left of the French that made their heroic stand in Paris. They have held off the Arabs for over a year and as a result saved what's left of Europe. We can't delay any longer. We have reason to believe that Paris has not fallen and they are fighting to the last man. To not try now would be like allowing the men in the Alamo to die. Let's not have another Alamo to remember. Let's have a success story. Now Congressmen, I would like to introduce Jim Claris. The recovery of the United States and our return to military power was engineered by him. I was only the instrument that brought him here to lead us. Gentlemen, Jim Claris."

When the applause died, Jim said, "You may not believe this, but I was very shy about talking in front of a group for years. All logic says that I should completely choke in front of this esteemed crowd, but I found that when I really have information to convey the shyness goes away in the effort to get the information out. So here goes. Cameras please." The room darkened and a one hundred inch high definition television screen lit up. "What we have here is a demonstration of a fighter airplane launching a rather large missile. The fighter has gained maximum airspeed and zoomed for altitude higher than it normally could fly. It then releases its missile that is shown here knocking down an Arab satellite with absolute precision. Now if you will watch screen two as we freeze the screen on television one. This is a satellite we launched last year in Geosynchronous orbit over the United States. The picture of our satellite is taken from the backup satellite for the one we see. On screen three you will shortly see two Red Chinese and two Arab satellites approaching the North American continent. Remember, this is live. We are recording it so we can play it back shortly. Ready...NOW! I see most of you didn't see what actually happen. Let's play what happened in less than one thousandth of a second. Our satellite here in Geosynchronous orbit is nuclear powered and has enough fuel for twenty years of operation.

It can generate its own electricity that is stored as a static charge throughout the satellite and on special capacitors not dreamed possible before. It is twenty-two thousand miles from Earth and is not to be feared. Through space its laser beam weapons can throw a devastating beam millions of mile with very little attenuation...loss of power. It's beams could destroy a city on the Moon. However, its beams would hardly be seen as a wink of light on earth because our atmosphere disperses the beam dramatically with most of the light actually being reflected back to space. The typical camera light meter could not measure the weakness of the light on earth.

Okay, now it is getting ready to fire. There was a quick four blinks of light. Did you see them? Let's slow it down more. Okay, there you can see the blinks. Now let's divide our attention with screen three. You can see the four enemy satellites explode simultaneous with the blinks on our satellite twenty-two thousand miles away. What you saw was one of thirty beams on our satellite firing four times and precisely destroying four enemy satellites. We have twenty of these now in orbit to protect North American from any further satellites or missile warheads that might be fired. In this same one thousandth of a second these twenty satellites could flicker four times from each of its thirty beams times twenty satellites. In other words, this one star wars system could shoot down twenty-four hundred missile warheads in one thousandth of second.

There is no way that any missile warhead will strike the North American continent. The additional satellites we are launching will be to protect the rest of the world from any future attack from space. To shoot down a high flying airplane at sixty thousand feet takes two minutes from one beam tracking and repeatedly firing. If all thirty beams per satellite are firing it takes one second to recharge and fire again. At fifty thousand feet the atmosphere attenuates the beam so it would take twenty minutes of firing with one beam. At forty thousand feet, all we could hope to do is give the pilot a sunburn. A question? Gentlemen, the question was what keeps the satellite from eventually crashing back to earth. The neat thing about a Geosynchronous orbit is that it would stay there forever. We figure it will be obsolete long before it runs out of nuclear fuel. When it gets old we will use the nuclear power plant to fire an ion engine that produces very little power, but will gradually accelerate the satellite to escape Earth's orbit and continue to the sun where it will cause a little pop of nuclear explosion. Compared to a typical solar flare that would be like a lady finger firecracker compared to a nuclear bomb. There will be no nuclear waste and no danger.

Now if you will turn your attention to screen one, I will show you what we are developing to stop cruise missiles and aircraft that might want to attack us. This one is only in testing. It is a similar satellite, but with a particle beam instead of a laser beam. It's particles are heavier than photons so they will carry through the atmosphere better to where we could actually hit ground targets although most ground targets are too hard to burn through. A cruise missile or airplane is thin and easy to burn through, making them practical targets. You would not see the beam because it would kill you too fast if it struck a living target. If you were wearing a helmet your head would be better protected than a cruise missile or aircraft. If the beam were directed at a concrete skyscraper it would burn through a floor every two minutes versus shooting down its intended target in a fraction of a second.

How do we launch them? A derivative of the National Aerospace Plane or NASP. It takes off with normal turbojets like an airliner, climbs and accelerates to a speed where the turbines can be feathered and the engines become ram jets augmented by separate ramjets allowing the aircraft to achieve a speed of over Mach ten. At that point it zooms into space releasing its satellites which are accelerated with booster rockets to orbit speed. Once out of the atmosphere it does not take much power to achieve great speed. The NASP is not designed to stay in space for even one orbit but return to Earth for an ordinary powered landing like any other aircraft. It has new metals making the tiles of the space shuttle unnecessary. It does not have the heavy life support systems of the shuttle.

Now, as we are going closer to the ground, watch screen two. Do you see it. On screen three is a radar picture of what you are trying to see. The radar sees it also, but not sufficiently for the radar operator to know it is there. A sparrow has a big radar picture in comparison. Keep watching. Now we see it because it is firing a rather large cannon from very short range. This is a live picture over Nevada. If you will look down on the floor you will now see the pilot wave at you. The airplane, having lost its human controller is programmed to fly back and land from the base where it took off from. It is a remotely piloted stealth aircraft.

Now screen one again. See the tank coming. It attacks and blows up an old American M-60 tank and now you see it drive up next to 1987 Lincoln which dwarfs it. You see this tank is a miniature remotely driven vehicle similar to the airplane. The tank, like the airplane will either return home or continue to a reprogrammed point without its driver. One driver could drive one hundred a day into battle letting the tanks get themselves there and back without human intervention. It takes people to fire the guns. It uses the Global Positioning System (GPS) to plot its course.

These last two weapons can actually attack in Europe while the people driving them are driving or piloting from here in the United States. These two weapons are so cheap that we can produce them by the thousands. Because they do not have commanders, drivers, and gunners we have fewer people to feed in battle. They take very little gas compared to the manned variety. Their ammunition is small and light weight while still deadly. Whereas a C-5 cargo plane can only carry two M1 tanks, it can carry forty of these small tanks or two hundred of the aircraft.

Gentlemen, we are ready." As Jim left the speakers stand he received a thunderous applause. He turned red from embarrassment and just kept on going until he left the room. The applause was still going as he stood outside the closed door.

MONTH 36 JUNE 17

Strange looking American airplanes had been coming in since Walter and Bridget got to London. There were also many F-15's, F-16's, and other aircraft. When they took off they headed toward the east coast of Great Britain. When they came back they immediately landed. He had noticed that frequently the same airplanes were airborne in less than an hour. The number of American aircraft flying east had been increasing day by day.

Walter had been assigned to a Army intelligence, but he was not given a job, all he did was check in once a week with them and to get his regular paychecks. When he went to the headquarters at an air force base, he found the skies full of airplanes landing and taking off. he recognized the C-5, the C-141, and the C-17 aircraft of the United States Air Force plus many commercial types of aircraft. He asked what was going on, but was told he was not cleared to have the information.

Bridget had noticed that things that were in short supply, including food were now abundant. "Has the United States recovered and now shipping all this?"

"Apparently, but I haven't been able to find anyone that is telling me anything."

"When you go in tomorrow, I suggest that you stay there and find out. All you have been doing is picking up a paycheck and running. Try hanging around awhile. I would like a little warning before my husband goes off to war again. There's the telephone again. Probably a salesperson, would you like to get it?"

"Hello."

"You're kidding? Then we're too late? Why do you say that? What are we going to do about it? Yes, I will call daily from now on. I hope so too."

Bridget could hardly contain herself, "What was that about?"

"Paris has been taken."

"How? They were defending the city so well."

"The leaders, in exchange for their own safety, pulled the guards on the Seine River which allowed minisubs right into the city where they gained control of the government offices and captured most of the French leaders."

"THEN THEY HAVE NOT CAPTURED PARIS, ONLY AN AREA AROUND THE SEINE. RIGHT?"

"I didn't ask. Would the French surrender because of their government being captured?"

"No. They would not. They know the Arabs have killed everyone they have come in contact with. A surrender would mean the end of France and the annihilation of the French people."

"I think you're right. I'm supposed to be a member of intelligence now, I'm going to the base and attempt to take my position."

"REMEMBER, I'M NOT MILITARY. WHAT IS INTELLIGENCE EXACTLY?"

"Intelligence means finding out where the enemy is, what weapons they have, and recommending how to beat them. I don't know how long I will be gone, but I'm staying until someone will listen to me." With that Walter left and went back to the air base. He went to the base commander's office and waited to speak to the Colonel. He was told that the Colonel did not have time to talk to Non Commissioned Officers, but he would not be dissuaded and eventually the Major informed the Colonel that there was some insubordinate army NCO that insisted on talking to the Colonel and no one else.

Walter was sent in to the Base Commander's office. The Colonel looked crusty lean and mean. More a man of action rather than someone sitting behind a large wooden desk. Like most Colonel's offices in the military, the office was a plain room with some print pictures of air planes hanging on the wall along with the Colonel's personal memorabilia such as plaques and pictures that had been given him as parting gifts from the many places he had been in the past. The office had a leather sofa and coffee table along with one over stuffed arm chair.

"OKAY SERGEANT, WHAT IS SO IMPORTANT?"

"Sir, I was with the expeditionary force that invaded southern France months ago to cut off the Arabs. My tank was the only one that survived the tank company that was totally destroyed before the retreat. I have been in France and know how the Arabs have been fighting. In fact, I spent many months there fighting with the resistance. Most importantly, we just came from Paris and know what was going on there not long ago. I'm supposed to be assigned to intelligence because of my experience, but all I do is come to the base, collect my pay and go back home. Paris has not surrendered, Sir. They will fight to the last man. We must do something to help them."

"Relax Sergeant. The major did not sit idly by. I have your brief right here." Patting a manila folder on his desk. "Sit down and lets talk. Here, I have a map of France." The Colonel sat on the sofa beside Walter and unfolded the map on the coffee table. "Tell me everywhere you've been and what happened at each significant point."

Walter recounted his last months in France right up to his escape to England.

"Sergeant, I think you and I need to go over to the command post and see what we can do with your information. When we get there, I'll introduce you and you just dive right in on this map. Circle and mark anything you think might be important on the map. You wanted work. You're going to work. Maybe we can show you what we have been doing too."

The trip to the command post was near the flight line and was a concrete block building. Walter had never been in a major military command post before. The building was relatively new and was the European command headquarters for the European theater of World War III. He had the same impression as most civilians about the ultra modern command post that one always see in the movies. He imagined that this was going to be a real treat with fifty foot high television screens surrounding a huge semi-circular room with real time views of the war theater. As he and the colonel drove up to the building, he was wondering if he was going to be he was going to be within one of the lavish glass rooms at one of the huge oval oak tables or down on the floor with all of the computer terminals.
"Colonel, why are you driving this staff car yourself, don't you have a driver?

"Sergeant. Maybe in the Army a Colonel has a driver because man power was cheap, but in the Air Force everyone has a job and there has never been enough to spare to provide drivers for mere Colonels. In fact, most Generals in the Air Force drive their own vehicles. Chauffeurs are only used for taxis for people that did not warrant the loan of a government vehicle, and visiting dignitaries that do not have government driver's licenses. The only exceptions are very high ranking Generals that have an armed driver for security reasons or when politics dictate. Some have drivers around Washington D.C. because of politics. We're here. Let me show you around your new digs. You'll be working here twelve hours a day from now on. You should know enough to not volunteer, but sometimes us professionals forget, right?"

"Yes sir." What else do you say to a colonel. As soon as they got in the building they were greeted by two security police. They were in a drab empty entry room with television cameras. There was also a thick window with more security police.

They greeted the colonel and the door buzzed them into a long hall. The hall was typical drab military. The hall was lined with small offices with the typical unexciting government paint. The offices had the typical government desks and cheap furniture. One thing Walter noticed immediately was that there were too many desks and people for even the military. They were packed in to the point that it looked like there were more people than chairs even. No one even looked up as they walked past.

At the approximate center of the building they came to another security area that was monitored by multiple television cameras and more security police guarding a heavy two foot thick vault door that was standing open. As soon as they passed the door, they were in another area with a thick glass window. The colonel placed his hand on some sort of sensor that lit up a green light and then the security police behind the window slid up a door in the glass and exchanged security badges with the colonel. The colonel slipped the badge in a slot while placing his hand on another sensor next to a metal elevator door. They went down. If it was a slow elevator they only went down a couple of floors, but it could have been twenty in a fast elevator. Walter couldn't determine how far they went.

With great anticipation Walter waited for the elevator door to open so he could see the fabulous technology in this European command headquarters that he knew was there. It was rather disappointing to find that it was more like an empty school gym painted with the typical government paint. The huge television screens were twenty to thirty inch screens that you had to walk up to in order to see. There were big glass rear projection screens, but they were mostly for man made view graphs and thirty-five millimeter slides. The oval oak conference table was stained oak, but was a large fifteen by thirty foot platform and made of plywood with multiple four by four posts for legs. There were telephones all around the table.

The colonel motioned him to a folding metal chair on the front row and then took a seat along one side of the table as more and more people filed into the room. From the name tags at the table, Walter could tell that the colonel didn't count for much. There was a four star at the head chair flanked by three and two star generals. There chairs were not standard government issue, but over stuffed leather conference chairs. The other chairs conformed to the standard plastic and cloth swivel chairs. The room came to attention when the generals came into the room. The four star said, "At ease." and everyone sat.

After the general sat he said, "Hold the briefings. We have a new man in the room. Colonel, would you like to introduce your friend and tell us why he is here."

"Yes sir. Sir, this is Technical Sergeant Walter Gaddis, US Army."

"So. Why did you bring him in here? This is a sensitive area with a very sensitive briefing. He is not on the security list for this briefing."

"Sir, I believe that Sergeant Gaddis has some important information that we all need to hear for ourselves. Sir, he was with the tank company that was wiped out in southern France. He was the one that fought with the resistance for several months before escaping to here. They assigned him to intelligence and then had him cooling his heals for months with nothing to do except draw a paycheck."

"Heard enough, Colonel. Sergeant, is that true?"

"Yes sir."

"Well God Damn it son. Where the hell have you been. We've been operating in the dark for months. Colonel, good job bringing him in here. Gentlemen, the main briefing will be postponed until thirteen hundred this afternoon. Now if everyone will clear the room, not you Colonel, I think this Sergeant has some information that needs to be discussed in private with us." The room cleared except for the generals and the colonel. The colonel whipped out the map that Walter had marked in the colonel's office.

When the general had first started talking Walter was wishing he was somewhere else and sorry that he had ruined the colonel's career. When the general was finished he was glad that he had picked that colonel to talk to and enthusiastic about getting himself heard. Maybe his hardship in France had paid for itself with Bridge's love, a child, and now his knowledge of the war in France.

The generals let him go at it except for a few questions like, "Sergeant, how steep is this hill really?" or "Sergeant, is this trail marked?" When Walter finished, there was silence for a moment and then the four star said, "Sergeant, I want to thank you for an excellent briefing. You convinced us that we have a lot of talking to do, but just between us generals. You will be welcome back here for all open meetings. In fact, I expect you here for each and every briefing. We will also want you to get involved in some other things. Colonel, thank you for bringing him here. Will you take him aside and give him some catch-up information? Please, feel free to provide other briefings using the staff briefers as you see fit. By the way, Colonel, clean out your desk as base commander. I want you here in the building. You are now in charge of intelligence. Move into the chief of intelligence office no between eight and ten tomorrow. Wednesday, you will be responsible for the daily intelligence briefing. Thank you both, you can go now."

When they got outside the Colonel told him, "Sergeant, You have two hours to find something to eat while I clean out my old office and then we are both going to go to work. I'll meet you back here in exactly two hours. I suggest that you call you wife and tell her you're going to be very late tonight. There's your car now. It will meet you daily at your apartment at 0600 each morning and take you home at 2000 each evening until we've pumped you dry. Remember, two hours."

As soon as Walter could get to the NCO club he went straight to the telephones and called Bridget. "Bridget, I'm in. It went beautifully. I briefed all the generals, I was assigned my own car and driver, you'd think I was an officer."

"WHOA. SLOW DOWN. DID YOU SAY YOU BRIEFED ALL THE GENERALS?"

"Yes. They asked why I was there and then they ran everyone out of the room. I'm afraid I talked for three hours straight and they hung on every word. I was told not to miss any more briefings."

"WHAT WAS THAT ABOUT YOUR OWN CAR AND DRIVER?"

"You heard me. They assigned me my own car and driver, at least for now. The colonel said, quote, until they pump me dry, unquote."

"WHEN ARE YOU GOING TO GET HOME?"

"I don't know. I'm meeting the colonel back at the command post at five PM to get caught up on intelligence. I might be here most of the night and won't be there long. My car will pick me up a 6 AM and bring me home at 8 PM every night. I guess I'm expected to work fourteen hours a day from now on."

"BEATS FIGHTING WITH THE RESISTANCE DOESN'T IT?"

"At least I'm not likely to get killed quickly. Yeah, its better. I asked to get involved. Well, I'm involved. No more just drawing a paycheck. Now I get to pay them back for all that free time."

"Well you had better get off the telephone and get to work. I'll see you whenever you get here. I love you and I'm proud of you. You never thought you could make a difference. Now is your chance to prove who you are, to make your mark."

Walter ate a lunch at the Non Commissioned Officer's (NCO) Club and then went back to the command post. He decided to try to go in and luckily the guards were looking for him to make his new identification passes to get into the building and then down to the underground command post. By the time the colonel arrived, Walter had his new identification passes.

"Sergeant Gaddis, I see you got your new ID. Good. Let me show you to your desk. This will be my office tomorrow. I want your desk to be next door where I can find you. Captain, would you mind letting Sergeant Gaddis having your desk."

"Sorry, Captain, not my idea." Walter managed to tell the Captain before he followed the colonel.

"It's all right, Sergeant. No harm done. I'm a professional too."

"Sergeant, take a seat there at the table where you can see the screens easily and just watch the pictures."

The pictures showed some new kind of fighter plane with another plane chasing it. The new airplane climbed into a loop with the other plane following. Suddenly the lead airplane flipped onto its back and killed the airplane chasing it. "This is the new Advanced Tactical Fighter or ATF. The airplane chasing it was an Arab MIG 31. The action took place over France. We only have fifty of them here yet because of a lack of trained pilots. It is very tricky to fly and take advantage of its capabilities. It is very stealthy, which means it is difficult to see on radar or heat sensors. It can do some very fancy flying as you just saw. Just when the enemy thinks he is in a tail position to shoot it down, the ATF can flip like you just saw to shoot behind itself as it temporarily flies backwards."

Another screen showed the stealth fighter of Iraqi war fame. Walter recognized it as the narrator said, "This is the F-117 Stealth Fighter. Whereas the ATF is an air superiority aircraft, the F-117 is a fighter bomber which means it is designed primarily to carry bombs into enemy territory to do damage without being seen on radar or heat sensors. Here are some sequences that took place in France yesterday. Here you see the target from the pilots view point. By flying in the clouds the F-117 is totally invisible. It can't be seen on radar. It can't be seen visually because of the clouds. The clouds help hide the very small heat signature of the engines. Now the pilot is over the target. Now you can see the video screen inside the cockpit that is taken by radar from the F-117. This is short burst radar that is hard to pinpoint, impossible for the Arabs to track. You can see the tank group on the radar. The pilot elects now to drop out of the cloud for the final few seconds rather than just use a radar drop. There he released his tank killers.   Now let's switch to screen three where we can show you what the tank killers did once released. This footage was taken at the development center at Eglin Air Force Base in the Florida panhandle. The sequence is very slow motion. There you can see the bomb. It flies itself directly over the tank group and then explodes releasing multiple bomblets that each pick a tank target and then explode directly above the six tanks parked below. Each bomblet releases four spikes that are driven downward by the bomblet explosion to penetrate the lighter upper tank armor. When the tip senses it has passed through the armor it explodes inside the armor. Now while five tanks were destroyed, the sixth seemingly survives, but let's zoom in closer. The spikes hit too near the gun and the front armor without penetrating the armor. Now the motion sensors take over. If anyone walks up to the tank or opens a hatch, the imbedded spikes explode into hundreds of pieces of shrapnel.

Once the attack has come there is terror inside the tank because no one wants to go outside the tank and no one wants to come help them. We have gained air superiority over all of northern Europe as far south as Paris and as far east as Berlin."

"Excuse me. I have been out of touch with any intelligence for the months that I was in France. Are you saying that the Arabs got as far as Berlin?"

"Actually they are just outside Munich in the south and almost to the old East - West German border in the north. They have swept up north to Finland and as far east as Saint Petersburg into Russia. Berlin was bypassed by the main Arab forces, but cut off from supplies.

"WASN'T THERE ANY RESISTANCE FROM THE RUSSIANS?"

"Not much. Most of their forces are in the east fighting the Chinese who have moved across most of Siberia. The satellite countries of the old Soviet Union simply didn't have organized military outfits without the Russian officers to lead them. They were chewed up immediately."

"I haven't heard that much about nuclear weapons."

"The Chinese used several and the Russians managed to get off one hundred and five missiles at the Chinese. The rest were sabotaged."

"WHAT HAPPENED TO THE SUBMARINE FLEETS OF THE SOVIET UNION AND THE UNITED STATES?"

"Well, that was kind of embarrassing. The Arabs knew the locations of almost every single one and had hundreds of Chinese made submarines that simply hunted them down and sank them. We didn't know what was happening to ours. We just lost contact with them. Our Air Force was essentially grounded and the Chinese used long range aircraft to hunt down our submarines with anti-submarine missiles."

"HOW DID THEY FIND OUR SUBMARINES?"

"Well. It seems our communications were not as secure as we thought they were and they just listened in over several years until they knew where they were as well as we did. We thought the STU-IIIs were secure telephones when the Arabs had the secret to listening in as soon as the STU-IIIs came out. What we later found out was that the time that a STU-III took to synchronize was actually dialing another number where Arab or Japanese spies working for the commercial telephone companies were listening in. It simply never dawned on us that we could not trust leased commercial telephone lines. Most of our communications were using these leased telephone lines and every one was tapped. All they had to do was wait for a STU-II or STU-III to use a commercial line and then synchronize for security and then they listened in. They had hundreds of spies in the active duty, but what really hurt were the all of the foreign born people that were working as civilians for the government. We now have a rule that all federal employees and congressmen must have parents born in the United States."

"What are we doing to get through to Paris before it is overrun?"

"Nothing so far."

It was midnight when Walter's driver dropped him off at his apartment and Bridget. She wanted to talk, but he was tired and had to get up to be ready to leave at 6 AM. He collapsed until Bridget woke him up with a cup of coffee and a kiss at 5:30 AM. "Wake up sleepy head. Time for work. You have thirty minutes to get dressed before your limo arrives."

"Love you, Bridget. It's not a limo. It's only a staff car."

"Only a staff car with your own driver. You say only?"

When Walter got to work there were more briefings. The open brief was delayed until 1400 or 2 PM. When the room was full the generals came in like yesterday but this time they were giving the briefing. "Gentlemen, we have decided to accelerate all plans to retake Europe. We want all actions taken to lay out plans for a counter invasion of Europe. Sergeant Gaddis and the Colonel will decide where and when and then brief us. Now everyone get to work. I need all inventories of all military equipment available for the invasion by tomorrow's oh eight hundred brief."

The briefing lasted all of five minutes and the colonel and Walter took over the conference room. They worked straight through until 5 PM.

Walter went to the NCO club and called Bridget to tell her he wouldn't be home. They worked through the night. Walter woke up with his head on the conference room table when people started coming in for the 8 AM briefing to the generals. The United States had five thousand M1A1 tanks and one thousand M2 tanks which had been developed and put into production in only a few months. It had multiple layers of armor, explosives, and more armor. The engine was turbo charged diesel. The gun was a recoilless 205 millimeter that could fire twenty rounds a minute.

To go against the thirty thousand remaining Arab tanks which had been supplemented by Chinese made tanks would take superior air power. The ATF could assure air superiority over the Arab aircraft, but close air support was difficult with man portable ground to air missiles. The colonel gave the briefing. When he mentioned the missiles, the four star said, "The invasion will not be stopped by man launched missiles. Does anyone have suggestions? ... Come on now gentlemen. Do I have to go around the room one person at a time?" Hands started going up around the room. The general said, "That's more like it. Now, I expect twenty fifteen minute briefings starting at 0800 tomorrow. I want independent thinking. Now the Sergeant here will hear your ideas and pick which twenty will be briefed. Sergeant Gaddis, it's all yours."

Sergeant Gaddis was a little taken aback by this attention. He had never before been in charge of anything more important than a tank. He imagined that they had picked him because of his experience, but didn't know. He wrote each idea on a view graph that projected onto one of the pull down screen as they were given. When he determined that one was a duplicate, he asked the two people to get together on a single briefing item. After paring down the ideas, he was hard pressed to come up with twenty and therefore had some ideas broken into two separate ones to come up with twenty. He was counting on the colonel to help him when he stubbed his toe.

The briefings were assimilated into a new plan for the counter invasion of France and then modified by someone back at US Military headquarters at the Alternate National Military Command Center. The plan was essentially unchanged except for extreme dispersal of forces and new tactics based upon independent but coordinated action. No longer would one send a company of tanks all bunched together to attack an Arab force. Now the same number of tanks would spread out offering many targets. Tanks might be sent, but they were forbidden from traveling together or even approaching from the same direction.

22 INVASION

III,9

The beach-heads at Bordeaux, La Rochelle in southwest France and Rouen in northwest France are secured and it will establish a hold on the ocean coast (England). by the allied forces of the French, English, and Dutch the enemy will be chased as far as Roanne in central France.

IV,46

It is an established fact! Those of Tours in western France, guard yourselves, your ruin is near. London will come from the Nantes and fight against the defenders of Reims in northeast France, but will be unable to proceed any further because of a drizzling rain.

IV,68

In a location not far from Venice, the leaders of conquered Asia and Africa will meet after taking the Rhine and the lower Danube, cries and tears at Malta and Genoa.

IX,38

The English will enter Blaye and La Rochelle and those from Macedonia, the Arabs, will withdraw. not far from Agen the remaining French forces will wait. One will be taken by commandos convincing the Arabs to retreat.

MONTH 37, JULY 14

The counter invasion of Europe was underway. This was nothing like D-Day from World War II. The port at Rotterdam, Netherlands was used to transport tanks and trucks that would be used to reinforce the Rhine river. As they were unloaded they simply trucked on down to the Rhine on the Autobahns that were not damaged. The decision was to defend what was left of Germany and to retake Paris that had the majority of all living Frenchmen still in France. If Paris wasn't relieved soon, there might never again be a France. Much of the equipment was simply trucked down the

Autobahns through Belgium to the front north of Paris. At the same time forces were landed on the beaches near Bordeaux where the expeditionary force had originally landed at the port. The idea was not so much attack the Arabs from the rear as to worry them about getting their supply lines cut. It also gave hope to the remnants still fighting in the mountains of Spain including what was left of Sergeant Gaddis's old tank brigade from other companies that escaped the fate of Sergeant Gaddis's company. The forces around Bordeaux immediately scattered and dug in to prevent a counter attack or an easy nuclear or biological target for the Arabs.

The forces in northern France immediately dispersed into loose fighting groups. There were no central headquarters or supply dumps for the enemy to target. Instead there were seven thousand different targets. Each tank had its own infantry and supplies separate from every other tank. This required more supplies, and was somewhat wasteful in that if a tank was killed, the supplies might not be near the next tanks refueling point.

In the past, when an Arab tank column was attacked, it was by a group of American tanks traveling together, attacking together, and sharing a common fuel and ammunition dump. Now it was attacked by separate American tanks coming at it from every direction sharing nothing except a common target.

In the past, the Arab tanks would turn and charge toward the American tank group and the American tank group would rely on firing from longer range to kill the Arab tanks before they could get too close. If the Arabs had good marksmen or enough concentrated fire the battle might be an even exchange. Now, even with American production lines running full tilt, the American forces were too out numbered for any even exchanges.

With the new dispersed attack, various tanks were told to attack a map coordinate at a certain time and proceed to that point on a direct line from their dispersal point. Fifty tanks attacking an Arab group would essentially come from fifty slightly different points of the compass. When the Arab tanks tried to counter attack, there was no one point to attack. There was no American strong point. Any direction they went resulted in an all out retreat of perhaps ten tanks while the Arab flanks were open to fire from the forty tanks not in the Arab path. This worked beautifully over and over.

Americans are brought up to be independent and to work alone. Arabs have to be led as a group. In theory, if the Arabs could have gone in the fifty different compass points to counter attack the fifty independently attacking Americans, they might have been more successful, but when they sent all one hundred or so tanks in their group off in one direction it was like punching air. The American tanks in their path went into all out retreat, while the other American tanks fired upon the weaker sides and tracks of the Arab tanks. Why fire at the strong front armor if you can hit the tracks or the engine? When the Arabs turned in another direction, the American tanks that had been in all out retreat, attacked the flanks while the new set of American tanks in the Arab path retreated. The Arabs called it chicken of the Americans to not stand and fight, but the Americans were reminded of their revolutionary war heritage, where the British tried to stay in a group while the Americans took pot shots and won the war.

MONTH 39, SEPTEMBER 1

It had not taken long for the Arabs to pull back away from Paris and try to set up a defensive line. As long as the Arabs were moving, the Americans ran and hit, ran and hit. A defensive line would require the Americans to come to them and fight a pitched battle.

The Americans let them retreat and set up a defensive line south of Paris to try to save as many French as possible that had been bottled up in Paris.

MONTH 43, JANUARY 15

It had taken three months to feed and clothe the French in Paris. Many were moved to tent cities outside of Paris now that it was safe to do so. There were public baths with treated water and sewage to put in. The amount of medical attention was astronomical as was the amount of food necessary to feed the people and provide for some excess storage. Tens of thousands were sick and five million suffering from malnutrition and dehydration as the result of the siege.

Even when the Arabs had taken the city centers, the French did not give in, but fought harder eventually driving the Arabs out of the city center and re-sealing the waterways from further invasion. Many of the outer suburbs were taken by the Arabs including one eight square mile section around the Versailles Palace. The advances of the Arabs had already stagnated as the result of American air strikes and air superiority in the area. When the Arab armored columns started suffering terrible losses as the result of the new American tank tactics, they pulled out of Paris, and pulled back fifty miles where they bull dozed earthen revetments for defense of a line across France.

Germany was now requesting the same type of effort to retake Berlin and East Germany. Berlin was not as bad as Paris, because there had been less time without allied air superiority. Berlin had been supplied mainly by air except for a two month period where the Arabs had air superiority. The Berliners had received minimal shelling, in fact, almost no fighting. They had ample supplies, but now that Paris was freed and the crisis on its way to recovery, the Germans were concerned about the many East German towns that were behind Arab lines. No one knew what would be found when the Arabs were driven back.

MONTH 48, JUNE 14

Germany now was back in German hands as was most of Austria. Nearly seventy percent of the Austrians that had stayed had been hunted down and executed by the Arabs. Never had the world seen such little regard to life, especially European life. If the Arabs had done this, what must the Chinese be doing to Soviets in the lands they had conquered. The main thing that had slowed the Chinese were the long winters and lack of supply lines from China. China had conquered most of India with the remaining parts becoming part of Pakistan. Pakistan said they were only taking back those lands that belonged to them in history. China got the entire southern part.

German cities were a complete disaster. The Arabs had not even bothered with mass graves but had piled the bodies a few miles from the cities they took over. Every stick of furniture and painting had been stolen or destroyed. Every eatable thing had been eaten. There was not a dog, cat, or rat to be found alive once the Arabs withdrew. There had been no such thing as a collaborator with the enemy. They killed every European they could find.

Some smaller, out of the way villages had survived extinction simply because the Arabs skipped over them without knowing they were there. The mountainous regions had been more than the Arabs wanted to deal with. Those that had hidden in the mountains had mainly survived. Germany and Austria had come through two previous world wars plus many other wars with Napoleon, the Huns, and everyone else sacking the cities, but never had an effort been made to kill everyone, just because they weren't Arabs. There could be no underground among dead people.

The East Germans had been similar to the old Soviet block Warsaw pact countries. They had been subjugated so long by so many different people from Hitler's Germany, to the Russians, that they simply just expected the Arabs to be just yet another ruler. By not fighting they figured there could be more coexistence. The Arabs simply lined up the people and shot them. They had a lot of left over Soviet military equipment, but never had the training and leadership to defend themselves. The only real defense against the Arabs in Europe had been remnants of Soviet forces not called to the eastern front, West Germany, and France. With the Arabs total air superiority over the battles, there was no doubt as to the outcomes.

Vienna had been ruined. It had not been shelled or bombed, but what wasn't stolen was defaced. Statues had either been shipped or broken. Buildings had been trashed by Arabs not knowing how to live in a building or caring. Most windows had been broken out and the water damage over two years of glassless windows had ruined most of the fine hardwood floors. The walls had been carved and painted with anti-European trash.

The West Germans were incensed. At the end of World War II people had been horrified at the Nazi death camps, but the Arabs had not even bothered. They just killed on the spot. Of the thirty percent that had survived the occupation nearly ninety percent were young women that had lived through physical and mental torture. They had all been repeatedly raped and most bore physical scars from tortures they had been put through. As you know any population is normally 50+ percent female. Now the population of East Germany and Austria was ninety percent female with nearly one hundred percent scarred for life. Any children born to these women had been aborted shortly into the pregnancies to prevent any half European children from being born. The only men that had survived were from the small villages or had hidden in the mountains. The women had been locked in basements except when in use during the entire occupation. Another reminder that these invaders had not had European heritage.

West Germany wanted to continue on throughout eastern Europe killing Arabs and liberating land, but now attention had to turn back to France and southern Europe. The U.S. high command had stopped the American support of West Germany to concentrate their forces on a move southward from Paris.

MONTH 50, SEPTEMBER 1

At long last, they were ready for their assault on southern France. The air superiority was so sure that many of the fighter bomber aircraft were flying off French, German, and Belgium air fields. Today was the day of the first air to ground mission to beat back the Arabs in France. They were using the same equipment and munitions used in East Germany and Austria.

The fighter bombers were a little different than the A-10s used in Kuwait against Sadam Hussein. These had no pilot on board. They were remotely piloted vehicles piloted through secure data links from the pilotless aircraft through the AWACS radar sentry aircraft back to ground stations where young enlisted personnel flew them like they would a video game. They sat at a television set with a joystick controller.

Some were little more than flying gatling guns. They used heavily insulated and cooled, supercharged internal combustion engines instead of jet engines to give heat seeking missiles less easy to find. They were quite small since there was no pilot on board with all of the required instruments, ejection seat, canopy mechanisms, oxygen systems, voice radios, etc. The entire front of the aircraft was a gatling gun and a TV camera mounted in the center of the gun. The remote pilot was naturally fearless since it was only a relatively cheap remotely piloted aircraft and not his life on the line. The enemy frequently never saw them until the gun opened up quickly firing all its ammunition killing tanks and then flying away at low altitude. It did not have much radar signature due to its size and construction. It did not have much heat signature for heat seeking missiles due to its well cooled and insulated internal combustion engine, and being very small it was not very visible for people either. It was practically impossible to shoot down. Even when people saw the guns firing, as soon as it quit firing most people lost sight of it. Because of its low price, the United States had manufactured thousands of them. For the same amount of money as one thousand of these you could buy only one ATF, advanced tactical fighter. Cruise missiles were very expensive in comparison. These aircraft were only large model airplanes.

A Saudi Arabian that had his degree from the University of Oklahoma in Journalism had left his unit and turned himself in to American troops. He claimed that as soon as he heard that the Americans were moving into Europe, he took his Saudi Arabian tank unit of ten tanks and just took off for the American lines with guns down and white flags flying. The following are excerpts from Captain Loni Fahled.

We were forced into service at the order of Prince Facil Saud. There were many rumors that the Saud family was being held hostage and Prince Saud has not been seen in person since the war started. We were ordered to move our tanks onto transports and were not involved in Italy. We landed in Marseilles after the landing was over. We were not involved in much of the fighting so far, but his entire tank company was very emotionally distraught at the total destruction they had seen. There is a big difference between Iraqis and Saudis. We have never had enough people and value life very highly. Most of us are well educated, not just the elite, but everyone, except for some of the Bedouins of course, but most have more than just high school.

From what we could see, it looked like the religious police had taken over the country and were working with the United Arab Nations. I can't believe that Prince Saud would voluntarily join this effort. We were loaded onto transports five months after the war started. We spent six months on the transport before being unloaded in Algeria. We lived in tents there without enough food or water and then a year ago we were loaded back on transports. We spent three months on the transports and then unloaded at Marseilles. After we eventually headed north we went through village after village that had been looted and destroyed with thousands of people killed. The bodies were just piled outside of town for the dogs to feed on. The stench was terrible. For us to know it was from human dead, was very disturbing, but what does one do when our group was only ten tank crews in the midst of hundreds that were celebrating the victory and were proud of the dead bodies. We were sickened and frightened at the same time, but nothing we could do except follow orders. We were behind the lines as a reserve unit until we got to Paris, and then pushed into the battle. We had been on the front line for only six weeks. We must have been called in when the leaders heard that the Americans had come back to Europe. As soon as we heard that the Americans were back, we decided that this war is not our war and we didn't want to get involved in the killing we had seen. When our company was ordered to attack the north side of Paris, we simply took off north and kept going until we found the Americans.

Ammunition? All of our ammunition is Chinese made and we have a good supply of it. It is not made as well, because the range on the cannon rounds is inconsistent. Yes, we were involved in shelling Paris from long range. We had to. We had no choice but to follow orders at that time. We never saw anyone to shoot at, but others say the Chinese ammunition keeps jamming the machine guns.

Air force action. Yes, our fighter bombers have been bombing continuously for weeks now, but they stopped when we started seeing strange new aircraft over the city. I don't understand how the French are holding out. They must have laid in huge amounts of supplies.

Yes, I saw an attack by some form of American aircraft on a tank unit. There were several of us using binoculars trying to look for American aircraft. We were right next to a mobile radar van and they never saw anything. I happened to have my binoculars pointed right at one. I thought it was a bird. All of a sudden there was a bright fire in the sky that seemed almost a beam of what must have been heavy cannon shells from a gatling gun. The fire was so bright I lost sight of the bird or aircraft or whatever it was. Tanks started exploding about five hundred yards to my right. Since I was in my tank there was no point in running. I kept looking through my binoculars to try to see the airplane. It flew right over my position at low altitude. I got a very good look at it. The front was the size of the gatling gun and it seemed to have a pusher propeller inside a circle. I think it was what I read about before the war called something like a ducted fan. It was too small to be a real airplane with a pilot so I knew for that kind of technology it had to be American. My tank company had three years to talk about it. Once we knew the Americans were involved, we started actively looking for an escape. We never wanted any part of this war and once we saw the destruction, we wanted out, but couldn't get out.

Oh. The aircraft. Yes, ten or more shoulder fired anti-aircraft missiles were fired at it, but only two got a lock on it. The others just ran off in one direction until they ran out of fuel and then crashed. The two that locked on were gaining rapidly on it, but it easily out-maneuvered it. It turned far more rapidly than the missiles with their little stubby wings. They overshot it when attempting to turn with it and then simply lost lock with one going straight ahead and the other hitting an Arab truck on the ground. From what we heard from other tankers, our ground to air missiles were hitting tanks, trucks, even chimneys on houses, but no one we talked with ever saw a single one of these miniature airplanes shot down by missiles. I did hear about one that was shot down by small arms fire. It blew up before it hit the ground."

Was it effective? The one I saw blew up eight tanks and four fuel trucks. The fires and explosions from the tanks and fuel trucks blew up ten supply trucks. It had no fear. It kept firing and coming in until it looked like it was going to crash before it pulled out.

"Yes, I believe all Saudis would pull out if they could without being shot by the others, as would many Egyptians and Moroccans. They were more interested in becoming Western than in being in a war of any kind."

The American tanks were moving south from Belgium toward Paris. Some of the Arab tanks moved north from Paris to meet them. A major tank battle was coming. The Arab tanks picked a rise where they could see the American tanks coming. What they saw were miniature tanks with big guns. They were moving about thirty miles per hour.

Back at the European command post Chief Master Sergeant Walter Gaddis was watching a room full of young privates and corporals playing what could be mistaken for video games. Walter had been promoted all the way to Chief Master Sergeant to give him the authority to deal with Colonels and be respected by younger non commissioned officers. Normal promotions had gone by the wayside with the war. The military had been drawn down to only thirty percent of its manpower during the Viet Nam war and now with a real world war going on the military had to come up to strength rapidly over the last two years once the United States had decided to get involved in the war for real.

Walter moved up behind one of the operators to watch the progress. There was a big screen panoramic picture on the far wall taken by a video camera aboard a remotely piloted hovering helicopter model airplane type vehicle. Walter alternately watched the "video game" and the panoramic shot from the battle surveillance cameras.

On the small video screen the private was driving a tank. At the bottom of the screen were digital readouts for amount of fuel and ammunition. The rest of the tank was monitored for mechanical health such as engine heat and if any came out of range it would pop up on the screen. If radio contact were lost with the tank the internal programming would take over and the tank would return to a pre-programmed rendezvous point. In the event that a tank became disabled and anyone tried to break into it the mini-tank would self destruct gutting itself beyond recognition. Maintenance men had to plug in a computer and put in a code for their own tanks to disarm them.

As Walter watched, the operator in front of him spotted the Arab tanks on his screen and accelerated his tank to sixty miles per hour. Arab tank shells started exploding around him, but sitting in front of his computer terminal hundreds of miles away, the one man remote tank crew was fearless. A shell exploded right in front of the tank and the tank fell into the hole it left, but the tank quickly ground back up out of the hole and continued its charge. As it got closer, its fifty millimeter gatling gun opened up and started chewing up the tank treads of the enemy immobilizing them.

Suddenly infantry appeared on the screen. Infantry can be very dangerous for a tank because they can sneak up and throw grenades in the tank treads, smear mud over gunsights, and otherwise disable tanks. The operator hit a key and the screen split into multiple views without magnification. He pressed another key and then pushed the button on his joystick. Miniguns opened up in all directions killing everything within hundreds of yards without doing more than scoring the paint on the other American tanks which were also firing. Infantry would think twice about approaching American tanks again. Because to do so was death.

Walter looked up at the big screen taken from above the battle as the mini-tanks retreated as fast as they were attacking. A few of the Arab tanks were pursuing but most on the front line were immobile. Then the view got wider as the hovering remote aircraft retreated. Then the immobile tanks started exploding as smart mortar rounds zeroed in on the tank shapes from twenty miles away. Some of the mobile tanks also exploded, but most kept chasing the mini-tanks without seeing the destruction to the immobile tanks behind them. The mini-tanks were out of ammunition and simply running now.

Then from the sides American M1A4 tanks came rolling in with their new anti-personnel miniguns and new one hundred twenty millimeter rapid fire cannon capable of one round every three seconds with laser aiming and cushioned for the shocks of crossing trenches while keeping a dead aim. They also had new armor over the old made up of a sandwich from the outside to the inside of reactive (explosive) armor to explode when struck hard without damaging the tank but to destroy ammunition that struck it. A two inch layer of a new steel alloy, and another layer of reactive armor before getting to the real tank armor. It wasn't pretty, but armored cooling vents and armored air intakes had been added to further protect the back of the tank and the engine. The engine was upgraded to provide thousands of horsepower to power the now heavier tank. The turbine engine would burn almost any fuel, but jet fuel would propel the tank at eighty miles per hour over open terrain in an emergency and when wheels were lowered from the bottom over one hundred miles per hour. The older Arab operated American M1A1, British Chieftain, German Leopard, Russian T-72 and French Alzar tanks had no chance against these superior gunned, faster, and better armored tanks.

The Arabs lost over one thousand tanks in this battle. The Americans lost one hundred mini-tanks with no loss of life and had twenty manned tanks disabled with no loss of life. The Arabs pulled back from Paris to preserve their forces and allowed the remaining French to survive and be relieved by the Americans. The Americans let the Arabs retreat in order to fly supplies into Paris and fly out the wounded and sick. Paris was in ruins, but two million French survived in Paris.

MONTH 50, SEPTEMBER 28

The relief of Paris was the big thing in the world news and had occupied most of the armor, but the relief of Berlin was also going on. Berlin had been surrounded but by-passed by the Arabs. With no Arabs that near Berlin and total air superiority, the people were not going hungry due to the Berlin airlift II. The French on the other hand were fighting street to street and being starved. There were fewer than one million healthy French left in France. Eighty percent of their military equipment was gone and sixty percent of their military dead.

Since most of the armor had been committed to the relief of Paris, the German front was fought mainly by air and infantry. The new intelligent mortar shells were very critical to the American success. There was also the problem caused by the Arabs being scattered along a very long line from the Alps to the Baltic. Too deep an advance in one area could expose the flanks to an Arab counter attack or getting the supply line cut.

A big help was the new anti-armor air to ground missiles that were launched by aircraft and then sought out the enemy tanks. They would have worked great if the all of the tanks were Russian, because Russian tanks have a distinct radar shape sound and smell, much different than American tanks. Because the Arabs had so many American tanks these missiles could not be used near any American tanks.

The close air support remote guided airplanes had been very effective when tanks were in the open, but the Arab tanks had learned to stay in the German forests as much as possible to hide from them. A manned aircraft simply could not survive the ground to air man-packed Stinger type missiles. The A-10 that had been so effective in Kuwait simply could not survive close to the ground where the miniature remote guided aircraft could. As soon as the Americans would try to come after the Arabs the Arabs would come charging out attack, mix in with the American forces and then run for the trees again.

Since there had not been enough armor to spare for two fronts the Americans had been attempting to use infantry to invade the forests. The anti-tank shoulder fired missiles which were so effective in open ground were ineffective in the forest with trees getting in the way. When the infantry got an aim the missile would automatically go toward while the infantry man hid, but the missile would frequently hit a tree in between the firing point and the tank exploding the tree or exploding against the tree depending on the size of the tree. At one hundred thousand dollars a shot it was an expensive way to cut down a forest. The heavy tank shell on the other hand would chop trees down enroute to its target. The Arabs had wisely stocked up their forces in Germany to allow them to fight for months without re-supply.

As the infantry tried to build up to take on the tanks in the forest, the Arabs released some more of their biological weapons. The Arabs had been inoculated, but not the American troops. The infantry had to try and fight in biological suits, but eating, drinking, and sleeping was difficult. The American forces rushed in special inflatable tents that sucked in air through special biological filters and then kept the tent filled with positive air pressure. The suits were washed with chemicals to kill any biologicals as the troops came into the tents.

Now that Paris had been relieved mini-tanks were rushed to the German front. The mini-tanks were safe from biologicals since they had no crew and the forty millimeter gatling gun was quite effective in chopping down forest while shooting at Arab tanks. There small size allowed them to slip through the forest much better than full size tanks. Arab infantry soon learned to stay away from the antipersonnel miniguns of the small tank.

The outer layer of reactive armor had to be removed when going through the forest to keep it from exploding as trees were hit or fell on tanks. The American forces were very frustrated and taking losses that no one had wanted. While five thousand men in a month in a world war this violent might not seem that many it was ten percent of all the men lost in ten years of the Viet Nam war and the United States had lost so many during the start of the war in the United States not to enemy action but due to Americans fighting Americans after the terrorist type HEMP attack.

The American forces had opened up a corridor to Berlin, and had managed to secure it, but the Arabs still controlled all of East Germany and most of West Germany.

MONTH 56, FEBRUARY 20

Now that the leaves were gone from the deciduous trees the tanks only had evergreens to hide under and the air power was becoming more effective. Also, the total air superiority had prevented resupply of the Arab forces and they were starting to surrender. They were running out of ammunition, fuel and food.

Walter was at home in the base housing unit built for him on base. Bridget and Walter had a second child now. Walter had his own staff car now, although not a new one. England had become a military encampment just like World War II. There were people in uniform any place you looked and had airplanes flying out regularly. The ports were full of cargo ships from the United States. The French, Italian, German, and all other fleets from the allies were all operating between the rebuilt industrial might of the United States and the coast of England and into the ports of northern Europe. He had the week off and he and Bridget had just come back from a tour of Windsor Castle.

The telephone rang, "Hello. Yes sir, I'll be right there."

"What is it Walter?" Bridget asked.

"It was the general. He said something was happening and that I should come in immediately to give them advice. Couldn't say on the telephone of course, but it must be important. I'll be home when I can."

Bridget waved good-bye, "I'll be here when you get home, whenever that is." They had been moved on base within two months of Walter's acceptance into intelligence for two reasons: their safety from terrorists that might be loose in London, and for convenience so Walter could get to the headquarters quickly. Walter had also had time to study at work in between battles and had completed his bachelors degree and was working on a masters degree in business. She was proud of him getting his education at the same time as taking the pressure of being a key member of the intelligence and battle planning team. Most of the new full colonels on base held him in awe. The colonels that were on base when they arrived were now generals.

The security people all knew Walter and he was quickly into the underground command post to see what the excitement was. The four star general welcomed him and then bade him sit and watch a series of recon photos of Europe. "These photos were all taken during your vacation. We're not sure what to make of it, but the Arabs are all on the move, but not towards us, away from us. What do you make of it?"

Walter said, "Show me recon south of the Danube. Ooookay. Now, on the other side of the Rhone. Oookay. Now show me some south of Paris, but on this side of the Rhone. Ooookay. I think I've got it."

"Got what, Walter?" the general asked.

"It looks to me like they have called a general retreat to cross over the Danube and Rhone rivers. They are still moving equipment north so I would say they are planning to regroup and defend the rivers on either side of the Alps to keep part of France, East Europe, and all of Italy."

"OKAY. I SEE WHY YOU SAY THAT, BUT WHAT WOULD YOU RECOMMEND?"

"We need to concentrate on taking out every bridge they try to build across the river and make sure their forces don't get across. We need to flank them and get a foot hold behind them. Is there any chance on making a landing in Italy for example?"

"No way, Walter. The Mediterranean is an Arabic sea. I don't think we can move any forces quick enough to get across the rivers before they can fortify it. They still have many times as many men and tanks as we have. Will you see if you can work something up?"

"Yes sir, General. I'll get on it."

vii,49

On February 6th those in northern France and Belgium will cause such a setback that the Arab will die on a red bridge.

Walter stayed there all night and had a plan when the generals returned in the morning. "Sir, I think we should take about three hundred mini-tanks and make an all out run for the these two bridges, one hundred and fifty tanks for each. We should disengage from all local battles and move tanks to toward those two bridges as quickly as possible. In the meantime we use our remote ground support aircraft to hit any forces that try to get in our way on those two routes. At the same time we concentrate our manned fighter aircraft to protect our rapid advance. We need the order immediately to have a chance."

"Okay, Walter. We don't have any better plan and I think you are right, as usual. We'll go for it."

Walter told Bridget about his plan when he returned home. "The order has already been given and our forces are racing toward those two points with all speed. Everything we have is committed. I hope I guessed right."

"I'm sure you did. I'll bet you never would have believed that one day the entire military might of the United States would be following your orders."

II,29

The Oriental will leave his seat of power and pass through the Apennine mountains on his way to France. He will fly over the seas and mountain snows. Everyone will be struck with his rod.

V,97

The one born deformed, the Chinese leader with one hand shorter than the other, will be suffocated in horror in the city once inhabited by kings (Carcassone). Severest command against the treatment of the captives will be revoked. The hail and thunder that came down at Condom caused inestimable damage.

II,57

Before the conflict when the great wall (of China?) will fall, a great leader will die, a death too sudden. It will be lamentable. He who will be born imperfect, when many will die in the water near a river where the land is stained with blood. (the Garonne river)

IX,73

A leader with a blue helmet will enter Foix (southwest France) and will prevail less than four years and an Arab Turk leader in a white helmet will die of a heart attack.

V,98

From the forty-eight degree, on June 21, will come an atomic attack, boiling the fish in the rivers and lakes. Bearn and Bigorre in southwest France will be from fire in the sky. apparently, his nuclear bomb caused a chain reaction in the atmosphere because lightening and hail spread through the air for hundreds of square miles.

VIII,2

At Condom and Auch and around Marmande fire from the sky envelopes them. At Mirande, tremendous lightning and hail caused the walls to crumble into the Garonne river.

I,46

Very near Auch, Lectoure and Mirande, a great fire will descend from the sky for three days and nights. It was a stupendous and marvelous event that caused around the world.

V,100

The one who created the conflagration was trapped in the fire that fell from the sky as far as Carcassone and Scotland

I,26

The great commander of lightning weapons will die in the daytime. Bad news will be brought to him by a negotiator. A second prediction, another commander will die at night.

MONTH 56, FEBRUARY 21

The red phone rang by Walter's bed, "Hello, you're kidding. How bad is it. Never mind, I don't trust this phone. I'll be right there."

"WHAT HAPPENED, WALTER?"

"A Chinese nuclear missile set off some form of special HEMP bomb and all radio transmissions are out. Our Star Wars weapons have shut down most possible damage from Inter Continental Ballistic Missiles, but this was launched from a truck in Europe and only went up and exploded. There was no trajectory to plot."

"HOW BAD IS IT?"

"It could be very bad. This housing was swept for bugs, but I can't talk about it here. Let me get into the office and find out what's going on. Don't wait up."

After Walter got to the command post he asked one of the generals about the status.

"Well, our remote tanks and aircraft are out of touch. The tanks are programmed to continue to the bridges and fire at anything moving ahead of them, but the remote aircraft are programmed to return and land. We can only presume our manned air cover is still providing air cover. We have no radio contact, even here in England on this air base. We dropped a film canister from a satellite and caught it with a C-130. What do you make of these pictures?"

Walter studied the pictures for awhile. "This looks like a spider web of lightning stretching over most of this half of the globe, but concentrated over the eastern half of what we used to call Free Europe. Look, you can see where the warhead exploded and the spider webs spread out from there. The HEMP is so bad you would think that it was designed for producing HEMP. You said Star Wars. I didn't think we ever had it."

"It wasn't public knowledge, but some was deployed under Reagan, more pieces under Bush, and a few pieces under Clinton. Once up there, we just let it sit. When we started recovering from the war in the United States, we accelerated production of a lot of the equipment developed under Star Wars, but never deployed. We have particle and laser beam weapons. Something called Brilliant Pebbles, and low altitude hyper speed ground to air missiles for point defense. None of them worked because we didn't have much over Europe, naturally. In addition, the beam weapons were designed to hit the missiles in space before they come down. This warhead was not designed to come down. Brilliant Pebbles would have worked, but we didn't expect a launch from within Europe and had no weapons in range. The hyper speed missiles only work on descending warheads that got through the other defenses. We weren't trying to defend Western Europe from Western Europe. We have the United States well defended now, but not Europe."

"NICE TO KNOW. YOU WANT TO KNOW WHAT'S FUNNY THOUGH?"

"What is funny about this? We're out of touch with our equipment just as we were trying your desperate run for the river bridges."

"I have seen the Arab equipment first hand when I was with the French resistance. They don't have very good maintenance. Oh they work, but I suspect that any HEMP protection they may have had, they don't have anymore. I am talking from radios to laser gunsights. We learned our lesson, even commercial radios are now protected if made in the states. In a day or two we'll be back in operation. I suspect the Arabs did more damage to themselves than to us."

"General, come here. They did it again." shouted a major from across the room.

The General and Walter went over to look at an instrument. Walter said, "I thought the electronic systems weren't working."

"General, can I tell him?"

"By all means."

"Sergeant, this is a special instrument that is remotely connected to an antenna outside the building. It's isolated from damage by diodes like most of our equipment these days, but it measures HEMP activity. Here you can see this very high spike before the signal was cut off and then you can see here on the tape how the electronic activity is still extremely high. Now look in the book here. A level this high is normal background electrical radiation in the country. This one is near a television station. This is near an airport radar. Now this one is a severe thunderstorm. This one is was recorded one mile from a normal nuclear weapon in the atmosphere. Now compare these with this tape and you can see this is multiples of any of these examples. This was a special nuclear weapon designed to produce HEMP, and fired at just the right altitude at the very top of the stratosphere for maximum effect. The nuclear even basically knocks loose electrons from the molecules in the air that are driven near the speed of light into other molecules that knock loose more electrons until the electron wave is attenuated by the earth. When this wave of electrons hits any length of conductor, such as power lines or long antennae, it causes a build up of electricity like a bolt of lightning, burning out all electronics along the wire or connected to the antenna. Prior to the HEMP attack on the United States we thought that portable radios were immune. What we discovered is that if they are not air tight the miles of wire on computer chips works just like a long power line. All American made electronics is now made completely airtight. Any antennae or earphones are isolated by specially manufactured Zenier diodes that immediately block any appreciable voltage."

"Whoa! I get the point. I believe that there was another HEMP bomb."

The general just laughed, but then sobered and asked, "Major, what did this one do to our electronics...just your personal opinion."

"Sir. I know that our electronics were all designed to protect against HEMP. The older stuff was protected against fifty thousand volts. The stuff made after the U.S. attack was made for protection against one hundred thousand volts. Sir, I estimate anything within five hundred miles may have been zapped by the equivalent of three hundred thousand volts. Just a minute, sir. Many things were tested to nearly a million volts. Oh, the civilian stuff would be gone, but a lot of the military equipment should have been protected. We'll have to wait a few days and see what happens."

"Thank you, Major. Walter, you might as well go home and think about alternative plans for our losing a high percentage of different kinds of equipment."

MONTH 56, SEPTEMBER 24

Walter was back in the command post listening to the results of the massive HEMP bombs that had gone off. The air was now clear of HEMP again and communications had been re-established with most of the American forces.

"The Advanced Tactical Fighter, being a very new fly by wire aircraft is unharmed. We lost all thirty percent or eight hundred F-16 aircraft that were never designed for HEMP. The testing that was done, was after the initial development of the F-16. It survived the relatively mild HEMP in the U.S. four and half years ago, but this overwhelmed it. Even those on the ground are temporarily grounded. The F-15 also survived the HEMP. Many of the M1A1 tanks survived as did all of the newer tanks. Most ground vehicles survived except for the truly civilian models. Seventy percent of all radios are operational. The remotely piloted vehicles all survived, both air and ground. The remote mini-tanks that were going to the river bridges continued on their way and stopped just this side of the rivers. Now that we have regained control of them, they have been sent across and have established major bridgeheads at both of the two target bridges.

In reviewing the recordings made by the remote tanks, they apparently went past hundreds of Arab tanks that just sat there and let them pass. The mini-tanks were only programmed to fire on moving tanks so they did not destroy the Arab tanks as they went past. The recordings also show many Arab troops just running away from the mini-tanks. Apparently they didn't care much for the mini-guns on the mini-tanks. For what ever reason, we now have totally secured both of the two bridgeheads with minimal casualties. Preliminary intelligence declares the mission one hundred and ten percent successful.

The manned tanks and infantry are now rounding up the Arabs on this side of the river. Apparently sixty percent of their motorized transportation quit and the remainder just ran for the bridges. If that percentage holds over central Europe, the Arabs just lost about thirty thousand tanks and two hundred thousand other vehicles. We may have won the war very easily as a result of their own HEMP attack on us. Our assumption is that they thought they would disable our very effective remotely piloted aircraft and tanks."

IX,85

They will march from Guienne to Languedoc in southwest France toward the Rhone and will hold Agen, Marmande, and La Reole in southwest France. In the hope of finding a way to Marseilles, the major base of the enemy, there will be a battle near Saint-Paul-de-Mausole in southeast France.

III,99

In the grassy fields of Alleins and Vernegues, in the Luberon range and near the river Durance in southeast France, the conflict will be sharp for both sides, but in the end the Mesopotamians (Arabs) will be defeated in France.

IX,63

Anger, tears, cries and howls near Narbonne, Bayonne on the Mediterranean coast and Foix. Oh what horrible calamities and changes. War will affect them several times.

III,4

When fighting will come close to here the lunar ones (Arabs) will fail. from one to another at no great distance, suffering from cold, dryness, and the danger of the enemy pushing at their frontiers. Where this prophecy had its beginnings (Salon-en-Province, southeast France.

MONTH 60, JUNE 4

Jim Claris had found an ally in a Walter Gaddis in Europe. Walter had been an NCO with an exceptional insight into how to fight this war. Most of what he came up with, Jim had also come up with. The two of them had managed to retake all of northern Europe and Paris and had recently convinced the Generals to take southern Europe back again. Walter was there in the midst of the action, whereas Jim was back in the states. Jim's ideas of mass produced remotely piloted/drive airplanes/tanks had worked wonderfully. It kept the crews safe from risk, while being very difficult to destroy. While they didn't have the sheer killing power of the full size items they delivered their ordnance very accurately with very few losses and dramatically less cost in manufacture, shipping, and support in operation.

The battles went fantastically successful and sent the Arabs running, but they ran so fast, they left behind so many people and so much equipment that the American generals stopped the American advance to regroup and collect the Arab stragglers. They were afraid the rout was really a trap.

MONTH 62, AUGUST 11

Walter had been very upset in that the United States had chosen to round up Arabs trapped on this side of the river instead of prosecuting their bridgeheads. The bridgeheads had been expanded to fifty miles in circumference and were safe with plenty of air cover and out of range of the Arab artillery. The Arabs had repaired a lot of their equipment and had fortified the passes through the Alps and along the French Riviera. An advance through the Po River valley from France or through the Alps would be very costly in men and equipment.

The generals had said, "We need to get more equipment from the United States before we spread out our forces and pursue the Arabs. We have to bring in supplies to what is left of France and rebuild some of Germany before we advance again. Besides, we are taking so many prisoners that their number is a big burden to our supplies. Do you realize what their submarines have done to our convoys?"

Walter had said, "The Arabs are disorganized, most of their equipment is broken, we can walk through them all the way to Yugoslavia and conquer seventy percent of their forces in the process. We might even win an early surrender."

Throughout the winter, the Americans moved supplies and some equipment, while the Arabs moved repair parts manufactured in Japan all the way through the Indian Ocean to Europe. All of the European cars were now in the same condition as the American vehicles had been five years ago. The difference was that there were so few older cars due to the salt on the roads, that they were even worse off than the United States had been. England was the exception because so many people from Great Britain enjoyed their older cars. The old Rolls Royces, Jaguars, MGs, Triumphs, and Austin Minis were in their glory again with the newer cars all disabled.

Walter and Bridget had plenty of time to visit all over Great Britain. They had been through every castle and palace open to the public along with many quaint little villages and busy cities. It was not easy traveling with two little ones, but he had plenty of free time. The area of Europe controlled by the Americans was very secure and until the offensive was ready to start there was nothing for Walter to do.

He spent his evenings worrying about the Arab buildup and where a flanking movement could be initiated. He scoured the maps of the Mediterranean, the Indian Ocean, the Red Sea, and the Persian Gulf looking for a landing zone. It would have been nice to have a landing zone on the Persian Gulf or at least somewhere on the Arabian peninsula, but that was too far and no way they could get air support. That left somewhere in the Mediterranean, but the Arabs controlled it.

Walter knew nothing about naval warfare, but then not so long ago he had known nothing of strategic planning for tank warfare and didn't even know that the United States was working on any remotely piloted vehicles other than battlefield reconnaissance. They couldn't just attack the bulk of the Arab army against fortified naturally defensible terrain. He had an idea that couldn't wait another minute. He went to the command post. He had in enough time for a retirement and he had his education now. There was nothing to lose. When he got there he demanded a hearing with the commanding general. The general saw him because of his past good advice.

"General, we have to get moving now. We can't wait any longer. We have to flank the Arabs. We cannot attack straight into their strength in mountainous terrain."

"OKAY, WALTER, JUST HOW DO YOU THINK WE'RE GOING TO FLANK THEM?"

"Sir, I've been studying the situation for three months now. Every day makes it more costly to attack straight ahead, therefore we have to develop another method."

"Keep going."

"Sir, our Air Force has to get air superiority over the Mediterranean immediately. An all out blitz to shoot down everything they have. That might take a month or two. Then we fly in mini-tanks into Turkey, right in their midst, air dropping them from C-5s and then controlling them from Joint Stars aircraft to create as much havoc as possible. A very small force can create a lot of havoc. Their fuel will last quite some time since they won't be driving to the battle. We'll have to be conservative with the fuel. We then drive them to separate strategic targets and use their self destruct systems to do more damage. We repeat the same thing at the same time in southern Italy, near Cairo, and in Syria."

"SLOW DOWN, SERGEANT. HOW MANY MINI-TANKS ARE YOU TALKING ABOUT?"

"A C-5 may only carry two M1 tanks, but it can carry mini-tanks three abreast. Say twenty tanks per C-5. With six C-5s we could hit six different targets and scare the devil out of the Arabs. That should convince them that their defensive positions are being flanked everywhere and make them pull back so we don't have to fight a pitched battle anywhere. In the meantime our aircraft should be able to take out any of their surface ships. The Air Force should be able to find and hunt down any submarines in the Mediterranean. By regaining control of the Mediterranean, we will be cutting off their supply lines by sea. As soon as possible, we land a major force in Lebanon and drive from there toward Iran, cutting their supply lines by land."

"WHAT ABOUT THOSE MONSTER LANDERS THAT THEY HAVE A SEA FULL OF?"

"If one of them comes up, we use one of the bunker busters we invented during the Kuwaiti, Iraq War. We also use them on every single Arab bunker we find as soon as we find them. We have twenty thousand mini-tanks in Europe and we need to commit most of them when we make the big invasion. That way, if the Arabs try to use poison gas or biologics, they won't do us any harm. The Arabs will expect us to land in Italy or Turkey. They will never expect a major attack right into their homelands.

We use stealth fighters and bombers to destroy as much in advance of the tanks as we can, using the Advanced Tactical Fighter and F-15s for air superiority. We can use rocket motors to launch the remote aircraft."

"Walter, are you proposing that we just bypass thirty thousand Arab tanks in Europe, leaving them at our back?"

"Yes sir. Why fight them outright when we can just cut them off? It won WEEK 6, DAY 35, September 21't take long before they run out of fuel and ammunition without any new supplies coming in. Then it will be just like those that we cut off on this side of the rivers."

"I think I said this over a year ago. Let me think about it. Now go on home. We'll call you when we need you."

Walter didn't hear from the generals for months, but the intelligence reports were clear enough. The Advanced Tactical Fighters and the F-15s were dog fighting over the Mediterranean. The F-117 stealth fighter was playing over the gulf at night, when it could not be seen, sinking anything afloat on the Mediterranean. A number of old B-52s had been resurrected out of the bone yard at Davis Monathon Air Force Base in Arizona, and were flying again with Harpoon III missiles, launching them from a distance into the Mediterranean sinking ships. They were also ranging over the Atlantic hunting Arab and Chinese submarines.

One thing that frustrated Walter was that the Pacific war was a total mystery to the European theater. It had been five years since the war started and he had no idea what was going on in the other half of the world. He knew that the Chinese had attacked Russia and India. He knew the Japanese were providing the industrial might and the engineering for China, but had no idea whether the Chinese were winning or losing. It wasn't over because there were Chinese known to be advising the Arabs in Europe, showing, if anything, an increase in Chinese involvement with the Arabs, and potentially, that the Chinese had won the eastern war and could now be moving new troops and equipment to Europe.

MONTH 63, SEPTEMBER 1

Walter was called in for a special briefing by himself. Some guy called Jim Claris was on the big screen television broadcasting from the United States by tight beam satellite.

"Walter, nice to meet you, all be it, by long distance. Apparently we are like thinkers. Unknowingly, you have helped me sell my ideas. You probably haven't heard of me, but I am currently the senior ranking civilian in the National Military Command Center and one of the key members of the strategic planning staff. Your plans have matched mine exactly, but your proximity to the situation has helped me sell my ideas. I decided it was time to bring you in on the big picture. By the way, you might be interested to know that you are now bird colonel Walter Gaddis and in charge of European planning."

Walter just sat there for a few moments trying to decide whether he heard this last sentence correctly and then asked, "Excuse me?"

Jim Claris cut him off, "That's right Colonel. A Chief Master Sergeant has a lot of pull, but not enough actual responsibility. You have done a masterful job of planning, but you haven't had the burden of responsibility. We all figured that you should receive your battlefield commission, but a second lieutenant would have been too big a step down. Even a major has a harder time communicating with the generals than a chief master sergeant, soooooo, presto chango, you're a full bird colonel! You have finished your college, so why not. Now, just sit back and listen."

"This first picture is the current political picture of the world. The blue area is controlled by what we think of as the allies, which you know are mainly American forces. The green are uncommitted areas that we think of as friendly even though they contribute little or nothing to our war effort. The red is Russian controlled. The yellow is controlled by the Chinese and Japanese which are in this war as allies. The Japanese have committed no military forces, but are key in engineering and much of the manufacturing of the Red Chinese forces. The lavender areas, not my choice of colors, is for the areas still under the control of the indigenous people still trying to defend that area from the aggressors. The orange areas are controlled by the Moslem countries. The black spots are areas made impassable by nuclear, chemical, or biological warfare. Bown is uninhabitable.

The next slide shows the impact of the war.

Cities	People Killed	Products
New York City	8,000,000	Stock market,banking, Grumman (F-14 Navy)
Boston	1,000,000	Military electronics, banking, insurance
Philadelphia	1,000,000	Military supplies
Washington DC	1,000,000	Government seat
Norfolk	500,000	Navel depot, ACC
Miami	700,000	
Cleveland	700,000	
Cincinatti	500,000	GE jet engines
Memphis	400,000	Mississippi Bridge
Atlanta	500,000	Disease control
Mobile	200,000	Naval Yard
Houston	1,000,000	Oil and NASA
Dallas	1,500,000	Oil management

Chicago	4,000,000	Stock Exchange
Denver	600,000	
Salt Lake City	400,000	Military Repair Center
Los Angeles	5,900,000	Military manufacturing
San Diego	1,000,000	Navy Yards
Seattle	500,000	Navy Yard
DIED in Nuclear	29,400,000	
DIED riots & disease	58,800,000	
Total Dead	88,200,000	
Remaining Alive	171,800,000	
Males Alive	68,720,000	
Sterile Males	54,976,000	
Females Alive	103,080,000	
Males not sterile	13,744,000	
Healthy Males	4,123,200	Ratio of healthy male to female=6
Healthy Females	24,739,200	

Fifty percent of the American males are sterile from the nuclear bombs that went off in the large cities and twenty percent of the women. More men than women died in riots killing off each other over some food morsel or some other thing of perceived value before the riots were quelled. The United States lost ninety percent of the minority races because they were concentrated in the inner cities and therefore were closer to the nuclear blasts, in the center of the worst riots, and suffered the most disease when the water and sewer systems quit working. Large numbers starved because they never got out to the farming areas where there was still food. A very high percentage of those that died of illness and starvation were children. Most of the older and more wealthy lived in the suburbs and survived. The wealthy in the U.S. were averaging only one point two children per family.

Most of those that did get out of the inner cities were considered looters because that's what they did and fought several pitched battles with most of the men being killed off. There is now a ratio of six fertile women to each fertile man. We are encouraging each non-sterile male to have two to three wives until our population can be built back up. It's considered to be the patriotic thing to have three wives and actually subsidized by the government through taxes. The fertile man with two fertile wives with one child from each woman pays no tax until income reaches fifty thousand dollars and sixty thousand with two children from each wife or with one child from three wives. With each child above that the family receives ten thousand dollars from the government for each normal child. If a man were to have six wives with three children from each, they would receive one hundred and eighty thousand dollars per year. Pretty drastic, but the U.S. lost most of a generation of children and with the high adult loss, we simply have to have more people. We are currently drafting only sterile men, but very few of the one million four hundred thousand men in uniform at the start of the war died or were sterile. At the current time there are only two million non-sterile men in the U.S. between eighteen and fifty and over twenty million fertile women between seventeen and forty for a ten to one ratio. See the problem?

There are many other factors not so visible. Many of the nuclear bombs went off in the bigger cities that had more doctors so the ratio of doctors is down dramatically. Add to that the doctors that are busy treating the wounded from the cities and the near wars with looters and the disease from the cities and the quality of medical care is only now coming up to what we had in the fifties. We are starting programs of artificial insemination to speed up the birth rate, but the multiple wives program easily exceeds the benefits to be gained from taking doctors away from treating the people that need it. The Mormons think it is great. Most men think it is great. The women are very understanding about it, at least the ones with men. With ten eligible women for each eligible man, there is a lot of competition. Many are living with non-eligible men, but they can't have children unless they can get a fertile man at the right time. Of the healthy people, naturally the fertile ones have priority with the doctors. It's all topsy turvy, but look what's happened to most of Europe.

The only consumer goods being produced in the United States are radios and a few televisions to be able to communicate in the United States. There are a number of new factories for military equipment to replace those lost in the first few days of the war. There is a very big consumer goods market in old and rebuilt parts for older vehicles. Many of the newer vehicles based on older designs have been modified to remove their fuel injections and electronic ignitions in favor of the old points distributors and carburetors.

As you could see from the map at the first, the Chinese have moved all the way to Russia. They would have moved further, but their supply line is very long and thin and the Russians fight very well when defending their own country. The Russians destroyed everything as they retreated making it very difficult for the Chinese. We're talking every building, road, railroad, and runway in Siberia. The Russian Air Force has no long range bombers left and only a few fighter aircraft, but the Chinese never had long range fighters and they are too far from the front to be of any threat. They have used up all their bombers and most of their missiles. With our Star Wars in place over most of Europe and more over China, missiles are not much good now anyway.

Now the Mediterranean. We have air superiority, but all the surrounding countries are controlled by the Moslems. We have jammed up the Suez canal and sunk everything in the Mediterranean. There are most certainly numerous submarines sitting on the bottom just waiting to see why we are clearing the sea. The Arabs have set up hundreds of pieces of artillery around the Straits of Gibraltar expecting our navy to come sailing in. You are getting this briefing today because we are implementing a modified version of your plan. I want you on a Joint Stars aircraft monitoring the main battle.

This communication channel is totally secure. I am using a tight laser to communicate with a satellite and the signal is going from satellite to satellite by laser and down to you by laser. A two inch error would lose the signal and anything trying to get in between points would totally disrupt it. The first set of mini-tanks will land in Turkey near Constantinopol to use the old name. Twenty four hours later another set will land near Venice to threaten their supply lines through the Po River Valley. Twelve hours later we will start a major push from the bridgeheads and another set will land outside Cairo, Egypt and in Morocco, and in Lebanon, and twenty C-5s full in northern Saudi Arabia. Five hours later forty C-5s, forty C-117s, and fifty C-140s will land in Saudi Arabia. This is it. We're hoping this will all be over in the next few weeks. Any questions?"

"How are you flying in all those forces right into Saudi Arabia?"

"Because Saudi Arabia is cooperating with us."

"Are you sure it's not a trap?"

"Yes. I know the prince. He is here with us and will be flying in on the second group to rally his people to support us. He was forced into cooperation and his own religious police took over the Saud family and held them hostage to get his cooperation. He found out that most of his family were assassinated and decided it was time to get out."

MONTH 65, NOVEMBER 1

Our attacks will come here and here and here, and the main force will land here. Because we cannot land our supply ships in the Persian Gulf, our landing will be here. We also have added more mini-tanks and aircraft because we don't have to feed their crews and they use only a fraction of the fuel of manned vehicles and will therefore be easier to supply. We have received a shipment of a new weapons.

This is a variation on the mini-tank except that it carries a new shell that is only ten millimeter. Yes, it is the same as in the current military pistol except that each round is a ten inch long spike and will travel at five thousand miles per hour. If it hits a standard Soviet T-72 tank, it would pass all the way through as if it were made of cardboard. Reactive armor will do no good, because this shell will pass through, before the armor layer can explode. Rather than exploding when it hits, it will sense when it has passed through sufficient armor and then explode inside the tank.

It has a new lightweight armor that is impervious to all known ammunition except our new ten millimeter shell. It's weight is the same as steel for a given thickness, but the armor on the new tank weighs less than one tenth of conventional armor because it is dramatically thinner. It is as big an advance in armor as any in history. It compares to steel armor as Kelvar would be to a cotton bullet proof vest. Even the tank treads are made of this new armor. It has been tested by firing one hundred twenty millimeter tank shells right into the tread with no damage. It cannot be painted, so forget using it for automobile bodies. It only comes in one color, sort of a greenish pink swirl. Because of its light weight the mini-tank is faster and makes considerably better gas mileage with a smaller engine.

In addition, all of the mini-tanks will be outfitted with extended range fuel tanks made of the same new material. The fuel tank wells are only one tenth of an inch thick, but it would take a direct hit from a seventy-five millimeter shell to penetrate it. If that happens, the tank is ejectable. In other words the tank can be jettisoned away from the mini-tank.

According to the written material, it is a blend of steel and plastic and, in honor of science fiction writers it is called Plasteel. Its melting point is classified, but much higher than conventional steel. It can only be manufactured upon radioactive bombardment, but is totally non-radioactive and any thin layer will provide one hundred percent protection from even cosmic rays. The process uses free electrons and protons to bond the plastic and steel into an entirely new substance. Once it has cooled and set in a shape it takes on this tremendous strength and protection from radioactivity. They have not yet found a way to weld Plasteel. The welds become weak links. It can be bolted together with Plasteel bolts, but then there is the need to seal the tank from HEMP and the sealing material is far weaker. The basic tank shell is cast in one piece. The only weak points are the maintenance access door seals and the engine vents. These are also made of Plasteel that is just as strong as the shell, the engine vents are scoops to prevent intrusion. They are covered with Plasteel screens to prevent grenades and such from entering, but have to be considered a weakness.

Because the new tank was based on the old minitank, it is the same size, but with the larger interior room and smaller gun with smaller ammunition it carries many more rounds and has a thousand mile unrefueled range. Actually, they could have built humvees that could protect the crew from anything the Arabs have got except a direct hit by the fireball of a nuclear bomb. The process uses a casting to shape the metal and only the tank has been tried so far, except for the long range external fuel tanks for the mini-tanks.

The B-2 stealth bomber was put back in production and we now have fifty of them. They will be used to bomb Teheran, Iran to empty out the town to give our Navy SEALS a better chance at breaching the security of the main command bunker. We have manufactured a number of bunker buster bombs to use on standard command bunkers, but we don't wish to use them on the main command bunker because Prince Saud claims that many of the Arab leaders are there by force not by choice. By keeping them alive they should be able to call off many of their forces allowing us to avoid hunting down every last Arab tank in pitched battles. The Arabs will fight until the end unless ordered back by their own leaders.

We have one thousand remotely guided aircraft that have been modified with the new tank killing gun. The gatling gun was the primary cause of wind resistance. The smaller gun makes the airplane considerably more slippery giving it more range and speed while making it even harder to see. The smaller ammunition also means more room for ammunition and fuel. The number of rounds of ammunition has doubled while doubling the range of the aircraft at a fifty percent increase in speed. The radar image is one tenth what it was making it extremely stealthy.

While these are great advances, we don't have the advances of World War II. The industry in the United States was weak due to the huge number of imports and with the war, our industry was really in bad shape. We didn't have to build up an industry from scratch during World War II, we already had it. Skilled people has also been a problem because of the deaths we had and the fact that so much industry had moved overseas. It did not help that Mexico nationalized all of the American factories. Technically they were not nationalized, but are controlled by the Mexican government who will not allow the manufacture of military hardware.

Because of the warmer climate and the historical lack of modern amenities Mexico was not as impacted by the HEMP as the United States. It also helped that the HEMP was directed mainly at the United States and Canada. Mexico City only lost their power and telephones for a couple of days versus in the United States everything electronic was destroyed. Mexico is a major source of consumer goods for the United States now with seventy percent manufactured there. This has been very beneficial to the United States. Remember that Japan and Europe are not exporting anything to the United States now.

As a result of the war there is no longer a welfare system and we have more jobs than people available. The flooding killed very few because of the warning that we had, but thirty percent of the population was displaced. Add to the number that lost their homes in the major cities and we have had a major problem. To solve that problem a lot of plywood prefab houses were built as in World War II. Assuming we can win this war without more major loss, there should be a financial boom similar to after World War II. By this report you can see there is optimism there. We had better pull through as expected.

Another major accomplishment has been to put Star Wars in place. Nearly fifty percent of the items researched in the 1980s actually worked. The laser beams and particle beams work so much better in space than the scientists thought they would. The key was the advance in nuclear reactor technology that allowed repeated firing of the beams with only milliseconds of recharge time between firings. By having three beams on each satellite, at least one laser is always firing. Range in space is unlimited. The only difficult shot is hitting lasers some distance away that stay low in the atmosphere. The particle beam is much better in this instance but we haven't managed the rapid firing of the laser beam weapons. The particle beam will cut through considerable atmosphere, but not enough to do damage to ground targets. However, any aircraft over twenty thousand feet can be hit and destroyed. The other major weapon is Brilliant Pebbles which basically consists of firing guided spikes into the path of a missile. The drawback is that the satellite can quickly run out of watermelon sized spikes whereas the beam weapons could literally fire continuously for a year until their reactor cores are used up. Brilliant Pebbles can fire for only about five minutes total which each firing being the equivalent of a laser flash. The advantage is that they don't miss. Again, they are no threat to ground targets because they burn up before they hit the ground. All three are perfectly capable of defending themselves. Computer speeds gained through parallel processing on all three would make the old Cray computers of 1990 look like toys. In fact, that desktop computer over there is faster than a 1990 Cray.

It was fairly common knowledge before the war started that we had the ultimate in spy planes. It can fly in the very edges of space faster than any ground to air missile. It has stealth technology making it very difficult to find. The SR71 was considered the fastest and best spy plane in the world when it was retired and it was retired because it was out-moded. The National Aero Space Plane (NASP) that was designed in the late 1980s and early 1990s was based on the existing technology of its time. It has been improved to where it now launches most of the satellites at a very low cost. Whereas the shuttle was fired into space by rockets and came down as a poor glider, the NASP is an airplane that takes off from a runway, flies to the edge of space a some speed above mach five (actual speed is classified), releases a small rocket with satellite that is basically the third stage of the old Titan Missile launched satellites.

The Russian war with the Chinese is getting very desperate. The only thing slowing down the Chinese is the supply line and the lack of total air superiority. We have four wings of Advanced Tactical Fighters in Russia now assuring that the Chinese will continue being second best in the air over Russia.

The B-2 stealth bomber has proven efficient in cutting Chinese supply lines and reducing the Chinese and Japanese supplies reaching the Arabs. They can't shoot down what they can't find, but smart bombs are finding the surface ships and rail lines. The air over China and Japan are considered too well defended for even the B-2 at this time.

India has been reduced to guerrilla warfare with millions hiding in the jungles. The Indian military has ceased to exist, but the guerrillas operating in South East Asia and India have prevented the Chinese from providing any significant men behind the Arabs who, we understand, don't want Chinese in their territory anyway.

23 ASIA

MONTH 68
FEBRUARY

VIII,10

A great leader from near Le Mans (south France), a doughty and valiant chief of a great army will come by land and sea with British and northern French forces. He will pass Gibraltar, take Barcelona and attack the isles.

III,88

From Barcelona will come a very great army by sea. All of Marseilles will tremble with fear when the isles are seized and help is shut off by sea. A traitor will swim on land (drown in his own blood).

III,79

The final order for destruction of the defenses will be passed down and its consequences the defenses of Marseilles will be broken. The city taken and the enemy captured at the same time.

X,87

A great military commander will capture the port of Nice. There will be a severe blow to the Arab empire. In Antibes the commander will place a monument of victory. Eventually plunder by sea will vanish.

I,28

The Tower of Bouc on the southern French coast will fear the Arab fleet, but much later will come the Hesperian (American) fleet. cattle, people and goods will be destroyed. Muslims and Christians, what a deadly quarrel!

I,71

The tower on the coast will three times be taken and retaken by Arabs from Spain and Italy, they will counter-attack against Marseilles, and Aix-en-Provence. devastation by fire, metal weapons, Avignon pillage from Turin in northwest Italy.

V,59

An English chief will tarry too long at Nimes in northern France and another chief named Redbeard will come to the rescue by marching toward

Spain. Many will die from a war started that day when a streaming star will fall on Artois in northern France.

VI,99

The knowledgeable enemy will be lost and confused. His great army will be sick and defeated by constant ambushes. He will lose control of the Pyrenees and Apennine mountains, finding only funerary urns near a river.

X,95

A great and powerful leader will attack the Spanish lands by land and sea he will conquest toward the south. This evil will lower again the power of the net (Arabs), and will clip the wings of those who worship on Friday (Muslims).

II,16

Naples, Palermo, Sicily, and Syracuse dominated by Arabs who will conquer them with fires and lightning from the sky. Then will come forces from London and Hesperium by way of northern Italy. There will be great slaughter then triumph will lead to festivities.

VIII,9

The eagle (USA) and the cock (French) at Savona in northwest Italy will be united, they will launch an attack by sea against the middle east and Hungary. Army will reach Naples on Italys west coast and Ancona on the east coast, and Sicily. Because of the Arabs there will be a great outcry from Rome and Nice.

VII,72

Oh what an enormous defeat on the fields of Perugia in central Italy, and another battle near Ravenna in northern Italy. Passage will be given to the religious to celebrate a feast. Once conqueror, now vanquished, they will eat horseflesh.

IV,34

A great leader of the foreign nation will now be a prisoner chained in gold and brought to general Henry. He who in Ausonia conquer in southern Italy and at Milan lose the battle, and all his forces burned with fiery weapons.

V,74

Of French blood will be born one of German background. He will rise to great military power. He will be instrumental in driving out the foreign and Arab legions, and he will return the church to Rome, to its former power.

VI,28

The great Frenchman will enter Rome leading a throng of exiles and banished citizens. The great pontiff will order the death of all who were united with the Arabs at the Alps against the French.

IX,42

Allies at the ports of Barcelona, Genoa, and Venice and disease stricken Monaco and Sicily, together they will coordinate action against the Arab fleet and the Arabs will be driven back into Tunisia

IX,30

At the port of Pola and San Nicole in Yugoslavia, and in the coast of Guarnero on the Adriatic the French will die. The captives in Turkey will cry in air, but help will come from Cadiz in Spain from a leader named Philip, Queen Elizabeth's husband from England.

V,27

Through fiery arms they will invade the Black Sea area. They will come from Iran to occupy Trebson in eastern Turkey, others will take Pharos Island (north of Egypt) and Mytilene Island of Lesbos off Turkey. When the sun shines brightly the Adriatic Sea will be covered Arab blood.

V,16

Weapons of death turn human flesh to ashes when the island of Pharos is attacked by the crusaders. The Isle of Rhodes in the Aegean will be restored.

III,47

The older leader will be chased out of his realm. He will flee to the east for help for fear of the crosses, he will fold his banner and will go to Mytilene Island to the port and then by land.

II,79

The Arab with the black and frizzled hair, by his skill, will with boasting and cruelty imprison many peoples, but the great Henry will travel far to free and save them, and all those captured by the banner of the moon (Arabs).

v,70

From the regions subject to the balance (Italy), forces in the mountains will cause great war. Captives of both sexes in Turkey will suddenly be overjoyed. the news of the fear will spread from nation to nation.

For seven years Philip will be fortunate. He will be one of those who will check the advances of the Arabs. But at the high point of his career, a French renegade, Ogmios will revolt, destroy Philip's base and take over his command.

VIII,83

The great leader of the fleet will leave the port of Zara in Yugoslavia. Near Turkey he will carry out his orders. Loss of life through battle on both sides not take place. Instead a storm will inflict damage on both sides.

VIII,91

Entering the fields of battle near Rhodes in the Aegean, the crusading allies will almost be united. Mars and Venus in Pisces, a great number will die in a depth of water.

V,80

The French general Ogmios will attack Turkey, the Arab defenders will be driven out. Of the two religions, the Mohammedanism will give way. Arabs and French never-ending battle.

VI,85

The great city of Tarsus in southern Turkey will be destroyed by the French and all the Arabs captured. Aid will come by sea from the great leader of Ugal, from urban's day of consecration to the first day of summer.

I,74

After being slowed down, they will reach Epirus (Greece). A great effort will be made against Antioch (south Turkey). The enemy leader with the black frizzled hair will strive with great energy to save his empire, but the commander named Redbeard will burn him with fire.

IX,62

Against the great leader of Usak (central Turkey) will come the crusaders with new reinforcements. The enemy leaders Oppi and Mandragora will hold for a long time, but on the third of October, the Benderik River will be crossed.

IX,43

Just as the crusading army is making a landing it will be crushed by Arab forces. It will be struck from every direction; the flagship Impetuosity attacked by 100 fast ships.

VII,7

There will be a battle involving large but light horses, the outcome will bring defeat to the great crescent (the Arabs). But by night they will return dressed as shepherds in the mountains to kill leaving pools of blood.

XII,36

A ferocious attack will be made in Cyprus. The Turkish and African fleets will suffer great loss, both will drive themselves upon the rock.

III,97

A new force will occupy the new world. The allies will march against Syria, Judea, and Palestine; and the great Arab army will crumble. All this will happen in a months time.

VIII,90

When one of the crusaders will be found with his mind disturbed. In the place of the holy one (Jerusalem, one will see a homed ox (Arabs). The place of birth in (Bethlehem) filled with swine. Order will not be maintained by the commander.

III,61

A large army of crusaders will take up positions against Mesopotamia (Iraq). A light company will defend a river and the enemy will hold his positions.

II,60

The cold-hearted powers will be destroyed in the orient. The empire that included the Ganges (India), Jordan, the Rhone and Loire (France) and Tagus (Spain) will be lost. The hunger of the conqueror glutted, then the fleet will disperse him, blood and bodies will swim in the sea.

IV,51

A military leader will eagerly follow the retreating enemy. He will penetrate their defenses and slow their army. They will be running on foot and be sued very closely. Finally they will stop and fight near the Ganges river.

C,59-last battle

III,31

On two open plains of Media in eastern Iran, Arabia and Armenia (in southwest Russia), the two sides will take up positions in all three areas. A great number assemble on the banks of the Araxes river in southwest Russia. There the great suleiman (Arab leader) will fall to earth in defeat.

I,52

The two wicked ones (Mars and Saturn) in Scorpio, the sultan of the middle east will die in the corridors of his command post. The church troubled by its new position; Europe still occupied from the north (US & USSR).

I,70

There will be rain and famine, fighting still going on in Iran. The enemy leader will be betrayed by those of his own Islam faith. The war will end there that begun in France. A secret sign made not to be harsh. Own Islam faith.

MONTH 68, FEBRUARY 12

Colonel Walter Gaddis was on board the Joint Stars (Joint Service Tactical Airborne Radar System) Aircraft. JSTARS works for the ground commander like the AWACS airborne radar system works for aircraft control and detection in the air war. By watching the screens he could see the battle on the ground. The mini-tanks were tracked from the moment they landed in Greece. The Arabs were unprepared and could only mount infantry and personnel carriers against them. The mini-tanks did terrible damage until the Arabs withdrew their troops and managed to send in some main battle tanks. The mini-tanks chewed through them more slowly and arrived at their destinations near fuel and ammunition depots where they were set to destruct from the JSTARS destroying their target. They were nearly out of fuel and ammunition by that time. The twelve mini-tanks had destroyed sixty armored personnel carriers and fifteen main battle tanks as well as five fuel and ammo depots. Seven mini-tanks had to be destroyed after prematurely running out of ammunition or being disabled.

The next attack was in Turkey with similar results twenty-four hours later. Twelve hours later, there were simultaneous attacks in Libya, Egypt, Italy, and in southern Iran. The drop area in Iran was in the high desert with no one around to care. C-5s, C-141s, and newer C-17s. Another large airdrop happened in Saudi Arabia with Prince Facil Saud flying in ahead in an American F-15 with Saudi markings. The American cargo planes were welcomed and the troops joined by jubilant Saudi troops. Within hours the Saudi religious police were purged from the system and the remaining Saud family members released from their years of mainly luxurious captivity.

The landings in Iran were mainly the new mini-tanks. Within twenty-four hours Advanced Tactical Fighter aircraft were operating from a prefab air base. They quickly established air superiority over the Iranian Air Force. The new mini-tanks proved deadly to the main battle tanks of the Iranian Army. Many mini-tanks received direct hits by battle tank shells and kept rolling. Their new ammunition worked almost as well as advertised. They were one hundred percent deadly when striking any flat surface nearly direct, but if the tank was at an angle and the shell hit the front armor where it sloped the shell sometimes ricocheted. Never-the-less, they were very effective and didn't put any American tankers in jeopardy since these crews were thousands of miles away directing their tanks from satellites. The Iranians found that the mini-tanks could not go through a concrete wall like a large tank so the American M1A4 tanks had to back them up and break through these with their large artillery and occasionally be driving through the walls. As soon as a wall was breached the mini-tanks poured through the breach leaving the M1A4 manned tanks behind. Another weakness of the minitanks was that they could not make it through wide steep trenches and the manned equipment had to plow dirt across the trenches. The going was not as fast as desired.

The huge submarine landers started coming ashore into Iran to counterattack the Americans, but they were stopped within feet of their landing by the huge bunker buster bombs from American aircraft. The Arabs tried to pull back their fighter aircraft to fight the American aircraft over Iran, but without aerial refueling, the Americans were well established by the time they got within combat range and by then their bases were within easy reach of American air strikes.

Walter was on the ground now at the main base in the Iranian desert with intelligence coming from many sources. The Iranians were apparently all fanatics sacrificing anything to slow down the Americans. The Arab armies were returning from Europe to counter the attacks from Saudi Arabia and the Iranian desert. The Chinese had launched one hundred missiles at the American desert base, but the Star Wars defenses stopped them during their boost stage trying to climb out from Chinese held territories.

Walter decided on a big end around. The remote guided aircraft all concentrated on Teheran, firing everything they had, to send everyone into hiding. Cruise missiles were also used as were F-15E fighter bombers. The old lumbering B-52s revived from the bone yard of Davis Monathon Air Force Base and B-2 bombers saturated numerous areas of Teheran. This was the first time that American forces had deliberately used saturation bombing on a civilian city since World War II. They used improved compressed natural gas bombs and conventional bombs. The natural gas bombs could easily be mistaken for small nuclear bombs. A canister under tremendous natural gas pressure is exploded to disperse the gas and then ignited with devastating effect. Some were used during the first Gulf war, but these were used in the desert. In a city the effect was devastation.

Under cover of this saturation bombing, a record large Navy Seal team descended on the main command bunker. Since the bunker was locked up tight from the inside, F-15s dropped bunker buster bombs developed quickly during the first Gulf war to knock holes into the inner sanctums. These were different because they carried no explosive. The SEALS dropped in through the holes, found where the under ground labyrinth turned, and then directed another F-15, with another bomb, to knock further holes into more areas of the huge bunker complex. The American Delta force followed behind the Seals. Experts on the Seal team managed to blow locks on some blast doors that were nuclear bomb proof and managed to electronically defeat others. The Iranian Guard, the elite launched an underground counter attack but only succeeded in sustaining huge losses and letting the Seals into new areas of the labyrinth. The drawings of Prince Facil Saud were indispensable in this underground invasion. The SEALS were quickly joined by Army Rangers who blasted their way through Iranian Guards until eventually the Americans had found the apartment areas where the Arab leaders were held captive. They were also joined by British commandos renowned for their fearless, almost suicidal dedication to warfare. The British joined the fray without even being seen by the Americans. They were just suddenly there as if they had been waiting for the Americans to need assistance. A SEAL would get surrounded by Iranians and suddenly there were three British fighting by his side. A group of Rangers would be under fire and the British would take out the Iranian position from behind.

The combined commandos killed off Iranian Royal Guards at a fifty to one ratio. Actually there were only three commandos killed, but a number were put out of action. Jabal Iscarnon and Sadam Hussein held out in the inner sanctum, but the other Arab leaders were all quick to surrender, all claiming to be glad of rescue.

The inner sanctum was protected by ten foot thick blast doors. The British tried explosives on the lock, but to no avail. A backup Seal team came in with a large, but portable laser. It was wired into the main power for the underground complex to provide power. They then used it to cut a small doorway in the huge blast door. The laser looked like a solid beam but was instead a series of small flashes. Each flash cut a tiny hole completely through the door. It took an hour to open a hold big enough for one man to crawl through. Anticlimactically, the two Arab leaders had been fried by the beam before the door was cut. The Arab elite troops within surrendered to the first American that poked his head through the opening.

As the Arab leaders were taken to the surface a fleet of armored helicopters flew in and whisked them off to safety. The helicopters were supported by saturation bombing nearby keeping everything in hiding, Advanced Tactical Fighters, remote guided aircraft, and the awesome fuel air explosives. The Iranian Army probably thought they were under nuclear attack and never discovered their command post had been raided and taken.

The Arab leaders using powerful communications called off the war. The combatants left their tanks behind and rode home in the trucks and jeeps, or simply walked. The Arab invasion of Europe was over. The terms of the peace treaty allowed the Arab rulers control over their own kingdoms once again, but without heavy weapons and open to American inspection of all research facilities. Iran and Iraq were removed as separate countries. The Arab rulers in conjunction with remaining European forces and American forces established permanent bases in these countries and took away their right of self rule. Egypt and Morocco took over joint rule of all of northern Africa with American bases throughout. These countries were allowed a limited democratic self government under Egyptian, Moroccan and American oversight. The European war was over, but Red China was threatening from the north and east through Russia.

When Walter arrived back in England, he was given his stars as a Brigadier General. His new job was to plan how to carry out the European defense against the Red Chinese. Bridget was there to pin on his stars, "I knew you had potential and was surprised that you were only a technical sergeant tank driver after I got to meet you, but a general? I do love you."

"And I love you. I'm still not worthy of you, but I'm getting closer."

MONTH 71, MAY 1

The Arab troops were back in their home countries and under the rule of their original rulers who had been forced to cooperate in the war, but now under American supervision and without any heavy equipment. The Arabs stockpile of biological weapons that could have destroyed life on earth more surely than an all out nuclear war between the U.S. and the Soviets at their peak of nuclear power, had now been destroyed. Never again would the arms makers be allowed to make one area of the world so strong. The majority of the American forces were now back in central Europe. The Chinese attacks were halted for winter due to the difficulty of getting supplies through to their forces in Western Siberia and into the eastern most parts of Russia. The Russians were repairing equipment damaged in the fighting like they had for past several winters.

The American Air Force from Europe moved to bases in Western Russia. While the Russians had become peaceful in the early nineties, American forces in Russia was a far cry from the uncomfortable peace before the war. The Russian people, as they have always been, were friendly.

Officially the Russian government welcomed the American help, the younger Russian troops were glad to see the Americans coming to help them after years of war with China, but the older Russian troops were not comfortable with allowing American forces in their land. Never in the history of Russia were foreign troops welcomed on Russian soil, and the senior leadership were well aware of it. Even the worst hard-liners against the United States had to grudgingly admit that any help they could get was needed.

Walter ordered the remote controlled aircraft to start round the clock raids on the Chinese troops with the bombers destroying the supply lines, roads, and railways through Siberia. There was no loss of life when remote controlled aircraft were lost, and the dollar cost was minimal compared to manned aircraft. The supplies were also less in that the small aircraft used less fuel and the new smaller mini-gun ammunition was much easier to move. The Chinese could not defend against the small aircraft and throughout the remainder of the winter saw fully forty percent of their considerable forces wiped out from the air raids. The American air crews never tired, because there were none. Each day saw Advanced Tactical Fighters roaming over Siberia escorting long range bombers and looking for Chinese fighter aircraft, but mostly just checked out the terrain and located potential targets.

24 PEACE IS ATTAINABLE

MONTH 72

IX,81

The crafty commander will understand his enemy's traps. His enemies will attack him from three directions. A strange number of tears will come in the eyes of coughing ones, when the empire will fail the leader of the foreign language.

epistle to Henri II

The leaders of Aquilon, two in number (the US & USSR), will be victorious over the Orientals, and so great a noise and tumult of warfare will they produce that all the orient will shake with terror because of these two brothers, who are not yet brothers.

MONTH 72, JUNE 2

Walter was explaining his plan to the generals in Europe and by satellite to the generals in the National Military Command Center in the mountains. "Let me direct your attention down here to Northern India which is one of the few areas held by the Indians. They held it because they were well fortified against Pakistani invasions that never came. The Arabs committed one hundred percent of their forces against Europe and counted on the Chinese to take India, but China concentrated their forces in Siberia and never succeeded in totally taking India. We have just gained twenty thousand serviceable main battle tanks from the Arabs and five hundred first line fighter planes. That is a small part of what the Arabs started with, but they give us a good boost. All of these aircraft and five thousand Arab main battle tanks have been moved to the Indian border over the past months. Add to this four hundred new mini-tanks and we have a sizable force to attack the Chinese with.

This is of course a feint. We will start with an air assault to keep the Chinese busy and then drive the tanks into northern India and disperse them in defensive positions that we hope will appear offensive to the Chinese. We will use our air craft and mini-tanks to appear to be attacking in India.

Forty-eight hours later the real attack will be launched in Russia. Our five thousand American M1 tanks with three thousand of the new mini-tanks and five thousand older mini-tanks will launch the major attack along with all of our remaining remote guided aircraft and our Advanced Tactical Fighters. We will leave four thousand manned tanks and two thousand of the older mini-tanks in Russia preventing the Chinese movement further into Russia. This will be supported by the Russians and of course air if need be. The remaining three thousand new mini-tanks, three thousand of the older ones and one thousand manned tanks will run south at high speed as if they were moving toward the southern front in India.

Instead after getting one hundred miles south of the main Chinese force these tanks will turn northeast coming up behind the main Chinese forces in a pinchers movement with the forces in Russia. The Chinese will not expect the entire force to run behind them because they have always had such a difficult time supplying their forces. What they will not count on is that we have so much air transport and the mini-tanks that require such little support compared to manned forces."

One of the three star generals asked, "You did not mention the infantry. How many infantry are going behind the Chinese line?"

"Don't get excited, I will explain. There will be no infantry." Walter waited for the noise to settle down and ignored the babble of questions before he continued. "This is a major risk, but one man can maintain one mini-tank leisurely or two working a twelve hour shift or in other words, two men can keep a mini-tank rolling nearly twenty-four hours per day. We will have six thousand mini-tank maintainers, four thousand tank crewmen, and three hundred maintenance men for the manned tanks for a total of ten thousand three hundred men. They will use air support and mini-tanks for their defense. The tanks will be near enough to Russia that we can use the venerable old C-130 aircraft and LAPES to supply these forces. I'm sorry, LAPES is low altitude parachute extraction system. As in Viet Nam thirty years ago, the C-130s will fly in low and close and use parachutes to extract the cargo out of the back on pallets. The Advanced Tactical Fighters will maintain total air superiority as the U.S. Air Force has done in every war since we got seriously involved in World War II. Do you realize that no American troop has been killed by enemy air since then?

We could just sit there and wait for them to run out of supplies, but the Chinese can last a long time with few supplies. We want this over with before winter. We are going to spread our forces out into fifty different camps to prevent the Chinese from thinking we can be attacked in force or knocked out with some super weapon. It will also allow us to launch attacks from multiple directions. Without aerial recon the Chinese will probably never find one of our bases."

"General Gaddis. What about Chinese satellites reconnaissance?"

"There is none. The last one was knocked down yesterday."

"How? I didn't know we had anti-satellite systems."

"We demonstrated the capability back in the early 1980s by shooting down one of our own. The Russians noted it, but there was almost no American news on it. They were too happy reporting the Russian successes. Whereas the Russian's effort to knock down a satellite cost millions per shot, the American solution was very cheap. We just never put them into manufacture until the war. That's one of many reasons the Russians gave up the arms race. While the news media complained of our military expenses the Russians were spending a lot more and getting further behind. That demonstration was before the news media even coined the name "Star Wars."

MONTH 72, JUNE 20

The attack started. Walter and the other generals watched closely via satellite television as the tanks headed south. The Chinese let them go. They were just turning east when the Chinese launched a major attack into Russia. The combination of American and Russian forces were holding them off. The American mini-tanks were dodging through gaps in the front line of Chinese tanks and hitting the twenty million Chinese infantry with their mini-guns. The remote guided aircraft again were strafing the infantry. The Chinese tanks were left to the manned tanks of the Americans and Russians.

The first day of the battle was definitely a Chinese victory, but the battle was far from over. The main American tank force did not get in position until evening of the second day. By that time the Chinese had gained fully twenty miles further into Russia at the loss of seven hundred thousand of their infantry and five hundred of their tanks. The Allied force had lost four hundred of their own tanks.

The other generals were very nervous about the Chinese advances and told Walter that he needed to get his other tanks into action. They recommended a slice straight through the back of the Chinese lines to get back to the Russia side of the battle.

Walter said, "Relax gentlemen. The Chinese are rushing headlong into our trap."

"WHAT TRAP? A TOTAL BREAKTHROUGH INTO EUROPE?"

"I'm sorry, you must have missed the briefings of last month when we showed the trap. Captain, will you roll the video of the ditch?"

"Sorry sir, it will take a few minutes to pull it out of the files."

"While we're waiting, I'll describe it. Then you watch the tape and see for yourself. Two months ago, we used the winter weather and our build up that was temporarily holding up the Russian to build our trap. It is a huge concrete and stone wall that is totally tank proof and not healthy for infantry. We used the manned tanks with bulldozer blade to build it along with train car loads of concrete. It is a minimum of ten feet high at every point and a maximum of fifteen feet. There are numerous temporary bridges for us to use, but they can be destroyed quickly to seal the trap. It forms a semi-circle fifty miles across."

"HOW DID YOU KNOW THE CHINESE WOULD ATTACK THERE INSTEAD OF SOMEWHERE ELSE?"

"The center of the semi-circle was the only area not heavily mined. As the Chinese attacked the center of the Russian line bowed inward to suck in the Chinese. While they, and you, thought they were winning, they were actually winning exactly what we wanted, the very center of the semi-circle. The tanks that withdrew under fire actually circled to the sides letting the Chinese have their advance into the trap. Fifty percent of their force is now inside the semi-circle."

"What about their infantry? Twenty million troops is a lot of infantry."

"Excuse me, general. The tape is ready. It will help explain."

The narrator said, "This is an animation of how we want the battle to go, but accelerated by a factor of one hundred times to be able to see the true movements of the forces. There you can see the right hand side of the battle bending to guide the Chinese forces to the middle of the trap. Again, you can see the middle of the line giving. Notice that what was once the main Russian and American force is now the weak point. For every ten tanks retreating slowly, one rapidly withdraws and then runs to the nearest side of the battle. Then another and another. To keep the Chinese thinking that is the main force in front of them there is a short burst forward against them followed by a bigger retreat as the Chinese bring even more force to that point of the battle.

The battle continues this way as the middle of our line weakens while the flanks build up without attacking. When the Chinese get within five miles of the apex of the semi-circle, our forces will go into all out retreat. The purpose of course is to get across the ramps and bridges so they can be destroyed before the Chinese arrive. When they come over this ridge they will get their first sight of the wall and will suspect a trap. By that time our forces that flanked them around behind will be in place to seal the trap.

We want this attack to take two days for them to reach the apex to let their infantry keep up. Fifteen million of the infantry carry supplies for the tanks, from fuel to shells. The five million true infantry carry all of their ammunition and food for two weeks during any attack. The Chinese tanks require a lot of maintenance and after two days of moving will need to stop for maintenance. The main attacks from the east will be by the older mini-tanks keeping the faster new ones to counter any power points the Chinese try to create. Even if some of their tanks make it out, their infantry never will.

Now take a look at some actual pictures of the wall and its construction. The walls have built in mines that will not be armed until our forces are back to the west side of the wall. Anyone trying to climb the wall will set off the mines killing themselves and anyone within fifty feet. In addition the wall has a pillbox built in every two hundred yards that will be manned with water cooled machine guns. We went with water cooling because we recognize that each gun will be firing thousands of rounds of ammunition. Air cooled guns overheat too quick. The worst result we expect would be for the Chinese to surrender. We really couldn't handle twenty million prisoners."

WALTER ASKED, "ANY QUESTIONS?"

There were none. The generals that had asked questions had just been embarrassed at not having been present for the briefings for the pass months.

MONTH 72, JUNE 22

The trap was complete. The Chinese tried a ninety degree run to the north only to hit the wall of their trap. Then they fought to the south passing the dead men and infantry they had left on their way north only to hit the wall to the south. They then attempted angling back to the point their main force had entered the trap. Their forces were strung out across the two thousand square miles of the trap. Hundreds of thousands of Chinese ground troops died trying to climb the walls. Pill boxes ran out of ammunitions and had to be evacuated while waiting for ammunition.

Within three days most of the mines built into the walls of the trap had been exploded. The remote guided aircraft killed tanks and Chinese. the mini-tanks made hit and run attacks into their midst. The Chinese tanks had to get off a lucky shot to hit a mini tank. The infantry ran at the first sound of mini-tanks.

The Chinese quit running after a week and regrouped their forces for a push back into Siberia. As soon as their eastern run started, the new mini-tanks joined in the fray. Instead of hit and run attacks the new mini-tanks charged right at the Chinese tanks. Their head on run made it easier for the Chinese to hit them, but these tanks were only temporarily slowed by a direct hit. A few were put out of action by being hit coming over rises where their light weight was not enough to stay upright when hit from underneath by a direct hit with the one hundred twenty millimeter guns of the heavy Chinese tanks. Their small caliber guns had to get in close to the Chinese before they had the velocity to penetrate the Chinese armor. At closer range the mini-tanks were deadly with Chinese tanks stopping with smoke coming out of their seams. The infantry tried charges like they had done in the Korean war, but they were run down if not shot by walls of fearless mini-tanks. Some older mini-tanks were killed by the newer mini-tanks until the allies learned to keep them separated and out of range of the mini-guns. The manned tanks stayed out of the battle lobbing in fragmentation anti-personnel shells by the thousand. Every operational truck in Europe was transporting ammunition and fuel to the front. Every C-130 was carrying supplies to the eastern force behind the Chinese.

The last Chinese tank was destroyed and fifteen of the twenty million infantry were dead. Walter decided to let them march on their own back toward China. They were beaten. They would likely starve in Siberia, but he had enough of the carnage in the battle. The battle had only lasted two weeks and had killed more than any battle in history. Not one American or Russian had died once the trap had been sprung. Walter hated that so many Americans had died in the first two days while springing the trap. Only two thousand older mini-tanks and one hundred of the three thousand new mini-tanks had been lost. Three hundred remotely guided aircraft had been lost, mainly due to remote pilot error in coming in too close and hitting the ground at high speed. The European war was over except for cleaning up the inevitable small pockets of resistance in both the Arab and the Chinese theaters. China was not defeated, but Walter's job was over.

Jim Claris called Walter, "Well Lieutenant General Gaddis, you've done a great job. I want you to get on the first transport with your family and report back here to the National Military Command Center. We have some housing waiting for you that your wife will appreciate. Your war is over, but we could use your advice on winning the Pacific war. The other Generals should be able to keep control of Europe. The rebuilding of Europe will take many years if it ever recovers. You have two weeks to report in here. Have fun." Jim hung up on Walter not giving him time to comment back.

The principal chief of the orient will be vanquished by the northerners and the westerners and the people they had stirred to war and had united with them will be put to death, overwhelmed and scattered, and their women and children will be made prisoners.

MONTH 72 JUNE 24

Hi Chung got the news that his European Army had suffered a terrible defeat at the hands of the Americans. He had sent one hundred million men and women into the battle and fifty thousand tanks and what was left was two thousand tanks and fifty thousand men. There had also been twenty million women that had been sent to carry supplies and please the men. They had been left behind the lines and the line of retreat had cut them off from the men. He had considered getting word to them to come back, but decided that twenty million women and their children would do more harm to the Europeans and China could do without twenty million women and children. Food was getting short with all of the people off fighting a war. In Southeast Asia there was plenty of food, but the years of having an army in Siberia had been very draining.

Now he could concentrate on India. The Japanese had developed a new aircraft that was stealthy, faster than what the Americans called the Advanced Tactical Fighter, could turn tighter, and carried their new Banshee missile. Their new fighter could lock on to the turbulence left by a stealth aircraft and guide the missile in from twenty miles away. The Americans had suckered them in northern India and they would pay now.

MONTH 73 JULY 7

General Walter Gaddis was getting his wife settled at the Army post near the ANMCC. "Walter, how old are you?" Bridget asked.

"Forty-three now. You know that. Why do you ask?"

"Did you read this orientation brochure?"

"No. Why?"

"It says here that all able bodied men capable of fathering children are required by law to take on three wives."

"No it doesn't."

"Close. Do you know what the tax breaks are for multiple wives? Actually, it says that it is the patriotic thing to do. The population of the

United States, actually all European countries is so low that there is some question as to whether we are still viable as a race. The Chinese or at least the Orientals may take over the world without fighting simply because so many of us have died both here at our own hands, from AIDS, and from the nuclear fallout of the bombs. Actually most of the deaths are from our own hands here. In Europe the Italian, French, and Eastern Europeans are almost extinct as the result of the Arab attacks."

"What's your point?"

"You should do the patriotic thing and find at least two more wives."

"I'm happily married to you. Why should I want more wives? Besides that, I wouldn't love them. In addition, they wouldn't be happy with someone that didn't love them."

"Walter. The point is that there are many women of child bearing age in the United States and not many fertile men that don't have AIDS. Women have needs too. One need is to have children. Another is to have a man, but a man dying of AIDS that will spread AIDS is not good. Do you realize how many people have died? Do you know how long it will take to return things to normal. With all of the men that have died the ratio of men to women will be off balance forever."

"WELL, I JUST WON'T HAVE THE TIME TO PICK OUT ANY EXTRA WIVES. OKAY?"

"No that is not okay. Do you want me to pick out some wives for you? I'm sure that I could pick some that I am compatible with."

"ARE YOU SERIOUS?"

"I think that you should pick out your own and then bring them home for my inspection. The past is gone. Now is the time for women to stop being jealous. Now is the time for men to have multiple wives and quit running around behind their wives back."

"I would never run around your back. My father didn't. My grandfather didn't and I won't."

"That's good. You don't have to sneak. When you see an attractive girl now instead of ogling her you can ask her to come home with you. While one of us is pregnant you can sleep with another until they are pregnant and so on."

"I'll pick my own. When I get time. Okay?" Walter went on to work.

MONTH 77, NOVEMBER 10

"Walter, we have lost India to the Chinese and now they have invaded Pakistan. With the Middle East disarmed they are being slaughtered by the Chinese. Our Advanced Tactical Fighters are no match for the new Japanese fighter the Chinese are flying. Our ground to air missile are ineffective due to their stealthiness. They are using chemical, biological, and napalm against us. We haven't lost that many people, but we have lost twenty percent of our mini-tanks and airplanes in the last three months and are retreating daily. Have you got any ideas?"

"Well Jim, a nuke would do nicely."

"We used up our missiles just to get them shot down by their space defense systems. We now hold space, but we have no more missiles. Our bombers would fall prey to their fighters with their new radar."

"Why can't we develop the same radar they have and an airplane to take theirs on head to head."

"Because we decided to cut the defense back in the early nineties. It takes years to develop a new aircraft."

"Okay, why not shoot them down from space?"

"We don't have the technology."

"Technology is what it takes. If we used every living person of European descent and each of them killed ten Chinese, China would still have plenty of people left. In the past, the Chinese used superior manpower to try to win wars. Now, with Japanese technology, they have the same or better technology than we have and enough of it for every Chinese to have a modern gun to shoot. There have been few times in modern history that the United States didn't have air superiority. One question. Do we control space right now?"

"YES. FOR NOW. WE CAN SHOOT DOWN ANYTHING LEAVING THE EARTH FOR ORBIT. WHY?"

"Then obviously we need to push for more superiority in space. Can we track their aircraft from space?"

"YES AND NO. WE CAN TELL APPROXIMATELY WHERE THEY ARE, BUT CAN'T PINPOINT ALTITUDE. WHY?"

"If we sent in all of our stealth planes at once, I'll bet they could not track them all."

"THAT MAY BE, BUT ARE YOU PROPOSING TO NUKE ALL OF THEIR CITIES?"

"Why not a raid on their biological and chemical warfare factories just to show them we could hit them with nukes and get them to back off?"

"I don't think it would be successful."

"Okay. One more idea. Could we somehow manage to blow up, let's say, their biological factories from space. I am really afraid of biologicals for which they may have a cure but we don't. That alone could kill all of us leaving the world to them. Chemical weapons can blow back in your face. Nukes can blow up a city here and there with some fallout that poisons the earth for centuries making it worthless to the victors too. Biologicals could have an inoculation for your own people by spreading from enemy to enemy until there is no enemy. You can then move your people in within weeks. You are not even sure what happened except people started dying off. What with AIDS the population of the earth may get reduced dramatically anyway. If we could hit their factories from space that would give them the idea that we can hit anything from space leaving them no where to hide and maybe bringing about an early surrender."

"That's a thought. Another is have our B-2s fly in fairly close to them and then release Advance Cruise Missiles (ACMs). They were deployed a long time ago, but the news media never picked up on them. They are like the regular cruise missile, but with a stealth design. If we added in some of our remotely piloted aircraft, we might just overwhelm their air defenses. They have nukes too though and right now neither side is using them. Give me some time to work and see if we could have a space attack."

MONTH 79, DECEMBER 25

"Walter, I called you in on Christmas to watch the show. I agreed with you that a nuke attack might just make it worse for us, and that an attack from space might get their attention. We used the National Aero Space Plane (NASP) to launch a new satellite last week. It took a week for its nuclear reactor to come on line and get stabilized. We have it operational. It has not been tested, but it should work."

"WHAT IS IT?"

"We have taken the particle beam weapon that we developed for anti-missile defense and boosted the output with a larger reactor. It should have the power to fire three times before the reactor overheats. We have picked three factories for our test. The reactor will be operating at maximum power for all three shots. By then the reactor will melt down. It is a very small reactor and will burn up in the atmosphere before it hits anywhere. It will not go nuclear."

They watched on video screens through high resolution cameras in space at one of the factories surrounded by huge vats as the beam came cutting through with no visible beam but cutting through the factory like butter. It cut a swath twenty feet wide from one side to the other exploding vats as it went. This one was located in Tokyo, Japan. Another was on the opposite side of the Island. Then the third was on the mainland of China. They never saw the tiny particle beam satellite turning red hot and then flashing out molten metal in all directions. It rapidly decayed out of orbit and burnt up totally in the stratosphere one hundred thousand feet up.

"WHY DID THE SATELLITE LAST SUCH A SHORT TIME?"

"It was originally created only as a defense against missiles. It was designed to fire a much lower power beam a thousand or more times with a very small reactor designed to last for years if the beam was not used. It normally would take only a few minutes to gin up the reactor which would then be allowed to cool back off for minimal power for communications in peacetime. We just removed the safety devices. The beam that would normally be only a pin point of light hitting a missile spread out due to the atmosphere. As you could see it cut through the factory like butter. Without the safety devices thirty percent of the radioactivity for a reaction was burnt up in minutes.

When Walter went home he found his wife with two other young women dressed in the very tight minimal clothing that had become very popular with the man shortage. "Merry Christmas, Walter." his real wife said as another very attractive slender young woman came out of the kitchen dressed in only string panties with a triangle in front and not much else and with a matching bra.

MONTH 80, JANUARY 20

The war was raging, but the Chinese were suing for peace. They asked for the land they had conquered to date plus retention of all their weapons.

Another two satellites had been launched by NASP in the past month. This time six more suspected biological factories were destroyed. The Chinese attacks into the Middle East stopped within a week.

MONTH 82, MARCH 10

Intelligence satellites had photographed mass graves being filled throughout Japan and China. There was almost no vehicular traffic anywhere in the region. Walter had settled in with his three new wives who had turned out to be a help to his real wife and kids. They had a foursome for Bridge. His wife had picked them for her compatibility with them and their general attractiveness to please Walter. She had no fear that he would not keep her as his favorite, and she was right.

MONTH 84, 1 MAY

Japan, never having admitted before that they were the brains in the war sued for peace. They offered up the inoculations against all of their biologicals in exchange for United States assistance in stopping and cleaning up the mass deaths. China and Japan had already lost at least half their populations and were in danger of losing three fourths or more. They had developed the inoculations at the same time as they developed the new viruses, but had not inoculated their populations As it turned out, China never received any of the serum until having lost over four fifths of their population. Japan lost two thirds by the time the diseases were stopped. The explosions of their breeding vats had spread the diseases within very quickly. By August, seven years after the start of the war, the last remnants of active war had been stopped. The United States had determined to keep the high ground of space as a location to spy on the world and destroy anything that looked like weapons on the ground. Any new factories were immediately brought under inspection for biologicals and nuclear weapons. The United States was determined, this time, to keep their military supremacy that they had enjoyed after World War II when only the United States had nukes.

POSTLOGUE

The United States used the threat of their space weapons to maintain the peace until a complete net of space weapons over the world was launched. After that was accomplished, it was no longer a bluff. The net of satellites was the insurance of the world that no one could ever again try to conquer the world. The particle beams left nowhere above ground safe, but made the world safe with the United States in sole charge of them. The advantage of being the only ones in the world with nuclear weapons had given the United States the capability of ruling the world at the end of World War II, and this time the United States was not going to let go of the high ground, space. The scientists of the world could develop what they wanted as long as it was peaceful and the United States would put it into space for their experiments to better the world. The only science allowed was either run by the United States government or over seen by United States personnel to assure that no one was creating weapons. The world was ready for a lasting peace and even if they weren't, the United States made sure that no one had a choice.

There would be no near term danger of over population again for many years. The job was repopulating the world. There really wasn't much interest in building war weapons when there was a world to rebuild. The old vehicles, tanks, and warplanes were melted down for use in building modern farming equipment for the world. This time around, the food production would stay up with the population growth. Without the possibility of war, governments could concentrate on feeding the people.

One interesting tactic, led by the United States, was the firm determination that there would be no welfare. Everyone had a job to do. The handicapped were given jobs they could do with their handicap. Even those severely crippled had jobs to do. The younger men and women did the manual jobs, the older ones held the desk jobs.

With total space superiority and a continual research to keep it that way, there was not much need for military. However, there was mandatory military service for all men and women, even the crippled. The military was used to clean city parks, plant trees in the forests, build houses for the poor, respond to natural disasters anywhere in the world. Houses destroyed by a hurricane were rebuilt. People injured were doctored. Roads were rebuilt. Unfortunately, many were stationed around the world to keep an eye on the research of the other countries. The United States military picked only the best for this duty and policed its own force for any abuse of privilege. They were joined by soldiers from every country as a United World peace force. Even civil wars were impossible. Any strong man that tried to take and hold a mountain, was reported, spotted from space, and eliminated. If any inspectors were prohibited from entering a research facility, a beam from space eliminated the problem. If a crime were committed against a U.S. inspector, that country was expected to pursue and investigate until the perpetrator was found. There was always the threat of the beam weapons. Only a few heavy ground weapons were kept stationed around the world by the United States.

Giving up our leadership in space would be giving up the high ground which is essential for our survival as a country.

ABOUT THE AUTHOR

Spent over 39 years with the United States Air Force in the USA, Asia, and Europe. He had some part in the development of most of the US Air Force development programs between 1980 and 1990. He taught classes on R&D program management techniques and R&D logistics as a guest lecturer for the Air Force Institute of Technology and various conference rooms from Los Angeles to Boston. Over 3000 future managers from all services and many government contractors attended his class on program scheduling. He served on many brain storming teams to come up with unique solutions to military problems from shooting down space objects to moving "dud" bombs off an active runway.

He is now retired from both active duty and civil service. He is still active and recently has been towing a Shriner parade float and been president of the local amateur radio club, going to almost weekly dances and generally enjoying himself.